*"If you throw me to the wolves,
I will come back leading the pack"*

~ author unknown

2

Moon Dancing

Volume 1

Iain McLachlan

**720 – Sixth Street, Box # 5
New Westminster, BC
V3C 3C5   CANADA**

Title: Moon Dancing (Volume 1)
Author: Iain McLachlan
Publisher: Silver Bow Publishing
Cover Design: Candice James
Editing: Janet Kvammen

© 2023 Silver Bow Publishing
www.silverbowpublishing.com
info@silverbowpublishing.com

Library and Archives Canada Cataloguing in Publication

Title: Moon dancing / Iain McLachlan.
Names: McLachlan, Iain, 1969- author.
Description: Second edition. | Contents: Volume 2.
Identifiers: Canadiana 20230561004 | ISBN 9781774032824 (v. 2 ; softcover)
        Classification: LCC PR6113.C49 M66 2023 | DDC 823/.92—dc23

Dedication

For Lynda.

Acknowledgements

I would like to give a big howl out
to all those who allowed me to use them
as a basis for several of the characters in the story.

6

Chapter 1

Belfast, 2008:

He was walking through the rain, hoping it would stop, but this was Belfast and here it seldom stopped raining. He dug his hands deeper into his pockets trying to find warmth. He did not see her until she spoke.

"Excuse me," her accent wasn't one from Northern Ireland. The girl who stood in front of him with her back towards the wall was dressed in black jeans, boots and a thick leather belt with a pattern on it that reminded him of something out of 'Lord of the Rings', one of his favourite films. His eyes moved up her body. The dark cotton top could have been sprayed on like a second skin. He could distinguish her abdomen muscles through the top; this girl liked to work out. Her body was crowned with a pair of very firm looking breasts. The thick black duffel type coat lay open revealing her body; the hood was down, and her jet-black hair seemed to melt into it. He didn't really look at her face until she spoke.

"Sorry," he was embarrassed as soon as he said the words,

"Do you know where I can find The Botanic Inn?" She repeated her question. She looked to be in her early twenties, her eyes the same colour as her jet-black hair. She had taken his breath away. Her accent was eastern European, but he did not know where; they all sounded the same to him.

"Ah, yes," he had to pause, turn around and point up the road he had just come down. "It is up there on the right-hand side, can't miss it." She spoke one word in a language he did not understand and left abruptly, quickly making her way up the road in the direction she had been advised. His thoughts started running wild; he started up the road after her but followed at a deliberate slower pace. She was hot, very hot; in fact, he wondered what she tasted like. He looked about at the other people walking back and forth through the rain and fading light. No one paid him any attention. A car horn blasted. He listened as the irate driver swore at the young teenager jay-walking across the road, who held up two fingers at the driver as he continued his slow walk to the other side of the road.

She walked past two security staff on the door, both, nearly six feet in height, regulation bald head, slightly overweight, ugly faces, black trousers and black jackets and an ear piece in their right ears with a cord that went into their jackets; but she doubted it did much else. Men like that believing themselves to be tough, 'ha,' she laughed to herself, if only they knew. The one on her right extended his arm, opened the door and gave the standard greeting she ignored as she swept past. A warm blast met her as the heavy door closed behind her.

The bar area was open with a semi-enclosed seated area to the right and a small set of steps which led up to the larger space. A flat screen TV was showing a local rugby match live, much to the excitement of those who were in front of them. The majority were men but the few girlfriends who were there did seem a little out of place among the rugby shirts and jumpers except for one who was wearing a similar rugby shirt as the men. To her left was a double doorway, leading to a smaller, quieter bar in a different room. The main bar ran from the double doorway along the back of the room. Several people stood along the dark stained wooden bar, most just ordering their drinks and returning to the quite full raised seating on the right. She moved amongst the crowd and made her way towards the bar, she was surrounded by larger males, two of them to her right turned to welcome the smaller, fit looking chick who had just walked between them and took up the small space at the bar. They both were tall, easily over six feet in height, wearing blue jeans and rugby shirts of the local team, and overweight. They closed together and rubbed up against her, the larger of the two leaned forward and spoke.

"All right love," his accent was local to Belfast. As he spoke he ogled her up and down, "buy you a pint?" he asked. She turned and scowled as she lowered her dark eyebrows and gave her one-word answer.

"No," she said it loud enough for them to hear. She turned back towards the bar. The one who spoke pushed forward with his shoulder, crashing against her to gain her attention back as he was slightly agitated by the fact she was ignoring him. The other one stood up to his full height in support of his friend.

"Well how about a chat then? A good-looking woman like you shouldn't be left all alone by herself you know," she turned again to face him.

"What? You mean I should be with a big strong man like you for example?" She was eastern European, a cheeky smile spread over her face taking him slightly by surprise. He tried to speak to her, but the barman attracted her attention. They did not hear her order but watched as she handed over a crisp twenty-pound note for the small glass that looked like it only had Coke in it. He spoke to her but was again ignored.

"I said," he nudged into her for a second time and leaned over so his mouth was near her right ear, "I would have bought that for you," his smile was hopeful, boosted by the words of encouragement that his friend had passed on while she was ordering her drink. Her nose was filled with the smell of his body, the cheap aftershave, body spray and sweat all mixed with the smell of stale beer. She moved her back up against the bar. She made a point of looking him up and down with an expressionless look on her face, the cheeky smile returned as she spoke.

"No, thank you," she moved to push past him, her smile vanished, "I have taste." His friend started giggling at the put down, she stepped between them and started to walk away. He reached out and grabbed her upper left arm with his right hand, she half spun around and he slightly lost balance, spilling some of his own drink over himself.

"Hey, I was only asking,"

"*LET GO NOW!*" she shouted, others standing around turned to see what was happening. He released her arm and held his hand up in mock surrender as she walked away to the other side of the bar.

"Lesbian!" he said as he slouched up against the bar in a vain attempt to regain his own social standing, "You can tell.," His friend was already laughing at him. She stopped at the top of the room, her keen eyes scanning every face, people walked past, she sipped her drink. The pub exploded in cheering, she watched as the two men at the bar walked over to the far side of the room away from her. She smiled again. Her phone bleeped. She fumbled around in her pocket. She read the message and replied with one word; she then returned the phone to her pocket. The entrance to the pub opened and the man that she had stopped in the street for directions walked inside a few paces and stopped. He was obviously looking for someone as his eyes bounced around the room. Slowly he started to walk over towards the bar. He didn't attract the attention of the bar staff to order a drink as any other customer would, he instead continued to search through the faces of everyone else. She shifted herself down a single stair. Her movement made his head turn towards the stairs. Shrouded in darkness, she stood alone, sipping a drink. He stared. She was tasty, and his mind went into overdrive, his pulse quickening as his eyes moved over her body.

She could feel him staring and pretended not to notice. She took out her phone, tapped in one sentence and placed the phone back in her pocket, grinning. The phone bleeped again, and she read the one-word reply. She deleted the messages without replying and made sure he could see her finishing her drink, then placed the glass down and headed for the door. His eyes followed her every move. She pushed the doors out of her way and hurried outside, oblivious of the security cameras above the entrance which captured everyone entering or leaving. In less than a second, he was at the door, past the security staff and into the rain. He surveyed both sides of the street, she had disappeared, he moved towards the edge of the road and continued his visual search up and down. He spotted the dark hair move from behind a white van as she was heading up the road away from the town. He started after her and got right up behind her when her phone went off. She turned to answer it, and *IT WASN'T HER.* He stopped where he was. He looked up and down and cursed himself for losing sight of her. He started back up the street towards the pub, towards where he had first seen her. Suddenly from behind a group of teenagers she stepped out, phone to her ear, chatting; his heart raced. She looked up and down the road moving between the parked cars and jogged to the pavement on the opposite side.

"YES," he exclaimed triumphantly. Crossing the road so that they were both on the same side, he followed her. He slowed when about twenty feet from her, moving around the few people making their way through the light rain, involved in their own lives and not noticing him. Her hair and clothes appeared to melt into the growing darkness of the evening. Streetlights illuminated the area. His eyes remained transfixed on her every movement, every sway, the way she walked, the way her head turned as she looked around; she apparently could not see him, but he could feel his own pulse beat in his neck. His heartbeat was racing with his excitement; he knew what he most desired. He had to force himself to slow down as he had gotten too close. She turned right down by the terraced street that led away from the busy road; had she just speeded up? Her phone beeped again, he heard a giggle come from her, it was so seductive. She put the phone away and carried on down the now empty street. He looked behind himself as he passed the shop on the corner. It was brightly lit; he could see people moving around inside. He turned back towards the direction that she was going. She pushed the phone into the back pocket of her jeans, showing off her behind; he liked that. The alleyway on the right led up between the terraced houses, most of these being accommodation for the student population of Queen's University which was less than a mile away.

The music vibrated from one of these, much as he knew, to the annoyance of other residents on the tightly packed street. The house seemed quite full as he walked past. He could never understand students that partied away what little money they had. Working his whole life, he was envious of how people with so little could party so much. Her phone beeped again, she read the short message and deleted it without a reply. She closed the phone and returned it to the rear pocket of her jeans.

The right hand clasped around her mouth, pulling her head back into his body, his left arm clasped itself around her, pinning her arms to her body and hoisted her clear of the pavement; her struggles seemed feeble and in vain, her legs swung in the air as he ran with her into the alleyway.

∞∞∞∞

Sean Parrish was awake already but the sound of his phone going off made him stir out of his bed. He reached across to the bedside table to read the time on the display. 5:54am. Sean looked back at the mobile phone and recognised the number.

"Luckily for you I was already awake," he said. The comment slightly took the male caller by surprise, the pre-planned apology did not seem to be received or acknowledged, "What's up?"

"Morning, anyway, a body was found in an alleyway near Queen's a few hours ago."
The male voice continued, "Male, but we are going to have probs with this one; he was torn to pieces," Sean was now wide awake.

"What do you mean, chopped up or what?"

"Head ripped off, massive injuries to torso, arms, legs, I'm telling you, it's a real mess this one." He gave the street name of where it had been discovered.

"I'm on my way."

An hour later Sean was standing at the police cordon getting changed into a white disposable paper suit and covering his shoes and hands so not to contaminate the forensic evidence around the area. The morning was trying to break through the thick grey clouds which covered the city; the long alleyway was blocked at either end by uniformed police and right in the middle was the familiar white domed tent covering the scene of the crime. He had seen many of these in his time as a police officer in Belfast but no matter how many death scenes he had witnessed it never got any easier for him. He did his best not to show it, especially in front of the junior detectives of the new Police Service of Northern Ireland.

Sean had been a police officer for 28 years and he never regretted his ambition to become a detective; he had policed the worst of the Northern Irish troubles and had seen more than his share of friends lowered into graves. Two more years, then he could retire. He had achieved his own personal goals and now had his sights firmly set on finishing his 30 years alive. Solving a crime and seeing a true conviction was something he always said was the greatest feeling. If his wife was around, he said it was the second best feeling only to the birth of their children. The detective sergeant waved at him from beside the white tent as Sean walked towards him.

"What have we got Mike?" Detective Sergeant Mike Dear was dressed in a similar white disposable suit and held open the entrance for Sean to step inside. Mike looked at the notebook he had been scribbling in.

"Mr Edgar Trotman, 42, rental address in the east of the city, he has lived there two weeks now, moved over from England. Simon is on the case with the rest of his background now." Sean looked down at the mangled mess in front of him, "Time of death, early evening; he was discovered by the owner of the corner shop walking his dog this morning." Sean knelt, the body was lying on its left side, the head was missing as was the right arm from below the elbow. The rest of the body had been torn apart. The body was naked and every body part had been violated.

"How do you know who it is?" Sean asked.

"The head and what's left of his clothes are up the alleyway. There's body tissue all over the place," he continued, Sean was looking at the wounds trying to picture what or who could be responsible for something like this.

"Sorry?" he said, Mike had just said something he heard but had not registered.

"I'm not sure what was used to carry out the mutilation, it looks like it mostly occurred pre-mortem," he repeated, Sean stood up, both turned and walked out of the tent into the alleyway. A small crowd had gathered at the bottom end, Sean recognised a journalist from one of Northern Ireland's big newspapers; they always seemed to arrive just as something was happening, almost as if they had prior warning. "Could it have been a chainsaw or something like that?" Mike asked. Sean had known him for the last 15 years, ten of those working with and for him. They had both come from the same part of Northern Ireland but had never met until they enlisted in the police. Their religious backgrounds were opposite but that was something which never was and would never be an issue; both their families had holidayed together in the past.

Mike had asked to come and work for him and this had been approved. They had seen very good results in the court room and helped put some dangerous and violent people behind bars. The only thing they really differed on was their choice of sporting teams which they supported, but the banter around the whole team had always been good, even in the dark days. Sean had been very glad of him in the past and knew that no matter what happened he had a friend for life in Mike Dear.

"Chainsaw? I think we can rule out the IRA or the UFF in this one," Mike agreed.

"*MIKE*" was shouted from the cordon, both men turned towards the voice of the middle-aged man with a receding hair line, bald patch on top and unshaven look as he walked towards them.

"Simon, what have you got?" Simon stopped as he got to them, produced the police issue note book and started to read. Simon was a Detective-Sergeant who had been on the team for just over two years now and was still as keen as the day he started.

"You're going to love this one," Simon was the newest member of the team but was also the eldest and was a lot closer to ending his 30 years in the police than Sean. He had spent most of his career as a detective and still enjoyed the job; he had been in a police station close to the border between Northern Ireland and the Republic and had spent most of that time investigating terrorist cases. He had been the section sergeant at Sean's first station in the early 1980's but the two had not seen each other in quite some time until Simon applied for this post after the team had suffered a death. "Mister Edgar Trotman, forty-two years old, address at one of the rented flats just across the road from the city airport. He arrived two weeks ago from an address in Manchester and paid two months' rent in advance," he paused.

"Welcome to *Norn Iron*," Mike used local slang and emphasised his own accent in doing so, Simon continued.   "Several arrests, two convictions for rape, one conviction for aggressive assault, possession of offensive material and is registered on the sexual offenders list." Mike and Sean looked at each other as Simon drew breath, "spent six years in Strangeways prison, suspected involvement in several other sexual assaults in Manchester, Birmingham and London, none proven due to lack of evidence." The three policemen had been slowly walking back towards the white tent as Simon had been speaking and they stopped at the door. Mike pulled back the door and all three looked in at what was left of the body lying on the ground.

"Vigilante attack?" suggested Mike.

"Don't think so," said Sean, "Well, let's hope not. We really don't need something like that in Belfast now." Mike dropped the flap and the tent closed as they turned to face each other. "Right Simon," continued Sean, "have a look at all the local CCTV footage from shops etc," Simon nodded in agreement as Sean spoke. "Get the rest of the team on that as well; we are going to need results fast on this one."

"OK, no probs," he answered.

"Mike, see what you can find out from forensics and the results of the post mortem, I really want to know what killed this guy." Mike nodded once. Sean continued, "Also I want to know who this guy hung around with, and what he's been doing for the last two weeks." Sean patted him on his left shoulder, "Find out if our Child and Adult Rape and Enquiry Team knew this guy was here in Belfast."

"Will do," answered Mike.

"I'm going to have a chat with the shop owner, and I'll see if I can get the uniforms to start door to door and get the press office to get a press release out" The three of them looked at each other, then Sean gave the final task, "Meet you back for coffee after lunch." With that, the three friends parted and set about what they needed to do. Sean would always start his investigation briefing for the team of detectives with coffee. He liked his coffee; no coffee, no briefing. It was widely rumoured that coffee ran in his veins and not blood as nothing seemed to shake him and any newly qualified detective would be told all about his nerves of steel. Sean liked this as it hid how he really felt most of the time. He had a coffee machine in his office which always had several bags of different types of ground coffee. Kenyan, Costa Rican, Columbian. Sean knew his coffee. Sean had parked his car behind Mike's and Mike was just opening his door when his phoned beeped with a message. Mike took the phone out of his pocket, it was from Simon. 'HE IS NOT AWAKE YET, MUST HAVE MISSED HIS COFFEE THIS MORNING' Mike smiled and tapped in a reply, then set about his work.

∞∞∞

Alexi was angry, very angry in fact, the others had not seen him like this in a while. They were sitting in the small living room, listening to him ranting. The two-seat sofa was up against the wall opposite the gas fire that heated the entire middle terraced house. The single seat chair that matched the design of the sofa was against the far wall and facing into the centre of the room. The tall lamp was in the corner beside the single chair, they had bought it cheaply out of a hardware shop only a couple of days ago. The door to the kitchen was on the left-hand side of the chair as you looked at it, it was painted the same cheap colour as the walls. The TV under the window was switched off and the small space in the middle of the room was being taken up by him as he was pacing and shouting.   From next door, she could hear the shouting, she hated noise, and she always had. The only noise she ever liked was the sound of her grandchildren coming into the house. The shouting started again, he was shouting in some foreign language, Polish or something. There was a lot of Polish in Belfast now, 'They should be made to speak English' she thought. They had all moved in recently and the old woman was hoping they wouldn't be staying too long before they moved on again. Back in the small living room next door the group of people were all sitting around, he paused from the shouting.

"What did you want me to do Alexi?" She was sitting in the single chair, the sofa had two men and another woman on it with two more men standing by the door. She flicked her black hair and finished her sentence. "Just let him rape me?" She was defiant. The man in the middle of the room stopped and looked at her. He put his hands onto his waist, he glared at all of them, he looked younger than the 45 he was. His thick black hair was combed back, his mouth only slightly parted to speak.

"No," Alexi paused again, "but you should not have been there in the first place!" Glances were passed amongst the group in the room. "We cannot go through this again, we have come a long way. *I WILL NOT LET THIS HAPPEN TO US AGAIN.*" His voice rose into a shout again. "You *WILL* do as you are told, all of you."

"Alexi," said one of the men as he leaned forward. Alexi cut him off before he could say another word.

"*NO* Davidov, I know what you want, what you think we should do *but that is NOT* our way anymore. We have done that before and look what happened to us. We are hunted by our own and we *MUST NOT* attract this kind of attention to ourselves." He turned his back to them and walked towards the window. "The west cannot accept our kind; they will not." He turned around to face them, "I am who I am; we will move from this place *AND THIS WILL NOT HAPPEN AGAIN.*"

Chapter 2

They had been driving around the town of Limavady for over an hour and not much had moved. The base station radio in the car had been quiet as well. The market town of Limavady in the northwest of Northern Ireland had its problems over the years but these days they were fairly minor. Situated only half an hour drive away from the city of Londonderry, or Derry as it was also known locally, Limavady itself was still a farming town. They were here covering the shift for two others who were at a police function in Belfast.

"So, what are you two doing for your holiday this year?" Kyle asked as he turned his head to the other police officer who was in the driving seat of the marked, un-armoured police car.

"She hasn't decided yet," his answer made Kyle smile. Tony Fallon's wife was the butt of a lot of banter between them. It had started after the first time Kyle had been taken out for dinner. Tony Fallon's wife's idea of a holiday was far different from her husband's. She was keen on going to a beach and lying there for ten days, Tony on the other hand would put up with that kind of holiday for nearly ten minutes before he was bored. Kyle was relentless in his baiting of his friend.

"So, two weeks of tanning for you then! bet she goes back to Palma again." They had been to Palma three times now and Kyle just loved bringing it up. Tony did not hide the fact that he was bored with the place and his suggestions of an active holiday fell on deaf ears, much to Kyle's continued delight.

"Not if I can help it,"

"Bet she's booked it already," Kyle used his hands to help picture his description. "The blazing sunshine, the cool lapping of the sea on the sand, the gay waiters checking you out from the bar..." This had happened on their last visit to Palma. Tony then made the mistake of telling Kyle about the advances of a gay waiter, who then told the rest of the section and Tony still hadn't lived it down, Tony turned and stared at him. A smile had spread across Kyle's face, "Well I think it's great that you can get blown out by both men and women."

"*I'M MARRIED! I DON'T GET BLOWN OUT,*" the bait had been taken,

"So how come after nine years of marital bliss you haven't any kids then?" Kyle grinned as he spoke.

"At least I have a wife. When are you going to get yourself a girlfriend, never mind someone to marry?" was Tony's retort.

"When I can find someone dumb enough to take the job on. When am I going to be an *UNCLE?*"

"Not for a while."

"So, you *STILL* aren't getting any then,"

"*PISS OFF,*"

Kyle laughed out loud. Tony got angry up until he realised that he was in fact being baited. "Piss off, one day you'll learn," Kyle was giggling and not hiding the fun he was having at Tony's expense. The radio suddenly spoke:

"Lima Delta Seven Three, Lima Delta," it was the control room of the police station in town; Kyle pressed the button on the side of the handset.

"Lima Delta Seven Three, send."

"Roger, reported disturbance outside THE INN Bar, four males, please respond." Kyle unhooked the handset from the base station and lifted it to his mouth, he spoke into it as Tony started the car.

".... Received." The car quickened up the empty street then slowed at the traffic lights. The lights changed to green and the car jumped forward, Tony piloted the car around the one-way system that took him around Limavady police station to another set of traffic lights that were already at green as Tony took the car around the 90-degree right turn. Kyle looked at the silver BMW that was stationary at the opposite set of traffic lights, the driver stared at them. He had been out of prison for over a year, but it was known that he was back and was seen associating with his previous contacts and that they were already continuing the supply of drugs in and around the entire north west of Northern Ireland. The car straightened and increased in speed before slowing again to take the left at the end of the street.

The INN Bar was on the right-hand side of the street with car parking spaces in front of it. Outside the white building were a group of young men who were fighting, both officers knew even before the car stopped that they were soldiers from the military base four miles up the road in the village of Ballykelly. Ten minutes later, after two more police officers had arrived on foot, four of the soldiers were sitting on the pavement with their hands cuffed behind their backs; other soldiers were keeping their distance as both Kyle and Tony had very quickly broken up the fight. Three of the soldiers were Fijian and were now refusing to speak English even though the other soldiers still spoke to them in English. This was obviously a trick they had used before. One of them had thrown a punch at Tony who had him face down with the cuffs on both wrists behind his back in less than two seconds. After that another was shouting at the other soldiers to back off. Kyle was always impressed at Tony's speed with getting the cuffs on and by the way he spoke to them letting them know that he was an ex-soldier himself.

An older soldier came out of the entrance of the bar, he obviously had some authority over them as the others who stood with their backs to the wall responded to him, Tony spotted this and zeroed in on him.

"Right you lot," he raised his arm and using two fingers pointed towards the older one, "you've had a good night out, no problems, but now is the time to get in your taxis and go back to camp." The older one stepped forward slightly and engaged Tony. Kyle was standing in front of the four intoxicated soldiers who all had swelling and bruising starting in and around their faces.

"Listen mate," his English accent seemed very out of place in Limavady, Tony recognised one of the bar staff who walked out the door and came towards them. "Yeah, we're off now, no trouble, no one's hurt."

"Good," said Tony.

"Now if you'll just let them go, I will take them back with me and we'll say nothing more about this."

"I don't think so," Tony waved his hand and indicated to the several other soldiers who were all the worse for wear from their night out and feeling a bit anxious. "You lot, get in your taxis and *GO HOME, NOW.*" Tony turned back towards Kyle; the other two police officers were standing off to his right.

The older one stepped forward again. "Now listen..."

Tony spun round and cut him off. Kyle stepped forward, so he was just in front of the four who were sitting in their line on the ground and the other two stepped forward in support and brought them back into view. *"NO, YOU LISTEN,"* Tony took a step forward and towered over the soldier. "These four are coming with us to the station, but if anyone else wants to join them go ahead, I have not got a problem with arresting all of you," a murmur of discontent went around the small crowd.

"I was just saying...." A second soldier stepped forward and took the arm of the older one. Tony informed them that he was going to phone their unit the following morning and after these four had made their court appearance they would be dealt with under military discipline.

"What have they done?" asked a voice from the crowd.

"Disorderly behaviour in a public place, but that is none of your business, however if you want to see your mate later come down to the police station," Tony said in a more official tone, "Then after they have been in court your CO will have a '*Bringing the military into disrepute*' to deal with," Tony paused, "Section 69 of the Army Act if I am not mistaken." Eyebrows raised among the young faces, except the older one who had obviously experienced that as well. Kyle had heard this before from Tony and was now smiling. "Yes, I do know about that, I was once a sergeant in *ONE PARA.*" Kyle smiled to himself. Tony had been in the parachute regiment where he had only served six years and never got promoted to sergeant, but the line was working with the soldiers. A white minibus pulled up at the far side of the police car and the soldiers moved forward and climbed in leaving the four sitting on the pavement.

"A Sergeant, eh?" Kyle made the verbal dig at him as the minibus pulled away as the second police car arrived. Tony glanced at him over his shoulder and returned the smile, then looked up at the full moon, paused then smiled. Neither of them could have known how much tonight was going to change the course of their lives forever.

Less than a mile away two friends were standing in another bar. They had known each other since school, one from Coleraine, the other from Limavady. Both were nearing their 21st birthdays and being out of work they were enjoying the last of the beer in their glasses; they could not afford to buy another. The large wooden counter extended round the bar, 'The Doah' was commonly known in and around the town as a nice place to drink. They looked at the 70-something man who was slumped at the bar; his clothes were old, tattered, thick woollen and well out of fashion. He was a local drunk who was regularly found sleeping around the nearby bus depot. Tonight, they had spotted him pulling out £20 notes, one after the other. This was unusual, where did he get this amount of money? He was already very drunk when the barman refused to serve him anymore and ushered him out the door. The two young men were soon out the door following close behind him with one thing in mind. They searched to the left and right until the younger of the two spotted the shape of him stumbling around the tall metal fence of the bus depot. They hurried after him and soon closed in on him. He staggered to his left and around the side of one of the small buildings. He didn't feel the first punch to his back but the kick to his legs brought him down. He rolled onto his back and faced his attackers, their blows rained down, he swung with his arms to fend them off, the pain in his chest struck like lightning, he made a gasp, the pain shot down his arms and all breath left him. He turned his body onto his left side, trying to hide from the beating; he almost was unaware of the foot that came down on his face, slamming his head against the hard ground. He couldn't breathe. He could taste his own blood in his nose and mouth as the foot came down again and again. The pain in his chest was excruciating. He tried to wrap his arms around the pain as he tried to breathe. Oblivious to the kicks to his body, he looked up at the raised foot and saw the look of hate in the young face just before darkness blacked out his world.

The two friends excitedly searched through the pockets of the badly beaten man on the ground. He smelt bad, he had not had a bath or shower in some time, his beard was thick with the blood pouring freely from his nose and mouth. The younger one stepped back to escape the blood. He stood up and over his friend.

"Ha ha, nice one Michael, how much have we got?" he asked, Michael handed him a roll of money.

"Count that," Michael ordered as he continued his search of the body, "looks like we struck it rich this time Liam," Liam was concentrating on counting the paper money in his hand. His excitement grew as he passed £100.

"Where did he get this?" He asked.

"Who cares, it's ours now..." Michael continued as Liam looked to his right, Michael punched his leg to attract his attention, "Grab an arm..." Michael moved and grabbed at the right arm, he looked up at Liam who was staring into the darkness, he punched him again. "I said, grab an arm,"

"What's that?" his friend quietly asked, fear evident in his voice.

"*OI, GRAB AN ARM!*" he turned to look up at him, Liam was staring into the darkness.

"What's that?" he was quieter than before.

"What's what?" Michael asked as he turned in the direction that Liam was looking and faced the same direction. He dropped the arm and slowly started to face what was in the darkness.

∞∞∞∞

The same minibus that had lifted the first group of soldiers had returned and after they had been processed was now taking the four soldiers back to their barracks in Ballykelly. Tony had watched it go as it pulled out of the police station and turned into the empty street; it had been nearly two hours since they had made the initial arrest. The duty Sergeant had not taken long to process them as the Fijians had suddenly remembered how to speak English; they would be in a local court before the end of the month. Tony walked back inside and made his way around to the kitchen. Kyle had his back to the door and was stirring one of the mugs of tea as Tony entered the room. The toaster popped, and two slices of toast appeared out the top.

"Butter them, would you?" he asked without turning around, the used tea bag made a thudding sound as it hit the bottom of the small empty bin. Tony opened the fridge, pulled out the butter and lavishly spread it over the warm toast. Kyle loved hot buttered toast and munched on it as the two of them talked together. He was making fun of Tony's use of military rank earlier with the squaddies.

"Worked as well," said Tony as he gulped down a mouthful of hot tea, Kyle smiled at him, the tannoy burst through the speaker mounted in the corner of the room.

"Crew of Seven Three report to enquiry office. Seven Three to enquiry office." The two emptied the remainder of their tea into the sink, swilled them out under the tap and placed them upside down in the metal sink. They lifted their hats and walked through the station to the enquiry office where the duty sergeant was speaking on the phone. Another police officer walked past them on the way out and headed slowly down the corridor; the sergeant turned towards them as they entered.

"Right..." He acknowledged towards them before continuing with his conversation over the mobile phone "yeah, no problem......... No, Belfast.............." They waited just inside the room for him to finish, "Ok, bye," suddenly the conversation was over. "Right, you two, take a drive around the bus station. We have had a report of a disturbance down there."

"What kind of disturbance?" asked Kyle.

"Kids," was the one-word reply, the phone sounded again, and the sergeant turned away from them as he answered it. He started talking then turned towards them and motioned with his eyes that they should leave, so they turned and walked out the door.

"I'm driving," said Kyle.

"No, you're bloody not," answered Tony as his pace increased.

"Yes, I am," retorted Kyle as his own pace quickened past Tony. This continued all the way to the car, and they were almost running by the time they got there. They pushed past a woman police officer who was walking away from the car park and heading into the main building. She shook her head as they flew past her.

"*KIDS,*" She half muttered under her breath, "My children are more grown up than you two *AND THEY ARE ONLY TEENAGERS,*" she shouted after them. Tony won and smirked as Kyle slid into the passenger seat. The car turned out into the empty street as they made their way around Limavady's one-way system, which was fine when it was empty but a pain on market day. They drove past the now closed pub where they had been only a few hours before. There was no one around the sleeping town. They turned right at the traffic lights and drove up towards the small county court house that was at the end of the street.

"Bet kids have broken a few windows in again on the buses," it was Kyle who spoke. He was deliberately not mentioning the way that Tony was driving so slowly compared to what he would have been doing, Tony picked up on this.

"It's *NOT* a 999 call, so *NO BLUE LIGHTS*, or had you just forgotten that bit of your advance driving course?"

"Piss off," Kyle responded.

"*WELL...*" Tony started, "I'm not the one who *failed* his driving course the first time," Tony stressed the word 'failed' as the car continued past the shops that lined either side of the street.

"That prick," Kyle folded his arms as he spoke. The two of them had met for the first time when Kyle was repeating his driving course at the police Driver Training Unit in Antrim. They were paired off on the course as they both had come from the military. Kyle had not liked the instructor at all as he kept making references about their past, which was something that Tony realized Kyle didn't like talking too much about that either..

Kyle failed the first course not on his driving but attitude. The instructor had discovered that Kyle had not served in the British Army as most people thought but in the French Foreign Legion. When Tony first enquired he was met with one-word answers but cracked through that when he shared that he was EX- Parachute Regiment. The instructor latched onto this and continued with outdated comments, jokes and misconceptions about the legion for the duration of the course. A couple of people had noticed that Kyle was starting to react but on the last two days he would always reply to the instructor in French. Everyone could tell that although Kyle was smiling he was swearing and abusing him. One other person from the police station in Lisburn could speak a bit of French and confided some of what he could translate to the instructor, so they failed him for it and made him retake the entire course. The car slowed and turned left towards the bus station; there was a closed petrol station on the right. The lights lit up a large mound of grassed area about twenty feet long to their left. Several trees had been planted there and helped to conceal part of the bus station. The large metal poled fence ran along the foot path and down the road leading away from the town, broken only by the entrance. The car stopped here and the two of them got out; they both were now silent as the moved through the open gates and into the darkness of the unlit park.

Tony had noted the time they arrived; it was just before three and the only light they had was that of the moon. The row of parked buses, nearly 40 metres away, were in shadow. To their left was a covered bus shelter with a small building that housed the station offices behind the parked buses.

Tony stopped.

Kyle stopped less than a second later. Whatever Tony could see he could not, but he knew he would have stopped for a reason. Tony slowly moved across the front of Kyle. It wasn't until he had passed him that Kyle spotted Tony's hand on his Glock Pistol, holstered on the right-hand side of his gun belt. Kyle's hand was on his as well as he stepped off to the right, enlarging the space between them. Something wasn't right here, he could feel it. His eyes searched the darkness as the two of them moved towards the shelter. He tried to pierce the darkness, but his eyes could only make out the basic shapes. They took another couple of steps before Tony stopped again; they had been in total silence up to this point. Kyle scanned the area around him. Something was lying inside the shelter, but he could not tell what it was. Tony murmured something. Kyle watched as Tony pulled out his black metal torch, pointed it towards the shelter and switched it on. The light cut through the darkness and lit up what was in front of them. Tony moved the beam around the inside of the shelter as the beam of Kyle's torch joined it.

They stepped closer towards the shelter where a body was lying on its right side and faced into the shelter. There was blood dripping from the walls. Kyle dropped the beam and found an arm lying on the ground. They both stopped where they were, Tony spoke.

"Kyle, do not step forward," he spoke quietly. Kyle dropped the beam of light to his feet and found the head lying face up and staring at the stars. The face was that of a young male. His mouth was open with large cuts and lacerations running across the left side of his face. The neck was a mess of loose ends and bits of flesh and a large piece of white bone that he recognised as part of the spine. The two beams of light scanned the area, picking up other bits of bodies; a leg, part of a chest; they had been ripped apart by something. Kyle swore under his breath at what he was looking at...MOVEMENT

The movement had been off to the right in the darkness and a sound had accompanied it. Both police officers had drawn their pistols and spun round to meet whatever was there. Tony moved off to Kyle's left, pointing the torch and his pistol in the same direction as Kyle now found himself moving. Kyle held the torch in his left hand but stretched his left arm out, away from his body. The pistol was firm in his right hand and was an extension of his right arm that guided his body, slowly and quietly into the darkness.

"*POLICE OFFICERS, LAY DOWN YOUR WEAPON AND STEP FORWARD,*" Kyle shouted, he could not see Tony, but he knew he was flanking to his left. He moved between the scattered body parts. Kyle repeated his warning as the torch searched for the sound. There was something right in front of them that sounded like something splashing gently in a small amount of water. Tony appeared without making a sound a few feet away from him. MOVEMENT

Both torches twisted towards were it came from at the base of a tree; Kyle dropped to one knee and brought the pistol up to his line of sight, ready to fire. The German Shepherd dog turned its head towards them, the lights caused its eyes to flash. There was blood all around its mouth as it continued eating the raw meat that it had found on the floor. Kyle relaxed as Tony jumped forward and scared the dog away with a shout and waving one of his arms. The dog ran a few feet then stopped and turned towards them again. Kyle stood up, turned around and surveyed the scene around his feet as the dog started to pace up and down. A light came on above the shop across the road. Kyle replaced his pistol in the black leather holster, fastening the clip that held the weapon in place. As he approached the shelter, he could hear Tony speak towards the body.

"Sir, can you hear me? Sir? Police officers..." Kyle was careful with the placement of his feet as they were now right in the middle of a major crime scene. Tony had turned the body of the old man onto his back. He had seen enough dead bodies to know that is what this was. The torch lit up the old face caked in blood. Tony looked at Kyle.

"Better call the duty sergeant and the duty inspector..." Kyle was already reaching for the radio on his belt.

"Lima delta, Lima Delta Seven Three," he released the button on the side of the black plastic handheld radio.

"Lima Delta send..." Kyle looked at the watch on his right wrist, it was ten past three in the morning and they were not going to get any sleep tonight.

"Lima Delta Seven Three, request duty India and duty sergeant to our location over," Hearing that, every police officer on duty in the Limavady District Command Unit turned up their radios as they now had something to listen to.

Chapter 3

The river bank, Coleraine:

"So, what do you think of Coleraine, Davidov?" The question brought him back to where he was. Anders approached and sat beside him on the black metal bench. Davidov looked around him.

"Ha, seen worse," Anders smiled. The two of them were seated on one of four benches that surrounded six triangular wooden flower beds forming a circular pattern around a singular tree in the centre. The black tar macadam formed the path way around the beds and off towards the main pathway that ran along the bank. The river flowed from the far side making its way towards the bridge on his left. Cars moved along behind them on the main road. A small hatchback coughed and shuddered as it made its way, slowly leading the row of cars behind it. The old church with its graveyard sat directly behind them. Each house had a raised concrete wall which was filled with small gardens that only measured a few feet across; the road at one time had obviously been higher.

"So, what do you make of the nice little houses he found for us then?" There was a hint of sarcasm in his voice. They had two of the houses to share between them all and Alexi had paid cash for them. The transactions had only taken place a few days before they all moved in just over a week ago.

"I still don't see why we left,"

"What? Belfast, I don't either. He was making too much of it," answered Anders,

Davidov looked at him. "No, not Belfast. *Home.*" Shouts from the river diverted his gaze to the four rowers in a long thin boat being given orders by a small man in a red jacket who sat at the end facing them. They were moving quite quickly, but obviously not quickly enough. Soon they were under the bridge and gone. His eyes came back along the far river bank, where a group of bushy green trees were stopped by a two-storey building that had a veranda around the upper floor. The bottom floor was plain red brick, but the first floor was painted a cream colour and lined in red. There was a set of concrete steps that led down into the water and he could see two men man launching a thin rowing boat into the water. The building was a Chinese restaurant, and a nice restaurant at that. They had been there for a meal the previous night. The evening had been good humoured, but they noticed that there were only a couple of Chinese who spoke English with a local accent, and most of the waiting staff were Polish. It was evident there was a large Polish community in Coleraine; that was something he could use to his advantage.

A dog barked; both stared at the small Jack Russell that was standing by the lamp post barking at them. It wasn't barking at anyone else, just at them. A teenager on a bike just missed the dog as he flew past, but the dog kept barking.

"Looks like we have strayed into someone else's patch; don't think he likes it much!" said Anders. They looked at each other.

"We 'are' in someone else's patch, and that could be a problem we may have to solve by ourselves," Anders straightened up.

"Do you think they know we are here? We would already know if someone strayed into ours without asking." The little dog kept barking as the grandmother came up and shouted at it to be quiet. She could tell the dog was barking at the two men who were sitting on the bench. She shouted again and went to grab the dog; it's barking increased in intensity. She had heard them talking and knew they were foreigners, Polish by the sound of them; she heard the way they said *"BEIL – FAST"* and *"Cal- ran"*. They were everywhere these days; they had poster displays just in Polish. In this country, they should speak our language; she had spoken her thoughts to others on several occasions and been told to keep her opinions to herself. The dog jumped forward at them, continuously barking.

Then to her surprise the one on the right, sat forward, pointed towards the dog with his hand and aggressively barked a word. Her Jack Russell suddenly stopped barking, retreated behind her and hid behind the flower bed. The dog was shaking, as the two men started smiling; one spoke, and they both half laughed. She felt fear towards them for the first time. These people were dangerous. Quietly she moved back to where the dog was hiding, blessed the dog with words of comfort, picked it up and walked away from them, not looking back. They watched as she walked slowly away with the dog in her arms.

"We will make this land *our own*," said Davidov,

"That is not what *our Alpha* has in mind," Anders replied, "in fact, we can thank our glorious Alpha for moving us from our homes to this wonderful, sunny place." He looked up at the cold grey clouds, the sun had been out earlier but none of them had ever been to a place where it rained so often. Was this why it was called the Emerald Isle? The land was green, but with so much rain it had to be.

"Our Glorious Alpha," Davidov repeated. He sat back deep in his own thoughts. Anders said something else that he missed but reacted when his phone beeped. He read the message, typed a short reply and returned the phone to his pocket.

"Who was that?" asked Anders. Davidov turned to him and asked him a simple question.

"Shall we go into town and get a cup of coffee?" Anders knew that he was being taken somewhere to do something, but exactly what he was not sure. What was he up to? Hopefully he would find out soon enough. They stood up and walked towards the stone bridge and into the town of Coleraine.

∞∞∞∞

Davidov sat down on the wooden chair in the coffee shop; there were three chairs around the small wooden table which was pushed against the wall. The large window was to his left, but it stopped at the table and the light green painted wall continued in front of him. The large coffee bar was now to his right with two attendants serving the other customers who were waiting; this was partially blocked by the back of a stand that offered packages of ground coffee and other foods for sale. He looked straight ahead at the glass double door entrance which was supported by a brown painted metal frame the same colour as the roof. Between there and where he was seated were several tables occupied by various people. He turned to look over his shoulder and looked around. From his table he could see Anders standing at the far side of the street.

Davidov's eyes scanned every person, every face, and every movement; he sat back and drank from the large white mug, the froth on top giving way to the hot fluid beneath. He sipped at it as he turned his head and looked out the window. He looked at the wall of the three-storey building across the narrow street, the occupant having tried to brighten it by painting the wall a light colour and the trims a much darker one. His eyes read the graffiti on the wall, pasted on the windows were billboard posters advertising a visiting circus; he looked up at the street name. 'SOCIETY STREET' he wondered how they decided on that. People walked past, he could not see into the main street from where he was sitting. He tasted his coffee again and continued to wait. A woman who looked in her late eighties slowly manoeuvred herself into a chair at the table beside him then took her seat before making slow movements to lift the coffee mug to her lips. The door opened,

"at last," Davidov said quietly as he stood up to identify himself.

∞∞∞∞

At the far side of the busy main street Anders was people watching, his head turned as his attention became transfixed on the two uniformed police officers that were walking slowly through the crowd up the street. His nose twitched, he stared straight at them. At least one of them was a threat. He would have no problem remembering both.

∞∞∞∞

Kyle walked past the green entrance to the bookshop and looked over his right shoulder into it and cast a glance along the line of shoppers waiting at the two busy tills. Tony suddenly stopped in front of him. He was staring down the street, he sensed something was happening. His friend had an additional sense that had fore-warned them of trouble before. It always fascinated him, and he was in some ways jealous of this skill; it was something he could have used many times in his past.

"What?" he quietly asked. Tony had started to walk slowly forward through the passing crowd. "Tony?" Tony half turned towards him.

"Mmmph??" was the noise he made.

"What is it?" He side-stepped a mother with a young child in her arms rushing out of the book shop. Tony didn't reply and walked on. Kyle moved up beside him looking around at the people moving back and forth; he knew something was amiss and this was not the place to discuss it. He could not see any 'local' faces who they had to look for, so he continued the foot patrol with his friend, but this had heightened his own alertness as to what and who was in the street.

"Not sure," Tony said suddenly as they got to the end of the street, "Not sure at all..."

∞∞∞∞

He placed the handset down on top of the body of the old phone and turned to face the room that was mostly full of people, all waiting for him to speak. He looked directly at the older man that was sat in the chair.

"Yes, it's true, they are here and hiding amongst the Polish somewhere in the North West; somewhere around Portrush, Portstewart or Coleraine."

"And they *are* who we think they are?" the older one asked,

"Yes, they are," all heads turned towards the chair which was pushed against the wall of the living room in the farmhouse. He paused, "Then I want them found," he paused again, "Then we will deal with them," they looked at each other in silence, a smile broke over one face.

Chapter 4

Cara-Marie Mc Kenna had enjoyed her 26th birthday; she looked at the face of her watch as she walked towards her car. Her mind flashed over the memory of the birthday which had been a week ago. She had a birthday meal at her parents with her sister, her sister's husband and kids and her brother with his family. They had gathered together for four o'clock in the afternoon and shared a meal and birthday cake before she headed to a pub in Portrush with two of her friends. She was the baby of the family, being four years younger than her brother, and was the only one not married, which was something her mother kept harping about. Her mother married her father when she was 18 and anytime she had dated for any length of time the comments about settling down would start again. Her dad was normally quiet on the matter only ever saying that it was her choice and not that of her mother. Her mother had always hoped her daughter would leave university with a degree in criminology and a husband. Well, she got it half right.

Her three-door hatchback rolled out of the driveway and onto the not too busy road as she headed into work; she flicked the CD player on and selected a recently purchased CD. The drive from her home in Portstewart to Coleraine did not take long. She enjoyed her independence, her own house, her own car and her chosen career. She started working for the Coleraine Herald two years prior; it was the smaller of two local papers to Coleraine. She had spent six months at the other paper but left as she hated it. All her assignments there seemed to cover old folk's homes and flower competitions. This job allowed her to be the investigative journalist she had always wanted to be, and some of the perks were not bad either! The amount of traffic increased as she got closer towards Coleraine. She made her way into the car park in front of the Tesco's superstore. She walked through the automatic doors and past the uniformed security guard who stood near the door. He nodded in recognition; she answered with a nod. She had published a story about a family day at one of the local schools and had used a photograph of him with his son. He always referred to how good the picture was. Such was the joy of working in a local paper.

She filled out the numbers on the lotto chit; she kept it secret how she made her choice of numbers. She placed the ticket and the receipt in her pocket and walked out the door, she would leave her car there until lunchtime and if one of the security staff approached her she had a receipt to say she had shopped there that day. Cara-Marie ran across the road, jumped through the traffic and walked the short distance into the main office of the Coleraine Herald. The office was buzzing. Something big had happened. She did not even reach her desk before the editor stopped her., He had that look on his face that whatever it was, it was a big one.

"Mornin' Cara," he never used her full name of Cara-Marie. He didn't give her a chance to answer, "Right, forget what you were doing. I want you to get up to Limavady and get onto what happened there; just found out that one of them was from Coleraine." Cara-Marie's face was blank, "You do know what happened there last night?" she half closed her eyes as she answered with a simple 'no.' The phone on the desk that belonged to one of their photographers rang. As he picked it up he spoke out loud,

"Some journalist you are," he was grinning as he spoke into the phone, "Coleraine Herald." She cast him a look with an angry grin. Their desks faced each other and the banter between them was always good humoured. Her attention returned to the editor, her right hand already fumbling in her pocket for her phone; it was off.

"Triple murder in Limavady, down by the bus station," her eyebrows raised at the news, no wonder the office was busy, "One of the dead is from here. I want full coverage on this, we got two of the names from the police press office half an hour ago, the other has not been officially named yet." She glanced up at the clock on the wall, she wasn't late for work. "I got two phone calls last night, one from a copper we know and another from a friend of mine down in Limavady, M.I.T. out of Maydown handling the investigation," M.I.T. The Murder Investigation Team, she had never had to deal with them before as Maydown police station is closer to Derry than

Coleraine and murder was not something which happened at lot around here. They had deaths, of course, traffic accidents, house fires, old age etc but not too many murders. Coleraine as a growing town had missed most of the troubles that had plagued their little country over the last thirty years and the occasion when the town centre was bombed was not the norm, unlike Belfast. This was something that all the office staff had once agreed was a very good thing. The team was a mix of both Protestant and Catholic but that had never been an issue amongst them. It was a subject that the editor never brought up, but he would normally send a journalist of the same faith to the family of someone who was dead. The phone on the editor's desk burst into life, he turned and walked towards it, his head turned and spoke to Mark the photographer, "Mark, bring Cara up to speed with the rest," Cara-Marie turned and sat down at her desk, Mark had finished his phone call, and was his usual cheerful self.

"*Morning,*" the grin spread over his face. Cara-Marie slightly turned her head to one side, pushed her lips together in a sarcastic grin in reply as she removed her jacket and placed it over her chair. "Well what a night I've had." They both relaxed as he shuffled through the pictures that were on his screen. He had printed some of them and handed them over towards her as he started in his official tone. "Three dead, two completely torn apart, just managed to ID them, the families *haven't* been told yet." She looked up at him then returned to the eight by ten-inch photographs. The first couple was of an older man who was lying on one side. She was not sure if she recognised him; her eyes widened at the ones underneath, her mouth slightly opened, and her eyes dilated at the images in front of her. Mark continued, "They were found by two coppers from Coleraine," Mark was now reading off a note pad, "Michael Watson, 20 from 102 Koolessan Walk, Limavady and Liam Paul Arthur, 20". Cara-Marie looked up at the name, "Riverside Walk, Coleraine." Her heart sank, as did her face. Mark lifted his gaze, "What?" he asked.

"Went to school with his elder sister," she replied, as another head was raised from the other side of the office. Cara-Marie stated she had met the elder brother once but did not know him very well. The editor approached their desks, addressing Cara-Marie.

"Right, still no ID on the third one yet, Cara, you know some of the family of Arthur's?" She nodded, "Get on to them; see if you can get a recent picture of him, one of them together would be better. I am interested in statements from family and friends, next door neighbour's etc," He was relating the action they would normally take, over a serious event like this. "Cara, find out the clergy who is involved. I want details of the funeral." His gaze moved around then returned to her, "Speak to the cops as to what happened and where; find out if they are considering a motive or paramilitary links." Mark and Cara-Marie looked at each other; 'Paramilitary links?' was not a normal one, "Plus, details of any arrests and speak to anyone who was in the area. Find out what they heard. I will keep in contact with the police higher up." He paused, "Any questions?" Cara-Marie spoke before Mark could.

"Could this be linked to that murder in Belfast two weeks ago; he was torn up as well?" the editor paused as he thought.

"*MMM,* just in case, yes, see what you can discover." With that he turned and walked away. Both Cara-Marie and Mark stood up at the same time. They agreed to speak later over the phone as they walked towards different exits of the small office. Time was of the essence as the other newspaper in Coleraine would also be after the scoop. For the first time in a while Cara-Marie walked with a spring in her step. She pulled the phone out of her pocket as she put the jacket on. Her left hand brought the brown leather handbag up on to her left shoulder as her right hand scrolled down through the numbers. She stopped at one and pressed the green dial button, pressed the phone to her ear as she crossed the road and into the car park.

"Hello," the female voice was quiet and subdued.

"Roisin? Hiya this is Cara-Marie,"

"Oh, hi, Cara,"

"I am so sorry to hear about Liam," the voice at the other end sniffled and muffled out a thank you, "May I call round?"

∞∞∞∞∞

Half an hour later in Belfast, Sean climbed out of his car, which beeped as he walked away from it towards the main building of the police station. He walked in through the entrance and glanced at the framed picture on the wall. It was a memorial to the 303 police officers who had been killed during the Troubles; his eyes picked out those he had known, scanned the dates of their deaths and sighed as he started up the stairs. He walked through the main office of Belfast M.I.T, most of the desks were already occupied by junior detectives, the unlocked door to his office moved aside to allow him to enter. The main office light flicked on as he pushed the switch down with his right hand, bent down to the small table and flicked on the coffee machine with his left. He walked around the desk and activated the police net PC that occupied the centre of his desk. It wasn't long before his login was accepted, and the first coffee of the day started to pass his lips. The door was filled by Mike Dear in a pale striped shirt and a plain tie.

"Morning Boss," he had a case file in his hands.

"Morning Mike," he answered, the mug returned to his lips. Mike started down a list of tasks that had been completed by the team since he had left yesterday. "Everyone here?" he asked as Mike finished.

"Yes, want to go for the morning brief?"

"Sure," he answered as he swung round and stood up. Mike left and loudly announced to the rest of the team to pay attention as he walked over toward the large white board at the far end of the long room. Sean refilled his mug, walked out and sat on the small chair beside Mike's desk. The other members of the team sat around their own desks, Mike started with a briefing of everything that had happened in the Belfast District Command Unit over the last 24 hours. In other M.I.T.s the inspector gave the morning briefing, but Sean had always been keen on giving the sergeants the experience of doing it, so much so, that it had been quite a while since he had done it himself. His team was coming along. Mike was giving updates on their own caseloads.

"We got an answer back in the Henderson case......" He paused and glanced at his notebook before continuing "And from forensics," he paused again, "They can 'confirm' a match and can place him at the scene of crime." A mild applause rippled around the room. Sean smiled as he took another mouthful of coffee.

"Questions?" Mike asked. Sean spoke up.

"What is the latest on the Trotman case?" Mike looked down at his notebook, flicked a few pages then answered.

"The DNA trace was corrupted so nothing there, the pathologist was able to put *MOST* of what was left together." Sean noticed some of the team had straightened up, passing glances between each other. "And his family didn't want to know."

"Pardon?" Sean stated,

"The family didn't want to know. Manchester police nearly wet themselves laughing when I spoke to them. I think they were going to have a party over it,"

"Yeah, I'm not surprised! *REAL NICE* guy," one of the younger members spoke up.

"Seemed they had nearly twenty sexual assaults they suspected him of, but they could not gather enough evidence to put him in court." finished Mike.

"So, what are we doing? How come the DNA was corrupted?" Mike looked across at Simon who sat forward at his desk as he answered.

"The shopkeeper who found the body was walking his dogs and forensics said there was canine DNA all over the place." Simon looked around the room and finished by fixing his eyes on Sean as he continued, "We got the CCTV footage from The Bott and the shop and the young woman that he was following never came forward and hasn't been seen since," he looked back at Mike, who finished the sentence,

"And still no suspects,"

"Paramilitaries?" Sean asked

"No Boss, definitely not from both sides,"

"Is that confirmed?"

"Yes Boss, confirmed through Special Branch," Sean took a deep breath in before finishing off his coffee, as he placed the mug on the desk Mike spoke.

"So, what are your thoughts Boss?" Sean stood up.

"Right we need to find this lass, so I want copies of the CCTV, a photo fit with description from the doormen and bar staff,"

"Already done, none of them remember her. From the time scale for her entering and leaving she walked in, was in for less than seven minutes, Trotman entered and left after her." Mike paused, "The pics and CCTV I have already got."

"Good," said Sean "We will take this a step up and do a 'crime watch' programme. I'll organize it" The team looked at each other. It was not often that a team would use crime watch, well not unless they had absolutely nothing, and it looked like they had absolutely nothing.

"Boss, did you hear about the killings up in Limavady last night?" All eyes turned towards the newest member of the team who asked the question.

"No," Sean turned towards him, the silence hung in the air with everyone looking straight at him as the seconds ticked by. Sean spoke again "Well, do not keep me in suspense, what killings?"

"Well, three people were killed in Limavady last night; apparently they were torn apart by dogs," Mike and Sean shared a glance. "The bodies were shredded over the bus station, bits everywhere." Sean shrugged. The last thing that they wanted or needed was a serial killer roaming the country tearing people asunder. The look in Mike's eyes said the same thing, Sean spoke to the young detective,

"Right, no problems, speak to M.I.T Maydown and see if there are any similarities between their case and ours! In the meantime, let's keep on with ours. Mike, you know the rest." Mike nodded as Sean walked back into his office, sat down behind his desk and picked up the phone. He flicked though the small notebook that never left his desk and he tapped in a number. The voice which answered was a young female with a country accent.

"Press office, Ms Anderson," Sean introduced himself by rank, name and department. The young woman replied with a simple, "Sir," then he stated what his plans were. He replaced the phone, walked around to the coffee machine and refilled it, just as he finished the phone rang. He picked it up and gave his professional telephone answer. "Sir, Ms Anderson, press office." He acknowledged her, and he was somewhat surprised to hear from her so soon, "We have a date for you sir,"

"That was quick," he said out loud.

She answered him as if she was expecting the comment.

"Well Sir, they had a cancellation from another service and needed to fill the gap."

"Just goes to show that some things are just meant to be Ms Anderson."

"That they are sir, that they are," he replaced the handset and shouted towards Mike and Simon, both walked in but didn't sit down. Sean told them the time scale of what was happening.

Chapter 5

The wheels of the plane hit the runway at Belfast City Airport, the cabin crew welcomed the passengers to Belfast. They soon walked off the aircraft and out into the cold Irish wind. Neither of them had ever been to Ireland before, neither North or South, they did not fully understand the border between the two nor did they care, as long as it would not affect their business. All the passengers were guided towards baggage reclaim, they stood in silence and waited for the baggage to arrive. They looked around at those congregated around the conveyor belt, both quickly identified the plain clothed police officers who were visible on one side. The baggage started to arrive on the conveyer belt, they were all shapes, sizes and some matching. A large rucksack probably that of a hill walker, a folded-up pram, and then the large plain holdall grip for which they were waiting. One of them moved forward and lifted it, without speaking they walked towards the exit. The glass paned automatic doors opened, they were almost the last to leave, when off to one side three people attracted their attention. The older man who had been in the chair at the farm house walked towards them, he was flanked by two more men who were younger than he was, but both appeared to be in their mid-forties. They stopped about five feet away; the older man bowed his head towards the two men, but he did not offer his hand.

"Welcome," he was answered with a nod.

The older man stepped back, extended his right arm towards the exit doors, and continued, "Please, if you'll follow me," he turned and walked towards the door with the two men following. The two men who were with him followed several feet behind. They walked outside and paused as the large Mercedes car pulled up. The older man opened the rear door and the two men climbed in. The holdall was placed in the boot of the car and once the old man climbed into the front they slowly moved off. The second car would follow close behind, it did not take long before the cars were out of the city and off up a motorway. One of the visitors spoke, his accent, very Russian, was a thick and heavy one.

"How long will journey take?"

"Half an hour at the most,"

There was a pause before the Russian spoke again." Are you sure it is them?"

The older man turned to face him. "Yes," the two men in the back of the car looked at each other before the other one spoke. "What have they done?" His accent was as thick and heavy as the first.

The older man answered. "They killed a sapien in Belfast and we think they killed two more in a town in the north-west yesterday."

"The sapiens?" he paused for a few seconds "what do they know about us?"

"Very little, we follow our laws," the older man stated.

"That is good, it has been a long time since there has been a problem from the green land," The car moved out into the fast lane and accelerated past another car, the second car kept close behind as they turned off the motorway and headed out into the green countryside. "When is your next moon dance?" The Russian asked.

"Tomorrow night."

"How large is 'The Northern Den'?"

"Forty full Garou," the old man smiled as he answered.

"And the Rua as a clan?"

The older man rested his head on the head rest of the very comfortable car before he answered. "Over three hundred Garou,"

"Have they been informed of our arrival?"

"Yes of course, you are guests there on Friday night. We will escort you down there for the feast, any requests you have will be attended to," the older man did not have to say the last part of the sentence as that would be taken for granted. The two men in the back sat in silence as the journey continued.

Soon the cars slowed and turned right into a country lane that could '*just*' fit two cars going either way. The lane went on for nearly half a mile, at the end was a country farm; the main building was two stories with the out houses being single story. The walls of the buildings were hand-built and looked like they had been painted recently. There were two large corrugated metalled barns, one painted dark green and the other a dark red. There were several neatly dressed people standing around who all reacted to the arrival of the cars. The Russians looked over the faces of those who surrounded the vehicle. The car stopped by the door of the main farmhouse. The door opened for them and as they stepped out those that were there slightly bowed their heads. The Russians acknowledged this as the older man guided them into the building. They walked through the door and into what was the living room; the open fireplace and the logs were burning brightly. The high chaired furniture was a dark emerald green material that would be very comfortable. The chair that the old man normally sat on was offered to one of the Russians, the other sat on the two-seat sofa that directly faced the fire. The small wooden table was bare and sat in between the sofa and two chairs; one being bigger than the other with the fireplace central to the entire room. There was another plain wooden door which was shut at the far side of the room. The room had been empty until they walked in and several of the men who had been outside joined them. A phone in one of their pockets bleeped and all heads turned, a red face fumbled in a pocket for the phone, the text message was read then the phone returned to the pocket. The Russians spoke to each other very briefly in their own language, the old man knew it was not for his ears. The Russian who was in the chair turned towards the older man, he was invited to sit, and he chose the smaller chair.

"Well, Godspodine O'Brien..." said the one who was on the sofa but the second one sat forward and spoke in English,

"Ha, in this country they say 'MISTER' not Godspodine!" He was half smiling as he spoke then nodded to the older man. The first one spoke again, restarting what he was saying, "Sorry, Mister O'Brien... about your visitors, tell me what you know," Carl O'Brien sat forward before he began.

"Just over two weeks ago a sapien was killed in Belfast; he was seen following a woman that has not been identified and was discovered the following morning by a shopkeeper walking his dogs,"

"Definitely not one of yours??" The first Russian asked.

"DEFINITELY NOT! Hunt as a pack or not at all," Carl repeated the law, "we had Garou in Belfast that night but nowhere near there."

"What were they doing in Belfast?" asked the one sitting on the sofa.

"Observing the Noctrailis," both the Russians raised their eyebrows, shared a look and returned their attention to their host. "The truce still holds here and has not been broken since the war." Carl had observed the reaction of the Russians, "We observe each other...."

"How strong is their coven?" asked the Russian on the sofa.

"Weak, less than ten in total, no threat and their feeding is controlled!"

"Tell us more about your visitors, where are they now?" asked the Russian in the chair, "Are they still in Belfast?"

"No," he said, "we believe their Alpha moved them near to a town called 'Coleraine', obviously trying to hide.'"

"Then it should be easy to find them," said the second Russian.

"We believe they are hiding among the Polish community living around there."

"Polish?" said the Russian on the sofa, they looked at each other again, "We did not know you had Polish here." he said.

"Yes, we have quite a few from Eastern Europe, Estonians, Latvians, Bulgarians, but the highest numbers are Polish," said Carl. Both the Russians spoke in their own language again, something was agreed then the one on the sofa spoke.

"Have you had any trouble with any of them?"

"Nothing involving us," with that the old-style phone in the corner rang. Carl looked at one of the others and motioned with his head towards the phone. He moved over and picked up the phone. He said hello into it and listened for a few seconds before turning towards Carl.

"It is for you," he said quietly towards Carl, "it is from the south," Carl stood up, walked over and took the phone; the silence in the room seemed to be thunderous until he spoke.

"Yes, no problem, seven pm," he replaced the handset and turned to the Russians. "My Alpha is looking forward to receiving you, Friday at seven."

"Friday at seven," repeated the one in the chair; the smiles that spread across the room started with the Russian on the chair.

ထာထာထ

Kyle turned the key in the metal locker in the changing room of the police station in Coleraine. The small door creaked open and he reached in and lifted out his police uniform and hung it on the top of his locker. As he was changing two more officers came in; it was shift change over. He didn't see Tony walk in but felt the friendly dig in his side as he pulled the door of the locker open; his head turned, and his face relaxed in recognition of his friend. The main topic of discussion among them was the triple murder, rumours were rife as to what was happening. Several of them would speak to both Kyle and Tony individually and come to their own conclusions. Both had written their shift reports about their findings the two nights previous. But the main scandal was that the police in Limavady were livid that it was two coppers from Coleraine that had found the bodies while in Limavady covering their shifts. They all filed downstairs and into the briefing room; this was a square room with chairs lined against the 3 walls facing a wooden desk with a chair behind it that was in the middle of the room. As he entered Kyle glanced at the glass cabinet with Polaroid photos contained inside; each listed details of people of 'Interest' to the police. Gone were the days when these would be suspected terrorists: now they were those in organised crime, drug dealing and sex offenders. Kyle scanned the same one every time, a drug dealer who lived in Portrush. Kyle took a seat as Tony sat down beside him; the other seats were filled with the rest of the day shift. The chatter died down when the duty inspector walked in followed by both section sergeants; the door was closed behind them. The inspector sat in the chair behind the desk and opened the hard backed A4 notebook that he always seemed to carry as he started the morning brief. The officers sat and listened to what had been happening during the night, concentrating on the murders in Limavady. Two of the shifts were tasked to go to Limavady to help with site security, others giggled, comments were made. The lucky two would be stationed at a cordon for most of the day and would be very bored. The inspector advised as to how officers should talk to the press. Since the murder was national news, various news channels had been at the site with journalists from most of the national and local newspapers.

"Some are already making connections to the killing in Belfast two weeks ago so nothing from any of you, *ESPECIALLY* to the press." More comments flowed; the inspector continued with his briefing. Belfast M.I.T. was taking the lead in the investigation. Kyle and Tony were paired off for foot patrol around the town, second day in a row. Once everyone knew their duties the briefing finished. Those who were in the station went to take over their desks and let those who were there head home. Kyle and Tony walked back up to their section office and just as they walked in one of the phones rang on the far desk. A police officer answered it; he looked round at Kyle.

"Yes, in fact he has just walked in," he sat back and held the handset towards Kyle, "Kyle, for you," his attention returned to his desk, Kyle stepped forward and reached for the phone.

"Who is it?" he asked.

"Some chick," Kyle took the phone and introduced himself.

"Morning," It was a female voice, "Cara-Marie McKenna, Coleraine Herald," she introduced herself, she very quickly got onto the subject relevant and wanted to speak to both him and Tony. His first reaction was to point her towards the press office for official comment, she had already been in touch with them and they had given her his name. He took down a number from

28

her then phoned the press office who stated they could meet up with her. They had talked through the current protocol for talking to the press and some of the 'Do's and Don'ts'. He never liked talking to the press, but it wasn't looking like he could get out of this one. He tapped in the number of the landline phone she had given him, she answered with a simple 'Coleraine Herald'. He identified himself and said that meeting up would not be a problem. He organised a time and she suggested one of the coffee shops for the meeting; she said it would only take half an hour.

"Oh, free coffee." said Tony after Kyle put the phone down.

"Mmm, she sounds nice too," said Kyle out loud. This got an instant response from the other coppers who were in the room, it was mostly abuse. Cara-Marie McKenna had either spoken or interviewed most of them, but not Kyle. "Isn't she the one with black hair?" he asked.

"Yeah and big pointy teeth too," said another,

"Watch yourself, she bites," Tony half turned his head and smiled at the comment as the two of them put on their padded outdoor jackets, then secured their gun belts around their waists. Just as they were leaving the voice of the eldest of them called his name.

"*KYLE,*" both Kyle and Tony stopped at the door and turned towards the most experienced police officer, who was in the corner. He was in his last year before retirement; thirty years as a police officer in Northern Ireland was certainly an achievement. The entire room stopped to listen to the quiet man who always had good advice to steer the younger officers in the right direction. "Watch what you say, everything can be taken out of context," both of them nodded and headed down the corridor towards the stairs. Kyle noticed that Tony seemed happier today than yesterday.

"So, what's got you so pleased?"

Tony looked at him and tried to suppress his grin as they walked down the stairs.

"*WHAT?*" he shrugged as they passed the double doors at the bottom, another copper was walking in as they were walking out.

"What indeed," Kyle paused, then turned towards him again, "So, you finally got some last night," Tony tapped Kyle's shoulder with a fist, "Hey, I'm married."

"My point exactly," retorted Kyle.

"Besides," said Tony, "It has been a full moon over the last three nights."

"Yeah and look what happened on the first one of those," Kyle did not notice Tony's reaction to his comment but did notice how he turned the conversation around.

"So, I take it from your obvious jealousy you are *still* single then,"

"Ha, bloody Ha," they waved at the police officer who was sitting in the front gatehouse, their wave was returned, and a buzz sounded as the two of them walked out of the police station, turned left and started their foot patrol around the town of Coleraine. For two hours they walked around the areas of the town centre that the duty inspector had instructed them to cover, stopping to talk to some locals they knew, some of the older ones just glad of a chat, most talking about what had happened in Limavady. One pensioner started telling them about the war, fighting in North Africa, seeing men torn apart by mortar and artillery fire. He went on his way slowly hobbling along, silent with his memories and the blackthorn walking stick, the only outward sign of his former regiment that the old soldier carried that still tied him to the memory of his friends. Most of who still patrolled the desert looking for Rommel's Africa Korps.

Kyle always spoke to the older ones; he had been brought up listening to stories from members of his family and friends, stories about the Irish civil war, the Free State, fighting both with and against Michael Collins. The tales of heroism had captured the young boy's imagination and gave him a love that would never leave him, even though now he had his own stories, some of them, however, would never be told. They walked on, they spoke to a shopkeeper who was outside his shop, the talk was still the same, the events in Limavady, very few people knew of their involvement in it and they were keen to keep it that way. They walked on past Tesco's along the riverbank past the Chinese restaurant and up to the traffic lights. Traffic was moving freely back and forth over the river Bann, they turned right into the pedestrian precinct in the centre of the town. The two of them walked side by side, they turned right into the entrance of the Diamond Centre shopping mall. The amount of people increased in and around the shops as they walked up the main concourse. They stopped at the top and Tony engaged in a conversation as Kyle walked up to the glass ice cream counter; he looked over the flavour of ice creams on display. They continued walking, as they went back towards the entrance a young woman with thick black hair walked around the corner, Tony straightened up, she reacted as if she had just walked into a wall. Her dark eyes widened, she stepped back looked at the two of them then walked on, not speaking.

"Do you know her?" Kyle asked as he stepped out into the sunlight,

"No," Tony was looking back at the direction she had gone, "No, I don't." He turned back and walked out into the street following Kyle. Kyle sensed that something was amiss.

"What is it then?"

"Nothing, what time is the coffee?" Tony's change of subject was as blunt, Kyle looked at his watch.

"Ten minutes."

Chapter 6

The door of the coffee shop, at the bottom end of Long Commons opened, and Kyle walked in followed by Tony, they removed their hats as they entered. They joined the end of the queue of people waiting to be served, shuffling slowly along. The young team who worked in the very brown coloured coffee shop had reason to be busy; Tony nodded at the owner who was stood overlooking the goings on behind the counter. Kyle ordered a latte and Tony a cappuccino then they walked up the stairs to the seating area. The room opened to the right with two small washrooms to the left, around the windows were leather sofas with small dark brown wooden tables in between them, the centre of the room was filled with tall chairs and tables, and it was quite empty, unusually so. Kyle had never seen it this empty. They chose the farthest window to sit beside so they could watch out the window at the comings and goings of people at the crossing, Kyle looked at his watch again,

"She is late,"

"She is a woman, of course she is late," Kyle looked up at the smiling face in front of him, "You would know this if you were married."

"Just because I am single does not mean that I'm not busy," Kyle fired back, they sniggered as both turned their heads towards the woman who had just walked in. Her hair wasn't brown, it was black, like her eyes and she was walking straight towards then with a handbag over her left shoulder and a notebook in her right hand, very confident. Both stood as she swapped the notebook into her left and extended her right hand in greeting.

"Cara-Marie Mc Kenna, Coleraine Herald." She had a firm grip and Kyle wasn't sure if the smile was real or not, she did not have a coffee so Kyle offered her one as they all sat down. She paused, looked at Tony then accepted a Vanilla Latte. Kyle walked across the room then down the stairs and joined the end of the queue, he shuffled along then ordered the latte.

"Oh, this is for Cara-Marie then," said the attendant who served him.

"One day she will buy her own," said another, Kyle smiled, funny... he thought it was a journalist's job to butter up the interviewee before trying to put words in their mouths.

"How did you know it is for her?" Kyle asked, the attendant was busying himself with the preparation of the drink.

"Spotted her walking in and that is what she always orders when someone else is paying." Kyle slightly shook his head and grinned at the attendant who placed the drink in front of him. Kyle paid for the drink and returned upstairs. Tony and Cara-Marie both looked in his direction as he placed the tall glass coffee cup on the table in front of Cara-Marie, they were both smiling.

"Thank you," she said as she reached for the mug,

"What?" asked Kyle.

"We were just reminiscing,"

"Reminiscing?" Kyle recounted, Cara-Marie sipped at the latte and let a small grin of approval slip out.

"Yeah," continued Tony, "I was at her sister's wedding a couple of years ago."

"Mmm," added Cara-Marie, "I thought I recognised you when I walked in, but I thought that you were in the army."

"I was," said Tony, "left just over two years ago when I got into the police."

"Really? What made you leave the army?" Her interrogation continued for several minutes without ever turning to Kyle, which was something that he was happy with, he really didn't have anything to input anyway. It seemed they both went to the same school and the same priest had married Tony as well as Cara-Marie's sister. Kyle finished his coffee without either of them noticing, Tony then produced the single picture of his wife and himself taken on their honeymoon. Finally, Cara-Marie got around to the subject at hand, she produced a manila envelope which contained several eight by ten photos; the tone of the conversation changed.

"Anyway, I hear you two were the ones who found the bodies in Limavady on Monday night," she started flicking through the photos, "Could you go through what happened?" She stopped at one photo and passed it over to Tony, Tony passed him the photo. Kyle looked at it, it was taken some distance away, and it was a broad view of what the scene had been two days previous. The cordon tape that had been flicking in the wind was still, the white domed tents covered where most of the bodies lay, white sheeting covered the rest, a police officer stood with his back to the camera with three very young teenage children, excited looks on their faces, one of them was looking directly at the camera when the photo was taken. Tony had started going through what they had been doing as they got the first call, he included the arrest of the soldiers. Kyle noticed that she wasn't letting them see the rest of the pictures, he wondered what was on them.

"Who took these?" He asked, both Cara-Marie and Tony stopped talking and looked at him, Kyle still had the first photo in his hands, she paused,

"Mark, the paper's photographer," she paused again, Kyle noticed that she had lifted her notebook but still hadn't written anything, "Why?" she asked, Kyle's eyes moved away from the photo up to her.

"No reason," he had lowered his voice as his eyes returned to the business in hand, "may I see the others?" he asked. She lowered her notebook and placed it on the table beside her half-finished latte, she turned and picked up the remainder of the photos and handed them to him.

"Are you the policeman in the picture?" She asked, Tony said 'no' and began to talk again but Kyle was not listening. He flicked through the photos, they had been taken from height, they showed the crime scene investigation officers and the murder investigation team, Kyle looked past them at the track of blood on the ground. His eyes focused in on the right forearm that had been left uncovered at that point: In his mind, he looked underneath the sheet at the body parts that were strewn over the ground, his nose filled with the smell, his body shivered at the chill of the night, the wind had increased in heat and the ground turned to sand. He felt the glow of the burning building off to his left that smell, that smell. Tony's touch brought him back to reality. Kyle sprang upright then looked at them, time had passed, and he had just missed it, Tony picked up on this.

"As I was just saying Kyle," it was said solely for Kyle's benefit, "all we did was find them then call in the duty inspector," Tony moved in his chair, "after that all we did was stand at the cordon and ensured that the scene remained sterile." Cara-Marie jotted down two lines as the radio barked into life. The voice echoed in the earpieces of the two police officers, by their sudden reaction Cara-Marie realised that something was happening, she waited to find out what it was. "Oscar Delta Seven Three, Oscar Delta, Over," the control room in the police station was calling. Kyle reached down to the radio on his gun belt and firmly pushed a button before he spoke.

"Seven Three,"

"Return to this location as soon as possible," Kyle and Tony looked at each other as they rose simultaneously.

"We have to go," Tony stated.

"Thank you for all your help," she said as they both moved past her on their way to the door.

"Seven Three received," they had only reached the door when her phoned beeped with a text message, Cara-Marie's eyes widened as she read it, as she rushed to the door she was instructing Mark, the photographer over the phone where to meet her.

∞∞∞∞

At the far side of the river they congregated in the front living room of one of the two houses, they had been listening to him for nearly ten minutes now.

"It wasn't us," Davidov said in answer to the question, "we were all here, in these houses Monday night," he paused as his gaze swept the room, "well, all except you two," with that Davidov pointed to the Alpha and the dark-haired girl.

"And we were at the cinema just up the road," she used the thumb of her right hand to point up in the direction against the flow of traffic towards where the cinema was.

"It wasn't any of us," Davidov repeated. Anders looked at him from the other side of the room then back to where the Alpha stood, he was quiet now.

"What about Belfast?" asked one of the others, Alexi put his hands on his hips and waited for a few seconds before he answered.

"The police here do not know about us, they think it was a vigilante attack." He turned slightly towards the electric fire which heated the room, "they do not know of our kind," he was quieter now, "as I have said, all I want for us is to be safe and live and grow old, we can do that in this land, we can be safe, our children can be safe," the others in the room exchanged glances, Davidov stared at the floor.

"We are safe here, we are not persecuted here, I cannot, and I will not allow that to happen again." There was a silence that hung in the air which was broken only by one of the younger one, he addressed Alexi directly.

"Alexi, what of the Rua? they will learn of us eventually," his nervousness came out as he asked the question and Alexi Chernov turned to him, a small smile spread across his face.

"Do not worry Viktor, I will deal with that in time, they will understand that we are no threat to them." Viktor looked over at Davidov who was still staring at the floor, Alexi spotted this. "If we had stayed, we would all be dead by now." Davidov looked up at him without speaking, "We would have Davidov, we could not have fought them all." Davidov semi-smiled and looked around, the dark-haired girl was staring at him, waiting for him to speak, but he didn't, Alexi changed in mood. "So anyway, I was in Portrush and found a place to eat by the harbour that I would like to sample...." he turned towards the dark-haired girl and started to extend his right hand, "Anna, shall we eat?" the dark-haired girl smiled, her eyes flashed over at Davidov.

"Yes, of course," she rose and took his hand, Alexi smiled as she stepped close. Alexi extended the invite to all of them and the room was filled with movement. Davidov's phone bleeped, he opened the picture to reveal two policemen, he studied the picture as Anna passed.

"The one on the left," she said, he stopped her by touching her arm.

"Are you sure?" he asked,

"Yes," she walked out the door after Alexi. Davidov forwarded the picture, the room had emptied except for himself and Anders, Anders looked at the picture on his phone.

"Problem?" he asked.

"Maybe," said Davidov, I wasn't expecting any Rua up here, I thought they were all in the South of the country," he paused then looked at Anders, "we may have a fight on our hands."

"No problem here," said Anders, "no problem at all."

∞∞∞∞

Sean looked at the name on his phone, smiled and raised the phone to his ear.

"Yes Mike," he said.

"Hi boss, just heard from the pathologist..." Sean turned his head towards the phone, "He had a cast made of the teeth marks and he sent them over to a *dental pathologist* in England."

"*A DENTAL PATHOLOGIST?*" said Sean," didn't know they even existed."

"Yeah, neither did I Boss but apparently, they do," Sean could hear by the background noise he was in the main office of M.I.T. "He said the teeth are Canine."" Mike paused again.

"Well that is one relief I suppose," Sean added. "So, we are looking for someone with a very nasty dog or dogs, did he say what kind of dog?"

"No boss, said that all he could tell was canine but not what type."

"Well it is a start I suppose, thanks anyway Mike."

"No probs," Sean hung up the phone and quietly cursed, this was not a direction he wished to go, but at least they did not have a psychopathic killer on their hands, this wee country had seen enough of them before. He glanced at the watch on his left wrist, he was already ten minutes late to meeting his wife and that meant he would be paying for dinner.

Chapter 7

The pain shot down the back of his right leg, it was electric, every movement made it worse. It started in his lower back, went sideways before shooting down his leg. The back of his calf muscle was numb as was the bottom of his foot and it had been like that for the past two days. Kyle slowly turned pushing the duvet to one side, he rolled himself toward the edge of the bed and slowly managed to get himself upright. Being laid down and static or standing upright were the only times when it was not painful. He had visited his doctor the previous day and had been given a sick line for five days, something he hated but there was no way he could carry out any duties presently. He eased his dressing gown up over his shoulders and knotted the belt around his waist; his movements were slow and deliberate as he moved through his home.

He had liked it as soon as he had seen it, three-bed roomed cottage with a garage. He had converted one of the bedrooms into a computer room/study, and he had almost completed converting the attic by laying flooring and sectioning off space around the attic, he had put down a cheap carpet and painted the chipboard walls a pale colour. The boiling kettle in the kitchen clicked off, he hobbled over to it, opened the wooden door of the cupboard above it and lifted down one of his mugs. He liked tea in the morning but would drink coffee at work, unlike Tony who thought that coffee was coffee and could not tell the difference between decaf and normal. He lifted the mug of hot liquid to his lips, closed his eyes and sipped. It tasted nice, he opened his eyes and looked up at the clock on the wall, it was just after half nine. He turned and slowly made his way towards the living room, the large flat screen television stood at the end of the room on the right. The Brown 'L' shaped corner sofa took up the entire end of the room on the left with a small oak and glass coffee table in front of it. Kyle had a matching single chair on the right, all faced the TV. Just past the single chair was another table made of the same wood as the coffee table, it was smaller but taller.

He shuffled over and slouched down in the middle of the sofa, lifted the remote control and switched on the 24-hour news. A news team had been spending some time with American troops in Iraq and was showing footage of them patrolling, Kyle smirked, they might have the most powerful air force but man to man they were crap, over aggressive and had no concept of defeat. He had only ever known one American in the legion, he was good but anytime they did exchanges with regular US Army he hated it. 'A Play Station Nation' a *Caporal Chef* in the legion had once said to the rest of the troop, they all agreed. His mind wandered back to the legion. He was still fiercely proud of the legion, he had loved his time there. He had kept in contact with some of them via e mail. The doorbell blasted and sounded much louder than it was. His sudden movement sent shock waves across his spine and down his leg, it spasmed and he nearly dropped the mug. He reached out and slowly placed it on the table, he could see Tony at the door through the window which was behind the TV. Kyle slowly got up and shuffled down the short hallway and opened the thick wooden door, as he did, the sunlight burst in. He squinted and moved backwards out of the way to let Tony in.

"*Morning*," he was cheerful as he walked past him. Kyle closed the door, Tony was taking off his shoes and placed them beside the two pairs of trainers that were neatly set by the front door, Tony seemed to jet off into the house and as usual headed for the kitchen.

"The kettle is just off the boil," shouted Kyle,

"Timing," said Tony as he moved through the door of the kitchen, the small plastic shopping bag Tony was holding banged against the kitchen door frame. Kyle made his way back into the living room to sit back down and muted the TV. The pain was again shooting down his leg, his right hand supported his aching limb by lifting it from behind the knee as he sat forward, his faced winced as Tony walked in with a steaming mug. Tony looked at him as he sat opposite him on the single chair.

"It's ok, you don't have to pretend anymore, no one is watching," Kyle looked up with facial annoyance at his comment. "*What*?" asked Tony shrugging his shoulders as he sipped at the mug. Kyle momentarily could not think of a retort but knew that more abuse was on the way, "Anyway, wimp, got this for you," Tony looked around for a coaster, lifted one from underneath the table and moved the mug onto it. He turned and opened the plastic bag and pulled out a rolled-up newspaper, it was a copy of the Coleraine Herald, the picture which the journalist had shown them in the coffee shop was on the front page, and the killings in Limavady had been the main news stories since they had broken. He had got The Herald the day after and the first five pages were devoted to the killings, it was as if this had been the only happening in and around Coleraine. They had interviews from people from Limavady, the families of both the boys who had been killed, 'police sources', he had noticed there was not much about the down and out who also died. Both the TV and newspapers were pointing out similarities between the killings in Limavady and the one down in Belfast a few weeks earlier. His right leg slightly jumped then twitched and he drew breath, Tony started with more abuse at his bad acting, it would have been much the same if it had been the other way around. "Turn to page five, you are famous," Tony dropped into the conversation, Kyle looked across at him then shuffled the paper over to the fifth page. Near the top was a picture of a line of police officers dress in riot gear, helmets, shields and body armour. Kyle grinned as he was able to recognise the line of police officers in the photo, one after the other, he picked out Tony but could not see himself.

"I'm not famous, you're the one in the photo," Kyle said back.

"Read the text," Kyle glanced at the words on the page, he started to read aloud.

"Police in riot gear deployed to the 'Heights' area of Coleraine to confront a hostile crowd that had gathered on Tuesday afternoon,"

"And disturbed our nice cup of coffee," Tony injected, they had left their interview with Cara-Marie in the coffee shop previously and gathered in the car park of the police station before they and the other police officers from the station deployed across the river to deal with the public order incident occurring. The PSNI did not like calling them riots, it was called a 'public order' incident in this politically correct world they worked. Kyle read on, it gave the details of approximate numbers involved, the length of time it took until the crowd dispersed with the final line which he also read aloud.

"Police say that one officer was injured," with that he breathed out, Tony looked up as he finished the drink from the mug in his hands.

"Well one officer found a way to get a couple of days off more like," he was smirking as he said it.

"One line covers so much, funny it does not mention me spending nearly four hours on a stretcher in casualty at the Causeway hospital," Kyle's eyes had returned to the newspaper that he held in his hands.

"Or the courageous actions of another police officer who managed to drag him to safety and lifted the heavy lump that he is *onto the stretcher,* putting his *own* back on the line," Kyle looked over at him.

"Yeah, right," the sarcasm in his voice was very evident, "on the line, my arse," Tony grinned, more friendly abuse followed, to the untrained eye it was personal, but it was a sign of respect; if you were not respected you were not spoken to. Kyle's eyes noted the name of the journalist who had written the article, Cara-Marie Mc Kenna, pictures by Mark Scott. The newspaper said the disturbance started between two families and was enflamed by heightened tension which had been evident around 'the Heights' housing estate over the the past few months. The next story underneath had a picture of an older man and a picture of a leg with bruising on it. Kyle's eyes scanned the story, this man had been walking past and had been hit on the legs by a police baton, he was insinuating that the police had used excessive force and that he had been lying on the ground when 'attacked' by the police. Kyle commented on what he was reading.

"Oh, him," said Tony, Kyle looked over as he folded up the newspaper, he slowly sat back as Tony told his short story. "He was at the side, we spotted him giving out commands to the younger ones, so we went to grab him, he put up a fight as did those that were around him, four of us against twenty of them," Kyle smiled, he could picture the scenario, "and just as we got things quieter these two DUP councillors appeared and started going mental about police brutality." Tony sat back into the chair.

"And the press was there as well," continued Kyle, he had noticed Cara-Marie off to one side near the start of the disturbance, there was a bloke with a camera with her, he guessed this was the photographer from the newspaper.

"Of course, they were, they were there *before* we got there," Tony paused, "some things never change." They looked at each other, Tony shifted in his seat and reached into his pocket, "plus, I have got something else for you," he pulled out a green piece of paper and handed it over to Kyle. "Got this from the section sergeant this morning," Kyle sat forward far too quickly and as he stretched out his hand to receive it a bolt of pain shot down his leg, his upper body tensed, and his face showed the pain he felt.

"Hey, always thought that you 2 ReP boys could ignore pain," Tony's smile spread across his face as Kyle answered.

"Yeah but Legionnaires have *got* brains to register pain, unlike the Paras, numb from the neck up from what I hear."

"Airborne," a grin spread across Tony's face again, "Parachute Regiment!" The regimental pride was still there. It was a connection that the two of them made, mutual respect, between paratroopers no matter what the nationality. An airborne brotherhood. Kyle was surprised at the number of former legionnaires who were in the UK when he went to his first reunion. Tony had been at the anniversary of the D-Day landings last year and loved it. He framed some of the pictures he had taken of some of the paratroopers with whom he had served, most were still in the regiment and he came back with more stories from Iraq and Afghanistan. Kyle suspected that part of him wished he was still with the regiment as part of Kyle still felt about the legion.

"2em Regiment Etrangere de Parachutists," Kyle said out loud not realising it.

"Second Foreign Parachute Regiment," Tony translated out loud in English. Kyle's head snapped up as he finished, "of the French Foreign Legion." Kyle smiled as he came back to the present, "but One Para is of course, the better," Tony finished as the newspaper hit him in the chest. Kyle unravelled the green piece of paper that he had been handed, he didn't recognise it at all. "It is a chit from the station that is sending you for an assessment by one of our physiotherapists from Sea Park," Tony looked over at the blank expression on Kyle's face, he continued to explain, "Sea Park, near Carrickfergus," he paused "Occupational Health and Welfare, you did pay attention to the welfare briefs, didn't you?" Tony asked.

"I didn't go to the welfare briefs," answered Kyle, "besides, I'm not going to Carrickfergus just to see a physiotherapist."

"You're not, they do a clinic up in Maydown," Tony paused again then dropped the bombshell, "and you are booked in at two this afternoon, I'll have to drive you up obviously." Tony folded up the newspaper and placed it in the middle of the table as he waited for Kyle's response, Kyle read over the A5 size green slip, he raised his gaze.

"Do I have a choice?" Tony laughed, stood up and walked into the kitchen and it was clear from the noise he was making another mug of coffee and would also be helping himself to the biscuits.

∞∞∞

Sean was sitting behind his desk reading over the recent emails, the majority of which were 'for information' which in his view was someone banging out loads of emails and feeling that their job, whatever it was, was justified by sending out all this crap. He lifted the mug of coffee to his lips, Mike appeared in the doorway. He motioned with his head for him to enter, the coffee tasted good in his mouth, Mike had a jotter in his left hand that was open and a black biro pen in his right. Mike had paused and was waiting for the right moment to speak, Sean placed the mug on the desk and closed the email without sending a reply, Mike looked at his notebook then up at Sean before he spoke.

"Got some answers from M.I.T. in Maydown on their killings," he stopped, paused, and then continued. "They have three dead, the first one died of a heart attack…" Sean turned his head and asked, "Heart attack? I thought they were youngsters?" Mike carried on,

"No, he is a down and out, they believe that he was being mugged by the other two, suffered a heart attack during the mugging." Sean raised his eyebrows, "He had injuries that would indicate recent trauma to the head…." Mike read from notebook "69-year-old, with a history of minor offences, mostly alcohol related, but it is the others that are the interesting ones"

"I bet they are," said Sean.

"Yeah, there are 'some' similarities, like in some of the injuries, they think that they were caused pre-mortem as well… massive trauma damage to all parts of the body, limbs separated, but there are some differences as well."

"Such as?" asked Sean.

"Well they think there was more than one dog involved, plus they have no idea as to why the down and out wasn't touched."

"Why do they think it was just dogs?" Sean continued with his questioning.

"Because there was still money lying all over the place, it appears that the drunk had won a couple of hundred on a lotto ticket and was spending his winnings, none of that was taken, plus, from the initial photos they sent me it is a different shape of mouth, so a different type of dog compared to ours." Sean thought over what Mike had said but before he could answer Simon appeared at the door.

"Boss, sorry to cut in, there has just been another one," both Sean and Mike turned towards him.

"What?" Asked Mike.

"Another attack, just heard about it in North Belfast, I've got the address, uniforms are there now," Sean was already standing up as Mike started to move towards the door.

"Ok, let's go." He pulled on his coat which had been lying over the back of his chair. Simon turned and headed towards his desk as did Mike, Sean spoke to the backs of the two men, "and I'm driving."

∞∞∞∞∞

Cara-Marie sat at her desk editing a page for the next edition, circulation of the paper had gone up with the stories from Limavady and the editor had made good comments to all the team for their work. They had the better coverage of the killings and had obtained and published a photo of both the boys together, something the other paper in Coleraine failed to do. She also got a personal word of thanks from the editor over the two stories from the riot in the Heights, she had seen two other journalists from the other paper, but the Herald were the only ones who got the police brutality story. Everyone knew that something was eventually going to happen up there as there had been minor public order problems for the police to deal with. The Heights are a council estate, 'inner city' was a description the local MP had publicly used, and it was beginning to stick. Coleraine police were never absent from there for very long before they were in again serving warrants, issuing summons or making enquiries regarding local crime. She went to lift the phone handset, but her hand found fresh air, she turned to the empty space where the phone had been, her hand had already closed around where the phone was 'supposed' to be. Her head snapped up and she stared at Mark who sat at his desk, talking on her phone.

He looked across at her with a smile on his face, she raised her eyebrows, batted her eyelids once and had a slight grin with a look of "Excuse me!". shrugged his shoulders and lifted his right palm up as if to say 'what?' Cara-Marie shook her head as she went back to the screen of her PC. Mark ended his conversation and put the phone down, he suddenly became engrossed in what he was doing. It was deliberate, Cara- Marie coughed slightly, Mark tilted his head and uttered a simple: "Uh?"

37

Cara-Marie drew herself up to her full height andtilted her head, so it was in line with Mark's. "May I have *'my'* phone back?" she was suppressing a snigger.

"Of course, you may," he lifted the phone up towards her, she snatched it back.

"What's wrong with yours?" she demanded.

"It's bust, plus, you never talk on yours as you are always on your pet mobile phone," answered Mark.

"SLANDER!" she shouted. She set the phone down on her desk and picked up the handset, she looked at the number in her notebook and as she started to tap the numbers Mark's notebook hit her. It fell onto her lap, fluttering. She looked around, Mark was engrossed, head down as if nothing had anything to do with him. The notebook hit Mark square on the side of his head, he turned and looked at the calm, , expressionless Cara-Marie. He looked around again. Cara-Marie ducked as it flew past her, this time it missed, "Ha," she said out loud, "missed" Mark looked up.

"Don't know what you mean, you pen pushing pansy?"

"Are you going to get any work done today??" she asked. Mark had one of his digital single lens reflex cameras in his hands and was scrolling through the pictures that were saved in the memory.

"Got loads done as *I wasn't* the one gassing on the phone," he tried to duck the notebook as it flew towards him, but he wasn't fast enough.

Chapter 8

Alexi pushed his right hand over his head as he stepped out of the bank and into the gusting wind, his eyes easily found Anna at the far side of the street. She was already moving towards him, weaving through the people who were walking past as he zipped up the black leather quilted jacket. He stepped forward and met her with a kiss on her right cheek, she smiled as her grip around him tightened before releasing him. She stepped back allowing him space as he moved off across the pedestrian precinct and away from the bank, he took her hand into his.

"Well?" she asked, Alexi looked into her eyes,

"Yes, all done," he stepped onward, they were heading down away from the bank towards the entrance to the Diamond Shopping Centre where Anna had seen the two policemen a few days prior. She had not told him about them and had decided not to as she knew how he would react. "All the money came across a few days ago, they were *very* keen to talk to me once they realised there was over half a million in one of their accounts."

"I bet they were," said Anna, Alexi stopped. Anna took an extra step before turning her head to look at him, "What?" she asked,

"I think we need a new car," he said,

"Let's get a good one this time, the Fiat is about to die," she said, Alexi chuckled. Anna had always liked the way he chuckled, her body moved towards him, bringing him slightly closer, his head turned to look into her face, the smile spread and lit up his face.

"You always think they are going to die," he started to move off pulling her along. Alexi turned to his right at a statue of a local man who had once played football for Northern Ireland in the 1950's and 60's. The figure was running with a football in front of him and a huge smile on his face. Alexi's eyes moved over the bronze statue as the pair turned right and down the street towards the library, Anna was still by his side and still nattering.

"So, what kind of car would you like to get then?" she asked with a hint of mischief about her.

"You'll see," he answered. They walked past jewellers on their right and past a couple who were also walking hand in hand, engrossed in their own world and ignoring all going the other direction, just the way Alexi liked it. The street was emptier than the main part of the pedestrian precinct. In front of them the main road flowed from behind the library that was on their left and onwards, the traffic slowed at the traffic lights and jumped forward when they changed. Alexi stayed on the right-hand side of the road, Anna smiled as she could see where he was leading her. They walked into the main part of the BMW showroom and walked around the cars, the large red one was big and powerful, the black 4x4 attracted Anna even more but what she really liked was the dark blue sports coupe at the back.

"Oh yes," she said. The blonde-haired salesman in a dark two-piece suit approached and as they turned Alexi could see him look them up and down, obviously by their attire there was no way they could afford one of these. He introduced himself and asked if he could help, Anna went to speak as she really liked the coupe, but Alexi cut her off.

"Where are the second-hand cars, I do not want a new one." The salesman noted that this man was blunt, and the younger girl was used to doing what she was told. When she spoke, she spoke in a kind of Polish or something which the older man answered with a shake of the head.

"The used cars are mostly outside," he extended his left arm towards the door they had just come though, he took an instant dislike to them. 'Tyre kickers' he thought to himself. People, who walked in, kicked the tyres, asked stupid questions and dreamed of owning a BMW, 'tyre kickers' never bought, never could afford it. These two would be no different; he had seen they're like many times. They held hands and there was an obvious age difference between them, the girl was younger, liked black and had a nice body. She was quite smartly dressed, black top, black jeans and a rather non-descript outdoor jacket; he was wearing blue jeans with a baggy jumper and a black leather jacket. They were not unemployed; they had some money, but he could tell they were not normally the kind of people who bought BMW's. BMW's were out of their league. They walked outside and started moving through the packed cars, the salesman was asked his name again.

"Brian," he answered, "What is yours?" The man turned and answered, Brian noticed that the girl did not.

"Alexi," was the one-word reply. Brian let the two of them walk around the green three series saloon before he tried to engage in conversation, breaking down the barrier and getting to know the client. This was everything needed to ensure the sale, exactly what he had been taught when he first got into this business. *'Be friendly and courteous, you want them to spend their money on your cars,'* Brian would never tell anyone from outside BMW how much commission he got for every car sold or how much percentage he got off when buying a BMW himself.

"So, you are new to the area then?" Alexi turned to face him to answer.

"Yes," The one-word answer seemed final; maybe he didn't want to get to know them. The girl spoke again, Brian could tell she was asking questions to which she was getting short sentences as answers. She liked the cars, that much was obvious to him. Brian looked through the window at the other salesman who nodded at him then turned back into the showroom, Brian tried again to get them talking as they headed around the dark blue five series.

"So, have you been here long?" Brian tried again, Alexi walked around the car, looking inside, he answered Brian plainly, leaving the girl at the rear of the car.

"Not long, we like it here, so we stay," English was clearly not his first language.

"That's nice," Brian paused before he asked his next question, "so, where have you come from?" Alexi's head snapped round leaving the question unanswered, "Poland?" Brian suggested, for a split second he thought he had just crossed a line, the girl spoke, Alexi seemed to relax.

"Yes, we come from Poland," his attention returned to the car, "can we look inside this car?" Brian noted the change of conversation and tone and knew not to follow on.

"Yes of course," he stepped back, "I will get the keys from the showroom, I will be back in a few moments." The falseness of his smile was answered by the falseness of the smile that was on the face that replied to him. Brian's suit jacket waved in the breeze that scooped around the car park as he strode toward the entrance. Alexi watched him go inside.

"He did not mean anything by it," said Anna, "he is just being a salesman," Alexi looked at her, smiled and relaxed, "not everyone wants to kill us," she said as she walked up and pushed her body close against him, he placed his arm around her and stared deep into her eyes.

"I know," he lowered his voice, "you know me better than I think and sometimes would like," she smiled again.

"As only a soul mate should," she raised herself up and kissed his right cheek. Brian walked around his desk and opened one of the drawers and fumbled through the bunches of keys that were in there.

"Got a sale?" asked the other salesman who was sat behind the desk across from where Brian stood.

"Tyre kickers," he replied, the other salesman laughed, the blonde-haired girl who sat on the reception turned her head and laughed at the joke, she looked over at the couple who stood arm in arm in the car park, yeah, they looked like tyre kickers to her as well, Alexi let go of Anna, and stepped away from her.

"This one," he said,

"I really liked the sporty one inside," she said.

"But it is new, expensive and will attract too much attention to ourselves," Alexi said.

"*Expensive?*" Anna reacted, "we can afford *any* car here."

"But it will attract too much attention to ourselves," answered Alexi, "we are in *hiding,* are we not?" Alexi laid the law.

"Yes, but can we not hide in comfort?" asked Anna. Alexi just looked at her, he had decided, and she would follow. Brian approached again, the smile still as fake as before, Alexi noticed another younger couple slowly walking into the car park, paying attention to the parked cars. Brian's head turned towards them, noted them but his attention returned to what he was doing, he pressed the black plastic key fob, the lights on the car flashed as the car bleeped then with a clunk, the car unlocked.

"Please, have a look inside," said Brian as he came to a stop in front of the car, his head again looking at the other couple that the salesman inside had not yet noticed. Alexi opened the driver's door and climbed in beside Anna who was already in the passenger seat, her approval was evident. Brian made his way around to the driver's side and filled the open doorway. Brian talked through the car, what it could do, how easier it made driving and so on, Alexi just nodded along with him but still noted that Brian's eyes kept going back to the other couple, Brian seemed to know his stuff.

"Would you let us discuss this between ourselves for a few moments?" Alexi asked, Anna's head turned sharply in surprise.

"Of course," said Brian and in seconds he was over introducing himself to the other couple.

"Discuss it?" asked a surprised Anna, Alexi just looked at her and smiled.

"I have already decided to buy this, I just wanted rid of him for a bit." Alexi reached into his pocket and pulled out his phone, he scrolled down the numbers and pressed the green button as he swung his legs out of the car and stood up. He lifted the phone to his ear and walked round to the back of the car, she knew not to follow him. Her eyes scanned the view out the car, she looked at the traffic on the road, the people who were standing at the bus stop on the far side, the small park that was full of flower beds behind the bus stop. Brian was talking to the woman as the younger man walked up to silver three series and promptly kicked one of the tyres, he shrugged and turned toward Brian, Anna watched their body language. The female was the more dominant, something she had seen a lot of since their own arrival first in England, then again here, which surprised her.

Brian continued to talk to her as the boyfriend returned, it was obvious that Brian did not have a sale with them, her eyes shot up to the rear-view mirror, Alexi was still on the phone, and he was happy and smiling and looked like he had just got some good news. Brian was on his way back over towards them, so she got out of the car and walked toward the front to keep him back from Alexi for the time being. As Brian approached she placed her hands on her waist and took a deep breath in, slightly lowered her head and allowed her hair to fall over her shoulders, it was all done to move his gaze to her chest. It worked, she could tell he was trying *not* to stare but that was all he could do, and he would be easy to control.

"I like this car," she said formally, Brian's eyebrows rose, he had not heard her speak English before.

"Umm, thank you, ahh," it took Brian a couple of seconds to regain his composure, "well, yes, BMW is one of the best cars around today..." Anna would keep him talking for a few more minutes. Alexi walked up to them and as he placed his phone in his pocket he looked Brian in the eyes. Brian looked straight back.

"We will take this car," he announced, Brian was surprised as that was not what he expected.

"Ok," he paused again, then stepped back and turned towards the main showroom, "well, let us go inside and complete the paperwork." He started to lead them inside, the blonde-haired girl at reception just smiled as they all walked past. Brian offered them the comfortable chairs in front of his desk, he started tapping at the key board that was in the middle of his very tidy desk and looked at the flat screen of his computer monitor.

"Ok, well here at BMW we have several finance plans that can suit all..."

"We pay total bill, out right," Alexi cut him off, Anna was silent. Brian stopped, the salesman from the other desk looked up, paused then returned to what he was doing but still listening to the conversation.

"Ok," said Brian again, "may I ask how you'll be paying?" he had stopped typing. Alexi let a smile spread but only as far as his mouth, the rest of the face wasn't smiling.

"Is cash ok?" The other salesman's phone rang, Brian paused, breathed in and answered with a smile and a simple:

"Yes," money talks, especially to a salesman. Brian took them through the required paperwork, registration and insurance for BMW, this would all be sorted by tomorrow, he would have the car serviced and valeted by then, they agreed on a pick-up time of 2pm.

"Would you like me to pay now?" asked Alexi as he reached into the pocket on the right side of his jacket and removed a large thick brown envelope.

"That would be fine," said a slightly stunned Brian. Anna could see his eyes widen as Alexi started to count out the crisp £50 notes, piling them 1,000 at a time until they reached the agreed £17,000. Brian was now a very happy man; it took another five minutes before they were done. Brian had noticed that there was still a large amount of money in the envelope after it had all been counted out and he wondered if he had just missed a bigger commission. Just as they stood up and started to walk towards the door Brian asked the final question that would satisfy his curiosity.

"So, Alexi, what is it exactly that you do for a living?" Anna and Alexi stopped, Alexi took Anna's left hand in his right and looked over his right shoulder at him, and he had nearly bumped into them when they stopped, the receptionist looked up at the sudden change in atmosphere.

"I will tell you what I don't do *BRIAN!*"

"What is that?" Brian asked, not sure what the answer was going to be, Alexi turned and as he walked towards the door taking Anna with him.

"I don't work in a bloody shop." The door closed swiftly behind them as they left, the receptionist was biting her bottom lip and had become engrossed in the file in front of her to stop herself from laughing at the put down. They walked up to the road and as if on cue the little Fiat with Davidov came around the corner and pulled in beside them, the car door opened and a smiling Davidov ushered them in. Anna climbed into the back seat by herself as Alexi took the front passenger seat, Alexi looked at him and Davidov smiled back.

"Yes, all done," he said as he pushed his way out into the traffic, "We can go there right now, and as I just said to you on the phone it is yours from ten this morning."

"What is?" asked Anna, she looked back into the BMW garage at Brian who was watching them leave. He was writing on a notepad in his left hand, probably their registration number on the small, old Fiat that they had climbed into, Alexi turned towards her in the back of the car.

"Got another surprise for you, Davidov has been shopping as well," said Alexi.

"And it has taken Davidov two weeks, but he has done it, *as usual*," Davidov finished off. Alexi was pleased with him, that much was obvious. The car turned right at the traffic lights that were just past the BMW garage and they headed up the hill. Davidov and Alexi were chatting, she let her gaze drift over the people who were walking up and down the street. She focused in on one girl who was very overweight but had still appeared out in clothes which were far too small. She was sickened by her obesity, how could a woman let herself get like that? She looked in front of the car at the pale coloured train station and the line of taxis that were outside it, one of the drivers stood by his car smoking a cigarette. He had not shaved for a few days and he probably smelt bad as it did not look like he washed regularly, the dead wood of this society. She felt her mouth water as another thought passed through it, she lowered her head to hide the smile and the rush of warmth through her body. The car stopped at another set of traffic lights at the top of a row of shops. The road turned around to the left and Davidov manoeuvred the car over to the left and pulled into the side of the road and brought the car to a stop, the two men looked at each other.

"Here we are," said Alexi as the car's engine died and both doors swung open. Anna stepped out onto the pavement and looked across the road at the police station and wondered what they could possibly be doing here? The two men walked over and faced the large, three storied terraced houses that were in front of them and opposite the police station. Davidov pointed his finger towards one of them then they walked down the pathway to the front door. He took out a set of keys from his pocket and handed them to Alexi who thanked him, Davidov then turned, smiled and walked back to the car. Alexi opened the door and lead Anna inside as the car sped off.

The house was empty except for the thick dark carpet that was laid in the hall and the living room, Anna was confused as to what was happening, and wondered what this could be? Alexi took her by the hand and led her into the middle of the main room; she looked around the empty room contemplating the space, and the white net curtains covering the open windows. The ground floor looked directly at the entrance of the police station.

"What is going on Alexi?" She asked, Alexi stepped closer and took her hands in his own, then looked into her dark eyes before he spoke.

"We have a house of our own Anna,"

"What?" she said, "what about the others?"

"The others will keep the two houses by the river, I have decided that you and I shall live here, in this house." Anna was not sure what to say.

"But..." she started.

"No buts," he moved closer, "I want us to be safe Anna, I want us not to feel threatened and we can do that here," Anna had heard this before but had not expected him to move away from the others. "Here we can all start afresh," he straightened up as if making a speech, "Here we will grow, we will flourish..." she certainly knew what he meant by that, "here... we can be what we were always meant to be, to be free." Anna looked deep into his eyes, they were wide with excitement, and he released her hands and stepped into a hug. She slowly moved her own arms up and around his shoulders and pulled him closer as he buried his face in her hair. His voice continued in her ear, "I will take care of you Anna, I will always protect my soul mate, here we can have a family of our own and raise them in *all* of our ways." Anna pulled her head back, his eyes nearly had tears in them, she could see the love there, and he was fulfilling his dreams and ambitions. She returned a smile and closed her eyes as their lips met, and then they devoured each other in the passion of the kiss. Their breathing quickened as did the kiss, their hands started moving over each other's bodies and as she pushed the leather jacket from his shoulders and onto the floor his teeth found her neck. She stepped back, looked into his face then stepped into another kiss, she knew their lovemaking would take over two hours then they would definitely be ready for lunch.

Chapter 9

Tony's car was flying up the road out of Coleraine towards Limavady, the mountain road expanded into three lanes as he accelerated past the slow-moving tractor that had kept the line of ten cars behind them waiting for the last mile. The road rose up the rising hill and Kyle scanned the tree line on the right; the gap was a favourite spot for traffic branch to sit with their little 'Hair Dryer' speed radar gun to catch those coming down. By the time the traffic cops were spotted it was too late, those caught would soon be £60 lighter. Kyle shifted in his seat as pain shot down from the base of his spine and down his right leg making him react. Tony looked at him and continued with the abuse as they went over the top of the hill. The sky was clear, and Kyle looked over the valley that was off to the right. The sunlight glimmered off Lough Foyle and the greenness of the countryside seemed greener to Kyle than before. The far side of the Loch was County Donegal in the Irish Republic. At the base of the Lough was the city of Londonderry, or just plain Derry depending on who you spoke to; however. the sight before him was a beautiful view that he loved every time he looked at it, that is of course when the skies were not low and grey and when the rain was not pouring.

The road turned to the right at the bottom of the hill and Kyle could see the truck which was making its way along the road with other cars overtaking when they could. The road was now surrounded by thick, dark woodland on both sides as the road rose and fell with the lay of the land. Kyle had once come down the road in his own car at four in the morning. For those first few minutes it was like he was in a rally car racing along trying to get the best time possible. The road opened as they came to Limavady. Tony carried on the by-pass as going through the town would take up too much time. Thankfully the truck had turned into the town and the traffic sped up. Tony passed the next two cars with ease and took the first left at the roundabout, Kyle had only ever been to Maydown Police Station once before and that was in the back of a car, so he only had an 'idea' of where it was. He could have found it if he had been looking but Tony had been up there recently. The car slowed again as they stopped in the traffic in Ballykelly. Kyle looked inside the recently refurbished chip shop on the left-hand side that had been open for over 30 years. The lights changed to green and as they moved over the crossing Tony pointed out the green metal gates of the army camp entrance that was down to the right. 'you could miss it if you were not looking'. The traffic carried on and the road opened again as they were leaving Ballykelly. They carried on the couple of miles to the Maydown round about, and took the right turn off the round about which led towards the police station that was now in front of them. Tony stopped at the main gate and waited for the police officer to walk out, looked in at Tony and the ID that he was holding and waved at them in recognition. As the heavy gate closed shut behind them Tony had already parked the car. Kyle hobbled out of the car and stopped as he put his hands on the roof to help himself stand up. Tony started clapping and shouting 'Bravo!' Kyle could do nothing except grin and let out a little laugh. If it was the other way around, then he would be doing the same.

The car bleeped as Tony locked it. As he walked away, Kyle limped towards the building. Tony knew where he was going, Kyle did not. Tony walked into the Gym and up the stairs with Kyle hollering abuse to slow down, which of course Tony took no notice of and bounded up the stairs. Kyle took one stair on at a time; he looked at his watch; he still had fifteen minutes to go before his appointment and did not know what the rush was.

"By the way?" Kyle asked, Tony turned half way up.

"What?" Kyle stopped as if to catch his breath, looked straight at Tony then asked;

"What is the name of this physiotherapist anyway? Is it that grumpy old one that used to do the police football team?" Kyle took a few more steps, he was moving his right lower leg as it was still numb, something that he still was not too happy about.

"No," replied Tony, "Kelly Vixen, she is a chick out of occupational welfare at Sea Park, I've told you that already!"

"Vixen? Interesting name," he answered, Tony had now turned and continued up to the top of the stairs. Kyle slowly made his way up to the top. Tony had walked on for a couple of feet to be stopped by a man in a track suit; it was the Physical Educational Instructor from Maydown, Kyle could spot them a mile off. It seemed that Tony and this guy knew each other.

"What are you doing down here?" he asked Tony.

"Just bringing this cripple down here to be seen by the physio; is she in?" Tony asked, pointing to the hobbling Kyle with his left thumb as Kyle just got to be level with the two of them as Tony finished his sentence.

"Nice one, yeah she is in." he slightly turned and stretched his arm towards the end of the corridor, "the waiting room is down there; she will call you forward."

"Oh," said Tony, "Stevie, this is Kyle, one of the other coppers from my section in Coleraine," Tony turned towards Kyle and introduced Stevie as he held out his hand.

"Kyle, Stevie is the PE Instructor here." Kyle and Stevie shook hands. "We went through Police College together," Tony explained.

Stevie finished the sentence off for Tony, "Yeah where I had to drag this Para's arse all the way through training as *'he'* couldn't keep up," all three of them smiled; this kind of friendly abuse was common.

Tony came straight back at him. "More like you couldn't keep up with me!! plus, better be careful!" Tony motioned towards Kyle, "This one here is ex-2 ReP, so that means that you are *surrounded* by PARA'S," Tony smiled. Kyle noticed the reaction in Stevie's eyes at what Tony had said about him. Stevie glanced at Kyle. His eyebrows raised as his body slightly tensed, he had obviously heard of Kyle's former unit.

"2 ReP, eh," Stevie left a slight pause as if he did not know what to say next.

Tony helped him on. "And Stevie is ex- bugger all."

"Anyway, I have to be off." said Kyle, "Nice meeting ya," he said toward Stevie as he moved off; he got a nod in reply.

"Good to see you again," said Stevie toward Tony as Kyle slowly limped off down the corridor. Tony said his farewells and took nearly five steps before he had caught up with Kyle. Kyle glanced at him.

"He is alright really," said Tony in defence of Stevie.

"I will take your word for that." said Kyle

Tony smiled as they entered the small room that was being used as a waiting room. "How come you know where this is?" Asked Kyle as the door closed behind him.

"Had an appointment with a doctor here and they gave me one of my vaccinations that was due at the same time," Tony turned his head towards Kyle. "The nurse was not what you would call gentle," Kyle sniggered as he moved up against the wall. Tony looked at his watch, "Well, you have ten minutes to wait so I will catch you in an hour."

"An hour?" asked Kyle, "Just how long is this going to take?" Tony smiled as Kyle's leg jerked again; his hands shot down his right leg.

"Ha ha, should take about three quarters of an hour; text me when you are free," and with that he was gone. Kyle shifted in his position, stood up against the wall, and made himself as comfortable as he could. He had been sitting far too long during the journey and had felt it when he was getting out of the car. He had tried to hide it as much as he could, but he knew Tony had seen it; for all of his abuse Tony was looking after him. Kyle closed his eyes and slightly moved his leg once more and breathed as his leg and lower back relaxed becoming pain free. He was suddenly jolted back to where he was by a female voice.

"Constable Foster?" She stood in the far door with one hand on the door frame. His eyes opened, and he looked towards the woman who was standing there. She was wearing black trousers, white blouse and a black woollen tank top that seemed to be the unofficial 'uniform' for civil servants who worked for the police. His eyes quickly moved up from the black slip on shoes, over the toned thighs and hips that filled the trousers. She had a natural waist that was in proportion to the quite large chest that was trying to burst out of the top that was far too small for her; perhaps that was her intent. The sleeves of the blouse stopped half way down her thin forearms and the collar spread wide away from her neck. She had dark-ginger hair that had been highlighted with blonde streaks and her bright smile that seemed to take up most of her face.

"Yes," Kyle said as he moved forward, and she moved back into the room that she had just come from.

"This way please," she turned and walked into the room as he entered. Her hair touched her shoulders and moved in motion with her natural sway as she walked. His eyes dropped onto her bum that he could tell was firm and was probably very nice to touch; this woman liked to exercise, regularly at that.

"Sorry?" he said. She had just spoken to him and he had been transfixed with her bum. A cheeky smile spread over her face.

"I said could you take a seat on the couch please," she stepped towards him as he held out the green slip in his hand; he felt his face go slightly red at being caught staring at her. The room was like a long doctor's room with the static plinth at one end that he was trying to sit on near the door. There weren't any privacy curtains around the plinth that you would normally expect to be hanging there, just a set of portable curtain screens held in a metal frame on wheels; real 21st century stuff Kyle noted. As he turned and slowly sat down, his eyes moved across the room. There was a small sink at the far end on the left-hand wall, the window in the back wall over-looked the car park where they had first arrived at. Her desk was on the right-hand side of the long room; on top of the desk was the computer terminal, the same make as the ones they used in Coleraine. The desk had a phone and a couple of document trays that had some folders in them. She was reading what was written on the green slip as he slowly sat down; he looked her up and down again. She had some freckles the same colour as her hair; but not too many and her eyes were a grey and blue mix. Kyle initially could not place her accent. She lifted her head and looked straight into his eyes, her pupils widened before she spoke.

"Hi, I am Kelly, I am going to be your physiotherapist today," Kyle held her stare as they shook hands.

"Kyle, Kyle Foster,"

"As in Bond, James Bond," she had broken the ice and Kyle dropped the gaze and laughed two breaths out of his nose; she was smiling as well as he lifted his head again.

"Yes, something like that."

"Well," she said as she straightened up. "What seems to be the problem?" A semi-serious look came over her face as Kyle went through what had been happening to him over the last few days.

"There is a shooting pain that starts at the bottom of my spine," he straightened up and motioned with his hands towards his lower back, Kelly had folded her arms and listened to him as he continued, "then it shoots down the back of my right leg," Kyle carried on the motion with his right hand.

"Does the pain go all the way to your foot?" She asked.

"No, it kind of stops round about the middle of my calf muscle,"

"Does it go down to the left at all?" The grin was gone, and the professional had taken over, Kyle was trying his best to keep his eyes looking at her face and not looking over the body in front of him; she had stepped closer as he spoke.

"No, not at all, which is a bit weird," he said. She nodded as if ticking off a list in her head.

"No, it's not weird, are you having any trouble with numbness or pins and needles in your leg?" That was what Kyle was going to mention next.

"Yes actually,"

"Where is it?" she asked. Kyle slowly bent forward but stopped when he felt a small acute stab of pain that told him to stop. The fingers on his right hand touched the top of his calf muscle as he spoke.

"From here down to my foot," he started to slowly straighten up again.

"And your whole foot is numb?"

"No, not the whole foot, just down the back and across the sole."

"Pins and needles?"

"None, just feels numb."

She stepped to near the bottom of the plinth. "Ok, let's have a look at you. Please take off your top and your track suit bottoms." Kyle slowly started to move; he was being watched very closely as he removed first his trainers, then his top and then his bottoms; he was wearing a pair of training shorts. As he straightened up, he looked into her eyes, they were wide and staring, she was playing with the tip of the fore finger of her right hand on her teeth. She started to move to the far side of the plinth as she spoke again, "Ok can you stand up straight," Kyle did so, "and try and touch your toes," again he slowly moved forward until a pain shot across his back. "Ok," Kelly was scrutinising every single movement he was making, "Lie on your front for me please." Kyle obliged. "Let me know where the pain is," she said as her thumbs started moving up either side of his spine. Kyle had his face in a small circular hole that was in the plinth which was quite comfortable to his surprise. She started at the very bottom of the spine. Kyle had expected her to start at the top.

"Nice tat," Kelly said. Kyle's eyes darted over to the right and focused on her feet. He only had one tattoo, his legion tattoo on his right shoulder.

"Thanks," he said as her thumbs got lower down his back; she was getting closer to where it hurt.

"Got one myself," she said

"Really?" he said in surprise as she did not seem the type that would have a tattoo. Her thumbs moved up to another vertebra in his spine; he was starting to tense as he could tell what was coming next.

"Yeah got one all the way down my back," for a moment Kyle tried to picture what kind of tattoo she would have. He did not realise he had just relaxed his back; her thumbs found the site of the pain. She pressed down. Kyle's leg, shoulders and his head all rose off the plinth as the pain shot across his spine and down his legs; she had found it. Another five minutes of prodding around his lower back continued; he had closed his eyes several times and had stopped speaking. Kelly had brought him back to where he was with questioning about the police but did seem interested in his time in the legion. She got him to turn over and lay on his back and placed a pillow under his head before she walked around to his feet and took his left ankle in her hands.

"Ok, what I would like to do now is see how strong the muscles in your legs are; could you bring you knee up and push against me?" Kyle started to lift his leg as Kelly stood close and with her left hand pushed against his leg; she placed her right hand behind his knee, "And the other way please." Kyle pushed his knee away from himself; he could feel the pressure from her hand all the way down his leg. "Can you straighten your leg now and raise it slowly towards the ceiling for me please?" Kyle slowly lifted his leg as Kelly moved to the far end of the plinth, he could feel her hand on his ankle, he could not lift it very far. "And the other leg." Kyle repeated what he had done and there was quite a difference. "Ok, could you bring your knee as close to your chest as you can for me again please?" she was very polite, Kyle started to lift his leg and bend it at the knee. Kelly moved beside him and placed her hands either side of his right leg this time. Kyle could feel her left hand slowly putting pressure on his thigh. Kelly moved closer until her left shoulder was nearly touching his knee. Kyle could feel the warmth of her chest that was pressed up against his thigh; he was trying not to picture what was underneath those clothes. Her questioning of where the pain was and what it was doing continued as she repeated this on the other leg, Kelly lifted his right leg up and went on to explain that there was less flexibility on this leg compared with his left and the pain was a lot more evident. "Are you getting any muscle pain? She asked, Kyle felt his face redden as he said yes. Kelly asked where.

"Well," Kyle paused, "It is in my arse cheek," she reacted with a nod.

"Thought so," she said out loud, "turn over again." Kyle moved slowly until he was face down. He made a joke about his movements which got a reply about how good movement was for him. "Could you hitch up your shorts?" she asked as she came around the side of the plinth. Kelly started pumping at the side of the plinth and it started to rise until Kyle was about a foot higher. Kyle slowly shuffled around until he had raised his shorts slightly high and revealed his bum; was she pausing or was she looking at something else, he was not sure, but it was several seconds before she spoke again, "Ok, where is the pain?" Kyle lifted the thumb of his right hand and pointed to the central part of his bum cheek.

"About here," he said.

"Just one side?" Kelly asked. He had not really noticed until now that it was just on one side. The prodding thumbs returned to both sides and Kyle felt himself the solid muscle on one side, "Oh yes, classic signs," Kelly said as her thumb pressed down on one side and sent another shot of pain, this time she did not release it but kept the pressure on. The pain was intense and hurt like hell, Kyle was already counting in his head as time passed, he was approaching twenty when she released the pressure, and relief swam over him. He had been holding his breath and he had a bit of a sweat over his forehead. She got him to turn over again; she was smiling.

"Classic signs?" Kyle asked.

"Oh yes, trigger points," Kyle sat up and Kelly brought the back rest up to support him. Her face was only a few inches from his and he stared into her eyes. His eyes glanced down, he really liked what he saw. As he looked up again she raised her eyebrows and the smile on her face grew in size and meaning. He had just been caught again, he looked away. Kelly turned and walked over to the desk and sat down behind it. As she spoke, she lifted a folder and started to make some notes on it. "Yes classic; your piriformis is in spasm and this is compressing the sciatic nerve, which is giving you leg pain, simple." She looked up at Kyle; his face obviously told her more than he said. "That means there is nothing serious and it is easily treated."

"Oh," answered Kyle. Kelly asked him a few more questions and Kyle noticed her reaction when she asked if he was married. Her eyes widened when he said 'single,' she continued to fill out the rest of the form in the folder laid out on the desk then she stood up and walked over to him. After demonstrating a few simple stretches for him to do she handed him a bean bag that he could use as a heat pack.

"Have you ever had acupuncture?" she asked.

"No," he said.

"Well I think that it would be a massive help for you as it will help relax the muscle but only if you agree. It is an invasive technique after all," Kyle nodded.

"Ok, no problems,"

"Plus, there is a consent form that you have to sign that allows me to stick things in you," Kelly had a piece of paper in her right hand and looked at Kyle as she spoke; his eyebrows raised.

"Really? sounds like fun, I will sign it later then," in seconds she had picked up a small box and made her was to the bottom of the plinth. She placed a small plastic tube near his big toe on his right foot and tapped the top; he hardly felt the needle going in. Kelly lifted the tube away and threw it into the bin near the head of the plinth. It only took Kelly a few more seconds and Kyle had two needles in the top of his foot, one at the side of his ankle and another in the side of his knee. Straight away he felt the entire leg relax and the pain lift, he rested his head back on the pillow and closed his eyes as he was comfortable for the first time since the disturbance.

"Ok, just one more to go," said Kelly as she took hold of his right hand and placed the needle in the web space between his thumb and first finger, his arm tensed as he felt it touch something, 'that hurt' he thought to himself, Kelly was quietly reassuring him, gently talking as she worked. "Right, now sit back, relax and enjoy," she said as she walked away.

"Ok, how long are these going to be in for?" he couldn't quite describe how he felt apart from very relaxed and pain free. She pulled up her chair and got comfortable behind her desk and picked up another folder. "Twenty minutes."

Kyle opened his eyes and looked at her as she looked up at the clock then toyed with the pen in her right hand. Her eyes darted over to him and they looked eye to eye, Kyle smiled as she blushed and lowered her stare into the folder. They both kept chatting as he just sat there with needles stuck in him and she kept looking at him then the folder. Kyle wasn't sure if she liked him or was she just being professional? He didn't know. Soon she was up with a yellow plastic box with 'clinical waste" printed in blue across the side of it. The needles came straight out, and she dropped them into the box, Kyle was slightly surprised to see that he wasn't bleeding at all. Kelly stepped close as he stood up; suddenly he felt light-headed. Kelly gripped his left arm and sat him down again.

"Not so fast," she reassured as she sat close beside him, Kyle looked at her before he spoke.

"Wow," he said. Kelly raised her eyebrows.

"Wow?" she repeated. Kyle's smile broke over his face, he slowly closed his eyes then reopened them before he spoke again. He looked into her eyes as he did so.

"Yeah, wow." Kelly let go of his arm, but she stayed close to him.

"Well," she started, in her hand, was a small business card, "I would like to see you again in a week's time." Kyle took the card and looked at it. It was a standard police card, with the police emblem on one side and her details of where she worked at Carrickfergus with a landline telephone number.

"Ok, what time would be good?" he asked. Kelly moved to the desk and lifted a dark coloured diary. She stood with her back to him as she flicked through the pages. Kyle's eyes moved up her body; she slowly turned towards him. The diary was open in her left hand and the black pen was in her right hand, pointing towards the open page; she stepped towards him as she raised her gaze.

"2 pm?" Kyle stood up again as she got closer, the dizziness was all gone, he nodded.

"That sounds ok to me," he looked at the card again then looked at her face, "If I have to change it, can I just get you at this number?" he turned the card towards her, a shocked look burst over her face.

"Oh no," she closed the diary and strode forward until she was less than a foot in front of him. Kelly took the card off him and to his delight she started to write on the back of the card. "This is my mobile number; you can text me on this," Kelly handed the card back to him and he smiled as he took it. Kyle slowly read over the number before he asked his last question of the very red-faced physiotherapist that was standing in front of him.

"Can I put my clothes back on now?"

Chapter 10

Sean was sitting back in the chair in the living room of his house, he pressed the button on the remote control and the TV flashed into life; he had the remote in one hand and a mug of hot coffee in the other. The local news was just starting; it was what he had been waiting for. The main stories were about the recent dog attacks in Northern Ireland; the cameras were at the house in North Belfast that they had just come from. A Pit Bull type terrier had attacked a ten-year-old girl who lived next door to the owner; this was the call they answered earlier. Behind the reporter Sean could see Mike walking away from the house and towards their car. He had spotted the news team arriving from inside the house and Sean always did his best to avoid them. He had been asked if any of M.I.T. wanted to be interviewed but they had declined; a uniformed officer would do the interview instead.

Sean and the others had been in the back garden of the house when the owner of the Pit Bull said good bye to the happy dog that was playfully jumping around the small back garden. The owner had a legally held shotgun and he destroyed the dog himself. Sean looked at him as he started to cry when he pointed the gun at the back of the dog's head, nearly breaking down afterwards. He had raised the dog from when it was a pup and obviously loved it, but he knew what he had to do. The next-door neighbours would settle for nothing less; they did not even have to quote the 1991 Dangerous Dogs Act (Northern Ireland) to him, so either way the dog was going to be destroyed. The owner agreed that the child had in fact trespassed and the dog had just done what came naturally to it, but he knew he would not win.

The news went on to another story as Sean drank some of his coffee, his phone in his pocket buzzed. Sean placed the mug down and took out the screen, he read the message from Mike asking if he had seen the news programme. Sean tapped in his reply then added that he had got approval to take him over for the crime watch programme. Sean had drunk most of his coffee before he answered. Sean pressed the dial button on his phone as a smile opened on his face just before a female voice answered the phone; it was Mike's wife.

"No, he bloody well can't!" he let out a small chuckle which she joined in with.

"Yes, he bloody well *CAN!*" Sean paused, "Well, I am not the police poster boy of the section." The phone got handed over to Mike, Sean and Mike spoke for a few minutes then said their goodbyes; the rest could be sorted out in the morning. Sean sat back again and looked out the window and wondered who or what could have committed the murder. They needed to be off the streets, but he knew deep down that this was not a one-off incident. Killers like this never struck once, they would strike again. Some claimed a cause, others claimed a god, some were mad, others were just bad. Sean finished the coffee just as the first drops of rain started.

∞∞∞∞

Tony dropped Kyle back at his house then drove to the police station in Coleraine. He found their section sergeant and informed him of Kyle's next appointment and that he had been stood down from duties for another week. The sergeant had not been too impressed but said ok 'not that he had much of a choice' Tony thought to himself. Kyle had started to text the Physio soon after leaving Maydown and his phone had been hot since. Kyle liked this one which made him smile, 'Finally,' Tony thought to himself when he was driving. Tony guessed that he would be texting her for a while.

∞∞∞∞

Tony was sitting in the front room of his house, the panoramic view out the large windows was amazing and it is what had sold the house to him when they first viewed it. They could see along the coast, all of the town of Portrush and most of one of the golf courses that attracted so many professional golfers from all over the world. Out on the water a small yacht with two white sails sat seemingly motionless, just a white dot in the blue carpet of the sea. In between the coastline and their house, the rolling grass covered hills rose and fell quite sharply, split only by the green hedges that separated the different fields. On a bad day, you could only see 50 feet in front of you but on a fine day you could see for miles, even catch Rathlin Island on the best of days. Tony turned his head towards the door of the living room as his wife walked in carrying a mug in each hand, she smiled as she approached, the weather forecast was on the TV at the time. She bent over and handed him a mug then leaned down and gently kissed him on his left cheek. Tony's eyes stared into her eyes; they shared the smile. The ringing phone stole it away from them as Karen turned and walked out to the phone by the front door, she answered it with a simple 'hello,' then placed the phone down and turned back into the room.

"It is for you," as Tony rose Karen walked away into the kitchen and closed the door, Tony lifted the phone to his ear and spoke one word. "Hello," he immediately recognised the male voice at the other end of the phone.

"Hello Tony; you say you think you saw the girl?" The voice was straight to the matter at hand.

"Yes, I am sure of it," said Tony.

"Tell me what happened," Tony described what had happened and described the girl he had seen at the entrance to the Diamond Shopping Centre in Coleraine a few days before.

"No probs, Slan," Tony said goodbye in Irish as he liked using it as much as possible.

"Slan go Foile," came the reply as the phone went down, 'farewell for now' Tony smiled again.

Dinner will be ready in five minutes," the shout had come from the kitchen and whatever she was making smelled good. He was going to enjoy his quiet evening in; all alone with his wife.

∞∞∞

Cara-Marie was heading towards the back door of the office as she had been there an hour more than she was supposed to. Just as she got to the door Mark shouted at her, she turned and faced him as her handbag fell from her shoulder and down to her elbow.

"Cara, are you going over to Tesco's?" It was not so much a question of '*are*' but '*could*', she smiled at him with a knowing grin.

"*I may be, why?*'" she said with a tilt of her head and a gentle closing of her eyes as she swung her handbag back up onto her shoulder.

"Brilliant," Mark jumped up to his feet and walked towards her, "could you get me a few things?" Mark then produced a list of fresh milk, bread and other items that any single person would need to have a meal by themselves. Cara-Marie's eyes scanned the list, she knew without saying anything that Mark and his other half had obviously just had yet another bust up and he wasn't going home just yet; how long would it be before he eventually left her? "I won't make it home for a bit as I need to finish this lot off," he turned his shoulder slightly and pointed his thumb towards his workstation. Cara-Marie knew it was a lie. She looked at him and smiled.

"Sure, that's no problem," she turned and walked out the door and let it close behind her without taking any money for the food. She looked over the list again just before she crossed the busy road that was full of cars and people bustling their way through the wind that was starting to nip. The list said so much more to her than just what he had written. Cara-Marie was jolted back to reality by someone walking into her. She sidestepped and uttered an immediate apology as the teenager stopped and blinked at her. He looked about sixteen, with spots, his black clothes did not fit but that was the style at the moment, his trousers were covered in dirt and had a rip in one of the legs. The leads of his IPOD led from his pockets up underneath his hood and into a mop of unwashed hair that nearly his covered eyes. He looked at her in annoyance, turned up his lip and muttered an insult and a curse before charging off in front of her in the direction he had been going. Cara-Marie went from apologetic to angry in seconds and stared into the back of the hood. The crossing started beeping and people either side of her moved forward to cross the road, she paused for a second then walked on.

As she entered Tesco's the security guard smiled and lifted his hand in recognition of her, Cara-Marie smiled a reply and walked on, trying very hard not to get into a conversation with him again. The wire basket soon filled with the few bits for Mark then she dropped in a few things for herself as she walked up and down the aisles. Cara-Marie stood in the queue and waited for the young girl at the till to finish with the pensioner that was in front of her. Each of the pensioner's movements were slow and deliberate, slowly taking in everything that was happening. The young girl was soon annoyed. As the pensioner dropped the coins into her empty purse the young girl had started to fill a plastic carrier bag with the few things that she had bought. The young girl finished before the pensioner as she slowly put the purse into her old cream coloured leather handbag hanging off her arm. Her shopping was being held out in front of her; the pensioner took the bag and whispered a thank you before slowly shuffling away.

Cara-Marie stared at the young girl as she fired her items over the scanner that bleeped at every item. Cara gazed out of the glass walls which looked over the full car park and wished she was somewhere else. Cara-Marie said nothing as she handed over a £20 note to the assistant who was avoiding eye contact and was saying everything bluntly and with a 'matter of fact' attitude. She held her in contempt and left without speaking.

The chilly wind hit her as she stepped out through the automatic doors and into the evening. She had an idea that Mark would love, she turned left and walked along the side of the brightly lit shop, keeping the car park to her right. She was moving quickly as she walked on until she came to the main road that ran around the car park and down towards the river, a light rain had started so she zipped up her coat to her chin. Cara-Marie stepped onto the pavement and headed with the flow of the one-way traffic. The wind was coming off the river and it grew stronger as she walked along the road. She was separated from the river by a small wall; on the far side of the road from her was a sport 'superstore'. She cast a glance across the river at the church on the far side; some of the trees blocked the view of the small graveyard, her eyes passed over the apartment flats that stood up from the road beside the church. The only thing that was moving over there was the traffic on the road in front of them. Cara-Marie walked on until she passed the large Chinese restaurant on the riverbank on her left; it shielded her from the wind a little as she ducked her head and walked just a little bit faster. The pathway split from the road at the far side of the restaurant; the shopping bag banged against her leg as she moved to one side to let a man walking the other way pass. Cara-Marie followed the path around a tree on her right then on towards the bridge; the smell from the Chinese restaurant filled her nose. The path rose to meet the bridge and was surrounded by a small wall which dropped over the far side. The sound of the light rain could be heard on the leaves of the trees above her and if it was not for the sound of the traffic it would probably be a very nice place to be.

The traffic lights turned to red and a silver car stopped. As the crossing beeped, she stepped forward as did a couple coming the other way. Cara-Marie darted over the crossing and onto the wider pavement at the far side of the road by the blue metal fencing. The phone in her pocket started to buzz with the new tune she downloaded only the week before. Cara-Marie moved the plastic bag of shopping to her left hand and fumbled for the phone. She pulled it out to read the number, pressed the green answer button and put the phone to her ear.

"Hello Mum," she stopped where she was and turned to her right to shelter from the wind. Cara-Marie looked over the car park in front of her as her mother started talking. Cara-Marie's eyes glanced over to the cream coloured building that was lined in green. The car park extended underneath the large building and was situated at the end of the building that overlooked the river were the large shops and open planed café. Her mother was talking to her about what she was doing for dinner that evening; invites like this from her mum normally led to her getting 'volunteered' do to something. The last time she ended up driving her mum and one of her mum's friends to Belfast and spent a day shopping before driving them back again. Cara-Marie said she would call round in about an hour's time and a very pleased mother hung up the phone.

Cara-Marie put the phone back into her pocket, moved the shopping bag back into her right hand and continued over the bridge. At the end of the walkway was a tall blue painted lamp post with a sign informing people of the bicycle/ pathway split; most people did follow the instructions, but some did not. The building at the end of the walkway was painted cream and white and was three storeys high, the blue lettering above one of the ground floor windows highlighted that it was now used by 'Age Concern'. Cara-Marie had written a story on them last year and she wondered if the same person was still in charge. As she got near the end her eyes looked to the right along the riverbank lined with trees. On the far side, behind the cream and green shop was a scrap metal yard that had closed for the day, the tall crane was almost a silhouette in the sky. Cara-Marie stepped to the left to avoid a middle-aged woman who seemed to be in a rush, she was wearing black trousers and a white waterproof jacket. Her makeup was thick, and her face was covered with an intense scowl that looked like it was probably permanent, or so she thought.

The pathway split at the Age Concern building, the right-hand side followed the river's edge and the left side curved around the front of the building. The pathway went against the flow of traffic and both sides of the street were lined with shops and take away restaurants. Cara-Marie was turning to the left when a young woman stormed past her. She had jet-black hair that sat on her shoulders. She was wearing a black duffel jacket that was open and revealed a fit looking girl dressed head to foot in black. Black jeans, black top, black leather boots, Cara-Marie looked at the young face that stared back at her.

Her eyes were very dark as was the look that she was getting from her. Cara-Marie almost stopped as the young woman stormed on, holding the eye to eye stare, slowly turning her head as she went on then with a flick of her head she turned and took off down towards the pathway along the riverbank, the wind slightly caught the bottom of her duffel coat and lifted it up and then flapped it down, almost in contempt back at her. Cara-Marie was opened mouthed in a slight state of annoyance, so much so that she did not notice the man who walked around the corner and past her on his way after the girl with the black hair. She closed her mouth, turned her head and walked around the corner in the direction that she was going.

Cara-Marie walked into the Chinese take-away, it was empty but those inside the Chinese itself were busy. She scanned the take-away menu and wondered what Mark would like for his tea; she placed an order of a meal and a soft drink. After she paid she sat down on the window ledge turning to pick up one of the magazines that was sitting there. It was one of the gossip magazines that she would never buy but would read if they were just lying around, like this one was. It was not real journalism; just PR and spin mixed up with a lot of gossip. She sat there and flicked through the pages, picking out faces she recognised.

"Hello, Cara-Marie, isn't it?" The male voice made her jump out of the magazine and look up at who was standing at the counter; it took nearly two seconds before she recognised the face.

"Oh, hello…" she paused before saying what she hoped was his first name, "Kyle," a smile broke over Kyle's face as Cara-Marie stood up to talk to him.

"And how are you this fine evening?" he asked. Cara-Marie lifted her left arm up on the counter to lean up against it; she was mirroring what he was doing. Kyle then shifted from one foot moving his weight to the other, and Cara-Marie noticed this.

"Yeah, I am fine," she smiled.

"*Fine?*" asked Kyle, Cara-Marie looked slightly puzzled at him before she answered with a simple, 'Yes,' "well my mum once told me that if a woman ever tells you that they are '*fine*' what they are actually saying is that they are F'd up, Insecure, Neurotic and Emotional!" Cara-Marie blinked as her mind went over the mnemonic, then she smiled with her mouth and her eyes.

"Ha, no, I am well, things are ok," she replied.

"That's good, so what is happening over at the Herald?" he enquired, she answered his question with a question.

"Not as much as your work place, care to tell?" Kyle smiled, he motioned with his head to sit down, she agreed. Cara-Marie noticed again the way he was moving, he had hurt himself and seemed to be in a bit of pain, "Are you ok?" she said as they were sitting down.

"Yeah, just damaged myself a little, you know, after the trouble up the heights a few days ago," She nodded in agreement but stayed quiet and allowed him to talk, "I read your article of the disturbance," Kyle glanced over at her as he continued, "there were a few at work who were furious at your photographer for the pictures and your story for not mentioning that a police officer was hurt!"

She raised her eyebrows. "Was that you?"

"Furious? Me? No, others," Cara-Marie knew that he was talking about some of the more senior police officers that were always so polite to her, but then they had to be. Kyle continued "Yes, I was the one who got hurt." There was a pause between them as the young Chinese girl appeared with two white plastic bags of food, she read out each order in turn, they both stood and walked out the door.

"Where are you parked?" she asked. Kyle pointed towards the car park across the river that was in front of the cream and green building.

"Over at Dunne's Stores," he looked at Cara-Marie, "You?"

"Tesco's, I have to take this back to the office as it is not actually for me," Cara-Marie half lifted the two plastic bags that were now in her right hand.

"Well since we are walking the same way", Kyle slightly turned towards her and extended his left hand in the direction of the footbridge, she smiled and accepted the invitation. She noticed that he seemed to be able to walk ok but there was discomfort there.

"So, is that it for you?" Cara-Marie asked as they got to the footbridge, Kyle opened his mouth to answer when they heard a sound they both would later describe as a cry of anguish.

They both turned towards the sound; it was a female voice and very high pitched; it had only lasted a second when there was another. They both started off towards the trees, Kyle leading the way, scanning the way as the darkness of the evening slowly crept over everything. Cara-Marie looked back over the empty foot bridge and knew that no one else had heard the sound.

The back of the Age Concern building was mostly derelict; the doors boarded up and wire mesh covered the windows. Anti-police graffiti covered the wall to their left as they passed another tall blue lamp post. Kyle had his hand on his right hip; Cara-Marie knew that he was carrying his gun, which at least made her feel a little safer, not much, just a little. The pathway led off in front of the trees and was known as a nice evening walk, unusually there seemed to be no-one else around. Behind the trees was another car park that served the community health centre, but it would be closed at this time in the evening. At the back of the building was an alleyway; the wall that separated the alley from the car park was a simple brick construction covered in moss and leafed bushes that grew all the way along it. The car park itself was empty.

A large green plastic council bin that looked brand-new stood up against the wall. Hung off the side was a woman who looked like she was in her late twenties, her right hand was hanging onto the bin and she was bent overlooking down at her feet. Her legs looked like they were about to give way as they were shaking violently. As she looked up her straight hair hung down past her face, she was covered in what was obviously blood, she burst into tears and collapsed when she saw two people run around the corner.

Kyle and Cara-Marie ran over to the now hyperventilating, panicked woman. Both tried to reassure her as Kyle scanned her, but he could not see any obvious wounds that were bleeding. She was grabbing at both Kyle and Cara-Marie, her eyes wide with fear, she rambled, and half screamed about running, she was scared out of her mind.

"This blood isn't hers!" he said out loud partly for Cara-Marie but more for himself. Cara-Marie straightened up and looked over the wall, she could clearly see the body of a dog lying in the middle of the car park, its head was lying further away and there was a pool of blood around the body; there was something else lying near it, but she could not make out what it was. Kyle was trying to ask the woman her name, she was trying to get up and run away; that was all she wanted to do, Kyle was trying his best to calm her down. Cara-Marie glanced back at her when her eye caught some movement. She looked over at the single-story building at the far end of the car park. Something had just moved beside it. Cara-Marie looked again at the edge of the building as a long arm covered in short black hair moved into view. What looked like a dog's head peered around the corner. It flicked out of view when it spotted her looking at it. Cara-Marie's left hand shot out and grabbed Kyle's shoulder.

"OH, MY GOD, THERE IS SOMEONE OVER THERE!" the head had come around at about six feet from the ground, but that wasn't possible, dogs didn't grow that tall. Kyle jumped up.

"WHERE?" he shouted. She pointed towards the building. He threw himself over the wall and commanded her to stay with the woman. The Chinese and the rest of the shopping was dropped on the ground. Cara-Marie went to take hold of the woman, she glanced up towards the building as she spotted two black dogs on all fours running up the hill and off behind the trees, with one movement Kyle drew his Glock pistol.

"POLICE OFFICER," he shouted as loud as he could. He had his phone to his ear and had started to half shout into it; he was talking to the duty desk officer back at the police station; all police officers had that number on speed dial. Cara-Marie did her best to try and comfort the hysterically crying woman. She still could not make any sense out of what she was saying. Cara-Marie pulled out her own phone and was counting the seconds and the rings before Mark answered his mobile phone.

Kyle had his pistol extended in his hands, leading the way as he half walked, half ran forward. He passed the dog; the head was several feet away and it had been gutted as most of the dog's internal organs were strewn over the ground. It looked like a Springer spaniel. This had been done with an incredible amount of force. A siren started up the built-up area that was over the far side of the river; the cavalry was on their way. Kyle's phone was returned to his pocket as his eyes scanned the area in front of him. He looked round at the tall trees to his right, at the end of these he spotted two legs lying out of a light-coloured bush.

There was blood on the bush, the ground and on the grass around the trees, Kyle looked over the top of his pistol and slowly turned around and looked all around. He looked up the hill, round the buildings, back at Cara-Marie who looked over at him. The woman's arms were wrapped around her torso, but Kyle could not see her head as he continued his arc and came back to the body in the bush just as the police car with the blue flashing lights and wailing sirens screamed into the car park.

Chapter 11

Sean waited for the number to start ringing before he put the phone to his ear; it rang three times before a female voiced answered.

"And I am telling you that he is *not* going to England with you," Joanne, Mike's wife said it with a comical tone, Sean smiled.

"Yeah, right, is the poster boy there?" He asked.

"Sort of..." She answered.

"Sort of?" Sean asked.

"Sort of," she paused before continuing her sentence, "he is on the toilet at the moment, I can pass the phone in if you want?" Sean closed his eyes at the picture that was now in his head, and chuckled slightly, to much delight at the other end of the phone.

"Thank you, no, just get him to phone me when he is finished."

"Ok, no probs," she hung up the phone. Sean scrolled down the numbers on his phone then pressed the green dial button; he again waited until it started to ring before he put it to his ear.

"Hi boss, I was expecting you to ring," Simon said as he answered,

"Hi Simon, you have seen the news then?" Sean asked,

"Yes, I can see the similarities already, do you want me to speak to Maydown MIT?"

"No," Sean answered simply, "No not at all, there have been other developments, could you meet us in the office and I will tell you face to face," there was a pause before Simon spoke again, he would of course say yes; saying no was out of the question, Simon showed once again that he was able to read events very well. "Ok, I will pack a holdall,"

"See you there," Sean noticed that Simon did not answer or say a farewell before he hung up; what was up with him he pondered. He was not his usual self, something was off. Sean put the phone down and as he stood up the phone went off again. Sean picked it off the coffee table and walked out of the door of his living room. He read the display name before he answered it leaving his wife on the sofa; she was reaching for the remote control for the TV even before he was out the door.

"Finished on the toilet then?" was the first question, Mike launched into a string of apologies that made Sean laugh out loud, and then he got down to business, "Could you come into the office? I have got things for all of us to do." The question was 'Could', but it really was not a question, it was a directive that Mike was not going to say no to.

"No probs, on my way," Mike answered.

"I have already spoken to Simon and he is going to meet us there," said Sean. Sean knew that the two of them would speak to each other on the phone and both would put forward reasons for a meeting in the evening that could not wait until the following morning.

"Ok, see you soon," answered Mike.

"Oh Mike," Sean said,

"Yes boss?" he asked, Sean paused; it was probably nothing and was now regretting giving his thoughts life.

"It's probably nothing. It's just that Simon was a bit off,"

"A bit off?" asked Mike.

"Yeah, I couldn't put my finger on it." Sean replied, now totally regretting saying anything.

"Ok, I will keep my eyes and ears open," Sean ended the chat and closed his phone, he looked out of the kitchen window as his thoughts of what the night held wandered. He opened the cupboard and removed one of the mugs neatly placed inside. His phone beeped with a message; it was from Mike. 'SPOKE TO JOANNE ABOUT SIMON, SHE SAID THAT TOMORROW IS TEN YEARS TO THE DAY SINCE SALLY DIED'. Sean read the message over again; of course, that made sense, it was ten years to the day that his wife had died of cancer. They had been married since he'd first met him, but Sean had never had much of a chance to get to know the wife. Simon still lived in the same house they had shared, and he heard Simon had turned the main bedroom into a virtual shrine. Sean knew Simon had a standing order from his wages that went to a cancer charity every month. The text had brought Sean back to where he was, and it was time to leave; the coffee would have to wait and by the time he got home his wife would have forgotten all about her annoyance at the empty mug that had been left on the side.

∞∞∞∞

Alexi glared at Davidov. The living room was heavy with atmosphere, the others were silent. Alexi didn't believe him, that much was obvious to everyone else. Alexi was sitting in the armchair with every single fibre of his being propelling itself towards him.

"Tell me again," Alexi quietly said, his tone however, was not. Davidov started telling all about the day's events, he looked at each one of them in turn, all except Anna who was sat to the left of Alexi and was staring at the new carpet in the small living room. They were in Davidov's house overlooking the river. Anders lived next door with the rest split between the two. It was cramped but they all enjoyed not having Alexi in the house permanently. Davidov spoke about meeting up with Anna, going shopping around Coleraine and how they thought that they were being followed. Davidov continued to talk, the others listening but Alexi just sat there. Anna was nodding occasionally in agreement. Davidov stated they had not killed the man who had been attacked earlier and, as if on cue, a police car with its blue lights flashing and its sirens wailing flew past on the road outside. Silence descended on the room, Anders cast a glance at Davidov then back at Alexi who was still glaring at Davidov. The silence seemed to go on forever before Alexi spoke.

"I want all of you out looking for the Rua." He slowly started to turn his head and cast his gaze around the room, "I want you to identify them then come and find me." He seemed as if he was restraining his anger, as if he was trying to hold back the beast inside him from bursting out. "I want you to identify them, come and get me so I can approach them and try and guarantee our safety." Everyone looked at each other with a look of shock on their faces as this was unheard of. Davidov and Anders looked at each other before Davidov looked back at Alexi.

"Alexi, this is something we cannot do, to identify ourselves to the Rua means certain death for us all," Alexi exploded. He sprang up from the chair and launched himself at Davidov. The palm of his right hand connected with the left-hand side of Davidov's face sending him spiralling onto the floor; the others jumped back at the attack, no one moved, no one intervened, they knew better. Alexi screamed at the top of his voice at Davidov.

"Do not *dare* to tell me what I can and cannot do, do not dare to tell me what is safe and what is not, do not tell me what you think certain death is, we would already be dead if it was down to you!" Davidov rolled over onto his right side and looked up at the shouting Alexi, his face was contorted with rage. Alexi pointed directly into the face of Davidov then straightened his posture up and his voice quietened from a shout. "Or if you want to challenge me," there was a pause to let his word sink in, his voice raised to half shouting again as he finished his sentence, "then do so."

All in the room took a breath in at the threat, '*A challenge?*' Davidov slowly raised himself up then knelt before him, bowing his head to the man who stood above him, Davidov spoke quietly, nearly in a whisper but loud enough for all to hear.

"No, I will not challenge you, I apologise if my actions were insubordinate and disrespectful to you." Davidov closed his fists and rested them on the carpet as his chin touched the top of his left knee. Alexi relaxed and stood back, his right hand turned and ushered him to stand. Alexi spoke one word. "Rise,"

The others could not believe what they had just witnessed. Davidov's contempt for Alexi was well known and he had just turned down what all expected to be his chance. Davidov stood in one motion, keeping his gaze looking down in front of Alexi who waited another few seconds before he spoke again. "Davidov," Davidov raised his vision to look at his face but he did not look into his eyes as Alexi continued speaking. "You are mine, in you I place my trust and that I hold dear," both their eyes snapped a glance at the very quiet Anna who looked back at them both. Alexi continued, "Davidov, in you I see my will; see to it that I am obeyed." Alexi stepped back again and relaxed his body; Davidov raised his head and looked at his Alpha. "Find the Rua, before they find us." Alexi said with finality.

Davidov nodded and answered with two words. "I obey," with that he looked at the others and with a small whistle of his lips and a nod he walked around Alexi towards the front door; the others stood and followed him out. Anna stood up and started to walk in the same direction, but Alexi stopped her with his hand in front of her.

"Wait." he commanded. She stopped where she was and stood waiting for the next instruction. The room emptied then the front door slammed shut; they were alone. The sternness and anger left Alexi's face as he moved close to her then pushed his arms around her waist and pulled her close. Anna slowly raised her arms and wrapped them around his neck; she felt herself being pulled tight into him before he released her, Alexi stepped back and turned away from her and walked over to the window.

"What's wrong my love?" she asked.

"Wrong?" he half laughed down his nose as he looked through the blinds at the moving traffic. "What could possibly be wrong? We are soon to become the hunted in a strange land where we have nowhere to hide. We cannot return home, or we face our own deaths. I am losing control of my own pack." He paused as she stepped up behind him, placing her hand in the small of his back. She stood close to him "I know the others will follow him before me..." Anna placed her head on his shoulder as he spoke, Alexi was staring out the window, "and I am losing control," he repeated but he could not say out loud the thoughts in his head as Anna reached up and gently kissed his left cheek. Across the road Davidov and Anders stood with their backs to the house, the others had been sent off in different directions into Coleraine, two had been sent in the car to walk around Portstewart then Portrush. Everyone was told not to be back before 4 in the morning.

"Is he still watching?" asked Davidov, Anders glanced back over his right shoulder.

"Yes," Anders looked at him, "He offered you a challenge, that was your chance!" Davidov looked at him before he turned and started to walk up towards the stone bridge and the uniformed policeman who stood by the tall lamppost.

"As the Irish say Anders, 'Tiocfaidh ar la' my friend," Anders looked at him with a confused look on his face.

"Chucky what?" he asked. Davidov patted him on the shoulder as they walked.

"It is Irish for *'our day will come'*, good don't you think? Very fitting for what we have planned!" A smile spread over Anders face.

∞∞∞∞∞

Carl was sitting back in the chair of the farmhouse. The killing in Coleraine was all over the news, he sat forward and brought his hands up, so his fingertips touched. He glanced over at the other chair where his friend of many years was sitting; the news coverage continued.

"We have to find them," Carl said quietly, across from him was another male of his pack. He was a similar age to Carl but, like him, did not look as old as he was. His friend looked up without speaking as Carl continued, "we have to find them and deal with them,"

His friend nodded, then spoke. "The Russians have not been very forthcoming with information for us,"

Carl looked over at him. "No Paul, they haven't," he said as his gaze returned to the TV screen. "We have told them everything that we know but they haven't answered any of our questions. Do they not know who this lot actually are?" Carl watched the TV for a few more moments, taking his time with his thoughts.

"Where are the Russians now?" Paul asked,

Carl waited a few seconds before he spoke again. "They have left the south and are spending a few days in Belfast." Carl's gaze returned to the floor in front of him before continuing, "At their request, they are to be left alone and they will get in touch with us when they wish too." Paul remained silent; he continued to watch what Carl was doing. Slowly, Carl stood up. Paul stood up with him, Carl turned to him as he pressed the off button on the remote and the TV screen died. "Paul." he said. The tone of his voice was raised to a command. Paul stood upright and stiff and listened to what his Alpha had to say, "Send six to search Derry city and the surrounding area." Paul nodded as Carl continued, "Send two to Coleraine, two to search Ballymoney and two across to Ballymena." Again, Paul nodded in understanding; most of County Londonderry would be searched by them in no time at all. "They are not to approach them, just find them then inform me." Carl paused, "This is our land, we will defend it."

"As we have always done." said Paul.

"As we have always done." Carl repeated with a friendly grin.

"We have a possible sighting of the girl in Coleraine," Paul stated. "The rumours are that they are hiding among the Polish there."

Carl placed his right hand on Paul's shoulder. "Of course," he smiled, "make sure whoever you choose to search Coleraine also covers the University, Portrush and Portstewart." he paused then spoke again, "In fact send six to Coleraine." Paul returned the grin then turned and walked out the door. Carl could hear Paul start to shout as he gathered those outside around him to carry out his masters wishes. Carl knew that his trust in Paul was not misplaced. One day he would let him take over. The dun and the whole pack would be safe under him. Carl sat back down in the chair and closed his eyes, his breathing slowed as he sank back into his own mind's eye. His nose twitched, his arms jumped then his body relaxed and rested as a small smile broke over his face; his head turned to one side as he started to relax and fall asleep.

∞∞∞∞∞

Kyle hobbled away from the entrance to the main building inside Coleraine police station. Tony caught up with him up in seconds.

"Want a lift home?" Tony asked. Kyle stopped and looked at him and smiled.

"Well, you did bring me in, and my car isn't here so, *yeah!*"

"Or I can call one of the patient transfer buses from the Causeway hospital for you," Tony half shrugged his shoulders as Kyle made his way around to the passenger door.

"Just open the door," the central locking of the car bleeped.

"I can help you if you want? You being a cripple and all." Another dirty look from Kyle was answered by something in French that Tony could not translate but knew it would have been very abusive. Kyle could swear at someone and make it sound like poetry. Tony loved it and made a mental note to learn some French sometime. As they drove out of the station Kyle's phone beeped. Tony got the car out into the traffic and took off up towards the Lodge road roundabout. Tony spotted a smile on Kyle's face as he read the text.

"Who's that from?" he asked, Tony could guess but he wanted to hear it from him.

"Oh, it is from Kelly."

"Kelly?" Tony asked.

"*Kelly, the Physio?*" the lights changed to green.

"Oh, her," Tony made his way around through the traffic and took off out into the dark countryside. Kyle was busy tapping away on his phone as Tony overtook the slow-moving tractor. They were alone on the dark, unlit country road. Kyle's phone beeped again. Tony looked at Kyle's face; he could see his excitement grow. Kyle's phone was to beep another three times before they pulled up outside his house. Kyle slowly got out of the car and made his way towards the front door. Tony looked over the top of his car. As Kyle was fumbling with his keys for the front door, he turned back towards Tony.

"Thanks, by the way."

"Thanks? What for?" Tony asked.

"The lift home," answered Kyle.

"You going to be ok tonight?" Tony asked, the front door opened, and the lights came on inside the house.

"Yeah, I am good," he replied.

"If you need anything then ask, ok?" Tony leaned forward over the roof as he had spoken. Kyle stepped into the house and turned in answer, he lifted his right hand that still held the phone.

"Well I am getting a home visit by a very nice physiotherapist from Ballymoney later, so no, I won't be phoning," the smile spread across both faces at the same time, things were moving fast.

"Ballymoney, eh? Well she doesn't have a cow town accent." said Tony as he started to lower himself back into the car. Kyle looked back bemused.

"Cow Town?" Kyle asked, Tony raised himself back out of the car.

"Yeah cow town." Tony paused as he realised that Kyle had no idea what he was talking about, he would have to explain, "Ballymoney is also known as 'Cow Town' as it is a farming town and they have a very large Cow market there so if you want to buy a cow,
you go to cow town." Kyle's eyebrows raised, and his mouth opened with the new information that he had just learnt. "Any local copper would know that," Tony raised his voice to just above speaking but not quite a shout at Kyle who was already starting to close the front door.

"I'm from Lisburn, how the hell would I know that?" Kyle was smiling as the front door closed shut.

Tony climbed back into the car, he reached out to close the door with his right hand as his eyes shot upwards. Tony stared at the first of the three-day full moon cycle, a smile of comfort spread over him as he felt the hair on the back of his neck, down his back and on his arms, stand on end. So much had happened over the past month since the last full moon. The car door closed, and as he started the engine his own phone bleeped. The message only said two words.

CALL ME

Chapter 12

The smell of coffee from Sean's office met them before he did. Sean looked up from the coffee machine as they walked through the main door of the section office; he waved them both over. Mike and Simon had phoned each other after they had spoken to Sean and arranged to meet in the car park of the police station. They had of course discussed what was going on; the killing in Coleraine had been paramount as they had discussed the similarities between that and their own investigations, Mike had not mentioned the text he had sent Sean about Simon but did notice Simon's mood.

"Come in, come in," said Sean, "help yourselves to a coffee," they did. They took their usual seats as Sean sat down in his swivel chair. "Right lads, I will get right too it," Sean lifted the mug to his mouth as the two men reached into their pockets and pulled out their notebooks and black pens, ready to make notes on whatever he was about to say. "I have had Chief Anderson on the phone earlier this fine evening." Detective Chief Inspector Anderson was Sean's immediate boss in M.I.T, and although they never had disagreements in front of them or the rest of the team, everyone knew about the differences in opinions between the two men. Sean continued "And he had been speaking to Super Sutcliffe before that so this one comes from upon high." Mike was nearly drooling at this piece of news, Superintendent Sutcliffe, Chief Anderson's boss, this was getting better. Sean paused as he took another sip of coffee, both men sitting in front of him exchanged glances at the information; something big was coming. "You both know about the killing in Coleraine?" Both men nodded as Mike spoke.

"How could we not? It's all over the news.,"

"Well," started Sean, "hold onto your hats boys as we have just been appointed to lead 'Operation Muirdris' and the investigation has been handed over to us." both Mike and Simon reacted.

"Operation what?" asked Simon.

"Muirdris," replied Sean.

"How do you spell that?" Asked Mike. Sean looked down at his own notepad and spelt it out for the two of them letter by letter.

"M-U-I-R-D-R-I-S." They both scribbled away on their notepads.

"What does that mean?" asked Mike again.

"No idea." Sean paused as they both looked up at him, "So Mike, get one of the youngsters on the team onto finding out that one."

"Ok boss, so what exactly are we taking over?" Simon was thinking it; Mike asked it. Sean took another mouthful of his coffee;

"This investigation has just gone province wide," Mike raised his eyebrows, but Simon didn't move, "and we are to be the lead investigation team in it." Sean paused to let the information sink in before he continued, "Chief Anderson has given us the lead because we have made the most progress so far and it is felt that there is a link between these murders, so," Sean paused again then slightly raised his voice *"we have to identify this link and we have to prove this link."* Sean lifted the mug up to his lips and leaned back in his chair as he watched the reaction of Mike. Simon still didn't move, he just scribbled in his notebook.

"How come we get the lead?" asked Mike. Simon cast a glance at him.

"We've made the most progress apparently." answered Sean.

"Apparently?" asked Mike.

"Apparently," said Sean, "I think the crime watch had a bit to do with it."

"What about M.I.T. Maydown?" Simon asked.

"Well Inspector Deswell finishes his 30 years in just over a month and there's no replacement yet, so I get the impression there is a continuity thing going on here and we don't want this thing coming back to bite us in another 20 years' time." Simon looked up from his notes as did Mike, they both knew that Sean was making reference to another team that had been investigating a bomb explosion and had not been what could be called professional. Sean continued, "So, we cross every 'T' and dot every 'I' in this case." Mike and Simon nodded as he spoke. Sean knew Mike would love this one. This kind of investigation very rarely came to an individual investigation team; this was normally a career making or career breaking job. "Right, to details. We need to drive up to Coleraine tonight and get a full hand over from the Maydown team," Sean looked down at his own notes, "Inspector Deswell will meet us there as will his two Sergeants." Mike let out an audible chuckle, both Sean and Simon looked at him.

"What?" said Mike as he looked back at the two of them.

"Maybe I should be asking you that?" said Sean.

"I know one of his Sergeants." Mike answered, and he was uncomfortable with it, Sean and Simon exchanged glances.

"Do tell," enquired Simon as he could tell there was something pretty good coming.

"Well," started Mike who had started to blush, Simon slightly turned in his chair towards Mike, "erm, well, you know Joanne," he said trying to explain.

"Joanne? as in your wife?" asked Simon. Sean started smiling as he suddenly guessed what was coming, he had first heard this a few years ago.

"Aaah, yeah,"

Sean lifted the mug as Simon lifted his and took a sip as they both watched Mike squirm in his seat, Mike paused again so Simon prompted him.

"Well go on, don't keep us in suspense!"

"Well, Joanne, my missus..." he paused again.

"We know who she is Mike," said Simon.

"Well she left him to be with me," a smile broke over Simon's face that matched the one that was over the face of the silent Sean, "and he kind of took it personally," Sean drank more of his coffee and the ribbing from Simon started.

"Which one? There are two?" Asked Simon.

"Dave Tattershall," answered Mike.

"So, you nicked his missus?" exclaimed Simon.

"No, I didn't!" answered Mike defensively.

"So, what was the time difference between her leaving him to start with you?" asked Simon. Mike paused; you could see that he was searching for a way of how to answer.

"Tell the truth," said Sean, Simon looked over at him.

"You know about this," said Simon as Sean nodded, "I had forgotten about it, but yeah I know what he is on about," Mike was going red fast as Simon returned his attention to him.

"Well?"

"Well, we had a bit of a connection, she left him, started with me and we got married 8 months later," explained the embarrassed Mike.

Married in 8 months?" said Simon.

"8 months." answered Mike.

"And how long were you married when Duncan was born?" said Sean. Mike gave Sean a look.

"Well?" asked Simon, "How long?" this was better than anything he could have expected. Mike muttered an answer that they both heard but wanted him to hear it louder. "Sorry I missed that Detective Dear, could you repeat your last statement again for the record." said Simon in a mocking official tone. Mike relaxed his shoulders, then turned his head and glared at the chuckling Simon.

"Four months."

"Four months? And I take it he is still a bit pissed, how long have you two been married now?" asked Simon, Sean was watching Simon, this was a really good distraction from what must have been going on in his head. This could not have been planned any better; Sean enjoyed this nearly as much as he was enjoying his coffee.

"Nearly 13 years." The baiting continued before Sean brought it to an end.

"Right, let's get back to what we're doing." both Mike and Sean adjusted themselves in their chairs as Sean got back to business, "We will all head to Coleraine tonight then tomorrow I want us to go through everything that we have for the crime watch with the whole team here at 11 am." Mike and Simon were scribbling again as he was talking, "Mike make sure the team knows and are they're prepped. Simon, get an update from forensics tomorrow morning on the Trotman case so we can see what similarities there are between this and the other cases." Simon nodded as he acknowledged what was being said, "Mike, I want the interview tapes gone over again to see if we have missed anything." Mike also nodded as he scribbled. Sean paused and looked at them, "Anything for me?" He asked.

Simon spoke. "Yeah, the killings up in Limavady were discovered by two coppers from Coleraine."

Sean raised his eyebrows at this. "Brilliant, the interviews should be easy. Get on to Maydown and request copies of the original transcripts." Simon nodded again as he wrote in the notebook, Sean continued, "Hopefully we don't have a serial killer on our hands." Mike and Simon looked up then their eyes glanced at each other. A serial killer, no one had mentioned it in any depth before. Sean looked at his watch, "Right, it's nearly 8 o'clock. We leave in ten minutes then." With that the notebooks were closed, the coffee mugs were emptied, and they shuffled out of the office; the ribbing of Mike however would continue all the way up to Coleraine.

∞∞∞∞

Kyle looked at the clock on his DVD player, '19:53'. Kelly was due to arrive in half an hour. He had not spent long in the shower and he had dressed quickly; well, as quickly as he could. He was wearing a black polo shirt with black jeans and matching socks. He tucked his shirt into the jeans to show off his abdomen. Kyle looked into the hallway mirror, his clothes matched the colour of his hair, he liked black, it was easy and didn't take much matching. The fewer decisions he had to make on it the better as his taste in fashion was not normally of a high standard, as different women had pointed out in the past. His phone that was sitting on the living room table bleeped. Kyle went down the hall, into his living room and read the message; it was from Kelly. 'RUNNING A BIT LATE, COULD YOU TEXT ME DIRECTIONS OF HOW TO GET TO YOURS SO I DON'T GET LOST PLEASE?' Kyle felt his pulse quicken as he read it. He tapped in directions of how to reach the bungalow then sent the message. He made his way back into the kitchen.

The kitchen was at the back of the bungalow; at the entrance door most of the kitchen lay to the left as you walked in. He had a totally new kitchen fitted only a few months ago. To the right was a door leading to the small dining room with a stained rectangle table and four matching chairs; the walls had been painted as well but did not have any pictures on them. This was something on Kyle's 'To Do List.' Directly opposite the entrance to the kitchen were the double doors that led out onto the recently laid patio. He opened the fridge and took out a cold can of 7-up, the door swung closed. As he opened the tin his phone beeped with another message. 'YEAH, NO PROBS, I SHOULD BE ABLE TO FOLLOW THAT. I WILL BE ABOUT 20 MINS, K' Kyle giggled at her text speak, he walked slowly back to the living room and tapped in his reply. 'YES, THAT IS OK, HAVE YOU EATEN YET?' Kyle always typed his question in full.

He drank a mouthful of his drink, put the tin down on one of the coasters on the table, he lifted the remote for his flat screen and started to flick through the channels. It didn't take long for the phone to beep again. 'NO, I HVN'T, NOT HAD CHANCE 2' a smile spread over his face as he sat back in the comfort of the sofa and faced directly towards the screen. 'WHAT WOULD YOU LIKE? PIZZA? CHINESE? INDIAN?' Kyle pressed the send button and cleared the text after it had gone. His eyes focused on the clock on the DVD player, another minute had gone by, '*great!*' he thought to himself '*she has me clock watching now, that's not good*'. The seconds ticked by as he waited for his phone to go off again, the channels flicked by, nothing, nothing, nothing, slowly tick by tick time just did not go any faster. The phone bleeped. 'WOW, CNSE OR IDN, NO PREF, U CHSE' Kyle read it a second time. 'Chinese or Indian, no preference, you choose.' He thought about it, took another drink then answered her. 'OK, I WILL PREPARE DINNER THEN, ETA?' The message was answered almost immediately, 'ETA?' Kyle giggled at her response, he slowly tapped in the reply 'ETA = ESTIMATED TIME OF ARRIVAL, WHAT TIME ARE YOU GOING TO GET HERE?' as soon as he had sent it Kyle wondered if he'd been too cheeky with it, but he was sure he would find out soon enough. The seconds ticked by until the phoned beeped.

'STUCK BEHIND TRACTOR, ½ 8 AT EST.' She was stuck behind a tractor and it would be half past eight at the earliest now. 'NO PROBS, SORTING FOOD OUT NOW, SEE YOU SOON,' the text wasn't replied to. Kyle stood up and went to go towards the door when a bolt of pain shot down his right leg and nearly brought him down; he was reminded why she was coming to see him in the first place. Kyle was surprised when she agreed to come out to his house, but she did say that she 'was up that area anyway'. She had told him in a text that she worked at a clinic nearby sometimes; the work was ok, but it was not regular and was only in the evenings, which infringed a little on the social life.

He walked out to the kitchen and opened one of the drawers near the sink that had a couple of basic cook books but more importantly menus from takeaways that delivered, Kyle shuffled through them and chose what he considered one of the nicer ones. After scanning through he settled on one of the set dinners, the choice was quite varied, and Kelly had said she had no preferences. Kyle dialled the number on the menu and ordered one of the set dinners to be delivered as soon as possible. He hobbled back into the living room and sat back down. The clock had not moved that far forward so he lifted the remote control and the soft drink again and started to flick through the channels; time was going slowly. He stopped on the history channel that was covering the ten years before the American Vietnam War when it was called French-Indo-China and the battles fought by the French army at that time. The Legion had fought well but the French lost the war; the French had wanted the Americans to use an Atom bomb, but the Americans refused.

Kyle drank from the tin again and settled down; he of course knew the history of his regiment. Kyle's interest increased, he knew the basics, but the programme was going into exact detail which impressed him greatly. He knew of the battles but didn't know this much detail and he loved it. The commentary was voiced over still pictures, some from the regiment's own museum and some footage of legionnaires at that time. *"March 1949 the battalion made its first operational jump northeast of Haiphong."*

The hair on Kyle's neck stood up; he remembered his first jump in training; then his very first operational jump, this was hitting a mark with him, *"then in April they jumped into Cha Vai to reinforce a French position that was under heavy attack by the Viet Minh forces,"* The still pictures faded in and out; these where his forefathers in the legion. The programme continued, *"In October 1950, the battalion was pushing the Viet Minh back past Dong Khe and ended on Hill 615, where the Viet Minh numbers proved to be overwhelming; the legionnaires were cut to pieces."* The still pictures showed faces of battle-weary soldiers who had seen too much; a bearded face had aged beyond his years, but he still had the white Kepi firmly on his head, his eyes looked deep into the camera. Kyle looked at the face as it faded to reveal another face; he could feel a sadness within him. *"A mere 23 survivors managed to reach the French lines"*, Kyle closed his eyes for a moment as he felt himself start to well up. He took a deep breath in as the programme moved to 1951; Kyle looked away. He did not know any of the faces on the screen, but they were legionnaires, they were his brothers, his brothers who had gone before, his brothers who had stood beside him and those that soldiered on. While they lived, the Legion lived, 'Vie La Legion' he heard himself say out loud. Kyle was almost in tears when his phone beeped with a message. Kyle set the drink down on a coaster and picked up the phone. He opened the message and read what was on the screen. 'TWO MINS AWAY, BE THERE SOON.' He smiled then sent a simple 'OK'. Kyle looked at the screen then pressed the menu button and the screen turned blue. The sadness started to leave him.

He stood up and hobbled towards the door as headlights filled the living room. Kyle peered through the spyglass in the door, the bright green Peugeot 107 came to a stop beside his own car, he waited for Kelly to get out before he opened the front door. The security lights attached to the outside of the house were already lit as the car door slammed shut. Kelly was wearing a black cotton track suit with white trainers that were lined in bright pink, her zip top was open, and underneath was a white polo shirt that was perhaps a size too small as it showed her chest off very well. She had her hair tied back in a pony tail and smiled as she walked towards the open front door. Kyle stepped back and invited her in. Kelly bounced past him, and her perfume filled his nostrils; *'very nice'* he thought.

"Turn right," Kyle said as she got to the door of the living room, she did. Kyle closed the door and walked after her. Kelly was sitting exactly where he had been only moments before; she looked up as he entered, and her eyes were smiling just as much as her face was. "Dinner is on the way," said Kyle.

"Really, wow, thank you," she answered. Kyle sat down on the sofa as Kelly took off a canvas shoulder bag that he hadn't noticed before.

"Is Chinese ok?" he asked.

"Chinese! Oh yes, love Chinese food." she turned and looked around the room, "Very nice. I like this." Kyle glanced around as well.

"Thank you, would you like to see the rest of my humble abode?" Kelly's body language was all going towards him, Kyle took it as a good sign. Kelly answered with an excited *'yes please'*. Kyle was conscious of the way that he stood up and walked towards the door. They walked through to the kitchen, then the dining room then back along the hallway; Kyle opened the small room that held the toilet. There were two doors left; one the spare room that Kyle opened and led the way in. The double bed took up most of the room. Kyle had changed the bedding earlier after Tony had dropped him off. The window was central in the far-left wall; the white painted wooden double door beside it faced the bed. Kyle opened this to show the empty cupboard space. Kelly glanced in and turned and walked over to the other door that was near the entrance to the room itself.

"The shower." said Kyle.

"Wow, it all looks really good." stated Kelly as she scanned the rest of the room. Kyle started towards the door.

"Well I have had a lot of work done to it; most of it has been completely refurbished."

"Really?" Kelly's eyebrows lifted in surprise. Kyle walked out the door as Kelly followed, "And the last room is yours then" she said. Kyle looked over his shoulder then reached out and opened the door to his own bedroom; he stepped to one side but didn't walk in. Kelly took one step inside. Kyle's arm reached round and flicked on the light switch. The bedroom was a reverse of the spare room; same size with a mirror layout of the doors and windows. His window looked out over the back garden, lit up by the security light outside. The curtains of the spare room where closed but his were open. There were two framed pictures with enlarged photographs. Kelly looked at them and asked who they were. Kyle stood very close to her right shoulder and noticed she didn't move away.

"This one is a sunset over some cedar trees in Lebanon." Kyle paused as Kelly turned and looked at him.

"Lebanon?" there was a pause as his eyes glanced across her face. She had folded her arms and the three buttons of her top were open, Kyle was trying not to look down at the exposed flesh.

"Yes," Kyle pointed at the other picture "and that is the mountains in Corsica." Kelly's eyes turned and looked at the view the picture held.

"They look amazing."

"They were," said Kyle.

"What were you doing there?" asked Kelly.

"Corsica is 2 ReP's home and we were in Lebanon a few times with the UN."

"I'm impressed," she said. Kyle turned and walked back towards the kitchen, Kelly followed but didn't close the bedroom door behind her.

"I've been hearing stories about you Legion boys," she said as Kyle turned to her.

"From whom?" he asked.

She paused; her eyes searched around the room before she answered. "Erm, I was helping out with the public order training and I asked some of the divisional support guys." Kyle smiled and turned towards the kettle as Kelly continued "A few of the ex-military ones there said a few things." Kyle said something quietly that Kelly didn't hear. "Sorry?" she asked. He turned towards her; the smile spread across his face.

"Nothing," At that the doorbell rang, the food had arrived.

Chapter 13

Cara-Marie sipped on her mug of hot tea, she sat back in her chair and looked around the empty office, she glanced up at the clock on the wall, it was nearly seven, the rest of the team would not be in at work for another hour yet. She had watched the sunrise from her house before she had gone to the office. She leaned forward and scrolled down the article again; she had written her own eye-witness account of the killing in Coleraine. She had been taken by ambulance to the Causeway hospital where the other woman was taken to but that was the last she had seen her. After four hours, she was allowed to leave. A uniformed police officer had spoken to her about what she had seen and had written the notes down. Cara-Marie started from leaving the Chinese with Kyle, she did not mention the girl with the black hair, how could that be important? Cara-Marie spotted a spelling mistake and groaned as her fingers sped over the keyboard to correct it. Another sip of hot tea and the article was done. Cara-Marie saved it in the shared area of the networked computer for the editor, and no doubt the editor of the daily newspaper that owned The Herald would be very interested in it as well as he had in the past taken stories from them. The arguments between their editor and the one from the daily were quite colourful. She smiled at the thought of it. She pushed the chair back and walked over to the back door of the office. The blinds were down but were open enough for her to look out over the street and watch different people walking past, engrossed in their own lives, walking too work, walking away from work, just walking, walking, walking. Her mind wandered; her eyes suddenly darted over to the far side of the street where a middle-aged woman was walking with her spaniel on a lead. Cara-Marie's eyes focused in on the face of the dog; it was a happy face, and it searched excitedly around, then looked lovingly up at the woman then bounced down the street. It was the opposite of the face she had seen the night before; her mind wandered back to what she had seen the night before. The state of the woman had shocked her; the blood, the butchered dog. Above all else was the face that had looked around the corner at her.

Cara-Marie had told the police officer every detail; it was obvious that he had not believed her. She had described the shape of the face, the edges of the face covered with white fur with a brown part that went up the face to the eyes. Those eyes; those eyes that had looked directly at her, blinked then ran away. The eyes were set in where the fur panned out and turned from brown fur to dark grey with two erect ears that pointed skyward, the eyes themselves were a deep, dark brown, they were powerful eyes. Those eyes had ensured Cara-Marie only slept one-hour last night and refused to let her sleep anymore.

Her mother had picked her up from the hospital and took her home. Mark had stayed at the scene with his cameras but went to the hospital later and drove her car home from the office. The Chinese was cold, but the memories were not. The doctor at the hospital had offered her counselling before she had left, '*normal reactions to abnormal situations,*' she had been told to watch out for nervous over-reactions, nightmares and signs of stress. '*Stress*' She had just found a hysterical woman that had seen someone getting ripped apart right in front of her. Cara-Marie suddenly realised she couldn't remember the name of the woman, or in fact the name of the dead guy. She cursed herself as it was written down on a piece of paper somewhere. Her mobile phone suddenly beeped with a message; she walked over and picked it up off her desk, the text was from Mark. "WHAT ARE YOU DOING AT WORK AT THIS TIME IN THE MORNING??? :-)" He had put in a small smiley face at the end of the text. Cara-Marie smiled then sat down as she tapped in a reply. "HOW DID YOU KNOW I WAS AT WORK?" Cara-Marie looked up at the clock, it was nearly half seven and where had the time gone. Her phone beeped again with another text from Mark. "I DROVE PAST THE BACK DOOR AND YOU STOOD STARING OUT THE WINDOW. JUST PARKED UP IN TESCO'S" she slowly blinked her eyes and smiled as she could just picture him driving and texting at the same time, which was going to get him into trouble one of these days. Her phone beeped again, "THANK YOU FOR THE CHINESE, I AM SURE IT WOULD HAVE BEEN LOVELY!" This time she giggled and relaxed as Mark started tapping on the back door.

"Morning!" he was very cheerful, she stood back as he walked towards his own desk.

"Morning," Cara-Marie smiled but she was a bit more subdued, the door closed, and she walked towards her own desk. Mark's computer burst into life as he landed on his chair, he was in a good mood, "so how come you are so happy this morning?" she enquired, Mark had opened a small blue and black backpack that he often carried with him. It had been left under his desk the night before. He glanced over at her as he was lifting his cameras out of the bag and placing them on the desk in front of his PC.

"Oh, not much, just happy to be here and enjoying work," Mark would never come in this early or in fact be in such a good mood at this time in the morning, unless.........

"So how much did you get for the pictures?" Cara-Marie did not ask about his relationship with his other half which had been strained of late. She did not ask about the number of hours he was working but she knew the kind of things that drove him like this. Mark had one of his cameras in his hands and was scrolling through the pictures on the memory card. Startled, he paused. His eyes searched around the room to help him with an answer. She sat down and placed her elbows on the desk and waited a few moments before he finally smiled, lowered his head, then lifted his eyes to look into her own.

"Enough to put a smile on the face of one certain woman, that's for sure." He turned back to his camera, "want to see?" he asked as he lifted the screen towards her. Cara-Marie turned to her own screen then started tapping on the keyboard as she answered.

"No thanks," she paused, "seen enough last night," she kept typing as she noticed the sudden stillness in the rest of the room. He was sitting staring at her, trying not to say the wrong thing to his friend. He may have whispered but it was loud enough for her to hear.

"Sorry, didn't mean to push." she stopped and looked up at him, he was sorry. They held a look for two seconds before he looked away and returned to his camera. "I left some exclusive ones in the editor's mailbox for him to play with later; the more explicit ones got sold on, ... did you get the name of the dead guy?" he asked.

She froze. No, she hadn't, nor did she have the name and details of the woman but had a copy of everything she had said to the police but that one piece of info she had totally missed, and she closed her eyes slowly at her mistake. Mark coughed. When she opened her eyes, he was holding a folded piece of paper, she leaned over to take it knowing full well that all the details she needed were written on it. Mark looked up at her and grinned, "Some journalist you are!" the two of them laughed together as she took the information and unfolded it. Cara-Marie read the information out loud.

"Andy Ferguson, 21, 34a Mountsandel Parade, Coleraine," it wasn't a name she knew, "anything else on him?" Mark didn't look up from the camera he was taking apart.

"Youngest of three brothers, lives at home with his mum and dad, police told them last night," Cara-Marie looked over at him as he continued, Mark lifted his gaze "The most recent family photo is under your keyboard!" Cara-Marie lifted the keyboard and took out the photo that was face down under it. "It's a couple of years old but it's the whole family, got it from the father last night, the mum was a wreck."

The mother and father were sitting on armchairs and were holding each other's hands, their knees touched, smiling. Three young faces were leaning over the back of the chairs informally. Two of them were wearing dark suits and the youngest was wearing the school uniform of Coleraine Institute. All the family shared the same smiles, a family resemblance. There was not much in age between the boys. The photo reminded Cara-Marie of a picture of her own family that was very similar. Cara-Marie suddenly became aware of the staring face of Mark; she looked up at him and let out a murmur as she raised her eyebrows to ask the obvious question.

"I said I will have to get you a Chinese to say thank you," Mark returned to his camera, she had not been expecting that.

"Yes, we will," she looked down at the photo then placed it to one side and continued tapping away on her keyboard.

ထဝ၀

Tony sat in the large chair staring out the panoramic windows, his eyes searching over every detail, every hill and every wave that broke over the water far away; he was tired, slouched on the chair, he had not been asleep all night, and his eyelids slowly closed, paused, then opened again. His body didn't move. The door to the living room opened and a recently awoken Karen walked in. Tony turned his head, the weight of it still lying back in the chair as he looked at her. She was wearing a warm fleeced dressing gown; she slowly walked towards him.

"Sorry, didn't mean to wake you," he said quietly,

"That's ok, I knew you would be out all night," she walked around his legs then turned and sat down on his lap. She turned herself round and laid her right shoulder under his left arm and rested her head on his chest, "did you find them?" she asked.

"No," came the one-word reply; it was obvious how tired he was. Karen pulled her arms in around herself and brought her knees up and off the floor. Tony moved himself so they both were more comfortable, then wrapped his arms around her. He looked down at her face and nearly cried. Her eyes were closed, and a peaceful, loving smile was firmly set on her face. She looked so loving, she looked so beautiful to him, and Tony moved his head and brought his lips together in a small kiss that he placed in the middle of her forehead. Her eyes opened wide and looked into his, love flowed between them as their lips touched and they shared a kiss. Karen broke off the kiss and said the only thing that she could think of at that moment, "I love you," Tony smiled and felt himself well up at the three words Karen just spoke.

"And I love you too," Karen smiled at his reply and rested her head on his chest again as they shared the warmth of each other's body. Karen soon drifted off to sleep, Tony felt the tiredness creeping over him again.

ထဝ၀

Kyle woke face down in bed, he slowly turned over and glanced around the familiar room, nothing was out of place. Everything was as it should be. The sights and smells of the nightmare drifted away into the daylight. He slowly made his way up and out of bed and made his way towards the shower, picking up one of the folded large towels than sat on the chair beside the door. He had not noticed yet that his leg didn't hurt, he could move easily without any shooting pain going up and down his back. It wasn't until he was getting out of the shower that he first realised it. Kyle leaned over the sink and stared at the unshaven face that looked back at him; the acupuncture needles had done their trick. Kelly had stayed for two hours, Kyle had wanted her to stay for longer, but her phone kept going off and she had to disappear to another client. Kyle turned and headed back to his bedroom. He took his dark grey dressing gown off the back of the door and pulled it around himself.

Kyle wandered into the kitchen and filled the kettle, he lifted a mug down from out of the cupboard and dropped a tea bag into it. He reached up and fingered open the small box that had the cubes of sugar, Kyle had two boxes of these, one with white sugar cubes for when he was drinking tea, then other with brown for coffee. Kyle waited for the kettle to boil as he stared out of the window. Yes, he had wanted her to stay longer, and time just seemed to fly by around her. The Chinese had gone down quite well. Kelly had got to work after the dinner. After prodding parts of his legs and back she sat him down on the sofa with his right leg stretching out along the sofa and had him roll his trouser leg up so she could stick him with the needles.

The effect was instantaneous, Kyle wondered how he could describe the feeling that passed over his leg and back; it felt like a weight had just been lifted off him. Whatever it was it worked, and he was impressed. They had chatted as he lay on the sofa, Kelly sat on the chair opposite him; it was a really light-hearted time which he enjoyed. The kettle clicked off and Kyle filled the cup, added some milk and walked back into the living room. His phone was sitting on the small coffee table and he had switched it off just before he went to bed about an hour after Kelly left. Kyle had sent a text saying thank you, but she had yet to reply. He placed the mug of tea on the coaster and as he slowly sat down, he picked up the phone and switched it on. Kyle watched the screen and waited as the phone booted up. No text came. Kyle placed the phone down and lifted the mug and the remote control; the TV burst into life. Kyle thought about texting her again but decided against it. He looked at the clock on the far wall; she would be in clinic in Carrickfergus now. It would be another two hours before his phone went off, but to his dismay it wasn't Kelly.

∞∞∞∞

An hour later Sean walked into the busy office; he briefly acknowledged the young policemen who were sitting at their desks or standing around and chatting away. The word had been passed that the murder investigation was now covering the whole of Northern Ireland and not just Belfast; the office was a-buzz, Sean walked on by and into his office.

"Let's see," he said out loud as Mike walked up to the office door, Sean looked up and beckoned him inside to have a seat. Mike sat down beside the gurgling machine which could now be smelt from the far end of the main office. Mike looked over at Sean who read from the screen. "Police sports day...... *delete*........ sponsor me I am doing..... *Delete*..... Inter-police football championships..." Sean raised his eyebrows and a smile broke over Mike's face "*Delete*......." Sean continued until his screen was clear and the coffee was ready. Sean stood and walked around his desk and started pouring out two mugs of coffee,

"Morning Boss," said Mike, Sean glanced at him and gave him a 'mmm' sound in reply as he handed him the coffee. Sean started to make his way back around the desk as Mike sipped on the steaming liquid then placed the mug down and helped himself to the sugar and cream in small packets in a bowl beside the filter machine.

"So how was your darling wife this fine morning?" Sean asked.

"Thrilled, I woke her up when I got home at one this morning!" they shared a laugh, Sean liked Mike's wife and enjoyed the banter they shared; he felt it made life with his senior detective a lot closer, he knew when something was wrong with Mike. Simon however was more difficult to read. Sean looked down the main office.

"Where is Simon?"

"You gave him the morning off!" Mike answered, "He will be in after lunch." Mike looked down at his notebook and continued speaking, "I did notice you didn't give 'me' the morning off, we all did get back at the same time." Sean smiled at the verbal dig.

"Well, he needed it," Sean didn't have to justify himself, nor was he making excuses; he didn't have to, he was the inspector. None of the rest of the team would know about the quiet memorial Simon would have at his wife's graveside this morning. Simon hadn't asked for the morning off but had quietly accepted it when they were leaving Coleraine the night before.

"Well, your name is mud with someone else, who asked me to pass on a message"

"Oh yes? And what was the message?" Sean could already guess what was coming next. Mike leaned back in the chair and tried to imitate his wife's city accent.

"Tell him for me that you are 'NOT' going to England with him, I'm not leaving you two alone again!" They both smiled then Sean got down to business.

"So, what have you got for me?" Sean drank again as Mike glanced down at his notepad, most of it was what the rest of the team had been doing; one was off sick with the flu and one of the married men's wives was now pregnant. "What time is the briefing set for this morning?" Sean asked, Mike looked at his watch before he answered.

"Eleven o'clock, in nearly an hour's time."

"Ok, brief them on what we covered last night up in Coleraine then update them on the latest with the Trotman case." Mike nodded in agreement, he had most of the notes on that done already. The phone on the desk rang as Mike stood up to leave. Mike indicated that he was taking the mug with him as he walked out the door. Sean had already started with the standard police method of answering a phone; it was about his presentation for the crime watch programme, Mike could hear as he slowed by the nearby desk that they would have to go through the entire presentation with senior officers before they would be allowed to go, Mike would get another coffee before the morning session started, Sean on the other hand would have two.

70

Chapter 14

In what seemed like no time at all the section was getting positioned for the briefing that was about to start, Sean refilled his mug with fresh coffee and headed out to take up the empty seat that was left for him on the right-hand side of the room near one of the desks. The chatter amongst the detectives quietened down as Mike stood up and started speaking. Behind him, four groups of photographs had been stuck on the white board that took up most of the wall at the far end of the office. The photos had been taken by the Crime Scenes Investigation team. Mike stood up with his notebook and started his briefing. He introduced a detective from Maydown M.I.T. who was going to give a brief on the Limavady murders later; most already knew him as he smiled and said hello, then all attention returned to Mike.

"Right then, as you all know, this investigation has gone province wide and we are the lead investigating team. This is to be called *Operation Muirdris*" Mike looked at the different expressions of the faces in front of him and spelt out Muirdris.

"What does 'Muirdris' mean?" asked one of the team, Mike looked at the back of the room, "Eddie, one for you, find out what 'Muirdris' means!" Mike was answered with an ok. Mike turned to his left and stepped back from the photos, "First murder here in Belfast," he looked down at his notebook, "Edgar Trotman, 42 years old, recently arrived from Manchester," most of the faces around the room looked over the pictures; they had all seen them already, "post-mortem report stated the body was healthy and there was no disease that accelerated death," Mike looked up at the assembled faces that were staring back at him, "death caused by blood loss following severe mutilation."

"So what avenues are we looking at with him?" Sean butted in. Mike looked at his notes, then back up at Sean.

"The DNA at the scene was corrupted by the two dogs of the shop owner that found him," a groan of disappointment went around the room. "There were no other tracks or traces left by the assailant at the scene, but…" Mike had emphasised the word *'but'* which raised some eyebrows, "we are getting a cast of the shape of the mouth from a dental pathologist." A few heads turned towards each other, "so that should open up a few avenues for us to follow." Mike used the word avenues as he knew Sean hated the word *'leads'* it sounded far too American for him; actors on cop shows followed leads, police officers made enquires, issued summons or served warrants. However, when Sean wasn't in the room with the rest of the team, they followed *'leads.'*

"When is that happening?" asked Sean.

"Not sure," Mike paused, "Davey, take that on. I have the details so speak to me after," Mike was answered with a nod of the head. "Our only avenue currently is the girl from the bar." Mike pointed with his left hand after he placed the notebook in his right. The still photo was of Anna leaving The Botanic Inn and a second one of her walking up one of the streets. "We have confirmed through CCTV that Trotman followed her into the bar, left just after her and was seen again in the background of this photo," Mike pointed to the shape in the background, "past the corner shop." Mike paused again as he looked at his notes, "Time, half past eight in the evening."

"Nothing on who she is?" asked Sean, he already knew the answer, but the information was more for the rest of the team to all be on the same page. This was the whole purpose of the briefing.

"None," answered Mike, "after enquires made in the shop, the pub and door to door enquires made on our behalf by our uniformed colleagues, nothing." A murmur of conversation went around the room, Mike carried on, "Time of death is estimated to be between half eight and half ten by the pathologist"

"And no one heard a thing!" said one of the team, Mike glanced over at him before he spoke.

"Door to door in the street where it happened turned up nothing. There was a student party going on in one house and in the house next to the alley is a pensioner who is 80% deaf, so no, no one heard a thing." A hand went up at the back of the room.

"Yes Eddie!" said Mike. At the back of the room the blonde-haired detective was sitting in a plain shirt with his collar open; Edward Cargill was the newest member of the investigation team.

"Muirdris," he started to read from the screen in front of him, "the name given to the lacustrine monster that was killed by Fergus Mac Leide. It was also known as 'The Sineach." Eddie finished triumphantly.

"When was that?" asked one of the others. Eddie went back to the screen as everyone watched his eyes speed read the information in front of him "Approx. 1000 years BC"

"Operation Muirdris, who thought that one up?" Came another comment before Mike brought everyone's focus back to himself as he introduced the Detective from Maydown.

"Ok, everyone, settle down. We have invited Detective Constable Irwin from Maydown M.I.T. to give us an up to date briefing on the Limavady killings that may be linked to our investigation." Mike smiled as the detective stood up and walked over to where Mike was standing. Mike nodded and walked over and sat down on the chair Irwin had just vacated.

"Morning everyone, I am Detective Constable Brett Irwin of Maydown M.I.T." a little cheer erupted with a hint of sarcasm along with a couple of claps from a few pairs of hands that echoed around the room, Brett was no stranger to a few of the team here, "Yeah, it's nice to see you too." Sean smiled, he hadn't expected the welcome, but it showed mutual respect between the teams. "Right then, to business," Brett turned to the next set of pictures on the board, his hand passed over the blue marker pen line that separated each set of photos "Triple murder in Limavady, first victim, this is Michael Watson, 20 years old, 102 Koolessan Walk, Limavady.," Brett pointed to an enlarged driving licence photo that was at the top of the board, a young face stared back at the room. "Second victim, Liam Paul Arthur, also 20 years old, Riverside walk, Coleraine and finally Mr David 'Septic' Simpson, no fixed abode, Limavady," notes were being scribbled down around the room as Brett started going through their injuries; the two young men had suffered similar fates to Edgar Trotman, very similar in fact.

"How similar are we looking at here?" asked Sean.

"We sent a cast off to the dental pathologist and are waiting the response from that,"

"Davey!" Mike half shouted, he was telling Davey to take this on as well, but he didn't have to say anymore. Davey understood.

"Aye, ok," was the answer, not that he had a choice in the matter, Brett smiled as he continued.

"Davey, I will pass you the details after this," Davey nodded, "The pathologist's reports on both deaths are the same findings as yours; the DNA was corrupted in the same way as yours." Sean looked up from his own notebook.

"Was it?"

"Yes." said Brett, he had paused when Sean had spoken, Sean and Mike shared a glance, that was news to them.

"Mike, follow that up!" stated Sean as he looked back at Brett. Sean nodded with his head to instruct Brett to continue.

"The killings also happened at night, but the bodies were found by two police officers who were following up on a call from a publican, *and...*" Brett let the word hang in the air, "two things that I didn't know until we shared this until today:, in both cases the victims had just left a pub and when discovered both were contaminated by dogs;, the two uniforms stated that there was a German Shepherd at the scene." It was not exactly what you would call hard evidence, but all seminaries had to be looked at. "What type of dog was at the Trotman killing?" Brett asked. Sean and Mike exchanged glances.

"The dogs were owned by the shopkeeper," said Mike, "I will chase that up today," Sean nodded, Brett went on.

"And I will follow up on the dog in Limavady; we have a name of the owner." Sean and Mike agreed in unison.

"What of the third body?" asked Mike, "what happened to him?" Brett let out a sigh as he glanced up at the next set of pictures on the board.

"Septic Simpson, he is a regular in Limavady." Brett had placed his hands on his hips, he obviously knew him, he turned to the team, "Down and out, nearly part of the towns monuments! Regularly seen around the town, a few minor civil offences, but nothing major." Brett paused again so Sean asked the question.

"So, what killed him? he wasn't torn apart like the other two," Brett looked over at Sean and subconsciously nodded.

"No, no he wasn't, his injuries were minor and facial mostly. He had won £200 on the lotto and was in the pub celebrating; the two boys followed him out and we believe attacked him with intent to rob him of his cash." Brett paused again, "The pub landlord had thrown Septic out for drinking too much and being too loud then the two boys went out after him. CCTV confirms this. Septic would normally sleep in the bus shelter nearby." Most of the team noticed that he had not answered the question, so Sean said it again.

"Ok, so what actually killed him?"

"Massive cardiac arrest brought on by sudden shock of the attack." Brett had quoted the post-mortem report exactly, Sean nodded.

"So, he wasn't touched by the killer?" Sean asked.

"Nope, and the killer wasn't after any money; most of Septic's winning were still at the scene." said Brett.

"Trotman's personal effects were untouched as well." stated Mike. The three shared a glance; more details that could be used for the crime watch programme.

"Next murder in Coleraine," Brett continued to the last set of photographs, "Mr Andy Ferguson, 21 years old, 34a Mountsandel Parade, Coleraine," again Brett stepped up to the next set of photographs, "this time the damage to the body is not so intense as it is 'mostly' intact, severe trauma to the head, neck, right arm and torso. We believe that this is because the attacker was disturbed during the assault."

"Who disturbed him?" asked one of the team. Brett was focused on one of the photographs, "Sorry?" he asked.

"Who was it that disturbed him?" Brett looked round at them.

"Him? Who disturbed him? Who disturbed the 'Attacker'? The sex of the 'Attacker' is not yet known." Brett turned back towards the photographs as he continued speaking, "Never assume knowledge, only collect evidence that proves fact!" Brett was quoting what they all knew and had learnt on their training courses. "The 'Attacker' was seen by a Mrs Jayne Brown, 28, from Coleraine who was walking her dog along the riverside. She was chased by the attacker who promptly mutilated her own dog before an off-duty policeman and a journalist intervened." This caused a ripple of conversation that spread around the room; Sean and Mike exchanged glances again, so Mike asked the question they both were thinking.

"You have a witness who can describe the attacker?" he paused, "and why were we not told that when we were up in Coleraine last night?" Mike was a little annoyed. Brett turned to face him, breathed in, looked at the floor, and then looked up at Mike.

"She's dead," shock burst over the faces in the room, "before you ask how, she survived the attack and was alive when she left the scene; from both statements given by the police officer and the journalist she was totally hysterical." He paused again to let this information sink in then allow them to take in what was coming next. "We are told that she suffered some kind of shock induced coma and she died in the Causeway hospital yesterday morning." Shoulders relaxed, people breathed out in frustration; they had just lost their best piece of evidence. Brett paused again but reacted when Sean stood up and walked towards the photographs.

"What time of day was this attack?"

"Approximately 6pm," answered Brett.

"And the other attacks happened later at night in a more secluded scene for the crime?"

"Yes," Brett gave a simple one word reply.

"Had the fourth victim just left a bar?" Sean waited a few seconds for an answer and when it didn't come he stopped pacing. Brett slightly blushed before he gave his embarrassed answer.

"I don't know," Sean looked at Mike who without speaking nodded, the team would go through the CCTV footage from the area and plot a last known route of Mr Andy Ferguson.

"So, motive?" there was a pause before he spoke again, "Anyone?" heads looked at each other; this is what Mike called *'The boss' coffee induced Brain Storming Sessions'*.

"Well. Trotman had several convictions for rape and other sexual assaults, could it be vigilante?" asked Eddie.

"What vigilante would mutilate like that?" Sean pointed to the Trotman photos, "plus there is no connection with the other victims," he started slowly walking again, "so far" he concluded.

"Tell me, what do you see?" He asked. Davey spoke up from where he was sitting.

"The *'Attacker'* is male."

"Why do you say that?" asked Sean.

"All the victims are male."

"Are they sectarian?" asked Eddie from the back. Mike looked down at his note book.

"Trotman, Atheist," he looked up at Brett who checked a page in his own notebook.

"Watson, Roman Catholic; Arthur, Roman Catholic; Simpson, Protestant and Ferguson..." he turned a page and paused as he read down his notes, "Protestant."

Sean turned and picked up the blue marker pen and wrote the religions down beside each photograph, he replaced the lid on the marker and turned towards the team again.

"What else? What is the 'Attacker' like?"

"Has physical strength," came another statement, Sean nodded; whispers sprung up as everyone discussed their own suspicions.

"Very good, what else?"

"Any Para-military involvement?" asked another. Mike turned and addressed everyone.

"No, confirmed with special branch, but they certainly are taking an interest."

"Why do we think that there is only one attacker?" asked Brett. Sean looked across at him, then again nodded in agreement.

"We don't" Sean answered, then looked over at Mike who was scribbling all of this down, this at least was something else for them to go on. "So, we are interested in finding this woman," said Sean as he paced towards her photograph, "and we have the footage of her from the pub and the corner shop, and we have next to nothing from forensics and we are waiting for the moulds from Dental Pathology." Sean paced towards where he had been sitting, he picked up the mug of coffee, sipped some then addressed the whole room but looked directly at Mike. "Right, so ensure that we collate all the CCTV footage that we are going to use, interview the shopkeeper again, go into detail about the dogs." Mike nodded as he wrote, a few others in the team also were writing as they knew the jobs were coming their way. Sean continued, "Go back over the statements of the two who were first on the scene in Coleraine and Limavady then Mike," Mike looked up, "both you and I will present all of this to Superintendent Sutcliffe and Detective Chief Inspector Anderson at 2 PM tomorrow." He stopped, looked around and waiting for everyone to finish writing, he made eye contact with everyone in the room before he spoke again. "Any questions, problems, queries?" There were none, "Fine, go to it." Sean walked down the middle of the office then stopped as he got to the door of his office. He turned and shouted back into the room. "Oh, one last thing," everyone turned to look at him, "Brett."

"Yes?" said Brett.

"Welcome to Belfast." with that Sean walked into his office and went straight to the coffee machine. Mike walked around the team allocating all the tasks that needed to be done., Eddie raised his voice and asked the one question of Mike that had been bugging him all the way through the briefing.

"What does 'Lacustrine' mean? anyone?"

Chapter 15

Cara-Marie walked through the quiet woods, the soft snow crunched under her feet, the light of the full moon lit up the trees and made the snow that had just fallen earlier sparkle as it lay on the ground. It hung off the branches of the trees and covered the fungi that she knew was on the ground. Cara-Marie could see her own breath, but she was not cold. She slowly walked through the forest in her jeans and woollen jumper. She could not feel the cold on her face or her hands as she normally could; her feet moved automatically. She wasn't following a pathway, but she moved through what seemed to be a natural opening that lay between the trees, almost as if they had moved out of the way themselves. She stopped where she was, stood still and listened to the stillness of the night. She slowly turned her head and looked around; her eyes moved over the ground, through the trees then up into the night sky.

The sky was clear, the clouds had gone, and the stars shone brightly in the night. She picked out the constellations that she had enjoyed as a child: Great Bear, Little Bear, Pegasus, Orion. She remembered sitting beside her father in the evening and he would tell her stories of how they came to be in the stars; tales from a time long ago. Cara-Marie closed her eyes as she felt the moonlight fall around her; she listened. Her right ear tilted upwards; she raised her right hand and brushed her black hair behind her right ear so she could improve her hearing but there was no sound. No birds, no animals, nothing. She opened her eyes then walked on, she had never been here before, but she felt like she knew where it was, it felt safe, it felt like home, but how could that be? Cara-Marie walked on following herself as she was guided through the moonlit forest.

Suddenly she stopped, a sound, her eyes bolted over to her left. The forest had changed, she felt her body tense up she slowly turned and started to lower herself as if she was getting ready to sprint; her pulse quickened. She could hear her own breathing, see her own breath. There was the sound again, it was to her left and from somewhere behind her; she turned her head towards the sound. It happened again, it sounded like a crunching sound, the sound of freshly laid snow being crushed under foot, her pulse leapt. Cara-Marie tried to hold her breath, she listened to the sound to see where it was coming from. Again, it happened, this time closer, another, another, closer yet. The footsteps quickened, she was not alone, but where could she run to? Where can she go? Who would hear her scream as there was no one for miles?

Cara-Marie could suddenly feel the cold, it bit her hands, it bit her face, it bit through her clothes; her breathing quickened as did her heartbeat; it was now thumping in her chest, the noise of which seemed so loud that whoever it was must be able to hear it; how could they not? Something moved in the darkness, she stepped back up against the tree. Whoever else was in the forest was walking straight towards her. Cara-Marie felt her fingers dig into the bark of the tree, her eyes widened in their search through the darkness, searching for what the moonlight failed to reveal. *MOVEMENT*

Cara-Marie's eyes fixed on a spot past the far tree, something had moved, the sound happened again, something was moving. Now she could see the pair of eyes looking at her through the darkness, they could obviously see her, but why were they so low, why were they lying down. The eyes moved towards her again and slowly out of the darkness and into the moonlight the grey wolf appeared. He was slowly walking around the tree, his head looking from side to side as he walked forward. Cara-Marie's heart slowed down, there was no danger here, this face was so calm, so gentle, and this gentleman would not hurt her. The wolf walked on until he was nearly 8 feet away then he stopped. His head suddenly looked over to the right, off in the darkness something had got his attention. Cara-Marie's eyes once again strained to see through the darkness, but its secrets remained hidden. She felt her body relax and she stepped forward towards him. Her eyes moved over his fur, he looked majestic in the moonlight; he was white around his legs but darker over his back, and his coat seemed to shine all by itself as he stood in the forest looking so very proud.

The wolf turned and looked Cara-Marie in the eyes, his eyes were bright, and his ears were folded back into his fur, he looked so calm. He blinked tilting his head to one side, did he just smile at me? She went to speak when his head shot back to the direction he had been looking. He lowered his head and breathed in a long breath through his nose, she looked on as he closed his eyes and lifted his snout into the cold night air, she could feel no wind, but he filled his lungs with it. The wolf lowered his head again then opened his eyes, he set off in a trot towards what he had been looking at then stopped just before he disappeared into the night. He turned his head to look back at her, slowly blinked and seemed to smile at her again. She lifted her right hand in a slow wave to say goodbye. The wolf opened and closed his mouth as if he was talking to her, but no words came out; then he turned away from her and was gone, off into the night.

She lowered her hand, she could no longer feel the cold, instead she felt warm, a strange warmth that she could not describe. Cara-Marie turned and walked on in the forest and for the first time she felt alone. She had not gone far when the sound of a long howl stopped her. She felt all the hair on her body stand on end at the sound, and a stirring in her spirit as her face turned to the left then up to the sky. Her protector was out there, she was not alone, she was not afraid, Cara-Marie found herself saying her thoughts out loud.

"How lonely is the night, without the howl of the wolf!"

Cara-Marie bolted upright, her hands fought with the duvet as her own room came into focus. She panted out of her mouth as her body fought for air. She closed her eyes tight and brought her knees up underneath the duvet. She sat upright and rested her arms over her knees. Slowly she dropped her forehead down onto them. Gradually her breathing slowed as did her heartbeat. Cara-Marie lifted her head and looked over at the digital clock on the small dressing table, it was just after 3 in the morning; she hadn't gone to bed until after 12 as she had been on the internet, searching since she got home.

Her mother had kept her on the phone for nearly an hour, she had wanted to call around, but Cara-Marie managed to stay that one away. She hadn't managed to get rid of her mother since the murder had happened. She took a deep breath and lay back down on the bed; she pulled the duvet up around her as she fought to find a comfortable spot to drift off, but sleep would escape her tonight.

∞∞∞∞∞

This was the second day in a row that she had been the first one in to work, in fact she had been there since before seven, but she said that it was just before eight. Cara-Marie had hidden the searches she had been doing before the rest of the crew had arrived, one half of her wanted to do more, the other half of her was telling her not to be so stupid and get some work done as she was in work time now; but try as she may she had lost the ability to concentrate on any job for any length of time and this had not been missed by the rest of the office.

"Where is Mark?" she asked generally.

"He went into the police station this morning; he is speaking to someone from Belfast," Cara-Marie stopped what she was doing and looked across the room.

"What is he doing in there?" or the real question that was in her head was why he hadn't taken her? He was just a snapper after all! The faces at the occupied desks looked at each other, paused then looked back at her, why was everyone staring at her?

"They are interested in his photographs!" this at least made some sense, "Oh he said that he left you a note on his desk!" Cara-Marie jumped up and nearly ran around the desks, again this had not gone unnoticed. She searched through the scattered paper that seemed to cover his desk, where was this message, why had they not told her about it before? She cursed under her breath at them. Suddenly her eyes focused in on the folded A4 sheet of paper with her name written on it, she grabbed it and stormed back to her desk. Again, glances were passed between the others as they went back to their own work. After she had left yesterday they had all spoken to the editor about her, in less than ten minutes he would get an email detailing how she was and had been acting this morning. Cara-Marie read over the handwritten note. 'GONE FOR A

CHAT IN THE COP SHOP, THEY THINK ALL THE MURDERS ARE LINKED AND A TEAM FROM BELFAST HAS TAKEN OVER. THEY ARE CALLING IT OPERATION MUIRDRIS (AFTER SOME BEASTIE THAT USED TO HUNT PEOPLE AND THEY SENT SOME BLOKE TO KILL IT) (I THINK).' Cara-Marie smiled at his use of double brackets, she read on 'THE WOMAN YOU FOUND AT THE RIVERSIDE DIED YESTERDAY IN CAUSEWAY FROM SOME KIND OF SHOCK, SO YOU AND THAT COPPER ARE THE ONLY WITNESSES SO FAR, FROM WHAT I HEAR THEY ARE LOOKING FOR SOMETHING TO DO WITH DOGS AND SOME FIT LOOKING CHICK WITH BLACK HAIR,' she smiled at the note again, how did he do that? For a photographer he had a gift for getting people, specially police to talk to him, was it the fact that he 'wasn't' a journalist that went in his favour? 'AND LUNCH IS ON ME, GOT SOME GOSS FOR YOU, HER NAME IS RACHEL, DETAILS LATER.' Rachel? Who the hell was Rachel? Cara-Marie was now in a good mood; she reread the message before tearing it up and throwing it in the bin.

Cara-Marie spent the next hour trying to finish the story she had been working on, this would have taken her fifteen minutes any other day, but today things just didn't fit into place. Every now and then she lifted the folder and read over what she had printed off the Net. She had spent over 6 hours last night then another two this morning, why wouldn't this leave her alone, but this wasn't possible, was it? Could it? Cara-Marie's fingers stopped moving over the keyboard, her face looked towards the screen, but her eyes moved to the pile of paper that was underneath the blue folder and again the face that looked around the corner at her appeared again, the shape of the head, the fur, the ears and the eyes, those eyes that looked directly at her. Her mind couldn't make sense of what she had seen. She closed her eyes and kept them shut for a few seconds then slowly opened them again, her desk came back into focus and suddenly she was back in the office.

"Cara?" The concerned female voice came from the other side of the office and with a slightly nervous jolt her body started moving again. Cara-Marie breathed in and turned her head to the right, one of the others had walked towards her desk and another stood behind his desk speaking her name. What did they want? What was going on? The woman closest to her stopped moving and spoke again.

"Cara, are you alright?" Her right hand was near her mouth as she spoke all other conversation in the office had stopped, everyone was looking at her, *'am I alright? what a stupid question! Of course, I am alright, I wouldn't be here if I wasn't now, would I?'* Cara-Marie wanted to shout out loud at them, but she paused, swallowed then replied.

"Yes, ok thanks, why do you ask?" the rest of the office slowly got back to what they were doing but the woman closest to her slowly backed away and turned towards her own desk saying "It's just that you were making some very strange noises there!"

Cara-Marie cast a glance around the room. No one made eye contact with her. What was going on? She turned back towards her desk, looked up and read over what she had just typed. She shook her head, deleted the last line then started typing again, another two lines and she closed the article down and sent it to the editor's mailbox. Her phone beeped with a message, it was from her mum wanting to take her for lunch, she quickly tapped in a reply that she was busy but would call her later, and she sat back in her chair. After a few moments, she swung from side to side then stood up and lifted her jacket and announced that she was just popping out for ten minutes. She grabbed her phone and search results.

Cara-Marie walked up into the town through the mass of people walking back and forth. Pausing at a coffee shop, she turned and headed over to the main door. A few minutes later she was sitting at the window with a large mug and the search results, her eyes scanned story after story. *'This cannot be'* she whispered. In mild frustration, she turned the searches over and placed them face down on the table. She lifted the mug with both hands, slowly sipped on the hot liquid and watched the world go by. People walked back and forth, her eyes jumped from person to person, she looked at them, but she didn't register them.

Out of the crowd at the far side of the street the girl was slowly walking past the metal railing of the church. She was walking a lot slower than everyone that was moving around her, she was in a very good mood and seemed very pleased with herself. Her hair was as black as her own as were her clothes, she looked around at the people walking past her. Cara-Marie watched as she took off her black duffel coat to reveal a shapely body which got the attention of the men walking past. She was definitely 'turning all the boys' heads. Her train of thought carried on when it felt like a brick had just slammed into her. That was the woman who had walked past when she was on her way to the Chinese, that is the woman who had stared at her as she walked past, 'FROM WHAT I HEAR THEY ARE LOOKING FOR SOMETHING TO DO WITH DOGS AND SOME FIT LOOKING CHICK WITH BLACK HAIR' the words of Mark's note suddenly rang true. Cara-Marie stared at her and made a mental note of everything about her, this was something she could take to the editor. In seconds she had finished the coffee and taken a picture with her phone. Excited, she bounced back to the office; all she had to do now is convince someone else.

Cara-Marie bounded through the back door into the main office of the newspaper; if she had been a minute earlier she would have seen the rest of the office staff walking out of the editor's office after having a chat about her. She took off her jacket and flung it over her seat dropping the pile of paper face down in the in tray on top of her desk. She had already separated the two sheets that she wanted, then walked over to the door of the editor's office. Cara-Marie didn't notice how everyone was so busy that no one spoke to her, she knocked on the open door with her left hand and the editor looked up.

"Can I have a word?" she asked. The editor closed the email that he had been reading and adjusted himself in his chair.

"Yeah, no problems, ok," Cara-Marie closed the glass door behind her as she walked in and sat down.

"The, um..." she paused, how was she going start this one? Kevin the editor picked up his phone.

"Hang on, I'll get Christine to hold my calls," that gave Cara-Marie a few more seconds to gather her thoughts, "Now we won't be interrupted" he said as he put the phone down.

"Yeah, the... um..." Cara-Marie didn't know what to say, Kevin just looked at her, "I think over the past week or so, I mean, I was in with the police yesterday, um" Kevin nodded his head as she spoke, "I don't know how to start this.... uh" she cursed herself; this wasn't how she did things. "I've got a line on the animal," Kevin's eyes widened.

"Seriously?"

"Yeah, seriously!" she replied.

"Go on," Kevin was now fully in his 'editor mode' as he would call it.

"I've done some searches, on this, um," she let that hang in the air as her mind fought for which bit to say next, what would the next logical step be?? "I mean, remember that whole 'Beast of Ballycastle' thing we had a couple of years ago," Kevin nodded and hummed a response of acknowledgement, "That's..." she paused again, "that was something different, you're not going to believe me on this... Um" again she paused, Kevin slightly tilted his head as he listened, he had never seen her like this before, something was coming, something different; she continued "It's what I think I saw." her eyes searched the room, Kevin breathed in.

"Right, try me," he said quietly, she took a breath in, looked at him straight in the eyes then let her thoughts fly.

"I think I saw a werewolf!" Kevin's pupils dilated, and his eyebrows shot up.

"Right, seriously? Is that what you think?"

"I think I saw a werewolf," she repeated. Kevin's face relaxed, his eyes looked down at the desk then back up at her, but the rest of his body didn't move, he was so hard to read, did he believe her? Cara-Marie didn't know; she slightly lifted her hands, "Hear me out...," Kevin's body relaxed as he looked at her, "this is a story, this is something I found on the internet," she sat forward and handed over a couple of A4 sheets of paper that had been stapled together, Kevin took them and glanced over the page as Cara-Marie launched into what she had found "It happened, in 1997 in Northern England, a woman was out walking her two dogs then, what she herself described as *'a large black dog, with no tail'* that was stood up on two feet that went for her and her dogs," Her excitement had returned. "She was running away, her two dogs turned around and attacked it; it shredded them. She managed to get into a main street and was able to give a description of it to the police." Kevin sat and listened as he eyes scanned over the bulletin from a county newspaper from Northern England that was much the same as themselves "She died of a heart attack in hospital that night," Kevin looked up from the sheet of paper that he held in his hands, Cara-Marie looked him straight in the eye, Kevin could tell that she believed what she was saying to be the truth. She leaned forward and pointed to the side of the print out, "look it even shows the links to the newspaper articles involved!" Kevin read the links, he slightly nodded as she spoke.

"Uh-huh, alright," he looked up at her again.

"That is a perfect description of what I saw!" She left it for a second before she became defensive in her statements, "Look, this isn't 16th Century stuff. I found loads of sites about sightings in UK and Europe. This was 1997." Cara-Marie pointed back at the page.

"But this is 1997, where? Lancashire? Yorkshire? you don't get werewolves running about, you maybe get an escaped 'Big Cat' from the zoo or circus!" Cara-Marie came back at him.

"She described a 7-foot dog that stood on its hind legs, that went for her and it moved at a phenomenal speed and it shredded her dogs, that woman in the car park, her dog had its throat ripped open!" Kevin had seen the photographs Mark had taken and that was a pretty good description of what happened. Cara-Marie stuttered a bit as she sat back, then lifted the next A4 sheet of paper and handed it towards Kevin, "Ok, Ok, that was 1997, that was about ten years ago," He glanced at what was on the page. "This one here is one I found, 2003 in North Wales," Kevin acknowledged with a nod and an 'Uh-Huh' as his eyes read what she was now saying out loud. "There was a couple on a holiday, right," she leaned forward again and pointed to the parts that she had highlighted from the text, "you see, he is a lawyer and she is a doctor and they were on horseback and they were going up a road, up a country lane when what they described as a 'Large Black Dog'" Kevin was reading from the page and was nodding as Cara-Marie spoke, "jumped through the hedge." Kevin looked up at her.

"Black dog!" he said quietly, Cara-Marie nodded.

"You see, this dog came out of the hedge."

"Right," said Kevin.

"It was running up the side of the hedge,"

"Right, ok," Kevin confirmed what was on the page to what she was saying.

"When it saw them, it stopped, and they said it looked 'surprised,' because the horses reacted to it, it suddenly 'stood up,' on its hind legs and it wasn't until it stood up that they described it as a 'humanoid figure' and at the shock of that, it made like a 'bark' noise, right." Kevin was reading down the page ahead of what she was saying as she continued, she had started speaking a little faster than she normally did. "Then in a startling reaction, it jumped back through the fence and ran off," Cara-Marie paused as she took a breath in. Kevin looked up at her as she said what was not on the page. "That's not a dog, dogs don't react that way, especially to horses!" Cara-Marie stopped and looked at his face, he just sat there. What was he thinking? Could he not see? she waited a few seemingly endless seconds. "Both their descriptions, describe a large 6 foot to 7-foot dog, humanoid in shape with no tail," she paused again, Kevin looked straight at her, "that's what looked around that corner at me!" Kevin blinked.

"But surely all you saw was a glimpse, around a corner."

"It stared at me," she said quietly.

"See, what I find most hard is that," he paused "well, you know me, I will stick a story up to its highest and I will lash everything at it, but you are the conservative one in the office and I just can't believe that you want to write a story and put your name to something like that!" Cara-

Marie went to butt in, but Kevin spoke over her, "because people are going to think that you are just crazy!" she bit her bottom lip, Kevin laid the print off on top of the other one and leaned slightly on his desk opening his arms as he spoke, she looked away from him as reality hit home with her. "I mean, I'll go for it, I'll splash it all over the front! but are you prepared to take the comeback on it?" She shifted in her seat, silence dominated the room, they looked at each other for a few moments, "it's just a witness, isn't it! there's no other proof, it's just you are saying what you thought you saw and that's why it's going to come back on you," he was just saying what she was feeling deep down now, she blinked a couple of times as he sighed. "You know, if any sort of a story came out like that, we would always run it, but it is an eye-witness account that is prepared to say, *I saw it, I was there, this is what I think*' we would always run that," he paused again as her eyes darted around, she lowered her head slightly, "but this isn't just some 'Joe Public' out in the street!" Kevin stopped, he thought he had gone far enough.

"There is something I found out yesterday," she paused, Kevin sat back in the chair, "something that I can't put into print, not just yet anyway," Kevin nodded to indicate that he was still prepared to listen to her. she looked up at him as she spoke, her volume moved up a notch as well, "The police are looking for a half-man, half dog!" Kevin bolted upright in surprise.

"Get outta here!" his mouth dropped open.

"That detective from Belfast, his team have DNA taken from the killing in Belfast, remember the killing in Belfast?" she asked, Kevin nodded.

"Yeah, course."

"That Trotman Fella,"

"Uh-huh,"

"They got a DNA trace from that, it is the same DNA trace that carried out the killing here in Coleraine," Kevin sat in silence, his mind raced as he sat forward before he spoke again.

"But that doesn't mean it a werewolf, does it?" Cara-Marie shrugged, she was losing this one.

"It isn't human DNA and it's not dog DNA, it's both,"

"Where did you get this information from?" he asked. It was her turn to sigh. She didn't want to say but to give her any credibility she knew she had to.

"A friend of mine who works down at the forensics' labs in Belfast," she paused "and one of the coppers on the investigation team, we all went to school together," Kevin shrugged his face, he couldn't really argue with her sources.

"I am assuming that they won't put their names to that then." she shook her head.

"No, they were telling me that this will come back and bite them."

"Did you go to the police press office?" she crunched up her face in reply,

"Come on!" Cara-Marie moved in her seat again, it was a subconscious nervous movement, "One of your police officers phoned me last night! They are going to want to know exactly who it is" Kevin looked at her over his hands.

"As you know then, we can't print it without the police saying something officially about it," she looked away as reality hit again, "If this was, just say 'Joe Public' out in the street, then fine, I'd grab it with both hands, but, I just think that you've been through a really, really bad shock and I'm worried that it's affected you in a way, just." Cara-Marie listened on to her editor. "I'm not going to splash you over the front of our paper and make you look like a fool," Kevin paused again, she looked down at the sheet of paper on the desk, "You are one of our staff and you know, there is only a small number of us and we look out for each other and you know I'll tell you, if you write a crap story!" Cara-Marie smiled, she had certainly been there before.

"Yeah, true," they shared a smile.

"So, equally I'm not going to let you make a complete fool of yourself either," Cara-Marie nodded towards him, "and I am not convinced 'yet' you have enough proof." Kevin emphasised the word 'yet' Cara-Marie felt her heart beat a little faster, did that mean that he believed her?

"I know, every educated fibre in my body says I'm talking out of my bum and says... um," she paused for a few seconds, Kevin could see her searching for the right words, "I mean, what am

I going to see next? Will it be UFO's?" Cara-Marie rested her elbows on her knees then placed her head in her own hands as she spoke, Kevin watched her slow deliberate movements.

"Do you think you need some time off?" the comment caught her off guard, Cara-Marie sat there and stared in front of her, then glanced up at Kevin as he spoke again, "I'll go with it, I will splash it across the front, no problem, but you have to think long and hard if you are prepared to take the comeback." she guessed he was just making his point, "Once this is all over, can you go out to the boring jobs where you gotta be straight, conservative and you have to sit there and listen to people who are thinking, *'that's your woman from the Herald, that's the looney who thought that she saw a werewolf!'* are people going to think you can be trusted to do the straight forward bread and butter we do, *'fair, accurate reporting?'"* Kevin was quoting from the very first class that would-be journalists get when starting at university, knowing it would strike a chord with her. "I know you, I've known you for years, we practically grew up together and I know you're not given to 'flights of fancy', as I've said of all of us in the office, you are the most conservative, I mean come on, look at the way we fight over headlines!" Cara-Marie smiled and let out a short laugh, Kevin smiled back, "We need someone in the police to say *'Yes, you are right!'"* she looked up at him, this was direction from him, the direction that any editor would give a journalist who had an incomplete story, but did he believe her? "Because they'll think we are only writing it for the headlines, they'll think we are only writing it to sell newspapers," she nodded as she knew where he was coming from, "which of course, we do want to do, but we need somebody in authority to come out and say, 'this reporter isn't as half-baked as you may think,'" Kevin shrugged. "Who that is I don't know, I mean, is it this mad Puma or 'Beast of Ballycastle' thing back again?" she shifted in her seat, she knew that story well. "It disappeared for years, it turned up in, where? In Omagh was it? County Tyrone, somewhere? Disappeared, turned up in Ballycastle! Disappeared, and nobody had seen it for years," she agreed with him.

"Coleraine's own 'Loch Ness Monster," she said, Kevin nodded.

"Plenty of monsters about the place then?" Kevin relaxed and nodded at someone out in the main office, Cara-Marie brought the conversation back to where she wanted it.

"The police have moved their entire incident room, from Belfast to Coleraine. That tells me they are on to something," Kevin looked up at her and agreed, she was still the journalist he had known all this time, Cara had something with that alone.

"Right, we need to get more onto this then, I'll get everyone to call in their police contacts, because it is a small enough town, nothing this big can happen in this part of town without somebody talking about it. You know what people are like, they love to be the first to tell you the news," It was her turn to agree. Kevin looked up at the much 'happier' Cara.

"But what if we find him before the police do?" her question made him think.

"Pictures, CCTV footage, video, anything that we can print!" Kevin moved some of the stuff that was on his desk, this was normally a sign that the chat was over, "but you have to go and have a think about this." Cara-Marie nodded,

"Just like the reporter from 'The Incredible Hulk' no one believed him!" they both laughed.

"Look, go out and get full drunk or lie in a heap for a day or two or just go out and bark at the moon," her face spread with laughter as she imitated a howl. Kevin laughed back at her.

"Ok, I will, my mum is still trying to set me up with one of her doctor friends,"
Kevin liked the change of topic. "Still trying to get you married off?" He asked.
"Ha, no one's good enough!" they both shared another smile,
"Touché!"
"Can I have tomorrow off??"
"No, definitely not," they smiled again, "of course you can,"
"Can I ask one last question?" she asked.
"Sure, of course!"
"Am I going insane?"
"You work here, don't you!"

Chapter 16

Mike was sitting at his desk tapping at his PC; he looked up at the document on the screen and read what he had just typed. Mike glanced at the concentrated look on Simon's face as he was totally engrossed in what he was typing. He looked around the busy office at the rest of the team; they were all working away, the conversations and abuse going on only pointed to one thing; they were all happy at their work. He looked back at his screen and started typing again.

"Ah, Mike, have you got a minute?" Mike looked up at Eddie who had just walked up to his desk. Eddie was half turned back in the direction of his own desk, "Hey, I think you might want to take a look at this," both Simon and Mike stopped what they were doing and looked at him.

"Ok," answered Mike as he saved the work that he had done. Simon was copying suite.

"Do you think you have something?" asked Simon, "Or is it a one to one chat?" Eddie started nodding as the two of them followed him back to his desk.

"Yeah, I've got something,"

"Right, what have we got?" he asked.

Eddie started going through pictures and brought up a still from the CCTV at the Botanic Inn, it was Anna leaving.

"We are looking for this lass here in connection with the Trotman murder as it appears that he was following her, right?" Eddie was pointing at the screen as he spoke, both Mike and Simon nodded, this they both knew. Eddie reduced the picture and brought up another picture of a busy street that had shops on both sides and one-way traffic coming down towards the camera. Eddie tapped the screen at a young man on the right-hand side, "and this is in Coleraine the evening of the Ferguson killing, would you say that is him?" Both Mike and Simon looked slightly closer at the screen.

"Yeah, I would" said Mike, Simon agreed.

"Well if I take this back a couple of frames..." Eddie tapped the keyboard then moved the mouse and the screen blinked and cars and people moved backwards in front of them, then the screen stopped. Eddie leaned over his desk and picked up his pen then tapped the shape of Andy Ferguson, "Would you say that he 'might' be following her?" Eddie stressed the 'might' as he tapped the screen on the black dressed female shape that was about 20 feet in front of him. Mike strained his eyes at the shape, Simon reacted as well.

"Can you enlarge the space around her?" asked Mike.

"You mean like this one," Eddie clicked the mouse on the bottom of the screen and Anna's face filled the screen, both Mike and Simon reacted.

"First class," said Mike as he patted Eddie on his right shoulder, "print me a copy off, will you?" said Mike as he straightened up. Eddie slowly reached over and overturned the A4 size photograph and handed it to Mike, in fact he had handed him several copies, a *'very pleased with me'* smile came over his face as he watched both Mike and Simon share them between themselves.

"Well done," said Simon quietly as he studied the picture, "well done indeed," all three paused then they all looked up at the same time.

"Result," said Mike as he started to turn and walk back to his desk. He glanced back at the grinning Eddie and smiled and nodded at the same time, this was good. Mike and Simon sat back down at their desks, Simon started tapping away again, "This puts her at the scene of both murders." said Mike, he was staring at the photograph. Simon looked up.

"Which makes her a suspect."

"That it does." Mike paused before speaking again, "That it does." his voice trailed off.

"Sean will be pleased with that," said Simon as he continued to type.

"Where is the boss anyway?" Mike asked, Simon stopped typing, waited, looked up at Mike and waited for Mike to look directly at him.

"With the Crime Watch people," Simon had a slightly sarcastic tone as if, *'you should know that anyway'* if it wasn't said, it was certainly implied. Simon continued, "We are meeting him for lunch." Realisation burst over Mike's face, yes, he did know that, Simon went back to his typing, "And by the way, you're paying."

"Why am I paying?" Simon stopped again and smiled.

"Well *'if'* you want to buy my silence and not have me tell him that you had forgotten, again," he tilted his head to one side, "then you buy lunch." Mike raised his eyebrows, he fought for something to come back at him with, but he couldn't think of anything, so he would have to concede. The phone on Mike's desk burst into life; he was glad of the interruption. The other members of the team had been around Eddie's desk looking at what he had found, the level of noise was raised slightly; the jigsaw was coming together.

"I'm sorry," said Mike into the phone. Simon stopped again and looked over at him, "can you not just tell me now?" Simon watched as Mike paused, he slowly nodded his head as he listened to whoever he was speaking to, "Yes, yes, I understand that, but can you not tell me why?" again he paused, Simon relaxed and looked over at Mike who looked up at him then pointed with his eyes to the ceiling, "Ok, no problems, 2 o'clock then." he paused, "Thanks, bye for now." Mike replaced the handset and looked over at Simon who was sitting patiently waiting and wanting to know what the conversation was about. "that was the forensic labs, they want the three of us to go up there for 2 o'clock."

Simon glanced up at the clock on the wall. "Why?" he asked.

"They have something that they're not prepared to discuss over a phone." Simon raised his eyebrows; it intrigued Simon, as it did Mike, why the forensic labs did not want to discuss something over the phone. That was very out of character for them; what had they found now?

"Ok, I'll tell Sean."

∞∞∞

Two hours later Sean was parking the car in front of the forensic laboratory just outside Belfast, Simon was in the front seat and Mike was in the back. Mike was going through more of the photos from Coleraine; he was very pleased with what Eddie had found. She was nearly wearing the same clothes; find her and they have found their killer. It was exactly what they needed.

"Have you ever met this guy before?" asked Sean as they climbed out of the car. Simon looked over at him as Mike was fumbling with the pictures spread over the back seat.

"Not met him; spoke to him on the phone," Sean nodded as they both closed the doors. Mike was now clambering out of the back door of the car.

"I have," he exclaimed. Sean and Simon both looked at him, then turned and slowly walked towards the main entrance.

"He is a bit eccentric," Sean continued. Simon was walking off to his left with Mike behind them. Sean continued, "but, very good at what he does,"

Simon nodded, as Sean pushed open the main door; he paused and stopped them both, "He is also deaf in one ear."

"Got loads going for him then," said Mike sarcastically. Sean smiled and walked inside. After introductions, they were led to a small conference room with only one small window. A long table took up most of the room and was surrounded by metal framed plastic chairs; they were not designed for comfort. The large whiteboard occupied the far end wall and a projector sat near it at the end of the table; they would be joined in a few minutes by their host.

∞∞∞

Alexi looked at his watch, it was exactly 2 o'clock. He sat in his BMW in the car park of Tesco's in Coleraine; the last of them walked up towards the driver's window. Alexi pushed the button and the window dropped inside the door. Anna moved into the passenger seat beside him.

"Well Viktor?" he asked. Viktor dropped down, so he was at eye level with him.

"Yes, one pair,"

"Where?" asked Alexi.

"Down near the train station, but they backed away when we approached them,"

"Did you get a photo?"

"Yes, on my phone, but it's not a good one," Viktor handed over the silver phone. Alexi pushed one button and the picture filled the screen. Viktor pointed at the two men in the picture, one had his back to the screen and the second was turning away. Both men had dark ginger hair and from the picture Alexi could see that at least one had blue eyes, *'very Irish'* he thought to himself. "What about the others?" Viktor asked, Alexi looked up.

"None, only you," a smile spread over Viktor's face, "Did they get a look at you?" Alexi asked, Viktor slowly nodded, "and they backed away?"

"Yes, as soon as they saw us," he answered, Alexi looked at him then over at Anna.

"So, they know we are here," Alexi paused as he stared forward. "Right go back to the house and tell everyone that I will address them later." Viktor nodded as Alexi started the car and closed the window; as the car moved forward Anna spoke.

"What are you going to do now?" she asked. Alexi slowly made his way through the mass of people who were walking back and forth through the busy car park. He paused and waited for the sports car to move past him and head for the space he had just left.

"Take you to Portrush for lunch," he said; Anna turned in her seat and faced him.

"No, I mean about the Rua? We cannot just sit back and do nothing!" Alexi brought the car to a stop at the exit of the car park and waited for a space in the flow of traffic from around the corner. Silence filled the car, Anna looked around at the people walking past them, "They know we are here now," she said quietly.

"They have known we have been here for a while," Alexi answered.

"So, what are you going to do?" the car jumped forward onto the street.

"What I would do the other way around, seek out their Alpha and go and face them," Anna turned away from him, Alexi could tell that was not what she wanted to hear.

"So, we will wait for them," they slowly followed the road past the Chinese by the river and stopped at the traffic lights, "then we will make our peace," he said. Anna smiled at him but didn't make eye contact, her anger was obvious. The lights changed to green and the car moved off.

∞∞∞∞

"Inspector Parrish!" The door had been flung open as the tall man passed through it. Mike stood up to greet the man who was holding out his hand toward Sean.

"Doctor Burns," said Sean as he stepped forward and took the hand of the doctor. Doctor Burns was in his late fifties with swept back hair and deep silver streaks. He had an old face that had seen too much but his grey eyes were filled with a strange fire that Mike had only ever seen in the eyes of patients on a ward of a secure hospital. His dress sense matched his age, it wasn't a tweed jacket, but it was close. He had a patterned open-necked shirt, no tie, and plain grey trousers. However, he was missing the white coat that was normally stereotypical of his profession. Mike agreed with Sean's earlier comment, this guy was eccentric. Sean turned and introduced the others.

"Doctor Burns, this is Detective Sergeant Simon McAllister," Simon's hand was clasped by the firm hand of the smiling doctor. Sean turned toward Mike, "and this is Detective Sergeant Michael Dear," again, the hand was shaken firmly. The Doctor had introduced himself by his first name as they had shaken hands, "Vic Burns, welcome," he then paused and looked at Mike, "have we met?" he asked, Mike smiled politely.

"Yes, you gave a lecture at the police college at Garnerville two years ago, we spoke afterwards." The doctor paused, looked at him with a slightly confused look as his mind searched for the face which was then dismissed out of hand.

"Sorry, don't remember the chat, but I recognise the face," they all stepped back and shared a glance as the doctor spread his right arm and invited them to sit at the near side of the table.

As the three men sat down the doctor walked around and sat at the other side of the table, facing them. He ripped open a large manila envelope and the sheets of A4 paper were placed face down on the table. It was obvious he was excited about something.

"Right then, gentlemen," he started by placing his hands on the table with his palms downwards, he continued speaking. "I have some news about the DNA samples from the killings in Belfast, Limavady and Coleraine," Sean nodded but remained silent to let this eccentric but very intelligent man continue, "when we got the samples from the first killings we were of the opinion that they had been corrupted and therefore could not be used," Mike glanced over at Simon, "then we got the samples from Limavady, which again were corrupted somehow," Mike could feel an excitement growing inside himself, "Then..." the doctor paused, Sean spoke for him.

"Then ... what?" The doctor sighed through his nose, brushed his hair back with his right hand, looked around the room then turned back towards the three policemen who were all staring at him.

"We got the samples from Coleraine," he stopped. Mike said it, the others thought it.

"So?" The Doctor shifted in his seat and it looked like he was biting the inside of his lower lip.

"Then we started looking in another direction," he paused.

"And what was this other direction?" Sean asked,

"Well, first I can confirm for you that the two DNA samples that we got from Belfast are the same two we got from Coleraine!" all three policemen reacted.

"Definitely?" asked Sean.

"Definitely!" said the doctor, Mike looked at the other two then back at the doctor.

"Well that's brilliant news!" Sean glanced at Mike and Mike looked back into his eyes. Sean's eyes moved back towards the doctor.

"So, what's the problem?" The doctor moved nervously at the question.

"Well, we at first did not believe our findings so they were tested, re-tested then again retested by a third technician, all got the same results." The three policemen glanced at each other, this wasn't a problem, this was a result. "The problem is... well..." The doctor started going through the sheets of paper and turned over one then placed it in front of them. "This is a normal human DNA trace," they had all seen a DNA trace before, "I know it to be normal because it is mine!" stated the doctor, Mike wondered if anything to do with this man was normal, another page was turned over, "and this is the first trace from Belfast."

"You said two traces," injected Simon.

"Yes, here is the second," The three policemen all looked forward and the patterns on the second and third pages, it was wildly different to the first, "here are the two samples from Coleraine..." they were the same as the two from Belfast. Sean wasn't quite sure what he was looking at, so he asked the question that was bounding around his head.

"Well this is good, can they be used in court?" The doctor sat back and grimaced.

"Well hear me out on this..." he sat forward again, "here we have the single trace from the Limavady killing, you can see that it's similar to the Belfast traces," he held the pages together, the pattern was similar but differed greatly from the 'normal' trace.

"So, we can definitely place these two at both scenes then?" asked Sean.

"Yes" answered the doctor, Sean turned towards Mike.

"Great, we find this girl and get a DNA sample from her," Sean was pointing with the thumb of his left hand to Mike who started nodding in agreement as he spoke "my money is on matching her to one of these,"

"Find her, find who else was there and bang, we got them," stated Simon, Sean agreed.

"What girl?" asked the doctor. Mike looked at Sean who nodded as Mike pulled out the photos and told the doctor of what they had found, the doctor sat open mouthed at the pictures.

He spoke to the girl with black hair in the picture, "Oh my God, are you real?" The three of them looked at each other again as Sean sat forward this time.

"Is what real Doctor?" The doctor's eyes flashed up, he pushed the chair back and started to walk up and down behind the chairs.

Look, it's what we think we have found," he stopped and stared straight at Sean, "If you find this woman, if she really does exist then we could be at a turning point in mankind." Mike glanced over at Simon, this guy really was bonkers, Sean spoke quieter than he had been.

"Explain then Doctor, what have you found?" the doctor hurried back to his pile of paper.

"Look, this DNA is not meant to exist!" he shuffled through what he now held in both hands.

"What's not meant to exist?" Sean asked. The doctor stopped, he arranged more traces face up on the table, he kept one that was wildly different off to one side.

"Right, De-oxy-ribo-Nucleic Acid, DNA," he looked up at the three faces in front of him to confirm that they understood what he was saying, as he was speaking he pulled a fountain pen out of his trouser pocket and hovered over a blank sheet of A4, "Is found in every single cell, it is the 'finger print' that is individual to each and every single living cell!" again he looked up, the three police officers remained silent, Mike wondered where this was going, "it is the blue print or code that is required to build and create life," Sean nodded at him as he spoke. "Right then, we can identify every living species by this code, each species being different and placed into different groups," the doctor was waving his pen around as if he was conducting an orchestra, "each group is then divided into sub groups,"

"Mammals, Amphibians, etc," stated Mike, the doctor pointed at him with the pen.

"Nearly," he sat down and pulled the blank sheet of paper towards him, he drew a stick diagram of a ladder and started pointing out the different parts of the DNA structure. "All DNA is divided into four parts, A, T, C, G," this was scribbled down at the top of the page, the doctor was not giving them a chance to butt in "A fits into T, C fits into G and they in turn are bonded together with hydrogen, this forms the ladder…"

"Doctor," Sean stated.

"So, from this we can see 'normal' human DNA, although each one being different in pattern all still falling inside the Homo-Sapiens group," the doctor paused at this "Homo-Sapiens," he paused again, "human, you and me," he explained.

"Yes, I know that," Sean got cut off again as the doctor carried on.

"So, when we first got your samples that contained other DNA, we assumed that it was corrupted and had been incorrectly taken from the crime scene," he was getting more excited as he got closer to his revelation that they now knew was coming. "Then when we got the other samples we went back over our work, then again, and again," the doctor looked straight at the three of them, "until we confirmed what we had found," 'finally' whispered Mike.

"So, what have you found?" Sean repeated, "what else was in the DNA trace?" the doctor nodded as Sean had spoken. "Canine DNA!" he looked pleased with himself.

"Canine DNA?" said Sean.

"Canine DNA," repeated the doctor.

"But the scene was corrupted by dogs before we arrived at the Belfast murder?" stated Simon.

"Exactly what we thought!" the doctor bounded in his chair, "well, at first anyway, then we were able to separate the different traces from the animals that we took from the dogs themselves." The doctor could tell that the three men sat before did not believe what he was saying; he reached over to the bottom of the pile of paper and pulled out three A4 sized pieces of acetate that had different DNA traces on them.

"Look, the first here," he placed it on the blank sheet of paper, "normal human DNA ok!" he got three nods in reply, he lifted that up and set down a second one "Normal Canine DNA," again three nods so he placed the first one on top of the second one and let the police men look in "combine the two then," he moved the DNA traces from Limavady to one side then the ones from Belfast to the other, three pairs of eyes scanned what was being shown to them, "what you are looking at is someone who has a combination of both."

"That's impossible," Mike said out loud, the doctor stood up and started walking again.

"No, no actually it's not,"

"Excuse me?" said Simon, the doctor walked back in front of them.

"It's called a hybrid, a mixture of two different sets of DNAs," The doctor was nodding. "it's not impossible, not totally proven in the scientific world but theoretically not impossible."

"Theoretically?" asked Sean as he looked the doctor straight in the eyes, the fire there was blazing, the doctor started tapping the table as he spoke.

Yes, but if we could confirm a living sample of such a person," a massive smile burst over his face as he fought for the right words, "then it would be like discovering an island of living breathing dinosaurs off the coast of Ireland." Mike was convinced, this guy is bonkers. Sean and Simon exchanged glances then looked back at the unconvincing doctor who now stood straight up, "we have identified the type of canine DNA that we are.... Sorry, you are looking for."

Ok," said Sean, the doctor paused so Sean continued, "What type?" the doctor looked straight at them.

"Canis Lupus," he replied.

"Sorry?" Mike crunched up his face,

"It's Latin for Wolf," Sean explained, an impressed look spread over the Doctor's face as he slowly leaned forward and picked up the photo of Anna.

"I would very much like to meet wolf girl here, very much indeed."

∞∞∞

The three men walked back towards the car in silence, Sean stopped at the driver's door and looked over the top of the car at Mike and Simon.

"Anyone asks we have a DNA profile that we are investigating, nothing more," Simon nodded back.

"He's off his head!" said Mike, "I mean totally bonkers," the three of them climbed into the car as Mike continued "absolutely barking mad."

"Less of the 'barking' comments please," said Simon as Sean started up the car.

Chapter 17

"Where are they now?" Carl turned his head and looked across the living room of the farmhouse, "Paul," the man across the room looked up at him.

"Mmm?" he replied.

"Where are they now?" Carl didn't like repeating himself, Paul looked at him.

"They're still in the hotel in Belfast," Paul watched as Carl walked around the room, he was engrossed in his own thoughts. Carl nodded his head and looked over towards Paul.

"Gather what we have collected and get a team together, we are going to have a chat with our Russian friends," Carl wasn't happy as he started towards the door that led outside.

"It is already done," said Paul as the door of the farmhouse opened.

"What?" questioned Carl.

"It is already done," Paul repeated, "your usual team is in the barn, two cars and the photos are here," with that Paul held up his right arm, lifting the small briefcase into view. Carl's eyes moved from Paul to the case then back to Paul.

"Well done," Carl turned and headed outside, "we leave in 5 minutes." The door closed behind him. Paul walked over to the old phone on the table. He pulled a small diary out of his pocket flicking through the pages before stopping and placing the little book beside the phone. He lifted the receiver, waited for the tone then placed his finger into one of the number holes and turned the dial, the number only rang a few times before it was answered by a young female voice. She introduced herself. Paul asked for the room number that was written beneath the phone number and the woman's voice was replaced by the 'on hold' music. Paul waited a few seconds before the male voice answered.

"Yes," the strong Russian accent was one of the two that had been at the farmhouse, but Paul could not identify which of the two it was. He introduced himself and mentioned Carl's name, the phone remained silent.

"Sir, we are coming down to the hotel as my Alpha would like to have a conference with you," there was another pause before the voice spoke one word.

"When?" It was more of a demand than a question.

"It is to happen at the earliest opportunity, we are leaving the farm in a few minutes to travel down to see you," Paul paused. There was silence again from the phone. "My Alpha requests would it be possible for both of you to be there."

"Fine, we shall be here," there was another silence from the voice before it continued, "just don't be late," with that the voice ended the conversation. Paul slowly put the phone back down on the table, turned and picked up the briefcase and headed out the door, he glanced at his watch as he did so, and it was just after five, this could be a very long or very, very short conference.

∞∞∞∞

All the way down the M2 into Belfast Carl sat in silence, he didn't speak so neither did Paul, he knew better than to try and make idle chat, that was something that Carl hated, especially when he was not in a happy mood. The traffic slowed, and the two cars entered the road works that had reduced the lanes down to single traffic. The traffic slowed to a crawl, the driver moved the car forward and the front passenger scanned everything that was going on around them. Paul looked over at Carl as the car broke free of the congestion and sped forward towards Belfast, Paul knew he was going over what he was going to say again and again in his head.

Twenty minutes later and the doors of the lift parted, Carl walked forward then turned left down the long corridor of the hotel; he was followed by Paul and two girls from the security team behind them. Paul noticed that Carl's pace had increased as they got nearer to the hotel room. Carl stopped and knocked three times; lowered voices could be heard from inside. A few seconds passed before a metallic clunk from the lock of the door sounded, the door opened and allowed them to enter. Only Carl and Paul walked forward, the others didn't, one would wait around the door and the other walked on to ensure that she knew where the fire escape and other exits were. The team in the second car would stay around the cars and the reception of the hotel. They were all there to protect their Alpha.

The door closed behind them and they stopped just inside the square room dominated by a large double bed that had its head to the right-hand side. They stood by the doorway to their right that opened into the en-suite bathroom. The open clothes rack was to their left, a bench ran the length of the left-hand side wall on which sat the TV set. In between the TV and the clothes rack sat a small tray with a white ceramic tea pot with matching tea cups and saucers. In a small glass was a selection of tea and coffee packets, none of which had been touched. The elder of the two Russians was sitting in the only chair in the room. He stood up as they entered. Carl made a slow nod of his head as the Russian stood up, the Russian opened the palm of his right hand and beckoned them further into the room.

"Thank you, Mr O'Brian, please come in," Carl and Paul stopped at the end of the bed, the other Russian walked between the two of them and past the first Russian. He turned and leaned up against the edge of the window that occupied the far wall. There was a slight pause before the Russian spoke again, "So, what is it that you want, Mr O' Brian?" he demanded. Paul glanced at Carl as he knew that the Russian was patronising him.

"You're enjoying your stay here in Belfast?" asked Carl. It wasn't a question, more of a statement.

"Yes, we are,"

"Your trip down south, did it go well?" the Russian slowly nodded, Carl already knew the details of their trip,

"Yes, it did. It is widely known how the Rua make good hosts," the Russian paused, "it was very impressive." The Russian over by the window shifted his position as the first Russian continued speaking, "But I do not believe you have called us together this evening for small talk? and if you have, this conversation is over." The Russian did not raise his voice, but there was no doubt it was a command. Carl looked over his shoulder and made eye contact with Paul, he nodded and Paul moved over toward the TV and opened the briefcase. Paul arranged the 5" x 7" photographs over the bench. Carl spoke as Paul closed the briefcase and stepped back. The Russians walked over and looked down at the pictures.

"I want to know exactly who they are, I want to know exactly where they have come from, I want to know exactly why they have come here," Carl took a single step towards the Russians as he finished the sentence, "And I want to know now!" the second Russian looked up and shouted back at Carl.

"What? Who do you think you are? You do not speak to us like this? We are council members, we ask the questions not you!" Carl didn't move, his voice remained at the same firm tone.

"I am Alpha of these lands and you are guests and you will be treated as such."

"What?" the second Russian went to step forward, "you forget who you are talking too," Carl remained calm.

"Your position and status are clear to me and will be respected as such," the first Russian turned his head to the left and looked at Carl and Paul, Carl continued "I want their names and I want them now Godspodine Tatamovich," Carl had used the polite Russian word for mister, he hadn't said his first name in the title as this would appear disrespectful, a fact that didn't go unnoticed. The second Russian went to speak but the first Russian stopped him by lifting his hand onto the centre of his chest.

"Calm Tatamovich, Carl is right, we are their guests and if this was our lands we would do the same." Tatamovich visibly backed down but still glared at Carl as the first Russian picked up one of the photographs, "Where and when, were these photographs taken?" he asked,

"Yesterday, around Coleraine." Carl answered, the Russian picked up a second photograph and paused.

"This one is their Alpha, his name is Alexi Chernov, this one is his second, Davidov Sprogis," The Russian went through each of their names in turn, but still was not giving anything else away.

"Thank you Godspodine Grishin," Carl was about to ask something else when the first Russian cut him off.

"You know where they are? yes?" he looked over at Carl.

"Yes," replied Carl, "but why are they here?" Carl repeated his earlier question. The Russian replaced the photos down on the bench.

"Well that will take more than a few minutes and I am hungry," Carl went to speak but the Russian lifted his right hand. "We will meet you down stairs at the reception in a few minutes, you will take us for a meal then we will return, and we will answer all of your questions." There was a pause of a few seconds before Carl nodded with his head and turned towards the door. Paul walked over and without looking at the Russians picked up all the photographs and replaced them in the briefcase. He followed Carl out of the room, as the door shut the two Russians relaxed.

"Answer their questions?" Tatamovich half shouted as he walked over and slouched in the chair, "Who do they think they are Grishin!" Grishin leaned back on the bench, he slowly smiled before he spoke.

"They are protecting their lands, as we would do, as they should do."

"So, what are you going to tell them later then?" he asked, Grishin looked up at him.

"Only what they ask, only what they ask," Grishin looked over at the entrance to the room as Tatamovich spoke.

"What of Chernov?"

"What of Chernov?" replied Grishin.

"What are we going to do about him?" he asked.

"We are going to let the Rua deal with their own problems their own way,"

"What if they kill again? What if they are caught before the Rua act?" Grishin looked up at him.

"The Rua know the law, we are just here to ensure that they follow the law, nothing more," Grishin stood up and walked towards the bathroom. "Well I'm going for a shower," he paused as he got to the door, "and you can go back to your own room." Tatamovich rose from the chair and walked towards the entrance of the room.

"See you in ten minutes," The door to the bathroom closed, they would make the Rua wait.

At the bottom end of the corridor the young woman who had been the passenger that was escorting Carl and Paul watched as Tatamovich walked away from the room and into a different room a couple of doors down, she took out her phone and tapped in a message. Down at the reception of the hotel Paul's phone bleeped, Paul read the message then told Carl.

"They will make us wait before coming down, but," Carl had stressed the 'but' "but they are going to tell us everything." Paul looked over at him.

"How do you know they will tell us everything?" he asked, Carl looked over at him.

"Because if they weren't, we would have left the room with just the names and nothing else, the meal is the polite way of saying, yes *you are right, but you will wait*." Paul looked back at him, "Politics, Paul, it's just politics." Carl could see that Paul was annoyed, "They are still council members and we must respect that, but we will have our way,"

"Where are you going to take them?" Paul asked.

"The Chinese in the Odyssey is very nice, get one of the team to phone ahead and book a VIP table." Paul nodded, turned and looked around, his eyes fixed on one of them then he stood up and walked over.

∞∞∞∞

As Cara-Marie closed the door of the dishwasher it jumped into life, it was half full of the dishes she had used to make dinner, most of which went into the bin as she couldn't eat it. She

90

poured a small glass of wine from the open bottle that was in the fridge then went through to her living room. She flicked the TV on, and the screen was filled by one of the shopping channels, her mum had been round and had been using her digital box to do some more shopping. Cara-Marie sipped on her wine as she flipped through the channels finally stopping on a movie channel. She had not seen 'Dirty Dancing' in a very long time and it was about half an hour into it.

"Excellent escapism," she said out loud as the remote got tossed to the far end of the sofa. The wine tasted well as she remembered, she recalled some of her earliest memories of dancing as a very young girl to the film's soundtrack. The bleeping of her phone brought her back to the present. She sat up and pulled her phone out from her pocket, it was from Mark, the photographer. She opened the message, 'HIYA CARA, HOWZ U?,' she told him where she was and what she was doing then at the end of her text asked the same question back to him. They had not long left work and they had been comparing notes about his last visit to the police and what he had written on the note, had he found out something else? What more news had he got his hands on? Did he have a photograph of the dogs? She placed her phone down on the coffee table and waited for it to bleep again in the next few seconds. Which it didn't. Cara-Marie lifted the glass of wine and tried to watch the film, but her eyes flicked back to the silent phone, she moved on the sofa and stared at the still silent phone. What was taking him so long? She tried to concentrate on the film, but it wasn't working and with a mouthful she finished her glass. She walked back into the kitchen and refilled her glass and just as she closed the door of the fridge her phone bleeped in the living room. Cara-Marie nearly ran through the house and grabbed at the phone, not even noticing that she had spilt wine on the carpet. She would be annoyed with herself later.

'YEAH IM FINE' was the simple message, was that it? *'yeah, I'm fine'* she said it out loud, sat back down on the sofa and started typing again, read over what she typed then deleted it without sending. She thought over the note that he had left at her desk in the office, 'something to do with dogs and a fit looking chick with black hair.' Her mind was in overdrive, again, she wanted to know who the woman with black hair that she had seen in Coleraine was, what was it that she saw over at Riverside, the same questions kept coming up, she lifted the glass to her lips and sipped at the wine. She re-read his earlier messages, one word had her reaching for the phone again; how had she forgot to ask this?

'WHO IS RACHEL?' This time it was answered in a few seconds, she opened the picture message that had just been taken of Mark's face with the face of a young woman pressed up against his. Both were grinning into the camera phone, she had dark-ginger hair and light green eyes. Cara-Marie started typing into her phone again, 'SO DO TELL, DETAILS PLEASE,' then she pressed the send button, the dancing continued on the screen as a smile spread over her face. She had known about the problems he'd been having with his now obvious ex-girlfriend and he had finally taken her advice and ended it. Not quite the way she expected but hey, journalists like scandal. The next text arrived and told her that they had known each other over two years, always liked each other, both their mums knew each other etc. Cara-Marie read over the message again, for all the information that was there and the way it was so freely given it was obvious this was a smoke screen.

'EXCELLENT! SO, WHAT ARE YOUR PLANS?' again she did not have to wait long for the answer. 'SHE HAS MOVED IN WITH ME AND I HAVNT BEEN THIS HAPPY IN A LONG TIME' wow, that was a quick move, unless.... 'SHE HAS MOVED IN QUICK? WHAT ABOUT THE EX? WHAT HAPPENED THERE?' this time the text wasn't answered straight away, she drank more of the wine and watched more of the film, and then finally the phone bleeped. Her mouth opened as she read the words. 'I AM GOING TO BE A DADDY' an hour later the doorbell rang, and she was introduced to Rachel. Mark recounted the last couple of times they had been out, and Cara-Marie made a mental note of the dates. Mark had still been with his ex at the time, not good.

She would wait until tomorrow then have a go at him and get the details of what he had been doing to his ex-girlfriend because regardless of what she had done, she didn't deserve that.

∞∞∞∞

Sean stopped at the set of traffic lights, it was dark and thankfully the rain had stopped. He had wanted to finish work on time but the presentation to Superintendent Sutcliffe had gone on longer than he had wanted. The Super had only wanted him and not Mike and the Crime Watch producers were on their way down into Belfast for a meal, maybe that wasn't the best idea after all, and he was starting to regret it. 'This is your biggest priority' the Super kept repeating, 'actually, no it wasn't,' the Henderson case was in court in two days' time and both Simon and he would be finishing off the preparation for that! It was a big priority to Super Sutcliffe as all he was concerned with was making sure that targets were met, and the service always looked good. Solving crime was nice but not really a priority. The horn of the car behind his jolted him, the lights were green, his car slowly moved with the flow of traffic, was it trying to rain? He wasn't sure. Sean had told his wife that he would be home for tea, that was four hours ago, this wasn't going to be pretty but that was the nature of the beast. As he pulled into his driveway his phone bleeped, it was Mike.

'I AM IN COLERAINE, ARE YOU COMING UP TOMORROW?' Sean texted back about the Henderson case and a brief description of what had been going on at work earlier this evening. The lights were on, but the house was quiet, no TV, which means there is about to be a shouting match. This part of the job Sean knew that he could not avoid and could easily do without, the phone beeped again from Mike. 'OK, NO PROBLEMS, NOT MUCH GOING ON HERE, JUST A COUPLE OF THINGS BUT NOTHING URGENT. GIVE ME A SHOUT TOMORROW.' Sean did not reply as he turned the key in the lock of the front door and walked forward into the stillness of the house.

Chapter 18

Kyle stared into the darkness, past the trees, they were there, and they were watching. Kyle slowly raised himself up from the ground and brought the sniper rifle up to his shoulder and looked through the scope at the wooden framed watchtower that stood up from the small bamboo camp. The dark African face of the soldier who stood in the tower was bored. Kyle could see the sweat drip from his forehead, the light green, dirty uniform hung from his body. He watched as everything moved in slow motion, the head of the soldier exploded, the rifle in his hands hardly moved. Kyle looked over to his right as the darkness was ripped apart by the movement all around him of dark shapes moving through the trees.

Kyle was running, but not moving, the faster and harder he tried the greater the force was keeping him back, the blackened face of a European appeared off to his left, the slow slurred shout poured from the open mouth, run, faster, run, faster. Bright orange balls grew from the ground and blossomed through the bamboo huts in front of them, his body was heavy, but he forced his way through the darkness, slow, slurred shouts came from all around, screams and cries mixed with the muffled sound of gunfire.

The door of the hut gave way to his right foot as the soldier threw in the small sphere. Everything was so slow, muted sounds all around as Kyle jumped through the open door into the dark empty room. A figure stood at the far wall with his back to him and Kyle watched as the bullet slowly carved its way through the thick dense air towards the figure which slumped onto the ground. He walked over to the body, kicked it over, then looked down at the twisted face.

∞∞∞∞

Kyle sat up in bed, the duvet was in a crumpled mess on the floor beside him. His bedroom slowly came into focus. He flung his legs off the side of the bed but did not notice the sweat that covered his body or the fact that he was still panting, out of breath. Kyle placed his elbows onto his knees then put his head in his hands, he lifted his line of sight slightly and waited for the clock to come into focus, it was nearly 5 AM and he wanted a drink of water. As he stood up the bolt of lightning shot down his leg and jolted the rest of his body causing him to fall back onto the bed, had he just shouted out loud? He wasn't sure now. He lay on top of the bed unable to move as he slowly waited for the pain to decrease, his breath slowed as did the thumping of his heart inside his chest. He made slow deliberate movements and raised himself up from the bed and walked very stiffly over to the door of the bedroom, the dressing gown slid over his torso as he opened the door and stepped into the darkness of the hallway. He made his way into the dark kitchen and without turning on the lights he poured himself a glass of water. As he stood taking a mouthful of water at a time he stared into the greyness of the back garden, he could easily make out the shapes that were there; this was a skill that had proved to be very useful many times in the Legion. It had been discovered very early on that he had a mild form of colour blindness, but this amplified low light and he found his night vision very quickly. That talent had saved more than just his own life, and it had got him a very high score on the sniper course the Legion had sent him on. Kyle smiled to himself as happier memories marched back into his mind. Being stood shoulder to shoulder with other legionnaires and singing as loud as he could, on the calming wind familiar voices sang with him again, his eyes opened, and he continued with the words of the song in English.

"But for the Belgians there's none left," the smile was firmly planted on his face as he finished the water then returned to bed, sleep would escape him yet again for the rest of that night.

∞∞∞∞

Tony Fallon walked up and pushed to doorbell on Kyle's front door, the door opened as he did so.

"You look like crap," he said as he walked past him and made his way into the kitchen. The kettle was empty but that could be rectified very quickly, Kyle was hobbling his way along the

93

hallway as Tony looked over his shoulder, "Brew?" he asked. Kyle paused by the entrance then nodded his head, Tony turned and continued filling the kettle as Kyle hobbled over to the table and slowly sat down. "What happened to you?" Tony asked as he spooned sugar into two mugs.

"I was climbing out of bed this morning and zap, my back went," Kyle looked up at him, Tony was grinning.

"You are getting old; your body cannot take much more," the kettle started boiling so Tony reached over for it.

"Piss off," Kyle replied,

"No, really, you are getting old,"

"And you really can piss off," both men smiled as the abuse passed between them, Tony handed over the mug of tea.

"Sleep well last night?" he asked.

"Yeah, not too bad," replied Kyle. *'Lie'* Tony thought to himself as he sat down.

"Nightmare again?" he enquired, Kyle looked up at him. There are some mirrors that you can disguise yourself in, but others that you cannot hide from, Tony was the latter. Kyle nodded as he lifted the mug to his lips, "So what time is your appointment again?" Tony asked, he already knew as he was here to give Kyle a lift there and back.

"Half 11," Kyle paused, "as you already know, or did the Para's totally turn your brains to mush?"

"At least we wash, smelly," Kyle looked over at Tony but before he could speak Tony continued "Or are you not going to have a shower,"

"Yes, I was...and I don't smell,"

"You smell just like me after I have been camping for two weeks," batted Tony back at Kyle.

"I am pretty sure that this classes as abuse," stated Kyle.

"Are you saying I abuse you?" questioned Tony.

"You're a funny guy Fallon..." Kyle paused, "that's why I am going to kill you last," Tony grinned as Kyle quoted from a film.

"I could stand in front of you and you would miss," retorted Tony, Kyle raised his eyebrows as he drank from the mug.

"I could get you in the head at 1000 metres,"

"You couldn't get me in the head at 10 metres never mind 1000,"

"Well you better get a move on, you don't want to be late for your date,"

"It's not a date, it is a Physio appointment," answered Kyle.

"With a very fit, good looking, professional woman who could leave you foaming at the mouth," Kyle went to say something but again Tony cut in, "you two still texting each other?" Tony falsely blinked his eyes and puckered his lips, mockingly.

"Yes, we are still texting," Kyle started to rise from the table, "but just to organise my appointments and discuss treatments," Kyle shuffled across the kitchen as Tony drank for his mug.

"Yeah, ok,"

"No, really, that's all,"

"Uh-huh," said Tony as he looked across at him standing there still in his dressing gown, "and you would not be interested in a fit woman like that, would you?" Kyle stuck two fingers up at him and turned and walked out of the kitchen. "Hey, that's not nice," Tony shouted after him, "Are you going to have a shower now, smelly?" The muffled reply from Kyle was more abuse, "you are going grey as well," shouted Tony as he stood up, finished the mug of tea and walked over to the sink.

"And you can really piss off," came the clear reply and the sound of the shower started. Tony washed up his mug and that of the half drank tea that Kyle had left on the table. The rest of the kitchen was immaculate, something that the legion had drummed into Kyle. Tony looked at his watch, it wasn't that long after nine and it was obvious that Kyle had been up for some time.

Tony dried the two mugs and replaced them on the wooden mug tree that sat near the kettle. The sound of the shower stopped, Tony walked through into the living room and switched the TV on, "has Karen decided on where you are going for your holiday yet?" Tony thought for a few seconds, it was something which he had forgotten totally about.

"Erm, no," he would ask tonight when he got home.

"Bet its Palma again," came the shout from the adjacent room, *'bet it's not!'* thought Tony, "don't know what she sees in you," Kyle continued.

"At least I *have* an 'other half'," again it was answered with a muffled reply. It would be another 20 minutes before Kyle would be ready to leave, dressed in a plain sweatshirt, track suit trousers and a pair of grey running trainers.

`   The drive from his house up to Maydown police station seemed to take longer than usual this time, even though there was less traffic. Tony parked the car and Kyle climbed out then made his way up to where the physio room was. Tony walked off in the other direction and would await the text message to arrive saying Kyle's physio had finished.

Kelly had a patient with her already. Kyle looked at his watch as he heard the voices come from the other side of the door to the treatment room. Tony had got him here fifteen minutes early which was not bad as he thought they were going to be late.

Kyle stood himself up against one of the walls at the far side of the room in the most comfortable position he could find. The fitness instructor from Maydown arrived at the top of the stairs, said a brief 'hello' then disappeared back down the stairs again; he was obviously looking for someone and that didn't include Kyle.

Kyle's mind wandered as he waited, his mind went over the dream from last night, he wasn't one for analysing dreams in the same way that others did, and he had stopped telling people what was happening in his nightmares as people just didn't seem to understand what it was like to have served, to be honest, he didn't really care. For a moment Kyle was back in the room just as the body turned over and just for a moment he could see the face again... Kyle suddenly was pulled through a kaleidoscope and back to reality, the door for the treatment room opened and a male figure filled the doorway.

As the figure came into view Kyle recognised the police officer as one from Limavady station, he thought that he was a dick and only ever spoke to him if he had to. Kelly shared a joke with him, and they smiled and said their goodbyes, he was obviously happy with the treatment that he had just received, *'walk on, walk on'* Kyle thought to himself.

"Oh, hello there," the voice started. Kyle reluctantly opened his eyes at the man walking towards him. Kyle kept his hands behind him as the less contact the two of them had, the better. Kelly stayed over by the door but grinned in recognition at Kyle, "If it isn't Beau Geste himself, how have you been? How is life in Ley Leegin?" his mispronunciation just got Kyle's back up even more.

"Hello Brian," Kyle really didn't want to be there at that exact moment in time. "By the way, I'm not in the Legion, I am in the police service," Kyle's reply was short. Kelly's eyebrows raised; Kyle's annoyance was obvious to all.

"Ha, well we all know you legion boys never let go," Brian did not pick up on the hint, Kyle's face slightly contorted at Brian's comment.

"Known many 'legionnaires', have you?" Kyle asked.

"Oh yeah, loads," Brian's boast did not sit well with Kyle. *'Lie'* he thought to himself. "What is it you all say?" Brian continued as Kyle stepped forward on his way into the treatment room, "once in the legion, always in the legion," Brian was now grinning at his own joke. Kyle stopped, turned and looked at him.

"No, actually, we don't say that." there was a two second gap before Brian, glanced at the ground then tried again.

"Ha, you guys, always making jokes,"

Kyle turned and walked towards the slightly embarrassed physiotherapist.

"Hello," she said as she stepped back and allowed Kyle to enter the room. Kelly quickly shut the door behind him, and he walked over and sat on the plinth; she walked around him and headed for her desk, "Sorry about that,"

"Sorry about what?" Kyle asked, "you didn't do anything to say sorry for." Kelly looked over at him.

"Not a friend of yours then?" she walked round the desk and sat down as Kyle answered her.

"I have met plenty of people like him, spent too much time reading comics when they were boys and have absolutely no idea who the legion is or what we have done." Kelly picked up the folder, flicked it open then scanned the paper that was inside. It was obviously about him, he stopped talking as she wasn't listening anymore, he waited a few seconds then she looked up at him and took a slight breath in before she spoke.

"Right, so what has been happening with you since I saw you last?" Kelly stood up and started to walk back round the desk towards the plinth were Kyle was sitting.

"Well the house is ok, it didn't take me too long to tidy from the Chinese after you left," Kyle paused as a slightly confused look gripped her face, then a grin with a slight blush spread over her face in realisation at what he was going on about.

"I was talking about your injury and not your very nice house." Kyle was looking directly into her eyes and she slowly blinked as she spoke, she stopped a few feet away from him.

"Very nice house!" Kyle repeated, Kelly had not actually realised what she had said.

"What?"

"You think I have a very nice house?" he repeated, she paused, flicked up her eyebrows then continued, she wasn't going to finish what was in her thoughts.

"Ok, so what has been happening with your injury since I last saw you?" a mischievous look spread across her face as she folded her arms under her chest. He let a small smile part his lips as he recounted the events of the last few days and what had been happening; as he was doing so Kelly was nodding occasionally and looking at the parts of his back and legs that he was describing. Her mind was ticking over the information that was being said to her. Kyle on the other hand let his eyes wander over her body and let his mind wander. Kelly looked up as he finished speaking and unfolded her arms as she took a step towards him. "Let's have a look at you then, just pop off your top and bottoms." Kyle started to slowly stand as she spoke and turned his head towards her when she paused, "You 'are' wearing running shorts under those? Yes?" Kyle let the grin open his face.

"Yes, I am wearing shorts under these." Kelly stood and watched as Kyle slowly undressed; was she looking at how he was moving and how much movement he had or was she just enjoying watching a fit bloke take his clothes off. Kyle was hoping for the latter. Although her face remained motionless, Kyle thought that he could see something different in her eyes. Soon he was only dressed in his shorts and was lying face down on the plinth. Kyle's face fitted into the egg-shaped hole at the head end of the plinth ensuring his back was in a neutral position. Kelly's warm thumbs began pressing different parts of his back.

The bolt of pain that shot down his leg let her know she had found what she was looking for as she continued down the back of his left leg. Kyle was made to turn over then perform leg raises, first with one leg at a time then both, after this Kelly would place her hands on his ankles and while only applying a little down force carried out the same procedures again, this time with slightly different results.

Kyle sat up and turned towards her, he let his legs hang off the side. Kelly took a seat back at her desk and started scribbling a few notes.

"Well there is massive improvement from your last session here," Kelly was looking down at the desk as she continued to speak, "Which of course, is really good!"

"Is that unusual?" he asked; she stopped writing and looked up.

"Every patient is different, but from a patient with your level of fitness I would expect a much faster recovery than most." Kyle noted that he was now 'a patient'. Kelly was back to being her professional self again. He waited for her to speak again, "So, let's see what we can do with you." Kelly wrote another few lines then closed the folder and walked back towards the table. Kyle remained silent as she walked towards him. Kyle lay back, face down. Her warm fingertips prodded around the top of his neck then over his shoulders, "What would you want to happen next?" she asked. The first thought that jumped into Kyle's mind nearly came out of his mouth, but he kept it to what treatment he wanted next.

"I want the pain to stop," he simply stated.

"Ok," she paused again. He was staring at the floor and heard her walk away from him; he heard a drawer being opened then a plastic container popping. She walked back over beside him and stopped. Kyle looked at the black canvas shoes that covered her feet, she wasn't wearing socks but then in these shoes that would not have looked right. Kelly had started talking before the acupuncture that she was about to do and moments later Kyle felt the first of the needles go into his shoulder, another followed soon after near his neck, then a third at the top of his spine. The next few went around his foot then the final one went into the side of his knee, already Kyle could feel the pressure lift from his body. The feeling lapped like waves over him, Kelly's voice started to drift away as he slowly floated into the darkness.

The poke of a finger into his side brought him back to the room where he was, a small film of sweat covered his forehead as his eyes focused in on the floor. Kyle slowly closed his fists then moved his toes, the needles were already gone from his body.

"Wake-a-wakey," Kelly's voice made him lift his head, Kyle felt the muscles in his arms and shoulders reluctantly start to move as he lifted himself up and sat over the edge of the bed. "Rise and shine," she smiled He lifted his right hand and brushed the sweat back into his hair as Kelly continued, "Time to go, my next patient is here." Kyle looked up at her, confused.

"How long was I out for?" he asked. Kelly looked at the watch on her left wrist.

"Just over 40 minutes. You obviously needed it," she said as she took a step towards him. Kyle got the hint that she wanted him out the door, so he jumped up from the plinth and reached over for his clothes. Kyle did not see the surprised look on her face as this was not a move she was expecting. Kelly slowly moved over to the far end of the plinth as she watched him getting dressed. He wasn't fully awake yet and dressed without speaking. He didn't notice how much more movement he had. He sat back and started tying up his trainers and looked up at the silent girl; their eyes met. As he stared deep into her bright, clear eyes, Kelly looked away.

"So, what happens next?" he asked. Kelly kicked into a debrief about what was happening to him, he could go back to work as there had been massive improvement, but he could make another appointment if he wanted to. He wanted to. The cheeky smile was back, which he liked a lot. Kyle stood to leave as Kelly walked back over to the desk and started turning the pages of the blue A5 Diary. Kyle's eyes were transfixed on her long legs and firm shapely bum that was up in the air, the black trousers once again proving that there certainly wasn't much cellulite if she had any at all. Kelly turned her head round and looked at him.

"Would that date suit you?" she asked. Kyle blushed as he forced his eyes out the window then back to her face, it was obvious what he had been looking at. Kelly's tongue moved inside her mouth as a nefarious grin made her eyebrows jump slightly. Kelly didn't move the rest of her body, she was letting Kyle have full view of her, "Two weeks' time? Would that date suit you?"

"That should be fine, but I will check with the Sergeant and get back to you." Kelly turned and scribbled on the page in pencil then stood up and turned around to face him.

"Brilliant, you can text me later if you want," Kyle smiled as he headed towards the door, at which he paused and looked back "I was wondering," he said.

"What were you wondering?" she replied.

"If I was to ask a beautiful woman for a meal on Friday night what would she say?" Kelly's eyes looked down then back up but she didn't look him in the eye, the smile faded from her face.

"She might be busy," Kyle nodded his head then turned and walked out the door; he never heard her asking him to send the next patient in.

Chapter 19

Cara-Marie was sitting at her desk and was reading the story on her screen; she was trying to fit the article onto page four, but it was starting to look like it would be moved to page five. The story was from the primary school she had gone to as a child and they had just held their sports prize-giving day. It had been raining, but Mark had taken some good portraits and he had made the rain not obvious in the pictures, which was a good eye to have for a photographer; however, she would never tell him that. Cara-Marie became aware of Mark staring at her from his desk; she slowly turned her head and looked over at him, his eyebrows were raised with an expectant look on his face, she paused.

"What?" She questioned. Mark pushed himself back into his seat and reached for a mug of coffee that was sitting on his desk.

"I said…" he paused, "have you not got that done yet?"

"Got what done yet?" she replied

"That school story," he took a mouthful of coffee, "you've been playing with it for over three quarters of an hour and it *should* have only taken you seconds!" Mark was having a dig as he was smiling, so Cara-Marie knew it was just friendly banter.

"At least I work for a living and don't just sit around playing with toys that go 'click'"

"Watch those paper cuts you pen pushing pansy" he replied, she returned to the screen as the friendly abuse continued; she edited the story down until it fitted over page four then saved her work, her eyes flashed up at the clock on the wall, he was right she had been at it for nearly 45 minutes and it was a task that would normally take her seconds, what the hell was she playing at? Mark finished off the mug and grabbed his jacket from the back of the chair as he stood up.

"Going somewhere?" she asked. Mark turned and looked straight at the clock on the wall, he was doing up the zip as he answered her.

"Yes, going to meet a young lady for a coffee as I am on my break now," he smiled,

"Mmm, anyone I know?" she asked as he headed towards the door; he paused turned to face her before he replied.

"Well you have met her only once so far…." her eyes dilated, and the muscles of her face widened in recognition as she clicked onto who he was talking about. She opened her mouth to speak when from behind her Kevin's door opened, Mark and Cara-Marie were the only two in that part of the office, the reception staff were sitting down by the front door and both were busy on their phones. Kevin looked around then summoned the two of them in. The small TV was on in the right-hand corner of the office as they entered, and the local news bulletin was only just starting. "What's up?" asked Mark as the two of them filled the doorway, the editor had walked back round his desk and sat down.

"Watch," it was obvious that he knew that an important piece of news was about to be broadcast, and they should hear it as well. The main news reader started by welcoming viewers to the programme and stated the date and time of the broadcast, the office descended into silence. The male news reader was a familiar face on Ulster Television and had been a news reporter for some time, he went straight to the main story. Cara-Marie and Mark perched themselves on the end of the desk and faced the screen of the television.

"Today at the High Court in Belfast, the trial of Mr Anthony Henderson finally came to an end when he was found guilty on all counts." Cara-Marie and Mark looked at each other, Kevin didn't move. The story was handed over to a young well-dressed female reporter who was standing outside the high court building. She had a stern look as she started to speak into the camera in front of her. As she read through the report, archive footage of police officers outside a house was being shown.

"Mr. Anthony Henderson from Ballysillian close, Belfast, was found guilty today of the double murder of Mr Joseph Stevens and Mr Daniel Hanlon, both of addresses in the Ballysillian area of Belfast," Kevin shifted in his seat, "both men were murdered in the alleyway of the estate two years ago; they had been beaten to death."

"Nice!" said Mark, the report continued with archive footage of several well-dressed men with briefcases walking up the marble steps of the building behind the reporter.

"Mr Henderson's lawyer put forward the case that the police investigation was part of a smear campaign against Mr Henderson following several other minor arrests and that the investigation itself was flawed, but the judge refuted this after seeing the police evidence."

"Yeah, like it isn't like the police to screw up an important investigation now is it!"

"Looks like they did it right this time," replied Kevin. The footage was now of several people walking out a door, Mike Dears' face filled the screen as cameras, microphones and dictaphones were held near his face, the voice of the reporter asked the first question.

"Detective Sergeant Dear, what is your opinion of the outcome of this case?" Mike Dear looked over to the side of the screen.

"This is the end of a very long and exhaustive investigation and we are pleased that a very violent man has been removed from society," the microphone was removed from view as the next question was asked.

"The defence stated that the police *'went after'* Mr Henderson from the start and this is all part of a campaign against him, what is the police view on that?"

"The investigation team was able to show evidence in court that Mr Henderson had been present at the time of death of both men, he had reason to wish for them to be dead or at least seriously harmed as they had evidence of Mr Henderson's participation in other serious criminal activity and the investigation believed they were preparing to come forward to the police with this."

"Clever," said Cara-Marie.

"Clever?" asked Mark,

"Yes, clever, he isn't saying 'I' or 'ME' he keeps referring to the team as a whole," Kevin moved in his seat and turned the volume down with the remote control; both Cara-Marie and Mark rose and started to turn towards him.

"Right, I want the Coleraine angle," he said, "Cara, Danny O'Hanlon's ex-wife and mother both live here so get around and see what you can get from them," he was pointing with his finger from his clasped hands at her, "Mark, you go with her, get some family shots, Ok!"

"Ok, but this is a Belfast murder, not a Coleraine one. An ex-wife and mother aren't really a Coleraine story," Kevin went to speak but Cara-Marie cut him off.

"Hanlon went to school here, he was born in the old Coleraine hospital and moved to Belfast when he got involved with Henderson's lot." Mark looked back at her, "More than enough for a local story,"

"By the way, it's Hanlon," Cara-Marie had slightly raised her voice to speak over the TV, both Mark and Kevin stopped and looked at her.

Kevin spoke. "What?"

"Hanlon, its Danny Hanlon, not O'Hanlon," she let it hang in the air, the editor's eyes darted over at Mark then back to her.

"Ok, Hanlon, no probs," at that Mark got pushed back into the office by the receptionist, she was flustered and was clutching a piece of paper in her hand.

"There's been another one, there's been another attack."

"Another what?" said Kevin in a raised voice, all eyes focused on her

"Just had a phone call...... Another dog attack... down near the marina.... by the council offices,"

Cara-Marie's eyes widened as images flashed in her head, Kevin rose from his seat.

"You two...... GO!" With that Cara-Marie and Mark turned and almost ran across towards their own desks, Mark had totally forgotten about his appointment in a coffeeshop that he would never make.

∞∞∞∞

Mike Dear was slowly making his way through the mid-morning Belfast traffic, he was in a good mood, in fact he felt better than good, he always felt this way after a successful conviction. It pained him to see men and women who had committed crime walk away from court all because they had a lawyer that knew how to bend the law and use technicalities to get them off. But on the flip side, Tony Henderson would not be squeezing money out of anyone again for a very long time; his little band of followers could not function without him at the helm. Belfast was a little bit safer now and that made Mike Dear love his job just a little bit more. The lights changed to green and he turned onto the M3 motorway and headed out past Belfast City Airport, the road split and Mike joined the queue of traffic heading up the Knocknagoney road; it was slow moving but at least it was moving. His phone beeped, he would read it when he stopped. The lights changed, and the slow traffic started to make its way up the steep incline of the hill, the large bright coloured Tesco's supermarket dominated the hillside and most people would not even notice the fenced buildings that were behind it.

Mike turned left, past the sign that had the emblem of the Police Service of Northern Ireland on it and the title of 'Criminal Justice Headquarters'; this was the home of M.I.T. Belfast. Mike parked the car and as he got out, he read the text message that had arrived earlier, it was from Sean.

'I AM IN THE OFFICE, GIVE ME A SHOUT WHEN YOU ARE FREE' Mike grinned at the message, Sean didn't do text speak, if fact Sean didn't really do texting and was being dragged both kicking and screaming into the 21st century. Mike didn't answer as he walked past Sean's car and headed towards the team's offices. Sean was sitting behind his desk, mug of coffee in hand as Mike walked towards him. Sean rose as he entered the office and held out his hand which Mike took in a firm handshake.

"Well done, well done indeed, good result," Sean sat back down into his chair and Mike took his usual seat, "I've had Superintendent Sutcliffe on the phone already passing on his congratulations." Mike smiled, a congratulation from Super Sutcliffe was rare.

"His face must have cracked doing that!" retorted Mike as he sat back in the chair opposite Sean. "So, what else has been happening back here?" he asked, Sean's face was transfixed on the screen of the desktop computer. Sean didn't move his face at all when he spoke.

"Well they finished filming the reconstruction,"

"Really!" exclaimed Mike.

"Yes really," replied Sean, "It was all done by mid-day and they were all packed up and on the half two flight from the city airport, and, we do the show tomorrow night!"

"Tomorrow?"

"Yes, tomorrow, the three of us are on a flight at half ten-tomorrow morning, we will be over there two days then back to de-brief Superintendent Sutcliffe." Sean changed the topic of conversation. "Where is the team meeting up tonight?"

"The Merchant Hotel, over in the cathedral quarter,"

Sean looked over at him, The Merchant was not the normal kind of place that they would all go for a team night out. "A bit posh there is it not?" he queried, "will they let the likes of us in?".

"Yeah, it is...." Mike had paused mid-sentence, Sean stopped typing and looked over at him.

"What?" he asked.

"The Merchant is Joanne's idea..."

Sean leaned back in his seat, the location of the hotel was something that Sean could clearly see was not Mike's choice, but it was certainly the choice of his wife. However, the venue was not what was troubling him, there was something else going on, Sean nodded.

"Yeah, it's very nice there, only been once myself."

"She wants me out," Mike's comment made Sean flinch in his seat.

"What?" Sean stated.

"She wants me out," he repeated, "she says she's had enough and wants me to spend more time at home," Mike paused, Sean composed himself and leaned forward to listen to what he had to say without interrupting him. "Apparently, I am not spending enough time with the kids, ignoring her etc, etc, etc," Mike held eye to eye contact with Sean as he finished the sentence.

"What do you think?" Sean asked. Mike had been expecting a 'we need you in the team' or 'stay on board' but asking what he thought? that caught him off guard.

"What do I think?" Mike's eyes searched around the room, "I think I love my job, but I love my children more," it was just the answer Sean was expecting.

"So?"

"So, what?" asked Mike.

"So, what are you going to do?" Sean finished his question,

"She really doesn't want me going away again." Mike continued, "She wants me home bang on half five in the evening, no late shifts and the like, you know," Sean knew only too well; too many times he had this same conversation at his own home.

"But you are not in a normal job, Mike," Sean spoke quieter than before,

Mike went to speak again when the landline phone on Sean's desk started to ring, in less than a second Sean had the phone to his ear. Sean listened to what was being said to him, slowly he nodded his head in acknowledgement then thanked the caller and replaced the phone.

"There has been another dog attack in Coleraine," Mike bolted upright.

"Dead?" it was more of a statement than a question.

"Not yet," Sean was already scrolling through his mobile phone." Sean put the phone to his ear. "One person is in intensive care at the Causeway Hospital"

"Right I'll get straight up there," said Mike.

Sean looked up at him as he spoke into the phone. "Simon, Hi," Sean gave Simon the details and the name of the section sergeant from Coleraine District Command Unit that was dealing with it, then asked Simon to go up there tonight. Sean nodded his head as Simon spoke to him, "Yeah, I have Mike here with me now.......... Yes, brilliant result, well done to the both of you....... No, I am sending him home now......" Sean raised his eyebrows at whatever Simon had just said, then a small smile broke, "Yeah, no probs, I'll tell him.... cheers Simon, give me a shout when you know the details.......... Ok...... Bye then," Sean dropped his phone and dropped back onto the desk where it landed near the land line phone, Mike spoke first.

"I could go as well,"

"After what you have just told me! no, go home and I will see you later at the meal,"

"Ok," Mike walked out the door then leaned back inside the office, Sean had started moving the computer mouse around the only space on his desk, and he looked up at Mike as he did so.

"What?" he asked.

"What did Simon say?" Mike asked,

"As he did most of the work on the Henderson case apparently you are paying tonight!" Both men let out a short laugh as Mike walked away. Sean shouted after him, "It's ok, I will do the washing up back here," although he could not see Mike face he knew that he would be grinning as the door to the main office shut. Sean stood up and walked over to the window and pondered what was happening up in Coleraine, this could be very bad and Super Sutcliffe had already told him that they wanted results and quickly. Sean's eye caught Mike outside walking towards his car, his phone was up against his right ear and Sean wondered if he was talking to his wife or to Simon. He picked up the jacket that was dressing the back of the chair, he had to get home himself before the meal later on then it struck Sean that Mike had not actually told him what time they were meeting, hopefully the wives had already disseminated that amongst themselves and the serious decision making had already been done, "happy wife, happy life," he found himself saying out loud as the jacket slid over his shoulders and with that he closed the computer down, locked the office and was on his way home; he would wait for the phone call from Simon later.

Chapter 20

Anders banged on the thick wooden door with his fist, the door could not be opened quickly enough for him as he barged his way inside, Anna was pushed back by the door, she swore at him as she pushed the door closed.

"Is he here?" he demanded.

"What?" she asked. Anders turned as he got to the door of the living room, he was searching and seemed to be nervous.

"Is he here?" he demanded again.

Anna's face twisted in annoyance, she folded her arms and stood defiantly in the hall.

"You forget whose house this is!" Anna lifted her head slightly, "you do not give the orders around here, you just obey them." Anna spoke with menace at him, Anders bounced over at her and grabbed both her arms, his hands gripping all the way round her biceps.

"Davidov, where is Davidov?" Anna pushed back with her arms as the palms of her hands hit Anders square in the chest, he was thrown back as a look of shock and pain shot across his face. The look on Anna's face fell as she glared at him, her voice lowered to a growl.

"Never place your hands on me," Anna paused as Anders regained his balance, he looked around then lowered his eyes as she glared back at him.

"You forget who I am and where I am in this pack," Anna took a step towards him as she continued, *"never* do that to me again." Anders nodded his head, he would wait until given permission before he would speak again. Anna slowly walked past him into the living room, Anders looked around the newly furnished room. Everything was new, the leather three-piece suite, the glass coffee table, the crème coloured carpet, the wooden rack that was full of newly purchased DVD's and the large dark coloured plasma TV that was perched over beside the window. Underneath it was the reception box for the satellite channels, Anna picked up the remote for the TV and it burst into life. A music channel filled the screen with an all-girl band who were dancing around and singing. Anna let him wait as she sat back and curled her feet up under herself before she spoke to him. It was all about power and position and Anders needed to remember that. Anders was still looking around at all the things Anna had bought with Alexi's credit card. "Now, what is it you want?" Anna kept looking at the screen as Anders replied.

"I need to find Davidov,"

"Why?"

"The Rua, they are everywhere,"

"What do you mean by *everywhere?"* she asked.

"I mean *everywhere,* we are under close surveillance, the house, in town, the shops, when we drive anywhere, they are there, they are all over us." Anders took a step inside the room as he spoke, his eyes darted around, it was already obvious that no one else was presently in the house. Anna reached over for her phone on the coffee table, as she flicked it open Anders spoke again.

"Don't bother, he isn't answering the phone," Anna glared over at him, Anders opened his mouth to speak then slowly closed his mouth again as Anna started tapping out a text message. When she was finished she glared over at Anders, then glanced out the window.

"Did they follow you here?" she demanded.

"No, they are busy crawling over the others, I took the usual precautions before coming" Anna waited a few seconds then stood up and walked over and opened the cotton drapes that covered the windows; it had been raining earlier but had stopped now. The barrier at the entrance to the police station across the road lifted and a dark coloured car drove out and stopped to wait for a space in the traffic. The music from the TV was interrupted by the sound of her phone beeping with a text message. Anna walked back to the sofa and slouched down as she read over the text then closed her phone and looked over at Anders.

"You are to return to the house and wait there," she instructed, "Alexi will be in touch when they have finished what they are doing," she looked away from the annoyed Anders who said nothing.

"You may leave," she commanded. She wasn't using her position with Alexi or Davidov, she was strong enough to establish herself and very few would challenge her to a fight. Anders had seen her last fight at the end of which Anna had shouted out that 'Men are brutal, women however, are vicious.' He recalled that she had more than proved her point as she washed the blood from her face. Jolted back to the present, Anders glanced up and made eye contact with her.

"I obey," with that, he turned and left. As the door slammed shut Anna stood up and walked towards the window again. She held her phone as she watched him dart through the crowds and head in towards the centre of the town, he was carrying out his anti-surveillance techniques that they all knew so well. The phone in her hand started ringing and with only moving her left arm she opened the phone and lifted it up to her ear.

"Has he left?" It was Alexi.

"Yes... just," she replied, "he is on his way back to the house as instructed,"

"Good, good, can you see any from there?" Alexi asked, she scanned the street, the cars, the people and the rest of the buildings that lined the Lodge Road in Coleraine.

"No, none,"

"What else did he say?" Anna recounted everything Anders had said but left out the incident where he grabbed her. She didn't have to as she knew that he would not do that again,

"That's good," he said,

"When will you be back here?" she asked. Anna glanced over at the small clock that hung on the wall.

"Not for a while yet, Davidov and I are still busy," Alexi had not said where he was going or what they would be doing. He was the Alpha, he didn't have to.

"Let me know when you are close, then I can prepare some food for you,"

"Thank you my dear, I will," Alexi had sounded pleased by Anna's comment and he hung up. She knew Davidov would not text her as he was with him, but he would be in touch later. She flicked off the TV and as she headed for the front door she chose a black cotton jacket to cover her torso before heading into town to spend some more money on her ever-increasing wardrobe.

∞∞∞∞

Anders danced through the shoppers as he passed the front of the Woolworth's store, a large delivery van blocked the view from across the street for a few seconds but when he glanced over again there they were. The two men had been following him earlier. He knew that he had lost them before he went to the house, had they only just found him? The darkness of the evening was slowing, creeping around the streets of Coleraine and it was slowly winning against the straining streetlights and shop windows that attracted the shoppers like moths to a flame. He walked on, keeping himself to the left side of the street, this time the two men didn't follow him, and they seemed to be looking at something else.

"Good," he thought as he got to the corner of the street, an old busker sat in the end doorway, he was well on in years and was dirty and unshaven. His thick clothes were certainly functional at keeping out the wind but didn't do much else. A small empty biscuit tin sat at his feet and, as Anders approached, the old man picked up the accordion which he placed on his knee. Without any introduction he began to make a noise that certainly wasn't a tune and started mumbling in a language that Anders didn't understand. People turned their heads and muttered and swore in his direction as the screeching continued. Anders walked on and glanced in the reflection of a shop window, his eyes moved back up the street to where the two Rua were still standing, thankfully they were not after him this time. Anders walked past the tall concrete memorial that stood at the end of the street. On it were the names of everyone from Coleraine that had been killed in a war that happened between 1914 and 1918.

103

'THE GREAT WAR' - this confused Anders as the only Great War that he had ever heard of was The Great Patriotic War, the defeat of Nazi Germany of 1941 to 1945. 20 million Russians had died fighting the Nazis, that was a great war, a costly war, but a victorious war none the less. Anders walked on, he felt his pace increase, he was moving faster. He kept looking forward, but his eyes moved everywhere, was he being hunted again? Anders felt his body tingle, his muscles tightened getting ready for the fight, his head looked right then left but he could not see where the danger was, but the danger was there. The thump inside his chest grew stronger, he felt his body yearn for the fight, he loved the fight, 'Come on,' he said into himself, 'Fight me,'

Anders passed the statue of a local footballer on his right then headed towards the bridge; the feeling of danger lessened then in an instant vanished all together. Anders stopped at the traffic lights and looked into the window of a sports store, he slowly looked back up the street. People moved about, some carrying shopping, mothers with children and teenagers dressed all in black with makeup on. His eyes looked at each face, none of these was the danger. His eyes searched the windows but still could see nothing, but the danger had been there. "Ha, they are afraid of me," he whispered then spun round and headed over the bridge and back to the house to wait as he had been instructed.

∞∞∞∞

The two men stood across from Woolworth's and leaned against the iron railings of the church, the gust of wind blew around them.

"So, what's it like being on the boss's security team?" the younger of the two asked.

"Only ever done it once when we went down to Belfast to see the Russians," he answered, he glanced down the street to where the busker was still creating a noise.

"I wish he would shut up," the first one said, they both looked over at the old man. "Why doesn't he just go back to Poland?" they both shifted where they were stood.

"Well John, that would be pointless as he is from Bulgaria!" John looked back at him then turned back down the street.

"Poland, Bulgaria or wherever he is from I wish he would just shut up and go back there." They moved off down the street keeping to the right-hand side of the street as the old man now had an open area around him as most of the shoppers were avoiding him, one man had walked up to him and asked him to shut up, but he was ignored; he still wasn't playing a tune, he was just hitting keys and half singing and half shouting in his home language. John used his right hand to zip up his jacket to try and keep the wind out. The two men carried on, they paused as they got to a phone shop. John turned in towards the shop and pointed with his right hand at one of the phones. He opened his mouth to speak but stopped before he uttered a word. DANGER

As both men spun round something hit them in the chest, it wasn't physical, but it hit them all the same. Their hands sprang out of their pockets ready to face their attacker, this was instant aggression. They both scanned the area in front of them, something was in amongst the people. They both felt the hair on the backs of their necks rise, their very souls were bearing their teeth and growled at whatever was in front of them, eyes looked deeper, ears strained for the slightest sound and every muscle in their bodies readied for the fight. They looked up and down the street. John walked forward a couple of paces and stopped. They could feel the anger that was pouring towards them, feel the hatred, feel the consuming rage that was there, however they could not see the source. They stood their ground, ready for the fight, wanting the fight, but the fight didn't want them. Slowly they felt themselves relax as whatever it was backed away. John looked round at him then turned back into the crowd, yes it was leaving, he heard the beeping of a phone then the voice from behind him spoke into it.

"Hi, yeah, it's me....... look something has just happened....... We are down from Woolworth's...... Ok. No problems," with that the call was ended, he stepped up beside John then spoke again.

"They will be here in two minutes," John nodded.

"What was that?" he asked, there was a pause before he got his answer.

"Evil, that was pure evil," John glanced over at him as he finished his sentence. "We are not alone in this town anymore," the phone in his pocket bleeped and as he reached in for it.

"So, what does that mean?"

"We have a fight on our hands."

∞∞∞∞

Cara-Marie was leaning up against her car scribbling on her notepad. She looked over the roof at the council buildings at the far side of the car park, she turned her head over to the left and looked at the small crowd that had gathered outside the smaller single storey building. Her eyes glazed over the blue letters that announced the residence of Coleraine's yacht club, the small marina was down the slope and out of sight, only the top masts of a few of the boats could be seen. She had never actually been inside but thought she should have a chat with the boat owners who had gathered outside and try to find out if anyone had seen anything.

"Hello there," she spun around at the male voice that had just spoken to her. She was greeted by the faces of Tony Fallon and Kyle Foster walking towards her.

"Hello back," her face smiled in recognition, they both stopped a few feet away, behind them at the edge of the grassed area was a police car. The blue flashing lights had now been turned off which she was pleased with as they had been giving her a headache. She wondered how she had not noticed these two police officers before, she had spotted two other police officers earlier, but they had now left. These two must have come from the far side of the cordon; either that or she was slipping up. As the evening was darkening the scene over by the bushes was becoming more obscure, there were four people standing around with another uniformed police officer, one of the four was a woman in her twenties who was visibly upset. Cara-Marie had just finished talking to her and had come back to the car for a bit of shelter from the wind that was picking up.

"So, what brings a nice girl like you out on an evening like this?" asked Tony.

"Oh, I got bored, thought I'd come out for a drive."

"What about you?" She asked. Tony went to speak but Kyle beat him to it.

"We were just parking the car and about to go for a coffee when this shout came in," he said, gesturing with his head half back over towards the cordon tape by the bushes.

"You were first to respond?" her interest in them just increased.

"Well if given the choice of staring at his ugly mug or come out to this, well no choice there really," said Tony.

"My ugly mug?" You looked in a mirror lately?" Retorted his colleague.

"Every morning!" Tony smiled back,

"Well you don't see much through a broken mirror!" she smiled at the friendly banter, but she wanted to talk about something else.

"Did you enjoy your Chinese?" he asked.

"Chinese?" she answered.

"Last time we met, it was in a Chinese," Kyle said prompting her memory, her expression opened as she remembered the conversation in the take away.

"Yes, yes, we did," memories of what happened next flashed in her mind, the screams, the blood then the face that looked back at her. Her eyes hunted around everywhere except into the faces of Kyle and Tony, both of which glanced at each other as she paused.

"We will have to do that properly sometime," hinted Kyle, the comment pulled her back to where she was; suddenly she was cold again.

"Yes, we will," her voice had lowered, then without saying anything else she suddenly turned and opened the car door. Cara-Marie leaned into the car grabbing her coat from the back seat. Kyle's eyes fixed on her behind, his eyebrows raised slightly as he murmured a quiet approval. Tony let out a small cough that brought Kyle back to where he was. Tony was looking straight at

105

him. Kyle shrugged his shoulders as if to say 'what?' Cara-Marie stood up and pulled her jacket on, turning back to face them both, "It is colder than I thought," she said out loud.

"I hadn't noticed," said Kyle.

"Said, of course, by someone who presently is wearing at least three layers, and that's including a bullet proof vest!" she answered. Tony smiled, Kyle paused as he counted the layers he had on.

"Four actually, and under this," Kyle said as he tugged at the yellow luminous jacket he was wearing,

"Anyway," she continued, "tell me more about what happened here."

Both Kyle and Tony slightly turned back to the crime scene as Tony stated talking, what neither of them had noticed was that Cara-Marie had pulled out her notebook and started scribbling.

"We responded to the call and drove into the car park and stopped here," Tony pointed to where the police car was still parked. He went on to describe that a male teenager was lying on the ground and a woman was trying to restrain a German Shepherd dog that was barking furiously at the injured man.

"What injuries did he have?" enquired the now focused journalist, Kyle butted in before Tony could answer, as he spoke his right hands would grab each part of his body that he was describing.

"There were obvious soft tissue injuries to his left forearm, upper arm and his left cheek," Kyle was about to say something else when Cara-Marie questioned him some more without looking up from her scribbling.

"Were the injuries life endangering?" Kyle looked over at Tony.

"Not really, the left forearm was damaged more than the others," he replied.

"So, what do you think happened here?"

"Well that is a matter for the detective over there," Kyle pointed over his shoulder with his right thumb towards Simon McAllister. She looked up and over at the plain clothed detective who was now taking an interest in the young woman with a notepad who was chatting to two uniformed police officers, their chat would be short, and they needed to be on a cordon, not chatting to the press.

As Simon walked away she climbed back into her car she lifted the phone to her ear, the ringing tone was answered by Kevin's voice, it took her less than two minutes to brief him on the situation. Mark was already back and editing his photographs. Kevin was pleased with the sources that she had got.

"And the detective is sure the two are not linked..." he asked,

"Positive," she answered.

"He is part of the team, but he did tell me that the crime watch programme about the Coleraine killing is going out tomorrow night and they have got a lot of good stuff!"

"Brilliant!" he exclaimed, "get back here and we can change page three..." with that he hung up, she started her car and pushed the power button on the CD player. As she swung the car around and headed for the main road, Kyle lifted his right hand in a wave, to which she smiled and waved back, the two of them were good sources, but that was something she would keep to herself.

Chapter 21

Paul took the phone out of his pocket, he read the text message aloud for those sitting round the living room of the farmhouse.

"Dog attack in Coleraine, twenty-one-year-old Joe Bryant," all those in the room stopped talking and turned to listen to what he was saying, Paul continued, "bitten by a four-year-old German Shepherd dog, owned by Jessie Critten from University Walk in Coleraine." Paul looked over at where Carl was sitting. Carl remained motionless and listened to Paul who carried on reading aloud, "Bryant is now in intensive care at the Causeway Hospital," Paul glanced again at Carl who then slumped back in the chair.

"Do the usual check on Bryant," as Carl spoke one of the younger men turned and walked out of the room, Carl turned towards Paul and carried on speaking, "find out if this Bryant might die or if not, when will he be released?" Paul nodded and started typing a text message, Carl turned to the two men who had been in the street in Coleraine.

"Now talk me through what happened earlier." Carl was given a description of what had happened, then asked them what they thought it was.

"Evil, pure evil," John answered.

"What was the source of this evil Paddy?" Standing beside John, Patrick M'Kane unfolded his arms. John shifted uncomfortably on his feet.

"I'm not sure," he paused, "but I have *never* felt anything like it before," John nodded from beside him. Carl looked over at Paul. Paddy continued, "it came from across the street."

"What was directly across from you?" Paul asked, Paddy and John looked at each other.

"Just a load of shoppers and a busker," answered Paddy.

"A busker?" asked Carl "Which busker?"

"That Bulgarian with the old accordion,"

"Yeah...the one he can't play!" continued John, both Carl and Paul let out a small laugh, the atmosphere in the room seemed to relax a little,

"Yeah, I know who you are on about," said Carl, Paddy folded his arms again as he let his face relax. "What I want you two to do is find where he is and see what you can find out about him and his background," both Paddy and John started nodding at the instruction, "Off you go, call Paul when you know."

"Ok, boss," said Paddy who then straightened up and half turned and pushed John towards the door. John opened the door and walked out first then Paddy closed it behind him. As the door shut Carl looked over at Paul; Carl took a deep breath in as Paul spoke.

"It's not like the Nocs to make it that obvious. I don't like the way this is going, it obviously wasn't the busker!" Paul sat forward as he spoke.

"How many Noctrailis are there in total?" Carl asked.

"Ten in total but they are spread over all of Ireland," Carl looked into his eyes as he continued, "as far as we know there are only five here in the north, and *he* agreed to keep them under control." Paul could see the spark of anger that was deep in the eyes of his Alpha, eyes that did not have to speak. "Carl, he would not break the covenant!" Carl stood up and slowly walked towards the door.

"Confirm the present locations of all the Noc's and where they have been feeding, I want to know which one that was and what they were playing at." Paul stood up as Carl was speaking and nodded "and remind them of whose land this still is," Carl opened the door of the farmhouse and as he stepped outside Paul's phone bleeped. Carl looked over left shoulder as Paul read from his phone.

"Bryant's condition is serious, but he will live," Paul looked up as he finished the sentence, "two weeks at least before he gets out." Carl paused,

"Let me know what the search finds and tell him to keep an eye on him," with that the door closed as Paul started typing in another text message.

∞∞∞∞

Sean's phone started ringing in his pocket.

"Better turn that off before we go on," said Mike who did not raise his head from the sheets of paper that were strewn all over the small, cheaply-made coffee table that sat in front of the blue cushioned chairs. Sean rummaged through his jacket then produced his phone. The small office had a single door that contained a glass pane that opened into the corridor of the television centre. They had been allowed to use this as their own office for the day, it was small, but functional, no windows and a group of chairs that were sitting in a circle around the small grey coloured table, Sean looked at the name on the screen.

"It is Simon," he said aloud as he lifted the phone to his right ear, Sean stood and walked away from the chair, "Hi Simon," he said as he leant up against the door. He paused briefly, and then stopped Simon from what he was saying, "hang on," he said as he looked over at Mike, "I am putting you on loudspeaker." Sean slowly walked over to the chairs and sat opposite Mike and placed the phone in the middle of the small table. "Right," Sean continued, "just Mike and myself in the room."

"Hi Mike," stated the voice from the phone, Mike relaxed back into the chair.

"Hello Simon, what's new back home?" Sean lifted the small plastic cup to his lips and his face contorted as he sipped the brown liquid, he made a disgusted noise just as Mike finished speaking.

"What was that?" asked Simon,

"Sean is just sampling the delights of the BBC's coffee machine," Sean cursed the foul-tasting liquid in the cheap cup.

"I know, I know, I should have brought my own before you two start," Mike raised his eyebrows and looked over at his boss, smiling as he did so.

"So where have they got you?" asked Simon from the other end of the phone. Mike's eyes glanced around the picture-less room.

"The penthouse at the Hilton," said Mike sarcastically.

"Really?" exclaimed Simon.

"No," said Sean, "he's joking" Sean glanced over at the grinning Mike.

"Ha, ha, ha" came the voice from out of the phone.

"No, really, they've given us a small room at television centre." Mike shrugged as he spoke at the phone, "however we met up with the team from Manchester in the hotel."

"Manchester!" said a surprised Simon, "What have they got?" Sean glanced around, Mike sat up in his chair as he answered Simon's question.

"Yeah, they have got an armed robbery of a security van, which by the way also included a high-speed chase," Mike was using his hands to talk as well, his fingers formed the shape of a gun and Sean could picture Simon nodding at the other end.

"Wow," was the only word that came out of the phone.

"Yeah wow," retorted Mike, "they also have a rape at a train station, however," Mike paused again "...they were really impressed with ours." Sean let a small smile break over his face, sometimes coppers behaved like children *'my daddy's bigger than your daddy,'* Sean's eyes focused on one of the pages on the table.

"I bet they were," answered Simon.

"So, Simon," Sean slightly raised his voice, "what else is new from over there?"

"Ok, the dog attack in Coleraine is *not* connected to our case at all,"

"At all?" asked Mike.

"At all," repeated Simon, "the DNA is nothing like ours, plus this was a domestic," Mike closed his eyes momentarily then slightly shook his head.

"A domestic! How?" Sean asked.

"The two-people used to live together until a few months ago, then she left after a couple of alleged physical attacks by him." This was no help to them at all and ended the interest of the two detectives, but Simon carried on, "so, this bloke put her windows in and then trashed her car. For that he got a caution and a five-month non-molestation order," he paused for a second then carried on as if he was reading it from a prepared script, "she bought the dog as protection after that, she is saying it was self-defence," Sean sat forward in his chair before he spoke.

"Right, not our problem...anything new for us?" There was a pronounced pause from the phone before Simon answered.

"Well, yes." he hesitated,

"Go on," prompted Mike,

"We sort of got the stuff back from the dental pathologist," Sean looked up.

"I had forgotten about him," his eyes darted back to the phone, "what do you mean by 'sort of'"

"We got a cast of one of the sets of teeth from the Trotman murder," answered Simon.

"Brilliant!" exclaimed Mike,

"What do you mean 'sort of' Simon?" Sean repeated his question "Will it help us tonight?"

"Boss, I will take a picture of it with my phone and I will send it to your phone then you can decide," this wasn't like Simon, he obviously had something.

"Send it to my phone," injected Mike, Sean looked up at him as Mike explained himself, "my phone has a better camera on it, plus...Simon"

"What?" asked Simon, Mike looked over at Sean.

"This is the boss we are talking about, I at least know how to use the camera on my phone!" There was a laugh from Simon down the phone at the ridicule and raised eyebrows from across the table.

"Do you want to be covered in cold, bad coffee, Dear?" Sean started smiling as he spoke to Mike, however it was loud enough to benefit Simon as well.

"Well its true" Mike was defending his comment.

"All I can say is that I am glad I am not stuck in a room with you two," said Simon.

"He's just grumpy," answered Mike. Sean slowly reached over for the now cold coffee.

"What else is going on over there?" Sean brought the conversation back to the job.

"Not much" said Simon, "Oh by the way, one more thing."

"What?" asked Sean.

"Just found out that most of the station here will be watching tonight, *so enjoy!*" There was a small sound that could have been a short laugh. The whole team would be watching, as would every M.I.T. in Northern Ireland. The show had been advertised on local television and was throughout the police gossip circles. Sean was living through his own personal hell, but then they had nothing, and they needed something and 'crime watch' at least could give them something, that at least was what they all were hoping for. Every copper watching would be watching for every slip-up and every missed or wrong word. Each slip would follow them for the rest of their police careers and depending on how big the slip up even after they had left.

"Ok, no probs," said Sean, "thanks for reminding me of that!"

A few seconds later Mike's phone bleeped with the arrival of the photograph. Mike pulled the phone out of his pocket and then looked at the screen. Sean watched as the pupils in his eyes widened before Mike looked over at him then offered him the phone.

Sean looked at the picture on the screen then breathed out a short sentence.

"Oh my God."

∞∞∞∞

Three hours later Kyle was just getting home. He reversed the car back at the front of the house, as he climbed out of the car the chill of the air bit his face, comforting warmth flowed through him; Kyle still preferred the cold to heat, he could work in the heat as he had done many times but there was something about the cold. A light from above shone down on him and he looked up at the clear night sky. The partially covered moon stared back at him from the heavens, the crisp wind whipped around him, and he felt comforted. It would be another two days until the first night of the full moon, the busiest time of every month for them, but the police were not alone in this; the hospitals and ambulance service always had more staff on duty, as there were definitely more lunatics running around.

The moment only lasted a second then Kyle walked up to his front door, the door gave a secure thud when he closed it behind him, and Kyle went into his 'just off duty' routine. A shower, a change of clothes and a fresh mug of tea. Kyle was walking back into his living room when his phone bleeped. Kyle picked it up from his coffee table, placed the mug of hot liquid on a coaster then sat back on the sofa, he opened the text message from Tony, 'ARE YOU WATCHING?'

Kyle paused then tapped in an answer, 'WATCHING WHAT? I HAVE TOLD YOU I AM NOT WATCHING YOU IN THE SHOWER! I WAS 2 ReP NOT PARACITE REGIMENT'. Kyle had deliberately misspelled parachute wrong as he knew it would get a rise from Tony. Kyle set the phone down on the sofa beside him and pressed the green button of the TV remote. The BBC news channel first came on, so Kyle started drinking his way through his tea. He held the large mug in both hands as the news went from story to story, most totally depressing. The mobile beeped again. 'NO DICKHEAD, BBC ONE. CRIMEWATCH. YOUR STORY IS ON,' Kyle read through the message and for a moment in time was glad there was no one else in the room to see his embarrassment as he had totally forgotten about it. The channels flicked over just as the titles first started, Kyle typed in a reply 'YES OF COURSE WHAT ELSE WOULD I BE DOING,' Kyle pressed the send button but kept the phone in his hand as the reply would be swift. Seconds later the phone beeped, 'I KNEW YOU HAD FORGOTTON, GOOD FOR YOU I AM HERE TO KEEP YOU RIGHT' Kyle smiled, Tony no doubt would bait him again tomorrow about it, then his phone beeped again 'UTRINQUE PARATUS' Kyle let out a short giggle as he read Tony's reply. 'Ready for Anything' the motto of the British Parachute Regiment. Kyle thought for a moment then decided against replying.

∞∞∞

Carl slouched back in his chair. Paul was sitting in the other chair across from him; no one spoke as the programme started. The others would be watching on the larger screen TV in the tearoom of the farm. He was not enjoying this, but the team had been assembled and they had been briefed on what he wanted them to do; several scenarios had been discussed and Carl had the final say on all of them. They all were left in no doubt as to what he wanted them all to do in each case.

∞∞∞

Alexi Chernov walked into his living room as Anna Nikitin looked up at him, she smiled as he entered the room. She had tied her hair up in a ponytail and she still wore the dressing gown she had first put on an hour ago when they had finished making love upstairs. Alexi had showered and changed. He returned her smile as he sat down beside her; she shuffled over and snuggled into him and murmured affection towards him as the show started.

"Now we will see what they know" he said out loud. Anna looked up, paused then lowered her head back onto his chest as the male presenter introduced the programme.

∞∞∞

Kyle swallowed more of his tea then picked up his phone again and started typing out another message, 'ARE YOU WATCHING CRIMEWATCH ON BBC ONE?' Kyle scrolled through his address book and stopped at Kelly's number, then he pushed 'send'. Kyle scrolled again then stopped at Cara-Marie's number, Kyle pressed the send button again and the message went.

"Let's see where this goes," he said out loud. Kyle's phone bleeped with a text message, Kyle hoped to see Kelly's name on the screen as she was usually fast at answering him however this was from Cara-Marie. Her message was a short one, 'YES, I AM AS I WANT TO SEE WHO IS PLAYING ME' she had put a small smiley face at the end of the message. Kyle re-read the message again before typing in his reply.

'PLAYING YOU? I DON'T GET IT?' Kyle set his phone down and drank the last of his tea. The police from Manchester were going through a violent armed robbery of an armoured cash delivery van; they were showing footage from CCTV and from their dramatization of the event.

Every couple of minutes they would flick back to the police team for more descriptions of what they wanted. Four still photographs from the CCTV were shown on the screen; all were angry looking, middle aged men.

"We would really like to interview these men, if you know their present whereabouts…" stated the English detective.

"I bet you would!" Kyle spoke towards the TV, his phone bleeped again, it was from Cara-Marie. 'THE DRAMATISATION WAS FILMED YESTERDAY BUT I COULD NOT GET NEAR THEM.' Kyle raised his eyebrows as he read the text. He had been at the Castlerock station, just along the coast from Portrush, and he had not even known they had been there. He typed his thoughts into a text and pressed the send button, she replied almost instantly, 'YES, IT WAS A FAST ONE, THEY WERE ONLY UP FOR A COUPLE OF HOURS THEN BACK TO BELFAST. THEY REALLY WERE IN A RUSH. MOST OF US FOUND OUT LAST MINUTE. NORMALLY WE WOULD KNOW THAT IN ADVANCE.'

Kyle smiled and thought about his answer, 'HA, YOU MUST KNOW MORE ABOUT WHAT IS GOING ON ROUND COLERAINE THAN WE DO, CERTAINLY FASTER ANYWAY.' Kyle put a smiley at the end but deleted it before he sent it, he looked at the phone again, he still had not had a reply from Kelly. The Manchester police were finishing off their part of the programme and they were breaking for advertisements, the presenter stated that afterwards they were going across the Irish Sea to Northern Ireland for their next case, this was what Kyle was waiting for. The phone beeped again. 'NOT SO SURE ABOUT THAT, PROBABLY FROM DIFFERENT ANGLES. ONE THING ABOUT BEING A JOURNALIST IS THAT PEOPLE ALWAYS WANT TO BE THE FIRST TO TELL YOU THINGS.' Kyle nodded to himself then started to write a reply: 'I BET THAT CAN BE ANNOYING FROM TIME TO TIME!' Kyle pressed the send button then watched the end of the car ad on TV, his phone beeped, it still wasn't Kelly. 'GOOD SOMETIMES BUT THE MAJORITY OF THE TIME USELESS CRAP OR JUST PLAIN GOSSIP' Kyle grunted a giggle then started tapping away again, 'ISNT GOSSIP PART OF THE FUN?' as Kyle sent the message the programme started again, Cara-Marie went silent on the texting. The presenter walked around one of the desks in the studio and started talking in to the camera.

"Northern Ireland, for so long a place where terrorism dominated the headlines with stories of murder, shooting and bombings," Kyle shifted where he was sitting.

"Good advert for Northern Ireland!" Kyle once again spoke towards the screen, the presenter carried on.

"Thankfully those days seem to be over, but criminality never seems to be too far away." The camera panned around to a stern-faced police officer who was introduced as Detective Inspector Sean Parrish. Kyle noticed that the Manchester police had all had their ranks abbreviated, from Detective Inspector to DI, Detective Sergeant to DS, the PSNI didn't do that at all and the presenter had obviously been briefed on this detail. The presenter carried on. "Detective Inspector Parrish and his team have been put in charge of Operation Muirdris," the presenter paused as Sean's face filled the screen, "welcome to Crime Watch, Inspector, could you tell us what 'Operation Muirdris' is for us please?"

Sean acknowledged the introduction and started to give a quick overview of what had been happening back home, as he spoke the name Muirdris it scrolled across the bottom of the screen and the crime watch phone number. Sean started with the details of the Belfast murder. A still picture of Edgar Trotman appeared on one side of the screen. The dramatization that had been filmed in Belfast then started, the difference in accents from the Englishness of the presenter to the Northern Irishness of Sean seemed to make Sean's accent stand out more. The dramatization followed the actress playing Anna walking up the street and into the Botanic Inn, Sean's voice over stated that the police believed that Edgar Trotman had been following her at this time.

∞∞∞∞

Alexi looked at Anna who sat upright as she watched the events on the screen. "She looks nothing like me," she said without turning her head, "we have nothing to fear here!" Next thing on the screen was footage from the CCTV from the entrance of the Botanic Inn in which Anna entered and was then followed by Edgar Trotman. The commentary stated the time difference from them leaving again. A still of Anna's face from the CCTV of her leaving was next on the screen, the picture was not the best quality, but you could tell it was her. Alexi's eyes widened.

∞∞∞∞∞

'WHAT DOES MUIRDRIS MEAN?' Kyle finished the text then sent it to Cara-Marie as he looked at Anna's face. There was more conversation between Sean and the presenter as the information scrolled again across the bottom of the screen, Mike Dear was then introduced.

"Detective Sergeant Michael Dear, also of the Muirdris team, welcome to Crime Watch," Mike looked as out of place as Sean. "Now for the next killings that are part of this gruesome case," Kyle noted that the presenter had said 'killings' and not 'murders' he wondered for a moment if was there a reason for that? Mike started with Limavady, the map on the screen showed where Limavady was then a picture of Liam Arthur and Michael Watson and a description of David 'Septic' Simpson. Mike gave the details of what had happened there. Memories flooded through Kyle's mind of what they had found in the bus station. After a few minutes, they started on the Coleraine murder with another dramatization of the route that Andy Ferguson had taken that night; Kyle looked into his mind's eye and remembered what he had found.

The same actress who had played Anna in Belfast was walking down the street in Coleraine, they passed the Chinese where he and Cara-Marie had been in at the time. The commentary only stated he had been found by 'two people' who got no other mention. Kyle typed in another message, 'LOOKS LIKE YOUR BIG SCREEN DEBUT WILL HAVE TO WAIT FOR ANOTHER TIME,' just before he pressed send, a text arrived. Kyle sent his then read the one from Cara-Marie that had just come in. 'MUIRDRIS: THE NAME GIVEN TO THE LACUSTRINE MONSTER THAT WAS KILLED BY FERGUS MAC LEIDE APPROX 1500BC. IT WAS ALSO CALLED THE SINEAD'

Kyle looked over the text with surprise, 'HOW ON EARTH DID YOU KNOW THAT?' he asked, his phone bleeped again, '

'THEY HIDE INFORMATION LIKE THAT IN THIS AMAZING INVENTION CALLED 'BOOKS,' a smile spread across Kyle's face as Mike's face once again filled the TV screen. Mike would really like to talk to the girl with the black hair, again the information scrolled across the bottom of the screen, Kyle's phone beeped again. 'YOU SHOULD TRY READING ONE SOMETIME. YOU WOULD BE AMAZED AT WHAT YOU COULD LEARN.' Kyle could not believe that he was being text abused by her, the baiting was about to start. It would be the following day before Kelly answered his first text when she said she had work to do and was busy.

∞∞∞∞∞

Alexi jumped up in anger. Anna sat back into the sofa as he started shouting and swearing as if the room was full of people. He spun round towards her.

"This will not happen to us again," his right forefinger pointed directly at her menacingly Anna lowered her head and did not speak, "You!" he shouted again, "you will not leave this house again until I allow it,"

∞∞∞∞∞

Carl looked at the screen, not hiding his anger at what he had watched. Paul stood up and awaited the commands he knew were coming. Carl slowly placed his hands on the arms of the chair and stood up, Paul took a single step forward, Carl looked at the far door as he spoke.

"It is time for us to act," Paul nodded. Carl looked directly into Paul's eyes, "You know what I want done?" he said.

"Yes," replied Paul.

"See to it," commanded Carl. Paul nodded, then turned towards the door. "Paul," said Carl just as Paul had reached the door. Paul turned towards him. "Yes?"

"I want them there in two hours," Carl paused, "make it happen,"

112

Chapter 22

"Davidov!" Anders shouted upstairs from the front living room, Davidov came running down the stairs. Anders was by the window; the light was off. There was one more person in the room who was standing a little back but was also looking out the window.

"Where?" Davidov had stopped just by the right-hand side of the window that looked out over the river, Anders started pointing out the window.

"Three over there by that red car, two by the trees, another eight at least in the car park over there," Davidov's eyes darted around at each indication that Anders was pointing out. "Four cars have all arrived in the last ten minutes and now that blue transit van," Anders looked at Davidov, "I have no idea how many are in there!" Davidov paused and looked back into the room.

"Viktor, get the others from next door, I want everyone in here," Viktor nodded and started towards the door as Davidov continued, "tell Pe'ter to bring his bags with him." Viktor stopped and glanced over at Anders who looked up at him then turned to look out the window again, Davidov was making a very quick assessment. The door slammed shut as Viktor ran out, Anders continued his briefing to Davidov.

"Yelina is by the back door, she said it is the same out the back," Davidov leaned back into the room, Anders followed suit. Davidov's eyes darted up and down the busy traffic.

"They would not try an assault, not in full view, would they?" Anders asked, Davidov cast a glance over at him.

"I am not prepared to take that risk," he paused for a few seconds then issued his commands.

"Anders, prepare here and upstairs to repel an assault," Anders nodded, "I want every possible way in covered, and everything ready as soon as possible." Anders stepped past Davidov as a key in the front door turned and the door started to open. Anders looked back at Davidov as he was looking at his phone. The front door burst open and the others all came running in and headed straight upstairs. Pe'ter and Viktor had been carrying two heavy rucksacks,

"Are you going to phone him?" Anders asked, Davidov glanced over at Anders.

"If the Rua want a fight, we will give them one." With that he directed with his head for Anders to go upstairs. Anders walked into the front bedroom and addressed the five men and one woman who were there. The two rucksacks had been laid out on the bed. Davidov's commands were repeated and Anders started giving out the directions.

"Pe'ter you join Yelina by the back door, Mia, you and Viktor stay up here," he paused as they all looked around at each other, "you all know what to do." They all moved at once, hungry hands pulled at the rucksacks then the metallic caches spilled out onto the bed. The small rifles bounced out of one and were grabbed by a hand and the loaded magazines for the rifles came out of the other. The weapons were new, and smaller than the AK-47 that they all knew so well but these were the AKSU-74s. A smaller, more compact version with a folding stock. Perfect for defending against a house assault. Several round spheres dropped out of the second rucksack and were passed out to everyone, the hand grenades may come in useful. The weapons were checked, loaded and cocked, each one doing their own preparation.

"Pe'ter?" Anders asked.

"What?" Pe'ter answered.

"Where are the vests?" Anders asked, Pe'ter nodded with his head.

"Under the bed," Viktor and Mia knelt down and started feeding the black military style assault vests to everyone, in seconds everyone in the room was wearing them. More were pulled out and laid down on the bed. A rifle was laid on top of each one and the pouches were filled with magazines and a single grenade in each, these would be passed out among the others downstairs. From behind Anders, an object flew passed his head and was caught by Mia who looked at the helmet, lifted the visor and pulled it over her head. She pulled a face as she adjusted it to fit, a small wave of quiet laughter rippled around the room as other helmets were passed around, soon they were filing back down the stairs.

Davidov pulled his vest over his body as others busied themselves preparing. Davidov pulled the thick plastic zip down the side of his chest and reached inside with his right hand. He pulled out the pistol and without speaking ejected the magazine from the bottom of it, checked the first bullet then pushed in back into the weapon, Davidov grabbed the top of the gun and cocked it with a loud noise.

"Ready!" He said out loud.

"Ready," Anders replied.

"Ready," came a voice from near the front door.

"Ready", it echoed around the house.

Davidov knelt down by the window, he had replaced the pistol inside his vest and attached the sling of the rifle around him, he held the pistol grip of the small assault weapon in his right hand but left the helmet on the chair beside him. Anders was kneeling between the window and the grey coloured television set. Anders had his right knee on the ground and was sitting on his right foot, his left elbow was resting just behind his left knee and he had a firm grip on the weapon with both hands, the butt of the weapon pressed firmly into his shoulder. Anders eyes were scanning the traffic and all the movement outside. Davidov turned and raised himself up to look out the window at the Rua who, were all over the place but didn't seem to have any weapons at all.

"Come Rua, come, these Mongols have a surprise for you!" Davidov whispered out loud as his eyes fixed on three Rua who were standing by a tree in the fading light of evening. Anders let out a short laugh from his nose as a ghoulish grin spread across his face as Alexi while Anna walked up to the front door.

∞∞∞∞

Over in the car park Carl was sitting in the back of his car. Paul Hawkins stood by the open rear door with Paddy M'Kane on the far side.

"Is everything in place?" Carl asked.

"Yes," answered Paul.

"And we are sure he is with them now?"

"Yes, we allowed him and the girl to enter ten minutes ago," Paddy answered, Carl paused as he looked over at the house, "they are renting the last two in the terrace, but they are all now in the end house."

"And we are sure they are armed and prepared?" Paddy looked over at Paul.

"Yes, with their backgrounds, we should expect nothing less," stated Paul, "but" Paul stressed the 'but' "If we were to assault the house we could do so in less than 60 seconds and eliminate all of them," Paddy nodded, Carl leaned forward and looked over at the end terrace house. He looked at the busy traffic that flowed down the road, his eyes moved over to the petrol station that was at the far side of the church and he thought for a moment.

"It would be so hard to explain that away in an early busy Coleraine evening," Carl looked up at the two men who were outside the car, "Do you not agree?" Paul nodded straight away but Paddy didn't. Carl could guess what the newly qualified, young, well-motivated body guard would want to do.

"Where is our assault team?" Carl asked.

"They are in the van," Paul paused as he looked around the rest of the local area. Once his eyes came back to the house he carried on speaking.

"The best assessment is a simultaneous assault onto both floors affecting an entrance from the rear of the house," Paddy turned his head from the van then over to the house as Paul kept speaking. "Cut off groups are already in place at the front of the house and at the end of the street both front and back," Paul slowly started nodding as his briefing went on.

"Starting with a distraction team which, is already in their house next door,"

"MOE?" he asked, Paul folded his arms as he answered the question.

"Explosive Method Of Entry not required, the survey of the house indicated normal rear door and window frames that will facilitate normal Method Of Entry for the assault team," Paul waited for a few seconds before he continued, "however, plan B is an EMOE, but that is starting in the house next door and affecting an entry through the upstairs wall then assaulting down the single staircase, through the front room then out the back into the initial cut off team in the back yard." It was obvious which one Paul favoured, Carl asked his next question.

"Police response?" Paul leaned back up against the car as Carl climbed out and stood beside him, Paddy shuffled where he was stood.

"One area car with one-foot patrol presently out around in the town centre. We have a distraction for them ready to go at the lodge road roundabout that would tie them up." Carl glanced over at Paul who was yet again confirming why he was chosen for the job.

"The station itself is minimally manned at present as the district commander wants the hours taken up by the part-time police to be cut down to reduce costs," Paddy looked over at him as he finished his last statement, "we would be in and out of here before they could react," Carl patted him on the shoulder.

"Well we will keep that on hold, Paddy!" Paddy turned to look at Carl as Carl gave him a single nod.

∞∞∞∞

Alexi was standing in the doorway between the kitchen and the living room, the house was buzzing. Everyone knew what they were doing. Davidov was down on one knee and kept a continual brief on what was happening outside. Everyone had been given an immediate target by Davidov; if the bullets started flying, then these were the first targets that they were to engage. Anna was over by the back wall adjusting her assault vest; her rifle was laying over her feet.

"Target!" shouted Davidov, everyone reacted, grips on weapons tightened and eyes focused on their own targets.

"Where?" shouted Alexi, Anna grabbed her rifle and jumped past Alexi into the kitchen.

"Single male, no obvious weapons."

"Direction?" shouted Alexi.

"Crossing the road and approaching front of house," answered Davidov.

"Report all contacts," Alexi shouted at everyone.

"Four targets at rear, no movement," came the shout from out of the kitchen.

"Four targets, forward left, no movement," came from upstairs.

"Targets, eight plus, forward right, one moving towards us," shouted Anders from the front window. Alexi wasn't wearing a vest but had a pistol clasped in his hands, his back was pressed up against the wall, something was about to happen.

"Standby!" Alexi shouted as the knock came to the door, Davidov jumped up and moved towards the door, his rifle was up in a firing position with its butt pressed into his shoulder, pointing directly at the door.

"Stop," shouted Alexi, Davidov stopped where he was, his body stood still but his eyes snapped over at Alexi. Alexi turned and shouted into the kitchen, "Anna," Anna appeared at the door beside Alexi, Alexi nodded towards her vest, "lose that and answer the door."

"What?" Davidov half shouted, Alexi looked into Anna's eyes.

"They are approaching non-aggressive, so then shall we also," Alexi turned towards Davidov who met him eye to eye, "let's find out what they have to say first." Davidov nodded and lowered his weapon. Anna stepped past Alexi and dropped the rifle onto the sofa. She unzipped the assault vest and pushed it off her shoulders dropping it by the far side of the rifle on the sofa. As she stepped forward through the centre of the room, she tilted her head to one side and, using her fingers as a comb, gave her hair a quick brush. Alexi managed a smile as this beautiful woman adjusted her top and remained the woman he would always love. Anna walked towards the front door.

115

∞∞∞∞

Paddy M'Kane used his fist to bang on the door for a third time, there was movement in the front room. He could hear them speaking in what sounded like Russian, they were silenced by one voice. That was the voice he was after. Paddy raised his fist to bang on the door again when a chain on the opposite side of the door was rattled, just prior to the door being opened. Paddy stepped back. The solid wooden door opened just a few inches and the face of a beautiful young woman appeared. Her eyes were filled with anger. He knew there was someone else behind the door. The woman was wearing a black jumper and blue jeans, her hands were hidden behind the door.

"What?" she demanded. Paddy's eyes shot up her body and looked into the dark eyes that glared back at him.

"Alexi Chernov and one other are commanded to come outside," Paddy tried to keep his voice as normal as possible.

"Never heard of him..." as she spoke the woman started to turn her head back inside and the door started to close. Paddy sprang forward and slammed both of his hands into the door. It jumped a few inches then it was halted by an immoveable object that was out of sight behind the door. Paddy shouted towards the gap in the door.

"Listen to me," the woman's head initially jerked back but she held the door solid, her face filled the gap in the door frame.

"Your name is Anna Nikitin," surprise registered in Anna's eyes, the living room behind her moved suddenly as well but Paddy carried on, "your Alpha is called Alexi Chernov and you are all from the Mongol Russian pack," all the movement behind her stopped. The door relaxed, Paddy stepped back, he had their attention. Anna moved her face towards her right shoulder as instructions where whispered to her, she turned and looked straight at Paddy.

"What do you want?

We want nothing from the Rua," he paused, they had both let each other know that they each knew who they really were and what they were dealing with,

"Alexi Chernov is commanded to walk over to those seats over there," Paddy turned and pointed with his right forefinger at the seats where Davidov and Anders had sat weeks ago. Anna's face contorted.

"You are in no position to command anything!" she raised her voice at Paddy. She was used to doing that as the Alpha female. Instructions from behind silenced her.

"This is *our land*, not yours," Paddy quoted, "My Alpha *commands* Alexi to meet him over there in," Paddy looked at his watch then looked back at her, "five minutes time," Anna paused, and more words were whispered from inside. Anna turned her head towards him again.

"And if we don't?" she asked. Paddy had been expecting this approach and relaxed his face. He let his eyes look off to the right, past the edge of the building as if he was making eye contact with someone else then turned back towards her.

"Then every one of you will not live to see the sun rise tomorrow," Paddy had lowered his voice to ensure that the level of his promise sunk in. Anna spoke again.

"We will never lay down our weapons," Defiance had returned to her eyes and her face. Paddy shrugged.

"We don't want you to," a look of surprise burst across her face as Paddy continued, "the only command is that Alexi Chernov and, if he wishes one other is to meet with him over there," he paused, "as commanded." she leaned back inside and was receiving more instructions, movement came from the room upstairs. Paddy looked up and from the way the male was standing Paddy knew that there was at least one weapon being pointed at him.

"When he comes across, he is to come unarmed," Paddy stated. He had just thought about that detail, this brought Anna's face back to the door with a look of resentment. "The rest of you can stay inside and keep what is yours!" A comment was whispered from inside.

"No weapons?" she repeated.

"No weapons," Paddy stated. Anna moved back again and after a few seconds of whispering the door opened a little bit more. Paddy caught a glimpse of a large male behind her in the darkness. Paddy was able to make out some sort of combat vest, a rifle and a military helmet. His eyes darted back to Anna who was issuing their response.

"He will meet your Alpha," she said. Paddy smiled and turned to walk away.

"Stop," she shouted, Paddy stopped and turned back towards the entrance to the house, Anna leaned back inside then turned back towards Paddy.

"What is his name?" Paddy smiled at the question, turned his head towards the car park then back towards Anna.

"Tell Alexi to come and find out," with that, Paddy turned, pushed his hands back into his jacket pockets and worked his way through traffic and across the road.

Chapter 23

Sean leaned back in the chair in the small room. The peace was broken by the sharp crack of the high heels of the woman who had made it her business to walk up and down the corridor every couple of minutes. She wore a dark grey trouser suit and her hair was tied up in a ponytail. Sean thought she was the stereotypical businesswoman. During the only conversation Sean had with her she came across as very English and very arrogant, she probably wasn't but that was the way she had just come across. He didn't really want to talk with her again. He opened his eyes and the small room came into focus. The strip light on the ceiling burned away and lit the room with a false light. The slight noise now was the only sound in the room as the footsteps faded into the distance, he knew however, that she would be back shortly. He looked down at the piles of A4 paper that occupied the centre of the coffee table. The police officer in him was going to have to read each single page first by himself, and then share them all with the team. Every single phone call, every single reported sighting that had come in during the programme would now be followed, so now he would have something to throw at Super Sutcliffe when he got back to Belfast. They had enough work to keep them busy for quite a while; he closed his eyes and wished he was somewhere else. The dramatization of the Trotman murder had been a good one which so far had got the best response. The Trotman murder, Sean's mind wandered. The smell just before the sheet was lifted, the feeling in his stomach when his eyes focused in on what was in the alleyway. Flashes of the blood burst through his senses, his mind kept imagining a face with a set of teeth that could do that much damage to a human body. The door of the room burst open and Mike flew into the room. Sean made a slight nervous jump at the speed at which Mike had arrived.

"Oh, sorry boss!" said Mike as Sean composed himself, "didn't mean to startle you." Mike landed in the chair opposite him. Mike was carrying two manila folders filled with more A4 paper. He produced a large decorated paper mug covered with a white plastic top. Mike held the first mug out towards "Full strength Kenyan coffee, with cream and one sugar," Mike beamed like a small boy who was showing off to daddy.

"What?" A surprised Sean asked.

"Proper coffee!" Mike motioned again with his right as the second mug came into view for Sean and Mike was performing a balancing act with it up against his shirt. "I found out there is a coffee shop just across the road from television centre; I thought you could do with one," an appreciative smile spread over Sean's face as he reached out and took the mug. Sean lifted the lid off the frothy coffee and let the sweet smell fill his nostrils. He took in a deep breath and allowed the aroma to blast away the thoughts in his head, his only thoughts were of the smell of the coffee beans. Sean wallowed in them for a while. Mike took a sip of his coffee then as he set the mug down on the table in front of him he stopped himself from speaking as he looked at Sean's peaceful face. It had been a very long time since he had seen that look. A look without a single care in the whole damn world, nothing mattered, nothing could come close to this peacefulness. The storms quietened, and the seas mellowed as Sean relaxed in the moment, Mike was reluctant to speak, but unfortunately, speak he had to.

"Err, Boss," Mike spoke quieter than he had been speaking previously and, as he did so, the elderly detective slowly opened his eyes and returned to planet earth. The younger detective smiled to himself, the coffee had been one of his better ideas. Mike placed the folders on the table and opened the top one. He started scrolling through the notes that had been scribbled over the top page. This was just one of the pages of notes that had been taken by one of the programme's telephone exchange personnel.

"Thanks Mike," Sean's whole body started to slump back into the chair as Sean first tasted the contents of the mug. He sat forward and started to take an interest in the paper work that Mike was playing with, "so, short version, what have we got?" Mike started sorting through the first folder that and started to pile the papers into each separate murder they were investigating.

"We didn't get a name, did we?" Sean asked,

"No, no we didn't," Mike's eyes darted over the mess of paper on the table as he searched for one certain piece of paper. "But, however, we did get sightings of her a couple of days before the Trotman murder in and around Sydenham," Sean stopped what he was doing and looked up.

"I wonder what she was doing there?"

"Well…" Mike started as he rummaged through the second file, "there is a lot of rented housing around there and if we find where she lives then," he paused,

"Bingo," said Sean, "we would have a name to put to the address!" Mike nodded,

"Ah, here we go," Mike handed Sean two sheets of paper that listed the details of the callers and the times and dates they said they had sighted the girl. It was going to be a lot of work for the team to cover, but that was what they liked, "one thing that we have got a lot of," stated Mike, Sean relaxed his hand that held the sheets of paper as Mike lifted up a separate bundle of paper.

"What this?" asked Sean.

"Phone calls from family, friends of victims who knew Trotman," Mike handed it over. Sean focused in on the top page, "most were overjoyed that he was dead," Both Sean and Mike had seen that reaction before in Northern Ireland, Sean felt his guts tighten again.

"Yeah, I took a couple of those myself, I had one bloke who wanted to help by setting up a reward if we 'didn't catch the murderer!' Mike shook his head.

"But then, with someone who has Trotman's background that is to be expected."

"Yes, I suppose it is," agreed Sean.

"Oh, did you hear about the Manchester team?" asked Mike.

"I was there when they all got excited, obviously they got a result in one of theirs" stated Sean.

"*Both of theirs*!" corrected Mike, "got the same name from over twenty different people about the railway rape and they got names and an address for the armed robbery."

"Well done them," Sean made a small congratulatory nod of his head.

"I was chatting to one of them on the way up here and they have an arrest team on the way round to the lock up where they are all holed up apparently!"

"A bit of action for the night," stated Sean.

"Yeah…" said Mike, Mike's face let it slip that it was one of those situations that he wanted to be at. Investigate a crime and then be the arresting officer at the scene, then see it successfully through the courts, a job well done.

Sean looked at his watch, "I don't know about you, but it is past my bedtime."

Mike agreed. "Ok, I'll tidy up here," he volunteered,

Sean stood up. "Grand, I'll pop to the toilet then see you downstairs."

"Yeah, no probs," Mike started packing the two folders as Sean walked to the door.

"What time is the flight tomorrow?" asked Sean.

"Half four,"

"So what time are you getting up at?" Sean asked,

"As late as possible, it's not often I get a lie in and I fully intend to enjoy it as much as I can!"

Sean smiled. "See you at the bottom of the stairs!"

ooooo

The front door of the house closed behind Davidov. Alexi walked to the end of the path and stopped. He looked over to his right at the men and women who were standing around. Some were looking at him, others weren't, more people were dotted around the far side of the road, some hanging around the trees, others walking on the path. To the passing eye they were just walking up the path beside the river, nothing illegal about that but Alexi knew what they really were. Davidov stopped behind Alexi's right shoulder, they had put on outdoor jackets. They didn't have any rifles, but they did have pistols inside the belts of their trousers. If these Rua thought that they were going to walk into this unarmed, then they had a surprise coming. Alexi looked back over his shoulder at Davidov, who looked back at him.

"I am here, we will do this together," he whispered, Alexi turned and inwardly smiled, he was glad Davidov was here. Alexi nodded then stepped through the gate and stopped to let a car pass from his right on the busy road, he didn't see Davidov look back into the house, or the face of Anna standing in the darkness with a longing look on her face. In the front bedroom upstairs Pe'ter pulled the sniper rifle out of the padded black canvas bag. Pe'ter got comfortable and knelt on the wooden chair. He lifted the rifle up into his right shoulder and pointed it across the road. He looked through the scope on top of the weapon Paul's face came into focus. The rifle was accurate up to 1000 metres, at 200 metres... well Pe'ter just grinned at the thought.

∞∞∞∞

Over by the circle of metal seating Paul stood with Paddy beside him, they were at the opposite side of the circle from the two men that had just come out of the house and were presently running across the road, in between the early evening Coleraine traffic.

"Do you think they are armed?" asked Paddy,

"Of course, they are armed," Paul stated in a semi annoyed manner, "if it was us what would we be doing?" Paddy folded his arms and looked at the two men who slowed to a walk as they reached the grass verge, both turned and started walking straight towards where Paul and Paddy were standing.

"I would have small arms on me..." Paddy paused as Paul cast him another glance, "and probably sniper cover as well as part of a reaction plan," Paul smiled as the two men came closer. The smile dropped from his face as they approached the far side of the circle of seats.

"Stop!" Paul said in a raised voice. The two men stopped right at the edge of one of the seats. It was obvious who the Alpha was as he was now a step forward in front of the second one, who, had moved over to the right side of his Alpha. If anything happened, he could react. These Mongols weren't stupid, the Alpha went to speak but he was silenced by Paul. One of the four men behind Paul opened his jacket and produced an object that was a similar shape to a small hair dryer and pointed it at the group.

∞∞∞∞

Anders jumped back and ripped the ear piece from his right ear with a yelp, the rest of the room turned around at his sudden reaction, Anders swore as he tossed the main part of the radio onto the sofa.

"What?" shouted Anna. Anders turned and stared at her.

"They are using counter measures," Anders spat, "we will not hear a word," Anna turned and stared over the road as several of the group closed in near the chairs. There was an obvious clear area around Alexi and Davidov, if the shooting started, they were both dead meat and there wasn't much she could do about that.

"These Irish," Anders said out loud.

"What about them?" asked Anna without turning her head.

"They are not that stupid," a coughed laugh came from the back of the room, Anders' head spun round and glared at Viktor who shrugged his shoulders in self-defence.

"What do you expect?" said Viktor, "they have been at each other's throats for thirty years, maybe they are more careful than we think?" Anders turned back towards the window and picked up his rifle. Anna turned and ran up the stairs and shouted at Pe'ter as she did so. Pe'ter turned his head and looked over his left shoulder at Anna as she bounced into the room. Anna flew round the side of the double bed and stopped between Pe'ter and the curtain of the window. She stared out the window and across the street.

"Don't worry they are *both* fine," said Pe'ter as his right eye looked through the rifle scope. The body armour absorbed most of the punch from Anna into his stomach as he recoiled from the force of the blow. He looked over at the stressed Anna who swore at him. Pe'ter looked into her face, 'but which one are you so concerned about?' Pe'ter thought to himself. He paused then lifted his left leg up and placed his foot on the chair. Pe'ter rested his left elbow just behind his knee and lifted the sniper rifle back up into his right shoulder and shuffled until his firing position was stable and comfortable. The rifle pointed directly at the head of Paul so all he had to do was operate the trigger.

∞∞∞∞

The Rua who had stopped Alexi looked over his shoulder at the two men who stood near the trees, one nodded and the Rua took a step forward. Alexi went to speak but was silenced again.

"Alexi Chernov." It was a statement and not a question from the Rua.

"Yes, I just want to say," said Alexi,

"SILENCE!" shouted Paul, Davidov twitched, "during the meeting, you will not make any sudden movements, is that understood!" Paul looked sternly at the two of them. Alexi paused and let his eyes dart over the men who stood in front of him.

"Yes, that is understood." Alexi nodded his head twice as he spoke. He had lowered his voice, so he spoke quieter than before, "may I ask a question?" Alexi hardly moved as he spoke, the others around them moved but kept their distance, the two men in front of him paused, and then the first one agreed.

"Who are you?" asked Alexi.

"I am Paul Hawkins, of the northern pack." Alexi answered him with a single nod of his head, "we know that you both are carrying arms, so during the meeting with my Alpha, if at any time we feel he is in danger.... you will be shot." Paul paused as he let the comment hang in the air, then he finished the sentence, "Do you understand?"

"Perfectly," answered Alexi, as he spoke a small red light flashed near his right eye, both Davidov and he twitched as the single red dot moved from their faces onto their chests.

"Very good," said an impressed Davidov, he glanced over the river.

"Where?" asked Alexi. Davidov's eyes darted over the buildings across the river.

"Fast food building... rear of building... large sports store... on top of roof of sports store... either side of the neon sign." Alexi's eyes followed the indications given by Davidov and soon his eyes fixed on the snipers that lay exactly where Davidov had said.

"Gentlemen," Paul took a step closer as he spoke, "English only, please," Alexi and Davidov both glared back at him as they had been speaking in their own tongue, Paul finished his sentence, "we would not want any misunderstandings, now would we?" Pe'ter looked over the top of the scope.

"What just happened?" asked Anna.

"I wish I knew," Pe'ter replied, "but something just got their ....." Pe'ter stopped mid-sentence as the single red dot of the laser sight touched his face and moved over the side of his head, Anna stepped back into the darkness to hide herself, "They can see us," Pe'ter said out loud. He relaxed his position as Anna made for the door of the bedroom.

"Keep your target," she half shouted as she moved, "they will know that they will take casualties if they try," The door flew open and in seconds Anna was down the stairs, there was sudden movement from everyone as they were being told of what had just happened. Pe'ter looked over into the darkness and knew that somewhere across the river someone was looking directly at him. The red dot had been to let him know that he would be the first to die, Pe'ter nodded at the darkness and the red dot vanished. Pe'ter kept his position and kept the face of Paul in the cross hairs of the scope on his rifle.

∞∞∞∞

"If you are not the Alpha of this pack, then who is?" demanded Alexi. Paul didn't answer, just looked towards the path by the river as three men walked to where they were standing. Two of the men stopped but the third carried on. He walked round the floor beds and stopped beside Paul, he left his hands in his pockets as he spoke, there was no offer of a hand shake welcome.

"Good evening, I am Carl O'Brien, Alpha of the Northern Pack of the Rua," he paused, Alexi made no attempt to speak, "and you are trespassing,"

121

Chapter 24

Cara-Marie's phone buzzed where it lay on the coffee table. Her right hand placed the remote control down on the sofa and she moved from where she was comfortable to reach forward and pick it up. She read the message. 'HIYA, WE R ON R WAY OVER 2 U. B THERE IN 2 MIN. MK' she thought for a moment; had she organised for Mark to come over tonight? she didn't think so, it annoyed her more than it normally would. She read the text again, her eyes fixed on the second word of the text, 'WE', Mark was not coming alone. She tapped out a reply, she had plenty of things to do tonight and being sociable wasn't one of them. She changed the channel of the TV when she heard the knock at the door. She slowly fumbled her way upright and dragged her feet over to her front door to let an excited photographer with his new girlfriend inside. Mark almost jumped in through the door, he was still wearing the same clothes that he had on earlier. Rachel however was looking good in her jeans and cream coloured cotton top that hung from one of her shoulders. The top was loose, and she knew how to show off her natural figure and perfect make up, if she hadn't been annoyed she certainly was now. She missed Mark's greeting but did catch Rachel's quieter, 'Hello' Mark headed straight for the sofa and Rachel dutifully followed. Rachel positioned herself beside him. Mark in total contrast just dropped himself right into the spot where Cara-Marie had been, he went to speak but was stopped by what was on the screen.

"What on earth are you watching?" Mark had a confused look over his face, "I thought you would have been watching the Crime Watch programme?" she closed the door and started to walk into her kitchen as she answered.

"I was," she paused, "that finished over an hour ago!" she started to fill the kettle.

"But what is this crap you are watching now?" Mark shouted from the front room, Cara-Marie slightly grinned when Rachel answered him as if she was being totally honest she didn't know what was on the TV as she had been searching the internet on her PC for most of the time since the programme had ended.

"Oh, come on, it's a top 100 iconic albums run down," she could hear that Mark and Rachel were chatting to each other with their next few comments. As the kettle was boiling she pulled out a tray and filled it with three mugs. She unearthed a small plate that she filled with a few biscuits from her ceramic biscuit tin that was shaped like a sleeping cat.

"Tea or coffee?" she shouted back into the living room.

"Do I have a choice?" Mark shouted back, she smiled and opened the cupboard by her head and lifted out her best coffee. She filled the mugs with the boiling water then added a dash of milk, she lifted the tray and walked back into the front room where Mark was comfortable as he slouched deep into the sofa, Rachel, however, was perched on the edge. Rachel looked up as she walked in. Rachel's eyebrows lifted as the tray was set down at one end of the coffee table.

"Wow, thank you," Rachel stated, Cara-Marie was not sure how genuine she was. Passing out the mugs the hostess took a seat in the single chair that looked directly at the TV. Mark took a sip of the coffee then stopped. Cara-Marie looked at him as he froze with the mug directly in front of his face.

"What?" she asked.

"Sugar?" he suggested.

Cara-Marie smiled, "If you want sugar you can get it yourself." Mark feigned looking hurt, she looked at Rachel, "I don't use it myself as I am sweet enough!" Cara-Marie and Rachel shared a girlie moment while Mark complained as he got up and headed into the kitchen, "and stay out of the fridge!" Cara-Marie shouted after him.

"Why? What's in the fridge?" he replied, this was followed by the sound of the fridge opening.

"He never does what he is told!" Cara-Marie said to Rachel as she took her first sip of the coffee. Cara Marie could tell that Rachel was trying to say something, her body language spoke more than what she did.

"Well," Rachel started, "he certainly is spontaneous!" Rachel paused then sipped her own coffee, Cara-Marie realized this woman was trying to make polite conversation and was failing as the pause hung in the air.

"When he asks you to do his ironing, just say "NO," said Cara-Marie as her eyes darted over to the TV.

"He can do that himself" Rachel's reaction was instantaneous. Two pairs of eyes looked over at the door as Mark walked back in. He stopped before he walked around the coffee table, he looked at the two women who were staring at him.

"What?" he asked. Cara-Marie and Rachel shared a smile.

"Nothing," they said in unison.

"I knew it was a bad idea leaving you two in a room together," he said as he reassumed his position on the sofa. The focus of the trio turned to the screen. The show was being presented by three people who were all facing each other and were discussing each piece of music in turn.

"Who are they?" asked Mark. Rachel spun round towards him.

"What?" Rachel had a shocked look on her face, "What do you mean 'Who are they?" Mark shifted beside her, his eyes darted over to Cara-Marie for support. Support he should have known in this situation he wasn't going to get.

"Ha, some journalist you are!" She teased. Mark went to say something but was cut off by Rachel.

"They are all DJ's from Radio One," Rachel lifted the mug to her lips, "didn't realise that I was dating such an ignorant!" Both the girls smiled again,

"Who?" was the wrong answer from Mark as he had never heard either. Mark then had to endure several minutes of verbal abuse from two directions now. Rachel had broken the ice with her, she glanced at the clock on the far wall as Rachel asked where the bathroom was, she pointed back towards the front door and gave the simple directions to her.

"First on the left," Rachel excused herself and made her way past Mark. Cara-Marie leaned forward and started to tidy the empty mugs on to the tray, Mark asked if he could change the channel on the TV.

"Why? What's wrong with this one?" Cara Marie asked.

"Not really my scene," Mark crunched up his face as he answered her question. Then without further asking he leaned forward and picked up the remote. Cara-Marie stood and lifted the tray then headed into the kitchen. She could hear Mark flicking through the channels, pausing only for a second on each one, which was such a boy thing to do. She started to load the mugs and the plate into her small dishwasher as Mark shouted something.

"What?" she shouted back.

"I said, did you recognise anyone from Crime Watch earlier?" Cara-Marie closed the door of the dishwasher as she stood up, her head turned towards the doorway that led back into the living room, she paused. She was not sure whether to tell what she thought or not, her hands started to tidy up the surface top that was beside her sink, she tidied and cleaned as her mind started to race. Flashes appeared in her mind, the body, the screaming woman, the blood, then the face of the girl that was dressed in black that she had seen in Coleraine, was this the same one? She was not sure, her hands stopped and rested on the edge of the sink.

"Cara," the single use of her name made her jump. Mark was standing just inside the doorway with his hands on either side of the door frame. She turned and tried to step back from the shock that she just had. Her right hand was pressed down on the top of her chest under her neck and the fingers of her left hand dug into the edge of the sink, she closed her eyes for a couple of seconds to compose herself again.

"Don't ... do ... that ... again..." she spoke quietly as the toilet flushed in the next room, her eyes focused in on Mark's face.

"Sorry," he paused, "I didn't mean to scare you," he looked at her face as it changed from white back to a light rose colour, "It's just that you stopped talking there for a bit," she half turned away from him before she answered.

"Yeah, sorry," she paused again, "I was miles away there for a minute,"

"Was it nice there?" he asked.

"What?"

"Was it nice there?" repeated Mark, she looked away from him as she gathered her thoughts before she answered him.

"No not really," she turned her back to him as she continued with what she was doing. "I printed off the press release photographs from the programme, they are quite good."

"Really?" he said, "Where are they?"

"Over by the printer," Mark turned around and walked over to the computer desk in the far corner. All around the desk was A4 sheets that were printed off from various websites, Mark moved a few of these, they were all the same subject.

"Werewolves," Mark heard himself saying aloud. It was obvious that she had been spending most of her time scanning through these websites. His concern for his friend grew even more. He would go for another chat with the editor again about her, he would have to do something this time, his eyes found the pictures from the programme, she had them all in a pile off to the right of the desk. As he lifted them Rachel walked out from the bathroom and came over to him. Rachel slid her arms around his waist and perched her chin over Mark's right shoulder, she looked down at what he was holding.

"I think it is time we were going," she whispered into his right ear, he looked into the eyes of his lover, a glint that he recognised was there, he smiled, then whispered back to her. "Ok,"

"I think I recognise one of them!" shouted Cara-Marie from the kitchen. Mark's attention was yanked away from Rachel. His head shot up towards the door of the kitchen then back at the handful of photographs that were in his hand. His body stepped across Rachel then took a step towards the kitchen door as Rachel released her hold on him. Cara-Marie appeared back in the room and took the photographs from him. As she shuffled through them Mark stepped up to her left side; she stopped at the photograph taken from the entrance to the pub in Belfast. The one underneath was from the footage from Coleraine, she held them beside each other, Rachel walked over and retook her seat on the sofa, this was not a conversation that she was a part of, "I agree with the police, this is the same person," she stated. Mark nodded as his eyes darted from side to side at both the faces on the prints.

"So how do you think you recognise her? Where you not in the Chinese when the murder happened?" asked Mark.

"Yes, I was," she started to explain, "but a couple of days previous I was having a coffee in town and she was in Church Street!"

"Church Street?"

"Yeah, she was there."

"Have you told to cops yet?" she lifted her head and looked into Mark's face, she looked back down at the face that was staring back up at her.

"No, not yet," she paused again, "I've remembered the time and the date, so she will be on the CCTV, and I got a picture of her on my phone."

"How sure are you?" he asked, she shuffled the photos again and walked away from him and headed over to the sofa, she turned her head back towards him before she answered.

"I'm sure," Cara-Marie then sat herself down beside Rachel who didn't want to be there anymore.

"You're sure!" Mark took a step forward, "no probs then,"

"What if?" asked Cara-Marie.

"What if what?" asked Mark, Rachel cast her a glance.

"What if," she let her question hang for a moment before she continued, "What if, we, find her first?" Mark could not hide his surprise.

"Find her?" Mark started to shake his head as he walked over and sat on the chair.

"Yes, what if we find her first? What a scoop that would be?" The excited journalist in her nearly jumped through her own skin, Mark glanced over at a silent Rachel who was not sure of what to say in the present conversation, Mark let a serious look fall over him before he spoke.

"If, and I do mean 'if' this lass is involved, then she is very dangerous." Mark glanced over at Rachel again before he looked straight at his friend, "and if she is, then she, and whoever else are involved are going to get very upset if we go sniffing after them!" Mark could see the excitement in Cara-Marie's face vanish as he spoke, she looked down at the photograph on her lap. "Cara!" he was louder than he had been so far, she looked over at him, "Cara, I can understand how you feel about this," he watched as her eyes flared, Mark had just touched a nerve and he knew it, "but leave police work to the police." Rachel's mobile phone bleeped, both Cara-Marie and Mark looked towards her as Rachel read the message then looked over at Mark.

"We need to be somewhere," her statement was however more of an order to him. The three of them stood and walked over to the door; they all said their goodbyes, Mark said he would see her at work tomorrow then the door closed behind them.

It was now much darker than it had when they went into Cara-Marie's, Mark looked up and down the road before he opened his car. Rachel said nothing until they got into the car then she launched into verbal abuse about the way that Cara-Marie had been dressed, her flat and the way she had been acting. Mark's car jumped forward into the main road without saying a word as the abuse continued. He listened as the car passed university corner, Rachel had not stopped with her bitchiness.

"I mean, did you hear the way that she was going on? You were totally right to shut her up with the 'police' comment!" That was enough for Mark, the car swerved into the entrance of Coleraine's university and he slammed the brakes on. Mark was furious, his left hand slammed into the release for the seat belt as Rachel recoiled in her seat. Mark was shouting as loud as he could, the couple who were walking their dog at the far side of the entrance could hear every word that he was screaming.

"Now let's get this straight!" Rachel's arms shot up around her torso in defence at Mark's sudden outburst. "Cara-Marie came across one of the worst murders this country has ever seen... and she 'STILL' came to work the following day...AND DID HER JOB...so don't you 'dare' criticise her!" Rachel said nothing as Mark quietened down. Mark gripped the steering wheel with both of his hands, so his fingers went white, he didn't know what was happening to his friend, but he didn't like it. He turned and reattached the seat belt then stalled the car as he began to move off. After he restarted the car he waited for a gap in the traffic and headed up the hill into Coleraine.

"What was in the text?" Mark asked.

"Nothing, it was a joke from one of my friends," Rachel looked at Mark, she had never seen him angry before, "it was just an excuse to get away from there." Mark stopped the car at the traffic lights, Rachel looked out the passenger window. "Sorry," Rachel whispered. Mark changed gear and moved off with the of traffic. Rachel was very conscious of the silence inside the car as Mark slowly placed his left hand onto her right thigh. That one-word got the response that she wanted, she would not be sleeping alone tonight. Mark caught a glimpse of the smile on Rachel's face and he felt his own spirit calm as she placed both of her hands over his with affection.

∞∞∞∞

Cara-Marie had watched them drive away into the night. She wasn't sure if she really liked Rachel or not, but she was surprised by what Mark had said. "Well I will just have to find them on my own then!" she said out loud. She looked up at the night sky and wondered what kind of moon was hidden by the clouds. "They are real," her eyes blinked as she stared at the clouds, "all I have to do now is prove it," she was not sure of what to do next. Then she had an idea.

Chapter 25

"To trespass was not my intent," answered Alexi as he slightly bowed his head. Alexi made the point of not looking Carl in the eye, Davidov's eyes jumped with every movement of the Rua who were all around.

"Intent?" echoed Carl as he stopped walking, Alexi tried to speak again but was cut short by an angry Alpha. "I don't care was your 'intent' was," Carl was staring into the lowered face of Alexi, Davidov was another matter. He was defiant, his hands tucked deep in the pockets of his jacket. Paddy had no doubt that he was gripping a pistol and was just waiting to pounce. "You have broken our laws!" Carl started walking slowly back and forth in front of them, "you have brought the attention of the sapiens to our kind," Carl stopped his pacing and glared at the two of them, "and I cannot allow that, not here, not in our lands." Alexi raised his head and brought his hands from behind his back and showed his palms.

"Please Godspodine O'Brien let me explain," Alexi was almost pleading with him.

"Explain?" Carl gripped his own side with his hands as his shouting continued, "And what would you explain to me Mr Chernov? That you were exiled from your own country by your own brother," both Alexi and Davidov reacted to what was being said, "and that if you return to Valka in Northern Latvia you will all be put to death after you challenged your own elder brother to the leadership of his pack," Alexi's mouth opened slightly but no words came out. Painful memories suddenly flooded back.

"What else would you explain to me, Chernov, that your brother after defeating you in a rightful defence of a challenge, a challenge by our own laws was supposed to end in death, could not kill his own brother?" Carl looked over at Davidov "or those who he knew supported your challenge?" Davidov looked at Carl then moved half a step forward. As the first word was being formed in his mouth Carl silenced him.

"Shut up, do not say a word Sprogis!" The sternness of the put down was matched by the look on Carl's face. Carl spotted the reaction in Davidov's facial muscles that gave away his surprise. Carl stepped closer to them as Paddy moved behind him ensuring that he still had a clear line of sight towards the two Latvians. "In these lands when I speak, you are silent," Carl paused then spoke again but in a quieter voice. "Do you understand?" Carl asked, Davidov remained silent but nodded in answer.

"Good," said Carl, he turned his head towards Alexi, "I know that your mate, Anna Nikitin was defending herself in Belfast," both of their eyebrows raised at the mention of Anna's full name, another reaction that was not missed by Carl. "I know more about you than you know," Alexi and Davidov shared a glance, "but what I want to know is what did you think you were doing in Limavady and again here in Coleraine?" Carl stopped and left a gap between them, Alexi straightened himself were he stood like a schoolboy in front of a headmaster.

"I can only apologise for our action here in Calrane." Paddy's head twitched at the mispronunciation of Coleraine. "But I can assure you what happened in Liymiyadie, was nothing to do with us." Carl slowly turned and walked back to where he had stood so they could not see his face, Alexi spotted that he did not seem surprised by this.

"Edward Grishin and Viktor Tatamovich are here," Carl looked at the reactions of those in front of him. "They are here to ensure our laws are followed," the two Latvians shared a glance as this Irish Alpha continued, "and our laws *will* be followed," Carl stared straight into the eyes of Alexi Chernov, "to the letter of the law." Alexi let his glance fall, "Is that understood?" asked Carl, Alexi nodded, "You will report all movements to us at the start of every week!" again Alexi nodded but Carl noted the change in Davidov. Carl turned and extended his right hand towards Paul, "Paul will let you know the details." Alexi looked over at him. Davidov was rapidly filling with anger. Carl caught Davidov's eye, "NO exceptions.... Or I will see to it that the law is applied *in full*" and with that, Carl turned and walked away towards the car park and back to his waiting car.

Paul stepped forward and smiled at the two men. "Right, obviously no more hunting for your little lot. Now for a few more details about how things are done here." Paddy moved over to his right by a few feet as Davidov was nearly at the point of exploding, but Alexi looked like a great weight had been lifted from him, relief filled his eyes and his body language spoke of total compliance. He would not be a problem, but Davidov, however could be a problem.

Across the road the atmosphere was still very tense as they watched Alexi and Davidov turn and start to walk back towards the house. Anna's eyes were fixed on the two faces as they stood at the far side of the road and waited for a gap in the evening traffic. Behind them all the Rua were disappearing into cars or up pathways towards Coleraine.

"They don't look very happy," said a voice behind Anna as Alexi and Davidov burst into a sprint to cross the road. Anna swore and jumped towards the front door, whatever had happened it had not gone well. All the heads in the end terrace house turned towards the opening wooden door. The door that would let both Alexi and Davidov back into the house and they would then in turn let all of them know about the meeting. What fate lay ahead of them? They had escaped death once, could it happen again?

∞∞∞∞

She watched as the car was carefully parking up in the driveway beneath her. She was standing by the open plan windows in the living room where she could see right down across the fields and out over the small seaside town of Portrush. The car door slammed; Tony started up the small set of steps up that led up to the front door of their house. He had his old canvas hold-all over his left shoulder. Her eyes watched his every move as if it was in slow motion, she watched the way his body moved as he jumped up two steps at a time. Her left hand gripped the top of the chair that faced back into the living room, even after all this time she still got excited to see him again, even though he had only been away a few hours. She did not rush to the front door as her instincts demanded she do. She fought them back as she stood her ground, sound in the knowledge that he would come to her. The front door closed behind him then she heard the thud of the holdall being dropped on the floor.

She turned her head back from staring at the entrance to the living room and looked out over the calm water that lay off Portrush. She had enjoyed her coffee earlier as she watched the sun slowly set over the distant hills of County Donegal. It was a scene she never got bored of enjoying; it was an amazing sight that touched all who stood in her living room and shared the view with her as well. Watching it made her feel warm and safe, as if somewhat removed from the pressures and strains of normal everyday life. When Tony wrapped his arms around her waist she closed her eyes and felt an unconditional love. Tony snuggled up to her and buried his face in the hair that hung over the right side of her neck.

"What are you doing standing in the dark?" he whispered. Karen thought for a moment before answering.

"Enjoying the sunset,"

"The sunset was hours ago," Tony stated. Karen opened her eyes and turned and snuggled into his body as she took a deep breath and spoke again.

"Yes, yes it was..." she paused as Tony lifted his head and looked out over the twinkling lights of the seaside town. She lifted her head and looked into his face, he responded by looking deep into her eyes. The light sparkled there and the small smile on his face let her know without speaking that everything was ok. Karen let her arms worm their way around his torso and she enjoyed the warmth of the embrace, then she felt a gentle kiss on the top of her head as she closed her eyes again.

"Ta gra agam ditch," she said softly in Irish, his arms slightly tightened around her as he moved his mouth, so it was directly by her left ear.

"I have love on me for you too," he whispered.

∞∞∞∞

127

Kyle lifted the empty coffee mug from the table and walked through to the kitchen. As he began to wash the mug in the empty sink his phone started to ring. Kyle looked over at the clock on the wall, who was phoning him at ten in the morning on his day off? The phone stopped ringing as Kyle turned off the running tap. He lifted the tea towel that hung from the handle of the gas oven and started to give the mug a wipe as the phone started again, he placed the mug on the side and walked through to the living room slightly annoyed, the number of whoever was calling was withheld, which normally meant it was from the police control room. Kyle didn't answer the call and dropped back onto the still warm sofa. The phone clicked off again. This time whoever was calling was now leaving a message. He closed his eyes and listened to the silence of the room. A small beep came from the phone on the coffee table as the caller ended their call. He activated the loud speaker and selected messages, he held the phone up as the automated voice talked through his voicemail just before the message started. The background was very noisy and Kyle instantly recognised voices from the police control room. The female dispatcher that started speaking had not been there long and was normally annoyingly cheerful, this time it was a very stern woman who spoke.

"Morning Kyle, all police officers are to report for duty immediately, major incident in progress," Kyle sat upright, the controller repeated the message then hung up. Kyle pressed the speed dial on the phone for the direct number for the control room in the police station in Coleraine.

"Good morning, Police Coleraine," Kyle stated who was calling but the voice did not relax, there was still a lot of noise in the background, only something big would produce that kind of commotion. "All officers have to report for duty immediately," she stated.

"Why? What's happened?" asked Kyle, the dispatcher paused, she obviously could not give too much information.

"A terrorist situation has developed; all officers have to report at once."

"I'm on my way," Kyle propelled himself upward, snatched the car keys from the table in front of him and pulled a pair of trainers on. Tony's number was engaged as his front door slammed behind him, the car alarm beeped off and he climbed inside. In seconds, he had attached the hands free for the phone and was on his way down towards the main road. The phone rang once, Kyle hit the receive button.

"Kyle," said Tony, he was driving too, "You're on your way?"

"Yeah" he replied, "any idea what's up?"

"No, just off the phone with Dave Tattershall, all sections are being called in," Tony paused, his full concentration going back to the road in front of him. Kyle turned right at the junction and was soon passing Castleroe, one mile away from Coleraine. "There was nothing on the cards at seven this morning for the shift hand over so whatever it is…"

"It has just happened," finished Kyle.

"Where are you now?" asked Tony.

"Just past Castleroe, what about you?"

"Just got onto the Ballywillan Road," Tony paused, I'll see you in the changing room.

"Done," he answered as Tony ended the call. Across at the next slip way four white painted armoured police land rovers drew up and stopped. They had their blue lights on but no sirens, the traffic slowed and one at a time they moved off and round the far side of the roundabout. The small silver car in front slowly bumped forward and started off round and into Coleraine as Kyle gunned the engine and took off up the short dual carriage way to the lodge road round about, which again was full of traffic. The car park of the station was full, cars were abandoned on pathways and blocking other cars in. At the far side of the entrance to the main building rows of white land rovers and transit vans were parked. The uniformed faces that stood around were not from Coleraine, in fact Kyle didn't recognise any of them. Kyle hemmed his car into a very small space at the end of the car park and started walking towards the entrance. Kyle suddenly noticed that when normal police have to go out with long barrelled weapons the only choice is the very reliable, German made MP5 which fires the same bullets as their Glock pistols. But most of these had the longer G33 rifle and some even had the brand new G36 rifles which meant that these were the special armed response units, something very big was indeed happening. Inside the corridors were full of uniformed police and others in plain suits. As Kyle got to the top of the stairs three men who were very scruffy compared to everyone else were coming the other way and they were not wearing any ID. The first one had what Kyle would call an 'El Gringo' moustache and his hair covered his ears, his jeans were clean, but the right knee was ripped, his dark hooded top had not seen an iron in a very long time.

"Excuse me," he said as he started down the stairs, almost pushing Kyle out of the way, the accent was defiantly English. The other two were dressed in a similar way but they didn't speak. Kyle turned his head as he reached the top of the stairs and looked back downstairs at them as they almost bounded down the rest of the stairs. They might want to look like unemployed workmen, but Kyle could spot a soldier when he saw one, or in this case, three. Kyle walked into the very loud locker room. Tony was already there, most were in various states of changing, the big question was what was going on. Different theories and rumours abounded around the room and Kyle started to push his way past towards his own locker.

"I SAID QUIET!" shouted the voice by the door, the level of noise died down, a mobile phone started to ring. The locker door closed behind Sgt Tattershall who was already in his uniform. "Briefing by sections, in the briefing room in five minutes," he shouted.

"What is up?" shouted a voice from the far end of the locker room, Dave Tattershall turned and opened the locker room door then answered him.

"Turn up to the briefing and find out," and with that the door slammed behind him. The flurry of the changing room made normal conversation difficult but a couple of minutes later all the section was in uniform and standing around the sides of the briefing room. The main door opened, and the inspector walked in followed by both the section sergeants. All three were already dressed for going out onto a patrol, they all looked very serious. The inspector stood behind the wooden lectern with the two sergeants standing just behind him as he first started speaking.

"Right then," he opened a paper folder that he had in his left hand, "Intelligence has just been received in the last hour that dissident republicans have brought a large bomb that they are transporting in either a transit or similar type van," The inspector did not look down but continued to look around the room and everyone started looking at each other, some exchanged single comments, others just listened as the inspector continued, "it is believed at this moment that it was manufactured across the border and was moved into Derry in the early hours of this morning," the inspector paused for a few seconds to let the information be digested around the room, Tony and Kyle shared a glance.

"Which one is it?" asked one from the far side of the room.

"Which one?" the inspector asked back. The police officer who asked the question had been leaning on the side, but he stood upright to complete his question.

"Yeah, which dissident republican group is it? Is it the Real IRA, Continuity IRA? Who?" The inspector glanced around the room.

"Right now, I don't really care who, what I care about is finding them and stopping them before they massacre anyone," the officer who asked the question relaxed and leaned back on the side again.

"Where is it now?" asked Tony,

"It is believed that it is being transported through Coleraine on its way to either Ballymena or Belfast," again, more comments from around the room.

"What is in Ballymena?" asked another, at that Dave Tattershall stepped forward and commanded silence. The inspector thanked him then continued his briefing, "it is believed they may be targeting the military barracks there, or the camp at Holywood."

"But it is empty? The army left there last year?" exclaimed one voice.

"And what we don't want is them leaving it in 'any' population centre if they cannot find a target." The inspector raised his voice, "Right, our response," he turned towards the large street map of Coleraine and started pointing out where the vehicle checkpoints were to be situated. These were the same as they normally are for any sort of incident in Coleraine. The tactic was plain to see, keep them out of Coleraine. The section was broken up into covering one section of the town, Tony and Kyle were put together with four others to man a checkpoint covering the main road outside the causeway hospital.

"What kind of 'van' are we looking for?" the voice was from the far side of the room.

"At this time, we do not have an exact description of the vehicle except that it is a van," answered the inspector as he looked down to read from the open folder on the lectern.

"Great, we have no idea! So, it could be in anything from a two-seat sports car to a truck." The comment came from the same officer who had asked the question, which in turn got him a look of disgust from the inspector.

"That's right, we have no idea, but what we 'do' have an idea of is that we want to find this bomb and stop these people from committing mass murder again....this situation is province wide, Ballymena, Antrim, Belfast, Lisburn and Portadown are all on high alert. Tactical firearms will maintain a rapid response here at the station ready to deploy if a situation develops." The inspector closed over the folder, "the press is already aware so be careful what you say," the section was already starting to stand up and move around, "plus, long weapons are to be carried by all those who have completed a competent long weapon shoot inside the last three months, which I believe should be nearly all of you." The inspector moved away from the lectern and started towards the door, "Deployment is to be as soon as possible as well."

"Where has this information come from?" The question had come from the same officer again who had asked the earlier question, he was now standing with his arms folded and he looked straight at the inspector.

"The Security Service, MI5," the room went silent again. The inspector then continued his way out of the room, closely followed by one of the sergeants as tuts and comments of distrust of MI5 echoed around the room. Dave Tattershall stayed and ordered the door to be closed as he would now give his own briefing to answer the rest of the questions that would be asked. Most already knew they were about to embark on a shift that would last at the very least the best part of fifteen hours, for some it would be a lot longer.

It took less than half an hour before Tony and Kyle were sitting by the open rear doors of the cramped armoured Land Rover with two other police officers behind them. The Land Rover jerked forward out of the police station and crossed through the busy traffic and on their way up the Lodge Road towards the Causeway Hospital. Both Tony and Kyle pointed their MP5's out the back of the Land Rover down the road; today was going to be a long day, then it started to rain.

Chapter 26

Simon was sitting behind the desk in the office they had been given the use of in Coleraine. His fingers tapped at the keyboard as he navigated his way through the web page on the screen, his desk faced the wall with the second desk over near the entrance. It also had a computer perched on top of it, he closed the page down as the phone on the desk started to ring. The voice at the end was looking for someone he had never heard of, so the caller rang off. Seconds later the same caller rang again and was now adamant that this was the right number and demanded to speak to the right person. Simon was just finishing speaking and hung up the phone as the office door opened and in walked Mike followed a close second later by Sean.

"And I am telling you that it is going to be brilliant, totally one sided," stated Mike as he walked round the desk and took up a position on the swivel chair that was sitting there. Sean walked past and acknowledged Simon with a nod and a wave.

"Keep dreaming," answered Sean, Simon turned around on his chair as Sean sat down on the single comfy chair that was pushed up against the back wall of the office. As Simon looked at Sean getting comfortable a bird landed on the outside of the ledge of the small window that was the only break in the wall.

"I mean we just love going to Lisburn, three easy points," baited Mike. Simon looked at him with a questioned look on his face.

"What are you on about?" he asked.

"Glentoran are playing Lisburn Distillery at the Lisburn grounds this weekend," explained Sean. Simon started to turn back towards the computer screen as Mike lifted his hands up and leaned back on the chair.

"Exactly, three easy points"

"I can get you transferred if you want," Sean had started to remove his outdoor jacket as he joked.

"My missus would love you forever if you did, you would get a year's supply of cake!" Simon looked over his shoulder towards Sean at Mike's retort, Sean mocked surrender.

"And that is a fate 'worse' than death itself," there was a comical moment shared between the three men. Simon grabbed the mouse and turned back towards the flat screen of the PC.

"By the way," he paused as the dark screen burst into life, "something I spotted this morning on police net." Sean and Mike stood up and moved to either side of Simon as the main police service website filled the screen.

"What?" asked Mike. All eyes followed the cursor as Simon moved it over the page on the screen, he moved it down the left-hand side. Right at the bottom was a new link that was titled *'operation muirdris'*

"You have been busy since we have been away," said Sean.

"It wasn't me," said Simon as he clicked on the link. A web diagram appeared at the top of the screen with the names of all three of them; a small interactive map of Northern Ireland took up most of the page with more links to each of the killings.

"Hey this is good," said Mike. Simon clicked on the Limavady killing and the faces of the dead filled the page, with details of who to contact on each page, Sean nodded his head.

"I like this," he paused,

"Yeah but the one thing that I just noticed about it that I think is wrong is," Simon paused as he navigated back to the main page. He clicked on the web diagram which had Mike and Simon's pictures with the team's details and above them Sean's.

"When did *'that'* happen?" Simon moved the cursor above Sean's and clicked on the face of Superintendent Sutcliffe. Mike leaned away and let out a noise at the same time. Simon moved the cursor over the face of Sean that did not move. "Since when was he *'Detective in charge of the investigation'*?" Simon did not hide his annoyance, Sean just let out a small unconvincing smile as he returned to the chair by the wall.

"News to me that... but it doesn't surprise me!"

"Someone is after a medal from Buck House," Mike almost spat as he spoke, "and wants his Chief Super at the same time," Mike wasn't happy. Simon closed the page and turned in his chair.

"What is going on here today?" Sean changed the subject.

"Well," Simon briefed the two of them up on the events in and around Coleraine; they would not get much assistance from Coleraine District Command Unit today. Sean made a command decision.

"Ok, scrub today, I want all the team for a full briefing at ten on Monday morning." Both Simon and Mike nodded, "Then we can sort out exactly who is doing what." With that Sean stood up and headed for the door, the other two watched him leave then Simon looked over at Mike who was grinning; he would be home early for once.

∞∞∞∞

The door to the Kevin's office opened and all the newspaper staff walked out after the briefing that they had just been given. Cara-Marie walked back over to her desk then picked up her phone and started to tap in a text message that would be sent to more than one, requesting inside information on what was happening around Coleraine that day. The phone on the desk beside her started to ring again but thankfully Mark reached over and answered it. News that a large van bomb was on the way had brought a stop to all the other tasks that the reporting team already had; their phones would be hot for a while yet.

"Ok, no problems... cheers see you soon," said Mark just as he replaced the handset. Cara-Marie landed in her chair then brought herself up to her desk and started tapping in her password for the PC. She made the point of not asking who it was on the phone as Mark was probably making a date with Rachel again. She turned her head and looked out the right-hand side of her eye. Mark had his head under the desk and was rifling through one of his new camera bags. Camera bodies started to appear on the top of the desk, the paper's webpage filled the screen, so she minimised that and headed for her inbox. Her eyes widened; she had not looked in her inbox yesterday at all. 93 emails! Most of them would be nothing but it would still take her time to get through them all. Time, she really did not have any to spare this morning. Her phone beeped with the first response to her text, 'I WILL LET YOU KNOW WHEN I FIND OUT' she answered with a thank you, but it was not the answer she wanted.

"Cara?"

"Mmph?" she could only muster a simple answer. Mark's face relaxed, then he dived under the desk again.

"See I knew you weren't listening!"

"What?" she asked, her phone bleeped again.

"I said that I just had a call from one of the snappers from around the corner," 'Around the corner' or simply 'them' was how the Herald staff referred to the other newspaper in Coleraine, "Barry is on his way to a coffee shop and wants me to join him," Her eyebrows rose, so she was wrong about the phone call, she cursed to herself, she was slipping.

"Why would he do that?" she asked as one of the other reporters darted past the two of them and headed out the back door. Mark stood up and started to pack a smaller camera bag than the bag on the floor, he was planning on being out for most of the day.

"Well," Mark started his explanation, "I have heard from somewhere else," her head darted back round towards him, "that he is actually thinking of jacking the job in!"

"Really!" she had spoken louder than she had intended as Kevin looked up from his office, then slowly lowered his head and went back to whatever he was doing.

"Yes, really!" stated Mark as he pulled his jacket from his chair and pushed his right arm down the sleeve. Cara-Marie raised her eyebrows at the sudden thought in her head.

"You're not thinking of leaving us... are you?" Mark zipped his jacket half way up as he reached for the camera bag and looked over his right shoulder at the editor's office.

132

"Now why would I do that?" the bag swung round him and hung off his right shoulder, he headed for the rear door. "Why would I want a job with better wages and fewer hours?" He grinned as he looked back at her, she watched the door close behind him. Cara-Marie lifted her notepad and scanned the notes she had scribbled on the pages, she was trying to hide what she was thinking. The journalist in her got excited again then she quelled the emotions, this is a local newspaper that is published at the beginning of the week, stories like that were for the investigative journalists from the daily tabloids. How many times had she heard 'Stick to flower shows and school fetes' said to her? She looked at Kevin's office, paused then walked over to his door. He looked up from the bundles of paper that he was holding as she politely knocked on the open door.

"Cara", she smiled back, "come in, come in," she stepped over the threshold of the office and closed the door behind her and took the first seat. Cara-Marie had her notebook in her left hand which she rested on her left knee; her right hand held the plain biro pen which tapped at the notebook. Kevin tidied the piles of paper then dropped them in one of the trays on his desk. "What's up? Have you found the bomb already?" her eyebrows shot up and her eyes widened with surprise, then in less than a second her face relaxed and she looked down at her notes.

"No, no I haven't," she paused, "I'll leave that one to the police I think!" She forced a grin which Kevin matched as he relaxed into his chair, he was regretting his first comment.

"It's about the Crime Watch programme," again she paused.

"Yeah, yeah, that was very good. I hear they got a very good response."

"Yes, I heard that too."

"Cara, what's on your mind?" he asked. She looked straight into his eyes.

"I am 'convinced' I spotted the girl they are looking for." Kevin's eyebrows shot up.

"Where?"

"Here in Coleraine," she had his attention.

"Where in Coleraine?"

"Church Street, to be exact." she paused, he pursed his lips.

"When?" His questions were short and to the point.

"A couple of days after the murder," she paused again, "I have the exact time and date in my other notebook,"

"How certain are you?"

"One hundred percent. I was having a coffee and I was chatting, so the time and date are on paper."

"Have you told the police yet?"

"No, I thought I'd tell you first," he looked around then glanced back at her, "then they could search through CCTV and see who else is around," he nodded twice.

"No probs, let me know what they say, ok!" He reached over for the bundle of pages again as she rose and opened the door, this was just his way of saying that the conversation is over, and she knew not to take it personally. Cara-Marie went back to her desk and hunted through the drawers of her desk until she found the details that she was looking for. She lifted the phone and dialed a number she knew well, there was a pause then it started to ring.

"Police Service Northern Ireland, Coleraine Station," the female voice answered.

"Inspector Parrish of M.I.T. please," Cara-Marie asked.

"Please hold,"

Cara-Marie started to sway from side to side in her chair as she waited on hold, the music was terrible and made her crunch up her face as she listened to it. The music was suddenly broken by a male voice.

"M.I.T."

"Hello, may I speak to Inspector Parrish please?" she asked.

"I'm sorry the inspector isn't here, who is calling?" she introduced herself, she thought she recognised the voice who had said sergeant, but it was not the one who interviewed her after the murder, "I'm sorry he is not available for comment; however, a full press briefing can be obtained from the press office who I can put you in touch with," she shook her head.

"Aaah, no, this isn't about a press briefing," she paused, the police officer didn't speak, "I would like to report a sighting of the girl from the Crime Watch programme," This had the desired effect, he was now very interested, "I'm sorry, who am I speaking to?" she enquired, the journalist was making sure she knew who she was talking to.

"Oh, sorry, this is Detective Sergeant McCallister," she remembered him from the yacht club. She wrote his name down on her notebook beside the time of the call.

"I am here in the office in Coleraine, I could pop round if that would help," any excuse to get inside the police station, especially today with a major incident going on.

"Yes, that will be fine, I will meet you at the enquiry office, what time are you free?" he asked, she looked at her watch then glanced at her screen.

"I am free right now,"

"Excellent, shall we say fifteen minutes?"

"Make it twenty,"

"No problems... twenty minutes." She bid him farewell and replaced the phone.
She walked back over to Kevin's doorway and leaned up again the door frame.

"How did it go?" he asked.

"Good... I am going around to the cop shop now for an interview with one of the detective sergeants and I am going to get a look round 'inside' as well," Kevin stopped what he was doing and looked up.

"Good girl Cara, good girl indeed," He knew she would walk away with more than she went in with.

Chapter 27

The drizzling rain dripped from the peak of his dark green police hat. Tony looked over at the white Land Rover and thought it needed painting. The side was scuffed and scraped and the grille around the edge was scorched, the wagon had obviously seen some action recently. The Land Rover was facing down the road and parked across one of the two lanes, so it formed a bottle neck which made the traffic easier to control. Kyle was standing at the side stopping traffic and listening to his 'Viktor checks' or vehicle checks in his earpiece; the two female officers propped themselves up against the back of the Land Rover. The driver was still sitting in the front seat, but the vehicle commander had got out and was leaning over the front of the bonnet, pointing the MP5 back up the busy road. Tony walked towards the central reservation of the dual carriageway and walked a few feet up, so he had a clear view of the cars that were stuck in the mini traffic jam the vehicle check point had created. Most were indifferent, some were hostile, it was easy nowadays to spot who was hiding something that would warrant a deeper look at the car and driver.

The traffic lights at the junction of the entrance to the Causeway hospital changed colour but the traffic did not move as more cars and vans joined the back of the line. Tony glanced at the watch on his wrist, it was nearly midday, they had been there for nearly an hour now and apart from booking one driver for illegal tyres they had not seen much. He went through the information that they had been given earlier at the briefing. 'If' the device had left Derry in the early hours then it would have already passed through Coleraine long before they were even being called into work, but then *what if…*'. All the main routes into Coleraine were covered, as well as most of the back roads, the overtime budget would be stretched thin this month; another car moved off.

Kyle held out his hand as the car slowed, the driver of the small hatchback already had his driving licence in his hand and stopped the car as Kyle got to the open window. The driver was a middle-aged man who was smiling; Tony could hear the conversation between Kyle and the driver, but he chose to ignore it; the earpiece came to life.

"All stations, all stations," the conversation between the two female police officers stopped, Tony felt his head slightly turn towards the voice in his ear. It was the main control room back at the police station.

"The device may be being transported in either a van or a BMW." Kyle was still chatting to the driver of the hatchback as the driver smiled again and shared a comment with Kyle as he started to wind up his window. Kyle took a step back from the car to allow it to pass.

"Kyle," Tony shouted, Kyle looked over his left shoulder at Tony, the grip of the MP5 was firmly in Kyle's right hand and the barrel pointed towards the ground. Tony continued "Did you get that about the Beamer?" Kyle nodded then waved the next car through without stopping it.

"Cars or vans? I wish they would make their minds up," said Kyle. Tony glanced down the line of traffic again and looked straight at the silver BMW that was now stuck in the traffic, he did not have to say anything as he knew that Kyle had spotted it as well. The drug dealer from Limavady was out of his patch,

"I wonder what he is doing down here?" Tony whispered. The line of cars moved again, Kyle waved the next two cars through then stopped the dark blue Ford that was in front of the BMW. Tony glanced over at the two female police officers who discussed between themselves what they should to do next, thankfully they made the right choice as one of them walked away from the Land Rover and over onto the far side of the pavement on the verge. She stopped by the large, long green hedgerow of trees that ran the length of the short carriageway, the butt of the MP5 moved up into her shoulder and she got ready to react. The Ford moved off and Kyle held out his hand, the angry face of the driver said it all as Kyle walked towards the slow opening window.

Movement over the far side of the entrance to the hospital caught Tony's eye. A media crew had just climbed out of a car that had stopped and were starting to set up a camera for an outside broadcast. A woman dressed in a well pressed trouser suit played with her hair then studied the microphone that she was trying to attach to her jacket. Tony hoped that the BMW was clean as they did not want to do anything in front of a camera now. The driver handed over his licence with a disgusted look on his face. He had been detained by the police so many times that this drug dealer probably knew police procedure better than most police did. Tony heard Kyle's voice in the ear piece in his left ear as he started the vehicle check.

"Oscar Delta, Oscar Delta, Delta Seven One over," Tony looked up the line of cars, Kyle walked round to the front of the car as the control room answered him.

"Send over..." Tony caught eye contact with the driver who looked back at him with venomous hatred. Tony knew the drug dealer well but had only ever arrested him once himself. An arrest which later got the drug dealer a caution in court, he had walked out free that time, but his time was coming; he pondered the thought as the well-dressed drug dealer looked away.

"Roger Delta, request Viktor check..." Tony moved round the singular signpost and glanced at the busy news team who looked like they were getting ready for a live broadcast.

"Roger Seven One, send details over..." Tony looked skyward, the rain had stopped but it looked like it was going to rain again.

"Roger, Viktor check please on..." Kyle read out the registration plate on the front of the car. He finished off by stating his police service number so there was an audit trail of who was carrying out the plate check, 'Big Brother' was watching them. The control room answered with a simple 'Received'. Kyle walked back round towards the driver's door as another call sign came up on the net and stated that they were in place and the check point was in operation, the control room answered as he got to the door.

"Delta Seven One, those details should refer to a silver BMW, three series," they went on to give the name and address of the drug dealer and stated he did have current road tax and insurance. It was up to Kyle if he wanted to search the car now or not. Tony heard Kyle ask the driver to step out of the car, he now wished that the rain had not stopped.

"Why?" the driver demanded before he moved anywhere. Kyle moved into the standard speech that he had given countless times now; Tony stepped forward in support, even though he knew that Kyle would not need it; he was just reminding the driver that he was still there.

"Under Section 23 of the Misuse of Drugs Act I have the power to stop and search a person or vehicle... now, Sir... please step out of the vehicle," with aggravated annoyance the driver did as he was told. The drug dealer wasn't stupid enough to carry the drugs himself as he had teenagers to do that for him. If they were caught, the drugs would be confiscated and little to nothing could be done against a minor. This low life knew it. Less than five minutes later Kyle handed him the completed small form stating that he had been searched and under what authority. It all fell in line with the Police and Criminal Evidence Act or PACE that they had to follow in every detail. Tony moved back beside the lamppost as the silver BMW moved off then accelerated down the road away from the check point as Kyle waved on the next car. He looked at his watch, it was nearly the bottom half of the hour, over at the news team the camera operator was set up and ready with the bright white light beaming from the top of the camera. A sound recordist held a long metal pole with a foam-covered microphone just out of camera shot. He had what looked like a very large tape recorder hanging from his shoulders that the large headphones he was wearing were plugged into.

"Maybe he should try an IPOD," Tony said out loud, Kyle turned and looked at him as the next car stopped.

"What?" he asked.

"Nothing," Tony answered.

Kyle turned back to the car then glanced back at him. Kyle mouthed 'weirdo' at him and returned to the driver of the car before Tony could answer him. The news team were now broadcasting. Tony lowered his head, so the peaked cap covered at least some of his face. Soon the car moved off, Kyle let the next few cars through then stopped a bright green hatchback. Tony noticed that Kyle had started beaming from ear to ear as he approached the driver's door. Kyle was blocking Tony from seeing who was driving so he walked forward a few steps then caught sight of the smiling face inside the car.

"Hi'ya Kelly!" said an excited Kyle. Tony grinned and walked back to where he had been standing, the female police officer at the far side of the road relaxed as well as the news team clambered back into their car, soon they too would join the queue.

"Hi Kyle... how are you?" said the smiling face inside the car. Kyle leaned over the open window and felt the beat of his heart quicken.

"Yeah... I'm good..." Kyle felt himself slightly blush, "Well, we better make this look good, have you got your licence?" Kelly held up the two-part licence and Kyle stood up and started acting as if this was a normal check.

"How is your back?" she asked.

"Yeah, it is good, I have a good Physio... what part of Ballymoney is this?" he asked as he pointed at the plastic card in his hand, Kelly's eyebrows rose.

"Why? You are going to pop round sometime?" Kyle looked up at her with a surprised look on his face.

"Well, you have been to my house," Kelly moved in her seat laughing back at Kyle as he shifted from one foot to the other, "plus, there is only one reason I would 'pop round'!"

"And what reason would that be?" Kelly moved her head slightly as she spoke, her voice slightly mocking.

"If the offer is there?" there was hope in his question.

"The offer is there," she said as she relaxed her face, Kyle handed her back the licence with a smile on his face. A cough came from behind him, Kyle didn't turn around as he knew it was Tony.

"Where are you off to now?" he asked, Kelly smiled as she glanced in her rear-view mirror.

"Well my clinic up in Maydown got scrubbed as only one person turned up," Kelly looked back at Kyle, "something to do with today's events," Kyle nodded in understanding, "so I phoned and asked for the rest of the day off but got told 'no way,'"

"So back to Sea Park then?" he asked.

"Not that I want to but yes, back to Carrick," he stepped back and motioned with his left hand that she could move on, this was more for the benefit for the car behind to let them know that they would soon be moving.

"Text you later?" Kyle asked.

"Text me later," she winked as she spoke then moved off. Kyle waved the next two cars through then stopped another. Tony looked down the road and watched the back of her car as the others shot past them. The news team drove past as did the next few cars. Tony glanced upward towards the darkening clouds; it was going to rain again. The radio net was now filled with vehicle checks from the other check points. Kyle's voice came up with another check and Tony settled down and observed his arcs, the soldier in him still lived and still looked round his 'Arcs of Fire'. His hands adjusted their grip on the MP5 as he looked around himself, his eyes checked everything inside 5 metres, then everything inside 10 metres, then 20 metres. He glanced over at the bored police woman who was walking back and forth. Tony's head snapped over to the left. His eyes shot down the row of cars as his spirit reacted... there was danger there. Kyle half turned towards Tony, something had just happened. Kyle spotted Tony's alertness and felt his own raise higher, he waved the next car on.

"Light green BMW... three up, four down," Tony spoke loud enough for Kyle to hear. Kyle spotted the metallic green three series BMW with three people in it, four cars down the line. Kyle looked around and got eye contact with the other police officers; they all reacted as something was about to happen. Kyle waved the other cars through but held out his hand to stop the BMW.

An older man was in the passenger seat compared to the driver but the woman in the rear seat was much younger. She had bleached blonde hair tied up into a ponytail and her arms were folded under her chest. She didn't look happy. The driver rolled down the window and with a heavy East European accent asked what was wrong.

"May I see some form of identification please?" asked Kyle. Davidov released his seatbelt and stretched out in the car as he fumbled in the pocket of his jeans. Kyle took a closer look round the inside of the very clean car. All three wore jeans; the two men were wearing cotton shirts and thin outdoor jackets. The woman had on a plain dark top that started on her shoulders and covered her upper torso. The sleeves stopped a couple of inches short of her wrists; the designer watch looked like it was probably a fake as the wrist band did not match. Alexi was uncomfortable and seemed angry at something. Davidov pulled out a blue wallet and started flipping through the plastic cards. He pulled one out and handed it to Kyle, who took it and stepped back. Tony moved to his left and Kyle spotted that all three had become transfixed with him.

The music inside the car was switched off and the older one said one line in a language that Kyle did not understand. Kyle walked to the front of the car and started the vehicle check, as he waited for the control room he glanced over at Tony. Tony was glaring into the car; his left foot was half a step forward and his body weight was on his left leg. The butt of the MP5 was nearly up by his right shoulder. Tony was ready to go and the three in the car looked like they wanted to as well. Kyle walked back round to the driver's door, he read from the licence.

"Mr. Spro...gis?" Davidov glanced up at Kyle then correctly pronounced his surname.

"SPROG..is" He looked away with annoyance, Kyle nodded his head then spoke again.

"Mr Sprogis... could you open the boot of the car please," Kyle took a step back to allow him space to exit the car. Kyle still gripped his MP5 with his right hand and held up the licence with his left. Davidov angrily got out of the car and walked round to the boot. The police officer that had been standing by the back door of the Land Rover walked up and stood near the passenger door. Alexi looked over at her then turned his stare back at Tony. The woman in the back seat shifted her position, something was wrong here and now the others knew it too. The ear pieces came back with the details of the car, it was not registered to the name on the licence, the boot was empty and was cleaner than what would normally be expected.

"Thank you," Kyle stepped back from the rear of the car as Davidov slammed the boot shut. "Is this your car Mr Sprogis?" asked Kyle, Davidov looked at Kyle straight in the eye.

"No... it belongs to my friend," Davidov went to walk past Kyle as he headed back towards the driver's door. Kyle stepped in front of him as Davidov bumped into him. Davidov snarled and threw out his right hand to push Kyle out of the way. A push that was stopped as Kyle dropped the licence and grabbed his right wrist with his left hand and stopped the push, there was only an inch between Davidov's hand and Kyle's body armour. The butt of Kyle's MP5 was raised as Kyle held the weight of Davidov's push and stared back as Davidov's angry face only a few inches away from Kyle's.

Tony sprung forward and raised his weapon, the rest of the police officers did the same, all of them shouting at everyone to stand still. Davidov opened his mouth but no sound came out, anger flared in his eyes, Kyle spoke firmly, directly and loud enough for everyone else to hear.

"*STEP BACK NOW...SIR*" A single shout came from the passenger seat inside the car.

"Davidov!" Davidov relaxed and stepped back from Kyle, Kyle released the wrist. Tony lowered his weapon as did the other police officers.

"Now... Let's try that, again shall we?" stated Kyle.

"The car is mine," The shout came from inside the car. Kyle held the gaze as Davidov looked down and showed Kyle the palms of his hands. He leaned back up against the car as Kyle took a small step back as well. Kyle glanced down at the licence that lay on the ground, and then looked over at the woman police officer by the passenger door. He caught her eye to eye then looked down at the car, she got the message.

"Excuse me, could you step out of the vehicle please?" she spoke directly to Alexi who was sitting in the passenger seat. The door opened, Alexi got out. Kyle looked back at the man who was standing in front of him.

"Could you pick up your licence please?" Kyle didn't smile, just kept a stern look on his face. Davidov looked around him then knelt down and picked up the licence. As he did so Kyle heard the personnel check being carried out at the other side of the BMW.

"Roger... Alexi Chernov..." Tony flinched, and Kyle noticed it but now was not the time, he read over the details again on the licence that had just been handed back to him, he looked up at the face that matched the picture that was on the licence.

"Latvia?" Kyle asked. Davidov looked at him, folded his arms as he answered him.

"Da..."

"How long have you been in Northern Ireland?" he spotted Davidov glancing over towards the older man before he answered.

"A few months,"

"Are you staying here for a while?"

"... Da..."

"Then, under current law here in Northern Ireland you are required to change your licence to show the current address of where you are resident," Tony moved back towards the signpost as Kyle took out his search pad. Another vehicle check came over the earpieces, Davidov still didn't look happy as the first drops of rain started again.

Kyle carried out a body search of Davidov and asked the other police officer to do the same on Alexi. They searched the inside of the car then finally searched the young woman who was in the back. Yelina did not speak at all and only handed over her licence when she was asked for it. All three names and addresses were written down in Kyle's notebook, all three lived in the same address in Coleraine. Kyle handed over the completed search form and stood back as Alexi climbed back into the car and Davidov walked over to the open door of the car. He stopped and rested his left elbow on the roof and placed his right hand on the top of the car door. Davidov looked straight at Tony, Kyle looked over at Tony then glanced back at Davidov who spoke a single word.

"Rua?"

"Pardon?" asked Kyle. Davidov looked over his right shoulder at Kyle, Tony didn't move or speak. He just stared back at Davidov who climbed into the car and once he had his seatbelt fastened he started the engine and slowly moved off. Kyle looked over at Tony who was staring at the BMW as it drove off towards the next round about.

"You ok?" asked Kyle, Tony simply nodded. Kyle knew that something had just happened. Tony remained silent. Another vehicle check came over the radio net as Kyle waved the next few cars through the check point, today was going to be a very long day.

Chapter 28

Sean looked at his watch as he arrived home. It was nearly half five in the evening. He had left Coleraine early but going into his office in Belfast had been a bad idea, yes, he had got a lot done, but if he was honest with himself it could have waited until Monday morning. Sean parked the car with the nose pointing towards the garage door, in seconds the engine died, and he was out of the car when his phone bleeped. Sean closed the door and secured the car before he turned and walked towards his front door as he fumbled for his phone, it was Simon. Sean stopped as he got to the door.

'INTERVIEW WITH THE JOURNALIST WENT WELL. CONFIRMED SIGHTING BY CCTV IN CHURCH STREET A COUPLE OF DAYS BEFORE.' Sean read over the message a second time then tapped in his reply. 'ANYTHING WE CAN USE?' Sean sent the message and opened the front door, the door closed behind him as he shouted a greeting to his wife but was answered with silence. Sean slid the jacket from his shoulders and hung it up beside the other coats that were arranged on a series of hooks by the front door. He walked into the living room and found the note on the table. His wife was out with one of her friends for a bite to eat as he had not shown up after lunch as he had promised. Sean felt a stab of guilt as he remembered his earlier text messages. The phone beeped, he sat down as he read it. 'YES, GOT A GOOD VIEW OF HER AND A BLOKE THAT WAS WITH HER AT THE TIME.' This at least was some good news, the screen blanked then the words *updating message* appeared. Sean scrolled through the first part of the message again then read the last line. 'I HAVE PRINTED OFF THE STILLS, SO WE CAN PRESENT THEM TO EVERYONE ON MONDAY MORNING' Sean leaned back into the comfort of the settee and listened to the silence of the room. After a few seconds, the phone bleeped again with another message from Simon, 'ARE WE GOING TO PRESENT THE CAST OF TEETH THAT WE GOT FROM THE DENTAL PATHOLOGIST?' Sean had forgotten about that, he thought for a moment before he replied. 'THAT IS GOOD, WE SHOULD HAVE A NAME SOON AND YES WE WILL SHOW THE TEAM THE TEETH.' The phone beeped to say that the message had been sent and silence descended on the room. Sean closed his eyes and listened to his heartbeat and wondered what the team would make of the evidence they had gathered so far, in fact what would a judge make of it was more to the point. His heart rate was starting to slow as he felt his body begin to relax. Sean enjoyed the moment up until the phone beeped again, the volume seemed so much louder than before and it startled him. It was Simon again.

'MIKE GOT A RESULT FROM THE RENTED HOUSE IN BELFAST.' Mike hadn't said anything to him. Sean tapped in a simple question. 'WHAT RESULT?' Simon's reply came almost immediately as if he had already been typing it. 'PENSIONER WHO LIVED NEXT DOOR STATED THAT A LOAD OF POLISH LIVED THERE AND DISAPEARED THE DAY AFTER THE TROTMAN KILLING.' He let the smile spread across his face, this was good. 'DID HE GET A NAME?' He stood and walked into the kitchen, as he was filling the kettle the phone bleeped again 'NOT SURE BUT HE WAS ON THE CASE' he could just imagine, 'WHEN DID YOU HEAR FROM HIM?' he flicked the switch on the kettle the red light came on, his phone beeped again. 'AN HOUR AGO, HE MISSED TAKING HIS MISSUS FOR LUNCH AND SHE IS MAD AS HELL' he frowned then answered, 'I KNOW THE FEELING, I DID THE SAME' Sean looked out of the kitchen window and looked around the tidy back garden and the low grey clouds that seemed to be permanently over Belfast, *What global warming?* he asked himself. Sean rested his hands on the edge of the sink, and listened to the kettle start to bubble, the phone again broke the silence. 'ONE OF THE MANY REASONS I AM GLAD I AM SINGLE' He slowly blinked and shook his head, his fingers tapped out the reply, 'JUST WAIT UNTIL YOUR NOT…' he paused and thought about what to say next. Simon had not been with anyone since his wife had died, well, not that he was aware of anyway. Sean reached his decision and finished the message 'THEN YOU WILL BE IN THE SAME BOAT AS THE REST OF US!' He pressed send, the words *message sent* appeared on his screen as the kettle clicked off. Sean reached up to open the cupboard to get a mug, his hands worked automatically as they prepared the coffee. As he stirred the hot liquid his phone bleeped again, 'HA HA LOL' he slowly walked back into the living room and re-read the message. 'Ha ha lol' this really raised his eyebrows, since when did Simon use text speak, 'LOL... laugh out loud!' He deleted the message then reached for the TV controller. He had just got comfortable when the front door opened. The female voices were louder than the TV, his wife was not alone and judging by the 'thump' sound of shopping bags being dropped in the hallway Sean's forgetfulness had just cost him dearly.

∞∞∞∞

Cara-Marie was the last in the office as everyone else had already gone. When she got back from the police station, she had relayed everything she had said to Kevin. She had been gone nearly two hours, not the half an hour that she had first said, but, he did not mind. It was a pity she had not been allowed to have a copy of any of the still pictures from the CCTV as that would have been a real coup for them. Kevin had finished and at just after half three told everyone to head home to enjoy the weekend. She had forgotten it was Friday. She stayed but the rest dived out the doors seconds after Kevin left, whatever they were working on was being left until Monday. Cara-Marie saved the story she had been working on and put it into the editor's mailbox, as she exited out of her programme; she paused, then used the drop-down menu to go onto a search engine. She typed in two words *'werewolf'* and *'Ireland'* then hit the return button. As she scrolled through the response, she mentally struck off the sites she had already seen, this took her to page three. She found one she didn't recognise, clicked on the link and in less than a second, she was presented with a web page displaying a background of a wolf's head howling at a full moon. She enlarged the photograph of the 'werewolf', it was nothing like what she had seen over at the riverside; in fact, what she was staring at was a man in what looked like a tailored monkey suit with some kind of prosthetic head.

"Friend of yours?" she jumped in her chair as Mark spoke behind her. She had not heard him come in through the back door of the office. She blurted out some friendly abuse and pressed both of her hands on the middle of her chest to try and help slow her heart rate down, Mark placed his camera bag on the floor and slid it under his desk, laughing as he did so. "Oi, language my lady!" he stated as he sat down in his chair. Cara-Marie cast him a glance that would kill a dozen mortals, "What?" he asked, she turned back to her screen and closed the web page. Mark started fidgeting with his camera bag on the floor.

"So how did your meeting go?" she asked, he looked up at her before he answered.

"Yeah, pretty good," he ducked his head back down under the desk then surfaced with a camera strap in his mouth. For a split second, he reminded her of a Grizzly bear fishing for salmon, the thought made her smile. He zipped the bag shut and grabbed the camera with both hands and started pushing buttons on the top of it. Mark froze what he was doing and looked over at her.

"You're staring."

"You have not told me about your meeting yet?" she retorted.

"Yes, I did... it was good." Just as he finished the notebook hit him in the side of the head, he threw his arms up in defence and cried *'assault'*, but it was far too late, Cara-Marie had struck her mark. When he composed himself, she was sitting with her fingers posed over the keyboard of the desktop computer and she was still looking at him, waiting for his answer, he shrugged his shoulders as he spoke.

"What?"

"Well... are you leaving us?" Cara-Marie's head turned back towards her PC, her right hand moved over to the mouse and she navigated herself away from the search engine.

"No... I'm not," she tried not to smile but a little of it slipped out, he paused again, the camera in his hand let out an audible bleep. "I did however find some interesting things," her head spun around, and her face crunched up into a scowl and waited for him to continue, he had the upper hand and he was going to enjoy this.

141

"Spill the beans or it will be more than a notebook that bounces off your head!" She glanced over, "well snapper?" he smiled then ejected the memory card from the camera.

"Ok, have a look at these," as Mark inserted the small card into the docking station she shuffled over in her chair until she was right beside him, his screen came to life. "Right, we swapped a few snaps," Mark started bringing up the pictures that he had got from the meeting "And Barry confirmed that he is not leaving just yet... the job that he was after in London has fallen through," she glanced over at the side of Mark's face. "So, he is staying here," the first picture filled the screen, it was a panoramic shot of the bus station in Limavady that had been taken from the main road the morning after the double murder.

"Old news, we can't use this," she cut him off mid flow, he glanced over at her as he started to scroll through the other pictures.

"No, not yet we can't," the next picture filled the screen, "but I am keeping these for future use," Mark returned to talking through the images. They started off at Limavady then moved to the murder scene at Coleraine, most of which she knew already. Then a picture came up of a row of houses that she did not recognise. The uniformed policeman who stood by the crime scene tape had his arms folded and several people stood near him, further down the street several people were dressed in white forensic disposable suits.

"Where is this?" she asked.

"The murder scene in Belfast nearly a month before the murder in Limavady," Mark let it hang in the air, she had that excited look in her eyes, he scrolled through the pictures taken at the scene then a picture which had been taken inside the dome tent of the mangled torso of Edgar Trotman, he expected her to recoil but she did not move.

"Next," she spoke quietly as Mark tapped the top of his mouse and the next picture filled the screen. A human head lay on one side with what was left of his neck hanging under it, again she did not move so he scrolled through the next ten pictures that documented every part of the body.

"Brilliant!" she said.

"I know,"

"Where did he get them?" she asked.

"I asked him that and guess what he said?"

"What?"

"*Don't ask!*" Mark did a quick American accent, they both smiled, "Plus, they are leading with the story that it is a couple of people who are using dogs to contaminate a crime scene 'after' they have committed the murders."

"Yes, I can see why they would go down that path," her vision never left the screen as he scrolled back through the photographs. Barry had obviously got them from a police snapper who would end up in court if it was ever found out he had passed images to a press photojournalist.

"How much did it cost him?" she enquired, Mark just looked over at her with the 'don't ask' look.

"You don't think it is a couple of people with dogs then?" he asked, it was her turn to cast him a look of contempt.

"I know what I saw Mark," she lowered her voice a few octaves, he stopped scrolling.

"And what did you see?" they both looked at each other, he could see the pain and hurt in her eyes, wondered what images now flashed in her mind. Cara-Marie said nothing, at first, then she looked back at the screen. Even if Mark did not believe her, she believed in herself and what she witnessed that night.

"Even if they are not supposed to exist!" she found herself speaking out loud, he didn't answer, how could he? 'Cara, my mate, my pal... you are off your head... you need help'... she would probably knock him out cold. Even though he had said his thoughts in face to face discussions with Kevin on several occasions, Cara was still part of the team and the team was still functioning, which Kevin had pointed out to him on both the occasions that he had gone to voice his concerns. Mark closed the screen. Cara-Marie tapped him on the shoulder, he looked over at her.

"You know what this means?"

"No... what?" Mark dreaded the answer.

"It means...I am hungry."

"What?"

"I am hungry," she repeated. He looked back at the screen as she jumped up, "and I fancy a Chinese." The back of her legs propelled her chair rearwards across the room, then collided with the far desk with a slight crash.

"Ok, but it is your treat," as he spoke the words *'shutting down'* appeared on his screen. Then much to his surprise she leaned in and pecked him on his left cheek with a quick kiss.

"Ok... my treat." A shocked photographer looked at the back of an excited journalist as she ran over to her desk and grabbed at her mouse to start shutting down her computer with her right hand as her left hand reached for her jacket. "Come on then... there will not be a second offer."

Mark turned and grabbed at his own jacket as well. It was now nearly seven o clock as the back door of the office closed behind them and it would be another half an hour before Mark got the first of several texts asking where he was as he was going to be late for his date with Rachel to the cinema. Rachel was not going to be very happy when she found out exactly who he was sharing a Chinese meal with or the fact that there was just the two of them. In her book, that was a date and if it was a fight that Mc Kenna wanted, well a fight she would get.

Chapter 29

Kyle pushed past the door of the changing room; it was quieter now than it had been earlier; Tony walked in behind him. Most of the section had already left. Kyle's right hand came out of his trouser pocket with the set of keys in his hand, in less than a second the locker door opened, and he started to take off his uniform, Tony was doing the same a few feet away. Two other members of the section were at the far side of the set of lockers and were boasting about the day's events. No bomb had been found near Coleraine, but they had caught a number of drivers with no road tax and other minor offences, one of the other sections had made an arrest of a suspect who was wanted for public order offences. Kyle did not say much but the two coppers from the other side did drown out the loud hum that came from the strip lighting running across the ceiling of the changing room. The thick, black bulletproof vest landed on the floor of the locker with a loud thump, a position which had been occupied by his grey holdall for most of the day.

"What time do you make it?" asked Tony. Kyle turned his wrist round and looked at the digital display of his watch; he inwardly groaned.

"Just gone half eleven..." half an hour until midnight, and this was the section's day off! "What time are we in tomorrow?" Kyle asked, Tony was pulling off his shirt, his eyes darted towards the back of his head as he tried to remember.

"In for half six, to deploy for seven," Tony turned and bent over his own holdall. The tattoo on his right shoulder of the British Parachute wings still looked as fresh as the day it had been created. All British airborne troops have the same tattoo., Kyle had something very similar on his own body. Tony stood upright as he pulled the clean tee shirt over his head. The two other coppers walked out of the changing room still making far too much noise for Kyle's liking. Kyle turned his head towards Tony as he did up his jeans, Tony had just said something.

"What?" Kyle asked, he was staring down at his phone. He was reading a message that had obviously arrived earlier, he started tapping a reply, then looked up with a stern look across his face.

"Three blokes from One Para were killed in Afghanistan late last night," Tony turned and faced the open locker. The comment caught Kyle completely off guard. Tony silently finished dressing then packing his things into his holdall. His phone bleeped again.

Kyle turned back to his own stuff, it had been a long time since he was in the same situation, as Kyle was locking his locker, he turned his head to see Tony tapping out another message. "Any idea who they were?"

Tony glanced over at him; a moment of understanding passed between them. "No, no names yet."

Kyle zipped his jacket halfway up and placed his Glock pistol into the waistband holster. Tony checked his then pushed it into the back of his trousers then adjusted his own jacket over it. The two men then headed for the door, Kyle glanced at Tony and Tony looked back at him, "they were from the FSG, so I may know at least one of them," he said as they both left the changing room and headed along the corridor, Kyle walked ahead and asked the obvious question. "FSG?"

"Fire Support Group... the support company blokes with all the support weapons, fifty calibre heavy machine guns, mortars, anti-tanks etc," Tony replied. Kyle nodded then asked the next question.

"They go on foot?" They reached the top of the stairs as a uniformed policewoman from the part time section raced up and barged past them. She was rushing towards her own changing room, Kyle and Tony started to descend the stairs.

"They can do, depends on the operation," they rounded the halfway stairwell as he continued, "but mostly FSG is in wagons," Kyle nodded as they headed towards the entrance.

Outside a row of white Land Rovers were parked end to end with the doors open. Crews were sitting in the front of each wagon with others just milling around. The tactical firearms unit did not react to the two going off shift, as they each veered towards their own cars. Kyle glanced over at Tony. "Keep me info'd," Tony stopped as he got to his own car, he nodded towards Kyle as Kyle's car alarm bleeped off.

"Yeah ok mucker... Slan Go Foil!" With that Tony climbed into his car, he looked in his rear-view mirror and watched as Kyle climbed into his and drove off towards the main exit to the station. "Farewell for now," Tony repeated in English. He only had to wait a short time when his phone bleeped again. He pressed the read button and scrolled down the text message.

'PRIVATE JASON ANDERS 19, PRIVATE MATTHEW POWES 19, LANCE CORPORAL BISHAN GURUNG 24". Tony looked over the names, he did not know the first two, but he had been in the same team in the sniper section as Bishan the Ghurkha. Tony closed his eyes and remembered this extraordinary little man standing beside his Nepalese wife showing all passers-by in the shopping centre in Colchester his new born baby. Tony felt his insides tighten as the memories flashed in his mind: on exercise on the Salisbury Plain Training Area, in the jungle of Sierra Leone and in Iraq in 2003. Ever the smiling Nepalese face, no matter what was happening. Bishan could spell the word 'fear' but the only fear he knew was how to instill it in those who opposed him.

"Oh, sacred heart of Jesus, whose heart was burst on the cross at Calvary, be with Bishan's wife this night..." Tony prayed out loud but was interrupted by his phone beeping again, his eyes read over the words of the text.

'CORPORAL TERRY THACHER 25, T1, COLOUR SERGEANT VINCENT BRANNION 32, T1... AEROMED BY TAC MED WING TO BIRMINGHAM THIS EVENING.' Tony looked up at the inside of the roof of his car as he let the information sink in. Tony sent a thank you back. T1... very seriously injured. This was just getting worse, Vince as well, just what the hell had happened? Tony started the car and reversed it back and swung it round into the one-way system that ran around the police station. He tried not to think about what was happening out there, the battalion had taken over from the Royal Marine Commandos whose losses were in double figures. The Paras had only been there a month, but it seemed in the last ten years they had been busier than the rest of the army and the number of casualties suffered showed that.

Bishan had a sixth sense for booby traps and he had been spot-on many times saving lives. In Sierra Leone they had only been out on patrol for twenty minutes when the 'West Side Boys' attacked. The 'West Side Boys' had over three hundred men, most of whom had just spent the morning chewing on a weed called 'Khat'. Khat had the same effect as rubbing opium on your teeth and got you high as a kite in minutes. The 'west side boys' believed that they were now invisible, and bullets couldn't harm them as they felt indestructible. The parachute company led by Vince Brannion had other ideas.

Tony moved his car out into the traffic and slotted in behind three Japanese made motorcycles then headed up the Lodge Road. Tony's headlights reflected from the registration plates on the back of the bikes. They accelerated to get through the traffic lights at the Lodge Road roundabout. Tony slowed and braked as the lights changed to red. The West Side Boys found out that Khat does not make you either invisible or indestructible. Tony remembered Vince recounting the story again just before the Airborne and Commando insert into Bagram airfield in Afghanistan just after 9/11, he remembered the laughing faces of the other paratroopers as they waited at RAF Brize Norton in 2001.

The lights changed to green and Tony moved off and headed towards Portrush, it was not long before he was turning off the Ballywillan Road and onto the Ballymacrea Road. Hedgerows lined the road as his headlights pierced the darkness of the night, the road rose and fell with memories that flooded back through his mind. Happy memories, memories of his friends, the memories that always made him smile. The car slowed as he came over the crest of the hill and his own brightly lit house dominated the hillside. A welcome sight to a tired man, he reversed the car up the gravel driveway leading to the house. As he slowly walked up the steps to the front door, the door opened, Karen stood there with a loving smile and welcoming look on her face. Both fell from her face when Tony reached the threshold, a gust of wind whipped around them.

"What?" Her right hand reached out and rested over his heart, "what has happened?" Tony lowered his gaze then slowly brought his left hand up and took her hand in his. "I watched the news… there was nothing on it!" Karen was almost pleading, she was dreading whatever he was about to say but the content still shocked her.

"Bishan was killed in Afghan last night," it was a simple statement, Karen's eyes widened.

"Little Bishan? No…"

Tony nodded, "Vince is serious…"

"Vince? Oh God no…" Karen's left hand came up to her mouth, they both stepped closer to one another then wrapped their arms around each other in the doorway. "How bad is he?" she asked. Tony pressed his right cheek against the warmth of her hair, the smell of which filled his nostrils, he closed his eyes before he spoke again.

"The Tactical Medical Wing of the RAF is flying him and a few others back to Birmingham tonight," Tony felt her arms tighten around him, "apart from that I don't know anything else," Karen released her embrace and the two of them stepped inside and closed the door behind them. In the morning Karen could phone Vince's wife while Tony was on shift. He would wait for more details before trying to plan any visit. Karen walked into the kitchen, but Tony just strolled to the bedroom. He undressed quickly then slid between the bed and the duvet, the room light was off and as he lay there he listened to Karen going around securing the house. He wrote out a short text message and sent it to Kyle, he had asked to be kept informed as Kyle was one of the few people who knew this situation as well.

Soon the heat from Karen's body would snuggle up beside him but his mind was elsewhere. At least Bishan had now got his greatest wish and would be able to stay in England forever. He wondered if, like the other Ghurkha widows, Bishan's wife and young child who were not British subjects would be sent on a one-way ticket back to Nepal; the very thought disgusted him. He wouldn't get much sleep tonight.

∞∞∞∞

Kyle was parking his car when his phone bleeped. He left the phone in his pocket as he turned the key and killed the engine. He released the seatbelt then climbed out of the car; his bungalow was in darkness, but the front was illuminated by the momentary flash of lights from his car as he activated the car alarm. Kyle walked over to the front door then paused and looked around before opening the door and walking inside. As the front door closed Kyle tapped in the sequence of numbers into the cream coloured plastic console that was partly hidden by one of his outdoor jackets which hung from several hooks on the wall. Kyle had placed them there deliberately, so the house alarm would be obscured by anyone stupid enough to break in. He had got the alarm set so it notified both him and the main control room at the police station at the same time. The small light on the console changed from red to green as the hall light came on. He kicked off his trainers, his jacket went on the one remaining empty brass coloured hook on the wall then he headed into the kitchen. In less than five minutes he landed on his sofa with a mug of tea in one hand and a freshly made sandwich of strawberry jam. The TV flickered into life and Kyle scrolled through a few channels before he settled on a 24-hour news channel. The presenter was talking about the latest political scandal that was rocking the British parliament but scrolling across the bottom was the story from Afghanistan.

'THREE SOLDIERS DIED IN SUICIDE BOMB ATTACK IN HELMAND PROVINCE. NEXT OF KIN HAVE BEEN INFORMED.' Typical of the British, Kyle thought to himself, everything so 'matter of fact' but then he did prefer that to the American 'shock and scandal' news

Kyle suddenly remembered the text that had arrived when he was in the car. He shuffled over onto his left side and pulled out the phone, he had two texts, one was from Tony and the other was from Kelly. Kyle opened the one from Tony first, he listed the dead and the injured, something the news had not. They report soldiers getting killed but not when soldiers are ripped apart and left crippled for the rest of their lives. He read over the ages of the dead and injured, 19 years old, 19 years old, 24 years old... boys and young men. That was where the legion was different, most who joined had life experience, most having already served in other armies, men who knew the dangers of what they were getting themselves into.

Vive La Legion," he whispered. Kyle paused then looked at his watch, it was nearly quarter past midnight, no he would not text Tony tonight, it could wait until the morning. Kyle saved the message to his phone then opened the message from Kelly, he smiled as he read it.

'HIYA, SPOTTED YOU ON THE SIX O CLOCK NEWS, DID YOU FIND ANYTHING? YES, TO POPPING ROUND WOULD TOMORROW NIGHT FOR SEVEN BE OK?' the sudden excitement in Kyle made his own body react as he bolted upright. An invite round to her house? Kyle spilled some of the hot liquid over his own foot which made him curse, he half dropped the mug onto a coaster then re-read the text message before tapping in his own reply.

'BRILLIANT, I CAN'T WAIT...' he stopped then thought about what he was writing then using his thumb he deleted the message a letter at a time before re-writing it. 'YEAH, THAT WOULD BE GOOD, SEVEN IS FINE BUT WHERE IN BALLYMONEY DO YOU LIVE?' Kyle pressed the button the screen read *'message sent'* he relaxed back. He glanced at his watch, maybe, just maybe it was a little too late in the evening to be sending text messages. Although his body didn't move when his phone beeped again his eyes did and they focused in on the name on the screen. *'Kelly V'* Kyle picked up the phone and opened the message.

'TEXT ME WHEN YOU ARE CLOSE, AND I WILL DIRECT YOU, CHINESE OK?' Was Chinese ok, didn't they have that the last time? he sent his response. 'CHINESE IS FINE.' He thought for a moment then sent a second message, 'WHAT ARE YOU DOING AWAKE AT THIS TIME OF NIGHT?' Kyle only had to wait for a few moments before he got a reply, 'HAD SOME WORK WHICH TOOK LONGER THAN I THOUGHT IT WOULD' Kyle looked at his watch again, 'YOU WORK AT MIDNIGHT???' His text was answered immediately, 'HA, NO ONE OF MY PRIVATE PATIENTS WITH CHRONIC BACK PAIN WHO COMES TO THE HOUSE... HE ONLY LEFT AT 11.' Kyle started to type out another message when his phone beeped again, curiosity got the better of him, so he cleared his message and opened Kelly's new message.

'OFF TO BED NOW, I'M BEAT, SEE YOU TOMORROW' Kyle wondered if he should reply but decided against it. Kyle finished his brew then decided to head for bed himself. He didn't know it then, but it was to be a restless night and he would spend most of the night back in Africa with the legionnaires who did not return. Kyle had also forgotten to ask Tony about the single word that had been said to him at the check point by the Latvian. Sleep was not something he was going to get a lot of tonight.

Chapter 30

"Anna is to stay in the house and not go out, the police are looking for her and if they find her..." Alexi let the comment hang in the air before he continued, "they find us!" He climbed back into the BMW and drove away from the front of the terraced houses leaving Davidov, Anders and Yelina standing by the front gate. They looked at each other before Davidov motioned with his head towards Yelina to go inside.

"What are we going to do?" asked Anders. The wind rushed past them as did a small hatchback that had three teenage males in it, the driver was wearing a baseball cap and the 'thump thump thump' of the music from the car's speakers surrounded it. Davidov paused then took a couple of steps towards the front door, Anders dutifully followed but bumped into him as he suddenly stopped, Davidov turned to face him.

"We may have to accelerate our plans," Davidov's statement brought a fire of excitement into the eyes of Anders. Davidov sat on the stone wall that separated the garden from the next house on the terrace, "but one question that I had to ask you?"

"Sure, what?" Davidov looked at him.

"Tell me 'exactly' what happened up in Limavady,"

Davidov paused and took a sharp intake of breath, he raised his hand and stood up, "no, wait until tomorrow, I don't want others to hear," he then turned and walked up to the front door, he opened the door with one of the keys that he had amongst a small bunch. Anders walked up behind him. Davidov stopped in the doorway and looked back over the river; another car sped up the road and Davidov looked at his watch. "It's nearly one..." His stare lifted from his watch to Anders then back over the river towards the quietness of the town that was broken by the sound of a police siren "We will make this land our own." Davidov turned and went inside.

∞∞∞∞

The question brought Carl's attention back to where he was. Carl glanced around the living room of the farmhouse. Paddy M'Kane had just left leaving only Paul in the room with him.

What?" he asked, Paul repeated his question.

"Did you believe him?" Carl raised himself out of the chair, walked over to the window and stared out into the darkness.

"Who? Paddy?" Carl half turned back to where Paul was leaning up against the far wall. "Why would I not believe him?" Paul lowered his head and gave it a slight shake.

"No, not Paddy," Paul looked up at Carl as he returned to staring out the window, "This guy, Chernov... do you believe him?" Paul folded his arms as he watched Carl pull his hands from his pockets and place them on his hips. Paul let the silence continue, he could also hear Carl thinking from across the room, the seconds ticked by, he was about to speak again when Carl turned around and faced him.

"I believe that he is scared." Carl started taking slow steps back towards the chair he had been sitting on as he spoke, "And I believe he did not sanction the Belfast killing." Paul watched as Carl slowly turned and walk back towards the window. "I also believe he is losing control of his little pack and they must be watched very carefully!" Paul agreed.

"Do you think they will abide by the terms?" Paul asked.

"Yes... I do," Carl turned once again, "What did you find out about the brother?" Paul took a subconscious breath in then divulged what he had found out.

"The brother, elder by two years took over their pack on the death of their father, a reign which lasted eighteen months before Chernov made his challenge,"

"A full challenge?"

"A full challenge," Paul repeated, "with two council members present held at their own den in Northern Latvia." Carl started pacing again as Paul continued, "The brother won, however at the end he refused to kill him." Carl once again stopped, "and in front of the whole pack banished him and those who had supported him, never to return." Carl already knew most of this and Paul wondered why he was going over it again, what had he missed the last time?

"Even though the law states that it must be to the death," stated Carl, Paul nodded.

"Yes, but the action was approved by both council members," said Paul,

"Which made it legal..." he muttered.

"Which made it legal," repeated Paul. "It has been rumoured that Chernov was put up to it by another," Carl listened.

"Sixteen of them left Latvia but only eight made it here," stated Paul.

"Where are the others?" asked Carl, Paul shrugged, "find out." The command was simple, "has there been any contact between them since?" asked Carl.

"Apparently the death sentence is still in place and should Chernov ever return to Latvia it is to be upheld... which kind of makes sense," said Paul.

"The law is there for a reason," he stated, Paul agreed, "What does the brother do?" Paul had to think for a second then he answered him.

"He owns two coal mines and several businesses around the country."

"Does he now?" stated Carl.

"Yes, which is one reason why he was able to transfer nearly half a million in US dollars to his little brother a couple of months ago." Paul expected a reaction to the money from Carl, but it did not come.

"Ransom not to come home..." Carl said out loud.

"Ransom?" asked Paul

"Yes, the elder brother has paid him never to go back as I would suspect he is reluctant to carry out the death penalty," that made sense to Paul, "who else did he bring with him?" Paul fished out his phone and went into his saved messages. The phone made several bleeps before Paul started to read from a text message.

"Alexi Chernov as Alpha, Davidov Sprogis as second... others include Pe'ter Shimikov, Anders Dusmanov and Viktor Shelaev..."

"Females?"

"Three... Anna Nikitin and Yelina Gurin," Carl looked up.

"Can we put names to pictures?

Yes, for most of them," replied Paul.

"Confirm exactly who is who with the Russians then make sure the entire pack has names to faces...that list is 7? Find the name of the other one," Paul nodded he had already started that, and would have it all finished by Monday.

"Are you going to let them keep their arms?" Paul asked.

"Yes... they have a right to defend themselves!" Paul's eyebrows rose before he asked his next question.

"And if the arms are found?" Carl stood up and turned towards the door.

"Then they will face a normal sapien court of law."

"Would you intervene? Paul asked.

"No... I would not." Carl turned again and took another step towards the door "We defend our lands... not govern them!" as he reached for the handle of the door the landline phone started to ring. They both looked at the clock on the wall, it was nearly two in the morning. Paul answered it with a simple 'hello' and listened to the caller. Paul said 'yes' and 'ok' a few times. Carl could hear the voice but could not make out the words then Paul finished the call.

"No problems, we shall leave this matter with you to deal with, thank you for informing us, Sir." Carl's eyes widened, there was only one caller that he would address as 'Sir'. Paul replaced the receiver and turned towards the middle of the room.

"Was that him?" Carl asked.

"Yes," Paul nodded.

"And what was said?"

"It seems they have a runaway," Carl sat back in the chair, "her name is 'Dani,' and she is a junior princess from southern England." Carl's expression did not move as Paul spoke, "she was supposed to take part in the last solstice but disappeared the night before."

"Why would a princess of the Noctrailis run away from a solstice?" Carl was not asking a question he was just speaking out loud as Paul carried on.

"They have a search team on the way," Carl's eyes shot over to him. "They arrive tomorrow night... if we have a sighting, he requests we inform him then he will leave."

"You have the number?"

"Yes, it's on my phone." Paul could tell Carl was not very happy with this situation.

"Pass the number to all...have you already told them about what happened in Coleraine with two of ours in Church Street?"

Paul nodded. "Yes, but I did not give identities away."

"Who is she directly related to?"

"We think... she is the second daughter of the Queen of the Black Witches," Carl looked over at the dying fire in the fire place, "from near Salisbury."

"Not like them to be so careless with someone so prominent," said Carl,

Paul agreed. "Probably hence the sudden rush to find her again," Carl nodded, Paul let the silence hang in the air as Carl rubbed his chin, then Paul had a thought, "why would they share this with us?"

Carl looked back at his friend, "Because if they had not at least asked us and we found either her or them... then we could have another war on our hands." Paul nodded as he sat down on the other chair as Carl continued, "and none of us want that again!" The fire crackled and Carl took in another deep breath, "Two-man search teams, deploy starting tomorrow plus a four-man team to observe the Noctrailis as I don't want any 'mistakes' with them." Carl looked into Paul's eyes. "I want identities, what strength, patterns etc, where they are and what they are doing during daylight, I want the whole scoop," Paul nodded, "Then inform the south of everything."

"I'm on it," replied Paul as Carl stood up and walked towards the door,

"As for me," he paused, Paul stood ready for another instruction, "I'm off to bed."

∞∞∞∞

The red deer lifted his nose and sniffed at the wind that blew through the forest; the sound of the birds had stopped. He blinked and stared out of his deep dark eyes for any kind of movement in between the trees. He could not see anything or smell anything that warned of danger, but he felt it. He turned and slowly walked away up the small track that led over the hill and down towards the river. His head was heavy with the weight of his antlers, but he did take care not to snap the lower branches of the trees that lined the edge of the path. His eyes caught the sight of a red squirrel running up the side of the tree. The squirrel stopped and looked back in terror then dived inside the tree. The deer bowed his head and tasted some of the grass, this would tell him who had passed by recently. Nothing. He slowly chewed on the grass then carefully chose each step so not to leave an obvious trail that could easily be followed. As he got to the summit of the hill he suddenly turned around and bowed his antlers at the danger that was down the path. The wind came up behind him and would only mask the scent of whatever it was, he was at a major disadvantage as they could now easily pick up his own sent. *RUN*

The instinct made his body react long before his mind did. Every powerful muscle burst into life as he galloped away, a crash came from behind him as his attacker broke cover. '*THE RIVER*'. Yes, the river, if he could cross the river he would be safe. The trail was open and faster than going through the thick forest that would slow him and cut him; having a fresh cut would only help what was behind him. The gravity of the downward slope helped him pick up more speed, faster, faster he had to go faster.

His breath was forced out of his nose and his mouth, but he could not breathe in quick enough. The smell from the water hit and filled his nostrils. Not far now, something shot away from the bottom of a tree to his left, his eyes glanced over as the small rodent dived for cover.

His right hoof snagged on an exposed root and his body slammed into the cold hard ground. Pain exploded throughout his body as he slid over the loose stones that sliced into his hide. He screamed as loud as he could, he struggled and fought with the root until he could get his own legs under him and he stumbled again as he tried to get up. He glanced behind him and the fear took him. The fear that he had felt before, the fear that he had to get away, he had to run, the fear that made him scream again as he started to run. The river was only metres away as the crashing sound behind him got closer, he screamed again as he lunged into the water. The river engulfed him, the coldness of the water was the exact opposite of the burning in his legs and thighs. The water stung his open cuts as his head burst through the surface, he kicked with his legs, a wave crashed over him the fear had returned. Oh, please no, please. Suddenly his front right foot hit something solid, 'YES,' he felt himself shout as his hoofs found the river bed, he kicked again and in seconds the water fell away from him. He felt his own magnificence as he stomped out of the water in victory. He stumbled a little over the cold rocks but soon he was up on the trail that led back into the forest on the far side of the river. He turned and looked back triumphantly at the far riverbank as he raised his head in a rut. He had done it; the fear was gone. The pain was gone he felt himself bathe in his own glory. This was a story to tell and tell it he must. His keen eyes searched the far bank, the bushes and through the trees. Nothing. His body relaxed as he turned his body and started to trot up the path.

He only saw the teeth just before they were sunk deeply into his neck. The fear took hold, he kicked and kicked as hard as he could, his antlers were useless now. His strength fell from his muscles, the pain slowly reduced and the panic slowly subsided as he gave into the snarling beast at his throat. The red deer lay at the side of the path as the naked dark-haired woman greedily fought at the neck. Cara-Marie raised herself up in triumph as the warm blood covered her nose and mouth and splashed down her neck.

∞∞∞∞

Cara-Marie's eyes widened in terror as her own scream woke her, she fought with the weight that covered her until the duvet was thrown onto the floor. She fought for breath as her own dark bedroom started to come into focus, she sat upright and steadied herself with her left hand and placed her right hand just under her own throat as she tried to breathe. She pulled the large tee shirt down from round her neck slightly, confusion reigned in her mind as her bedroom entombed her. Slowly she reached for the side light that was on the small dresser beside the bed. As the light flicked on the darkness died, she closed her eyes and slowly calmed herself down; she started to breathe slower and the pounding pulse in her neck slowed and faded.

Cara-Marie took a long slow breath in through her nose then opened her eyes. She raised herself up from the bed and stepped over the crumpled duvet that lay on the floor, she did not know how a coffee would help her, but it was the only idea she had. The kitchen light came on and she glanced at the clock on the wall, it was just after half three; she reached out and lifted the kettle then looked at the clock again. Her gaze went over to a brown and white toy dog that took up one of the wooden chairs placed around the small wooden table. She looked the toy in the eye.

"I thought you are supposed to guard me while I am asleep?" her question went un-answered as she started to fill the kettle. "Glad I am not at work tomorrow," she placed the kettle onto its stand then reached for the biscuit jar, it would be a while before she slept again tonight.

Chapter 31

Kyle had been awake since before nine, which for a Sunday when he was not working was not good, not good at all. But that was three hours ago, and he had only just got dressed. The shower felt good, but he reckoned he had only had a few hours of sleep again last night. Kyle strolled through into the living room with the mug of tea in his right hand, the TV was already on and as he landed back on the sofa where he had been earlier, he started to flick through the channels on the digital TV. Nothing seemed to catch his eye, he was bored, he continued to scroll. He stopped at a black and white World War II film about a German general in the African desert in 1942. Kyle enjoyed the two hours of escapism, the film told the story well, he remembered talking to the old man outside the Diamond Centre, the frail old man with the black walking stick and the memories he had been so keen to talk about. The very same old man who had fought against the Germans in the Western Desert during 1941 to 1943. Kyle wondered if the old man was still alive. His mug was empty and a slight rumble from his abdomen reminded him that he had not actually eaten yet. His breakfast of a mug of tea would not suffice for the rest of the day. He rose and lifting the empty mug walked through to the kitchen. He hunted through the cupboards and eventually decided what he wanted and started to prepare himself lunch. His phone beeped in his pocket.

'HI, ARE YOU STILL ON FOR TONIGHT?' Kyle's heart made an extra beat as he read Kelly's message. He stopped what he was doing as his right thumb flew over the keypad. 'YES, I AM REALLY LOOKING FORWARD TO IT.' '*Message sent,*' filled the small screen. Kyle placed the phone down near the kettle and started making himself a plate full of strawberry jam sandwiches, as his hands worked away his eyes kept darting over to the silent phone. He waited patiently for her next reply. The kettle clicked off and Kyle made yet another mug of tea. With his lunch he returned to the living room, it was two minutes until the top of the hour, he reached for the remote and pressed in the number for the 24-hour news channel. The headlines were readout by a stern-faced newsreader who looked bored, the soldier's deaths were not headline news, it was right at the end and two of the names of the soldiers who had been killed in Afghanistan were read out.

Kyle looked at the young faces, the smiling face of the Ghurkha looked back at him. Tony had often talked about the Ghurkha's, but Kyle had never actually met one. 'They are like marmite...' Tony explained, 'you either love them or you hate them!' The newsreader had already moved on to another story. The beep of his phone brought him back to the present, he leaned forward and set the plate of sandwiches and the mug down on the table, he fished the phone from out of his trouser pocket. 'OK SEE YOU LATER THEN!' Kyle wasn't sure, but he had expected something different in her message but decided against sending a reply. Kyle's eyes flicked over at the clock on the wall, he would leave to go to Ballymoney in a couple of hours, after he had got himself ready.

∞∞∞∞∞∞

Karen walked into the living room with a mug in each hand. Tony was sitting back in the swivel chair and was staring out of the large windows at the landscape in front of him.

"Isn't this view amazing?" he asked. She stopped beside him and held out the mug in her right hand, he looked up and took the mug in both hands and sipped the steaming liquid; she noticed he closed his eyes as he did so, she moved around the coffee table, tucked her right leg under herself as she sat down in the middle of the sofa and looked across at her husband. Tony opened his eyes and looked out the window.

"Yes, it is," she answered before she sipped from her own mug.

"I will never get tired of looking at it," Tony was not exactly speaking towards her, he was more just talking out loud. She stood up, walked over beside him and placed her left arm over his shoulders. Tony looked up into her face and they shared the moment; he stared back out over the fantastic view; he then had an idea.

"Fancy a picnic?"

"A picnic?" she questioned.

"Yeah, you see a picnic is when you get some food... and something to drink," Karen punched him in his side.

"I know what a picnic is," she stated,

"And then you go to a really nice spot and 'eat' the food... and guess what?" She propelled herself upwards and turned to walk away. Tony's right hand shot out and grabbed her hand, the movement pulled her back towards him and she fell back onto his lap, she was giggling as she did so. Tony shifted where he was sitting so his face moved up close to her face.

"What?" she asked, he closed his eyes and gently kissed her lips breaking between each kiss to speak a few words.

"Well......you get to...... drink the drink...... then afterwards ......" Tony held a slow passionate kiss, as he did so his arms tightened around her and she found her own arms pushing their way around him. The fingers of her left hand drew lines down the right-hand side of his cheek after the kiss.

"Then what?" Her question was intimately spoken, his nose glanced her cheek.

"Then..." he paused, "then you get to enjoy the wonderful place you are in!"

"Sounds like fun," she answered.

"It is,"

"The picnic will have to wait until tomorrow," he lifted his head back at her comment.

"Tomorrow?"

"You are off tomorrow are you not?" she asked,

"Yes... I am." Tony was puzzled by the direction of this as he knew that she was fully aware of his shifts. Karen then let a seductive look fall over her face as she spoke again.

"Yes, tomorrow...... as I have plans for you for the rest of today!" and with that she lifted her head up and they locked in a long passionate kiss.

"I have another idea!" said Tony between a kiss.

"Shut up," Karen ordered in reply then devoured him with her mouth.

The picnic would wait until tomorrow.

∞∞∞∞

Kyle moved his car over into the faster lane and carried on behind a Renault that was towing a small trailer with a lot of wood secured to the back of it. The blue twined rope strained as they followed the lane around the roundabout. A baseball cap in a dark green Vauxhall pulled up beside him. Kyle looked over at him, but the young driver was more concerned with the car directly behind him. The Vauxhall's engine revved in a challenge to race and the car behind answered in kind. They sped off when the lights changed to green. The town fell away as the green of the land opened either side of the road ahead of him, the car in front of him picked up speed as did Kyle. He passed a signpost on his left that was written in white letters with a dark background stating that Ballymoney was only 6 miles away. The amount of traffic coming the other direction had now increased and prevented him from overtaking the very slow hatchback that was driving at exactly 40 miles an hour. Kyle had to stay where he was as the road rose and fell and twisted and turned with the land and he knew that there was not a long straight bit for a few miles yet. He flicked through the text message again with the directions to Kelly house, he put the phone down and carried on driving.

The road expanded back into a dual carriage way and a red Citroen went to overtake, but he was already accelerating, he indicated then moved into the fast lane and over took the small car. Kyle kept the car at 70 as he moved back into the slower lane, the driver of the Citroen was obviously annoyed that he had not overtaken Kyle sooner and floored his accelerator pedal and overtook him in turn. Kyle glanced over at the smirking young face that was sitting in the driver's seat, Kyle shrugged and slowed down to 60. It would not be long before the young driver found the police speed trap that lay ahead just over the next rise in the road.

153

The road narrowed once again back into a single carriageway, the traffic had lessened off once again and there was a lot more space as Kyle watched the Red Citroen disappear into the distance. The dark road stretched out in front of him as it cut its way through the different shades of the green from the fields. After a bit, the traffic in front of him slowed as he passed the red Citroen on the side of the road with a police car parked right behind it. Kyle did not recognise the police officer who was stood by the driver's open window; he could imagine the conversation that was going on, then he wondered about the evening that lay ahead of him.

An excitement grew in him, it was an excitement that he did not know, why was he excited? Was this not just another girl after all? The first rain drops landed on his windscreen as he looked up at the dark, grey clouds that hung over the town of Ballymoney. At the top of the hill was a large sign that directed him off to the right towards Ballymoney town centre, the traffic slowed again then came to a stop at the roundabout. He passed a large blue and white sign that welcomed him to the 40 mile an hour zone in Ballymoney. 'Enjoy our town' the greeting on the sign declared. He picked up his phone and scrolled to the directions on the text message, he read out loud.

'Take the Ballybogy Road towards town until you reach the first small roundabout, then take the first left into Margaret Avenue…" his eyes found the road sign at the entrance to Margaret Avenue, so he slowed and turned in the built-up area. The green of the fields had gone, an old couple were standing by the first set of gates, talking, the woman was standing at the far side of the metal gates wearing her pyjama's and an old man in brown jumper and brown tweed trousers was pointing at the sky and probably complaining about the weather. Either side of this road were rows of terraced houses, mostly cream coloured but some were painted white. Various makes and colours of cheap cars were parked in driveways and filling up the side of the road, Kyle slowed and read from the text again.

"Terraced houses will be on your right-hand side… come all the way down until you get to number 123." Kyle counted down the houses as the car crawled along the street. Outside a house on his left were parked two ice cream vans that had seen better days. Kyle's eyes kept counting down the numbers until he spotted the numbers on the door, 123. He parked in a space beside the pavement across from the ice cream vans. In his excitement Kyle nearly forgot the wrapped box of chocolates that he brought for Kelly.

The brightly painted front door of the mid terrace opened as he walked towards it. Kelly stepped back and opened the doorway, welcoming him in. Kelly's eyes looked him up and down, she smiled as she did so. Kyle wondered if the plain shirt, jeans and new trainers were sufficient as Kelly had obviously spent time on her hair and facial makeup as it matched her patterned cotton top that hung from her neck and exposed her left shoulder. Her trousers were of a much darker colour than the top, but they still matched.

"Hi, come on in," she greeted him. Her smile was matched by a smile from Kyle as his right hand extended with the gift, which she took as the two of them exchanged pleasantries. The door was entrance to a hallway with a small landscape painting that Kyle did not recognise. The staircase to the left disappeared upstairs as the hallway led down into a kitchen at the rear of the house. Halfway between the entrance to the house and the entrance to the kitchen on the right-hand side wall was a doorway which would lead into the living room. The warmth of the house was matched by the strong aroma of simmering spices from whatever she was preparing. The door closed behind him and Kyle found himself being directed towards the Chinese meal that was already out on the round wooden table in the kitchen, dinner was going to be first.

Chapter 32

Grishin was enjoying the hot shower. He let the force of the water hit him full in the face. He shook his head from side to side and turned around, so the water could thrash into his neck. Grishin lifted one of his arms and started to wash away the worries of the world; he was he could not hear his phone ringing beside the hotel room bed. It would be another 20 minutes before Tatamovich would get any form of reply from him. Grishin kept his eyes closed as the water poured over him, his movements slowed while he just enjoyed the feeling the shower was giving him and he started to relax a little bit more. Soon they would be going home so they could report back to the council in person that O'Brien was following the law and things in Ireland were under control. His right hand moved to grip the heat control of the shower and with one movement turned it fully over to the left and down to the bottom on the blue line. The temperature went from boiling hot to ice cold. He opened his mouth as he felt his heart pound in his chest. The muscle groups in his back tightened and moved his shoulders rearwards; again, he started to turn around under the water. He loved this.

After the shower, his movements were slow and deliberate as he dried himself with the large towel. He had already picked out what he was going to wear for the rest of the evening and the jeans, collared polo shirt and socks were lying neatly along the end of the bed. He took his time getting dressed as he was savouring the moment when his eyes picked up the flash of the screen on his phone. Grishin pressed the redial button and waited for the ringing tone to start.

"What?" Grishin demanded when Tatamovich answered his phone.

"What are you doing?" he asked, Grishin turned his head and looked around the room.

"Well I am standing here just out of the shower with a towel wrapped around me dripping wet and presently wondering what you want at eight in the evening." There was a titter of laughter down the phone at having caught him at such a moment.

"I've had an idea," he stated, "how about we go down to where the first one happened and have another look ourselves," Grishin twisted his face as he listened.

"But we've done that already?" retorted Grishin.

"Well..." replied Tatamovich, "I want to look again,"

"Or do you just want to get near the waitress of the restaurant we found across the road from the bar?" Grishin relaxed as he guessed the real reason for Tatamovich's sudden idea.

"Well... we are leaving tomorrow so I just thought one final night out in Belfast." Grishin knew from experience which part of Belfast he wanted to explore. He agreed but made him wait nearly an hour before he met up with him in the lobby of the hotel. The taxi would drop them off near The Botanic Inn and they would walk from there; tonight, it was going to be a fun night.

ooooooo

Kyle followed Kelly from the kitchen back through to the small living room at the front of the house. The single window dominated the room from the right as you entered. The view was of the houses at the far side of the street and nothing more. Kelly had paper vertical slat blinds as well as a white cotton net curtain, she obviously enjoyed her privacy. Hanging on the wall to the left was a single framed picture of a landscape with a large hill central.

"Wow," Kyle spoke without meaning too.

"Wow?" enquired Kelly as she plonked herself down without spilling a drop from her wine glass at the far end of the two-seat sofa. There was a matching single chair directly opposite the sofa by the window. Kelly had a small wooden coffee table that did not match the wooden bookcase holding a collection of CDs and DVDs; it was cheap but functional furniture. The TV was sitting in the corner with a digital box attached underneath it; he pointed with his right hand, holding his wine glass, at the picture.

"Yeah," he extended his right forefinger as he did so, "where is that?" he enquired, a surprised look burst onto her face before she raised the glass of white wine to her lips.

"Ha, you aren't a local copper, are you?" Kelly lowered the glass and motioned for him to sit down beside her on the sofa. Kyle's eyes glanced at the picture again then slowly lowered himself down into the corner of the sofa, she turned her body, so she was at an angle towards him, he looked into his glass before sipping from it again.

"No, no I'm not," he drank from the glass again as a playful smirk of '*I know something you don't know*' flashed on her face.

"It is Slemish Mountain near Ballymena,"

"Slemish?" his head turned to look up at the picture, "as in where Saint Patrick used to herd sheep?"

"The very same"

"Oh."

"So how come a Coleraine copper didn't know that?"

"Because this Coleraine copper actually comes from Lisburn."

"Lisburn?"

"Yeah, Lisburn...it's this town 12 miles south of Belfast..." a quick punch landed on his left shoulder, he mocked a look of hurt back at her.

"I know where Lisburn is, my ex-husband comes from there,"

"I didn't know you used to be married?"

"I didn't know you used to live in Lisburn!" she answered.

"Well it seems we have a lot to learn about each other then," Kyle shifted forward slightly as he spoke and to his great pleasure she followed suite.

"That we do," they stared into each other's eyes for a few seconds and for those few seconds he did not know what to say next; suddenly she leaned back and spoke for him.

"So why join the legion?" the unexpected question made him think for a second.

"I wanted to be the best," he sipped at the glass of wine again.

"Is that it?" she asked.

"Why did you want to be a physiotherapist?" he asked back.

"I didn't," she stated.

"What did you want to be?" Kyle had turned the conversation and she had not noticed.

"I really wanted to become a vet."

"So, why didn't you?"

"Simple really, I needed four straight A grades to get into Veterinary surgery and I got three A's and a B." Kelly paused and took a larger sip of wine than she had before.

"And physio was your next choice?" Kyle asked. Kelly looked over at him again. Kyle watched as her eyes mellowed.

"Something like that, yes."

"Do you regret it?"

"Regret what?" she asked.

"Regret doing physio?"

"Not at all, it is nice after all when my patients are able to *tell* me that they are in pain and not find out by getting kicked in the head," he smiled as she finished speaking.

"Well there is that I suppose," he paused as his eyes moved over her, "and you get to inflict pain on people," his eyes continued their journey.

"Yes, I do!" she perked up with her answer, "legally as well,"

"Kelly's house of pain... it has a ring to it."

"Hey..." another soft punch to the shoulder, he noted that it was the second time she had touched him, "Keep that up and you will find out about pain..." she answered.

"Excellent... some parts of France you have to pay for services like that!" a third punch that was harder than the first two landed on his left shoulder.

"Keep that up and you will find out," Kelly's grin turned into a small laugh.

"This evening just keeps getting better," said Kyle as he leaned forward, Kelly did the same, their faces came close to touching.

"Thank you for dinner by the way," he leaned forward and gently kissed her lips.

"You are welcome," she answered with a deeper kiss but broke off when he nearly spilled his wine. They both broke apart, he apologised, as she made a joke about him cleaning it up later. He placed the nearly empty glass on the table, Kelly brushed her body against his as she placed her glass right beside his, she looked straight into his eyes as she moved her head closer to his again and locked her face onto his in another passionate kiss.

∞∞∞∞

Kyle's eyes opened and looked at the pale colour of the ceiling in the darkened bedroom. His body twitched as he became aware of his surroundings, he was on the right-hand side of the double bed. The duvet was lying in a crumpled mess over the bottom of the bed. He was only covered from the waist down but wasn't cold. His left arm extended along the pillow that her head lay on, he listened to her slow breathing and slowly turned his head to look at her. She lay face down over his arm. Her right arm lay across him and her hair covered most of her face. She moved slightly where she lay and murmured at the same time. His eyes moved around the room searching for a clock as he now had no idea what the time was as his own watch was in a pocket of his jeans. She moved again, and he looked over at her. Kyle moved himself, so he was now lying on his left side and he moved his right hand up to the base of her naked spine. The tattoo that covered her back was one of the most amazing he had ever seen, it was exceptional in the detail. She had mentioned on his first visit she had a tattoo, but he had not expected anything like this.

The tattoo was of three red roses whose branches started at the base of her spine and had been drawn to look like they were twisted around her spine. The tattoo was in fact one large one and four smaller ones down her back. The three roses bloomed in a crucifix shape, the largest rose just under her neck line and two smaller roses branching out towards her shoulders. The branches with green leaves and thorns twisted in a clockwise direction downwards and it was at the very bottom where Kyle let just the very tips of his forefinger touch her skin. He slowly started to draw his finger up the direction of the main branch and Kelly's back reacted, she murmured again, he stopped and looked at her half-covered face, slowly, her eyes opened.

"Don't stop," she whispered.

"What?" he asked. Kelly lifted her head a little from the pillow as she tried to focus in on his face.

"Don't stop... I love my roses being touched," a gentle smile spread on her contented face as she closed her eyes and rested her head back on the pillow. Kyle let his fingers make their slow journey up her back, he paid attention to each rose leaf. The higher he climbed the more the response he got from her. Finally, after drawing his fingers over the petals of the flowers he let his fingertips slowly graze over her spine as he let his hand travel directly over her spine; as he lifted his hand away Kelly lifted her head and brushed away her hair, she was now fully awake and smiling.

"That was nice," she teased.

"That is some tat!" he stated.

"Yes, it took nearly six sittings of over two hours each..."

"Wow," he answered.

"Mum and Dad went mental when they found out," she turned her head, her hair dropped to cover her face again.

"They didn't approve then?" Kelly lifted her head and looked at him.

"No, they didn't approve of their only child leaving home and going to university," Kyle rested his head on the pillow as he listened to her as she continued, "they didn't approve of me getting married... they didn't approve of me getting divorced after only a year... 'how could they show their faces at church when their daughter is running around behaving like a harlot'..."

157

"They said that?" she stared straight into his eyes before she answered him.

"Yes, they said that, to me and anyone else who would listen." Kelly turned her head back and rested it on her pillow, she was looking directly at him.

"Do you still talk to them?" he asked.

"Sometimes..."

"Sometimes?" repeated Kyle.

"Sometimes to Dad... Mum not really," Kyle paused before continuing.

"Why not your mum?"

"Well..." she started as she made him lift his head, so she could lay her right arm under his neck, "Mum was raised as a strict 'Free Presbyterian,' so marriage is for life etc..." Kyle nodded his head in understanding as she continued, "Dad is as well but it was something that I just never got into."

"Why not?" Kyle's question was direct, and it was Kelly's turn to be caught on the hop.

"Why not?" she asked back, she paused as her eyes looked up and to the left as her mind searched for the answer. "Well they believe that on a Sunday a woman's head must be covered when on holy ground, only a woman prepares food on a Sunday and is *only* to wear a dress or skirt on a Sunday,"

"So, if that is what they believe, that is what they believe," he shrugged his shoulders, she pulled her head slightly rearwards.

"And only lose your virginity on your wedding night!"

"Most of the world's religions say that same." Kyle answered, she retorted with a disgusted look on her face as she pulled the duvet up over them.

"Not for me thanks," Kyle smiled and decided not to pursue the subject any further.

"So now you know my life and family history, what about you?"

"What about me?"

"Well... any family?" she asked, he shifted himself onto his back; she could tell this was not a comfortable subject for him.

"Both Mum and Dad are dead, I had a younger brother..."

"Had?" she asked, "as in past tense?"

"As in past tense, he is dead as well," Kyle pulled Kelly into a hug under the duvet and she responded by placing her head on his chest, so she wasn't looking at him. "Both him and Dad died the same time." Kyle paused as if he was searching for words, but none came.

"What happened to them?" she asked, he shifted again, whatever was coming Kelly knew was the truth and was still painful.

"The two of them were heading into Belfast as Dad wanted to buy a new car and they were at the wrong place at the wrong time," he paused, she moved her head but didn't look at him. "No warning car bomb... the IRA killed them both and seven others in the middle of Belfast..." he felt the tightness of her hug increase as he continued, "Mum dropped dead when she went to identify the two of them... I was six years old." Kyle felt the warmth of her body against his, she lifted her face from his chest, so she could speak.

"So, what happened to you?" Kelly replaced her head on his chest.

"I went to live in Canada with my sister in Ottawa until I was 13..."

"Then what happened?" she enquired, Kyle took a deep breath in as her fingers started to trace their way over his abdomen and around the right-hand side of his chest.

"Well... we moved back to Lisburn for five years...until I was 18,"

"Why only five years?"

"They were moving back to Canada and I didn't want to."

"So, you joined the legion."

"So, I joined the legion..." she kissed him again, "and I have never looked back," she held another long kiss as she moved on top of him.

Kelly broke off the kiss and leaned over him as she reached into the top drawer of the pine dresser beside the bed and pressed the button on the top of the small white plastic clock. The light from the face lit up the room, Kelly replaced the clock on the side where she had lifted it from. Kyle moved his hands up and started caressing her chest. Kelly fished about then positioned herself over him, again revealing the shape for her naked body.

"It's 2am," she stated, he looked at the face above him,

"So?" he asked.

"So... your taxi is coming at 3... so we have an hour..."

"You booked me a taxi already?" a surprised Kyle asked.

"I booked it before you arrived..." and with that she dropped her body weight onto him again, it would not be until he got into the taxi before he thought about how he was going to get his own car back to his house.

Chapter 33

The sunshine had dried the ground during the day and the rain clouds that had dominated the sky over the weekend were now long gone. The six teenagers spilled out the doors of the small car as it skidded to a halt in the nearly empty car park of the small council run forest. As they escaped from the cramped conditions inside the car they stretched, then slowly congregated back around the doors; one of the teenagers walked up to the parked green BMW car and peered inside.

"Oi" shouted one of the others, the surprise made him jump back and spin round towards the ripple of laughter that was now coming from the teenager that was just closing the driver's door, the car was left unlocked.

"Made ya jump Heighton!" Ashley Heighton's face turned from one of shock to one of anger as he gestured back at Jony O'Keefe with his left hand. Verbal abuse came from the others as they all headed towards the single path that led away from the car park and into the forest. Jony O'Keefe had enjoyed his status as top dog over the last few months and his new earring and short highlighted spiked hair was statement to the fact that he was the one to emulate, but his reign was coming to an end. The six young teenagers hurled abuse at each other because there was no one else around to abuse instead. All of them had left school the year before and none of them were going on to university. It wasn't good to be known as a 'swot.' 'Swots' were the stuck-up teachers' pets who never got detention or who never had their parents called into school after they set off the school's fire alarm system; that day had gotten Ashley out of his maths homework that he had not actually done.

"Ash?" The question made him turn his head towards the largest of the group, Davie Mc Gonigle. Davie had just been released from the young offender's centre down near Belfast after spending three months there, the position of top dog was now his again.

What?"

"Have yea forgotten sumpin?" Davie had more of a country accent than the others as his family lived outside Coleraine,

Ash looked around himself. "No,"

Davie pointed to his back. "Weren't you supposed to bring the drink?" A look of realisation burst over his face as one of the two girls that were with them started laughing at him. Ash swore again and turned back towards the car, he pushed Keri Ingram and Matthew Boyd out of his way as he burst into a run back to retrieve his small backpack that he had stolen out of a camping shop in Ballymena less than a month before.

"Did he get the tabs?" Davie glanced over at Jony as he asked the question.

"Oh yes… that 'we' both did," Davie gave Jony a congratulatory slap on his right shoulder as his grin showed off the off-white teeth in his mouth. Davie was taller and a heavier build than others the same age as him and he would use this to get what he wanted. Davie Boyd had played rugby for school and the local rugby team in Coleraine had started to take an interest in him. It was at a trial for them that he had got the new nickname 'Wookie' as they all pointed out that he was more than a little bit hairy as well. The interest from the rugby club however came to a sudden stop after he was arrested for assaulting a police officer outside a pub in Portstewart. They found the ecstasy tablets in his pockets when he was searched back at the police station, the judge gave him three months and today was his getting out party. Ash had got the cans of lager from the cupboard where his Dad kept his alcohol and Jony had got the bag of ecstasy 'tabs' from his usual supplier in Portrush. He was quite pleased with himself as the supplier was two years older than him and had done him a special deal when he told him what he wanted them for.

Keri Ingram bounced along beside him, the height difference was massive as the top of her head was just above Davies's elbow. Her light-brown hair bounced off her shoulders in rhythm with her walk, the paleness of her round face was set off by the bright rose colour of her cheeks.

The black hoodie top was the standard and she had bought the pale jeans only two days before hand to show off the bum he had always liked.

Katie Gillespie was the quieter one of the pair of girls. Her hair was a darker brown than Keri's and was naturally straight. Keri had better curves and boys naturally always went for Keri before looking towards her. Katie was slimmer and normally wore baggy clothes that hid more than what Keri showed. Katie was jealous of her friend but there was a pecking order in the group, and she was lower down it. Her small glasses made her look serious whereas Keri's face just said 'fun.' Katie looked over at Matthew. This was the boy she had a crush on for first year biology class, his hair was short, and he didn't speak much and was the subject of most of the ridicule from the other boys. He had shown a flair in computers, but his high scores cost him much in social standing and that was the reason that he did not turn up for any of his final exams, much to the fury of his parents.

Katie wasn't wearing the same hoodie top as the others and this time had slightly overdone her makeup, her jeans were rolled up to expose her ankles and her white tee-shirt was deliberately too small. She didn't have much of a chest but what she had she wanted to show off today. The rest of the boys would be looking at Keri, and she wanted Matthew to be looking at her. Katie had chosen a yellow cardigan that only went to the bottom of her rib cage and sleeves that only went to her elbows. She had borrowed the thin gold necklace and gold-plated bracelet from her mum; she would not miss them would she. Ash jumped back into the middle of the group with a two-tone canvas bag in his left hand.

"Let the party begin!" he shouted into the empty forest.

∞∞∞∞

Tony watched as Kyle reversed his car up the driveway until it was parked beside his own, both cars were pointing back out the driveway and out over the green field's then out to sea. Tony felt his gaze lift out towards the setting sun. A noise from the kitchen turned his head towards the living room door.

"You ok?" he shouted, there was a couple of seconds before Karen answered.

"Yeah, no problems...we are not taking the eggs!" Tony smiled then glanced back out the window as Kyle bounded up the steps. Karen already had more food than they were ever going to eat, even with his appetite so they could do without the eggs, no matter what mishap had just befallen them. Tony walked through the living room to open the front door.

"Hi mucker," Tony greeted him,

"What-a-bout yea- big man," Kyle stepped forward and overdid his own accent in reply, Kyle threw a short jab with his left hand towards Tony's abdomen which, he spotted in just enough time so that the blow only hit a wall of solid muscle, he responded by landing a punch on Kyle's left shoulder as he walked past. Tony closed the front door as Kyle turned into the living room.

"Karen... your husband is beating me up again," he shouted as he slipped his jacket off. Kyle made his way towards the sofa as Tony headed towards the chair the two of them had been sitting in the night before.

"Well beat him up back again," she replied.

"Self-defence," shouted Tony as the two of them landed back into the furniture at the same time.

"That will be a first, he's only a paratrooper after all," Karen's comment made Kyle laugh out loud.

"Oi" Tony shouted.

"Oi, what?" answered the voice from the kitchen.

"Remember whose side you're on!" There was a muffled answer that was not fully heard by the occupants of the living room.

"Did you get the flights sorted?" asked Kyle, Tony paused for a second then nodded an answer before he spoke.

"Yeah the first of the funerals is happening Wednesday so I am flying to London tomorrow."

"Sorted," said Kyle.

"Yeah, yeah it is, I am being met by one of my old section at the airport." Tony fell silent when he finished his sentence, Kyle let his thoughts and memories wander. After what seemed like only seconds Karen appeared in the doorway with a hold-all in one hand and a day sack over her right shoulder.

"Right... ready to go?" Even though it was posed as a question both of them knew that it was more of a statement. Both the boys got out and jostled each other as Karen opened the front door, the moment of sadness had passed as Kyle knew Tony needed happy thoughts before the week that lay ahead of him. Karen stopped and looked back as they both crowded the doorway behind her, she smiled, turned and almost jumped out the door. Tony relaxed and headed after his wife.

"Where are we going anyway?" asked Kyle as he followed him down the steps toward the cars, one of which had the hatchback open.

"Some picnic area in Castleroe that the wicked witch has found."

"I heard that," she shouted.

"You were meant to," Tony answered. The rear of the car slammed shut as a smiling, very happy wife walked round and climbed into the driver's seat. Tony and Kyle exchanged a glance and without speaking Kyle climbed into the backseat as Tony got into the front.

"So, Kyle... where is your girl?" Karen asked as the engine roared into life. Kyle paused as his mind searched for an answer.

"Aaaah...she could not make it as she is working tonight."

"Oh... lady of the night I see." It was Tony's turn to smile; his wife had turned on Kyle.

"What?... eerr, no." Before Kyle could say anything else Karen continued her assault.

"But you did score with her last night, didn't you?" Kyle relaxed his shoulders and looked out the window as Karen turned the car onto the empty Ballymacrea road.

"No... I didn't"

"Lie," shouted Tony.

"Anyway," Karen continued, "tell me more about this girl," Kyle had nowhere to hide, the interrogation would continue for several minutes. It did not take Karen long before she had motored her way through the Coleraine traffic and was now making her way down the Castleroe Road towards their final destination. She slowed the car down at the entrance to the woodland park. 'SOMERSET, EXERCISE CLUSTER'. The letters on the signpost were painted white and really stood out against the dark colour of the background.

"I have never been in here before," Kyle spoke but his eyes were transfixed on the surroundings outside the car, "I didn't actually know this place existed to be honest."

"One of the many little secrets of Coleraine Borough Council," answered Karen as she reversed parked the car into a space in the right-hand side of the car park, Kyle guessed that it would only hold about twenty cars. He unlocked the seatbelt and climbed out of the car; Tony was getting out as Kyle closed the rear door. There were two other cars in the car park. A small French hatchback that had extra spoilers that had been cheaply bought and fitted as they were a different colour to the car and they looked totally out of place, it was probably done to try and hide the car's real age.

"Rear tyre," Tony stated as he lifted the holdall out of the boot of the car. He had been looking over the old car as well, Kyle's eyes scanned the treadless bald tyre that was obviously illegal.

"Would you two stop that... you're 'off duty,'" Karen half shouted as she shoved Tony in the back and propelled him away from the car. She swung the day sack over her shoulder, smiling as she did so, she was obviously looking forward to the picnic. Tony followed her with the holdall. The other car was a light green BMW and was parked in the corner of the car park at the edge of the wood. Kyle didn't recognise it as the one he stopped at the VCP only a couple of days before, but then he had stopped hundreds of cars, he could not remember each one. Kyle was enjoying the sense of peace that this place had, his eyes looked around. His head slowly nodded, this was a good spot, when it was not raining of course. "This one," decided Karen, she headed towards the nearest wooden table, the two boys following behind as sheep to a shepherd. It did not take her long before the three of them were sitting around a table full of food. Karen had prepared snacks, nibbles, sandwiches, a bowl of sausages and another of chicken that was still warm. Tony served up the soft drinks as Karen started filling their plates, the two boys tucked in and enjoyed their food in silence. Karen glanced at the two of them, smiled, then bit into a chicken leg. The sun slowly started to drop behind the trees as the light started to dim. The edge of the sunlight crept up the side of them. Karen commented that they should have arrived sooner. Tony waited until Kyle had a mouth full of food before he blamed him. Kyle half choked then gulped at the paper cup full of cola. The banter between the two started again, she smiled, she could see the bond between the two friends.

Tony paused then looked around the edge of the clearing. He looked down at his watch, they had been there about 40 minutes he thought to himself as his eyes darted up at the tall trees that acted as a barrier between the eating area and the wood itself. He felt himself stir, the hair on the back of his neck started to rise, something was out of place here. Kyle was across from him and had his back to the woods, but he picked up on Tony's reaction.

"What?" he asked, Tony didn't answer. Karen stopped mid-sentence then looked at her husband's now emotionless face. She looked over at Kyle who met her glance, she did not seem overly worried, almost as if she had been in this situation before.

"Tony?" Kyle had slightly raised his voice. Tony's body broke from the stare and looked Kyle in the face.

"What?" he asked.

"I just asked you that," Kyle stated. Kyle turned on the bench to face the same direction that Tony had been looking. Kyle shifted in his seat then turned back at Tony who slowly lowered his hands and placed his paper mug and half eaten sandwich back on his round paper plate.

"What did you see?" Kyle asked, Tony's concentration had returned to the wood.

"Not sure... something in the woods," Tony was almost stammering as he spoke. Kyle spun round and let his eyes search the tree line, they fixed on nothing. He could not see what his friend could. Tony's body suddenly flicked up and Kyle reacted to his movement. Tony did not realise it, but his right hand now covered the grip of his Glock pistol that he carried hidden under his top, Karen drew back.

"What's there?" Kyle raised his voice slightly. He knew Tony was reacting for a reason, from inside the woods they could suddenly hear clapping, cheering and jeering.

"Are you armed?" Tony asked as he started to rise from the bench.

"Yes of course I am," Kyle also started to rise. Tony stepped away from the bench and took a couple of steps towards the woods. Something was wrong. Something was very, very wrong. Kyle glanced over at Tony, he knew that something was about to happen. Kyle had in the past been able to sense danger, but Tony seemed to be able to pick it up strongly, Kyle knew it and since they had been working together he had learnt to trust it as well.

"What is it?" Karen asked. Neither of them turned towards her, they both faced the woods, "Tony, what is it?" Karen almost shouted the repeat of her question. Kyle picked up on the slight nervousness that had crept into her voice. Tony no doubt had heard the same. Tony had stopped, and Kyle looked over at him, was he sniffing the wind?

"Karen" Tony spoke quietly before he stepped forward with his right foot, his hand was now under his top and his right hand now had a secure grip on the pistol. Kyle's right hand unconsciously did the same, and his attention became fixed on the woods. A feeling of danger was creeping up on him, there was something dangerous in the woods. He could make out the quieter, muffled sounds that they could now hear after the cheering had suddenly stopped.

"Yes," she answered.

"Pack up the things and wait in the car," Kyle glanced back at Karen who he expected to protest at least against what Tony had just said but she wasn't. She started throwing the food into the holdall and cleared the top of the table as fast as she possibly could. "Stay in the car and lock the doors," Tony continued to say as his eyes hunted the gaps in the woods. Kyle stepped closer to him but kept facing the trees.

"Mucker... what do you see?" Kyle had lowered his voice to ask the question.

"I am not sure... but..." Tony was suddenly cut off by the piercing sound of screaming. The screaming was a mix of male and female voices and it came from inside the woods, they were already running towards the path that led into the woods as the screaming continued. They ran past the BMW and through the wooden posts that dictated the perimeter of the car park. The pathway snaked through the short grass and parted the trees.

"This way," shouted Tony as he shot off down the left-hand path and into the wood. Tony stopped beside a small brook that came down from the right and flowed under the pathway. Kyle stopped himself a few paces on, Tony extended his left hand.

"Stop!" he shouted. Tony looked back into the forest. He had his weapon out of the holster and by his side. Kyle lifted his pistol out and stepped away from him so he could see what he was facing. Kyle tried to control his breathing as they listened to the forest but the only sound he could hear was the running water and the thumping of his own heart inside his chest.

"Where?" he quietly asked. Tony turned away from him, so he was facing into the wood. Tony's left foot was a pace forward of the right and both his knees had a slight bend in them. Tony was ready to engage whatever was out there, Tony slowly brought his left arm round and took a two-handed grip on the pistol.

"We've come too far," he answered, and then he slowly started to walk back up the path. Tony was completely focused on the forest, Kyle kept up with him as he started to walk faster "Yeah...over there," As Tony spoke Kyle suddenly realised that there were no birds or the sound of wildlife, the woodland had become very quiet and still, both of which amplified every sound. The silence was broken by the sound of snapping wood which came from the far side of this patch of trees, Tony's pace quickened again.

"Up there," Tony pointed up with his left hand to the slope of the hill that the trees covered. Right in front of him his eyes caught a single leaf of a nettle plant that had been sprayed blue. Just a single leaf, no other, just simple vandalism or a marker left for someone. Tony looked over his right shoulder as Kyle followed on, he now broke into a trot, his attention never left the trees that were now up to the left. They passed the bench again and carried on back down the way they had first come, slower more deliberate this time. Kyle's breath was returning as the pathway straightened out, Tony halted at a small path that led through the trees.

"Over there," Kyle followed him as he went down the trail. The floor of the forest changed from green to brown under the canopy of the tall trees. Tony had slowed, and Kyle still wanted to know what was up ahead but if Tony knew would he not have told him? Tony raised his pistol up so both his arms were extended in front of him, Kyle did the same, he kept back and to Tony's right as they made their way up the hill.

The sound of a car horn on the Castleroe road made Kyle glance back over his right shoulder as they continued. Tony had slowed down, almost as if he was on a military patrol and expecting to find the enemy at any moment. Neither of them made a sound as they moved deliberately up through the trees, Kyle tightened his grip on the familiar black plastic grip of the weapon. Patches of green on the ground pointed to the obvious trail that had been trodden on many times. Final beams of light from the setting sun lit patches of the ground around them as the darkness grew deeper. Kyle looked over the large mound of earth that was up ahead, to the far side of this mound was a clearing that was more brightly lit than where they currently were, the greyness of their surrounding seemed to welcome them both. Kyle could now smell something, he wasn't sure what it was, but he was picking something up. Tony was slowly breathing in and out of his nose as he moved, he seemed to absorb everything.

Another small brook stretched across in front of them and a small bridge had naturally formed over it. The bridge was about 2 feet wide, but it served its purpose. A single tree was standing in the middle of the path at the far side of the brook with a mound of earth either side of it. The clearing was now off to their right. Tony jumped first and Kyle seconds later, both without making a sound. As they passed the mounds they both could see a black duffel coat that had been outstretched on the ground, a few other clothes were scattered around, a pair of jeans, a single trainer, underwear, a crumpled shirt, a woman's red top. All were new, all were clean and totally out of place, but up ahead was a deeper brook and the area behind that was much darker and they were drawn towards it.

The far side of the brook was much higher, and the ground formed a natural barrier as if it was a different level. It had a natural entrance to a small area behind it that was about 20 metres wide and was surrounded by trees. The far side of the clearing stopped at the very steep rise of the hill that went straight up nearly 70 metres. The entrance to this clearing was guarded by a tree round the bottom of which a left hand stretched around, a strip of bark where the hand had gripped was missing and blood was slowly dripped from it. They jumped the small brook and landed either side, Kyle landed with Tony on his right, another fallen tree was by his left side and four other trees formed a box in front of him. Tony moved a pace round the tree with the hand and found the body of a young male without his head. Kyle didn't have to move as he could clearly see what lay in front of them both.

A large thick oak tree was off to his left with the body of a young male slumped up against it, his back was towards Kyle however he could already make out the massive trauma to the side of his head, neck, shoulder and right arm. Kyle stepped forward; he was already dead. A few feet to the right at the far side of the fallen tree was a young female who lay on her left side. Her feet and legs were bare, but she still wore her dark hooded top. Her head looked up towards the hill as if to expose how much of her throat had been ripped out. The dark red earth around her was in sharp contrast to the pale whiteness of her young, shocked face. Kyle moved over the fallen tree and looked at the young male that lay on his back with his arms and legs outstretched, there was blood all around them. Most of his face was missing as was most of his throat. His chest had been ripped bare and his torso was covered in deep lacerations made with great force. Dead eyes looked up at the darkening sky as Kyle stopped at his feet.

Tony moved behind Kyle and placed a reassuring hand on his right shoulder; he took a couple of paces towards the female. Kyle looked down at the body in front of him as he heard a couple of beeps. He looked over at the back of Tony as he started to tap at the number pad on his phone, Kyle looked up the hill and into the pair of eyes that looked down at him.

The dark eyes stared into his, the figure was standing upright with well-developed arms by its side. It was perfectly silhouetted against the sky behind it. The head was a weird shape and the greyness darkened around the face and teeth that seemed to shine in the darkness. The hair fanned out from the sides and two ears pointed upwards, was it smiling at him? Kyle had looked at it for about two seconds when his own body reacted by dropping down onto his right knee and pointing his pistol at the figure as it turned and vanished.

"POLICE... STOP!" Kyle screamed as loud as he could, he blinked, and it was gone and again his body reacted by jumping forward to give chase when Tony cannoned into him sending him crashing into the earth.

"Kyle, NO," Tony jumped to his feet, turned up the hill, standing over the startled Kyle.

"IS MIS RUA... IS MIS RUA," Tony shouted as loud as he could, then stepped back to allow Kyle to his feet.

"What?" was all he could muster. Tony turned away and put the phone to his left ear.

"Wait, please wait," Tony said as he holstered his pistol.

"Now just wait a minute," Kyle was nearly shouting and bounded towards Tony's back. Tony spun round and stopped him with his outstretched right hand.

"They are gone," it was almost a whisper.

"They? Who..." Kyle's head slightly shook from side to side in confusion as he spoke. "Wait for what?" Tony lowered his head and his arm as he started speaking to the police control room and started to describe what they had just found. Kyle looked up the hill at the gap in the skyline where the figure had been standing. Confusion reigned in his head as the only sound he could hear was the sound of Tony's voice. His eyes looked across and found the missing head looking back at him. It was lying beside a tree and looked as if it had been placed there.

Suddenly at the far side of the oak there was movement and a young girl with blood dripping from her face stumbled and fell to the ground.

"Survivor," shouted Kyle, Tony looked up at the fumbling girl.

"There is one still alive... we need an ambulance as well," Kyle rushed over to her, she was mumbling, her wide eyes darted back and forth in shock. Blood was splashed over her face, neck, arms and body but as she rolled on to her back her hands waved in a hysterical way. Kyle could not make out any visible injury to her body; as he knelt beside her, he struggled to reassure her. He looked up at Tony who was still talking to the control room.

"Injuries?" he shouted, Kyle shook his head.

"None I can see, this blood is not hers," Tony relayed this down the phone. Kyle looked back at the girl who fixed a look at him; he had seen fear before but never like this absolute terror. Her rambling continued as her feet fought with the earth and her hands fought with Kyle's.

"Police officer... it's ok, it's ok... we are police officers... you're ok... you are safe now..." the word safe made the girl suddenly go from mumbling to full on hysterical screaming. Kyle looked over at Tony who was nodding his head, then he ended his call. In the distance, a siren started as Tony knelt beside Kyle to help with the girl.

"What is going on?" Kyle demanded, Tony didn't answer. Kyle released his grip on the girl who was trying to stand up. She fainted.

"Grab her," shouted Tony. After the girl was laid out in the recovery position Kyle turned on Tony again demanding to know what was happening. Tony sheepishly shook his head, Kyle exploded with anger to which Tony just stood upright and said nothing.

"Well, what are you going to say?" Kyle continued, Tony looked straight at him.

"Kyle, mucker... I can't"

"Can't?" Kyle paused "What do you mean "can't?" Tony looked around.

"One of us better get down to the car park and guide them up," said Tony as he turned away from him. Kyle threw a punch which landed at the rear of Tony's right shoulder, the force of which propelled him forward. Tony spun round as Kyle threw a second punch with his left hand, Tony righted himself and stopped the punch by catching it in his right hand.

"We don't want to do this..." Kyle's face came close to Tony's, Kyle relaxed as Tony released his fist.

"Then tell me what the hell is going on.... What on earth was that? You know, don't you?" Kyle stepped back as Tony nodded his head, more sirens could be heard approaching them.

"Yes... yes I do... but Kyle," Tony looked up at him.

"What?" Kyle did not hide his anger.

"You must not say a word. I promise I'll tell you later what I can." Tony let the comment hang.

"Don't push yourself..." answered Kyle. "You better go down to the car park as your missus is still down there," Kyle didn't hide his anger as Tony nodded and turned away from him. The long howl that pierced the night was soon joined by another, they were not far away.

"Stay here... or they will kill you too," stated Tony as the sound quietened down. Kyle stared at him then turned back to the young girl that lay on the ground.

"Do not mention him to the other coppers either," Tony was walking away as he spoke. Kyle glared at his back. '*HIM*' he said out loud.

"Or you'll do what?" he snapped. Tony stopped, turned and stared back at Kyle.

"Because I am asking you to..." Kyle stared back at him as he continued "I must get permission first," and with that Tony turned and ran off down the slope towards the approaching police cars. '*Permission?*'

Chapter 34

Sean Parrish drove past the uniformed police officers who were standing in the middle of the entrance to the forest park on the Castleroe Road. He had been told about the situation by Mike nearly two hours ago over the phone, much to the great annoyance of his wife. The car park was full of police cars, he recognised the two dark Ford transit vans of M.I.T., who the uniformed police officers called the Murder Investigation Team, '*MURDER IN TRANSIT*'. Sean liked the term. Mike already had most of the team there and they were busy carrying out the tasks that he had set them. Two raised a hand in welcome as they walked around the back of one of the vans, the ambulance drove past him and headed for the exit. Sean stopped the car on the left-hand side then opened the door as a cold gush of wind jumped inside and swirled around him, he undid the seatbelt and stepped out. Two uniformed police officers walked past him and headed for the entrance; one of them was carrying a large roll of blue and white police cordon tape.

Sean picked out Mike who was over the far side of the car park near a green BMW that had a cordon around it. He raised his right hand in recognition, Mike replied the same. Sean walked over. The flash of a camera from the Crime Scene Investigators kept going off round the car. CSI officers dressed in white paper suits were inside the cordon. Mike was also wearing one, but he had the hood down and wasn't wearing the mask. Sean's eyes flashed over at a small group of people in civilian clothes that were off to the right-hand side of the car park. He picked out one member of his team talking to them and taking notes, Eddie Cargill was concentrating on what he was doing, Mike's smile welcomed him as he approached.

"Evening," Sean raised his eyebrows then looked up into the night sky.

"I can think of better things to be doing," he answered. Mike nodded and raised his notebook.

"Ok... messy one this time,"

"Go for it," Sean answered, Mike flicked through the pages.

"Ok, five sudden deaths, all local teenagers and one survivor," Sean raised his eyes from the notebook to look Mike in the face.

"A survivor?" he exclaimed,

"Yeah, not a mark on her."

"Her ... excellent a living witness at last," Mike grimaced back as Sean spoke.

"Not sure how useful she will be,"

"Why?"

"Well it seems that they got together this evening to celebrate the release from the young offender's prison of one of their friends, a one..." Mike looked back at a previous page then continued reading "David McGonigle... 17..."

"Never heard of him," stated Sean.

"Two arrests, got three months in Hydebank for assaulting a police officer and possession of ecstasy," Sean turned his head towards the forest as Mike continued the briefing, "he got out yesterday."

"Where are they?" Mike pointed with the notebook towards the path.

"Up there in the forest, put a suit on and you can see for yourself," Sean turned his head towards the pathway. A woman in a white disposable suit was walking back down and she was covered in mud. "You don't want your suit ruined... your missus will kill me if I let you go back home caked in mud,"

Sean turned back towards him, "I have news for you."

"What?"

"I think she wants to cause *you* pain for dragging me all the way up here at this time of night." They both smiled, Mike waited for Sean to go into the back of the dark coloured transit van and start to pull on the paper outfit.

"Where is Simon?" Sean asked from inside the van.

"Up at the scene with CSI."

"Tell me about the others," Mike looked back down at his notes.

"Ok... Jonathan O Keefe, 17... in fact they're all 17... Ashley Heighton..." Sean climbed out of the van and stood beside Mike.

"What about the survivor?" Mike started to walk away from him and headed towards the pathway, Sean followed. Up ahead in the darkness the bright lights of the crime scene pierced through the trees.

"The survivor? ... Oh yes..." they parted on the path to let another woman, who was dressed in the same white suit as they were wearing pass between them. She was also wearing the mask and small protective visor so only her eyes showed. She was carrying a clear forensic bag in each hand and the weight of each was making her strain. the two of them closed in and carried on up the path.

"Katherine Gillespie ... she is in the Causeway Hospital, but I don't think she will be a lot of use."

"Why not?" Sean asked as they turned at the small junction.

"Because she was so hysterical that they had to sedate her and from what we managed to get from her she was also smacked out of her skull at the time." Mike led Sean off the path and down a pathway that was marked out through the trees by blue and white police cordon tape.

"What have you got from her so far?" Sean asked. Mike swayed his head as his gloved hands adjusted his hood then the paper mask over his face, Sean followed suite.

"Not much, just something about the grass turning blue, something about the clouds then nothing."

"Nothing?"

"Well hysterical screaming,"

"We can interview her tomorrow."

"I have a uniform guarding the room ... her parents arrived about an hour ago and nearly got lifted themselves."

"Why?" Sean asked, as they walked up the rise Sean could make out the shrug of Mike's shoulders.

"They took one look at their daughter and went buck mad ... they tried to pull her out of the bed as they decided that they were taking her home, the hospital staff were glad, for once, that we had people there."

"Understandable I suppose,"

"Right then ..." started Mike as they arrived at the scene, several figures all dressed in white moved around the edge of the area with plastic bags. Sean looked up the top of the hill as the camera flashed again.

"What is up there?" he asked.

"That's where we found body number five," Sean looked over at him, "also where Simon is."

"Ok ... let's go." Mike stood near a tree and started by pointing at the body that lay closest too them.

"Number one: David McGonigle ... 17 ..." he then pointed over at the young male body that was lying facing the dark sky, "body number two: Jonathan O Keefe ... the half-naked girl is a Miss Kerri Ingram and that one over there ..." Mike pointed to the body that was lying over by the tree, "is Ashley Heighton ..." A camera flashed again at the top of the hill. Sean's eyes moved over the bodies of the mangled and in one case headless teenager, they had died very violent deaths, he felt his insides churn at the horror that lay in front of him.

"Who is up there?" he asked. Mike flicked the page of the notebook over before he answered.

"Matthew Boyd ... apparently they all hung around together in school."

"These ID's are confirmed?" Sean studied the scene in front of him.

"Yeah, two of them have driving licences, one provisional licence ... other personal stuff on them ..." Mike paused then turned back towards him.

"Oh!"

"Oh?" exclaimed Sean.

"I nearly forgot … the green BMW down in the car park we believe belonged to them." Sean looked over at him.

"How can a bunch of 17-year olds afford a BMW?" Mike crunched up his face and slightly raised his hands.

"No, no, no, not 'them'… the suspects … the killers," Sean reacted to the good news.

"Fantastic, if it is,"

"Then we have a good forensic clearance 'AND' can place them at the scene of the crime," Sean nodded.

"Something else"

"What?" Sean asked.

"They were here to party, we also have found tins of lager, a bottle of vodka and quantity of ecstasy and it seems, our little friends here were experimenting with Crystal Meth." Several of the heads of the white dressed bodies all looked over at Mike, 'Crystal Meth' was very addictive and very deadly.

"How sure are you?" Sean asked.

"Simon found the small backpack over there," Mike pointed to the far corner, "he first identified what was inside it … Mark from the drug squad is on the case." Sean looked around the scene again as one of the forensic team left with another plastic bag.

"Mark?" asked Sean.

"Mark, dark-haired scruffy fella, from Belfast, you know," Sean thought for a moment then remembered the face of the Detective Constable from the Drug Squad who had given a presentation only a few months before to the rest of his team. Mike carried on with his briefing.

"They will be here to remove the bodies inside the hour," Mike scanned his notes again.

"So, talk me through what happened," stated Sean. Mike walked over to the mounds of earth and flicked back to the opening page of the notebook, Sean followed and listened to what he had to say.

Right, our friends here apparently come up here all the time for their little drink and drug parties and …" Mike paused, he didn't say sex, but Sean knew that was the next thing on the list of the teenagers, "They had been up here for approximately an hour when our two killers arrived over there," Mike pointed to a spot that was just a little down the hill.

"How do you know there were two of them?" enquired Sean.

"Two sets of footprints and two sets of clothes," stated Mike.

"Two sets of clothes?" repeated Sean. Mike glanced over at him as two white clad figures were making their way up the path towards them.

"Yeah, not sure why but they came up to here behind that rise and those trees there …" Sean nodded as Mike spoke.

"Out of sight from anyone on the pathway," he stated.

"Yes," agreed Mike, "and took off all their clothes, we found them lying around that area there."

"Any idea why?"

"Not yet" he paused "I am going to wait to interview the young girl tomorrow and see what she has to say." Sean nodded.

"Something then happened as the two coppers who found them told us that they heard what sounded like clapping and cheering for a few brief moments before prolonged screaming,"

"What?" he exclaimed,

"Yeah, they were down in the car park having a picnic with one of their wives when it kicked off." Sean moved out of the way to let the two figures pass as Mike continued, "I have one of the team getting a full statement from them now."

"Ok, no problems, did they see anything?"

"Not that we know so far, seems when it kicked off they ran up here, found this then phoned Coleraine control room."

"What happened before that?" asked Sean.

"Before," Mike continued, "our two suspects came up here and did this," he turned and opened his hand over the area, "in a very short space of time."

"What about him up there?" Sean pointed up the hill towards the flashing of the camera. Mike's head moved from side to side slightly.

"Well ... judging by the blood trails he was killed down here and dragged up there, so they could have a feast."

"Feast?" asked Sean.

"Oh yeah ... he's half eaten that one," exclaimed one of the white suits.

"Yeah ... real mess." Mike stepped around Sean and started to lead the way towards the taped pathway up the very steep hill, "it makes the Trotman killing seem like a hit and run." Sean briefly closed his eyes, Mike glanced at him before he moved away then a shout came from the pathway behind them.

"INSPECTOR PARRISH," Sean turned and walked back over to where they had been standing. Sean could just about make out the uniformed police officer that was standing at the far end of the taped pathway that led back down to the tarmac path. "INSPECTOR PARRISH," he repeated his shout.

"YES," Sean replied.

"The station commander has arrived and would like a briefing before he speaks to the press, sir." Sean acknowledged him and said he was on his way.

"Have fun," said Mike as a figure came running down the hill out of control. Mike caught the figure to stop him from careering through the crime scene.

"Boss," the two figures briefly fought for balance and composure before Sean recognised the out of breath face of Simon. "Hello boss,"

"Hi Simon ... what is happening up there?"

"Well..." Simon was trying to breathe between his words, Mike held a steadying hand on his right arm for a few seconds until he could stand by himself, "well ... CSI has just finished ... and we are good to go ... we can move the body ... whenever you are ready."

"No problem," answered Sean, "thanks guys," Sean spoke to everyone who was there as he turned and started to make his way down the hill.

"How is he?" asked Simon once Sean was out of earshot.

"If we don't get results soon Super Sutcliffe will go bananas," Simon looked at Mike.

"What about his missus?" Mike shrugged.

"As usual he didn't say ... are you going to take this all back to Belfast?" Mike asked. Simon watched as Sean walked out of the light and fade into the darkness.

"Yeah, got some stuff to sort out tonight as well." Mike turned and walked a few paces back inside the crime scene.

"I'll get the rest of the team to bring the tents up," Simon said, Mike agreed.

"Plus, could you find out if the two coppers who found this have stopped arguing yet."

"Sorry?" Simon asked.

"Yeah, the two who found this were having some sort of argument when the uniforms arrived, Eddie is with them now."

"Who are the two coppers? Local?"

"Yeah," replied Mike "same two that found the bus shelter lot."

"Really?" Simon exclaimed.

"Yeah really," Mike answered Simon quieter than he had been speaking "I was thinking that myself," Mike moved closer so only Simon could hear.

"I will do the check on them but keep this between us."

"Sure, no probs," answered Simon, bringing local police officers into an investigation always had internal police politics and they knew it.

"Plus, there is another reason why I want to do this myself and keep it quiet,"

"Apart from the obvious?" asked Simon.

"Yeah, there section sergeant may not take too nicely when he finds out I have been cross checking his coppers."

"Why would he get upset?" Mike moved further away from the ears of the CSI team.

"Because of who he is and the history between us," Mike lifted his notebook, so it looked like they were discussing something written down there, Simon looked confused.

"Who is his section boss?" Mike straightened up.

"Dave Tattershall," Simon reacted.

"Dave Tatter …. I thought he was up at Maydown M.I.T.?"

"He was. When DI Deswell left he was replaced by a bloke from the Met Police in London,"

"Yeah, I heard that but what's that got to do with him?" Mike looked around then back at Simon.

"Inside a week the two of them were punching each other in the office over the way an investigation was going … ended up with the divisional commander getting involved."

"Dave lost," stated Simon.

"Dave lost and found himself posted back to uniform and guess where he got?" Simon shook his head.

"Coleraine," Mike nodded, they both knew the obvious problems that this could cause.

"What happened between you and his missus was a long time ago," stated Simon.

"Well judging by the look and response I got when we walked past each other in the top corridor the other day I don't think he has forgotten,"

"Ok, what do you need from me?" Simon offered, Mike smiled, this wasn't what he was asking for but was glad of it.

"Could you do all the face to face in the station for me?"

"Of course, I will … consider it done." Mike's left hand gently squeezed Simon's right arm.

"After I get back from Belfast with this lot that is," both men grinned.

"Right let's get back to work."

Chapter 35

Kyle had parked his car in the Long Commons car park in Coleraine and was walking down the street towards the town. He had a few things to get, well that was what he was telling himself. The real reason was, he had only had two hours sleep the night before and being in the house by himself was doing his head in and he wanted to spend some time around people. Kelly had been texting him last night, but she didn't want him to go around as she said that she was working. She had been working a lot recently and he had found it frustrating; she on the other hand did not seem to mind at all. The world slowed for him as more cars passed by on the road, the people around him walked and moved slightly slower. He felt his eyes fix on one person who seemed wrapped up in their own life. Kyle felt himself turn to face the coffee shop and with what seemed like a slap in the face he woke from his numbness and crossed the road. He walked through the single door of Coleraine's best coffee shop. The ground floor was quite busy with people bustling around but it was not as full as Kyle had seen it before. As he joined the end of the queue he became aware of the conversations going on around him. Everyone was talking about what had happened up at Castleroe the night before. Try as he might not to hear what was being said he could not help overhearing several discussions. One couple were saying how awful it was, another couple of women were discussing that drugs had been found and they were drug users and so deserved what had happened to them. The mental pictures of what he had seen last night flashed in his head as the two women remained engrossed in what they were discussing, encouraging and agreeing with each other.

The sudden taste of bile filled the back of his throat, he suddenly wanted to turn and scream at the two of them. He wanted to show them how wrong they were, no one deserved to die like that and most of all it had nothing to do with drugs. Drugs had not killed them, that thing ... that thing that had looked down at him from the top of the hill had destroyed them. Kyle felt his fingers curl into fists as he glanced round the room. He tried to control the rage that was bursting to get out of him and shower the room. The queue moved forward a few steps and from above the counter a young pretty face smiled back at him and with that look he felt the rage subside.

"Morning, what can I get ya?" Kyle had been served by her before and he liked her. She always had a smile on her face, her personality could be described as bubbly, but she wasn't today. Today she was dressed in her usual head to toe black which seemed to be the unofficial uniform in here. Her hair was tied back in a bun and if she was wearing makeup it was not obvious, as he ordered a latte his phone beeped.

"Is that everything?" she asked.

"Yes, yes thank you," he replied, there was a sadness in her eyes that was not normally there, but the face was covered in a pleasant smile. Kyle opened the message which, to his surprise, was from Cara-Marie. 'HI WHAT ARE YOU UP TO THIS MORNING' he replied where he was and that he was about to have a coffee. Cara-Marie replied almost immediately. 'FIRST CLASS, MAY I JOIN YOU?' she was always so polite, this brought a smile to his lips. 'OF COURSE,' Kyle pressed send as the latte he ordered was placed in front of him. Kyle caught the eye of the young woman as she told him how much it would cost.

"May I have a vanilla latte as well please?" he was answered with a smile and an 'of course'. Kyle typed out another text as he waited for the second coffee 'GOT YOU A VANILLA LATTE' Kyle pressed the send button Kyle's phone beeped again with a reply from her, 'OH THANK YOU, I AM ON THE WAY' Kyle did not answer and just deleted the message as the second coffee arrived in front of him. The young woman bid him a pleasant morning and gave Kyle the impression that she meant it. Kyle answered the same then made his way up the single passage staircase at the end of the long room.

The nearly empty room opened to the right at the top of the stairs as the different shades of brown theme continued. The dark brown wooden tables matched the light brown chairs for the first half of the room with light brown leather sofas around dark brown coffee tables in the second half of the room. Windows along the left-hand wall looked out over the junction of Long Commons and Church Street. Small black plastic speakers were fixed at points along the top of the left-hand wall. Quiet easy listening music filled the room with an ambience that was deliberate. At the far end of the room a man was sitting by himself engrossed in the book he was reading and the only other people in the room were two women over by one of the windows. Both the women he guessed were probably mid-forties and both had overdone their makeup. Kyle chose a table on the left side facing the entrance. He got himself comfortable as he waited for Cara-Marie to appear.

Kyle looked at his watch, it was just past eleven in the morning, he wondered if Tony had got the flight, so he reached for his phone and started to tap out a message. 'DID YOU ARRVIE ALRIGHT?' Kyle pressed the send button and watched as the *'message sent'* appeared. Kyle placed the phone down on the table and lifted the mug of coffee. He sipped at the liquid a few times, the smell of it filled his nostrils each time the mug was raised to his face, then Cara-Marie arrived at the open double brown doors. Her face lit up in recognition as she started to walk towards him, he rose from his seat to welcome her.

She was dressed in a pair of flat shoes, blue jeans and the same pale coloured outdoor jacket that she was wearing the last time they met. Her brown leather handbag hung from her right shoulder and she was carrying her notebook in her left hand, her smile filled her face as she extended her right hand that Kyle took in a firm grip, they exchanged smiles.

"Hi'ya," he welcomed.

"Hi," she paused as she shuffled her shoulders and arms to remove her jacket revealing a lime green cotton top. They exchanged pleasantries as she took her seat, Kyle waited for a second to allow her to sit down before he sat down as well.

"So how is life at the Coleraine Herald?" he asked, Cara-Marie shifted in her seat as she placed the notebook down neatly on the table and tasted the coffee as Kyle had spoken, she briefly closed her eyes.

"Mmm," escaped from her unconsciously, he grinned.

"You like the coffee then?"

"Yes, yes, I do," he noticed as her eyes darted around the room and in less than a second, she had made a mental note of everyone in the room, "this place does the nicest coffee in Coleraine."

"Yeah it does, doesn't it?" The two women stood up to leave and adjusted their long coats. The two of them walked out still chatting and still without taking a breath in, her eyes followed them as they left.

"Friends of yours?" he asked, Cara-Marie's eyes shot up and to the back of her head as her mind searched for how to answer the question.

"Friends? ... no, but I do know who they are."

"Anyone of interest?"

"Not to anyone outside the business community, no,"

"So, no real scandal on them then," Kyle's head turned slightly to the right as the workman on the roof of the opposite building came into view.

"Nothing that would interest a police officer, no," she took control of the conversation, just the way she liked it. Kyle noticed that she had not actually answered his earlier question about the newspaper.

"So, what have you been up to lately?" It was his turn to sip from his coffee.

"I asked first," Kyle folded his arms as Cara-Marie lowered her eyebrows at his statement.

"No, you didn't,"

"Yes, I did ... 'how is life at the Coleraine Herald?" he repeated the question, she grinned as she held the mug in front of her face, she liked the way he played.

"Chaos, we have media outlets from all over the world wanting information from us,"

"Really?" Kyle stated.

"Yeah, I just had a newspaper from Hannover, Germany on the phone just before I came out,"

"Wow,"

"Well 'wow' wasn't my first reaction to last night's events," he turned his head slightly and she spotted it, she had control of the conversation back again.

"Yeah, me neither,"

"So," she paused before she pounced, "what were you doing out at Castleroe last night anyway?" Kyle looked up into the staring eyes in front of him, "not one of your usual haunts?"

"Err, no, no it isn't." Kyle watched as the journalist in front of him slowly drank from her coffee and gave him the time to answer, "Ok I was having a picnic."

"A picnic?" she stated as Kyle's phone bleeped with a text message, he lifted the phone and read the message.

"You don't seem the type to take yourself off for a picnic by yourself."

"I wasn't by myself," he replied.

"Who were you with?"

"Tony and Karen," she moved in her seat, "it was Karen's idea as she found the picnic area a few days beforehand."

"And you just went along for the fun of it?"

"Press ganged would actually be a better description," Kyle had started to reply to the message.

"So where is Tony now? It isn't like you two to be separated for any length of time?" Kyle lifted to phone and wiggled it slightly.

"He just arrived in England,"

"England?"

"Yes, England, Leeds/Bradford airport to be precise," Kyle pressed the send button as she drank her coffee.

"And why has he gone to England?" Kyle placed the phone down and considered how much to actually tell her.

"Funeral of a friend of his and to visit two more friends who were seriously hurt." Cara-Marie visibly reacted, was that actual concern in her eyes?

"Oh no," the coffee mug lowered slightly "Who?" Kyle relaxed, this was a friend of Tony's after all.

"A couple of squaddie friends of his in the Paras," the concern was real, Kyle was sure, "Roadside bomb in Helmand, Afghanistan."

"Please pass on my condolences," Kyle nodded once and tapped out the message. "Thank you" she said as *message sent* appeared. A group of five teenagers started up the stairs, the first two carrying trays with an assortment of drinks and food on individual plates. Both their eyes scanned them as they went past. They crowded onto two of the sofas at the far side of the room, the volume of their conversation drowned out everyone else and the only thing they were talking about was how much they knew about each person who had died the night before.

"So, what else has been happening with you?" Kyle asked in an attempt to change the conversation, he was half listening to the conversations of the teenagers at the same time.

"Me? Oh, not much."

"Now that I don't believe," stated Kyle, she smiled.

"Well mum is still trying to get me married off."

"Who to this time?"

"I gave up asking questions like that a long time ago!" they both smiled then both attentions diverted across the room.

"And they had their heads ripped off and they could not recognise any parts of them ..." shocked responses came from the others as the young male embellished his role as storyteller, "Wookie had just got out and Jonty and Matt had got some tabs for them," other questions bounced between them as the injuries got worse and the destruction more intense with each telling.

"Oh my God ... what about Katie?" asked one of the girls.

"Oh, she is still out of her skull in the Causeway." The storyteller was speaking loud enough for the whole room to hear, the waitress from downstairs smiled as she walked past and proceeded to clear one of the tables.

"Is that right?" asked Cara-Marie quietly.

"Is what right?" retorted Kyle.

"The survivor is sedated in the Causeway Hospital," Kyle felt uncomfortable and shifted in the seat, his eyes looked around him as the images flashed in his mind.

"I'm not sure to be honest, she was in a state when we found her,"

"I bet she was ... I hear the family went bananas when they got to the hospital."

"Really," said Kyle "Why?" It was her turn to look around, her voice lowered again.

"The family didn't know she was there, they didn't like who she was hanging around with and wanted to take her home, right then and there." Kyle crunched his face in such a way that it told Cara-Marie that what she said sounded right, she would keep on watching his body language.

"I mean they were all smacked, everybody knew Keri was banging Jonty the whole time that Davie was away," the storyteller moved up onto the arm rest of the sofa and had his back to the wall, he was darkened as the light of the window illuminated the others. Several heads nodded, and other comments passed between them about Keri Ingram and her history with other boys. The comments made Cara-Marie's face churn, Kyle lifted his head slightly and made a noise, he was asking the question of 'what?'

"It has always annoyed me," she explained, her regular volume returned, "that if a boy sleeps with lots of girls then he is a stud," Kyle relaxed back in the chair as she spoke, "but if a girl sleeps with lots of boys then she is a slag, a slut," she was about to say something else, but Kyle got there before her.

"It's an unfair world."

"Yeah, everyone except Matt Boyd," stated one of the girls, she looked past Kyle at the waitress who just stopped what she was doing and glared at the back of the head of the teenage girl who was speaking.

"Katie Gillespie had a big thing for him,"

"Yeah pity he didn't have a 'big thing' at all," the storyteller laughed at his own joke, the others joined in. The look in Cara-Marie's eyes made Kyle look over his shoulder at the young woman who was standing with an empty glass in her hand, her face reddening with anger and tears forming in her eyes.

"I heard that the dickhead never even turned up to any of his final exams, he left school with nothing," another round of laughter made Kyle slowly push his chair back, the waitress was about to explode, and she had a weapon in her hand.

"What a tool," the storyteller never finished his sentence as the glass exploded on the wall beside him, showering him with glass. The girls of the group screamed, and all raised their arms. The screaming waitress was being pulled back by Kyle towards the opposite end of the room.

"*DON'T TALK ABOUT MY BROTHER LIKE THAT... YOU DIDN'T KNOW HIM ... WHO ARE YOU TO TALK LIKE THAT...*" The waitress broke down and gripped the arms of Kyle as she started sobbing. The teenagers had jumped up and moved away from the table, Cara-Marie positioned herself between Kyle and the group of people.

The storyteller had started shouting back at the waitress as other staff members ran up the stairs. The waitress had now completely broken down as the teenagers were thrown out by the rest of the staff after they heard what had been said, the other man that had been there left very quickly. Cara-Marie was sitting beside the weeping girl as another waitress appeared and started to comfort her. The owner was now on the way and the other waitress said they had stopped anyone else from coming up the stairs.

"Rachel, it's ok, Rachel," the second waitress wrapped her friend in a hug as the two arms locked themselves around her in response. Cara-Marie backed away slightly as Rachel started to compose herself. Kyle walked over to the broken glass and started to pick up the larger pieces, this situation could be left to the girls.

"Your name is Rachel?" Cara-Marie asked; a red face with red lined eyes turned and looked at her.

"Yes, Rachel, Rachel Boyd."

"Elder sister of Matthew Boyd," Cara-Marie stated in recognition, a slightly surprised waitress looked back at her.

"Yes, how did you know that?" she identified herself as a reporter for the Herald, both the girls reacted in recognition.

"I know you," stated the other waitress, "I read your stuff in the paper all the time." Cara-Marie kept the conversation going as Kyle slowly walked down the room and headed towards the top of the stairs. A younger man, dressed head to foot in black, arrived at the top of the stairs; he looked over at the three women who were sitting down on the sofa at the far end of the room.

"What happened?" he asked.

"Who are you?" Kyle asked. The young man was employed at the café, Kyle filled him in briefly and said that it was probably best to leave the girls to it.

"Yeah, yeah," he nodded, "I heard about what happened last night, the boss phoned me and said to cover her shift this morning, but she phoned him back and said that she was coming in." Kyle looked over as the three of them stood up and the two-waitresses started making their way towards the stairs., Cara-Marie followed a few steps behind.

"I think you need to get someone to clean that up," Kyle pointed to the remainder of the broken glass.

"Yeah, sure, I'm on it," Kyle watched as he stepped back to let the girls pass then followed them down the stairs.

"Have you finished your coffee?" Kyle asked.

Cara-Marie was surprised by his question with its change of direction away from what had just happened. "No, have you?"

"No, then shall we?" They returned to their seats in the now very empty room.

"So, what actually happened last night?" she asked. Kyle settled and went through the basic details, most of which she would already know, he left out about what had happened between Tony and himself as there were far too many questions that still had to be answered, she started questioning him about what they did, she was trying to get details out of him that she would not get from the press office.

"Hey, I got interrogated last night," he said as he finished his coffee, she smiled back, then she had a thought.

"How long did it take you to find the body up the hill?" Kyle pushed the chair back as he prepared to leave.

"I didn't."

"Didn't what?" her inner journalist reacted to Kyle answer, he was hiding something.

"I didn't find Boyd's body, the Murder in Transit team did," she looked puzzled.

"But you said that the obvious trail led away from the scene?"

"Yes, it did,"

"So, why didn't you?"

"I was with the survivor, I couldn't leave,"

"Tony?"

"Tony went back down to the car park to meet the arriving police," Kyle went to stand as he spoke, "anyway I have to go to Woolworth's to do some shopping."

"Woolworth's?" she raised her voice then smiled, "do you ever actually read my newspaper?" she asked; he took a step away from the table then started to replace the chair he had been sitting on.

"Yeah, why?"

"The entire Woolworth's chain closed throughout the entire UK last week after 99 years of trading ... you never heard of the world financial crisis?" he was taken aback.

"Well ... yeah ... of course, Ok, so I have to shop somewhere else then," Kyle grinned as he started to walk away, Cara-Marie turned towards him.

"You didn't tell me why you didn't go up the hill?" Kyle turned back towards her.

"Yes, I did."

"I mean what did you see that stopped you from ....." she stopped herself as the realisation hit her as she watched the reaction in his eyes. He did not have to say anything, his eyes said it all. "You saw it, didn't you?" Kyle turned and got a step away from her before she landed in front of him. Both her hands gripped the sleeves of his top as she stopped him from leaving. "You've seen it too ... haven't you?" Her voice was quieter, as she loosened her grip and stepped back from him. The tears of relief swelled in her eyes as she stared towards him, he looked down at the ground before he spoke in a whisper.

"I don't know what it was I saw," he lifted his head and looked straight into the relief in her eyes, "but not a word to anyone, clear?" The police officer was back.

"Clear," she stepped back and let the weight rise from her shoulders.

"You haven't told the police what you saw, have you?" she asked, he looked around the empty room then looked back into her eyes.

"I will when I know what it is that looked down the hill at me,"

"I know," she started saying.

"You know what?" he asked.

"I know what looked at you, the same thing looked at me." From his body language he did not want to be there anymore, "It stared at you for a few seconds then turned and ran away, didn't it?" she said. Kyle slightly dipped his head before he replied with a very quiet single word.

"Yes," he looked up and thought she was going to start crying, a look of genuine relief spread across her face as she reached out with her right hand and placed it on his left arm.

"We'll chat again," Kyle nodded then walked past her and left the coffee shop.

Chapter 36

Mike walked into the office in Coleraine. Sean was talking on the phone and the conversation was not going well; he was welcomed with a nod. Mike walked round the other desk and moved the laptop out of the way before he landed on the chair. It was obvious that Sean was trying at least to have a conversation with a very angry Superintendent Sutcliffe. Mike removed the jacket of his suit and hung it over the back of the chair. Sean was being cut short with every sentence he tried to say. Mike could hear the shouting that was coming down the phone. Sean replaced the receiver of the landline telephone back onto the main body receptacle at the end of the conversation. Mike waited for Sean to speak first.

"Apparently, we have a very angry Mayor here in Coleraine," it was more of a statement that a conversation starter,

"Why?" Mike asked.

"Well ... he was on the phone to the DCC and he was put through to the Super ... then it all went downhill from there." Mike watched as Sean's face changed, was that a giggle as he finished the last sentence? The mayor of Coleraine phoning the Deputy Chief Constable of the Police Service to complain then being passed down to Super Sutcliffe. That wouldn't have been a pretty conversation at the best of times. Mike had watched the news the night before and listened to the local politicians going on about how these killings had to be stopped and that the police seemed powerless to stop them. One politician made a call for the Chief Constable to place a more senior detective in charge of the investigation, a call Mike knew that Sean would have been told about. However, from his experience of Super Sutcliffe he knew that the position of 'in charge' was not something the Super would give up easily; at least he was not down here personally overseeing the investigation, which would cause more problems that it would solve. Super Sutcliffe was renowned for being a very hard man to work for. Sean looked over at Mike, "So, what else have we got?" he asked. Sean did not tell Mike the details of the conversation he just had but it was obvious that Sean had just been on the receiving end of a ferocious man demanding results.

"We have confirmed a name," Mike leaned forward as he spoke, "we got it from the details from the green BMW and matched the same name and address down in Belfast from a rented property," Sean's face seemed to light up at the news.

"Brilliant," he said.

"Simon is following it up down in Belfast and hopefully we will have a bigger picture from that info by the close of play today," Mike continued, Sean smiled.

"Do you want some better news?" asked Mike.

"There's more?" Sean answered, Mike nodded.

"The DNA taken from the car is a match for the Trotman murder and the Riverside killings here in Coleraine," Sean closed his right hand into a fist and gentle punched the air as he listened to Mike. "... So, we can place them at all three crime scenes... and ..."

"And?" asked Sean.

"And the BMW was bought right here in Coleraine." A relaxed look spread over Sean's face as Mike continued, "I've got two guys down there at the moment; they have confirmed the girl from the security cameras and are getting copies, so we can see if the same bloke is in that from the address in Belfast." It was some good news at last, the investigation was making progress, all they had to do now was find them.

"What about the Limavady murder?" he asked.

"Nope," Mike shook his head "The DNA recovered from there is different."

"Pity," answered Sean.

"But ..." said Mike, Sean glanced over at the 'but', "the trace there shows the same abnormalities as the others, so we are looking for three killers in total." Mike let the information sink in, Sean of course already knew this, "plus Doctor Burns down at the labs is still having kittens about his wolf theory."

"He has a 'theory'?" Sean asked. Mike looked around before he answered.

"Yeah, he is even more convinced that the people we are looking for are part-dog," Sean coughed into a laugh that Mike joined in on.

"Imagine the press conference ... *'We are looking for Lon Chaney and ask him to give himself up,'*"

Mike crunched his eyebrows. "Who?" he asked.

Sean looked over at him in disbelief. "Lon Chaney? ...the very first person to play the part of the wolf man in the 1941 classic black and white film *'THE WOLF MAN'*?"

"Oh," said Mike "I wasn't born in 1941." The phone rang; Mike answered the it and after a few seconds looked over at Sean. "Hold on please ..." he covered the mouthpiece then held the phone away from his head, "The Mayor of Coleraine ... for you," Mike watched as Sean's shoulders sank; then he nodded as this was a call that he would have to take. Sean reached out and lifted the handset to the phone on his desk. After a brief conversation Sean looked wearily at Mike.

"Get the whole team together down in Belfast from 10 tomorrow morning. I want a full update from everyone, to everyone," Mike nodded and reached into his pocket for his phone. What they had been talking about was all evidence they could use in a court of law and gain vital prosecution; this was good progress; soon they would have an arrest and that would get a few people off their backs.

∞∞∞∞

Paul walked out of the farmhouse and closed the door behind him. He headed for Carl who was standing over by one of the large barns; he stopped just a little behind him.

"Chernov has lost total control of his pack, he was with two of ours when it happened, so we know it wasn't actually him.," Carl did not turn around;, he kept staring out over the field of deer, "Who was with him?" he whispered the question.

"Alan Morrow and his son." Paul waited a few seconds then spoke again, "We believe it was probably Sprogis and Dusmanov,"

"Where are they now?"

"Chernov went back to the two houses and battered two of them ... Alan was outside, however Sprogis has not been seen."

"I want Chernov brought here, tonight." The command was only a whisper, but it stirred the spirit inside Paul; it could mean only one thing and the solution would be final. Carl was still very angry, and Paul knew his Alpha would not allow this to happen again in his lands.

"That is already happening," he stated, Carl slowly turned his head and looked into Paul's face, "Inform the south; and what about the Russians?"

"They have agreed to stay an extra week and I will phone down south right away." Paul turned and walked back towards the farmhouse with the same urgency that he had left it, yet again he was proving his worth. Carl watched the farm door close behind him then he turned back towards the field. He moved his head in a beckoning motion and from over to his right and down the side of the barn Paddy M'Kane stepped forward. Carl kept looking forward as he spoke.

"Paul will be busy for a while, but you will have one job and one job only." Paddy didn't speak, he just continued to look towards Carl although he wasn't directly looking at his face. "Find Sprogis ... and destroy him," Paddy's face did not change as he listened to the instructions.

"Paddy ..." Carl had raised his voice to a command, Paddy looked up and into eyes that burned with anger. "The police are looking for two killers ... make sure they find them." Paddy nodded, "these are *'our'* lands ... not theirs ... and we will defend them." Paddy nodded again and walked behind him and started off towards one of the parked cars.

"Paddy," Carl called after him. Paddy stopped in his tracks and turned to face him, "No guns."

"No guns," Paddy repeated; nodding as he did so, "the old-fashioned way," Paddy stated,

179

"The *'proper'* way," corrected Carl, "the way we have done for centuries." A massive smile burst over Paddy's face as the realization of the task he was being given sunk in. Carl motioned with his head towards the parked car and a very excited Garou bounded over towards the car. Paul walked out of the farmhouse and headed towards Carl.

"He is up to the task," stated Carl as he turned back towards the field.

"Yes, it is time for him."

"What about the order for Brazil?" The change in conversation made Paul pause as Carl went back to running a business.

"No problems we can fulfil their needs, however they have said that they will only pay the remainder of the bill after they have received the stock," Carl started to nod.

"That isn't a problem," Paul thought for a second that he was about to say something else. "What about the order for Scotland?" There was something else bothering him, that much was obvious, but Paul would wait until he brought the subject up before he would go into it more.

"Scotland? ... Yes ..." Paul followed Carl as he walked down the side of the large barn. What had happened in Coleraine would be dealt with, finally.

∞∞∞

"The police are looking for the same people who carried out the Riverside murder for Castleroe as well," Cara-Marie was out of breath as she arrived in Kevin's office, he stopped what he was doing and looked up at her. To his right the very pregnant woman in charge of advertising stared at Cara-Marie, the A4 sheet of paper in her left hand hung motionless in the air.

"Thank you," he said as he took it. The woman left the office without saying another word, "Come in, please sit," he motioned with his hand towards the chair that was sitting opposite his desk. The door of the office was closed as he lifted the handset for the phone and pressed a button that would divert any calls to the front desk.

"So, what have you got?" he asked, she was sitting upright, and her hands spoke as much as her voice did.

"A witness,"

"And what did they witness?"

"They saw what I saw," her statement had an obvious reaction with him, "they saw the animal," confidence poured from her; vindication at last.

"Who is the witness?"

"One of the policemen, Kyle Foster."

"Foster? The same one you were having a Chinese with the night of the Riverside murders?"

"Yes,"

"And he is prepared to say all this and put his name to it publicly?" she paused at the question, "I didn't think so," he continued. She felt her elation fall as she let the words sink in, Kevin relaxed back into his chair, he extended his left arm.

"Cara ..." she bit her lip and wished that he would not shorten her name; it was really starting to get to her, "we have got one of the biggest stories ever to happen in Coleraine and I need you to focus."

"I am focused."

"Try focusing on your job."

"I am focusing on my job," Kevin sighed after she had spoken, "What?" she asked, he shifted in his seat and looked around the office before looking back at her.

"No Cara, you're not." The comment hit her like a brick, never had her work been called into question.

"Excuse me?" her voice was irritated, he seemed uncomfortable, which was unusual for him.

"You are only concentrating on what you think you saw that night." She felt her own mouth slightly open in shock at what was being said, "not long ago you were sitting there, in this office telling me you saw werewolves running around Coleraine and I need you to be focused on reporting the news not writing science fiction stories." She felt the anger in her soul rise and her eyebrows lower as his face turned into a scowl, "I want good unbiased reporting from you, that's all I want of any of my staff," he paused as he could see the obvious reaction in her happening right in front of him. "Look the international press is descending on us and I want this newspaper to be a source of good, accurate reporting, not something that will totally discredit us for years to come." So that was it, he was just protecting himself; she felt her fingers tighten into fists as he continued. "Now can you tell me anything about this whole mess that we can seriously report as a legitimate news story?" He let the question hang in the air. Was he preparing to send her home and away from her job? She was not sure, but she kept her movements slow and deliberate as she reached into her clutch bag and lifted out her notebook. She started to read from her notes as she fought to control the rage that was bursting inside her.

"Well … the police have recovered a green BMW from the scene that has DNA traces of the suspects from the Castleroe murders … it is the same as the Riverside murders … so they can tie the two of them together," she looked up as she continued "and the car was bought here in Coleraine … the police have got a name of a Polish national from the registration details of the BMW," his face started to drop, "they are looking for an '*ALEXI CHERNOV*' and they plan to release a photograph of him at a press conference scheduled tomorrow at 3pm." Cara-Marie wanted to scream this at him, how dare he accuse her like that, who did he really think he was? "and the forensic labs are looking at some sort of scientific breakthrough which they may be going public with later in the month." She slowly closed her notebook, "Now," she said as she stood, "if you don't mind I have got some more journalism to focus on." Cara-Marie slowly turned, opened the door and walked back over to her desk, the rage inside her screaming to go back and tear him apart but she kept her self-control. Kevin did not move in his office. He would have preferred a screaming match as he could win them, but against this there was no defence, he was wrong, but it would be a long time before he ever admitted it.

The screen on her desktop came to life and in seconds she was typing out an email including all the details she had just given to Kevin. She copied it to the rest of the reporting staff and then added the information about the survivor that was still in the Causeway Hospital. At the bottom of the email she listed the names and dates of birth of the young teenagers who had been killed and asked one of the other journalists to follow up on two of them and stated she would do the other three. She made a footnote to the photographer that he would need to come with her for the house visits which would begin after lunch time, then as she added her signature block; then she clicked the send button. The email was addressed to everyone and everyone would know that this was Cara-Marie virtually slapping Kevin in the face and doing it professionally.

"You are so cute when you are angry."

"What?" her head snapped to the right as Mark fiddled with his camera,

"You are so cute when you are angry," he repeated, she shifted in her seat, glanced at the desktop screen then back at the smiling snapper.

"I'm not angry," she stated.

"Really?" Mark was almost laughing as he answered her. His right hand reached out and moved the mouse on the desk, she glanced over at the changing expressions as he read the email, "you even 'write' angry."

"I do not."

"You do so."

"Not."

"So,"

"Not,"

"So…" as he tried to answer a journalist's notebook hit him in the face. He yelped as he tried to keep a hold of his camera and fight off the notebook and keep some composure all at the same time. The outburst made the rest of the staff look round at him as they were all reading the email as well.

"I believe that is 'assault,'" he spun round in his chair as he raised the notebook up to throw it back. She was sitting with her fingers posed over the keyboard, her head turned, her face gave him a *'don't even think about it look.'* Mark paused and thought about his actions for a second them flicked the notebook over onto a space on the side of her desk.

"Anyway," continued Mark, "It's time for lunch." Cara-Marie's eyes shot up to the clock on the wall, it was nearly half past 12.

"Lunch isn't for another half an hour?" She stated.

"I'm paying," he answered. Her eyes glanced over at the smiling face as his shoulders lifted in a shrug, "It's my turn ... plus I owe you."

"Yes, you do," she conceded. "Won't your other half mind?" he caught her question as he spun out of his chair.

"What?" he asked as he was reaching for his jacket hanging over the back of the chair.

"Rachel? Your other half. You know the one who doesn't like me very much." Mark stopped as his eyes darted up and to the left as he searched for an answer.

"Ah ... yes she does like you," as she reached for her own jacket, she answered him.

"No, she doesn't."

"What makes you think that?" he asked.

"I am a girl ... you may have noticed."

"I had, mostly, yes."

"Well, we girls are very good at letting each other know when to back off and stay away from their territory."

"Territory?" he even looked confused as he said it, "she doesn't do that," he continued as he pulled the jacket over his shoulders.

"She is a girl; yes, she does"

"No, she doesn't..." and the notebook hit him again.

"I am a girl. I am right." As she turned towards the door she looked back over her right shoulder at the flustered snapper and finished her sentence, "... and the sooner all you men realise this fact, the better."

Chapter 37

Anders walked through the shoppers as they moved back and forth across Church Street. His eyes flicked over every face, seeing all but registering none, his mind was elsewhere. The windows of the Woolworth's store had been whitewashed as the insides of the shop were now empty. He had never actually seen Alexi as angry as he was last night. Viktor had initially stood up to him but the beating that Alexi had poured on him had been something else, then Pet'er had tried to break them up and Alexi turned on him. Thankfully Yelina had stayed out of it all. Suddenly he jumped into the open doorway of a shop to hide. He watched the people going by and started to grin as the two young men who had been following him walked past, they had yet to notice that they had lost him. He kept his eyes on the back of their heads as they walked on up the street. He stepped back out into the street and darted off in the opposite direction, away from his followers. He glanced at the watch on his wrist, he was three minutes late and that was not good. He quickened his pace as he flew past the War Memorial then past the local banks on his right. A small group of teenagers were huddled together nearby, and the only topic of conversation was what had happened over at Castleroe.

"Yeah and that they were torn apart by two massive dogs..." Anders eyes flicked back at the teenagers as their conversation continued.

"I heard that it was a bloke with an axe and that big Davie owed money and he couldn't pay," Anders dismissed the gossip and pushed his hands into the pockets of his jacket as he quickened his pace. The grey metal railings surrounded the two-storey building that housed the local library to his left; he paused as the crossing in front of him started beeping as it held the rush of busy traffic flowing from the old bridge and around the town; he broke into a dash to get over the road before the traffic started again, he made it, just. The phone in his pocket bleeped with a text message, he stopped where he was.

'WHERE ARE YOU?' He paused then replied, 'I WILL BE THERE IN TWO MINUTES.' He sent the message then carried on. The pavement split into two and was separated by a hedge that blocked out the view of the traffic from the busy road. Anders glanced across the road into the BMW showroom as a tall salesman in a clean pressed suit walked past one of the sports cars with a young couple in tow. Something attracted his attention off to his left. His eyes looked past the black painted metal wire fence that ran along the edge of a small football pitch. The white painted goal posts stood at either end, both stood without their nets. People were standing at the two bus stops on the opposite side of the hedge, a couple were arguing but they were out of sight, however their stench reached him, unwashed flesh. These people had no self-respect.

Again, his eyes darted over to the far side of the small football pitch, there was something in or near the wall that separated the small field from the scrap metal yard that lay to the far side of the wall. Along the wall stood several trees but no bushes so there was nowhere to hide however something was there and whatever it was, it was watching him, and he liked that even less. His pace quickened up the empty path, the feeling that he was being watched grew stronger and it was definitely coming from the far side of the bushes. He carried on as there wasn't much he could do about it anyway. Finally, he reached the entrance to the garden. The entrance itself had flower beds on each side of the short red brick wall which formed the natural barrier between the pavement and the park. Either side of the entrance stood two brick posts just over six feet in height which housed the mounts for the two black metal gate posts. On the right-hand side of the entrance, 'Anderson Park' was mounted on the wall in large metal letters. The pathway that he was now on was about ten feet wide and turned right towards the fountain located in the centre of the small park.

Leading to the fountain the pathway was covered by two metal archways that were painted the same black as the gates, the fountain was comprised of hexagonal blocks that rose up to a metal bowl with a large black painted metal bird of prey rising up out of it. He stopped and looked around, first at the traffic on the road, then over the small car park that was at the far side of the fountain then over at the trees. He could no longer sense whatever had been there, whatever it was, it had retreated.

"You're late." Anders spun round to see Davidov standing only a few feet away. "And you shouldn't let anyone get this close to you," Davidov had his hands in his pockets and glanced from side to side as he spoke.

"I was being followed by two Rua," Anders said.

"You got rid of them?" enquired Davidov.

"Yes," he answered as Davidov relaxed, "Of course I did." A silence hung in the air for a few seconds before Anders spoke again. "The Rua are all over us now," Davidov glanced over his shoulder at something behind him, "Alexi is losing his head over this," Anders paused, "he knows about you and Anna now."

"Well it's a bit obvious, now isn't it?" Davidov turned and sat down on the main monument, facing towards town.

"Alexi wants to know where you and Anna both are."

"I bet he does," Anders noticed movement in the small car park and spotted Anna walking around a three-door hatchback car.

"He wants your head," Anders stated, Davidov glanced over at him them looked away.

"What happened at the house?" Davidov asked.

"Two Rua were with him when we heard about what you had done," Davidov didn't move as Anders continued speaking, "he came flying into the house and Viktor said the wrong answer," Davidov nodded his head a few times but did not interrupt him. "Then Pe'ter tried to break it up . . ."

"Wrong move on Pe'ter's part," Davidov answered, Anders nodded.

"It was, Alexi nearly killed the two of them, and Yelina was standing by the kitchen door and didn't do anything."

"What about the Rua?" Davidov asked.

"Well they know that it was you at Castleroe," he stated.

"What are they doing about it?"

"Alexi has said that he will bring you to them,"

"Really?" exclaimed Davidov.

"Yeah," answered Anders, "he has the rest out looking for you now," Davidov thought for a moment.

"Ok, tell him I am down by the Mountsandel fort, you followed me there, but I did not see you," Anders nodded at the instructions, "it's time to do things 'our' way." Davidov looked over his shoulder towards Anna.

"Can you tell me what actually happened last night?" asked Anders,

"Simple really, we went to the woods and these teenagers appeared and started clapping and cheering when they found us naked," Anders did not have to ask what they went to the forest to do. "So, we changed and dealt with them," Davidov paused then looked over at him, "Good fun really."

"Others didn't think so," Anders stated, Davidov just shrugged.

"So?"

"We hear the police have found the car and some of your clothes," Anders kept looking straight ahead as he spoke. Davidov shifted where he was sitting.

"I went down to collect Anna's backpack and things she had, we got that, most of my clothes but I had to leave quite a bit of it when these two policemen appeared," Davidov seemed a little annoyed at that bit.

"Which is how I could phone you."

"Where are you staying?" Anders asked, Davidov stood up and turned towards Anna.

"I will tell you tomorrow, if he asks you, you can give the honest answer that you do not know," Anders smiled. The plan seemed a good one, "remember, tell him where you followed me to."

"Right," said Anders. Davidov started to walk away then turned back towards him.

"We will make this land our own," he stated. Anders smiled back. Anna lifted her head in acknowledgement towards Anders as Davidov turned away from him and headed off towards the smiling beautiful woman who was leaning over the cheap car.

"Where did you get the car?" he asked after him,

"Stole it, you don't think I actually paid money for it, do you?" Anders turned away and started to walk back towards the town. He stopped by the entrance to watch the small car turn left then out of the car park heading away from Coleraine. Things were going well, and he was excited about the future. This was the first time he had felt like that in a long time. He turned away and walked into town to find the two Rua who had been following him earlier. He could lead them back to the house and tell Alexi what he had found.

∞∞∞

It was eleven o'clock when the briefing started, there had been a hold up with some of the pictures from Coleraine, but they were ready now. Sean walked over and took his place at the side of the room; a nod and Mike started the briefing. Mike let each detective give an update on the investigations they were carrying out. Most had turned out to be dead ends, but some added more to the investigation and could be used in court. The green BMW had caused the most interest and had provided the best evidence so far for the whole investigation.

"Right," started Mike after the last detective finished, "a few things we are going public with at our 3pm press conference this afternoon," he turned towards the pictures that he had put up earlier. "This is a mister '*ALEXI CHERNOV*' who we believe to be in the Coleraine area and is officially 'wanted in connection,' to the murders in Belfast and Coleraine." Comments rippled around the room. Mike continued, "So with this we should expect an arrest pretty quickly."

"What nationality is he?" asked Eddie, another who was sitting near Sean spoke up.

"I interviewed the pensioner who lived next door to them in Belfast who said Eastern European," another spoke as well.

"The salesman in the BMW garage said he asked where they were from and they said Poland," Another ripple went around the room.

"Right," stated Sean, "Mike, while you and I are doing the press conference I would like that followed up." Eddie spoke up again.

"I have already spoken to a representative of the Polish community in the North West and I have her number, so I can take that on." he offered.

"Good." Sean looked back towards Mike who carried on with the briefing.
"We now can place the same DNA at the scene of the Belfast and Coleraine riverside murders and a similar DNA that would point towards a family member or close relative to be involved with all three."

"Do we have an address?" asked another,

"The address from the BMW garage was false,"

"What about the Castleroe killings?" one of them asked.

"We don't have a 100% answer back from the labs yet, but we are heading back down there this morning." this made Sean look up.

"Are we?" he asked, Mike smiled as he looked over at him.

"Yes Boss, check your email itinerary." A small laugh rippled around the room as Sean looked round with a fake look of discontent.

"Any final questions?" Mike asked the room, heads were shaken in reply as Sean stood up for the final word.

"Right then, I want all of you to have a copy of the picture from the CCTV from the car showroom that we are handing to the press and I want you all to be fully familiar with it; anything that comes your way pass straight to either Mike or Simon," he paused for a second as heads started nodding in reply, "Ok, the survivor who is still in the Causeway Hospital is being interviewed today? Yes?" Mike answered him,

185

"Yes, after the press conference I am heading up to do it and I am taking Eddie with me." Sean nodded.

"Are you?" exclaimed a surprised detective.

"Yes, I am then you can meet this Polish person face to face," Eddie was about to say something but decided against it.

"One last thing." Sean announced. Mike looked at Sean as it was his turn to not know what was coming next. "Something that you all will keep totally to yourselves is a piece of evidence that has come to us from a lab in England." Mike looked around the room at the faces looking back at the two of them and Sean motioned to the team members on his left. "If all of you would drop the blinds on the door and windows as I don't want anyone outside this room to see or hear anything about this." a ripple of excitement bounced around the team as the door and windows were closed.

Sean whispered to Mike, "Get the cast from my office." Mike walked towards Sean's office. "I want to stress the importance of this piece of evidence and that its existence does not leave the room." This got the team sharing glances and whispered comments, "I do not want any of you talking about this outside of this room; am I making myself clear?" Sean was answered with a flow of nods and 'yes boss' as Mike appeared in the doorway of his office. "This is not to be even talked about over phones, either in spoken words or text messages, which goes for emails too." More excited glances passed between the team who were now eager to find out what this was. "If anyone, and I do mean *'anyone'*, compromises this your career in the police *'will'* be over." Mike looked up; Sean had just made the ultimate threat. In the 15 years that he had worked for him he had never heard it before. Sean was taking this one very seriously. "Mike?" Sean motioned to Mike to walk towards him; every eye looked at the plain cardboard box that he placed on a small table at the rear of the room. "Right, gather round." said Sean and the excited police officers clambered around their desks and chairs to see what Mike had. Mike slowly opened the box and removed some cotton wool to reveal the white plaster cast of a set of non-human teeth. The team reacted with surprise as the cast was lifted out of the box and was passed around the detectives.

"What is it?" one of the team asked.

"That," Sean started, "is a cast from a dental pathologist in England who has made this model to show us the shape of the mouth and teeth of whatever killed Trotman in Belfast." The comments flowed between the younger men as Sean listened to what they were saying to each other. Each one of them took turns in lifting the two parts and opening and closing them in a biting motion, A stern-faced Eddie turned and looked at Sean and Mike.

"So, what exactly are we dealing with here?"

"We have at least three murderers on the loose and it is our job to stop them." Mike noticed Sean had not actually answered Eddie's question. Eddie had picked up on it as well.

"Alright, grab your seats everybody," stated Mike and slowly they all returned to where they had been sitting, Sean waited for them to sit down before he continued.

"Exactly how they are doing it, I, for one, am not certain but," Sean paused, "we've let a Vet look at these and he could not identify which breed of dog it is in the attacks." Mike nodded.

"Well we will just have to ask Mr Chernov when we get him what he has been up to then," stated Eddie.

"That we will Eddie, that we will," answered Sean.

"Right you all have your jobs allocated to you; let's crack on," ordered Mike and with that the room came alive with movement. Sean walked over to where he had left his coffee and took a sip as Mike walked past Sean stopped him.

"What time are we down with the mad professor?" he asked. Mike looked at his watch.

"In 20 minutes." Mike spotted Sean rolling his eyes. "So, you better get a move on."

Chapter 38

Paul walked into the farmhouse and closed the door. The small fire had been lit and was gently burning, Carl was sitting in the main chair with his laptop in front of him, tapping away. Carl looked up and nodded for him to sit down, which he did without interrupting him as his fingers furiously typed. Paul was sitting in silence and looked around the room; the only sound was the occasional crackling from the fire and the continual tapping of the keyboard. Carl kept his eyes fixed on the screen as he spoke.

"I see we have received the payment from Scotland," he stated.

"Yes," answered Paul, "they have paid for the entire order in advance."

"Pity the South Americans could not be so precise," Paul smiled,

"Yeah, that would be a plus. Have you read the email from Tony?" Carl stopped what he was doing and looked up at him.

"Yes," he replied, then started typing again. Paul paused as Carl had obviously already decided. Carl stopped typing then closed the laptop. He leaned back into the chair and looked over at Paul, "Ask Tony to come around tonight so we can chat about the other police officer." Paul looked over at him, questioningly,

"What?" asked Carl.

"That will be a problem," Paul answered.

"Why?"

"He is over in England for a couple of days at least," Carl's face questioned the remark as Paul explained, "He is over for the funeral of one of his friends who was killed in Afghanistan last week,"

"Of course, yes, I remember..." he glanced around the room, "Ok when he gets back, I would like to know more about the other police officer before Tony tells him anything." Paul nodded, "It's already done, he is coming up here tomorrow night, straight from the airport before going home." Carl nodded in satisfaction at Paul who smiled back at him. The phone in Paul's pocket suddenly burst into life, he stood and headed towards the door as he answered it stopping at the door with his left hand on the handle as he just repeated, "Yes" and "Ok". He turned back towards Carl who was again working on the laptop.

"No problem, thank you Alan."

Carl stopped typing and looked up. "What?"

"They have found Sprogis," Carl's face lit up as Paul continued, "apparently he is at Mountsandel and Chernov has already left to deal with him,"

"Then?" asked Carl.

"Then they'll bring the body here; he has asked Alan and his son to stay back and allow his pack to handle this.," Carl nodded twice.

"Yes, happy with that,"

"Alan will bring him here once Sprogis has been dealt with."

"What about Dusmanov?" Carl asked.

"He didn't mention him," he answered with a shake of his head. Carl placed the laptop on the coffee table then stood up.

"Right pass all this onto Paddy and keep the surveillance on the others. I want to know where they all are at all times." Paul nodded then stepped back as Carl walked towards the door, "Any obvious problems then they are to deal with it on the spot," Carl stopped just before he opened the door.

"I have had enough of this lot." Carl opened the door and stepped outside only to be met by two excited Irish wolfhounds who were bouncing around him. Carl started playing with them a little before he looked back at Paul.

"I want it dealt with and over with." Paul nodded as Carl continued speaking, "Finally, once and for all."

"I agree." Paul answered as another male walked around the corner of the building and brought the two dogs to heel.

"Tell the Russians as well." Carl ruffled the hair on the top of the head of one of the dogs, "So, are you two lovelies hungry?" Carl was smiling as the two dogs became excited once more, "Let's go," Carl would spend at least the next half an hour with the dogs and their handler, playing mostly before they would be fed, but it was time that he would enjoy as there were preparations to make before this evening.

∞∞∞∞

Cara-Marie was typing at her desk; she was trying to concentrate on the story in front of her, but her mind kept wandering.

"What do you think of the front page?" asked Mark. The distraction of his conversation was almost welcoming.

"Well it is definitely one for the archives," she replied. Mark lifted the freshly delivered newspaper, the front page was covered with just one word, *'MASSACRE'.*

"Any idea what the others are doing?" he asked.

"Yeah," she replied, she reduced the page she was working on and enlarged the web page of the other newspaper; their front page was similar, *'SLAUGHTER'*

"Catchy," Mark had wheeled himself over beside her as he read the headlines, "but we have better pictures."

"Of course, we have; we are the better newspaper!" she pointed out.

"Pity we don't have their budget," answered Mark as he pushed himself back towards his own desk; she glanced over at him again then enlarged the story she was working on.

"Well if it is a bigger budget you want," she paused as a loud bleeping noise started coming from one of his cameras, "just ask the editor." Mark stopped what he was doing and let out a small laugh, "I am sure he will listen to your every request," the sarcasm in her voice was very evident.

"Yeah, I'm sure he will," Mark's attention returned to the camera that was in his hands, "and I will get to date Britain's Next Top Model," she smiled as she looked back at her screen.

"Are you looking forward to becoming a daddy?" The question totally caught him off guard, the fact that his girlfriend was pregnant had not even been mentioned in weeks.

"Yeah, yeah, I'm really looking forward to it," she stopped typing and looked directly at him.

"You could at least try to sound convincing." He smiled in reply then became engrossed in the camera, she let the comment hang then went back to her desktop, as she saved her work Mark spoke again. "The ex was at the door last night," he quietly said, she stopped what she was doing and turned towards him.

"How was she?" she asked. Mark looked up then dropped the camera onto his desk.

"Hysterical ... crying ... all the things you girls are great at that us boys hate," she watched as his face fell as he was talking, this was hurting him.

"Why did you two split?" she was speaking quieter than before, ensuring that only he heard the question.

"I didn't want a family," he answered; her eyebrows raised.

"But you are starting one with someone else?" The guilt over-took him as he shifted uncomfortably in his seat.

"Well, it wasn't exactly planned you know," he breathed heavily, "Rachel wants to get married before the child is born,"

"So, what are you going to do?"

"Avoid her parents,"

"Why?" Mark stopped and turned towards her.

"Her father has only three words for me,"

"Which are?" she asked.

"Murder, death, kill," he managed a smile that she shared with him. "I got their daughter up the duff before I had met them *and* outside of a marriage. I'm not top of the popularity stakes," he turned back towards his own desk. "You missed the excitement in here this morning," she turned her head, something had happened that she had missed?

"What?" she enquired.

"Ex's mum appeared at the back door about two minutes after you left this morning," again Mark's face fell.

"What happened?"

"Loads of tears and pleading to go back to my ex, etc," Cara-Marie's mouth opened slightly as he continued. "*I am the one for her daughter...she already looked on me as a son in law, etc.*"

"So, what happened?" she asked as she was now wondering why he had not told her this over lunch; a depressed Mark looked over at her,

"It took Kevin to throw her out,"

"That could not have been nice," she said, her phone that was sitting on the desk in front of her burst into life, she glanced at Mark as she reached for it, he nodded, this conversation would have to wait. She looked at the screen, it was a withheld number, she answered it with a simple 'hello'.

"Oh yes, hiya ..." she said in recognition, Mark looked over at her as her conversation went down to one-word answers, this may not have been a conversation for him to hear. He lifted his mug and indicated that he was going to make an instant coffee, she nodded and mouthed a 'thank you', as he rose from the chair her conversation got intense.

"Really?" she exclaimed, "When?" Mark was walking towards the kettle with two mugs in his hands, "brilliant, could you send that to me?" He lifted the kettle and started to fill it from the tap, "oh, ok, yes that makes sense," that was a no, and she had just got one. "That is fantastic," she paused again, "thank you '*very much,*'" she said her goodbyes as the kettle started to boil, he looked over at an excited journalist.

"Good news?" he asked.

"Yes, very good news indeed," Mark noticed that she did not expand on what the good news was and there was only one subject that she no longer spoke to him about these days, her phone went off again and this time she ran out the door to answer it. He sipped his coffee as he watched her through the glass then his own desk top bleeped with the arrival of an email. It was from the editor; the police would be releasing the following photograph of the main suspect in the killing at a press conference in an hour's time, the photo of Alexi Chernov was attached. Mark clicked on the attachment and the CCTV frame came into view. The picture was taken at the entrance to a car showroom and the man in the middle of the picture looked to be in his late forties and he had a young girl with jet-black hair beside him. Mark recognised her from the other pictures the police had released. He was marked as 'dangerous' and the public 'should not approach,' now they had a name and it would not be long before he was found.

Mark's phoned beeped with a text message, it was from Rachel, his pregnant other half. 'COME HOME NOW, WE NEED TO TALK'. Mark was taken aback by the text, he read it again before he answered. 'I AM AT WORK, I CANNOT JUST LEAVE. I WILL BE HOME JUST AFTER FIVE'. Rachel would not like his answer. Cara-Marie came bounding back into the office so Mark told her about the email from the editor.

"Really? At last," she said as she landed in her chair and opened the email. As she was reading the email Mark looked at his phone. Rachel didn't answer straight away, and would no doubt be at the very least, annoyed that he didn't just drop everything and hurry home. She printed off the picture of Chernov and as she was looking at it she asked Mark the obvious question.

"Where was this taken?" Mark was swaying gentle from side to side in his chair.

"Well let's see," he started, "there are BMW cars in the background, there is a BMW sign by the door, the salesman I know actually works for BMW at the showroom here in Coleraine," this time he was able to catch the notebook that was thrown at him, as he threw it back his phone beeped again, "Some journalist you are!" She shot him a quick smile before she returned to studying the picture. Mark lifted his phone to read the text message. It was from Rachel, 'WHAT WERE YOU DOING HAVING LUNCH WITH HER? I WANT TO KNOW NOW.' This was going to take a long time.

∞∞∞∞

Simon walked into the small room where Sean and Mike were sitting; he was holding a large file full of papers.

"Right the briefing is all set. I have copies of the picture of Chernov that will be distributed to the journalists before we go live," Simon dropped the file on the wooden table in the centre of the room. Sean and Mike were sitting facing each other. Sean nodded as Simon was speaking; Simon did not notice how quiet the other two were being, "We have quite a group this time." he stated.

"Really?" said Mike, "Who?"

"International, we have reps from all the daily papers from here, from down south, England, France, one from Germany and we think one from the US as well." Simon seemed quite excited, "And we have the family of Michael Watson from Limavady who are going to appeal to Chernov to give himself up."

"Where are they?" Sean asked.

"Two rooms down; I have been with them for the last two hours going over the briefing and the kind of questions that they may be asked by the Press."

"Are they ready?" Sean asked.

"Yes," Simon relaxed back into the chair, "I am going to escort them after the briefing and make myself present at any interviews they give one on one with the press. After that I'll ensure they are sorted for the journey back to Limavady tonight." Simon now noticed the tension in the room, "Ok, what?" he asked.

"What? What?" shrugged Mike.

"What is up with you two?" Simon remembered where they had just been. "How did the meeting with Dr Burns go?" his question had the required response, both men shuffled in their seats and Mike started a long line of how deranged the doctor was, "So, what was said?" Simon asked.

"Ok, the good Doctor has a theory," Sean started.

"That we are looking for someone who somehow has canine DNA mixed in with his own, yes I know that," injected Simon, Mike leaned forward, Sean lifted his hand to stop him.

"No, it's a bit more than that," Sean said.

"Go on then, don't keep me in suspense,"

"Well ... apparently we are looking for at least three 'things' that may have the ability to actually change their shape."

Simon recoiled. "What?"

"Dr Burns brought another scientist over from England and they went through all our stuff and they are getting ready to publish a paper on the existence of 'shape shifters,'" Simon's mouth dropped, "he has confirmed that the DNA from all the crime scenes is the same,"

"Except Limavady," said Mike.

"Except Limavady, but the entire collected DNA evidence in this case had active *memory cells*." Sean continued, "He went off on a tangent about new species being classified all the time."

"Apparently underwater biologists have recently discovered over 5000 new creatures in the last year alone." Mike looked back and forth between Sean and Simon as he spoke.

He then told us a story about tales of strange black and white creatures in China at the turn of the last century, we now know these as Pandas but at the time, until they were classified they

190

remained just tales of explorers." Sean did not sound convinced by what he had been told less than an hour before.

So ... we are looking for a Panda?" asked Simon.

"No ... no we're not," answered Sean.

"So, what does he think we are looking for then?" Simon asked.

"*A previously undiscovered part of human evolution,*" quoted Mike.

"Can someone talk to me in English please?" retorted Simon.

"Dr Burns thinks we have stumbled upon a previously unclassified DNA strain that would enable a person to be able to change some or even all of their own appearance." Sean seemed less convinced than before, Mike looked sheepish and Simon was more confused than before.

"Ok," Simon started, "What exactly are we dealing with?" he asked. Mike looked straight at Sean who turned to look Simon in the eye.

"We have stopped Dr Burns from going public with this and this information is only between the three of us," Sean's face wore a stern look. Simon nodded. "Our official line is that we are looking for three people who've been using dogs to attack people that will of course, continue."

"I agree," answered Simon, "but that isn't what they think is it?"

"No," replied Sean, both Sean and Mike weren't too happy about what was coming, "it isn't." Sean took a deep breath and said something he never dreamt he would ever say.

We may be dealing with a werewolf," Mike didn't move but Simon jumped out of the chair and stepped back towards the door.

"Excuse me?" his obvious shock did not surprise Sean, silence held the air for several seconds as the information sunk in.

"That is why we are keeping this 'theory' of his under wraps, if this gets out..."

"Whoa..." Simon stopped Sean as he was speaking, "are you actually entertaining this idea? I mean really? Werewolves?" Mike shrugged.

"No Simon, we are not," stated Sean, "we are investigating several brutal murders and we will continue to do so," a very shocked Simon retook his seat, "which is why we cannot have this theory of Dr Burns compromise our investigation," as Sean continued Simon relaxed a little bit more. "I don't want this getting into anyone else's hands, I don't want the two of you even talking about this between yourselves where you may be overheard." Both of them nodded.

"Yeah, of course," Simon said quietly.

"Do not discuss this over a phone, or put anything into an email that could be retrieved later," Simon looked at Sean, this was serious, but it made sense, "I do not want any of us held up to public ridicule for even thinking this, ok?"

"Ok," they both agreed.

"We will let Dr Burns indulge his fantasies 'after' we have our convictions." This relaxed Simon a bit, Mike was still not himself, "Right," said Sean, "what's happening after the briefing?",

Mike spoke first. "I am going to the Causeway hospital and taking Eddie with me to interview the survivor then liaise with the uniforms in Coleraine and follow up any sightings of Chernov,"

Sean nodded. "Good, that's good."

"I will be with Watson's family sorting them out," answered Simon.

"First class," said Sean, then there was a knock at the door.

"Come," shouted Sean and the door opened and a young police officer in a dark suit half stepped into the room.

"Inspector Parrish?" he asked.

"Yes?" answered Sean.

"Superintendent Sutcliffe has asked me to inform you that things will be getting under way in ten minutes and he would like another word with you beforehand."

"Ok, we are on our way," as they all stood up Sean placed a hand on each of their shoulders, "and we will meet up in the office in Coleraine at ten tomorrow morning."

Chapter 39

Kyle was walking across the old bridge in Coleraine heading back into town. He was on foot patrol with Alison. Alison had been in the job a long time and had originally joined the Royal Ulster Constabulary before it became the present PSNI. She had a very strong 'no nonsense' way about her that he liked, you always knew where you stood with her; if you annoyed or upset her, you would know about it. Her arrest record showed the same. He cast a glance as he side-stepped out of the way of two pensioners who were making their way across the bridge. They were both ignored by the pensioners who just shuffled along their own way, she looked over at him and nodded for him to cross over the road.

"We aren't going into town?" Kyle asked.

"No," she paused, "head down into the car park." He shrugged then looked over his left shoulder and walked across the road and onto the pavement at the other side. As the two of them walked around the corner, she led the way down the small set of steps and into the busy car park of the department store. The two of them had been in the rest area of the police station with most of the section and they had all watched the press conference on TV. They already had the same pictures that were given to the press, so they all knew who 'Alexi Chernov' was and he was for immediate arrest. However, that had been two hours ago, Alison just seemed to take off, past the cars and headed over towards the metal fence that was near the river bank.

"So, we are not checking car tax then?" Kyle suggested.

"No, we're not." Alison stopped at the fence and leaned over it, Kyle stopped beside her. She was looking directly over at the age concern building and along riverside where he had discovered the body. He looked around himself, the traffic on the bridge was flowing, and people busied themselves going to and from the cars in the car park. The shop had a constant flow of people walking in and out and Alison just seemed to stare ahead and said nothing at first.

"So, are we here for a reason? Or are we just enjoying the view?" he asked. Alison made him wait several seconds before she answered.

"I was away the night of the Riverside murder," she paused, "could you talk me through what happened?" She turned and looked at him, the brightness of her crystal blue eyes reflected the sunlight, then as she blinked, she removed her hat and brushed her right hand over her short blonde hair and looked back across the river.

"Yeah, sure," he started, "I was in the Chinese over there getting dinner and in walked the journalist from the Herald,"

"Why were you meeting her there?" she asked.

"I wasn't," Alison glanced over at him then looked away again as he continued, "I had never eaten out of there and thought I would give it a try on the way home … I 'm not sure why she was there."

"Really?"

"Yes, really," he paused, "we walked out of there, I was coming back to my car that was parked just over there," he pointed to the corner of the car park, "when we heard a very loud scream."

"What did you do then?" he was thinking this was starting to sound like an interrogation.

"We came around the corner," he had started to point with his right arm to the far side of the river, "and when we got to that corner there, we found the woman." he paused. Alison was intense; she was trying to picture every detail as if she had been there herself.

"Was she already dead?" she asked.

"No," he answered, "she was completely hysterical and died later at the Causeway before anyone could get anything out of her."

"Pity," she whispered.

"Yeah, I found what was left of her dog just over there in the middle of the car park."

"What had happened to the dog?"

"It was torn in half,"

"Did you see what did it?" she asked, Kyle looked at her.

"No, no I didn't," she seemed happy with that then looked back over the river.

"Where was the body?" Her question seemed obvious, but Kyle obliged and pointed past the tree that was off to their right by the metal fence.

"Do you see where the line of trees ends over on the far side?"

"Yes," she replied.

"See the large bush?"

"Yes,"

"She was lying just there," Alison was alone in her thoughts.

"It's awful being first on the scene to something like that," her statement was quiet, but she meant it and was obviously speaking from experience.

"When was the first one for you?" Kyle asked. Alison twitched slightly at Kyle's question; he spotted a little quiver of her bottom lip. He had touched a nerve, and silence hung in the air between them before she came out with one word.

"Mayobridge," he was slightly confused, he had heard of a small village in South Armagh called Mayobridge, but he didn't know what the connection was, she spoke quietly, "It was late 1989; I was just out of the college and I was at my first station ..." Kyle relaxed and listened to what she had to say, "I was out in one of the armoured Ford Sierra's when the call came in," tears welled up in her eyes as her mind remembered what she had seen, "an army paratrooper patrol had been hit by a massive bomb, they said later that it must have been at least a two-hundred-pound device." 200lb's of explosive. Kyle did not have to imagine the size of the blast. Alison went silent.

"Were you the first there?" he asked, Alison's head jerked towards him, then looked away again.

"Yes, the second Land Rover was in the field on its roof but the first one had been right beside it..." Kyle went to say something but stopped himself, he let her carry on. "There were body parts all over the place, there was this sodden lump that managed to live through it," Kyle's eyebrows rose, "lost all his limbs but apparently he lived, one of the soldiers in the other Land Rover was a combat medic." Alison looked at him and he nodded, he knew what a combat medic was and what they could do. "A helicopter arrived shortly afterwards but it took us hours to scoop up all the body parts and shove them into plastic bags," she drifted again.

"So, what happened then?" Kyle asked. Alison was brought back to reality by the question.

"We had to keep the scene as sterile as possible, the plastic bags got flown to Belfast, but the soldiers were sent back out to patrol again that night... no rest."

"I meant what happened to you?" he asked.

"Well the other constable I was with that day I married five years later

"From one traumatic situation to another," he said, she laughed in agreement.

"So where is he now?" Kyle asked, "I have never known you to talk about him before." Alison straightened herself up then turned and faced the town centre again.

"I got traded in for a younger model a few years back,"

"Sorry, I didn't know," Alison smiled and patted him on the shoulder.

"Of course, you didn't, those that do know also know to keep their mouths well and truly shut," Alison started to walk away from him and headed back towards the bridge.

"Thanks for that," she nodded back to Kyle's right as he arrived at her side.

"No problem," he said as the radio in their ears came to life.

"*Six Five from Control, six five from control,*" the main control room was calling the area car.

"*Six Five go ahead,*"

"*Six Five, Control where is your present location? Over,*"

"*Six Five, we are just passing Tesco's on our way towards the old bridge, over*"

"*Six, Five, Control, make your way to the Mountsandel site; we have just received reports of a body over,*"

"*Six Five, roger on our way,*" The siren of the car was flicked on as the police officer was finishing his transmission; as he finished speaking Alison's voice started in Kyle's earpiece.

"*Six five, Seven Two, we are on the old bridge presently and we can join you, over*" Alison was already running towards the steps and the near end of the bridge.

"*Seven Two, Roger, we will pick you up there, out*" Kyle made sure he beat her in the race to the steps.

∞∞∞

Cara-Marie walked towards her car she had left in the Tesco car park. A middle-aged woman with several bags of shopping walked past and said 'hello'; she had passed her before she was able to react. Her train of thought was broken by the siren of a passing police car suddenly being switched on. The car sped off around the corner and headed towards the old bridge. She wondered where that was going, she glanced at her watch, and it was nearly quarter past five. Her eyes caught the police car on the far side of the river heading out of town, her nosiness was getting the better of her. Mark stopped a few feet away from her and turned so his left shoulder was facing her; she looked past him then spotted his car parked in the line of cars opposite.

"So, what are you up to tonight?" he asked.

"Oh, not much," she looked from side to side and did not make eye contact with him, whatever she was about to say was a lie, "just going to relax and not do much." She had been excited all afternoon since getting those two phone calls and Mark really wanted to know what they were about, he could guess but it would be just that, a guess.

"What about you?" she replied, Mark shrugged his shoulders and looked around.

"Well it looks like I am in for a fight when I get in."

"Why?" she took a step closer to him.

"Well it seems that Rachel's spy network is up to its usual high standard," she looked puzzled, "she knows that we had lunch together and she is not happy about that." Mark explained.

"I told you she doesn't like me," she grinned.

"Ok, that is my gossip for the day, now what's yours?," she went to speak but Mark cut her off, "and don't tell me you don't have any because those two phone calls you got today have turned you into a bubbling teenager,"

"Ok, but you are not going to believe me when I tell you this..." Mark's interest just doubled with her reply.

"Maybe I will?"

"Maybe you will ..." she looked around herself then slowly stepped forward, then met him eye to eye. "I have a source in the forensic labs that has confirmed that the police are looking for at least one, possibly three werewolves,"

"*WHAT?*" Mark almost shouted.

"Yeah, they've brought another scientist over from England who carried out his own tests and he's come up with the same results," she couldn't hide her excitement.

"I don't believe it," he put his hands on his hips "that is confirmed, is it?" she nodded.

"They are going to release a scientific paper on human DNA that can change shape, they are calling them 'shape-shifters'," Mark's mouth opened.

"You are being serious, aren't you?"

"Yes, I am, they believe they can confirm and identify the active memory cells that can change from one shape back into another," he looked round himself then shook his head, "A shape shifter is someone that can change from human into..." Mark stopped her.

"I know what a shape shifter is; I do get the Sci-Fi channels," a confident woman folded her arms.

"They have also confirmed that the DNA they have is a human/canine mix."

"And they are planning to go public with this?"

"The police were informed this afternoon," Mark turned and took a single step away before turning around again.

"They believe this 'Chernov' that they are looking for is the one doing all the killings, changing shape to do it, then changing back to human form and then just walking away."

"This is incredible,"

"Isn't it," she smiled as she spoke,

"And you can get copies of all this before they go public?" she winced at the question.

"Not yet," he sighed then the disbelief flooded back over him, "but when I do," her phone started ringing. She answered it "Hello."

"Really!" she exclaimed, "When?" she nodded in agreement to whoever she was listening to, "OK, thanks, I owe you one," then she hung up, "they have found Chernov," she stated as she rushed around her car.

"Where?" shouted Mark.

"Mountsandel Fort, *GET IN,*" she commanded and seconds later they were on their way to the old fort. Cara-Marie would fill in what details she knew except who it was that had just phoned her. It was, however, to be

Chapter 40

"All the other council members have returned over a month ago," Tatamovich liked to remind Grishin of little details like that.

"But the other council members have not had to deal with what is happening here?" Grishin answered.

"Yeah, how come we get to spend so much time in a place that rains as much as it does here?" Grishin smiled, the two of them walked on through the grounds at the front of the Belfast city hall. The large white marble building stood proudly at the top end of Royal Avenue and seemed to be a magnet for people drinking coffee, and sitting in groups, it was not the kind of thing that Grishin would normally do. They occasionally would hear someone speaking Polish or another Slavic language, which is why they stuck to Russian, no one could understand them, and he liked that.

"What are we going to do about Chernov?" Tatamovich asked, "Sprogis 'has' broken the law," he said, Grishin nodded.

"The Rua are following the rules and I agree with the way O'Brien is handling the situation," he looked over at him, "it is right for Chernov to punish Sprogis then take him before O'Brien, I agree with that," Tatamovich nodded, "so how much longer shall we stay?" he asked.

"We will stay in Belfast until the end of the week then move to a different hotel ..." it was Tatamovich's turn to nod, "but not too far, you have a waitress to keep in touch with, have you not?" the two men smiled at each other.

"Speaking of which," he started, "you and I can have a meal then go to the bar for the evening." Tatamovich looked at his watch as he spoke.

"I like that idea, where shall we eat?" answered Grishin.

∞∞∞∞

Sean had not been home an hour yet as his phone started going off. His wife had just gone up the stairs and he was enjoying his real coffee that she had made for him in the coffee machine. Dinner would be ready in about half an hour and he really didn't want to answer the phone; he read the name on the screen.

"Yes Mike?" the noise in the background indicated he was using the hands-free in his car. Mike had left Belfast an hour ago and would not have made it to Coleraine just yet.

"Hi'ya boss, sorry to take you away from your coffee,"

"Have you got surveillance on my house now?" Sean joked.

"Ha ha, now why would I do that when I seem to spend most of my time around you anyway?" Now that sounded just like Mike's wife talking now, how many times had she said that to him, "besides when do you 'not' have a mug of coffee in your hands?" Sean conceded that one.

"So apart from telling me that I have a caffeine addiction why else are you phoning me?" Sean noticed a change in the tone of Mike's voice as he spoke.

"I have just heard from the duty sergeant in Coleraine, they think they have found this Chernov fella," Sean reacted immediately.

"Brilliant! Have they got him in the custody suite?" he asked, Mike paused.

"No, what I have got so far is that they have found a body and they think it is him."

"What do you mean?" This was not good news.

"A couple out walking their dog found a body down near the Mountsandel Fort about an hour ago," Mike paused then carried on, "they have opened a scene log; armed response is on standby and ATO has been tasked. I am on the way there now."

"Armed Response and ATO?" Sean asked, "why would they need a specialist firearms team and the army's bomb disposal?"

"They are telling me they have found a pistol at the scene," Mike explained,

"Where are you?" He asked.

"Just passing Ballymoney, I will be there in 20 minutes, approximately," Sean nodded to himself, Mike was telling him all he knew presently.

"Ok, give me another call after you know more."

"Will do Boss," Mike hung up. To say this was not good news was an understatement, in fact this was worse than not finding him at all. The press conference had been a good one and they were getting a good and positive response from it. Finding Chernov had become the priority; but finding him alive would have been far better. Sean thought over what Dr Burns had told the two of them this afternoon, this could not be right, these things could not be real, could they? Of all the things that he had seen over the last few decades of his time in the police nothing could have prepared him for this. The coffee tasted sweet in his mouth as he heard his wife coming down the stairs. He knew she had also watched the press conference, but she would only talk about it if he brought the subject up, this time that was something that he would not do. How could he? 'Hi honey, we are looking for monsters that do not exist' they would be laughed out of court and laughed out of the police for even entertaining the thought.

He lifted the controller and scrolled through the digital films selecting the first channel he came to and after a few seconds the film filled the screen. He laughed to himself at the werewolf film that had just started. It was set in England and two American backpackers were on holiday when they were attacked by the werewolf. Sean could hear his wife in the kitchen as he watched the werewolf attack the two men on the moors. Suddenly he was picturing the crime scenes they were investigating. 'Could it be?' he thought to himself, his wife appeared round the door, the screaming on the TV had just stopped.

"What are you watching?" she asked.

"Just an old film," he answered, she twisted her face as the werewolf attacked for the second time and the screaming started again.

"Do you have to?" she asked. Sean flicked the channel over, no he didn't have to watch a film, as he had now seen it for real.

"Real," he said out loud.

"Pardon?" she asked, Sean looked up at her then shook his head.

"Nothing," she disappeared back into the kitchen and muttered something that he did not hear, which was probably for the best.

∞∞∞∞

Cara-Marie weaved her way through the evening traffic, she knew the Mountsandel site, and every school child from anywhere around here knew it. School visits were a must. Mark was hanging on for dear life. While he enjoyed a 'white knuckle' ride at a theme park his present experience differed from them as they were safe with an illusion of danger, the present ride had an illusion of safety. Being a passenger in a car with Cara-Marie driving when she is in a rush is the opposite of safety, these were not good odds. He wished he was driving. The courthouse passed in a flash on his left, they didn't have far to go. The next roundabout sounded to the chorus of the car horns of annoyed drivers she had just bullied out of the way. Relief poured over him as she braked and turned right into the entrance of the Mountsandel Park. The police car was already there as was another dark coloured car.

A small group of people had gathered by the entrance gate that reached across the natural road; two uniformed policemen were with them. It took Cara-Marie seconds to park the car. Mark would say that it wasn't parked, it was abandoned, but she was focused on getting past the two police officers which for some reason she wasn't able to do at first. What she did find out was that two of the people who were standing there had been the ones who found the body and that they had used their phones to take some pictures of where the body lay before it started getting dark. Mark's business head suddenly came to life.

∞∞∞∞

Mike had followed the road signs towards Mountsandel and had driven past the courthouse as he had been directed to by the control room in Coleraine Police Station. He almost missed

197

the brown and white signpost that advertised the entrance of what had looked to him like a driveway leading to someone's house. It was just before he had turned into it that he first spotted the un-armoured police car with two police officers and a small crowd of people. Mike was shaking his head as he walked away from the car park and the crowd that had included the journalist from the Herald. She had gotten here before them again.

The large plaque welcomed everyone to the Mountsandel wood and was proudly standing at the fork in the pathway, behind it was a stump of wood that was directing towards the upper path with 'Fort Walk, 0.6km' and the lower walk with 'River Walk 1.8km'. He had already been told to take the upper path. The pathway swept through the woods like a river and it was surrounded on both sides by the darkening trees, above him and to his right was a fence line that marked the edge of the woods. He followed the pathway along, he was dressed in a two-piece suit with a dark blue Gortex jacket. He always kept the jacket in the boot of the car in case of rain. He glanced down at his shoes which probably weren't the right footwear for going for a walk in the forest, maybe he should have changed before he left Belfast.

The path dropped down and passed over a small culvert, the left-hand side of the path was protected by a wooden fence that was meant to stop someone falling into the brook that cut its way down the side of the hill towards the river Bann. He stopped as a grey squirrel ran out into the middle of the path and paused to look at him. The squirrel blinked then took off up the bank to the right and scooted up a tree. Smiling he walked on up the pathway as it continued to weave its way through the trees towards where the uniformed police officer was standing. As he got closer the police officer turned towards him, over the crest of the mound a female police officer appeared and raised a hand in welcome, Mike waved back, the male police officer welcomed him with a nod of recognition, he stopped beside him.

"Constable Foster, isn't it?"

"Good evening Sergeant," Kyle was very polite in his reply. Mike looked around the area. Small steps led down the side of the bank from where he was standing then up the far side of what was obviously Mountsandel Fort. At the top of the steps the female officer was standing, silhouetted against the skyline.

"So, what have we got?" he asked Kyle.

"A body," Kyle answered, "just over the rise where she is standing," Kyle had turned and pointed up the hill towards Alison. Mike noticed that Kyle had not given the name of the other police officer who was waiting patiently for him.

"Cheers," he thanked him as he took the first couple of steps then stopped and turned back towards Kyle, "Did you find him?" he asked.

"No," Kyle shook his head, "a couple out walking their dog heard something and came looking." Mike nodded as he listened to Kyle, "then they phoned it in, and we all came straight here."

"Cheers again," Mike said to Kyle.

"No problem," Kyle answered, Mike walked away,

"You must be Sergeant Dear?" she said as he approached.

"Yes, Constable ...?" the introductions were being very formal so far.

"Constable Wallace, he's over here," she turned away from him and walked a couple of steps down into the bowl that the fort was shaped in. Mike stepped down beside her, she was staying well back from the body that lay on its back with the head turned over to the right-hand side, the right arm was underneath the body with the left slightly out to the side.

"I have not been any closer as we are waiting for ATO to arrive to clear that," she pointed over to the right towards the grass, Mike didn't see what she was pointing at.

"Clear what?" he asked, she gave him an annoyed look.

"The short-barrelled weapon that is lying just there," she leaned slightly over and emphasized her point again, the small black pistol was lying in the grass. Mike nodded as she turned and walked away from him. He didn't go any closer either, so he followed her back up to the edge of bowl. She was looking down at Kyle who was speaking on his mobile phone and waiting to attract his attention.

"How do you know it is the same guy we are looking for?" he asked, Alison glanced round her.

"The couple that found him, found a driving licence on him and recognised the name, but we will have to wait for the formal identification later," Mike nodded.

"So, have you touched the body?" he asked, the glare he got back told him her answer before she started speaking.

"Apart from the couple, no one has, we are keeping the scene of this crime as sterile as possible."

"So how do you know that he was dead before you got here?" he enquired.

"Because..." she placed her hands on her gun belt, "the retired doctor and his wife that found him said so... they are down at the area car with the other officers if you want to talk to them."

"So," he started, "what do you think happened here?" he asked, she stared at him then looked away as she spoke.

"Well," she breathed in, "we have a male with a gunshot wound to his head that looks like it was fired from point blank range," she looked over at him again, "so until you see what forensics can tell you that is all I can say." She was just stating the facts and was not answering his question of what she thought, she was getting annoyed with him, was he rubbing her up deliberately?

"You're not Alison Wallace, are you?" she stopped and turned her head towards him.

"Yes, why?" she asked,

"I have heard of you," he stated.

"Have you now?" she said, "and what have you heard?" Mike looked at her.

"That you applied to become a detective and passed the selection to begin training then turned around and elected to stay in uniform," Mike spotted her face tighten, "...and did not give any reason why at all; at the time, it was said that you would have passed the course with flying colours..."

"Others are 'entitled' to their own opinion," she was not happy about having to explain herself that much was obvious.

"Yes, yes, they are ... and far too often express their opinions when they should keep it to themselves," he heard her take in a deep breath.

"Is there any other way I can assist you Detective Sergeant?" The formality of her question was laced with annoyance and she was not going to let this conversation go any deeper.

"Where is the station duty sergeant? I was told he was here with a scene log?" Alison started to walk away from him, she didn't turn around as she answered his question.

"He is sitting in the area car and is organising the arrival of the ATO from Maydown, I will tell him you are looking for him." She confidently strode away from him and exchanged a few words with Kyle Foster before she walked away back down the path. Mike watched her go; she did not look back.

"Touché," Mike said quietly, he took out his phone, scrolled down through his numbers then stopped at the one he wanted. He lifted the phone to his ear as it started to ring.

"Eddie? ... Hi, ... yeah I am there now ... no, I am not going to make it ... sure no probs ... well we can read her statement tomorrow ... oh and I hear that the family are not police friendly ... sure, see you tomorrow ... cheers, bye." Mike cancelled the call and turned back towards the body that was lying in the hollow. Mike wondered what he would have been able to tell them. The phone started to ring, he saw Sean's name on the screen.

"I was just about to call you ..."

Chapter 41

Kyle looked at his watch, it was nearly ten o'clock, he felt the tiredness creeping over his body as he walked into the changing room of the police station. Two police officers walked past him as he opened his locker and started to remove his body armour, slowly he stripped off his uniform and started to feel human again. The busy changing room had emptied after the shift change was over; he had been told that some of the sections were heading to a pub in Portrush before they were heading home. Kyle had declined the offer of a few beers and lots of banter between policemen. He had never been keen on socialising in large groups as he felt it drew attention to them when they were out and about. He slowly made his way out through the station to his car. He was in no rush as he drove out past the front gate house, waving at the on-duty staff. It only seemed like moments before he was pulling up outside his house. The crisp air nipped at his ears; the car door closing seemed to echo in the darkness that enveloped the bungalow; he stopped by the front door to look out over the fields. The farmhouse over on the opposite hill was brightly lit up but the rest of the land was in darkness. The darkness was quiet and still and gave him a feeling of peace and was strangely reassuring. The Ivory Coast it certainly was not, the contrast was immense, the thought made him smile then he opened the front door.

The beeping of the security system blasted out as he kicked the door closed and reached out with his right arm and tapped in the deactivation code and the noise stopped. He flicked a switch that was underneath the console and the heating system kicked into life, in ten minutes the house would be warm enough for him to walk around in just his bathrobe. Over the next half an hour he would shower, fill a mug with coffee and half fill a small side plate with biscuits, he padded his way into the living room and flicked on the TV. The first mouthful of hot coffee tasted good and he was about to reach for a biscuit when he heard his phone going off; it was still in the bedroom.

Kyle placed the mug down on a coaster then walked over to the bedroom. The ringing had stopped but it only took him seconds to dig the phone out of the pocket of his trousers, it had been a 'withheld' number which, probably meant it was work. Kyle dropped the phone into his pocket and returned to the comfortable sofa and started to flick through the TV channels. The phone in his pocket bleeped with a message, it was from Kelly. His body reacted with a sudden jump of excitement, he was pleased to hear from her. 'HEY, HOWZ U' her text speak had not changed. 'NOT TOO BAD, JUST GOT BACK TO THE HOUSE,' he answered. Kyle looked up at the clock, it was nearly quarter past eleven, and he typed in another message, 'WHAT ARE YOU UP TO?' He placed the phone down and waited for the answer that did not come straight away. He drank more coffee and made a start on the biscuits, he stopped at one of the music channels that was doing a feature on Foo Fighters. The remote was dropped on the sofa as the phone finally bleeped. 'I HAD A HOUSE VISIT EARLIER DAT TUK LONGER DAN IT SHOUD'V' Kyle read over the text again and just as he was starting to reply the phone buzzed again. 'DID U HVE A BUZ DAY?' Kyle read the message out loud as it made more sense then.

"Did you have a busy day?" he wondered for a moment then typed in his reply. 'SORT OF, WE WERE ON FOOT PATROL THROUGH THE TOWN THEN WE HAD TO DEAL WITH A DEATH UP AT MOUNTSANDEL FORT IN COLERAINE' he sent the message then took another sip of coffee. The phone bleeped immediately, but it was Tony's name on the screen. 'HI, I WILL BE FLYING BACK TOMORROW NIGHT, AM I WORKING ON FRIDAY?' Kyle thought about it for a moment then typed in a reply, 'NO, YOU ARE OFF FRIDAY, MORNING SHIFT SAT MORNING' he sent the message then typed in another to Tony. 'HOW DID IT GO?' his phone bleeped as he was typing the second message, he opened the text that had arrived from Kelly. 'WOW, I HRD DAT ON NEWS, WOT HAPPENED?' Kyle's sense of humour answered the text for him.

'WELL I GOT TO STAND BESIDE A TREE FOR FOUR HOURS AND WAS TREATED LIKE I WAS INVISIBLE BY THE MURDER TEAM ... OH AND SOME GUY DIED' he was smiling as he wrote it, his phone beeped as it was sending, 'THANKS, IT WAS OK.' Kyle shrugged and took a breath in before he answered the text. He knew what Tony was feeling after having just attended to the funeral of a friend and visiting two more who had been torn apart, it just wasn't nice, but there was something very pressing for him, Kyle decided on the less tactful approach, 'WE NEED TO TALK'. The screen changed to message sending so he passed the phone over to his left hand and lifted the mug of coffee with the right.

He drained the last of the coffee as the phone beeped again, this time it was Kelly. 'LMAO' Kyle thought for a bit then typed in the obvious question as he had no idea what her text meant. 'LAUGHING MA ASS OFF, DUMMIE' he smiled, 'WHAT ARE YOU DOING TOMORROW NIGHT?' he replied. The phone bleeped again, this time from Tony, 'YES WE DO, FRIDAY LUNCH?' Kyle was already typing in the answer before the nerve impulse had left his brain, 'I AM WORKING UNTIL 3PM, WE COULD MEET AFTER THAT?'

Kyle left the empty mug down on a coaster and turned the TV up, he really loved this song, the phone went off again as two texts arrived, he glanced at the screen, one was from Tony and the other was from Kelly. He opened Tony's first, 'THAT WILL DO, LUNCH IS ON ME'. This at least was sounding more like him, Kyle decided against answering as he may say something that would only make things worse. Tony had a lot of explaining to do, what was that on top of the hill? And more importantly, why had Tony acted the way he had. They had almost started fighting, first at the crime scene then again in the car park and that wasn't good.

Kyle opened Kelly's text 'DER IS A FILM ON AT DA CINEMA IN CRAINE DAT WUD LUV 2 C'. Kyle smiled as he typed in his answer 'I COULD PICK YOU UP AT HALF 6, GET THE TICKETS THEN GO FOR A BITE TO EAT?' Even as he sent the message, he could feel himself getting excited as he waited for the phone to bleep again with her answer. 'DAT WUD B GUD, C U L8R DEN' again he had to say it out loud for her message to fully make sense.

"That would be good, see you later then..." Kyle then headed off to bed as he felt the tiredness creeping over him again; tonight, would be one of the best night's sleep he would have in a long time.

∞∞∞∞

Sean was sitting behind the desk in the small office at the police station in Coleraine, it had just gone nine in the morning and his first coffee hadn't taken effect yet. He had opened the laptop and just entered his password when there was a knock at the door.

"Yes,"

The door opened at Eddie appeared with some paper in his hands. The three bars of music welcomed everyone to the now activated computer as Eddie closed the door behind him. "Mornin' Boss,"

"Mornin'" Straight away Sean knew there was something wrong, Eddie's body language was all wrong, it was not the young, confident and eager detective that he normally was. "What?" Sean questioned.

"Err," Eddie looked down at the paper in his hand, "Well Boss," this really was not like him at all, and "It's just..."

"Well out with it man, don't keep me in suspense," it wasn't said as a demand but that was precisely what Sean wanted.

"Ok," Eddie shrugged, "I got the statement from the survivor from Castleroe last night..." Eddie held out the pages that Sean took, as Eddie continued speaking he started to read over it, "and I don't think this will stand up in court as a reliable witness," he stated.

"Why not?" Sean asked.

"Well," Eddie paused again, "she admits that they all had been drinking and taking Ecstasy ..." Sean looked up at him.

"So? That doesn't make her an unreliable witness."

"No, no it doesn't, but they had all been experimenting with Crystal Meth and she was out of her tree at the time," Sean looked down at the pages but wasn't reading anything.

"Crystal Meth? How do you know?"

201

"Well Boss," Eddie thought for a second, "a small backpack was recovered at the scene with Ecstasy and Crystal Meth still inside it, plus," Eddie stepped forward and took the statement out of Sean's hands. He shuffled through then pointed out one of the pages as he handed it back to him, "she describes that she watched as all the grass turned blue, then the clouds changed into horses that were running across the sky…" Eddie breathed in before he continued, "then she says she watched as a man and a woman who were having sex nearby change into dogs," Sean looked up, "I know, I know," Eddie said, "completely out of her brains," Sean looked down at the statement.

"What did she say happened next?" Sean asked. Eddie was a little surprised by Sean's question, but then this was one of the most experienced detectives in the whole force, he had dealt with this kind of thing before obviously.

"She passed out," Eddie answered, "next thing she knows she wakes up, all her friends are dead and there are two coppers with their guns out." Eddie shrugged then finished his sentence, "the rest, we know, is history."

"Cheers Eddie, thanks for this," Sean lifted the statement up with his right hand then placed it down beside the laptop, Eddie looked around.

"I was looking for Mike, but I couldn't find him, and he isn't answering his mobile either." Sean looked down at his laptop and placed his right hand over the mouse.

"He's in with the station chief," Sean replied without looking up.

"Really?" Eddie got excited again, "Why?" Sean briefly glanced up then let his eyes return to the laptop.

"I am sure you will find out soon enough," Sean was nearly smiling as he fed the inquisitive mind of the young detective that was already racing.

"Oh…" Eddie let slip out. Sean placed his right hand on top of the statement and caught Eddie eye to eye.

"Thank you again for this," Eddie knew when he was being dismissed and not to ask anymore. "Ok, no problems boss," Eddie was already on his way out of the door as he spoke. Sean's face dropped as he read over the witness statement. The young girl was only 17 and was describing why they were all in Castleroe that night. The descriptions continued as Sean tried to picture what she was saying; the effects of the drugs were obvious but the description of watching a man and a woman change into large dogs did not seem that of a drug fuelled hallucinogenic vision. The rest would be laughed out of court. Eddie was right, they could not use this as evidence.

The phone call he had received from the station chief inspector earlier had not been a pleasant one. Mike had some explaining to do and had to do it face to face. The door opened, and Mike walked in. He had a graze to the left side of his face and the right side was swollen. It didn't take much detective work to determine how he received the grazes over the knuckles on both of his hands. Sean nodded a welcome to him as he raised his own left hand towards Sean. Mike looked dejected after being on the receiving end of the Chief Inspector's wrath for nearly 20 minutes. He landed on the seat behind the other desk and let his eyes bounce around the room.

"So…" Sean began, "what did you tell the Chief?" Mike stretched his head back and let his arms extend behind him.

"The truth." Mike's answer was simple.

"Did he believe you?" Sean asked, Mike glanced over at him and crunched up his face.

"Don't think so, he…" Mike was cut off by Simon walking in. Simon stopped at the desk and let the door close behind him. Simon looked surprised at Mike.

"What happened to you?" he asked. Mike eyed him with an equal look of surprise.

"Funny I was about to ask you the same question?" Simon turned towards Sean and revealed his own swollen face and pronounced bruising around his right eye.

"What the…?" Sean let slip out of his mouth.

"Yeah Boss," Simon started, "I have something to tell you."

"Really?" exclaimed Sean, "Well after his exploits last night," Simon walked over and sat down on the comfy chair that was beside the coffee table then turned on Mike.

"And what exploits were they?" Simon asked.

"No way, you are not turning this on me... what happened to you?" Suddenly the door burst open and Eddie and another detective suddenly arrived in the room.

"Morning Sergeants... *Sergeants?*" he exclaimed as the two battered and bruised sergeants stared back at them. Mike went to speak but Sean beat him to it.

"You two!" Everyone in the room turned to look at Sean as he raised his voice, "Out." Sean directed his thumb of his clenched fist that was now his right hand back in the direction that they had come from, the two giggling men muttered a chorus of *'yes sir,'* then headed back out the door.

"See, I told you," all three of them heard the comment Eddie made as the door closed.

"Well it seems I'm the only one who doesn't know about you, so you first!" said Simon.

"Ok, last night after I got back here I bumped into Dave Tattershall in the car park..." Mike looked over at Simon.

"And?" asked Simon, Mike looked away then glanced back towards him as answered.

"Scores were settled." Simon glanced over at Sean who just raised his eyebrows.

"So, what is the fallout from that?" Simon asked.

"I got a phone call last night from first the duty inspector then the station Chief Inspector about two sergeants having fisticuffs in the station car park." Simon glanced over at Mike who sheepishly looked over at him.

"I was in with the station Chief at half eight this morning," Simon nodded as Mike continued, "He isn't taking it any further but if it happens again ... blah blah blah."

"Why no further?" Simon asked, "That isn't like a station Chief these days?" Sean leaned back in his chair and answered for Mike.

"Well the fact that if he disciplined Mike he would have to hand the same punishment to Tattershall..." Realisation sparked in Simon's eyes.

"And he has just finished probation for fighting with the boss at Maydown M.I.T..." Mike looked up.

"Of course, ..." he nodded, "I never thought of that, maybe that is one reason why you are not an inspector yet," he joked.

"I like the way you put that, *'yet'* anyway enough of me now what happened to you?" Mike's attention turned towards Simon

"Well, I was having dinner at the Wellington Park Hotel and as we..." Sean and Mike stared into each other's eyes, 'We', was Simon on a date? "...were coming out we headed up the road towards where the car was parked..." he continued.

"Who is *'we'*?" It was Mike who asked the obvious question, they noticed the slight blush.

"Well..." he was uncomfortable with this, that much was obvious, "Margaret and I just wanted to go out for a meal together."

"Margaret who?" Mike pushed, Simon gave him a death stare before he answered the question.

"Margaret Withworth, you know, works in Community Relations at Garnerville," Mike and Sean shared a glance.

"Never heard of her," stated Mike, Sean didn't move but his eyes flicked between the two. He knew who it was. Sean had carried Colin Withworth's coffin on the day of his funeral 15 years ago. Colin had been part of the 'Organised Crime Team' and they had several very high-profile successes. His killing, it was rumoured was not just terrorists killing a police officer but a paid 'hit'. It was to be several years before the team had any more 'high profile' convictions. Sean said nothing, he had known Colin well but had only met his wife once who was also a serving police officer, she was very pretty, from what he remembered.

"So, we were passing 'The Botanic Inn' when suddenly this massive fight erupted," Simon started using his hands to add explanations to his descriptions, "bodies were literally being thrown around like rag dolls when this bloke was rugby tackled by two young fellas and slammed against a parked van." Simon's head was excitedly bouncing back and forth between the other two as in his mind he replayed what had happened. "One of them got flung off and the other got an elbow smashed into his head, his face just exploded with blood and then he went flying..." Mike glanced over at Sean then back at Simon.

"So how did you get a kicking?" he asked.

"Well," said Simon "I got stuck in... to make an arrest and well..."

"Well what?" asked Mike. Simon paused as he tried to think of the correct words to explain what happened next.

"Well, let's just say he resisted arrest," Mike burst out laughing and Sean smiled.

"Were uniforms not there?" Sean asked.

"They were just arriving as Margaret pulled out her Glock," said Simon.

"Margaret did?" exclaimed Mike, this was getting better for him.

"Yes, I wasn't carrying mine at the time," Mike laughed as Simon continued, "but there is something strange about the whole thing."

"What?" asked Sean, the smile fell from Simon's face, "It was the way he stood over me as I lay on the pavement and Margaret shouted at him to stop..."

"He stopped?" injected Mike.

"She did have a pistol pointing at his head at the time, that normally helps." Both men shared a smile as Simon returned to the moment, "something happened to him..."

"What do you mean?" asked Sean,

"Something about him .... changed," Sean and Mike shared glances as they let Simon continue, "His posture, his voice... he actually growled at me..." Both Mike and Sean knew that Simon was telling the truth, he totally believed what he was saying. "Then his friend pounced on him and put his arms around him, he was shouting in what I thought was Polish or something..."

"He's Polish?" asked Mike. Simon shaken from his memories looked around himself.

"Polish? No, he's not as it turns out... he's Russian."

"Russian?" said Sean.

"Russian," confirmed Simon.

"Where are they now?" asked Mike.

"Custody suite at Musgrave Street Station, we're holding them for public order offences and assaulting a police officer," Simon started shaking his head slightly, "but I'm telling you, it was weird..."

"How?" Sean's question seemed to cut Simon off.

"If we are looking for someone or *'thing'* that can change shape...... I am telling you, he is it." Simon did not mean for it to be as explosive as it was but that was the shocking effect that it had on the other two, as the room calmed down Sean reached over and lifted the statement that Eddie had given him.

"Well we will look at them in more detail of course, in the meantime both of you need to read this..."

Chapter 42

Cara-Marie clicked the print button on her screen and her printer whined into life. She had written two articles about last night and saved them to the editor's inbox. He had seemed pleased with them. Mark on the other hand had been chatting to one of the daily tabloid newspapers over in London last night about the pictures that he had got of the crime scene from the phone of the retired doctor. The price of them had been going higher and higher as the evening had worn on. She had interviewed the Doctor and his wife, they had asked not to be photographed but they were happy for their names to appear in print.

 She glanced up at the clock on the wall, it was nearly 11 and Mark had been in Kevin's office for close to an hour. The editor in charge of the group of newspapers that they belonged to had not been happy when he found out that a photographer from one of the local weekly newspapers was talking to an English daily. In his opinion he should keep all photographs for their daily newspaper. The difference in the amounts of money that were involved in the purchase of the pictures differed only by the place of the decimal point.

The door of the office opened, an angry looking snapper walked out. Kevin was on the phone again, that conversation had not gone well. Mark landed in his chair and spun around in it. Cara-Marie scanned through the pages that she had just printed off.

She looked at what was on the pages, but she didn't read them, her attention was solely on Mark who had stopped spinning in his chair. He stared at her, she moved her head and lifted her eyes to meet his. Intense anger burned in his eyes. Cara-Marie raised her eyebrows to ask the obvious question of 'what'? Mark glanced over his shoulder towards the editor's office.

"Fancy a coffee?" he said as he looked back at her, she smiled in reply.

"That depends?"

"Depends on what?"

"Depends on who is paying?" she had a playful look on her face, he had a short laugh that lifted the tension.

"Well that would have to be me then," he said; she spun round and lifted her bag and jacket both at the same time.

"I'm in ... let's get going."

"Hang on, I haven't even said where we are going yet?"

"You don't have to, just follow me," she was smiling as her jacket slipped over her shoulders. Mark propelled himself out of the chair but stepped back out of the way as a handbag that was being thrown over a shoulder intentionally nearly hit him. He reached for his own jacket as the back door of the office was already open and if he didn't hurry up she would be off up the street and he would have to run to catch up. "So, you got a good deal on the pictures then?" she asked as he caught up beside her, the one-way traffic moved past and when a break appeared they both darted across to the other side of the road and headed towards the pedestrian precinct.

"Yeah, pretty good,"

"So, what was the shouting match about then?" she asked.

"What shouting match?" he answered, she glanced at him, she did not have to state which shouting match she was talking about. "Oh 'that' shouting match," he conceded, she raised her hand and mouthed a silent 'hello' to a middle-aged woman who was walking in the opposite direction at the far side of the street.

"Well?" she said, "what was said?" Mark's eyes bounced around the faces of the people who were walking back and forth in the street.

"It started when the big boss in Belfast phoned...it all went downhill from there," she glanced over at him. 'The Big Boss', the chief editor of the newspaper group that they belonged to; it could not have been a pleasant conversation. "They wanted the photos exclusively for one of our daily papers and I was told that he would pay £600 for them, when I told him that I was in discussion with one of the tabloids in England and they were offering ten times that," Mark looked over at her, "well you can probably guess the rest," she could, they walked on.

"What did he say to that?" she asked.

"I got reminded who I worked for, who pays my wages etc," he shrugged, "I then got a lecture on something about loyalty to the company and all that,"

"So, what was your answer to that one?" her question kept his flow going, just as she intended.

"So, I pointed out that I was in my own time, using my own camera and that I had been approached by another newspaper for a position with them already," they both slowed down, "He didn't like that... not one bit."

"Chalk one up to you then?"

"Yeah, something like that," they turned the corner into busy Church Street and headed towards the white painted café that was on the opposite side of the street. "When are the funerals?" The change in conversation from him was deliberate and she got the hint not to ask any more. He was asking about the funerals for the teenagers who had been killed over at Castleroe.

"Not until next week, the coroner has not completed the post mortems yet," a busker with a guitar started playing a song from the far side of the street, they glanced over at the man who looked to be in his fifties, the guitar was out of tune as was his singing voice.

"There is a problem with the DNA evidence collected on the night of the attack and..."

"You still think it is some kind of wolf thingy?" Mark's question nearly stopped her in her tracks.

"Yes, yes, I do..." Cara-Marie was really surprised by his out of context question.

"Any help I can be Cara," he stopped as he got to the door of the café, "...then please, just ask." He looked straight into her eyes, his offer was genuine, "and I mean that," she placed her right hand on his shoulder and stepped half a step closer to him.

"Thank you... that means a lot," the door of the café opened.

"Now just what the hell is going on here?" demanded a very angry girlfriend who was just coming out of the café.

"Rachel?" Whatever Mark would say now would be wrong, the coffee would have to wait.

∞∞∞∞∞

Paul nodded then ended the phone call as Carl came back into the room, he was less than happy.

"Is it him?" he asked.

"Yes," his short answer was not what Carl had wanted to hear, but it was the truth. Carl turned and walked back out the door of the farmhouse, Paul followed him. The news over the last 24 hours had not been good. Carl walked over towards one of the large barns, pulled back the large door and walked inside. The metal building opened into an arena that was over 200 metres long and over 100 metres wide. The wooden framed barrier stood nearly five feet in height and ran all the way around the barn in an oval shape with a ten-metre gap between the barrier and the frame of the building. The barrier was broken by four double gates that were at the corners of the barn. All four gates led to entrance and exits. Inside the arena several red deer stood or slowly moved around, only one of them raised their heads to acknowledge the two men who had just walked in. Paul pulled the door shut behind him.

"Most inconvenient," Carl said quietly as he rested his arms on the barrier, Paul was not sure if he was talking to him or just talking out loud.

"We have confirmed that the body at Mountsandel is Chernov," Carl looked over at Paul, "single gunshot to the head... confirmed dead at the scene." Carl looked back at the deer. Paul walked up beside him and leaned on the barrier. "Police think it was suicide," Carl just shook his head.

"And it wasn't Paddy?" he asked.

206

"No," Paul shook his head, "I was just speaking to him, and he was the far side of the old bridge at the time."

"What was he doing there?" Carl asked.

"He thought he had spotted our missing princess," Carl's head shot up.

"In daylight?" Paul looked over at him then nodded his head.

"That can mean only one thing with her," Paul said, "she isn't fully Noctrailis, she must still be part sapien."

"Which is why they are going to so much trouble to find her,"

"If she can move around in the day then she can avoid them after dark," stated Carl who thought for a moment then spoke again, "Where is their search concentrating on?"

"Well," Paul shifted where he was standing, "they have finished in Belfast and Antrim and are slowly moving up towards Derry. We have been keeping an eye on them which, has turned up some good news." Carl raised his eyebrows, some good news at last.

"Which is?"

"We know where they are all sleeping during the day so, any problems with them and we can deal with it in one swoop!"

"Yes, ... yes, we could," said Carl, "but they would know that and while they are here, they will not provoke us," Carl glanced over at the far door that had just opened and one of the girls had just walked in. She waved across at them both and Carl raised his hand in greeting back again. The deer started over towards the trough that was at the side of the arena, it was feeding time.

"So, what about the Russians?" Paul asked.

"They broke the law of the land," Carl paused, "what is happening to them?" he asked. The phone in Paul's pocket started to ring, he answered Carl as he fumbled to pull it out of his jeans.

"They are being released this afternoon, but they have to surrender their passports," Paul spotted Carl's eye dart over towards him, "as it turned out the first police officer on the scene is one of the detectives on the Muirdris team." Paul looked at the screen, "It's Paddy again, what do you want me to tell him?" Paul asked, Carl turned away and pulled back the large door again.

"If he spots her then let us know before they find her," Paul nodded, "but his first task is Sprogis ..." Paul nodded again, "all other tasks come secondary."

Paddy would have no problems with the update on his instructions. It was Paul who was not sure how Carl was going to deal with a member of the council who started to change in a public street, in a major city, covered by CCTV camera's and now as it turns out in front of a local police officer. That was a break in their rules and could not be ignored.

∞∞∞∞

Viktor was sitting on the small stool looking out of the window of the bedroom as Yelina walked in. He glanced over at her and acknowledged her with a nod then continued to look out the window.

"Are they still there?" she asked. He looked up and down the lines of traffic; his eyes picked out the figures standing around the car park and the figures in around the trees.

"Yes." Yelina stopped at his left shoulder and placed her right hand on it.

"What do you think they are going to do?" there was a slight nervousness in her voice. Viktor looked up; he could see her eyes darting around the far side of the road along the figures on the riverbank. He lifted his right hand and placed it over hers, she looked down into his eyes.

"Hey, things are going to work out; all this will settle soon," he had not answered her question and his reassurance didn't help. Yelina Gurin leaned forward and looked over at the figures standing around the trees.

"If they had done what Davidov did in our country then they would be dead by now," her blonde hair was touching the top of his hand.

207

"Davidov will sort everything out with them," his lowered soothing voice followed his hand as his fingers glided through her hair, his fingertips brushed over her cheek, his touch made her look down into his eyes again.

"We cannot fight them all," her voiced had raised an octave as she straightened herself upright, "It is not a fight we can win."

"He will not let it come to that," Viktor stood up behind her and grabbed her around the waist with his left arm, the action jolted her backwards into him, he pulled her tight up against him and used his right hand to brush her hair away from the right-hand side of her neck before he landed his lips there in a kiss, Yelina playfully struggled with him and let out a laugh at the same time. The concern on her face had been replaced by a smile. Her head fall back onto his shoulder and opened her neck to allow him to continue kissing her there. Her hands had gripped his left arm at first but now relaxed and her right hand moved along his arm, around her own body and started touching his body, she murmured a response as his right hand started to move over her.

"We have the house to ourselves," he stated, a playful giggle came out of her as she turned around to face him, "for at least the next two hours," she moved her arms up around his neck and closed her eyes as they shared a passionate kiss.

"No one must know," she stated, Viktor answered by kissing her neck again and moving his hands down her back to the top of her jeans and then pushing his thumbs upward under her top. His hands moved upwards over the skin on her back. In his pocket, his phoned bleeped with the arrival of a message but it would be over an hour before he would read the message from Davidov telling him to come and meet him.

∞∞∞∞

Kyle was walking down Church Street, Alison was on his left and had just seen someone she knew, they had exchanged a few pleasantries as they passed each other going in opposite directions. The two police officers continued their foot patrol making their way back towards the Lodge Road, as they got near the pedestrian crossing Kyle recognised the old man with the black walking stick. He caught his glance and observed the look of recognition in the old man's eyes, and his face lit up. Kyle stopped as the old man approached, they both shook hands and Kyle engaged in a warm and friendly conversation with him. Alison was introduced, she was polite but stayed out of the chatting. It did not take long before the old man was again telling tales of the western desert in 1942. A warm feeling flowed over Kyle, the old man never talked about family and only ever mentioned a friend who had served with him in the desert who still lived in Ballycastle. A story of them meeting every year was told to him, it was just the two old soldiers remembering a battle that was minor in history but was major to them. A battle that was still as clear to him as if it had only happened yesterday. Kyle listened as the old man described the chill of the freezing desert night air, the scream of the German artillery and the sense of fulfilment when they had taken their objective.

"The panzer was on fire to the right, it was a mark three, you know the type?" Kyle nodded, the old man continued, "and as we looked over the ridge where they had been we could see Torbruk for the first time, it was amazing." The conversation was broken by the voice in Kyle's left ear, Alison turned slightly and acknowledged the call from the control room.

"Return to this location, M.I.T. have requested statements from you reference last night," Alison glanced over at Kyle who nodded back at her.

"Roger, received," she answered, Kyle looked over at the old man.

"I am sorry, but we have to go," the disappointment was obvious in the old man's face, "but we are wanted back at the station," Kyle explained, a nod of understanding came back from the old man. Kyle offered out his hand, which the old man took in a handshake with a smile.

"We will chat again soon," said the old man.

"That we will," reassured Kyle. The old man released Kyle's hand and Kyle turned away from him, as they crossed the road Alison gently bumped into him.

"You have a fan there," she smiled as she spoke, Kyle playfully bumped back into her.

208

"It's an ex-soldier thingy," Kyle grinned, "you civvies wouldn't understand." Alison side stepped to bump into him again, but Kyle moved so she missed her collision.

"I'll get you next time," she whispered.

"Really?" answered Kyle.

"Yes, really,"

"We will have to see about that one," Kyle said loud enough for her to hear, Alison grunted out of her nose and raised her eyebrows at Kyle's comment.

"Many have tried before legion boy...and failed."

"Legionnaire!" he corrected, Alison noticed he even said it with a French accent. The old man paused, his mind was still in the desert, as was his conversation.

"Then there was that Foster fella, a Coleraine man you know, ..." the look on his face changed, "and what happened to him at the full moon .... tear the Germans apart he could."

Chapter 43

Sean looked over at the clock on the wall, it was nearly half three as Simon walked in and sat down behind the other desk.

"They have been released," he stated.

"Who has been released?"

"The Russians..." Simon looked like he was about to say something else but decided against it.

"Who were they?" The question made Simon stop and open one of the folders on the other desk beside the closed laptop. Simon scanned one of the sheets of paper before answering.

"Edward Grishin and a Viktor Tatamovich," Sean glanced over the page that was in his hand, "And are in court in Belfast at 10 am tomorrow morning," he paused, "we got a Russian interpreter from the university."

"They couldn't speak English?" asked Sean.

"Perfectly, in fact the interpreter stated that we were wasting his time as their English was better than his." Sean knew that they had just been following the correct police procedure with the interpreter so that the police knew what the foreign nationals were saying to them and to each other.

"What are they looking at?" he asked.

"Just a fine, they both said that they were being verbally harassed and then the fists started flying, the door men from the pub confirmed all of that so they are in the clear." Simon looked around then slightly lowered his voice, "and they are connected as well," he stated.

"What makes you think that?"

"Last night we had people from the Northern Ireland Office on the phone asking after them and wanting to speak with them. It seems that the Russian consulate in London was 'very' concerned about them." Sean went back to what he was doing, he thought for a moment before he asked the next question.

"So apart from their ability to beat up off duty policemen and defend themselves from a group of drunken teenagers, what else do we know about them?" As he asked the question Sean reached over for the mug of coffee that was sitting near the landline phone on his right, there was obviously something more about these two men.

"Hi..." Mike paused as he entered, then landed on the soft chair that was positioned between Simon and Sean as Simon continued.

"Well, both are Russian nationals and seem to be quite well-off businessmen."

"What makes you think that?" Sean asked,

"Firstly, they were both well dressed and have been over here for a while now,"

"How long exactly?" Sean's question cut Simon off.

"Well I'm not sure,"

"Find out," Sean was being abrupt.

"I can get one of the team onto that one," said Mike,

"What else?" Sean was engrossed with sorting out the paperwork in front of him, but his voice was more concerned with what Simon had to say; were they touching a nerve?

"Well..." Simon stated, "they said in interview that they have been touring Ireland both north and south and were heading back to Russia next week."

"I thought they were meant to be flying back today?"

"Yes, to London," Simon started, "then on a direct flight to Moscow a week later..."

"Have you done background checks on them?"

"Just some bits, a deeper check will take time,"

"Do it," Sean commanded as he dropped the paperwork onto the desk. "What bits did you find out?" Simon flicked the page over and read from handwritten notes.

"Both claim to be senior executives for a Russian built Trans-European gas pipeline,"

"I've never known executives to get involved in punch ups outside a pub" stated Mike.

"Me neither," said Simon as he looked over at him, "and when I asked them about that they both stated that they were former members of 'Alpha Squad'..."

"Who?" asked Mike.

"And what is 'Alpha Squad' exactly?" the tone of Sean's voice had relaxed a little. Simon shrugged. "Neither of them was keen to discuss details but the only thing they said was that it was part of 'Spetsnaz'... apart from that, nothing," as Simon finished off Mike turned and went into one of his folders.

"Wait a minute," both Sean and Simon glanced at him as he thumbed through the paperwork that he had. "Here we go..."

"What? You got something?" asked Simon.

"Yeah," said Mike as he stopped at a page of hand-written notes, "Alexi Chernov..."

"Chernov? The suicide at Mountsandel?" asked Simon,

"The very same..." said Mike as he looked up, "he is also a former member of this 'Spetsnaz' group."

"Where did you find that out?" asked Sean,

"Eddie did a background check on the Latvian driving licence that we found on him... it seems he received some sort of award for being in Chechnya."

"So, who are this 'Spetsnaz' lot?" asked Sean.

"I 'think' from what I can gather, they are some sort of Russian special forces."

"So, could they have known each other?" Simon asked the question but all three had thought it, all at the same time.

"Possible," said Mike.

"We could have our killers," Simon's face lit up as he spoke, all three men exchanged glances, and a small excitement entered the room.

"Find out exactly when they arrived here," Sean's tone had dropped again, he had already told Simon to do precisely that.

"Boss?" asked Mike, Sean looked over at him.

"Yes?" Sean answered.

"You ok?" Mike didn't move as he spoke, but Simon relaxed back in his chair.

"Yeah, I am good," Sean shrugged, "just fending off Super Sutcliffe and his constant updates are annoying me!" Neither Mike nor Simon believed what he had just said. The landline phone on Sean's desk started to ring and as he lifted the handset Mike and Simon lowered their voices and continued their discussion. Sean spoke into the handset then recognised the familiar voice of Chief Inspector Anderson. Chief Anderson was back at work in Belfast after he had completed a three-month course in Mass Incident Strategy with the Metropolitan Police in London, and he wanted an update on the investigation. Sean leafed through several sheets of paper with the witness statements.

"So, what do you think of this?" he asked, Mike held out his hand and took the statement from him. Mike leaned back and looked over the handwritten notes. Sean started laughing into the phone as he shared a joke with Chief Anderson. It was obvious he was pleased to hear from him, at least the team could go to him before annoying Super Sutcliffe.

"Well," Mike started, "there isn't much here we can use,"

"If any of it at all..." stated Simon,

"Her description seemed quite detailed after all."

"Yeah if I ever want an authority on clouds changing into horses then I know who to ask," they shared a smile, "What did we get from the drug squad?" Simon asked.

"Not a lot," Mike mused, "at first, they wanted the case but changed their minds after they saw the crime scene and read the witness statement," Simon looked perplexed.

"What did they want the case for?" Simon had stopped what he was doing as he asked the question, Mike glanced over at him.

"It was the quantity of Crystal Meth and X that they were interested in. After they read the statement, they kinda lost interest." The phone on the desk in front of Simon started to ring, Simon answered it with the standard police answer. Mike lifted the folder that was sitting beside the coffee machine as Simon thanked the caller and said that he would be right down, as he replaced the handset he glanced over at Mike.

"The two coppers are back from their foot patrol and are on their way to the recreation area, so we can get statements from them both." The recreation area was a large room inside the police station that has a TV in one corner and a few rows of cushioned chairs, it has many uses, this time for interviewing two police officers in a relaxed environment, which was precisely the situation that Simon wanted.

"Is Foster one of them?" asked Mike, Simon pushed his chair back,

"Yes,"

"Him again," said Mike.

"Him again," echoed Simon as he walked around the desk and headed for the door of the room.

"Simon," Mike called out. Simon stopped by the door and looked back at him, "Get what you can from him, and we will chat later." Simon nodded and reached for the door handle.

"That is the plan," Simon opened the door, "I have done this before you know…" Simon was smiling as he spoke, a smile that Mike returned as his phone beeped with a text. Sean suddenly laughed out loud as he shared whatever had just been said down the phone, both Simon and Mike looked over at him as he finished off the call and replaced the handset of the phone; he was very pleased about something.

"Well?" Mike asked,

"Well what?" Sean answered.

"Well what has got you in such a good mood?" Sean looked back down at the sheet of paper in his left hand.

"Not much. Colin really enjoyed his time in London," Sean had called the Chief Inspector by his first name. The whole team knew that Sean had known the Chief for a long time, and it was also widely known how much Superintendent Sutcliffe and Chief Inspector Anderson openly despised each other. "Oh, and he has taken over from Super Sutcliffe and he wants a full team briefing in Belfast next Tuesday at 10." The good news would flow through the whole team in minutes.

Chapter 44

Cara-Marie pushed open the back door of the newspaper's office, Kevin was in his office on the phone and the other reporter was down at the reception with the three members of staff, her desk was empty. Cara-Marie was taking off her coat when her phone bleeped with a message; it was Mark. 'SOZ ABOUT DAT'. The simple message made her smile, she replied saying it wasn't a problem as she took her seat and opened her desktop computer. Kevin's voice raised to a shout at whoever he was having the conversation with, the other members of staff stopped what they were doing and looked around as well. The conversation was not going well for him, so far no one had noticed that Mark wasn't with her. Her phone beeped with a message again. 'I AM TAKING HER HOME, C U 2MROW'.

Rachel had exploded with rage outside the small café at the sight of the two of them together, she hadn't accused them of sleeping together but the suggestion certainly had been there. Cara-Marie had left the two of them to their shouting match, well actually it was Rachel's shouting match with Mark trying to calm her down. She sent the smile answer of 'OK', she had thought of putting something else but decided against it just in case he was not the only one reading his texts. Kevin slammed his phone down then cursed it as it was sitting on his desk, it had been a while since she had seen him that angry. Her eyes scanned down the list of email addresses then stopped at the one from her friend at the forensic labs. She clicked on that one first. 'HI CM, YES I CAN GET YOU WHAT YOU WANT BUT I CANNOT SEND IT IN THIS FORMAT, SHALL WE MEET? YOURS, ME X'

Her eyes read over the short email a second time, this was brilliant news. She could get a copy of what the forensic labs were doing. Her heart started to beat faster as her mind started to race over what this could possibly mean. If she could prove what she had seen that night at the riverside was real and the police knew it... she clicked on the 'reply' button and started to type out her answer. 'HI, THANKS FOR GETTING BACK TO ME. YES MEETING IS PROBABLY BETTER, I CAN BE IN BELFAST TOMORROW AFTERNOON. WHERE AND WHEN WILL BEST SUIT YOU? CARA-MARIE'. She smiled as she typed out her full name and not what her friend's abbreviation; someday, people everywhere would get the hint.

She started going through her other emails, and her desktop pinged with the arrival of the reply from Belfast. 'COOL, 1 PM AT THE FRONT OF THE CITY HALL. LATERS, ME X' she read it again, '1 PM tomorrow, no problem.' It took her seconds to write the email to the editor saying she would be going to Belfast tomorrow morning and would be back the following day; her excitement was back. The phone on her desk started ringing. It was one of the receptionists putting a call through to her. "Thanks," she said as the line clicked then went quiet, "Hello reporters, Cara-Marie speaking..." the line was quiet for a few seconds then a male voice sounded.

"Umm ... err ... hello," the voice was unsure and was uncomfortable, but he continued, "can I speak to Cara?" The accent was a local one, there was no please or thank you.

"Yes, speaking, I am Cara-Marie," she corrected.

"Umm ... hello..." The line went quiet as he stopped speaking.

"Hello, ... can I help you at all?"

"Umm ... yeah ... I ... I got something that you might ... umm ... you might kinda like ... umm ... yeah ..." he paused then spoke again, "there's something I want to show you."

"OK," she paused. Silence remained on the line and the seconds ticked by as she waited for him to speak again and since nothing came she took charge of the conversation again.

"OK, who is speaking ... please?" The next answer had better be good, or the handset was going down.

"Oh ... ahh ...I'm ... I'm Martin Gillespie, erm ... I'm Katie's brother." He stopped speaking again, it took Cara-Marie seconds then the name registered, it was the brother of the only survivor from the Castleroe killings.

"Oh yes Martin, hello," her voice picked up as did her interest, "how are things?" Her concern was partly true, but this was an excellent source of information and every bit of information had to be collected.

"Well ..." he started, "well little Katie is outta hospital now, like you know, ... umm ... and the police have finished talking to her, but ... you know ..." Cara-Marie did not interrupt this time, she was just letting him flow and hopefully relax a bit more before he got to the real reason why he was phoning a local journalist, "but anyway ... I've got something that you might like to see,"

"OK," she was not sure where this was about to go.

"I've got Katie's phone ... and there are some really strange things on it..."

"Right ..." she replied, this was something else and the journalist in her drooled at what could possibly be on that phone, "so how do you want to play this? Do you want me to come and see you? Do you want to come to the office? Or ... do you want to meet someplace else?"

"Well ... well I'm in Coleraine, you know, what's ... what's good for you? I mean are you busy?" he asked.

"No, no I can see you right now, but do you want to come to the office, or would you prefer somewhere else?" She was letting him decide so he felt as safe and comfortable as he could; experience had taught her that when an interviewee feels safe and comfortable then they are more likely to answer all your enquiries.

"I would prefer somewhere else."

"Right, no problem," the somewhere else would be well populated as she was not in the habit of meeting strangers somewhere that was not.

"There's a wee brown coffee shop down the bottom end of Long Commons, do you know it?"

"Yes, yes I know it."

"Oh, OK ... well I can be there in about ten minutes, can you be there in ten minutes?"

"Yes, that's no problem," to her right Kevin appeared, it was obvious he wanted a chat, "it wouldn't be too busy or too noisy, no?" she glanced up into Kevin's face, "you are happy enough to go there?" she asked.

"Aye, aye no problems," he answered.

"No problem, I'll see you there in ten minutes then,"

"Going somewhere?" Kevin asked, she reached out and picked up her notebook and as she was turning in her chair she spoke.

"Yes, the brother of the survivor from Castleroe wants to talk to me," she stood up and pulled on her jacket again, the editor could not stop her with this one.

"Where is Mark?" She swung her shoulder bag over her left shoulder and paused to think before she answered.

"I think..." she paused "he is taking his pregnant girlfriend home, we met her down in Church Street." He nodded and muttered something about being the last to know then turned and headed back into his office, she was already out the door.

As she walked down Church Street towards the coffee shop she easily could spot the nervous young man who was fidgeting near the entrance. He noticed her as she started to cross the pedestrian crossing. He was wearing a dark hooded top that advertised a music group that she had never heard of, he had not shaved in a few days, but he had the same colour of hair and eyes as his sister. He was quick to introduce himself and then dive through the single doorway, she followed on behind him, he was in an obvious rush. The coffee shop was quite quiet downstairs and it didn't take them long to get their coffees and head to an empty upstairs. Martin Gillespie took a seat at the far side of one of the tables that were on the right as they entered, he was facing the entrance to the room at the top of the stairs, Cara-Marie took the seat that was directly opposite him and lifted out her notebook.

"Well, what about Katie?" she asked at first, this would get him taking comfortably, "how's she keeping?" Martin took a breath in and looked down at his coffee.

"Katie's ... Katie's not good, erm ... they are putting her in with some shrink people from Derry," Martin Gillespie also spoke with his hands, each word that he spoke was also formed for extra emphasis and meaning, "I mean she was completely out of her ... I mean when we first went to the Causeway she was in a real mess, she was like, hysterical," he shifted in his seat as he relived the encounter, "proper screaming like, you know, they kept on having to inject her with these..." his right hand motioned in a stabbing motion towards his left arm, "this stuff ... and then ... like, the police were there," he looked around the empty room, he carried on, she let him.

"There were other people coming up ... and there were these people trying to get in to see her like, we didn't know who they were," she nodded as she visualised the situation that was being described to her, "and they were saying that they were family, and we were like 'who are you?' it was ..." he paused again.

"Did you tell the police about that?" the question was out before she even realised it, the question didn't stop his flow.

"The police were 'there' you know, in fact there was a couple of times we thought it was the police." His hands just missed the mug of hot coffee on the table, his eyes continued to dart around the room, "it took two days before the doctors said that the police could actually talk to her and," his voice stumbled through the sentence, "you know, she was ... Mum was there and the police actually threw her out of the room because Mum kept on changing what Katie was saying and ahh ... kept on saying that Katie was lying and ..."

"They put your mum out of the room?" Cara-Marie was surprised by that, the mother must have been really getting in the way.

"Yeah!" he eagerly answered, "they put Mum out of the room," he repeated.

"Grief," she whispered,

"Katie's 17 you know, she's ... a modern 17-year-old and ahh ..." his hands were all over the place again, "in Mum's eyes, she has raised her as a good girl, a good daughter and doesn't believe," the pause was longer, she could guess what he was about to say but she remained silent. "Ok, yeah, they were drinking, a bit of shagging and they were dropping tabs,"

"Mmm uh," she just nodded her head, it wasn't anything that she had not heard of before.

"That's ... well, Katie had gotten into that about the last 18 months, two years ago, but hey, who hasn't had a bit of X" he explained.

"But it's still stuff a mother doesn't want to hear," she replied.

"What mother does?" Martin explained, "I mean, I," this time he stopped himself and again shifted in his seat, the coffee remained untouched. "Katie was infatuated with Matt Boyd, absolutely head over heels about him, um," again he paused and took a deep breath in, then he started to speak again.

"That little tart Keri, you know, she was just a little bitch," Cara-Marie wondered for a second how Keri Ingram's family would describe Katie Gillespie, "She hated her, you know, I mean ... Yes, when Keri copped off with Matt Boyd, Katie was in tears for weeks about that," he paused again, "they were all getting together that night because the big Wookie was getting out of prison, it was a little celebration for him."

"Do you think that had something to do with what happened up there?" Her question brought his train of thought to a standstill.

"Well that is why they were all there," he paused, "they would actually go up there quite regularly because it is somewhere not a lot of people went," his hands were back to over emphasizing what he was saying, she nodded, "They would drink some beer, drop a few tabs and ... have some fun."

"Do you think the jealousy thing had anything to do with what went on up there?" By the look on his face it was not something that he hadn't even considered, so she expanded her question. "The jealously over this guy or ..."

"I ... I don't know," his body language said that he was telling the truth, he genuinely didn't know, "But I know the whole time ... wee Keri was seeing the big Wookie before he was in prison and the whole time he was in there she was copping off with Johnny, you know," she nodded, she did know who he was talking about from the family pictures that they had been given. "This was supposed to be his best mate and obviously that ended the day that he got released from prison." The web of teenage scandal continued to thicken, "I think, actually he knew about it ... but you know ... then ... 'that' happened." Martin stopped speaking his eyes were looking but not seeing as he was picturing something in his mind, she changed the direction of the conversation.

"What about the people who had been trying to see her, in the hospital?" she paused as he came back to reality with a flash, "Cause that's not right if somebody's pretending to be a member of your family. It's quite worrying, don't you think?" Martin was back and on the defensive. "They just wanted to get in, they had small tape recorders with them and Dictaphones."

"Ahh, reporters," she explained.

"I don't know," Martin answered, "but the police that were there said that they weren't' and there was a few of them who were English and claiming they were cousins', but ..." she listened to his explanation, she could picture what had happened. "But we haven't got 'any' English family," his head darted around the empty room once again, "it was a really bad time for ... I mean, Mum had to get pills from the doctor ..." This was a painful memory, it was time to get him on her side.

"That's a bit worrying, really." Martin's face reacted, "press trying to get in."

"Journalists just taking advantage ..." he answered.

"*Some*, journalists," she replied.

"Oh aye, I've got these photies are ... are a bit ... are a bit weird," he reached into his pocket and produced a small flip open phone in a pink case, very feminine and not the type that someone like Martin would have. The journalist inside her fought to break through her calm exterior, this was what she wanted to see, was this finally the proof she needed?

"This is her phone?" She asked.

"Aye," he confirmed. He flipped the phone open and moved his right thumb over the keypad and handed the phone over to her with a picture of two smiling teenagers filling the small screen, "she's given it to me as she says that she doesn't want it anymore." The picture had been taken in the woods, the smiling faces were pressed up against each other, the selfie had been taken at arm's length, in the background she could clearly see a side view of a tall young man with dark hair who had a can of cheap beer in his hand. She pressed the down button and after a few seconds the next picture filled the screen. Martin kept talking but she wasn't listening now. The second picture was of Katie, this time she had her left arm around Matt Boyd. He was smiling but she was the more excited of the pair, she scrolled on. The next picture was taken at distance and was looking down the hill, she had to look closer before her eyes could make out the shapes of a naked woman who was on her knees and a naked man behind her. Even though she could not make out the faces her mind flashed back to the young dark-haired woman in the duffel coat that she had seen in Coleraine, was this the same person? It certainly could be, the next picture filled the screen.

The picture was blurred as whoever had taken it had moved as they pressed the button, the trees were out of focus as was the dark shape at the bottom of the screen. Cara-Marie's eyes tried to focus in on the shape, it was on all fours with its head lowered, and it did look like a large dog. The head was lowered and the white of teeth could be seen but there were not any real features that she could make out, it was moving up the hill.

"What is that?" she asked as her eyes studied the screen, she looked up into his face and her voice raised an octave as she repeated the question, "*what is that?*"

"This is what she has told me she saw," he pointed towards the screen.

"A dog?" It wasn't so much a question but more of her own brain trying to make sense of it all, "Is it?" Memories of what had looked at her from around the corner of the building in the car park at the river flashed in her mind.

"She said ..." his hands were back to emphasising what he was saying, "that there was a man and a woman there ... and they watched them become these ... *things.*" The look of shock on her face matched what she was feeling inside, "they ... they changed in front of them ..." The shock passed from her as fast as it had come, "and this is what the police don't believe," it was Martin's turn to be silenced for a second. "The part of her story obviously that they just don't believe." He didn't know where to look, it wasn't the response that he was expecting, "have they seen these photographs?" Martin's eyes searched around as his mind fought to find an answer that he could explain.

"No."

"Have they seen that photograph?" She held the phone up in her right hand.

"No," at least he was telling her the truth,

"Why not?" he was stuck again.

"They don't believe it ... they ... why would they believe it?" she kept her gaze on the nervous young man in front of her as she listened to him, "they are saying she was smacked out of her skull,"

"But ..." she interjected "someone giving a statement saying one thing is very different from photographic evidence of what she thinks ... of what she is saying she saw."

"So why didn't she show that to the police?" she asked. Martin's body language became very defensive, this conversation was not going the way that was expecting it to, "to prove her statement?"

"She forgot that it was on her phone," she didn't move, it was a poor lie from him, after seeing what she says she witnessed no one could 'forget' that they could prove that what they were saying was true. "It wasn't until she got home, and she got her phone and she went through it," his hands were back to doing most of the talking again, "and she was sitting on her bed flicking through them ... she was crying ... you know ... she's been crying a lot." Martin wasn't looking at her, a sure sign that he was lying even more.

"Have you shown this to the police?" He looked in amazement at her question.

"No,"

"Why not?" she asked. '*Why not?*' he crunched up his face.

"I'm not walking into a police station saying, '*look there's this person who can change into a dog and then rip five people apart'.*" This part was the obvious truth. "I'm not doing that!"

"So, what do you want me to do with this?" At last she was getting to what he wanted to know, "because this ..." she pointed with her left hand at the phone but kept her gaze on him, "could be construed as withholding evidence." The look of shock was back on his face, '*evidence*' wasn't the word he expected to hear either.

"So, you are saying we should go to the police?" he asked.

"I'm not saying what you should or should not do, I'm just trying to get all the facts straight and find out what it is you want me to do with this?" He was totally confused now, "and more importantly what you want our newspaper to do?" Cara-Marie already knew that the editor of the newspaper group would grab this, and it would be on the front page of every single daily newspaper in Northern Ireland the following morning.

"Well I was chatting to Katie ..."

"If ..." she stopped herself, something was about to flow out of him, so she let it come,

"About it ..." he paused again, "and she doesn't want anything to do with it, she's going to throw the phone away," he glanced up at her, another lie, of all the things that they were going to do, throw the phone away certainly isn't one of them. "She's trying to forget it, she's ...." The sentence stopped, and he didn't know what to say next.

"So, the bottom line is ... why are you showing me this photograph?" His eyes bounced around the room, "do you want us to publish this and say, *'this is what killed those kids up in that wood?'*" She could just imagine the headlines, Martin nodded.

"That's what Katie told me," another lie, "she said that she saw, ... there was a man and a woman that arrived up there ... they took off all of their clothes and started having sex near where they were." This bit was probably true, but she didn't interrupt him. "Johnny started clapping and cheering but it was when the rest of them joined in, they started clapping and cheering and they took about 30 seconds she said ..." she could picture what was being described to her, "then they became these ... *'creature - things'*" he pointed at the phone at the end of the sentence, "then they came running up the hill and," his face contorted in a grimace as he pictured what happened next, "and tore them apart."

"Will she stand over her claim?" she asked,

"Yes," It was more of a whisper than a spoken word.

"So, she is happy to put her name to this photograph and say, *'here's the photograph that I took'*" Martin looked around the room again before he answered her.

"Look, Mum wants her to never talk about it again. Mum has said that very clearly. When people have come to the door Mum has 'shoved them away with a brush'" this was becoming a waste of her time, she cut to the chase.

"Right, bottom line, if we publish this ... which we would grab with both hands ... if someone is willing to say, *'I was there, in Castleroe wood, that night and I took a picture ... of this creature ... who did this to those people,'* it's going to come down to one person." She looked into his nervous eyes, "your sister," he thought for a moment.

"Aye ... do you want me to sell you these photos?"

"Is that your decision to make though?" she placed the phone on the table, "Is that not hers?" Cara-Marie wanted these photographs and part of her could feel them slipping away, her professional side kept her going, another side wanted to grab the phone and run out of the shop.

"She can't make decisions," he finally answered.

"Where does the grey area lie?" she said, he didn't know what to say and this wasn't at all what he wanted. He had expected her to almost bite his hand off but that had not happened.

"I mean she is ..." he started saying quietly.

"Because at best ..." she interrupted.

"She is still adamant about what she saw," he spoke over her, "She is still adamant that she was there," this was big brother defending little sister now, "yes ... when these 'dogs' started coming up the hill ... she lay back and that's when she passed out," his hands didn't know what to do, "I mean ..."

"She won't?" injected Cara-Marie.

"She didn't ... I mean," he corrected as she glanced down at the untouched coffee in front of her, then glanced back up at him as he continued speaking. "The next thing she knew ... she woke up and there were two men there with guns."

"You see ..." she started, "publishing that photograph without her permission or her best wishes is at best for us, withholding information from the police in a 'live' murder investigation," she paused slightly, "from our point of view," he could tell he probably wasn't going to like what she was about to say, "possibly 'at worst' it is manipulating somebody who possibly isn't in a fit mental state to make the decision to give us that photograph."

"Ok," he answered, it was never his intention to *'give'* the photograph anyway.

"Don't get me wrong ... this is dynamite, absolute dynamite and I would publish it like that," she clicked her fingers as she said 'that'.

"OK, I'll square it with Katie then," he was nodding as he answered her, "I'll go back and speak to her."

"That's OK," she said.

"Is it ok if I call you later this afternoon?" he asked as they both stood up.

"Absolutely, yes,"

"Will you be in?" he asked.

"Yes, ring the office anytime, it's not a problem, if I'm not at my desk the reception staff will find me."

"Aye, grand so, grand so," he turned and walked towards the stairs, she followed on behind him.

"Did you like your coffee?" he asked over his right shoulder, she glanced back at the still untouched coffee that had been sitting in front of her, then she noticed that his had been half consumed. 'When did he do that?' she thought to herself.

"Yes, it was grand, thanks very much," she answered. Once outside Martin watched Cara-Marie walk away down Church Street as his right hand pulled his mobile phone out of the pocket of his jeans, he turned away and started to slowly walk up Long Commons as he put the phone to his ear, the call was answered very quickly.

"Hi'ya, it's me," he said.

"Did she see them?" the female voice asked, Martin looked around himself, there wasn't anyone around this side of the street.

"Aye, she did," he answered.

"And?"

"And what?"

"How much did she offer for them?"

"Nothing,"

"Nothing?" The female voice almost shouted, "doesn't she know what they are?"

"She knows," Martin answered.

"Well what did she say? She isn't getting them for free!" Martin looked down the road, the traffic lights up ahead had changed to red and brought the traffic to a stop.

"No, no she isn't, she said that we should take them to the police," This made the voice angry.

"We're not going back to the police ... no ..."

"Katie," he stated.

"We're not, not them,"

"*Katie.*" This time it was almost a shout.

"What?" her voice softened.

"I have told you that I will take care of it, haven't I?" he walked on as Katie was silent for a few seconds.

"Yes, yes you did."

"And I will."

"So, what are we going to do?" she asked.

"Simple," he started, "the English newspaper offered ten grand for them, so we take the ten grand,"

"What about Mum?" Martin thought for a few seconds then answered his sister.

"Well I am sure the ten grand will change things," he reassured.

"If you say it will," Katie sniffled from the other end of the phone.

"It will, plus after they have them they will offer more for your story. Everything will be great, we're in the money now Kat. Katie wasn't convinced but at least they didn't have to go back to the police again.

Chapter 45

Tony Fallon slowed his car down at the entrance to the lane that led up to the farm complex. Although he could not see them from inside the car, he knew very well they were there, and they were watching. The car passed him and headed off back down the road he had just driven up. He turned the nose of the car into the entrance and started up the lane lifting his hand in welcome to the unseen eyes that were watching and guarding the entrance.

The top of the lane opened out into the main farm complex; the two-storey farmhouse was on the left with the first large hangar in front of him. The second hangar was at the far end and was standing in line with the first. A small courtyard that lay between the farmhouse and the hangar extended round the far side of the hangar and continued to the other out-houses: the slaughterhouse and the granary where most of the food stuff for the deer was held. All the out-houses had been converted into living quarters, some permanent, and some temporary. It had been a while since he had to stay over at the farm, he reverse-parked the car over by the first hangar. The Irish wolfhounds barked as he climbed out of the car. A small group of people walked past and headed towards the large field that separated the farmhouse from the main road.

"Tony," he looked over to the corner of the hangar, it was Paul, he smiled and nodded toward him, he started walking over to where he was standing. Paul was smiling and held out his right hand as he got close. The two friends shook hands and shared a warm greeting, Paul turned and started to walk towards the farmhouse.

"How are things?" Tony asked,

"He is keeping his temper," he answered. Tony's eyebrows shot up in surprise.

"Really?"

"Yes, really."

"That's a first."

"Yes, yes, it is." Paul paused for a second, "but it isn't going to last much longer."

"Tell me," he asked.

"Later ... after you have spoken with him," they reached the door and Paul led the way inside. The fire was lit, and the room was warm and welcoming. Carl was sitting in his usual chair and was tapping away on his laptop. His eyes widened in pleasure at Tony's arrival. Tony smiled and closed the door behind him. He stopped where he was standing and waited for the invite to further enter the comfortable room. Carl asked him to sit down in the chair opposite from him. Paul moved over to his master's right-hand side taking the laptop from him and placing it near the phone as they started talking.

"Tell me, how was it?" Tony was just getting comfortable as Carl asked the question.

"It was OK as funerals go,"

"Sad, sad time ..." he looked up at Tony, "you knew them well?"

"Yes ... yes, I did, all of them," Tony sat in silence, the sound of the fire being the only sound.

"Did you get to visit your friends that are in hospital?" Carl's concern was real, Tony nodded.

"They are permanently disabled now, but the regimental association is on the case.

"They will be looked after, yes?" asked Carl.

"Yes," answered Tony, "as best as they can be,"

"Anything we can do ..." stated Carl, "then please, just ask," Carl was looking directly towards Tony as he spoke; Tony knew that he meant every word of it. Tony shifted in his seat, there was one thing he just thought of, Carl had spotted it as well, "tell me," said Carl.

"Well," he started, "there is one thing I think is a bit off ..." Carl's interest was real.

"Yes?" he enquired.

"It's Bishan's wife ..." Tony started.

"What about her?" Carl asked,

"She is being deported back to Nepal," he started, Carl and Paul shared a glance then Carl spoke.

"There isn't anything we can do about that!" he stated.

"Yes … yes, I know," answered Tony, "I just want her to be ok when she returns to Nepal, I mean there a widow isn't worth anything and will be considered an outcast," Carl could see the pain in Tony's eyes, Carl raised his right hand.

"Do not worry … we can ensure she will be comfortable." Carl looked over at Paul and Paul nodded in answer, Tony smiled a comfortable smile as the emotional weight was lifted from his shoulders.

"But the reason we are here …" said Paul.

"Yes, the reason we are here," copied Carl.

"Yes," he said, nodding at the same time.

"In your email, you said that we may have a problem with another police officer." Carl stated.

"Yeah," Tony started, "it's the other one who was with me at Limavady,"

"What about him?" asked Carl.

"Well, we were together at Castleroe and one of the Mongols was at the top of the hill," Carl and Paul shared a glance.

"What happened then?" Carl asked. Tony relaxed and went through the events of the night, from the picnic, to their discovery, including the survivor. Tony described how he had stopped Kyle from opening fire.

"He wasn't very happy about that then?" Paul's question was more of a statement.

"No, no he wasn't." answered Tony, "but at least I got him to agree not to mention it to the investigation team." Paul raised his eyebrows.

"Really?" Paul glanced first at Tony then over at Carl who was listening to what Tony had been saying, "that is something at least," Tony looked at him.

"For a police officer, yes, it is."

"Well," Carl moved in his seat as he started to speak, "we will have to do a full check on this guy as usual."

"No problem," stated Paul, Carl went to stand as he continued speaking.

"Give his details to Paul and he can do the rest," Tony stood out of respect as Carl rose from the chair. "Excellent, Paul will bring you up to speed on what else is happening as well." Carl smiled, Tony smiled back, Carl seemed happy enough. Carl started towards the door as Paul lifted a refill pad out of one of the drawers of the small table in the corner.

"Right, what is his name?" Paul pulled a pen out of his trouser pocket and Tony took a step closer to him.

"Constable Foster." Paul started scribbling as Carl reached the door.

"First name?"

"Kyle," The room stopped. Carl spun round as Tony said Kyle's first name.

"What?" Carl snapped,

"Kyle … Kyle Foster," Tony's eyes darted between the two as Carl and Paul stared at each other for several seconds.

"What is his father's name?" Carl's question seemed strange.

"I don't know … I believe his parents are dead," Carl took a step closer and Paul straightened up.

"What family has he?" Carl asked, Tony had to think about it.

"He has a grandmother somewhere near Kilrea," he answered.

"Kilrea …" Carl had said it just as Tony did.

"Could it?" asked Paul, an excitement had risen in the pair.

"But he doesn't really talk about them," Tony said.

"What's his middle name?" he asked.

"His middle name?" repeated Tony.

"Yes, you know not his surname and or his first name …" started Paul.

"I know what a middle name is!" said Tony, "but I don't know his middle name."

"Ask him," Carl had lowered his voice slightly for the command, Tony nodded.

"OK, I am meeting up with him tomorrow ... I can ask then."

"No," said Carl, "ask him now," Tony paused, Carl spoke again, "you have his mobile number, don't you?"

∞∞∞∞

Kyle looked at the clock on the wall of his living room as he entered, it was nearly 9 o'clock and there was a film starting on one of the movie channels that he wanted to watch. The trip to the cinema with Kelly had been cancelled as she 'had work to do' he had tried to hide his disappointment, but Alison had spotted it. The freshly made tea in his right hand splashed a little over his hand as he sat back on the sofa. He quietly swore as he felt the burning liquid drip over his knuckles. He placed the mug down on the coaster and licked it from his hand. His left hand lifted the controller and he scrolled through the channels and stopped on the one that he wanted. He dropped the controller back onto the sofa and lifted the mug to his lips. The phone in his pocket bleeped with a message, his heart thumped as he read the name across the screen. 'HIYA WAT YA UP 2?' The message from Kelly made him smile as he replied, her response came quickly. 'BORING' the cartoon face at the end of the message was sticking out its tongue at him, it made him smile more.

'WHY WHAT ARE YOU DOING?' he asked. He watched as the message sending profile changed to message sent as the adverts filled the screen of the TV, the credits of the film started. The phone beeped again, 'GOT A CLIENT CUMIN IN 10' she answered, 'BORING' he sent back, 'HA HA U DNT NO DA ½ OF IT. CHRONIC LBP ... V BORE' Kyle read over the message a second time, this time he said it out loud, so it would make sense.

"You don't know the half of it ... chronic ...." He paused then replied, 'WHAT IS LBP?' The film started, the seconds ticked into minutes. He wasn't watching the film, he was watching the phone for it to beep with another text from her, another mouthful and the drink was gone. His eyes looked over at the clock and fixed on the time, his eyes glanced back at the phone, it was just sitting there doing nothing. Kyle looked back at the film and tried to watch at least some of it but none of it was going in. The phone beeped. His right hand grabbed the phone and opened the message. 'DO YOU HAVE A MIDDLE NAME?' The text caught him off guard, what did she want to know that for? Kyle closed the message then saw who it was from.

∞∞∞∞

Carl had retaken his seat and Paul was now over by the fireplace, their excitement was obvious, but how could they possibly know Kyle? Carl looked straight at Paul, smiling as he spoke.

"At last!" Paul smiled and nodded back at him. 'At last' what? thought Tony. His phone beeped, everyone in the room became engrossed in the message. Tony read it and coughed a small laugh.

"What?" asked Paul. Tony looked up.

"I asked him if he had a middle name..."

"And?" started Paul, "What is it?" Tony turned the phone round and Paul read Kyle's answer aloud. "Yes, I do have a middle name," Paul was annoyed, "ask him what it is then," he waved his hand as he turned back away from Tony.

"Is he at work?" asked Carl, Tony paused, he had to think through the shift pattern.

"No, working tomorrow morning then off for the weekend."

∞∞∞∞

Kyle's phone bleeped again, this time he read Kelly's name before he opened it. 'LBP: LOW BACK PAIN' her previous message now made sense, the phone beeped again, the next message was from her as well, 'I AM FREE DIS WKEND. WAT BOT U?' Her text speak was the usual. Kyle thought through his shifts then started to tap in a reply. 'I AM FREE SAT AND SUN MORN, WORKING SUN NIGHT.' He sent the message then started to tap in another when his phone bleeped with another message, it was probably from Tony, so he decided to finish sending this

222

one first. 'WOULD YOU LIKE TO GO FOR A NIGHT OUT IN PORTRUSH SAT NIGHT?' After the message was sent he read the text from Tony. 'WHAT IS YOUR MIDDLE NAME THEN?' the question was simple enough, the real, deeper question was why?

"He wants to know why?" Tony read aloud.

"Because we want to know!" Paul demanded, Tony looked back at him.

"That will not wash with him … if I send him a text like that I will be told to '*piss off*' and we will get nothing from him."

"How do you know that?" Carl asked calmly.

"Because if it was the other way around that is the answer that he would get from me."

"We need to know," Paul said towards Carl.

"That we do," answered Carl who then looked back over at Tony, "tell him you might be speaking to a friend of his father's…"

∞∞∞∞

Kyle's phone beeped again. 'BRILL, SOUNDS GUD. NEED 2 B IN BMO SUN PM.' Kyle smiled as he read over the text, she needed to be back in Ballymoney Sunday afternoon. 'EXCELLENT, YOU CAN CRASH HERE, SHALL WE SAY YOU TO BE HERE FOR SEVEN?' Kyle watched as the screen again paused as 'message sending' filled the display. 7 PM would give them enough time to have some time here then head up to Portrush. The phone beeped, Tony's message hit him like a brick hitting a window. 'I AM TALKING TO SOMEONE WHO 'MAY' HAVE KNOWN YOUR FATHER SO JUST TO MAKE SURE, WHAT IS YOUR MIDDLE NAME?'

Kyle was out of breath as his eyes bounced around his living room, his eyes read and re-read the message. The phone bleeped in his hand, but Tony's message was still open. Kyle typed in the one-word answer and sent it. He breathed deeply and slowed his breathing and calmed himself down before he opened Kelly's, 'OK, C U DEN' the cartoon face was winking at him, Kyle didn't reply, he was now more interested in what Tony had to say.

∞∞∞∞

Tony read from the screen, a puzzled look came over his face, he had obviously never seen a name like this one before. The excitement grew in Carl as he listened to Tony trying to pronounce the name.

"He says it is … '*John … nus' … john … ass'*…"

"It is pronounced Yohannus," Carl stood up as he spoke, "the 'J' is pronounced as a 'Y' …" He looked straight at a very pleased Paul, "We have him," Carl placed his right hand on Paul's shoulder as Paul answered him. "At last,"

They looked at a very confused Tony who was standing looking at them with his phone still in his outstretched hand. "Could someone tell me what is going on please?"

Carl walked over towards him, smiling as he did so. "When is the next time you will see him?"

"Tomorrow … we are meeting for coffee so I could tell him whatever was decided by you to tell him about the Mongols," Carl nodded then placed his right hand on the outside of Tony's right arm.

"Bring him here instead,"

"Here?" Tony questioned,

"Yes here, … we have a celebration to organise," Carl turned and walked towards the door, "Kyle Johannes Foster," he stopped and turned around to look at Tony, "younger son of *David James Foster,*" Tony's eyes widened, and he breathed in at the same time in surprise, "and he will be most welcome here," Carl opened the door and walked outside, Paul rushed after him leaving a stunned Tony alone in the farmhouse. Yes, the only surviving son of the previous pack Alpha would be made welcome. Kyle obviously had no idea who he was or what he could be. Now that was going to be an interesting conversation.

Chapter 46

Mike was looking out of the window of the office in Coleraine police station, the grey clouds had parted, the morning was turning out to be quite a sunny one. The coffee machine coughed and spluttered as it finished off preparing the pot of hot coffee, he rose from his chair and walked over towards it, as he lifted a mug Simon walked in.

"Ah, timing. Yes please," he stated as he went around the desk and sat down behind it.

"Morning ... by the way," said Mike,

"Morning ... Coffee ..." he answered as he lifted one of the files that was in a plastic tray on the corner of the desk.

"What's the magic word?" said Mike as he was pouring the first mug, Simon stopped, looked over at him and caught him eye to eye.

"Now,"

"Ok, ok ..."

"And don't spit in it this time," Simon retorted.

"Yeah ... I'm just off to the toilet ... I'll be back in a minute with your coffee."

"So, what has got you in such a good mood?" Mike was sitting down beside the coffee machine and Simon was leaning back in the chair behind the desk as the door opened and Sean walked in.

"Who's in such a good mood?" Sean was wearing a long outdoor coat and carrying his briefcase.

"Just happy to be here boss," stated Simon.

"Yeah, right," said Mike. Sean walked past them and round behind his desk, he took off his coat and hung it over the back of the chair. He glanced up at the clock on the wall, it was five minutes to nine. The three men chatted for a bit but were disturbed by a knock on the door. It was the eager young detective, Eddie.

"Morning Boss," he acknowledged Sean, "Sergeants ..." Sean nodded at him over the rim of the mug, his caffeine levels were not at the right balance yet for him to fully engage in a new conversation.

"Morning Eddie," answered Mike, Eddie stopped in the middle of the small room, his gaze flicked between all three of them.

"Just to let you know ..." he started, "we are just about to interview a bloke who walked into the enquiry office last night,"

"What about?" asked Mike.

"Well, the desk sergeant said this morning that this guy claims to have seen two large dogs at the far edge of the woods at Castleroe the night of the murders"

Mike nodded. "Ok, give us a shout after the interview and let us know the full details of what he saw."

"Will do," Eddie turned to leave but Sean stopped him as the door opened.

"When?"

"Sorry?" Eddie asked.

"When are you doing the interview?"

Eddie looked at his watch, "Couple of minutes," and with a grin, he was gone.

"I remember the days when I was like that," stated Mike.

"You were *never* like that!" retorted Simon.

"You didn't know me in my '*keen*' days."

"The only time you were '*keen*' was when you were potty training!"

"At least I am potty trained," Simon went to answer but Sean cut in.

"Guys!"

"What?" asked Mike.

"I have a really good idea," said Sean.

"Take the rest of the day off and have lunch on you?" injected Mike before Sean could finish his sentence.

"No ... how about we do some work instead?" Mike and Simon looked at each other, Simon passed Mike a folder from the desk.

"Well, update from me ..." Mike started, "the two Russians are in court this morning,"

"Fine?" Sean interrupted.

"And we are expecting a fine, yes." Mike flicked through the folder and read over the notes that were on the page in front of him. "I spoke to the Russian consulate in London yesterday and they were not helpful, to say the least."

"What do you mean?" Sean asked.

"Well," Mike looked up at him, "all they would confirm was that the two of them were in fact Russian passport holders and both had served in the Russian army."

"And since they still have national conscription that isn't giving much away," Simon commented.

"Yes, absolutely," answered Mike.

"Did you ask about the rest of it?" asked Sean.

"Yes, and they refused to comment on anything to do with national security" said Mike.

"The British government have a similar 'no comment' policy as well," stated Simon.

"So, we have no idea if Chernov or these two served in the same unit or not then?" Sean asked.

"No, we don't," answered Mike, Sean nodded to Simon to speak.

Simon started reading from his notes, "Both the coppers who seem to be around when things happen and are both ex-soldiers as well," Sean didn't move except to sip some of the coffee. "One ... Fallon spent six years in the Parachute Regiment and the other ..." he looked down at his notes, "Foster, was in the French Foreign Legion for four years ..." Simon paused.

"Foreign Legion ... wow," said Mike, Simon looked up.

"Yeah, 2 REP ... 'Second Foreign Parachute Regiment' to be exact,"

"I've heard of them," said Mike who then looked over at Sean the back at Simon. "Toughest of the tough ... really good."

"Then this is the funny bit ..." said Simon and he flicked the page over, "he then spent two years in 'Le Crap' ..."

"He spent two years in the crap? What did he do?" asked Mike.

"No, no, not 'in the crap', he was a member of 'le crap'"

"And who are they?" asked Sean, Simon shrugged.

"I have no idea ... if I was to guess ..."

"Anyone can guess ..." Sean cut him off, "I don't want guesses, and I want to know exactly who and what we are dealing with." Sean sat upright and placed the mug on the desk. He looked at the two of them then reached into his pocket and pulled out his mobile phone, "I have an idea," Mike and Simon glanced at each other, "I want something decent to put in front of Chief Anderson on Tuesday ... not guesses," Mike drank from his mug and Simon leaned forward and rested on top of the desk. Now they knew where Sean was coming from, cross every 'T' and dot every 'I', they would have to continue to do just that. Sean lifted the phone to his ear and waited for a few seconds.

"Darren ... Hi Darren, how are you?" Sean smiled as whoever he was talking to answered Sean's question. The seconds ticked by and Sean started to nod. "Ok ... actually this is a work call ... have you a landline number I can call you on?" Again, silence filled the room, then Sean started scribbling on one of the pads of paper on the desk in front of him. "OK ... got that ... yeah ..." he let out a short laugh, "Speak in a moment ... bye then."

"Darren?" enquired Mike, Sean didn't look up from the numbers on the pad as he pushed a button on the landline phone on his desk. The dial tone sounded from the tiny speaker; Sean spoke as he tapped in the numbers he had just been given.

"Detective Superintendent Darren Forester … Special Branch," both Mike and Simon breathed in, they knew who he was.

"The grey fox," Mike whispered. Very few people in the police had met him but most had certainly heard of him; he had spent most of his career working in undercover and surveillance units with the police and the army. His arrest rate was high; he was also credited with being involved in shooting dead three-armed terrorists in a joint police and army operation in the 1990s. The SAS took the credit, but it had been the police officer who opened fire. The line started ringing; after three rings the call was answered.

"Hello …" there was no standard police introduction, nothing to say who you were talking to or where your call had ended up, just 'hello'.

"Darren?" Sean asked, the voice changed to a very cheerful tone.

"What about ye mucker,"

"I'm grand, what about you?" Sean asked.

"None so bad big man, none so bad," Darren answered.

"Darren, just so you know you are on speakerphone and we are in the temp office inside Coleraine station," said Sean, "the other people in the room are Detective Sergeant Mike Dear," Sean looked over at Mike then glanced over towards Simon, "and Detective Sergeant Simon McCallister," the line was silent for a few seconds then Darren spoke.

"Mike Dear … as in 'The Mike Dear' from the Henderson case that was all over the news?" Simon and Mike both turned towards each other and smiled, then Mike turned back towards the phone.

"Yes … Sir," he paused, "The very same," Sean glanced over at the two surprised men, and then looked back at the phone as Darren continued speaking.

"Well done on that one, I followed it on the news."

"Thank you, Sir," replied Mike who went to say something, but Darren beat him to it.

"Ach no need with the 'sir' bit … just call me Darren,"

"OK," said Mike.

"So, Sean, any progress on your investigation? You didn't look too comfortable at your last press conference!"

"I hate those things," he replied.

"Sutcliffe is being his usual self then," they all heard the short laugh come down the phone from Darren.

"Anyway," Sean was changing the subject again, "the reason that I am phoning you,"

"You just wanted to hear my beautiful voice?" Darren's comment made all three of them smile. Both Mike and Simon could tell that Sean and Darren knew each other well.

"Dulcet tones more like!" retorted Sean.

"I take it you're still following crap football teams then?" Sean's face contorted.

"Oi!"

"Thought so, I mean 'Lisburn Distillery' come on," Darren continued his baiting. Mike let out and audible laugh to which Sean looked over and raised his eye brows.

"I should tell you that Mike is a Glentoran man … as well!" Sean sighed as he spoke.

"Is he?" Darren almost seemed excited by the news. "I like a man of good taste,"

"ANYWAY …" injected Sean.

"Anyway …" answered Darren.

"Back to the real reason I am phoning you,"

"Go for it,"

"Do you still work around the army lot?" Sean's question was not specific, but Darren would know what and who he was talking about, there was a pause from the phone before he answered.

"Yes."

"Good, this is probably more for them actually," a slight pause from Sean was answered by silence from the phone, so Sean continued, "We want to learn more about the background, more specifically the military background of some people who are part of the investigation," another pause.

"Mmm ... interesting," answered Darren.

"Yes, I want to know *'precisely'* what we are dealing with ... and asking saves a lot of guesswork."

"Absolutely!" Darren's answer was instantaneous, "send me an email with the questions you want answered and I will let them have a look and get back to you ... OK?" Sean smiled again.

"Cheers Darren ... thanks once again," said Sean.

"No problems, till then," the line went dead, Sean pressed a button on the phone and reached for the mouse of the desktop computer.

"That at least will be something," stated Simon.

"We should know a little bit more about our 2 Russian friends," answered Mike who then looked over at Simon, "are you still convinced they are the ones?" Simon leaned back in the chair again. Sean's screen came to life as Simon spoke.

"It was the way he ..." Simon's hands jumped up from the desk to near his face. His palms were towards his chin and his fingers outstretched "he just started to ... you know."

"To ... what?" asked Mike, Simon looked away and his eyes darted around the room and his mind relived what he had seen.

"To ... change," Mike and Sean exchanged a glance, Simon was still outside the bar in Belfast as his fingers closed into fists to defend his face. "The other one was throwing people around like rag dolls when he just ... *flew* into him." Sean started to click on the mouse as his eyes moved away from Simon and onto the screen. Simon stopped speaking and looked over, first at Sean then at Mike.

"Change into what?" Mike had lowered his voice to ask the question. Simon shrugged his shoulders and looked away.

"I've no idea ..." he looked up at Mike, "we will have to ask him that!" Mike nodded.

"Right then," Sean said towards the screen. Mike stood up and walked round by his left shoulder and looked at the open email message. Darren Forrester's police email address was in the 'send to' box. "What do we want to know?" Sean asked.

"Who are 'Alpha squad'?" asked Mike, Sean nodded and started to type a greeting and started to read aloud as he was typing. Simon rose and walked over to the coffee machine and refilled his mug then refilled the nearly empty mug that Mike had left beside it, "*We would like to know 'who' and 'what' are the following military organisations ...*"

"Refill?" asked Simon. Sean stopped typing and looked over and nodded.

"*From Russia: Alpha squad and the spets... how is it spelt correctly?*"

"S-P-E-T-S-N-A-Z," Mike spelt out for him, Sean typed each letter as he did so.

"*... and from France who are 'le crap'?*" Sean was looking up and down from the keyboard to the screen as he was typing. He tapped the return button twice then continued to type. "*We would like to know what kind of skills former members of either of these ...*" Sean paused and looked at Mike.

"Can do ..." said Mike.

"Possess ..." said Simon, "What kind of skills they 'possess'" Sean nodded,

"*Possess... yeah I like that,*" Sean finished off the email and clicked on the 'send' icon, Mike straightened up and walked back to his fresh coffee.

"Do you think we will get anything?" Simon asked.

"Well anything is better than nothing," said Mike as he sat back down, Sean agreed. His computer pinged with the arrival of an email, Sean opened it and glanced over the 'read' report that had just arrived.

"We will know soon enough ... he has just opened it."

Mike was over with Simon and they were discussing something from one of the folders. Sunlight poured in through the window. Sean was lost in thought, *'just two more years to go'*, he enjoyed the thought, but it also scared him. He had been a police officer for over 28 years now and he had another 15 years before the state pension started, what would he do? What could he do? *'Well at least the wife will be happy,* the computer pinged.

"He has answered," Sean said as he reached for the mouse, both Mike and Simon stopped what they were doing and crowded round to read the short email.

'NO PROBLEMS, THEY SAY IT IS TOO MUCH TO PUT INTO ONE EMAIL, BUT THEY CAN GIVE YOU A FIVE MINS FACE TO FACE ON EACH ONE IF YOU LIKE. SAY AT YOUR PLACE, MONDAY AT 2PM?' Sean looked at the other two, both were nodding as they read the text of the email.

"When are we doing the presentation to bring Chief Anderson up to date on where we are at?" Sean asked.

"Tuesday at ten," Mike answered.

"Belfast at two on Monday then," Sean tapped in the reply and as he sent it a second email arrived from Darren.

'YOU ARE GOING TO GET TO MEET 'THE DUKE' AND 'THE UNHOLY TRINITY'WE ARE ALL GOING TO BE IN BELFAST FOR A FEW DAYS ANYWAY NEXT WEEK. 2 BIRDS, 1 STONE. :-)'

"Who is 'The Duke' and 'The Unholy Trinity'?" asked a confused Mike.

"No idea ..." answered Sean, "but I think we are going to find out." Sean re-read the email and smiled at the smiley face Darren had put at the end; some people just never grow up and, for a moment, Sean was jealous.

Chapter 47

Davidov was late. Anders looked at his watch again. Davidov had told him to be in Anderson Park at 9am and it was now nearly half past; of all the things that he wanted to be doing this Friday morning standing around waiting was not one of them. Now that Davidov was Alpha he had been quick to enforce his authority; last night he had gone around to the houses and shouted everyone down. The Rua were to be ignored and Viktor had been given the task of organising the cremation and return of Alexi. Yelina had asked if his brother had been told back home. Anders knew it would not take long for the bruise on her face to disappear. Anders was sitting on the monument and was facing towards the town. The two Rua who had been following him were standing over near the bus stop. They were mostly hidden on the far side of the hedge, but he knew they were there. His phone bleeped with a message, it was from Davidov.

'ARE YOU THERE?'

'YES,' he replied, Davidov asked another question almost immediately.

'ARE THE RUA THERE?'

'YES, TWO OF THEM,' he kept the phone in his hand but this time Davidov didn't answer straight away. Anders glanced over at the two Rua who were chatting, they seemed really pleased about something, was it the death of Alexi? The traffic on the road flowed in both directions, he felt his eyes moving upwards to the low grey clouds; it wasn't raining for once. The phone beeped again.

'OK, WAIT UNTIL I GET THERE,' he looked around, of course he would wait, he knew better than to go against a newly promoted Alpha who would love the chance of making an example of his dominance.

DANGER

Anders eyes shot over to his right, his body reacted, and he felt his wolf bear its teeth. There was danger over there, he glanced over at the Rua, they were reacting as well. Whatever the danger was, it clearly wasn't them. The danger backed away and subsided, He felt his body start to relax as walked around the monument noting everything and everyone. The people walking along the far side of the road, the empty cars in the small car park, the two Rua, his mind sharpened. His hands reached inside the pockets of his jacket and his right hand firmly gripped his pistol. If they wanted a fight, they'd get one.

After several minutes, the two Rua walked off towards the town; he watched them go. His head moved to his left as a small hatchback pulled into the car park; he did not recognise the car, but he recognised the shape of Davidov inside it. Davidov parked in the last remaining space and walked confidently towards him. Viktor turned to face him and removed his hands from his pockets.

"Where are the Rua?" Davidov demanded. There was no greeting, just a question, he turned to his left and pointed with his left hand.

"They had been by the bus stop over there, but they just left."

"Why?" again he demanded, Anders looked back at him.

"I don't know, but,"

"But what?" Davidov fixed his gaze onto Anders.

"But there was something over there," Anders pointed over to where the danger had been, "but it backed off."

"Rua?" Davidov asked he shook his head.

"No ... the two that were over there reacted to it as well," he paused, "it wasn't one of '*our*' kind," he explained, Davidov nodded.

"Fine, leave it for them then." Davidov relaxed a bit, "we have a problem of our own," Anders turned back towards him and listened. "The Rua have sent one of their own out after me," that could mean only one thing, they wanted Davidov dead. "His name is 'Paddy M'Kane' and he is good,"

"M'Kane ... the first one who came to the door?" Anders asked.

"The very same," answered Davidov.

"I will take care of it," Anders said confidently; anger flashed in Davidov's eyes.

"Do not underestimate him, he is after both me and Anna ... and that cannot be allowed," he did not ask how Davidov knew about this, but Anders knew the meaning of that, and the very thought brought a smile to his face.

"We are at war with them now?" he asked, Davidov tensed as if he was about to strike.

"No, no we are not," Davidov took a couple of paces forward and walked past him, "we are not strong enough yet to defeat them."

"We will follow you," answered Anders, a look of pride shone from his face. Davidov looked over his left shoulder and smiled, he turned to walk away towards his car.

"Yes, I know you will," Davidov stopped, "but first they will learn that we will not be subject to them," Davidov stated.

"What do you want me to do?" Anders asked. Davidov looked directly at him.

"Find M'Kane and stop him, he must not get close to my Anna," Anders picked up the '*my Anna*' comment.

"I obey," Anders had straightened up as he answered Davidov. Davidov nodded and waked away. Anders was excited by this task and walked towards the house. By giving him this task Davidov was making him higher in the pack that any of the others. Things were now falling into place, just as Davidov had told them all before they had left home. They were going to make this place their new home, this was the new den and Davidov would rule with him by his side. Viktor was very excited indeed.

∞∞∞

"So how much sleep did you actually get last night?" Paul's question made him look around. Carl had been watching the herd of deer that was being moved by three men on quad bikes. His eyes moved over the surrounding fields; he always loved the different shades of green that filled his vision with a strong bond of belonging that kept him tied to this land. Paul was standing beside the 4 x 4, he was wearing rubber boots and water-resistant trousers with a matching jacket, the mud was nearly up to his knees.

"Enough," Carl's gaze returned to the moving animals that were at the bottom of the hill, one of the quad bikes roared and started to circle the beasts and change the direction they had tried to go. Paul walked over beside him.

"All of our present stock is being re-checked this morning," Paul said. Carl nodded in acknowledgement twice.

"So, what happened in County Down last night?" he was asking about the other deer farm in Northern Ireland, a farm that had nothing to do with them, but was in the news.

"Well it appears that two of the farm hands tried to stop an elder male from mating ... both are still in hospital," Paul answered, Carl turned his head towards him, and a small smile spread over his face.

"They tried to stop a male from mating?" Paul let out a small laugh as Carl spoke.

"Yes," he answered, "I don't think that they will do it again!" Both men smiled, and Carl's attention returned to the deer at the bottom of the hill.

"You cannot teach experience," Carl stated.

"No, you can't," answered Paul, "the Health and Safety Executive went there this morning."

"What state are the farm hands in?" asked Carl.

"One is quite bad, but he will live."

"That is good," answered Carl. Paul noticed that Carl wasn't looking at the deer any more, he was gazing out over the hills again, his mind was elsewhere.

"Tony is bringing him here for 3pm," Carl already knew this and slowly turned his head away to look over the hills again.

"His son is coming home," it was no more than a whisper that Carl had uttered. Ever since Tony had told them the name of Kyle Foster, Carl had been more unsettled than Paul had ever seen him before.

"Then we will welcome him as '*his*' son, he will know he is amongst family here," Carl turned and walked past him, he was heading towards the passenger door of the 4 x 4.

"What if he doesn't actually know?" Carl asked, "What if he has no idea who ... or what he really is?"

"He must!" stated Paul.

"From what Tony has said we must assume he doesn't, he was only a child at the time, remember?" Paul nodded and let his eyes drop, "We must establish what he remembers, then ... and only then will we know what the rest of his family told him." Paul raised his eyes. Carl was looking straight at him as he had been speaking. Paul nodded and the two of them climbed into the warm vehicle; as Paul slammed the door his phone started to ring.

"It's Paddy," he said. Carl adjusted the heater as Paul answered the phone, "Hello," he nodded his head as the phone was by his ear. "Look I am with Carl ... hang on ... I will put you on speakerphone," Paul took the phone and placed it into a black plastic mount and connected a small black wire; the speakers inside the vehicle burst into life, "Right, we are in one of the wagons and there is just Carl and I," Paul stated.

"Hi," Paddy's voice seemed distant.

"So, what is happening?" asked Carl.

"Well a few things ..." started Paddy, "I can confirm that Sprogis is '*not*' with the others at the two houses,"

"That makes sense," said Paul.

"Yeah, it appears he does have the support of the others for his challenge and the female 'Nikitin' is with him."

"She is dangerous," stated Carl, "do not underestimate that one," he advised.

"I won't..." answered Paddy.

"What else?" Carl asked.

"Well I was observing Dusmanov this morning when he had a short meeting with Sprogis in Anderson Park in Coleraine, but it was cut short."

"Why?" asked Carl.

"I think it was that Princess you told us about."

"What makes you think that?" Carl asked.

"That same thing that happened at the bottom of Church Street, well I felt it again."

"What happened then?" Carl asked.

"The Mongol reacted, and she backed off."

"Did you see her?" Carl had breathed in as he asked the question.

"No ... but she was definitely there." Carl nodded his head.

"What did the Mongol do?" Paul asked.

"He headed off in the opposite direction."

"Did he not go after her?" Carl asked.

"Dusmanov returned to the house, Sprogis headed off towards Portrush, so no I don't think so, what do you want me to do about her?" Carl looked out the windows of the 4 x 4.

"Only engage her if you are directly confronted by her ... she may not be alone,"

"Ok," answered Paddy.

"Intercept Sprogis and deal with him as you have been instructed to,"

"I will," Paddy answered immediately.

"Paddy ..."

"Yes,"

"Stay within our laws," Carl commanded.

"I will."

Carl reached up and pressed the red button on the phone and ended the call.

"Let's go back to the farmhouse ... we have a guest to prepare for." Carl turned his head and looked out the window; this evening was going to be a very eventful one indeed.

∞∞∞∞

Cara-Marie looked at her watch, 12:50, she was ten minutes early; she looked around the front of the busy City Hall in Belfast, the white Italian marble looked as elegant as the day it was first laid. The large 'Belfast wheel' slowly turned; from inside the viewing pods people looked out over the rooftops of the city. Her mind wandered.

"Cara?" she snapped back into the present and looked into the swarm of people who were crossing at the traffic lights at the junction with Royal Avenue. From behind a man in a dark suit stepped a young woman who was much shorter than the business man. She was wearing a dark coloured, woollen beret and a thick black jacket. A pale canvas shoulder bag hung over her right shoulder, and she was cradling several folders in her arms. Her bright smile welcomed Cara-Marie.

"Hiya," she welcomed her in a brief hug as the two friends met.

"Hiya," her friend smiled.

"It's really good to see you again Fiona," Fiona slowed down so the two of them walked side by side.

"Yeah ... and you," the two of them passed through the gates of the City Hall. Fiona turned to her right and Cara followed her towards the open space. Several small groups of people were sitting around in small circles and were enjoying the sunshine, but a summer's day it was not, the wind made sure of that.

"How long has it been now?" Cara-Marie asked.

"Oh ... nearly three years, I think," Fiona answered.

"Three years?"

"Yeah, three years ... it was 'that' engagement party," Fiona had a mischievous grin on her face, a grin matched by Cara-Marie, the two women exchanged a knowing glance.

"Oh yes .... but we're not going to talk about 'that' party," she was almost laughing as she spoke, Fiona let out a little chuckle as they walked on.

"Do you keep in touch with him?" Fiona's question was direct, and it made the smile on Cara-Marie's face reduce to a polite smile.

"No ... I haven't heard from him since that night," she paused then asked, "What about you? Do you keep in touch with .... him?" The smile spread across her face.

"Not since that night ... no," she looked around the ground as Fiona answered, "some things are best left in the past ... do you not agree?" she asked.

Cara-Marie looked over at her. "Yes, I do,"

"Do you miss uni?" Fiona asked.

"One part of me does miss university, another part, no," she replied.

"Anyway, the reason we are here," said Fiona as she stopped at a patch of grass. Fiona took off her shoulder bag and sat down on the grass and laid the folders down in front of her. Cara-Marie looked around, there was no one nearby and she sat down opposite her. Fiona started to sort through the folders until she came to an A4 brown envelope.

"Here we are," Fiona picked up the envelope and held it out towards Cara, she eagerly took hold of it, Fiona's grip of the envelope tightened; she looked up at her.

"What?" she asked.

"I want to be clear," Fiona started.

"Ok,"

"You did 'not' get this from me ... I am in 'no way' connected to Dr Burns or his research," Cara-Marie nodded.

232

"Of course," without a named source she could not use whatever was inside as a reference in a published story. Kevin would probably not allow it. Fiona's grip loosened, she went to open the envelope, but Fiona stopped her.

"Don't open it here," she was serious.

"Is it *'that'* bad?" she asked, Fiona looked around at the other people, she did not look back at her as she spoke.

"Dr Burns is an exceptional forensic scientist," Cara-Marie relaxed back and looked directly at her friend, this was not like her, "but the direction he is going in," Fiona stopped herself, "they *'cannot be real'*..."

"What cannot be real?" she asked.

"Were ......" again Fiona stopped herself, she nodded towards the envelope, "well you look at that and make up your own mind."

"I will," Cara-Marie answered, Fiona rose to leave so she stood up.

"Look, I have to get back to work ..." Fiona bent over to collect her things and adjusted the bag over her shoulder.

"Yeah, I have to get back to Coleraine,"

"We have to do this again," stated Fiona then smiled.

"Yes ... next time socially .... and include wine as well," Fiona let out a short laugh.

"Yes, absolutely," the two of them turned and walked back towards the main entrance.

"So, is your mum still trying to get you married off?" Fiona's question was answered with a shrug and a noise of frustration.

"She is doing my head in ... it's nearly every bloke I talk to is *'oh he's nice'* or *'he's in a nice job'* ..." the two of them walked on and chatted all the way back out of the City Hall. Finally, Fiona stopped, the two of them shared a short hug and Cara-Marie watched as her friend disappeared back into the crowd. As soon as she was out of sight Cara was ripping at the envelope. There were several sheets of printed paper, the first was a press release that was dated for next week, the next sheet of paper was a pathology report on a death, she recognised the name from the riverside in Coleraine, but it was the next set of pages that were stapled together that stopped her in her tracks.

"Oh my ...." she breathed in as she read the words on the page, her eyes scanned the words, *'AND WE CAN SHOW THAT THESE ARE IN FACT REAL.'* She shoved the pages back inside the envelope as she almost broke into a run to return to her car, "God bless you Fiona," she said aloud.

Chapter 48

Tony glanced over at Kyle who was in the passenger seat. Kyle was not impressed by any stretch of the imagination, Tony looked back at the empty country road.

"Where are we going again?" Kyle asked.

"It is a deer farm," answered Tony.

"And why do I want to go to a deer farm?" Tony thought about Kyle's question.

"Well ... your dad used to own it." The car rose over a small hill and Tony caught a glimpse of the farm a few miles away, he could feel the stare he was getting from the passenger seat.

"My Dad?"

"Yes ... the present owner is really looking forward to meeting you," answered Tony.

"And who would that be?" Asked Kyle.

"Carl O'Brien," Tony glanced at Kyle, "your father and he were good friends."

"Apparently," stated Kyle. "I don't remember anyone called Carl," Tony decided to leave it at that. Carl had said that he would make his own introductions. The car slowed as he approached the entrance to the lane that led up towards the farmhouse. He turned the car into the entrance and started off up the lane. The hedges on either side guided them all the way up to the complex where a large group of people were waiting. Tony slowed the car as they approached the courtyard and reversed parked his car in beside two parked cars.

Across the yard two parked 4 x 4's had people sitting on them, others were gathered around the yard. Tony knew all the faces, Kyle was less than comfortable, all attention now turned towards the new arrivals as Tony turned the engine off.

"Who are they?" asked Kyle. Tony released his seatbelt and slightly smiled at him as he reached for the door.

"They? ... they are family."

"Family?"

"Yes, family," Tony looked around at the faces of the mixture of men and women who were staring at them. The group ranged from teenagers to the middle aged, "they are the farm hands who live and work here," he opened the door of the car and climbed out, Kyle followed suit.

"Hi Tony," one of the men who was standing nearby spoke. A ripple of excitement flowed through the crowd; they were excited at Kyle. Kyle caught a few of them eye to eye as Tony shook hands with the older man who had stepped forward to greet him. Tony was on familiar ground that much was clear. Kyle looked around the yard glancing out over the field. For a moment, the land flashed, and it was no longer overcast mid-afternoon but a brilliant sunny summer's day. The old tractor appeared, and Kyle felt himself running towards his brother who was climbing up it, they were only children.

"I've been here before," Kyle felt himself suddenly say.

"You have been here before." The male voice brought him back to where he was. An older man was walking towards him with another man just behind him, the older man held out his hand as he approached.

"It's good to see you again Kyle."

"Who are you?" Kyle had not taken the offered hand.

"I am Carl O'Brien ... and I have been looking forward to this day for a very long time." Kyle slowly reached out and took the offered hand, "Welcome home," Carl said.

"Home?" Kyle reacted with surprise.

"Yes, home ... this is your ancestral home."

"How do you know me?" Kyle demanded, a hush had descended over the gathered crowd.

"I know you very well, your father used to bring you and your brother here for your summers when you were children." Kyle's head twitched towards the field.

"There was a tractor over there," said Kyle and raised his right hand to point in the general direction, Carl paused.

"Ah yes ... I remember, it was broken down, you and your brother played on it for nearly two weeks."

"It was burning ...." Kyle did not finish his sentence.

"That's right, it caught fire," injected Carl, Kyle looked around then fixed his eyes on the man who was standing in front of him.

"I don't remember you,"

"I'm not surprised," Carl stepped back and extended his hand directing Kyle towards the farmhouse, "come, let us go inside so we can talk some more." Kyle paused as everyone else seemed to move at once, voices in the crowd directed some to tasks that still needed to be completed, others moved off out of sight. Tony moved and seemed to fall in behind the little group of men that now headed towards the door of the farmhouse, a group that Carl was leading. Kyle didn't move, it was Carl who stopped.

"Kyle ... this way," he directed. Kyle's body reacted without him even thinking about it. Something made him follow the command he was given by this man, there was something about him that made Kyle obey, this man was a stranger, yet he was very familiar. The group of teenagers who were hanging around the far side of the door of the farmhouse seemed to be in a state of mild excitement; Kyle was the topic of their conversation that quietened to a whisper as he approached. One of the older one's straightened up and grinned at him, he was really pleased to see Kyle. Kyle returned the look with the same near stare that he saved for drunken teenagers outside pubs after closing when he wanted them to do exactly what he wanted. The door of the farmhouse opened, and the small group entered.

"He's an Alpha alright." It was one of the teenagers who had spoken just as Kyle walked through the doorway to the warm room of the farmhouse. A voice outside shouted further commands and the groups dispersed in different directions; there was still work to be done around the farm. The log fire was crackling as Carl sat down in the larger of the chairs that were positioned around the centre of the room; some biscuits were on a round plate placed on the coffee table. The other man took up a stance just behind the high-backed chair on the right-hand side and Tony walked over to Kyle's right as he entered, the door was closed from the outside, leaving the four men alone inside the room.

"I can only say how pleased I am that you are here," Carl said, Kyle noticed he had a very gleeful look on his face. Kyle however was far from that, in fact he was very uncomfortable. Carl was about to speak again when Kyle cut him off.

"Can you tell me exactly who you are and what I am doing here?" Kyle demanded, "I want to know exactly what that was at Castleroe the other night!" Judging by the reaction of everyone else very few people spoke to Carl like that. Carl paused, took an audible breath in then stood and held out his hand. Kyle didn't take it at first but slowly stepped forward and grasped the firm handshake.

"You are right, of course, just like your father was. I am Carl O'Brien. I am the Alpha of the Northern Dun of the Rua clan of the Garou," Kyle's face widened in surprise.

"You're the what?"

"The Alpha ... the leader ... the one in charge of the Northern Dun," Carl explained.

"And what precisely is the northern dun?" Carl relaxed and returned to his seat. The rest of those in the room relaxed as well, Carl extended his right hand towards one of the other chairs.

"Please, sit," Carl offered.

"I feel like standing," Kyle's tone had not changed.

"This may come as a surprise to you Kyle," Carl spoke as he sat back down on the chair. "But you are part of a family that can trace its history back over 6 millenniums."

"What?"

"Yes ... your ancestors built the original foundations here quite some time ago."

"Dun is the Irish word for old fort," another commented.

"I haven't come here for a history lesson," Kyle stated, "I was told that you would be able to tell me what I saw on top of the hill at Castleroe." The man behind the chair twitched and crunched his face in annoyance. Tony glared at Kyle as well. They didn't like the way Kyle was speaking to Carl. Carl held up his right hand in a message to the two men who instantly backed down.

"But first you must know who you are, you are on safe ground here," Carl explained.

"Answer my question ... or I am off and heading straight back to Coleraine police station." Kyle was adamant, Tony glared at him. Carl looked at him and slowly nodded.

"Ok ... his name is Davidov Sprogis and he is from the Mongol pack," Kyle's eyes widened as Carl spoke.

"A Mongol?" he asked.

"Yes, from the Mongol pack, they are mostly spread across modern day Russia and Mongolia ... obviously, but they are also found in other countries such as Poland and around Scandinavia, Sprogis ... for example is from the Baltic state of Latvia,"

"You have actually met him, we stopped him at the VCP outside the Causeway Hospital," Kyle looked over at Tony, Tony nodded his head, "yes, you remember," Kyle did, "He recognised me and sized you up... you did very well not to back down." Kyle pulled his hands out of his pockets and held them up.

"Wait a minute ... I saw an animal at Castleroe," the man behind Carl smiled.

"He would be pleased to hear you say that," Tony smiled at Paul's comment and let out a short chuckle.

"Excuse me, who are you?" Kyle demanded.

"This is Paul Hawkins, he is my number two around here," explained Carl, "he knew your father as well," Kyle looked up at the serious man who was looking directly at him.

"I am sorry at the loss of your father, I considered him a friend," Kyle didn't react to Paul's condolences but looked back at Carl.

"Well as I was saying ..." Carl stood up again and started to walk around the room.

"Sprogis is a Mongol and has recently killed his own Alpha ... I understand that you know about the death of Alexi Chernov." Kyle tried not to react, but his eyes twitched as his mind flashed through the images from Mountsandel.

"Killed? ... I thought that it was a suicide."

"No, Sprogis usurped his Alpha and has taken control of the other Mongols."

"Others?" Kyle's mind had so many questions but that was the only one that came out.

"Yes," answered Carl, "less than ten of them; they have been misbehaving recently, such as the riverside killings, which I hear you know first-hand." Kyle didn't like being in this situation, this man obviously knew more about Kyle than Kyle did about him.

"I didn't see a man at Castleroe ..." Kyle whispered, Carl stopped walking and turned to face him.

"You saw a Garou, not a man," said Carl.

"Garou?" questioned Kyle.

"It comes from 'Le loupe Garou'..." injected Tony, "it's French for ..."

"I know what it means..." Kyle almost shouted, taking a step forward as he did so, "I do actually speak French ... remember!" Tony went to react as did Paul, but they were again stopped by Carl.

"Yes, so we hear,"

"So, you are telling me that this 'thing' is a man wolf?"

"Is that so hard to believe?" asked Carl.

"You expect me to believe that all these murders have been carried out by ..." Kyle's voice trailed off.

"A Werewolf," Carl finished the sentence, "yes, actually I do," Kyle's head spun round towards Tony.

"You don't really think these things are real? Do you?" Tony didn't answer.

"They are as real as you and I." Kyle looked over towards Carl as he spoke.

"What are you saying?" Kyle could see that something was coming.

"You are a part of a family that has survived against all persecutions for centuries," Kyle suddenly realised where this conversation was going.

"I am not an animal."

"Neither are we," Carl started slowly pacing around the room again, "what if I told you 95% of what you know about our kind is just middle age paranoid and Hollywood fiction?"

"They aren't real ... they can't exist," Kyle's statement was met with a smile from all three of them.

"You are different ... you have always been a little different," Carl started, "let me guess, you seem to be able to see a little better in the dark than everyone else?" Kyle's mind flashed back to one of his first training exercises in the Legion. '*How can you see them from here?*' remarked one of the other recruits. Kyle could see the other recruits who were the enemy force but no one, not even their instructors could. "Your sense of smell just seemed to be slightly better than most," Carl continued, again memories flashed in Kyle's mind. "Many of us do find ourselves as hunters and trackers ... you were a sniper I understand?" Carl question forced Kyle back to the present.

"I was, yes ..." Kyle paused.

"Yes, many of us find our way into jobs like that." Tony and Kyle looked eye to eye, he remembered that Tony's last two years in the Parachute Regiment had been as a sniper.

"We are not animals," Carl looked over at Kyle, "We don't hunt our own for our own sexual gratification ... we do not sell chemicals to children to inject into their own bodies ... we do not traffic our own kind into the hands of evil for our own financial gain." Carl shook his head at his thoughts, "they call us evil just because we are different,"

"You only fear the dark because of ignorance," said Kyle.

"Yes, precisely,"

"Who said that?" asked Paul.

"An instructor at Calvi," Kyle quoted.

"We lost track of you after your sister took you to Canada, does your grandmother still live near Kilrea?" Carl brought the conversation back in the direction that he wanted, Kyle was stunned into silence, "I will take that as a yes then," said Carl. Carl looked down into the flames of the fire, "she never could accept any of us for what we really are,"

"Granny ..." Kyle stopped himself this time.

"Yes, your grandmother knows all about us, but well, ... she isn't keen on us."

"Us?" asked Kyle.

"Yes, your father was the Alpha of the Northern Dun," Carl turned toward him, "do you know what happened to your grandfather?"

"He was killed in Italy in 1944 during the war," Carl smiled as Kyle spoke, "Somewhere near Monte Cassio."

"Yes, that is true, but do you know 'HOW' he died?" Carl asked, Kyle shook his head.

"Well, your grandfather had been part of the British forces that were surrounded by the Germans at the siege of Torbruk in 1942,"

"Where he was decorated for bravery," stated Kyle.

"That's right, he was, we know that he revealed who he was to his unit commander and he would lead raiding parties at night to attack the German positions."

"It was believed that the Germans thought that they were facing a much larger force and therefore did not try to assault the city," Kyle stated.

"Again, you are right, his commanders kept what he was secret, he used his strengths until he was captured at Monte Cassio by German paratroopers." Kyle didn't move, "and the only way he could have been caught was if he was captured by German Garou ... by his own kind." Kyle listened, Paul slightly bowed his head and Carl looked away.

"Your grandfather was butchered for what he was; Garou are ruthless with our own."

"I have never heard that before," said Kyle.

"I am sure that you haven't" answered Carl, "not the kind of thing that is discussed over the dinner table."

"I am not a monster," said Kyle quietly,

"Neither are we," said Carl.

"Well if I am one of these ...." Kyle paused,

"Garou," said Tony, Kyle looked over at him.

"How come I don't get all hairy and things..." Carl chuckled at Kyle's question, "Don't I have to be bitten or something?"

"It is in your DNA and your Garou DNA has to be activated first... not everyone has this and only people who carry the DNA strands can ever become one of us." Kyle was slightly confused.

"You are assuming of course that I believe that they are in fact real!" Kyle looked around the room at the others who all exchanged glances.

"Ok, let me prove it to you," Carl started to walk towards the door, he stopped as he reached Kyle, "Follow me,"

Carl opened the door and walked outside followed by Paul, then Kyle and Tony who closed the door behind him. Carl was walking briskly over towards the large metal barn. A small group of farm hands were standing over behind the parked cars, they all turned and acknowledged the party as it passed them. Paul and Tony pulled back the large entrance door and Carl asked Kyle to follow him inside, they closed the doors behind them. The arena was lit up and standing inside the arena were four men, all the men Kyle noted looked like they were mid-twenties. Three were dressed like the rest of the farm hands and the fourth was wearing a two-piece track suit. They had all been joking and were in an obvious good mood when the door opened, and they stopped whatever they had been doing to amuse themselves beforehand, all eyes looked towards Carl. Carl nodded his head and all four of them walked towards the arena fencing.

"Ready?" Carl asked. The one in the track suit smiled and nodded his head, "Begin," Carl commanded.

"What is going on?" Kyle whispered towards Tony.

"What is happening," said Carl, "is John here is going to show you what we are." As Carl was speaking the man in the track suit started to undress, he flicked the trainers off his feet and wasn't wearing anything under the track suit, which was folded and handed to one of the others, he looked towards Carl who nodded, he closed his eyes. The naked man twitched his head and Carl started speaking what seemed like a prepared speech.

"We are the Rua, and we have protected these shores for nearly six thousand years," the man in front of Kyle started to twitch all over. Kyle moved towards the fence as he watched the man fall to his knees and onto his hands, "we exist to ensure our own survival in this modern world," Kyle noticed that hair had started to appear all over his body, muscles twitched, he was in obvious pain, "we are not animals," the head jerked as the front of the face seemed to pop and snap forward, "our kind survive all over the world," Kyle watched as slowly the hair over the man's body continued to grow, his muscles slowly changed with each twitch, "we defend our lands against all aggression," Kyle watched as the hands slowly cracked and widened, the hair around his head and shoulders started to grow faster and thicker, "from wherever the aggression comes from," Kyle was standing mesmerised by what was happening in front of him, the creature yelped in pain as his spine popped and cracked again, loud cracks came from his chest as some of his ribs seemed to pop, the creature's ankles were longer and the ends of the pads of his feet had slowly spread, "we pass on our laws from generation to generation," The elbow snapped back as his jaws slowly pushed forward, his teeth pushed farther out than Kyle had ever seen before, "we are the Rua," the three men standing nearby stepped forward and helped him rise to his feet. Kyle watched as he stretched his arms and legs, moved his shoulders from side to side, opened and closed his mouth and turned his head from side to side. Then the three men stepped back, and the creature took a step forward. His face was more wolf than human. The hair around his head fanned out and hung over his well-developed shoulders. His fingers stretched then clenched into fists and this now calm creature looked deep into Kyle's eyes, he blinked and slowly nodded his head towards Kyle.

"And, we are your family," Carl finished. Kyle's confusion was mixed with fear, he hadn't seen anything like this before; he grabbed the Glock pistol secured on the belt of his trousers, Tony intercepted him as the wolf bared his teeth at this aggression.

Paul came at Kyle from his left side, kicking at Kyle's legs. Kyle fell to the ground with Tony and Paul on top of him, pinning him to the ground. Kyle felt pain scream from his right hand as Tony pried the weapon from it. Kyle fought and kicked with all his strength, but his legs soon felt the pressure of three more people until his entire body was unable to move. Kyle was screaming at them to get off as Tony was trying to reassure him that everything was ok.

"ENOUGH," the command from Carl stopped everything. Everyone was motionless for a few seconds before Carl spoke again. "Release him," slowly all the men relaxed their grip on each of his limbs one at a time and stood up and stepped away, Tony was the last to do so. Kyle was allowed to stand, he moved back against the wall. Tony kept the pistol in his right hand. Kyle hadn't wanted to obey him but something about Carl made him comply, "You have no idea who you really are?"

"I am not a monster," Kyle almost shouted,

"Neither are we, Kyle, neither are we." Carl turned towards the creature and motioned upwards with his head, the face of the wolf seemed to smile as he took a step back and took a deep breath in. Smiles broke out over everyone's face as the wolf pointed his face towards the roof and through his open mouth let out a long, powerful howl. Kyle watched as the hands of the wolf closed into fists and his eyes closed, everyone standing around him closed their eyes and looked upwards in ecstasy.

Kyle felt the howl swirl around him, it made him close his own eyes and instinctively he held his own head towards the sky, his body tingled, his fingers twitched, his eyes filled with tears as the howl ended. Outside the barn other howls continued in the distance, he opened his tear-filled eyes and looked towards Carl. Carl walked over to him and placed his right hand onto Kyle's left shoulder.

"We are your family and we are here for you, you have nothing to fear ever again," Kyle's body shivered.

"What are you doing to me?" he whispered.

"I am doing nothing, it is your own wolf answering the call of the pack," Kyle dropped his head and Carl moved forward and embraced him. Kyle could not understand why he was crying but he could feel his own body start to curl up. He suddenly felt secure, he suddenly felt safe, like a young child in a loving father's embrace. Carl released him from the hug and looked into his face.

"We are your family," Carl was nearly crying himself as he spoke, "welcome home," Kyle's world went blurry, then went dark.

Chapter 49

Paddy M'Kane looked at his watch. It was just after half six in the evening and the sun was setting over the hills, the land would soon be dark. He heard that the son of the previous Alpha was coming to the farm today and he wished he could have been there for that. The clan still talked about the previous Alpha with the utmost respect, he had been a true Rua. Paddy moved in his seat inside the car as his phone bleeped, it was from Paul. 'FOSTER IS ASLEEP IN THE FARMHOUSE, JOHN CHANGED IN FRONT OF HIM THEN CARL TOLD HIM TO CALL TO HIS WOLF,' Paddy read the text then smiled, he had seen that before, he replied, 'NICE ONE, WHAT HAPPENED THEN?' Paddy dropped the phone in the passenger seat, he looked around the empty car park then over at the two houses where the Mongols were. He had followed Sprogis here in the small car three hours ago. He would wait until he was alone then he would carry out his orders. Several cars passed him and headed towards the traffic lights beside the petrol garage, Paddy looked over his right shoulder and out across the river. The Chinese restaurant was brightly lit up and already had customers in it, more cars moved along the road at the far side of the river bank, his phone beeped again. Paddy reached across and read the message. 'FIRST, HE PULLED HIS GUN, TONY, MARTY, DAVIE AND I TALKED HIM OUT OF THAT ONE,' Paddy chuckled at the image that the message put into his head, 'THEN HE SPARKED OUT. WE HAVE BEEN TOLD TO WAKE HIM AT 7.... WHAT IS HAPPENING WITH YOU?' Paddy started to tap in a reply but changed his mind and called the number.

"Hello,"

"I thought that I would phone instead of texting, takes less time," said Paddy.

"Aye, no problems," replied Paul.

"So, he is out cold?"

"Oh yes,"

"So, he didn't know then?"

"Well we weren't expecting him to. Tony has worked with him for nearly two years and he didn't suspect anything ... and Tony, as you know too well has a nose for things like that." Paul's comment made Paddy smile, it was Tony who first found Paddy and it was Tony who helped him through his first change.

"Yeah, he is good like that, but anyway," Paddy paused, "just to let you know I am in Coleraine and I am watching the house."

"How long have they been there?" asked Paul.

"Couple of hours now, they all seemed to arrive shortly afterwards."

"No one leave?"

"No, Alan and one other are watching the back, it is covered," stated Paddy.

"You know what to do?" said Paul.

"Yes," was the one-word reply.

"Stay within our laws," stated Paul.

"I intend too," smiled Paddy.

"Good," said Paul, "Call me when you are done." Paddy cancelled the call and tucked the phone away into his trouser pocket. The front door of the house opened, and a single figure walked out, Sprogis had not changed from what he was wearing earlier. He pulled the woollen cap down over his head as he had walked out the door. Paddy watched as he quickly climbed into the small car that was parked outside the house, the engine coughed into life. Paddy pressed a button on the hand-held radio.

"November, Oscar over," the transmission was short and precise.

"November," Paddy recognised Alan Morrows voice.

"Oscar, Primary one now mobile, I will take control, maintain present task, over." Paddy let the hand-held radio drop into the compartment in the driver's door as he heard Alan answer him.

"November, roger, out." The primary target was on the move and he was going to follow him, they should stay here and continue to watch the house. There were several cars in between them as he stopped near the traffic lights. Paddy couldn't see the car, so he pressed the top of the CD player in the car and the digital display came out and flipped up. He scrolled through the menu of the music that was on the system where at the very bottom of the list was one word. 'FIND' as he pressed it a small GPS map appeared and located the small button transmitter that he had placed on the car yesterday. The two-dimensional road map of Coleraine had a red dot on it and at the bottom of the screen were the words '47 METRES AHEAD', he was not going to lose him in traffic.

"Now let's see where you are going this fine evening?" Paddy said out loud as the traffic started to move off. Davidov had moved over to the right-hand lane, so he was not going to Castlerock but heading back into town. The lights changed and slowly the traffic began to move, Davidov was at the far side of the bridge and was heading off towards the university, he was soon following, occasionally glancing at the screen on the dashboard. Anyone looking into the car would only make out a satnav display, only a trained eye would spot the moving red mark that was also showing. Paddy followed the dot up the road past the BMW garage on the right and Anderson Park on the left, Davidov continued onwards underneath the railway bridge. The volume of traffic lessened, so he made ground on the target car, but he made sure that he didn't get too close.

The dot on the screen turned left before the next bridge and took the road towards the University. The space to his left opened, Paddy noticed that Davidov had speeded up, he would keep pace. He flew past the entrance to the University but slowed at the next junction, he wasn't going to Portstewart at least. Paddy followed on as Davidov turned left and followed the road up to the next roundabout. Left would take him to Portrush, right back into Coleraine or straight on, Davidov went straight on. The right-hand side of the road was now lined with trees, behind which was the Ballysally housing estate, or 'BallyBosnia' as it was also known. Davidov carried on over the roundabout at the end of the road and onto the next roundabout, Paddy was starting to think that his surveillance had been compromised and he was being taken on a wild goose chase or maybe Davidov still didn't fully know his way around town.

At this roundabout Davidov turned left into the countryside and away from the town. His was the only other car on the road now and Davidov had probably spotted him by now as he speeded up considerably. Paddy decided to keep to his own speed and let the GPS do its work. His headlights illuminated the road and the hedgerows. The red taillights of Davidov's car disappeared into the grey of the night.

"Don't worry ... I'll find yea," he whispered to himself, the hand-held radio crackled into life.

"Oscar, November, over," said Alan.

"November," he released the button then Alan spoke again.

"Just to let you know all targets have left location one and are all heading in separate directions," Paddy thought for a moment then Alan continued. "Primary four is in Charlie two and heading towards Red route two, over," Paddy realised what he was saying. Primary four was Pe'ter Shimikov and Charlie two was the second of their cars, now why was he heading off towards Derry City?

"Oscar," Paddy confirmed that he understood what Alan had said so far.

"November, all other Primary's except two and three who are still stationary, are mobile on foot. I am following Primary four and November two is maintaining current task," Alan was following Shimikov to see where he was going, his son will continue to monitor the house.

"Roger," Paddy confirmed that was ok. Paddy continued down the road all the way to the village of Ballybogy. He glanced at the screen, Sprogis had turned right onto the Ballybogy road and was heading down towards Ballymoney. A couple of cars passed him at the junction as he waited to turn right and continue to follow the car, Sprogis was now nearly half a mile ahead. He reached down for the radio again.

"November, Oscar," he said, Alan obviously still had his in his hands as he answered it immediately.

"November,"

"Oscar, I am still mobile following Primary One in Charlie One and I am just turning onto Blue route one now, over,"

"November two, Oscar," a few seconds later a younger voice answered him.

"November two,"

"Oscar, copy all in a datalink and inform the farm, over," Paddy released the handset, Alan's son replied.

"November two," Paddy gunned the car and it jumped out across the road, the car slowed down behind the white Ford as they passed the petrol station in Ballybogy, glanced down at his petrol gauge, it was still three quarters full. As the road cleared he over took the couple of cars and sped off down the long straight road after his quarry. The hand of the speedometer moved up in one steady motion as the ground passed faster underneath the car, the road rose and fell as he could see that he was catching the small dot on the screen. The distance dropped to 300 metres, so he slowed down until he was doing the same speed as him. It was an open straight road and Paddy could see him now and he could also see that there was nothing in front of him so why had he slowed down?

Paddy carried on, behind him the cars that he had passed earlier were starting to catch up with him. They were now coming towards the Ballymoney roundabout and Paddy wondered which way was Sprogis going to go? He could turn left and head towards Ballymena, right and head back to Coleraine or straight on into Ballymoney, he slowed the car down again as he was now less than one hundred metres behind him.

Sprogis was sitting at the junction waiting for a gap in the flowing traffic that was coming from the right, that ruled out Ballymena, Paddy slowed the car right down to a stop right behind the car he was following. The rear-view mirror was twisted so he could not make eye contact with Sprogis, he looked to the right at the traffic. The line of cars and vans ended and Sprogis jumped forward. Paddy took his time and moved forward one space to the junction as the car came all the way around the roundabout and headed back the way that they had just come. Sprogis still had the hat on and was talking on the phone so his hand was covering his face.

Paddy knew that his surveillance was compromised as Sprogis suddenly accelerated past him and back up the Ballybogy road. Paddy was now eager to get after him as the device was only effective up to two miles away, any more than that and he would lose the signal. A gap appeared in the traffic and Paddy shot forward and turned around the roundabout and headed back up the Ballybogy road, Sprogis had got a good head start but he was in the more powerful car. The night was closing in and it was getting darker, but the red dot was still on the screen, he was 3/4s of a mile up ahead, he was nearly at Ballybogy again, dropped a gear and the car sped up. Suddenly as Sprogis got to Ballybogy he slowed down, in fact he slowed to a crawl, he would have no problems catching him, then he turned off to the right.

Paddy looked up ahead, the lights of the village were closing fast, and the road was still clear, he felt his own heart beat a little faster, he loved the chase. Sprogis had picked up speed again and was navigating his way along the dark country lane. This was good news, he knew the road, and Sprogis didn't. It only took Paddy seconds until he was turning down the road as well, Sprogis was only 300 metres in front. The headlights lit up the country road as Paddy took off after him.

Suddenly Sprogis slowed right down and turned off to his right. Paddy was now right behind him and slowed to a stop at the entrance to the fenced car park. The car park itself was used for car boot sales every Sunday afternoon but Paddy had only been there once, but what was Sprogis doing here? He watched as Sprogis drove the car over to the far side near the trees and stopped the car. As the lights of the car went out Paddy made his decision and turned his car into the car park. A smile came over his face as he now guessed why Sprogis had come here. He wanted a fight, well a fight he was going to get. The headlights of the car found the left-hand side of the parked car, Sprogis was still sitting in the driver's seat. Paddy stopped the car some distance away then turned off the lights and then the engine. As he opened the door he reached over in to the foot well of the passenger's side and lifted out the small daysack that had been sitting there, it contained only one thing.

Paddy confidently rose out of the car and slammed the door. He dropped the keys into one of his pockets as a massive grin spread across his face, he was going to enjoy this so, so much. He held the daysack in his left hand as he started to walk towards the parked car, the driver's door opened, and the figure stepped out, he kept his head down and slowly walked around to the rear of the car.

"So, Mister Sprogis … it's time to teach you a lesson," shouted Paddy as he slowed to a halt, the figure was only a few metres away now and was still looking towards the ground.

"No, M'Kane of the Rua … it is you who will be taught the lesson," The figure lifted his head and with his right hand took off the hat and Anders looked straight at him, it wasn't Davidov. Paddy let the surprise wash over him, then after a breath in Paddy answered him.

"So, he can't fight for himself … well after I have dealt with you I intend to deal with him," Anders just smiled back at him.

"Again, you are wrong," suddenly Paddy felt himself look to the north as the Wolf rose up from the under growth, a wisp of wind made his head dart towards the east as the second wolf stood up on its hind legs. Paddy slowly turned his head to look to the west as the third wolf rose up, he closed his eyes briefly and listened to the approaching wolf from the south, he opened his eyes again, this time they blazed with anger.

"This is our land," he shouted, "you will obey our laws." Anders slowly removed Davidov's outdoor jacket and took a step towards him, laughing as he did so.

"Wrong, wrong, wrong," Anders smiled and held out his hands, showing him the pistol, "we are going to make these 'our' lands, and when we do …"

"The Rua will not allow that," the venom in Paddy's voice flowed over his tongue. His right hand went towards the daysack as the four approaching werewolves came ever closer.

"Ah yes, the Rua, famed for their music, dance and hospitality… well do you know what we Mongols are renowned for?" Paddy dropped the daysack but held onto the grip of the short Japanese sword with his right hand.

"Yeah, for being unreasonable and unco-operative," Paddy's comment had the required effect as the approaching wolves snarled and barked at him.

"Warriors," Anders stressed, "respected by all Garou for our strength as warriors in battle." A smile came across Paddy's face, he had got him to react. Slowly with his left he firmly gripped the sheath of the sword and slid it off to reveal the shiny straight blade. In one movement, he gripped it with both hands and with a ferocious shout jumped forward and pointed the sword towards Anders.

"I am Fi – ann – a," Paddy was shouting, "we rule these lands …you are subject to us," Paddy looked around at the creatures that were walking step by step towards him, he looked around at each one in turn, "two male and two females," Paddy counted before he fixed his gaze on Anders, "and you," Paddy raised his head in a slow nod as Anders slowly shook his, they all understood, this Rua would not be subject to them.

"Too bad …" said Anders, "I kinda liked you," Anders let out a short ghoulish laugh "but I will like your females even more," he boasted. Paddy showed his teeth and growled, he would not have time to call to his wolf, he felt his grip on the handle of the straight sword tighten. He brought the sword straight up beside the right-hand side of his own face, he was ready to strike. Paddy felt his lungs fill with breath as he got ready to scream and charge at Anders.

"Take him," Anders commanded.

Chapter 50

Cara-Marie was sitting behind the computer desk in her house. Several sheets of paper were lying over the desk, more were spread across the floor, she was in deep concentration studying the information she was reading. The noise of the door chimes brought her back to the present; as she rose from her desk the door chimed again.

"Coming," she shouted. She glanced at her watch; she had been home for about four hours. She opened the door and Mark stepped forward into the hallway.

"I have got half an hour to be back at the house ... she will go mental if she finds out I am here," he said as he headed towards the sofa, "Is the kettle on?" he asked.

"Did you put it on?" she answered as she closed the door.

"No,"

"Then the kettle isn't on," she walked back to the desk and as she sat down she looked over at him, "I'll have a tea,"

"What?" he said.

"Milk, no sugar ... thank you," she lifted a handful of sheets of paper and started shuffling them. She stopped what she was doing and looked over at him, "have you forgotten where the kettle is?"

"No, I just..."

"Milk, no sugar," she butted in, Mark smiled, rose from the sofa and walked into the kitchen.

"So how was your trip to Belfast?" he shouted.

"Very, very good," she answered, she started to put the pathologists' report back in to chronological order.

"Really? What did you get?"

"I wasn't shopping,"

"Why else would you go to Belfast on a Friday then?" he asked, she glanced at the paper work in her hand and smiled.

"I was meeting up with someone,"

"Your mum finally set you up with a boyfriend then?"

"I don't need my Mum to set me up with anyone, besides I would rather be single than have two on the go at once," she smiled at her own retort.

"I don't have two on the go ... just got the one up the duff," she paused, she had not liked his ex-girlfriend and his present one hated her but that was his choice, he appeared in the doorway with a mug of hot liquid in each hand.

"So," he said as he walked towards her and handed her one of the mugs. She smiled and took the mug in her left hand; her right hand still grasped the report. "Why did you go to Belfast and why is it so important to get me round this evening?" he walked over and retook his seat on the sofa, she sipped at the hot coffee.

"Too much milk," she said.

"What?"

"Too much milk," she lifted the mug towards him then sipped some more.

"You're welcome," he said lifting his mug to his lips, she turned the chair towards him, stood up and walked over to where he was sitting; she held out the report as she did so.

"I went to get this," she said. Mark glanced up at her then took the sheets of paper, she sat down at the far end of the sofa but had turned her body, so she was facing him. She watched as he started reading over the report, the look of surprise started in his eyes, then moved up to his eyebrows then spread over his face.

"Where did you get this?" his voice had raised an octave.

"An un-named source," she answered, smiling as she did so. Mark didn't look up but became more engrossed as he went from page to page.

"Oh my," he paused, *"Real?"* he looked over at her as he said the last word, she winked at him.

"He is going public with this next week," Cara-Marie lifted the mug to her lips again as shock spread over Mark's body.

"I mean he is going to publicly say that these are in fact ... real"

"So, it seems," Mark paused and looked over at her.

"So, what are you going to do with this?" he asked, she looked him square in the face.

"Put this in front of Kevin on Monday morning, then the front-page Tuesday morning," he wasn't convinced, his eyes looked over the words on the page again. "We will be the first paper to break this story, just think what that will do for our circulation!" he glanced over at her as he read on,

"Well ..."

"Well what?" she demanded.

"Well this is a good source but ..."

"But?"

"But do you really think people will believe that these things are real?"

"People believed the threat from Iraq was real and look what happened there."

"Well you have a point there," he became engrossed with what was on the page.

"So..." she glanced over at the computer desk where her phone bleeped with a text; she rose and walked over towards it, "do you think I have enough there for a front page?" Mark looked up at the back of her head.

"With this? ... Yes ... however," she suddenly turned and cut him off,

"TWO CARS ON FIRE WITH A BODY TORN APART NEARBY," she was reading from the screen as she was reaching for her jacket,

"Where?" he asked as he propelled himself up from the sofa.

"Out past Ballybogy," she was already heading towards the door as she was tapping into her phone, she stopped and turned towards him as they both reached the front door. "You got your stuff?" she asked.

"In the boot of the car," he answered. "Who is telling you this?"

"Brilliant," her front door was already flying open as her jacket slid over her shoulders and her large leather handbag hit him as she spun round and dived out the door.

"Where did that come from?" Neither of his last two questions were answered the way he wanted.

"I'm driving," she shouted without turning around. He slammed the door behind him as it was useless to argue, and it would be a few hours before he remembered that he had told his girlfriend that he would be home in half an hour, another argument was coming.

ooooo

Kyle's eyes slowly opened, he looked around the unfamiliar bedroom, he was lying on an old iron framed double bed, he was on top of the thick duvet and was fully dressed. He looked around at the solid wooden furniture that was around the room, it looked like the bedroom was furnished for one person. The single window let the lights from the farm complex flood in. The curtains that looked handmade were drawn back. On the opposite wall there was a landscape print he didn't recognise. He tried to stand up, but his body felt exhausted. His muscles ached as he slowly made himself sit up on the edge of the bed. He closed his eyes and lowered his head. The single wooden door opened, and a cheerful Tony walked in holding a mug. The smell of coffee filled Kyle's nostrils with a strength as if it was being held directly under his nose, he opened his eyes and slowly lifted his head.

"Look at the state of you," he was smiling as he closed the door behind him. Kyle raised his hand and took the offered mug.

"How did I get here?" he asked

"I carried you," answered Tony.

"What happened to me?" Kyle asked.

"You found out who you really are," he answered. Kyle looked up.

"What?" Tony smiled a reassuring smile.

"John called to your wolf and,"

"And what?"

"And ... your wolf answered," confusion reigned inside Kyle's head his face twisted.

"What?" Tony smiled and walked over towards the door.

"Don't worry, it will take a while, but you will soon pick it up."

"What if I don't want to pick it up?" Tony stopped with his hand on the door.

"You are definitely your father's son alright."

"And what's that supposed to mean?" he was getting angry again, Tony opened the door to the bedroom and stepped forward.

"When you are good to go, make your way downstairs and I will meet you there." Tony closed the door as he walked out. Kyle closed his eyes then painfully stood up. He walked over to the window and looked out over the busy farmyard. Kyle stood looking out the window as his mind started to flash back to memories of running through the farmyard. The cars were different, the clothes were different, but the buildings were the same. For a moment, he could see his Father standing in the middle of the farmyard and shouting towards his brother, then in a moment it was all gone. His eyes took in the present, the cars, the clothes and the people who were walking back and forth.

His body moved before his mind told it to do so, he turned towards the door. The memories of what he had seen earlier hit him and made him jolt. He had watched as that man, that human had slowly changed into something, but what? The thing he had seen at Castleroe was similar, but it was also different. Different in the same way that two men are different, but they are still the same. They are both men, but they are different. Kyle's mind was still racing as he made his way down the small staircase and through the wooden door at the bottom that led into the living room of the farmhouse. The room was empty, but he heard movement outside. The fire had been restocked with blocks of wood and it crackled away, happy in its own existence. Kyle gently closed the door behind him. His movements were slow and deliberate as he walked over to the fireplace.

"Are you ready to go?" Tony asked. Kyle spun around; he hadn't heard Tony enter.

"Ah, yes, I think so," answered Kyle.

"Don't worry you'll feel better in a bit," Tony opened the door and headed outside, "Come on then," he stepped out into the darkening night. Kyle followed him into the farmyard. Over to Kyle's left were two transit vans that had their side doors open. Several people were loading black holdalls and grips of different sizes in through the open doors. Kyle looked at them, then looked over at Tony who was waiting for him to catch up.

"What's going on?" Kyle asked, Tony looked around the farmyard as a Land Rover drove up and stopped near the vans; the passenger jumped out and started telling the farm hands to hurry up.

"One of ours was on a job and he hasn't been heard from in a couple of hours," Kyle looked over at him, "that's not like him," said Tony.

"And you are just popping out to look for him," said Kyle.

"Something like that," answered Tony, Kyle looked back at the small group of men who were now climbing into the back of the transit vans.

"Going out to look for one of your own with tactical equipment." Tony didn't answer him. "I do recognise weapon bundles when I see them," Tony looked over at the vans as one of them turned on their headlights and started the engine, the second one followed moments later.

"Carl has told me to tutor you in our laws," he turned away from Kyle and started to head towards his parked car.

"You didn't answer my question," shouted Kyle, Tony stopped as he reached the driver's door of the car and looked back towards Kyle.

"No, I didn't." The first van drove in front of Kyle and headed off down the lane. The side door of the second one slammed shut and followed on from the first. Kyle walked over towards Tony's car as the Land Rover reversed back around the large barn. Tony opened his door and climbed in before Kyle could speak again, his body was getting faster with each step, as he climbed into the passenger seat he spoke again.

"So, what is the first lesson in your 'tutoring?" Kyle adjusted his seatbelt.

"I want to offer you an apology," Kyle stopped what he was doing and looked straight at his friend. Tony held the steering wheel in both hands and stared straight out the windscreen, "I am sorry for not realising who you were sooner,"

"That's not your problem," Kyle started.

"But it is … if I missed the son of an Alpha who else have I missed?" Tony seemed annoyed with himself.

"I don't see what the problem is!" said Kyle.

"This is a massive problem … what if someone I miss gets bitten and changes without the pack?" Tony had raised his voice.

"How is that a problem?" asked Kyle, Tony looked back out the windscreen as the Land Rover full of people drove past them and off down the lane.

"That is our biggest problem … someone who changes while they're alone," Tony's voice trailed off, he was realising his fears inside his own imagination, "they have no knowledge of who they really are, what they can do," he looked over towards Kyle, "power, without control is very, very dangerous."

"How?" Kyle asked, "how is it so dangerous?"

"Well just imagine a 17 or 18-year-old suddenly finds out they can change into a Garou," Tony glanced back at him again, "everyone who has ever picked on them, they attack, everyone who has ever said anything against them … they attack … they reveal what they are just to impress people," Kyle spotted Tony's grip on the steering wheel tighten, "their wolf would dominate them instead of them dominating their wolf."

"And that is bad?" Kyle asked.

"What?" Tony nearly shouted back at him, "Yes, it is." Tony's body almost turned in the driver's seat, he had touched a nerve, "Society will never, can never accept what it does not understand; to them we are nothing but …"

"Animals," Kyle finished off the sentence.

"Animals that should be exterminated or used for their own ends … we are not a freak show or a weapon …" Tony's voice lowered, "and that is all we would be to them."

"Have you ever tried?" asked Kyle.

"Tried what?" answered Tony.

"To be accepted," Kyle wasn't sure where the question had come from, Tony glanced over at him and let out a nervous short laugh.

"All through our history we have tried, we defend sapien kind and still every time they turn on us," Tony lowered his head.

"When?" asked Kyle.

"What?" answered Tony.

"When? I have never heard of anything like that in history," he looked at Tony.

"The last time was in 1899,"

"1899?" answered Kyle.

"Yes … in 1899 in America,"

"I can't say I have heard anything about werewolves in America in 1899," answered Kyle, Tony smiled and started the engine and headed off down the lane.

"Well it happened," said Tony.

"What happened?" demanded Kyle.

Tony turned the car out onto the main road and headed off towards Coleraine, "The pack Alpha was realising the dream of the 'new world' and revealed who they were to the local town," Kyle looked out over the dark fields that passed on either side of the road, "the 'new world' turned on them."

"What happened to them?" Kyle asked.

"Slaughtered."

Tony's one-word reply made Kyle look over. Tony concentrated on the road but continued talking, "They had a state law passed that gave bounties to any hunter or trapper that killed a wolf," Kyle looked back out the window, "thousands of innocent wolves were slaughtered, the grey wolf almost became extinct in America, most only survived by crossing the border into Canada... it is only recently that they have been re-introduced back into the wild in the US." Kyle listened as Tony seemed to relive events that obviously hurt him. "Paranoia and fear helped make it a federal law across the entire continent ... as for the Garou ... well ... practically none survived."

"You're all immortal then?" Kyle's question made Tony's face crunch up in dis-belief.

"Ah ... no,"

"Oh," said Kyle.

"Where did that come from?" asked Tony.

"Well I watched a werewolf film a while back and they were all immortal." Kyle's explanation made Tony smile and cough another short laugh.

"Hollywood has a lot to answer for!" said Tony.

"Why?" asked Kyle.

"Well at least 95% of what comes out of Hollywood is totally inaccurate."

"Example?"

"Well ... for example," explained Tony, "We aren't immortal ... and we don't infect every single person that is bitten."

"I thought if you survived a werewolf attack you became a werewolf!"

"Hollywood has it wrong, totally wrong, if you have it in your DNA then yes you will ... if not ... then no." Kyle nodded his head and looked up the road that was being illuminated by the car headlights. "That is why we investigate every single dog attack to see if there is a possibility of it."

"Nice job for someone, ever found any?" asked Kyle.

"Yes," Tony answered. "Me,"

"You?"

"Yes, me, that is how the Garou found me."

"What happened?"

"Well ..." Tony paused, "I was on an army cadet camp in North Wales when I was a teenager and I found what I thought was a sleeping dog in the middle of a group of trees," Tony paused and glanced over at Kyle, "by the way if you see a sleeping dog ... don't wake it ... especially with a big stick," Tony grinned and changed gear as he went around a corner.

"Jonathan managed to stop himself before he killed me," Tony was grinning as he recounted the adventure.

"Jonathan?" Kyle looked puzzled.

"Yes, he changed and him and the others from the local pack took me to hospital ... saved my life."

"You know this guy?" stated Kyle.

"I haven't seen him in a while but, yes, I do know him." The car passed through a small village then Tony took a right turn off the main road towards Coleraine.

"Where are we going?" Kyle asked.

"My house."

"What's wrong with mine?"

"Your wolf was awoken," Tony glanced over at him, it will not be wise for you to be left alone tonight." Tony looked back up the road as Kyle pondered what he had been told.

"Just had a thought," said Kyle.

"What?" said Tony as the car came over a hill and Portrush's lights came into view.

"This guy ... who did the Castleroe murders..."

"Sprogis," stated Tony.

"Yeah, you all know who he is?"

"Him and the rest of his little runaway pack,"

"There is one thing you are missing here," said Kyle. Tony looked slightly confused as he could not imagine what was coming next.

"What?" he asked.

"You are a police constable, and you know important information in one of the most serious investigations that has happened around here in years!" Kyle's voice had raised an octave.

"I must obey my Alpha," he answered.

"That excuse will really stand up in court," Kyle was annoyed.

"That is Carl's decision, not mine,"

"You are still in the police ... or had you forgotten?" Tony paused again as he turned right onto the Ballymacrea road, "you are not above the law,"

"I will speak to Carl about that tonight," as Tony spoke his phone started to ring.

"He isn't above the law either," Tony slowed the car down just before he turned into his driveway at the front of his house. Both the living room light and the porch light were on which meant Karen was in.

"No, he isn't." Tony's answer wasn't exactly what Kyle wanted to hear.

"So?" he asked, Tony parked the car.

"Yes, you are right," Tony answered.

"You swore an oath ... remember?" Kyle was staring at Tony as he switched off the engine and then the headlights, Karen would be watching upstairs. Tony paused and looked back at Kyle.

"But you have met him as well," said Tony.

"What? Sprogis?"

"The VCP outside the Causeway hospital, remember the bloke you thought was Polish who sized you up?"

"Yes,"

"That is him, his Alpha was in the car."

"And they knew what you are?" Kyle asked.

"Yes ... that is why he said what he did."

"And it was him on top of the hill at Castleroe?"

"Yes," answered Tony, Kyle paused as pieces started to fit into place.

"But you still swore an oath to uphold the law!" replied Kyle.

"Yes ... but I also swore an older one before that ... and I must obey my Alpha." Tony opened the door of the car and climbed out. Kyle followed him out of the car and up the steps to the front door; Karen was waiting for them and was very happy to see Tony.

"Grab a seat in the front room and I'll put the kettle on," Karen was beaming as she spoke, Kyle could only smile and nod his head in reply. Kyle switched off the light to the living room as he entered, Tony and Karen went into the kitchen. Kyle was sitting in the dark room looking over the twinkling lights of the town, Tony was in the hallway talking on the phone.

"Right, no problems I'm on my way," he said as he hung up the call. Tony walked into the room. "I have to go, the spare bed is made up for you already,"

"Thanks," Kyle looked across at him as he answered.

"We will chat more tomorrow, and we will get this sorted," Tony let a small confident smile spread across his face; tiredness swept over Kyle.

"Ok," Kyle paused, "Are we not on shift tomorrow?" he asked.

"No, we have the weekend off and have made plans to go out tomorrow night." Tony went towards the front door, "see you at breakfast," and with that the door slammed shut. Kyle watched as this man he thought he knew jumped down the steps and in seconds was in his car and off out the driveway onto the empty road towards Coleraine. Kyle sat there in the darkness. His mind raced over all that he had seen in the last few hours.

"It's not that bad," said Karen as she entered the room, a mug of coffee in each hand.

"What?" asked Kyle as he took the offered mug. Karen walked over to the window and looked out over the view, her shape was silhouetted against the lights of the town.

"He will never leave me," she lifted the mug to her lips then spoke again, "he will never be unfaithful to me," she turned and smiled at him, "they mate for life after all, so I can trust him completely and," she turned and looked out the window again, "he will sacrifice his own life to save mine against any danger." Kyle watched as she sipped more from the mug, "no matter what that danger is and if anything ever happens to him the pack will take care of me ... what more could a girl want?" Kyle was sitting and just listening to her. "And if anyone ever dares to harm me ... well ... heaven help them," she turned her head back towards Kyle, "because only heaven will be able to stop them ... they are very protective of their own," she explained.

"What?" said Kyle quietly, Karen stared out the window.

"I am totally secure ... nothing will ever harm me."

"Are you ...?" Kyle started to ask his question, but Karen guessed and ended it for him.

"A wolf? Ha, no, I'm not," she drank more of her coffee. "I got a bit of a shock the first time I saw his wolf."

"What do you mean?" Kyle asked.

"It's a dog eat dog world Kyle, ... and he has bigger teeth than most!" Kyle looked at her with disbelief.

"How can this be?" he quietly asked.

"You'll find out, you've had a very big shock today; now come on, let's get some food in you."

Chapter 51

Tony was in the back of the transit van with several others and all of them were looking past the two men in the front seats. Everyone was watching the front door of the two end houses. Conversation murmured around the others as a beeping noise came from a box that was lying near the feet of the passenger. The box looked like a small hand-held typewriter with a digital display, the keyboard showed a lot of use; the passenger pressed a button on the right-hand side and the small screen lit up.

"Datalink message from the others," he said.

"Well, what does it say, Numbnuts?" answered a voice from behind Tony, he smiled. The passenger looked over his right shoulder and fired abuse back at his assailant. The verbal bantering continued until Tony shouted above the rest of them.

"Guys!" The inside of the van fell silent, he looked at the passenger, "What does it say Dermott?" Dermott McMurrugh glanced at Tony then looked down to read, the light from the screen illuminated his face.

"It's from the others, they are in position and awaiting the 'go'. Dermott handed the device over to the driver.

"Copy it to Paul back at the farm," he instructed. Tony looked at him then looked at his watch, Dermott spoke again, "Inform Paul we are ready and in place to assault both the houses and to inform us when the decoys are in place." The driver nodded and started to type into the keyboard of the data link device. The murmur of conversation grew louder inside the van. Everyone had been told about the instructions that Paddy had been given to kill Sprogis. An excitement filled Tony's ears, but dread filled his mind. Something was wrong, something was very wrong as it was out of character for Paddy to be out of touch during an event with such a high profile.

"He is probably lying in a bed somewhere with one of those Latvian chicks," said one of the voices from near the back of the van.

"That wouldn't surprise me," answered another, Dermott watched as the driver continued typing then as he looked up he acknowledged with a nod that the message had been sent.

"Right," he said, "get yourselves ready." Everyone inside the van moved and started opening the black coloured grips that they had been sitting on. Tony pulled off the plain coloured jacket and accepted the heavy black coloured vest he was handed. The rest of the team started to dress in similar Kevlar body armour then cover themselves in their outdoor jackets. Various colours of baseball hats were pulled from inside the bags and passed around. Everyone adjusted their own dress until they settled down again, the atmosphere inside the van was starting to fill with tension. A bleep came from the Datalink and the light from the screen illuminated the driver's face again; he read the message then looked up.

"To Dermott, from Paul, the decoys will be in place and ready to go in a few minutes, Red teams to go on your discretion," Dermott looked out the windscreen towards the end terrace houses.

"Right, copy that to the other team and add on that they are to deploy their sniper cover at the rear of the house," he nodded and started typing into the machine, "inform the other team to move into direct communications," Dermott nodded his head without looking up, a tap on Tony's left shoulder made him look round, he was handed the small device that looked like a hands-free device for a mobile phone. Tony took the personal communicator and fitted it to his right ear, no one would speak now unless they had to. Dermott fitted one to his right ear and pressed a small button on the side of his mobile phone, his words reverberated in the ears of all the team. "All stations, all stations this is Red zero, I have control, Red two zero acknowledge over," a voice from the other team answered him.

"Red two zero, our Sierra will be in position in figures zero two," Tony nodded at Dermott, the other team would have their sniper in place in two minutes.

"Roger, Red two zero you will act as cut off to the rear of both locations and only engage identified x-rays. Red one zero will complete method of entry over." The other voice acknowledged what Dermott had said. Tony smiled slightly, Dermott spoke again, "get the others from the 4 x 4," the driver nodded and climbed out of the van. The door slammed shut as Dermott opened out a sheet of paper, the bodies in the van moved out of the way to give him some space so they could all see the layout of the houses. Seconds later the side door opened, and they were joined by four others all wearing their body armour under their clothes.

"Nice night isn't it," said one of the new arrivals with a grin, Tony shuffled over to let Dermott move past him and into the centre of the space. Dermott divided them into two teams of six, both houses were to be assaulted at the same time with each team splitting into two so both floors could be cleared at the same time as they had practiced.

"Questions?" he asked as he finished his short briefing.

"Opposition?" asked one of the men.

"Could be up to six x-rays," Tony glanced over at Dermott who was still calling them x-rays and not Mongols.

"Any news on Paddy?" asked one of the men inside the van.

"None," heads nodded. Dermott talked through how he wanted them to go through the houses, "as soon as you are through the door, Team One clears the ground floor and Team Two goes straight upstairs and clears the upper floor," as he finished speaking Tony's phone started to ring, Tony took it out and looked at the screen. "Who is it?" he asked,

"A journalist with the Herald," he replied.

"Answer it," Dermott looked down at the floor plan again as Tony raised the phone to his ear, everyone else remained silent.

"Hello," Tony had lowered his voice slightly.

"Tony? Hi'ya, it's Cara-Marie here," Tony could tell that she was driving and that she was driving fast.

"Hi'ya," he replied.

"Just wondering if you had heard about what is happening in Ballybogy?" Tony looked over at Dermott, he knew what the decoys were doing but he wondered how she could have heard about them so quickly, "Ballybogy? No idea, why, what have you heard?" Dermott glanced over towards Tony.

"Well," Cara-Marie started to explain, "I heard that there is a body that has been torn apart and two cars have been burnt out at the old car park and I wondered if you knew anything yet?" Tony paused.

"I'm not working but I will see what I can find out for you."

"Cheers, you're a pal," and with that she rang off.

"What's happening?" he asked, Tony was scrolling through his phone before he held the phone up to his ear.

"Not sure, but Paul might be able to piece it together."

Dermott nodded, discussions burst out among everyone, it seemed to take forever before Paul answered his phone.

"Tony!" he exclaimed. Tony told him about what he had just heard from Cara-Marie, Paul paused as he absorbed the information, "Is Dermott there?" he finally asked. Tony looked up at Dermott.

"He is."

"Put me on speakerphone," Paul instructed, Tony held the phone away and pressed a button on the phone.

"Ok, you're on speakerphone," said Tony.

"Dermott?" asked Paul.

"Yes, I am here," he answered.

"Carry out your task as previously instructed we are now in zero option." Everyone reacted to what Paul was saying. 'Zero Option.' We have no other options but to kill them all, everyone there knew what Paul was saying, several smiles broke out amongst the men.

"No problems," he replied, "What about Paddy?" he asked, Paul took a deep breath in which was audible down the phone.

"The last Datalink we had from Alan was that Paddy was in the Ballybogy area and was following the Mongol," everyone shared glances as Paul continued speaking, "Which means we have to assume that this body could possibly be him and the Mongols got to him before he could carry out his task."

"I agree," said Dermott.

"The decoys are now in place and the police are reacting, carry on with your own task," Paul instructed, all eyes turned towards Dermott.

"No problem, I will send you a Datalink message when we are done," he glanced from the phone up towards Tony.

"Brilliant, I will confirm what is happening at Ballybogy," Whispers bounded around the inside of the van, "Oh, and Tony?" said the voice from the phone.

"Yes?" he answered.

"Just as a thought, phone the journalist back and give her some bits about the decoys; the last thing we need is a journalist sniffing around us." Tony nodded as Paul spoke.

"I'm on it," he answered. The line went dead, and Tony started pressing buttons on the phone again. The back of the van emptied, and they gathered in a bunch around the side door of the transit van.

"Right, make your way over to opposite the targets," most turned and looked at him then turned and started to walk away, "Make the call," he instructed, Tony scrolled through his phone until he stopped at Cara-Marie's name, as he pressed the call button he lifted the phone to his ear. Dermott got into the driver's seat as Tony heard a familiar voice in his left ear.

"Tony!" Cara-Marie's voice was pleased to hear from him at least.

"Hi'ya, where are you now?" he asked, she paused, Tony could still hear the noise of the car in the background.

"Mmm, we will be in Ballybogy in a few minutes, what have you heard?" Tony smiled. 'We' She wasn't alone.

"Well nothing about Ballybogy but I do know that the police are currently reacting to two incidents, one in Portrush and one in Coleraine."

"Oh?" she didn't know about these, "What's happening?" she asked. Tony thought for a second before he spoke, he could tell by the echo that he was on speaker and someone else was listening in.

"Well, at the moment there is a van on fire near the Mountsandel community centre and something about a fire arms incident in Portrush," Dermott looked over his left shoulder towards Tony, Tony looked over at him in response.

"Really? What kind of fire arms incident?"

"No idea ... I'm not at work, but when I know I will let you know, ok?"

"That's brilliant, you're a pal, I owe you," she replied.

"Yes, you do," smiled Tony, "a coffee at least," she thanked him and rung off, the other voice in the car had said something but Tony didn't pick it up.

"You didn't mention Sainsbury's car park," said Dermott.

"If I give her too much information that will only let her know that I know more than I am letting on,"

"I like your thinking," he smiled, "right we have work to do here."

∞∞∞∞

Cara-Marie had her phone attached to the dashboard and with one hand on the steering wheel she quickly scrolled down to the name of one of the other reporters and hit the call button.

"What are you thinking?" Mark asked, she glanced over at him.

"Simple," she started but was interrupted by a female voice from the phone.

"Hello?"

"Hi, it's Cara-Marie here," as she was speaking, she slowed the car down as they passed a speed limit sign.

"Cara, you do know it's Friday night, don't you?" was said straight away before she could say another word.

"Yes, I know, something is going on round the Triangle area tonight,"

"What?" the voice sounded like she had been sleeping.

"Look, I am on my way to Ballybogy with Mark. There's been another murder and I've just heard that there is a firearms incident going on in Portrush."

"What kind of firearms incident?" she asked.

"I don't know, but there is also a van on fire near the Mountsandel Centre," the excitement in her voice was only matching her driving as the car entered the small village of Ballybogy.

"Really?"

"Yes, really," she answered.

"The Mountsandel Centre is just down the road from me," the other reporter explained.

"Yes, I know, that's why I called you first,"

"Ok, I'm on it."

"Stay in touch,"

"I will," the line went dead, Mark had his phone in his hand and was tapping away at the keyboard.

"Who are you texting?" she asked.

"No one, I am phoning Davie Graham," she thought for a second as she turned the car left into the road that led into the dark country side.

"Davie Graham? The freelance snapper?" she asked. The car speeded up again as she took the first turn; up ahead the sky was illuminated by blue flashing lights.

"The very same, who also lives in Portrush, if anything is going on he will know or at least be able to find out very quickly," she didn't answer but gunned the car over a small hill, "Don't worry, you won't have to talk to him," said Mark.

"What do you mean?" she asked.

"I know how much you can't stand .... Davie, hi," Mark spoke into the phone and in seconds had ended the call with a word of thanks. Mark felt the car speed up again as she came out of another small corner, up ahead the lights from the marked police car blocked the road.

∞∞∞∞

Tony walked towards the nearest of the two groups of men that were standing near the trees opposite the houses. Dermott's voice filled his right ear.

"Decoys in place and we have confirmation of reaction of police," no one responded, no one had to. Tony nodded towards the nearest of the small group of men as he approached, the face smiled at him and was about to speak when Dermott cut in again.

"All stations, all stations, I have control, I have control, wait ... out." The two groups of men all turned and hurried across the road each heading towards a front door. Tony filed into the space between two men as they got themselves into order on the pathway. Almost in unison everyone produced an automatic pistol, each weapon had a black metal tube attached to the front of it to suppress the noise. The uneducated in the film industry called them silencers. Those who knew what they were doing called them suppressors. From the far side of town police sirens started up, the voice returned inside Tony's ear. "All stations, all stations ... standby ... standby ... standby..." the voice paused, and muscles strained waiting to be released "GO, GO, GO,"

Even before the second 'go' had echoed in their ears the front door was already crashing to one side. Tony followed the first figure through the doorway and then right into the living room, the figure behind him immediately spun round and cleared the area as they all entered the house. Everyone had their weapons firmly held out in front of them, the weapons pointed in the direction that they were looking, searching for targets to engage.

"Ground floor, first room *clear*," Tony heard himself speak in his communicator, the sound of doors crashing open came from upstairs.

"First floor, first room, *clear*," Tony was already moving towards the door at the back of the room that led into the small kitchen at the rear of the house. Tony slammed into the far wall as the other figure slammed in behind him, the room was clear. They moved with speed, aggression and surprise, just as they had been taught.

"Clear," said one voice.

"Clear," answered another.

"Clear," repeated Tony. Everyone relaxed, Tony looked out of the kitchen window at the two men from the other group who had occupied the back garden as they had gone in through the front door, the whole thing had taken less than 10 seconds.

"All stations, all stations all clear, complete SSE then ... stand down, out." Everyone reacted to Dermott's voice and in less than sixty seconds from going through the front door there were all filing out having completed the Site Sensitive Exploitation and heading back to the vans where Dermott was leaning up against the transit van waiting for them.

"No one's home," said Tony.

"And they are not coming back," said another voice.

"What makes you think that?" Dermott asked.

"The cupboards, the drawers ... they're all empty."

"Nothing?" Dermott crunched his face as he asked the question.

"Nothing personal so they weren't in a rush when they left," answered a different voice.

"Which means they wanted us to go in," Dermott was annoyed, he pushed himself away from the van and started to walk around the front of it. "Mount up, everyone head back to the farm." Tony pulled the communicator from his ear as he climbed into the back of the van, the others followed. Short conversations bounced between the others as they slammed the side door shut. The body armour would be removed and stowed away, weapons would be checked and once everyone was in some degree of comfort in the back of the van they moved off. Tony's phone bleeped with the arrival of a text message.

"Who is that?" asked Dermott. Tony shifted over onto his side and reached into his pocket.

"I've no idea, hang on," after a few seconds Tony had his mobile phone in his hands. "It's from another copper from Coleraine station," Tony looked up at the back of Dermott's head. Tony opened the message then read it aloud, all conversation in the van stopped as he did so. "WE ARE UP THE FAR SIDE OF BALLYBOGY, 2 BURNT OUT CARS AND ONE BODY THAT HAS BEEN RIPPED APART, AND THERE WAS SOME KIND OF FIGHT HERE," the message electrified the back of the van, Dermott didn't move.

"We should go up there," said one voice.

"No," he commanded, "we are to go back to the farm someone else is on the way there already."

"But we might be able to help Paddy?" the voice looked around the others for support.

"If it is Paddy," answered Tony.

"If it is Paddy then he is already dead and there is nothing we can do for him." Dermott's statement silenced all conversation.

"We need to find these Mongols," the voice said again, loud enough for everyone to hear, Dermott looked straight at him.

"And when we do find them, we will tear them limb from limb.

Chapter 52

Davidov was sitting on the sofa in the living room of the house on the Lodge road when his phone beeped. His eyes glanced out the window into the street as the traffic slowly moved past, he wasn't really watching the news channel on the TV, he read the short message he smiled, Anna walked in wearing only a thin dressing gown.

"Who is that from?" she asked,

"Anders," he answered as she positioned herself beside him on the sofa.

"What does he want this time?" Davidov read from the message.

"The Rua assaulted both the houses as you said they would, but they only used pistols. We would have slaughtered them if we had been there." Anna smiled and relaxed back into the comfort of the sofa.

"Well they will back away from us when they find what is left of their 'hero' they sent after you," she was smiling as she uttered the words. Davidov remained emotionless, he deleted the message without answering it.

"How would we act if they had come to Latvia and done that there?" he quietly asked, Anna reacted.

"Hunt every one of them down, they kill one of ours, then we kill all of them."

"Precisely," he replied.

"But we are Mongols! We are warriors, not music loving Rua, they are beneath us," she rose from where she had been sitting; defiance burst out from her. Davidov smiled a gentle smile, there had always been something about her that made him want her more every day, every single day from the first time he had met her, but she had chosen another before him. He had made a choice and now that choice had finally paid off, what he wanted most in the world was now his.

"It's a dog eat dog world," the words just came out as a whisper, Anna looked confused.

"What?"

"Do not underestimate the Rua," he said as he stood up and started to pace over towards the window, "they have survived here in the west when others could not,"

"But we have killed their best!" she cut off the end of Davidov's sentence, he stopped and looked back at her with a look that left her in no doubt not to do that again.

"But what have we awoken?" he said, "that is why I had everyone find their own place to live, if we stay together as a group they will find us easily, by moving around it makes it harder for them to follow us," she relaxed.

"His sword does make a fine trophy," she exclaimed. Davidov turned and looked out of the window and stared at the front of the police station.

"Yelina has already been instructed to return the sword to the Rua. Anna jumped up and walked up behind him, she intimately pushed her arms around his waist.

"Why?" she nuzzled her face into his back.

"Why? Well if we return it we can argue to the council that they were aggressive, and we defended ourselves. If we can get them to back off that may give us the time we need,"
Davidov turned and embraced this woman. He could feel the warmth of her body and he sensed she was smiling; he kissed the top of her head. She lifted looked at him lovingly.

"I will follow you to the end," her smile beamed, "and beyond my love," Davidov stared into her eyes and locked his mouth on hers in a passionate embrace. She pulled her head back away from him then pushed her hands up inside his top pushing it up over his head, they were kissing again even before it landed on the floor; their love making would last long into the night.

∞∞∞∞

Kyle's eyes opened, the bedroom screamed to a halt around him. His lungs were fighting for breath in the dark room; his right hand moved up and the tips of his fingers touched the material of the thick curtains. They were real. Kyle was lying on the spare bed in Tony's house. His clothes lay in a crumpled heap beside the bed, and the duvet was pushed up against the wall under the window; slowly his breathing calmed down. He swung his feet around and sat upright on the side of the bed. He placed his hands on the edge of the bed. Closing his eyes, he forced his breathing out of his nose, forcing it slow down.

As his chest calmed down he opened his eyes to look at the small clock sitting on top of the chest of drawers. He had only been asleep for an hour; he felt the sweat slowly run over his skin. Something moved him; he projected himself upwards. He was only wearing his boxer shorts and without thinking his left hand reached out to grab his tee shirt off the top of the pile of clothes. Pain jolted through his arms and shoulders as he lifted it up over his head; had he just yelped in pain or had it just been in his head? He wasn't sure, pain shot down his legs as he stepped forward towards the door of the spare room. He opened the door and a coolness swept over him, the darkness of the hallway receded as his eyes became accustomed to it. He felt his body move forward step by step, the pain in his arms and legs lessened with every step as he made his way up the short hallway and into the cool air of the living room where he flopped into one of the chairs that faced out the windows. The sound of his own breathing became the only sound in the room as his eyes looked out at the lights of Portrush; his eyes moved over the landscape.

"You ok?" The sound of Karen's voice startled him; he had not heard her walk up to the doorway.

"Yes ... I suppose so ... I think," he didn't know what to think if he was being honest with himself.

"Well that probably isn't surprising ... I didn't sleep for nearly three days after I found out about his wolf," she was smiling, and the smile reassured Kyle in a way he would never have guessed.

"Did you consider a divorce after that?" he asked. Karen stopped by the edge of the large window, she looked at him.

"Divorce?" she let out a short giggle after she had uttered the single word, "I married him 12 months later!" She folded her arms as she turned her head and looked out over the dark landscape.

"You still married him even though you knew he was cursed?" he asked.

"Cursed? It's not a curse," she had raised her voice slightly, he had obviously touched a nerve.

"What is it then?" he asked, she paused.

"It is a blessing,"

"A blessing?"

"Yes, a blessing," she looked at him sitting in the darkness, "it is one of the greatest blessings that could ever happen to you,"

"I bet there are others who don't think so," stated Kyle as he tried to stand but a shot of pain jolted him back into the sofa.

"How are you doing anyway?" she asked,

"I want to say 'ok' but to be honest ... I'm not sure," he then projected himself upwards, so he was standing fully upright. Karen watched as he took several steps over to the window, he was now standing beside her. He was looking out the window, but she was looking at him.

"This will pass shortly," she reassured,

"If you're not one of them .... how do you know then?" she smiled a gentle smile.

"It was the same with Tony," Kyle shrugged, he couldn't really argue with that. A silence descended over them for a few moments before she turned and started to walk away towards the entrance of the living room, "fancy a hot chocolate?" she asked. It wasn't until she walked through the door that Kyle noticed that she wasn't in a dressing gown but was still wearing the same clothes as earlier.

"Yeah … how did you know I was awake anyway?" he raised his voice after her. The hallway light clicked on and the light blasted into the room and he heard the sound of a kettle being switched on.

"You stopped screaming," she shouted back in reply. Kyle turned and stared back out of the window as he didn't know how to answer. Flashes of images filled his senses, appearing and disappearing in the fraction of a second. The greyness of the landscape came into view again as he took a deep breath and tried to quiet his mind. Inside his chest Kyle could feel the rhythmic thump of his heartbeat. Kyle stood and felt his body relax as the coolness of the room surrounded him; slowly the memories of the nightmare faded from his mind. She reappeared in the doorway with a hot chocolate in each hand.

"Here you go," her smile was infectious.

"Tony's not home yet then?"

"No, he's still at the farm," she didn't elaborate any further on what he was doing. It would be another half an hour before the two of them would finish their drinks and Kyle would make his way back to the spare room, she would stay up until her husband came home.

∞∞∞∞

"Well?" Carl asked as Dermott and Tony walked into the front room of the farmhouse. Tony closed the door behind him and acknowledged Paul with a nod. Tony moved over to the left-hand side of the door, so he was behind Dermott's right.

"Well," started Dermott, "we assaulted both houses at the same time, but no one was there," Carl's face contorted, he already knew that, "and it was obvious that they didn't leave in a hurry," Dermott finished off.

"What makes you think that?" asked Paul.

"There was no disturbance in either house and all their personal belongings were gone."

"Everything?" asked Carl.

"Everything," replied Dermott.

"So where are they now?" he asked.

"I've no idea," shrugged Paul.

"I want them found … every one of them!" Tony nodded

"Is it Paddy at Ballybogy?" asked Dermott, Carl's face filled with anger.

"Yes," answered Paul.

"I want Sprogis dead before sunrise," Carl demanded. Dermott and Tony both made a single nod and turned to leave just as the farmhouse door burst open, the teenager's face was red with excitement.

"They're here!" he shouted, "They're at the bottom of the lane," the teenager was stopped by Dermott's right arm. Everyone in the room reacted, Carl launched himself from his chair.

"Who's here?" he demanded.

"The Mongols," The teenager had quietened down in Dermott's grasp, but he was released as the four men ran past him. The back yard of the farm was alive with movement, the two transit vans lights all came on and people were shouting at each other as they reacted. The 4 x 4 came around the corner and was stopped by the bodies that were running back and forth. Some ran to the vehicles, others ran towards the barn. Dermott immediately stepped forward and started to issue commands, two men ran from the first transit vans with hunting rifles, Dermott shouted at them to go to the top of the barn.

"What is going on?" shouted Carl. The yard paused, and every head turned towards their Alpha.

"A blue sedan with at least one Mongol has stopped at the bottom of the lane," answered one of them.

"When?" demanded Carl.

"Less than a minute ago," he answered, Dermott looked round towards Carl but only had seconds to wait for his instructions.

258

"Dermott, full area sweep, I want all four directions watched and guns out going around our perimeter," Dermott nodded and headed towards the first van. Stalker teams would be looking to the north, south, east and west with teams of Garou doing a full sweep of the farm lands looking for any sign of an intruder.

"Paul!" Carl commanded, Paul stepped forward, Carl did not have to turn his head to know that Paul was standing just behind him. "I want an escort team kitted up, here and ready to go in one minute," Paul was already moving, Carl started to walk towards the edge of the farmhouse. "Tony," Carl commanded. Tony had started to follow Paul towards the transit van where people were already dressing themselves in dark body armour, but he changed his direction instantly. Tony stopped beside Carl. He was standing by the corner of the house looking over the green field at the car sitting at the bottom of the lane with its lights on. Tony was looking over his shoulder as the sound of the car's engine was extinguished.

"Do you still have your weapon?" Carl asked. Tony's right hand made an unconscious move to touch the firm object that was just under his top by his right hip.

"Yes," he answered, Carl just stared at the car and did not move. Tony's eyes darted over to the four dark shapes that were hunched over and moving along the hedge row, they had on the thick full plate body armour, helmets and face protection. Each one expertly carried the G36 rifles up in the alert position as they moved without making a sound.

"Confirmed, only one person in the car," came Dermott's voice from behind them.

"Anyone else nearby?" asked Carl, Tony turned his head to look at Dermott who was listening to his earpiece, then started to walk over towards them.

"No, the road is totally clear for a mile in each direction," Dermott stopped just behind Carl and nearly level with Tony. "We have two teams moving down the path, either side of the road, two snipers in the observation tower on top of the barn," Paul's voice came just after Dermott's.

"We have the primary escort team in the vans and the 4 x 4 and I am in comms with everyone else who is out sweeping their areas." Carl nodded.

"Driver's door opening, one female getting out," Dermott relayed to everyone, the sound of a car door being deliberately slammed shut echoed over the quiet farm.

"Who is it?" Carl quietly asked.

"TWO THREE, Can you ID?" Dermott was speaking into the communicator, there was a pause as he waited for a response, "Roger, maintain option …" Dermott paused again then spoke to Carl, "they think it is the female, Yelina." Carl nodded.

"Good," answered Carl, from where the three of them were they could easily make out the single figure walking up the lane towards the farmhouse. The four dark shapes on this side of the hedge row had stopped and were not moving, all four rifles pointed towards the lone figure that was slowly walking up towards the house. Dermott clicked his fingers and four armoured figures sprinted past and took up positions either side of the end of the lane, one kneeling and one standing, all four pointing towards the woman who was just staring ahead of her as she took slow deliberate steps.

"She has something in her left hand," stated Dermott.

"What is it?" asked Carl, again Dermott waited for a few seconds before answering.

"A small daysack and by the way she is carrying it, there isn't anything too heavy in it," Carl had calmed down considerably from when he was in the farmhouse.

"Dermott, I want a full thermal sweep, I want to know every living thing inside a mile of here," Dermott turned and walked back towards the transit vans, "Paul," Paul took a step forward, "stop her 30 metres from the end of the lane … and Tony," Carl looked over his right shoulder, "with me." The lights of the farm lit the lane up very well as all the different pairs of eyes watched the woman approach. She was wearing a plain red sweat shirt and jeans with dark training shoes. The small dark canvas bag swung gently from her left hand as she walked towards the end of the lane.

"*Halt*," shouted Paul. She stopped, bowed her head and went down on her right knee. Carl walked forward with Tony and Paul on either side of him. Carl stopped in line with the four black clad rifles that pointed down the lane, if she did anything then everyone had a very good field of fire and she would not survive, the fact that she wasn't moving meant that she knew that as well.

"Rise," commanded Carl, the girl stood up but stared at the ground, not lifting her eyes as that could be mistaken as challenging.

"My Alpha has instructed me to bring you this," as she spoke her hair moved from the side of her face to reveal the recent bruising around her left eye and down the side of her face, she moved her left arm but only slightly.

"Open it," Carl's command had an instant reaction. She slowly raised the bag and used her right hand to open the black plastic catches and reached inside. As she slowly lifted out the short sword a gasp then a murmur of quiet comments passed between those that were still in the yard. Tony felt his body react as every single muscle tensed up and was ready to strike as he recognised Paddy's sword. Carl didn't move. Yelina held it out in front of her with her right hand and went down on one knee again.

"Leave it on the ground," said Carl. She did. Carl waited a few seconds before speaking again. "Rise," she rose but continued to look down. "What does your Alpha think he is doing in our lands?" the woman in front of them all winced and blinked several times before reciting a prepared speech.

"My Alpha is returning this to you as an act of reconciliation," Tony felt his right-hand move under his top and feel for the familiar grip of the pistol, every fibre of his body wanted to spring forward. He wanted her dead, he wanted the kill, but his body could not move until his Alpha commanded it. "My Alpha would like you to know that he only defended himself from aggression and wishes nothing further and ...."

"And?" shouted Carl who took a step forward as he spoke, Paul and Tony kept up on his shoulder. "And ..." he repeated cutting her off. Fear swept over the woman in front of them as Carl's anger rose, "Your Alpha is in no position to say or do anything ...This is 'our' land and I am Alpha ..." The woman bowed her head even further as Carl shouted at her. The four figures by the end of the lane also rose and moved in line with Carl, their rifles never moving from the target in front of them.

"He wishes to be presented to the council members," her voice was now no more than a quivering whisper, the fear that is only known by those who know that they are about to die gripped her every word. Carl stopped halfway between her and the end of the lane, everyone around him did the same. Carl watched as the woman started to tremble.

"And your Alpha sends you instead of coming himself?" Carl had lowered his voice, but his words were full of contempt.

"I must obey my Alpha," she whispered. Carl paused and let the silence surround them. "I have also been instructed to tell you that the owner of this sword fought well, and my Alpha has the upmost respect for this warrior," Tony could feel the emotion of the rest of the pack sweeping over him, their desire to taste their revenge for their friend.

"Tell me," said Carl, Yelina lifted her head slightly but looked down again before she spoke.

"He fought off four of us ..." as she spoke slow motion images of the fight flashed in Tony's head, "he injured all four, one seriously,"

"How long did it last?" asked Carl. Yelina paused, her eyes darted from side to side at the figures in the hedge row.

"Nearly half an hour," her comment caused a wave of reaction among everyone. Yelina looked up at Carl, "he was very brave," she finished off before lowering her head again.

"Tell your Alpha to present himself here with one other Wednesday night," the girl nodded but she didn't lift her eyes from the ground at her own feet. Tony shot a glance over at Paul, "until then he is commanded to stay indoors," again she nodded, "Do you understand?"

"I do," she whispered.

"Leave," Carl commanded.

"I obey," she answered before she rose and walked back five paces before turning around and almost running down the lane. Everyone went to move but with a wave of his hand Carl stopped them. He walked forward and stopped beside the sheathed sword that lay on the ground. He waited until the car door slammed shut and the car took off up the road. Everyone relaxed, and Dermott started shouting again calling everyone back over to the vans. Carl turned and faced the farm, Tony and Paul came close. Carl was silent as he held the sword in his right hand, his eyes never leaving it.

"That was very smart of them," said Paul.

"What?" asked Tony. Paul looked at him.

"Returning Paddy's sword, it means they aren't keeping it as a trophy and then asking for the council members, very smart."

"You have lost me," answered Tony. Carl remained silent as Paul explained.

"By not keeping a trophy, they can claim self-defence and ..."

"And any Alpha can ask for council members to preside over any dispute between them and another Alpha," Carl finished off.

"Which means between now and then we can't touch them!" Tony was annoyed.

"Very smart of them," said Carl as he pushed past the two of them and walked towards the farmhouse.

"So, what next?" Tony asked

"Next?" said Paul, Tony looked over at him.

"Yeah, what happens next?" he repeated. Paul looked at his watch then looked over at Tony.

"Well I don't know about you, but I'm off to bed. I am knackered!"

Chapter 53

Sean's eyes glanced over at the clock on the dashboard as the numbers clicked over to 08:30. He had been driving for an hour now on this dry Saturday morning and the roads were surprisingly empty, which was a good thing since he had not had time for his morning coffee and this was still far too early. Mike had woken him at exactly 7am from another crime scene.

"Where?" he remembered asking in the darkness of his bedroom.

"Ballybogy," Mike had replied.

"There really is a place called Ballybogy isn't there?" he had asked. The very thought of the question now made him smile slightly as he drove up Frosses road and made his way past the town of Ballymoney. The voice of a radio presenter suddenly came on with the news headlines, 'A vicious murder in the town of Ballybogy near Portrush' was the main story, a reporter on the scene spoke and described little bits of what Sean knew already.

"And local people here describe several cars coming back and forth last night that were not from the area, police are appealing for any witnesses to come forward to assist them with their enquiries" A smile appeared on Sean's face, 'well done Mike, got that in early,' he thought to himself. The radio presenter continued with the next story about a traffic collision near Belfast that had killed a teenager. The empty road in front of Sean opened as he looked up the straight road that sliced its way through the green of the fields surrounding it. He looked up ahead at the approaching small town that he hadn't ever heard of.

"Go into Ballybogy then take the first right," Mike's directions echoed in his ears. The village soon passed behind him as the road changed from long and straight to a much smaller one that rose and fell with the lie of the land, hedgerows and trees lined each side. Acting as natural boundaries they guided everyone around the small hills that seemed to dot the landscape here, he easily spotted the marked police car up ahead. An open area to his right was now full of vehicles, he spotted the teams transit vans, and people walking back and forth dressed in the one-piece paper disposable forensics suits. He slowed the car down further and indicated that he wanted to turn right into the car park. The entrance had the police car sitting on the right-hand side and faced outwards. The plastic police tape had been stretched from the back of the car across the entrance to a metal post on the far side, both the doors of the car opened, and two uniformed police officers got out. Sean started to turn the car off the road and stopped at the tape, he pressed the button and his window slid downwards. The nearest police officer approached holding out his right hand indicating that he wanted him to stop, the second shut the passenger door and rested his arms on the top of the car. Sean reached into his inside pocket and pulled out his wallet, the young police officer spoke first.

"I'm sorry sir, but this is a crime scene," he stopped as he reached the window of the car. Sean smiled at him as he showed him his police ID.

"I know son, that's the only reason I am out of bed this early on a Saturday morning," The police officer returned the smile as Sean introduced himself. "Inspector Parrish, M.I.T." The police officer looked at the ID

"Good morning Sir," he answered.

"I'm looking for Detective Sergeant Dear," the police officer straightened up and took a step backwards, he raised his right hand and pointed towards the nearest transit van.

"You will find him over there, he has just got back."

"Just got back?" Sean repeated, "Where has he been?" The young officer smiled before he answered.

"He was out getting coff ...." he cut himself off as he just realised what it was he was saying, "I'm not sure, Sir," the police officer paused, the other police officer at the far side of the car cringed at his colleague's lapse. "You may go right in, Sir." Sean released the brake and let the car move forward, he waved and thanked the officer as he passed him.

"Idiot!" shouted the police officer from the far side of the car as he opened the door. Sean pressed the button in his door and the window slid upwards, he was still smiling at the young officer's gaffe as Mike appeared round the side of the van. Mike lifted his hand in welcome then pointed to a space behind the vans, this was where he wanted him to park his car; he parked beside the growing collection of vehicles at the far end of the open area. Sean climbed out and as he closed his car door the casually dressed Mike approached.

"Morning,"

"Why are you so cheerful?" Sean asked.

"I'm just loving my job," Sean cast him a glance of disbelief as he quickly pulled on the white paper forensic suit, boots and gloves.

"You got grief from your missus as well then?" he asked. Mike smiled as the two of them turned and started to walk towards the two burnt out cars. The fire appliance and a parked ambulance were over on their right as the two men walked towards the several people who were dotted around inside the police tape carrying out their own detailed tasks.

"Yeah pretty much, been here since gone one this morning," Mike answered.

"One?" Sean seemed surprised.

"Yeah, I got a call from one of the desk sergeants on my mobile who said that this may be coming our way."

"Was he right?" Sean asked, Mike didn't answer until Sean looked over at him. Mike nodded his head. "Ok, what have we got?" Mike took a breath in then started to brief Sean on what was happening.

"Two burnt out hatchback cars, the one on the right was stolen yesterday from the Heights in Coleraine," Mike was pointing with his right hand as he spoke, "The other one is registered to a Patrick M'Kane," a figure in a white paper suit waved at them as they approached, "and there is Simon."

"What is this place normally used for?" Sean asked as they slowed down by the strip of plastic tape.

"Apparently it is used as a site for a car boot sale on a Sunday," he answered.

Sean looked at him. "Apparently?" he asked.

"Yeah ... I'm not sure exactly,"

"Confirm that," said Sean, "Morning," he greeted Simon.

"Morning boss," Simon looked tired as did Mike, Sean came straight to the point.

"Do we know who the body is yet?"

"We think it is Patrick M'Kane," answered Simon, "but we are in the process of confirming that," Sean nodded.

"What else?" he asked. He listened to the two of them as they described their findings.

Simon started, "The body is in pieces, spread over a wide area between the two cars,"

"And there was some sort of scuffle," injected Mike.

"Yeah, we have confirmed three other blood types and a couple of different sets of prints all over the area," Simon continued,

"Our first van there," Mike turned and pointed to the transit van that was close to Sean's car, "is nearly full of evidence already,"

"Have you had any sleep yet?" Sean's different track of question caught them of guard,

"Ugh ... no," Simon answered.

Sean turned away from them and started back towards the vans, "right let's go have a look at this body," Mike led them towards the first of several white forensic tents.

"Well this one is just as dismembered as the very first one down in Belfast," Mike started his briefing, they slowed as they approached the front entrance. Sean counted five tents in total. Mike answered his question before he asked it. "Yes, there are body parts in each one, but that's not the scoop," he said.

"What is the scoop?" Sean asked, the three of them all pulled up the hoods and started to arrange their face masks as Mike spoke.

"What do you think happened?" Sean asked.

"I think there was some sort of fight, the various footprints and traces suggest there were at least two assailants."

"Why do you think that?" asked Sean

"Well," Mike pointed at the far hedgerow, "It seems something came from that direction and another from that direction," he pointed up past the furthest tent, "as we have found disturbance in the ground around those sites and we also believe that we have at least two different blood samples,"

"And we are just waiting to confirm who this Patrick M'Kane is," Sean's glance asked the obvious question. Simon added, "We have uniforms on the way to a deer farm that he lived and worked at."

"Right," he said as they all stepped forward and Mike pulled back the entrance flap. "You two will hand over what you have done then head home to bed, I want everyone who has been here since the wee hours stood down and replaced by fresh sets of eyes as soon as we can," Sean was direct with the instruction.

"Most of that is already done, but we would like to stick around for a bit yet," Mike indicated towards Simon as he spoke.

"Who's in charge of this investigation?" there was sarcasm in his voice as Sean posed the question, Mike stopped with his back to the frame of the tent, his arm holding open the flap.

"You are," he answered.

"Excellent," Sean's reply was almost joyful, "and since I am in charge how about you two do as you're told ... for once," Sean stepped forward and entered the scene. "Besides I don't want any more grief over the phone from your missus now do I?" Sean was smiling from behind the mask as he looked back over his left shoulder towards the very tired detective.

"No, I suppose you don't."

∞∞∞∞

Cara-Marie was reading over what was on the screen of her desktop in the very quiet newspaper office. Her eyes glanced up at the clock as the hands clicked onto the Nine o'clock position, she paused. The photographer had long since left after several very irate phone calls from a pregnant girlfriend in the early hours of the morning. She reached into her handbag to take out her phone and scrolled through the names until she reached the one she wanted. Her thumb pressed the green button then she placed the phone to her ear. She waited for several rings before she hung up without an answer, she dropped the phone on the desk and slouched back into the chair. Cara-Marie closed her tired eyes and rubbed them with her hands as she tried to wash away the tiredness. She jumped at the sound of the back door to the office flying open and a buoyant photographer bounced in.

"Morning!" he exclaimed. Cara-Marie gave him a look that totally expressed her feelings at that moment. "My Mum always said that if you pulled faces like that your face would freeze, and it would remain like that forever," he bounced past her and landed in his chair by his desk, she glanced over at him.

"You're cheerful this morning," she said.

"And you're not!" he was almost laughing as he typed his password into his desktop.

"I'm fine," she answered as her attention turned back to the story she'd been writing.

"You know I was once told ..." he started, her head shot over at him again as she knew what was coming next, "if a woman tells you that they are 'fine' they are really saying ..."

"DON'T ... I know what the acronym means," Mark stopped what he was doing and looked over at the side of her head as she was going through word after word.

"What time did you finish in here last night?" His screen had come to life, but she wasn't looking up at him at all.

264

"Not sure," her answer was almost a whisper," he looked at the wall clock then back at her.

"You haven't been home at all have you?" he asked, her glare in answer said it all. "You know Medusa would have been proud of that one." She tried so hard not to giggle but it burst from her uncontrollably, he joined in. Cara-Marie started to close down what she was doing, "what are you up to anyway?" he asked, she glanced at the screen then over at him.

"Just saving all the stuff into the shared area so hopefully some of the dailies can use them."

"What did the boss say?" Cara-Marie let out an audible sigh as the sound of Mark tapping away at his keyboard seemed louder than usual.

"Ballybogy comes under Ballymoney and they can cover it," he could hear the disappointment in her voice.

"What did he think of the rest?" he asked.

"Well," she started, "he liked the incident report about Mountsandel, but there isn't much about the burnt-out van near the cinema."

"Why?" he injected.

"Nothing much to say ... it happened in the only spot that isn't covered by security cameras and no witnesses," she took a deep breath in and for a moment wished for her own bed.

"Did you hear about the firearms incident in Portrush?" he asked.

"Yes," she paused, "Your 'friend' was cursing something chronic down the phone when his scoop turned out to be two idiots with water pistols running around Glenmanus," she looked over at his smiling face, "he was not pleased to say the least."

"Yeah, I heard ... I thought you would find that funny," he didn't look up as he spoke, she enjoyed the few minutes of silence before she spoke again.

"So, what happened to you when you got home?" her mouth moved but the rest of her body didn't at all, he shrugged his shoulders.

"Apparently, she spotted me on one of the news channels before I got in,"

"So, she was happy then?"

"Evening ruined, blah blah blah, if she had an Indian name it would be Four Horses!"

"Four horses? I don't get it?" Cara-Marie crunched up her face.

"Nag, nag, nag, nag," The previous uncontrolled giggle mixed with tiredness turned into a burst of laughter at the joke.

"Very good,"

"So, what's the update with what happened at Ballybogy?" he asked.

"No change from last night but I know someone who will know," Cara-Marie reached for her phone and started to tap in a text.

"Who are you texting?" Mark asked and started to scroll the pictures taken last night.

"A copper in Coleraine," she answered

"And what do you think he will tell you?" he asked,

"Well hopefully, just put a few more bones onto what we have already," as she finished speaking her phone bleeped with the arrival of a text message, eagerly she picked it up.

"That was quick!" he stated, she sat back in her chair.

"And so is the answer,"

"What did he say?"

"He says he has no idea," Cara-Marie subconsciously bit into her bottom lip.

"What are you thinking?"

"One of two things ..." she said quietly,

"And what are they?"

"Oh, either he genuinely has no idea or he's lying, and he knows something significant."

"Or you could be barking up the wrong tree totally," his smile this time was mischievous, which in turn got a notebook thrown at him.

"Haven't you got a girlfriend to keep happy or something?"

"Haven't you got a husband to find or something?" the notebook was followed by a stapler.

Chapter 54

The heavy knock came to the door of the hotel room. He turned around from where he had been looking out the window over London. He unlocked the door, turned and walked back towards the window. The voice behind him filled the room as the door shut behind him.

"So, we are going back to Ireland then?" asked Tatamovich, Grishin stopped as he reached the window.

"Yes, we are," he answered without looking round, Tatamovich took the only seat in the room.

"O'Brien is doing everything he is supposed to be doing, we have nothing more to do, we should just be heading home; it has been long enough," he stated.

"Davidov has killed again."

"Who?" Tatamovich's voice lowered for the question.

"They killed one of the Rua ... and in public as well,"

"So ... O'Brien has the justification he needs then to destroy them all," he said. Grishin shook his head twice.

"It's not that easy ... unfortunately."

"Why?"

"Well, it seems that the Rua had one of theirs following the Mongols and they lured him to a car park and killed him."

"So?" he stated, "It is their lands, they can do what they want!"

"So," Grishin continued, "before the Rua could act and wipe them out."

"As we would have done," Tatamovich injected.

"As we would have done quite correctly," Grishin started to walk over towards the bed away from the window, "Davidov returned the Rua's sword and asked for a council ruling," Grishin paused, "which means you and I," Tatamovich nodded in reluctant understanding.

"Which means the Rua cannot act against them because it would go against any ruling from council members."

"Exactly ... Davidov knows how to use the law to his best advantage," said Grishin.

"Just like his Father," answered Tatamovich.

"I only knew 'of' Davidov's father," answered Grishin.

"I was involved in that ruling," said Tatamovich, Grishin looked over at him in slight surprise.

"Were you? ... I didn't know that,"

"Well it was a long time ago," he answered, "and you were in China at the time."

"Ah yes," he said remembering, "that was a bit of a busy time."

"So, when are we going back to Ireland?" he asked.

"Monday afternoon."

"So, we have the weekend here in London? ... again?" Tatamovich didn't like the city much, Grishin smiled.

"No, my friend, we are invited guests of the Garou in Dartmoor, we are leaving after lunchtime."

"Excellent," he then thought for a moment, "Where's Dartmoor and how long will it take us to get there?"

∞∞∞∞

Karen walked into the living room towards where Tony was standing, he smiled as she approached, she slowed and slid her right hand across his back then over his shoulder, and they gazed over the landscape.

"So, what is happening now?" she quietly asked, Tony started to explain.

"Well, two of the guys from the other section at the station have been out to the farm to officially inform Paddy's sister that he is gone."

"He is one of the ones who has a house at the farm complex, isn't he?" Karen asked, Tony nodded in response.

"Yeah, he's one of seven families who live on the land, shares it with his sister, Lynne."

"She must be going out of her mind," Karen snuggled into his chest as she spoke, he lifted his left arm and wrapped it around her.

"Yeah, I bet she is," a silence descended over the room as they held each other a little tighter. Both their heads looked up at the sound of a door opening down the corrido. Kyle slowly made his way up towards them, he had dressed, but his movements were slow and deliberate. Tony smiled as he hobbled through the doorway and Karen broke off her embrace.

"Morning," she smiled.

"Ugg," Kyle replied,

"Anyone ever told you how rough you look in the morning?" he asked.

"Could be worse," Kyle answered as he made his way over to them.

"How?" asked Tony,

"I could look like you!" Kyle could not move fast enough to avoid or block the left-handed punch that landed on his right shoulder. The force would not usually have made much of an impact however, the way he was feeling the result was worse than it would normally have been. Kyle landed on the sofa as Tony feigned a hurt look on his face.

"Guys," Karen lifted her hands as if in a mock surrender, they were smiling as Tony stepped forward and reached out his hand to help Kyle upwards. "I'll make some breakfast, so I can leave you two to flirt in peace," she said as she started to walk away.

"You said it was 'our little secret'" Kyle exclaimed towards Tony as he got to his feet.

"Only in your dreams legionnaire," retorted Tony as Karen looked back over her left shoulder before she disappeared out of the living room.

"So, what's happening?"

"Karen's making us some breakfast," Tony answered,

"I meant," he paused, Tony knew what he meant.

"Well there was a reported firearms incident in Portrush," he answered,

"Really? What happened?" Kyle asked, Tony shrugged.

"It was reported there was one male, running around Glenmanus in Portrush with a handgun so they responded."

"And?" Kyle enquired, Tony glanced at him with a grin.

"It turned out to be some idiot with a water pistol," Kyle let out a short laugh.

"I bet he got a bit of a shock when people started pointing real guns at him."

"Yeah apparently, he did, but the photo journalist was funnier," answered Tony.

"What journalist?" Kyle asked, "your friend from the Herald?"

"Cara? No, it was one of the freelancers from Portrush, he was livid when he found out it was a wild goose chase."

"So, what happened at Ballybogy?" Kyle's question made Tony glance at him.

"Paddy was murdered," Tony's answer was short as it was precise, adding no extra details to those Kyle already knew. Kyle nodded and turned to walk over towards the sofa, "Murder in Transit has been on the scene since the early hours; they are dealing with it."

"So, what about your little 'pack' of friends?" Kyle had raised his voice an octave for the word 'pack', Tony glanced around at him.

"Two of the lads from the other section have been out and officially informed Paddy's sister that he is dead. Carl has organised for two of the lads to take her out there," Tony turned back to the window.

"That's not what I meant," Kyle retorted, Tony turned and went over to the main armchair, he spoke as he sat down himself.

"I have spoken to Carl and the matter is now with him," Tony took a breath in then quoted his Alpha, *"We defend these lands, not govern them."*

"You are still a police officer."

"And you have only just found out what you are," Tony's answer was quick and sharp.

"So, what is going to happen next?" he asked.

"That's up to Carl, but the Latvians returned Paddy's sword and asked for a ruling."

"Brilliant," answered Kyle, "What does all that mean?" they reacted as the smell of cooking food came from the kitchen, both sniffed the air before Tony looked over at Kyle.

"Normally after a kill, a Garou will keep a trophy; they didn't, they returned the sword."

"And that is significant because?" he asked.

"Because they can claim it was self-defence. If they openly attacked us, we would be within our laws to wipe them out." Tony was very matter of fact about what he was saying.

If Kyle was shocked, he wasn't showing it. "Our laws?" Kyle questioned.

"Yes," Tony moved in his seat, "The laws that govern all of us are written in our sacred scrolls." Kyle reacted by sitting up and nearly burst out laughing.

"Whoa, whoa, whoa," he was holding his hands up to stop the direction the conversation was going in, "Sacred scrolls?" you really expect me to believe that you have ancient scrolls ... that is very farfetched."

"Two days ago, you were 100% convinced that werewolves only existed in fantasy fiction yet here we are." Tony's voice was quiet and calm, but his words left Kyle momentarily speechless. The sound of Karen moving around in the kitchen became the only sound as Kyle's mind fought with the words Tony had just uttered. Kyle's body relaxed as he could not answer from what he had witnessed at the deer farm then, what had happened next to himself.

"You said something about a ruling?" It was the one thing that Kyle grasped onto; the one thing that Tony said that would get an answer he could comprehend.

"Yes, we have two council members coming over to listen to each side then they will issue a ruling; that is our way."

"Council members?" Kyle repeated.

"Yes," Tony replied, "every clan can put forward two members to the ruling council, their membership changes every ten years; they themselves are then governed by the permanent higher council."

"Higher?" Kyle uttered,

"Yes, the higher council has five permanent members that govern over the council to ensure they enforce our laws."

"Sounds a lot like the UN in New York," the words had left Kyle's mouth even before he realised he had uttered them,

Tony laughed a short laugh. "What do you think the UN Security Council is based on?"

"What? Are you going to tell me that this council has made secret pacts with the world's governments or something?" Tony propelled himself out of the chair.

"No, not quite, as far as we know the world governments don't know we exist for real," Tony paused, "and that is the way we want to keep it."

"Why?" Kyle asked.

"Why?" the question stopped Tony who looked back over his left shoulder. "I don't know about you, but I have no intention of ending up as some experiment somewhere in some lab that doesn't officially exist." Kyle nodded in agreement as Tony continued explaining, "We do our best to avoid exposure to the world. The modern world will never accept us, we are different; in their eyes we are monsters who should be put to death just for being what we are. The council exists to ensure that all Garou follow the same law." Kyle stood up as the smell of food filled his nostrils.

"So how large is this council?" he asked.

"48 members, five higher members," Tony answered as his stomach grumbled, "and I am hungry," he turned and walked out of the door, "are you still on for the night out tonight?"

"Tonight?" Kyle asked as he followed Tony out of the room.

"Yes," Tony said as they entered the kitchen, "We are meant to be going out to the Harbour Bar in Portrush tonight, us two, with you and your Physio friend."

"Tony has been telling me more about your new romance," smiled Karen as the two of them came to a halt by the neatly laid out kitchen table.

"It's not a romance."

"Let me guess, she's just '*a friend*'," Karen mocked as the two of them sat down around the table. The atmosphere had lifted somewhat. The questions in Kyle's head could wait until later when Tony could tell him more about the new world that was starting to open up to him.

"She is just a friend,"

"I am looking forward to meeting her, finally," Karen smiled.

"I will text her after this and remind her," answered Kyle as Karen turned around and placed a full cooked breakfast in front of each of them. Kyle was going to enjoy his meal and for a short time anyway he would forget the things that were going on elsewhere.

∞∞∞∞

She could not see them, but she knew that they were there. She paced along the footpath that lay to the side of the road; the path separated the coastal road from the golf course to her left. The golf course took up the ground between her and the blustering sea. The wind was getting stronger and swept up around her. She felt her black full-length coat fly open as if it was trying to take flight. The feeling returned. The Garou were at the far side of the golf course and they were moving parallel with her, the very thought angered her. She glanced over to her right at the empty car park, at the far side of the road was a sign welcoming those that passed it to the town of Portstewart.

"Mornin'," the greeting made her head spin round as the middle-aged man walked past her. He was wearing a waterproof jacket, thick trousers and a pair of walking boots. His smile beamed across his face as he bounced along his way; she didn't answer him. In disgust, she turned back up the rising hill and followed the road towards Portrush. Her eyes glanced over the markings on the road, they were small boxes that were formed into lines as if it was the start of a race, but what could race here? She dismissed the thought as her eyes shot over to the edge of the small cliffs that lined the coast between the two towns. They were moving. They had started to move quite quickly so she quickened her own pace until she reached the top of the rise.

From here she could see the harbour at Portrush and make out people who were walking along the small beach to the east of the town. The Garou were now behind her and were approaching more cautiously, but they were still out of sight. She closed her eyes and brought a stillness over her face. Two younger men passed her as they made their way towards Portstewart. She slowly breathed in and let her arms drop by her side.

"She's gorgeous," one of them remarked. Her jet-black hair settled as the wind around her died down. Suddenly she forced her breath out and clenched her fingers into fists as she let out a small yell; power surged from her and for a moment weakness grabbed at her but as she breathed in her strength returned. She opened her eyes and looked back down towards where the Garou had been. One of them was hurt and they were backing away; they had felt her power and that brought a very satisfied smile to her young face. Confidently, she turned and started down the hill into Portrush. The phone in the pocket of her black trousers started to ring, she considered not answering the withheld number. The phone continued to ring, she had de-activated the voicemail as she knew that you could trace the location of the phone by the voicemail, however something made her thumb move and she pressed the green button then held the phone to her ear.

"Dani," the male voice had an American accent that she did not recognise, she didn't answer him as he continued to speak, "I have been looking forward to meeting you."

269

Chapter 55

Kyle was leading the way through the crowd of people into the side street beside the pub; it had just gone half past midnight and it was time to go. They moved through the couples standing around smoking and all talking louder than they needed to. Up against the white wall at the opposite side of the alley to the entrance a young couple were having a full on shouting domestic argument which was starting to draw more attention from the rest of the crowd. The end of the street was blocked by a waiting taxi while a second taxi sat close behind the first one. Both were mini-cabs organised by one of the local firms, Kyle had dealt with them on many occasions and not all of them were good examples, but at least they were ferrying people home safely, for the moment anyway.

The second car was at a slight angle as the turn at that end of the very small car park was quite a tight one. The car park could only hold about twenty cars, so it didn't take much for it to fill up. Kyle looked across the cars that were parked there; most of them were black with an occasional silver or red. There was a mixture of BMW, Toyota, Lexus and a top of the range Jaguar. The two girls were chatting away merrily, he was glad that they were getting along so well. Kyle held back as Tony spoke to the driver in the first taxi, it was not theirs, so they would have a wait on their hands.

"Over there," Tony pointed away from the taxis and the shouting couple who were getting louder. The four of them made their way to the front of the pub where a mass of people had formed. The pub had two wooden benches up against the wall and they were proving very popular with the smokers who were standing and sitting around them who were themselves waiting for their own taxi's. The Jaguar slowly moved off and made its way through the mass of drunken people who had spilt out over the road. Kyle made his way to the end of the building and stood with his back up against the wall. Kelly was standing near him and was very amused by the text message she had just got.

"Who?" Kyle asked, Kelly glanced up at him and giggled again.

"Just harmless flirting," her attention returned to answering the text message. *'Just harmless flirting?'* Kyle thought to himself, he didn't think such a thing existed. Tony and Karen were standing close in as the wind was starting to pick up.

"Maybe I should have driven?" Tony said. Karen said something that Kyle didn't hear. The crowd around them was slowly dispersing, some heading up the hill and others over the bridge at the far side of the car park. The bridge was a walkway over the shallow part of the harbour that was used by the owners of the yachts and boats moored there. Kyle could see the masts of the yachts moving back and forth in the wind, his eyes moved across at the blue and white painted pub at the opposite side of the inlet from where they were.

"Maybe you should have!" Kyle looked over at Tony who smiled in return. Kyle let his gaze follow up the road that led away from where they were standing. He looked at the row of terraced houses that all faced the harbour and out to sea, the lifeboat station stood dark and empty, on guard with its solitary radio mast sticking up from the near side of the building. The stone wall that ran along the side of the road separated the cars, motorbikes and vans that filled the road and all the people who were in various stages of drunkenness that were making their own way home. Two uniformed police officers were walking up with the flow of traffic towards the pub. Karen and Kelly stepped closer and continued chatting, obviously what had been on the text wasn't for the ears of men.

Suddenly Kyle's attention transfixed on the dark blue transit van that was parked in the space directly opposite to them and was facing up the hill away from the pub. The driver was constantly looking around him and seemed nervous. The driver had a baseball cap on that advertised an American football team; it was pulled down as if to cover some of his face. Kyle was already making notes on him. He hadn't shaved in a few days; this was made obvious as he took a drag on a cigarette.

"Tony," he said aloud. The inside of the cab was slowly filling up with smoke. The driver physically jumped when two girls who had been inside the pub knocked on his window, he didn't roll it down. Kyle looked at Tony, who was also looking at the goings on at the far side of the van. Something was not right here, and Kyle sensed danger. Tony nodded towards the van confirming that he could feel something as well. Kyle's eyes flashed back at the two girls, one had a short skirt on and the other was wearing jeans but they both had similar tops on.

They thought he was a taxi and they wanted a lift. They were both being loud and getting more obnoxious towards the driver of the van for not rolling down the window. Kyle could not believe that two young girls after a night out would get into a van with someone they did not know, *'are they stupid?'* did they want to become another statistic? The driver was refusing to roll down the window or even open the door as the girl in the short skirt tried the handle and pulled at the door, it did not move. The two girls then walked off out of view at the far side of the van and off towards the bridge, unstable in their high heels and their alcohol consumption. They still managed to shout abuse back at the driver for not doing what they wanted as the aim of their evening had not obviously been met. Kyle straightened up as Kelly's phone bleeped. Tony took a step forward, and then it happened.

The engine of the van sprung into life and the van jumped forward to the next parking space and stopped. The driver's door suddenly swung open and he jumped out and ran around the front of the van, leaving the driver's door open, his jeans were dirty, and his jacket was unwashed. Both Kyle and Tony stepped up the road towards him. Kelly burst out laughing at what she was reading but Karen who was now looking up at the van was not sharing whatever Kelly had just found funny. From the far side of the entrance to the ten-pin bowling alley they spotted a girl with long black hair being grabbed by two men.

Her feet were thrashing back and forth as she struggled to get out of their grasp. The two men were dressed similarly to the driver of the van, unshaven, baseball caps and unwashed jeans. Nobody else seemed to even notice the abduction that was taking place less than twenty feet away, but both Kyle and Tony did and jumped forward towards them.

"Stop!" shouted Tony. Tony was on the right and Kyle on the left as they arrived at the girl just as the driver was trying to grab her feet. The abductor at the girls left side had his right arm around her waist and his left hand clamped over her mouth, pushing her head back into his shoulder, her left arm was pinned to her body and the abductor that was closest to Kyle now had her by her right arm, all four pairs of eyes turned and looked at the two men who were moving very fast towards them.

The sole of Kyle's right foot landed square in the chest of the man who had released the arm he was dragging to face what was coming towards him. The force of the front kick propelled him back into the girl and the third man; all three sprawled out over the ground. The driver of the van lashed out with a punch but as it flew towards Tony he glimpsed the flash of metal, Tony reacted to the knife before he had totally recognised it. Tony clamped his grip around the wrist with the knife and stepped backwards continuing the forward momentum of his attacker, then jerked the wrist further still, pulling the driver off balance and into Tony's body. Tony pulled his right hand back past his head and keeping his left foot firm moved his right rearwards again, the driver was exactly where Tony wanted him.

Nobody in the fight registered the female scream that occurred in the crowd behind them as heads turned to see what was going on. Karen pushed Kelly up against the wall and commanded her to stay there. Kelly had only screamed once but it was enough to stop the arguing couple and get heads turning. Karen stood in front of Kelly and faced the fight that was going on in front of them both, she had learnt from experience not to intervene and let the fight finish.

The drivers back thudded up against Tony's body as Tony's left hand firmly slapped into the side of his face slamming his head in towards Tony's chest. With one movement Tony spun round to his left, twisting the driver so his legs fell from underneath him and felt the full weight of Tony land on top of him as the driver's chest collided with the wet tarmac road. The driver did not at first realise that his right hand had already released the knife but felt the sharp lighting pain as Tony pushed his wrist up his back and stopped between his shoulder blades. In one swift movement Tony was kneeling on him keeping him firmly restrained on the ground, he was not going to play any further part in the fight, Tony glanced at what Kyle was doing.

The girl had rolled away from the second man who was about to launch an attack at Kyle. Tony's eyes picked out the blade in his right hand that was pointing towards Kyle. The first abductor rolled on the ground with his arms cradling his chest, the threat from him was gone. Kyle had stepped back; his right foot was rearward, and his left hand was slightly forward with his right arm defensively protecting his torso. The attacker jumped forward and thrust the knife at Kyle's face. Tony could see what was about to happen, but the abductor was about to get a very painful surprise.

Kyle ducked a few inches and moved his body to his left; the blade passed his face with about an inch of air between it and the flesh. Kyle's right hand was already asserting the grip around the attacker's right wrist. Tony looked on and as if in slow motion Kyle twisted his body and pulled the attacker forward. Kyle brought his left arm up in a vertical line in front of his face and as the attacker gasped Kyle pushed all the force he could muster and propelled himself forward. Kyle's left arm connected with the straightened right arm at the elbow, he pulled back with his right hand extending the arm further as he heard the smash of bone as the elbow joint gave way to the sudden application of force pushing the lower arm over 30 degrees the wrong way. Every fibre of his being suddenly became totally transfixed with what was happening to his right elbow. He forgot everything else existed as his brain was hit hard by the pain. Kyle released his grip and stepped back. Everything had taken less than a second as the hysterical man now fell to the floor.

From around the van appeared another four men who suddenly became the next threat. Whatever had been going on they were part of it. All of them produced knifes except the fourth who had a shoulder bag that he was frantically trying to open, even the members of the crowd could see that this abductor was going for a larger weapon, perhaps even a gun. Karen ran up to them, dragging the stunned and now silent Kelly and shouted the one-word command that they all reacted to. *"RUN"*

Tony released the driver that he was kneeling on and turned towards the dark-haired girl who was trying to stand up. Tony recognised her face and he realised that Karen was right, they had to get her away from here. Tony's left hand caught her under her right arm and propelled her forwards.

"Kyle … grab an arm," in less than a second, they were dragging the girl away for the scene behind them. They all ran past the white painted restaurant that was on their left and up the small incline to the first set of steps that led up and away from the road. The stone wall stood over eight feet high and dominated that side of the spiralling road. Single filed steps were cut into the hill and faced back down towards the small car park in front of the harbour bar. They were too narrow for them both to carry the girl, so Kyle let go and Tony lifted her upwards. Kyle stopped to look back at what was going on down by the van, there was a crowd gathering around the men and a lot of shouting had just started. Kyle sprinted up the last few steps and joined the others.

At the top of the steps was an open area, the wooden framed entrance to the white restaurant was now on their left, a few people were coming out and were totally oblivious to what had just happened below. Tony led them past the cars and onto the road. Kelly was already out of breath and panting but her mind was racing as she could not totally take in how fast things were moving, Karen however, seemed to be taking everything in her stride. Tony pointed past them and directed them up the darker road to their left, away from the town centre and away from the shouting that was getting louder and closer from behind them. "That way, go," he shouted, he released the black-haired girl who was regaining the use of her own legs. Kyle started off with the other two girls in tow. Kelly was still looking lost and shocked and Karen now had an intense scowl on her face. Kyle looked back at Tony who had his phone out and to his ear. Tony ushered him on with his free left hand. The girl regained herself with every step and soon Kyle released more of his grip. A large blue sign directed them on the road towards the recreation grounds, Kyle knew the road but the girl in tow obviously didn't. Karen started to encourage and reassure her while Kelly stayed silent following two steps behind. Tony was still on the phone but at least he was now coming up the road after them. The group made its way around the corner. Kyle paused to let Tony catch up. Karen nodded towards Kelly and they both took the girl over to a wooden bench that was built into the concrete as the young girl continued to come around more.

Both Karen and Kelly were both now talking to her without much response. Kyle looked her up and down, she was wearing black leather ankle high boots and dark black jeans that were tight around her legs. They stopped halfway between her knees and her ankles. On her right leg, wrapped around the leg was a tattoo of a branch with leaves coming of it, they spread out and wrapped themselves around her leg and led off into her boot. The tatt was green and lined in a very dark blue, Kyle liked it and he wondered where else the tattoo led to. The jeans were held up with a leather belt, and she wore a black cotton hooded zip top. As she sat forward, the zip opened and Kyle could see that she had a red top on underneath. Her jet-black hair hung straight down towards the ground and covered most of her face. Kyle stepped forward as she spoke, he didn't understand what she said as it was not a language he had ever heard before, it was clear from her body language that she wasn't speaking to any of them. Kelly and Karen were now sitting on either side of the girl, talking to her and trying their best to reassure her that everything was going to be alright. Tony walked up and stopped beside the sign that stated RAMORE HEAD in large letters. As Tony spoke the girl sat upright.

"Karen, take Kelly back to the car and we'll meet you both there in a few minutes," Karen stood to leave but Kelly didn't move.

"Hey, wait a minute, I want to know what the hell is going on here!" Kelly demanded. The girl in black looked around her and Kyle looked straight into the dark brown unreadable eyes that glared back at him. Tony walked over and was about to speak to Kyle as Kelly spoke. He stopped and turned his head and looked back at her, he paused before he spoke; Karen had taken two steps and stopped.

"Kelly, we have just stopped this girl from being abducted and Kyle and I are going to ensure that she is alright, and then send her home." Kyle knew he was lying about sending her home.

"Come on, Kelly" said Karen, she nodded with her head and headed back down the direction they had just come from. Kelly looked around for support, pursed her lips then stood up.

"Kelly, we are police officers," Tony said, "it's all part of the job," again Kyle knew it was a lie, but he didn't react. Kelly was deliberately not being told about something which he hoped he would discover shortly. Karen waited for Kelly to join her and they both started off down the hill. Tony waited until they were far enough away before he turned towards the girl. "You are to come with us," Tony said sternly. The girl looked at him, raised her eyebrows and her top lip in disgust.

"I don't have to do anything you say!" Kyle could not place her accent but her utter contempt towards Tony grew with each passing second. "I will do what I want ..." Tony stepped forward to speak again and as he did so she stood up and squared up to him. She was quite tall, taller than he had first thought, he guessed that she was about 5'11 maybe even 6 feet, defiance radiated from her. "I certainly don't have to do anything that 'YOU' say," With that she started to turn to her right and push past Tony. Kyle stepped forward as Tony's hand shot out and grabbed her, stopping her in her tracks. His voice rose to nearly a shout as he barked his order.

"You will come with us and yes, you will do as I say." The side of her mouth raised, and a small noise came out, she tried to pull her arm free.

If only you knew who I am, you...." she started, Tony cut her off.

"I do know who you are ... Dani," A look of shock burst over her face, "and yes I do know 'what' you are ... and yes you are 'STILL' coming with us." Tony released her and allowed her to step back. She had not been expecting that, whatever it meant. Dani was not from around here, but that still didn't explain the strange language that she had used earlier, Dani paused and stared at him, after a few seconds her face relaxed slightly.

"I do not take orders from an animal," she spat. Tony grabbed her left arm, spun her around and shoved her up the pathway towards Ramore Head.

"You may not," Tony started, "but you will do what we want right now!" The hill rose up and the pathway cut through the green of the grass as they walked either side of Dani. The sea lay ahead of them in the distance, it was calm, and the moonlight reflected off it. Dani was silent as they walked on. Kyle wasn't sure what was about to happen, but something was, he had picked up on her 'animal' comment, and *how could she know what he is?'* he thought to himself. The grass rose into a mound on their left, the wind and the sound of the waves on the rocks let you know that you were near a cliff edge. Tony walked on, taking her with him. Over the mounds to their left in the distance were the lights of Portstewart, the pathway rose again sharply as they drew level with the box shaped building down below. Tony stopped as his phone bleeped, he read the message then looked down towards the car park that lay at the end of the row of houses. "We are to go to the car park," said Tony as he put the phone away in the pocket of his trousers. Dani muttered in the strange language again to which Tony reacted, "Shut it." The command was direct and to the point, he shoved her again. Could Tony understand what she had said? What was the language? He couldn't even speak French, how could he know this? As far as Kyle knew Tony only spoke English and Irish but as he had been finding out there was a whole lot about his friend that he did not know. As they were making their way down the hill Kyle asked the most obvious but seemly most irrelevant question.

"Are you going to tell me where we are going?"

"Yeah sure, the car park," Tony nodded as he spoke, he smiled as they walked on into the empty car park, Tony was back to being himself again. They stopped in the middle of the car park, Dani was still being defiant, whatever was about to happen she was not happy about any of it. They stood in silence and Tony was looking around, his grip on her arm never relaxed.

Kyle noticed that both Dani and Tony both straightened up as the two cars drove into the car park. Both were four door sedans, one a Volvo and the other a Ford, the cars turned and stopped twenty feet away. The cars pointed towards the exit, they were not planning on being here very long. The doors of the cars opened, and a group of well-dressed men and one woman got out and started walking towards them. Dani let out an audible tut and sigh, then relaxed into a shrug. Some of the group slowed and held back, some fanned out and a group of four men and the one woman walked towards them. Kyle could see that if they were armed, every one of them kept a clear line of sight on himself and Tony. The woman was tall and thin with bright blonde hair that was nearly at her elbows, like Dani she was dressed head to foot in black. All the men wore dark clothes, Kyle aged most of them to be late twenties and there was something about them that he did not like, in fact his own body was reacting to them. Tony was like a statue, but Kyle could tell that his whole body was tensed up, ready to attack.   'DANGER'

∞∞∞∞

The group stopped a short distance away, they were not happy, not happy at all. The shorter man was standing with the three others behind him in a semi-circle. Whoever he was, he certainly was in charge. All the men were standing in a non-aggressive way but in a way that they could easily bring their weapons up and into use. Kyle's mind noted each one as his eyes bounced from face to face, this team knew what they were doing.

The blonde looked Kyle up and down as the shorter man spoke in the strange language. Kyle looked at him and blinked, whatever that was it did not make sense. He was direct in his tone and it seemed like a command of some kind. Dani slowly moved forward and walked past them towards the car, two of the men behind the shorter man turned and followed her. Dani looked back over her right shoulder and silently swore at Tony with her mouth, now that, Kyle could understand. Two of the other men that were standing near the cars walked up towards Dani and opened the rear door, she climbed in and one of them got in after her, the Blonde spoke.

"This is the one I was telling you about," now that was a weird accent, Kyle thought to himself, the shorter man's eyes opened in recognition.

"Ahh ... you are Tony Fallon then," he said, his accent was similar to the one the blonde had, Tony looked at them.

"Hello Sabine," he said, a smile broke over the face of the blonde.

"Hello Tony," the shorter man then spoke cutting off any further conversation.

"You have done us a service, for which you have our thanks," every alarm was ringing in Kyle's body, something was very out of place here as the shorter man continued, "the child will be punished of course for causing so much trouble," Kyle glanced at Tony whose face remained expressionless, Kyle had never seen that before. "I am in your debt, now isn't that something unusual for our kinds?" the shorter man smiled at his own joke but no one else moved. If a fight started Kyle guessed that they were dead, they couldn't fight off all of them. Tony spoke.

"I have but one request," The greying eyebrows of the shorter man lifted.

"And that is?"

"The two sapiens that were with us tonight," Tony stated, the shorter man turned to the younger man who was stood to his left, he nodded, and the shorter man returned his stare to Tony.

"Yes, what about them?"

"They are with me, under my protection," Tony breathed in as he continued,

"They are never to be touched ... no hunting, ever, whatever the reason." There was a pause from the group in front of him, the tall blonde reacted to what Tony had said. Kyle searched those in front of him for any sign that they were about to attack but the only sound was of the wind around them. Tony spoke again, "agree to this and I will consider the debt repaid," The shorter man raised his eyebrows before he answered.

"You will of course inform your Alpha of this?" the older one asked.

"I will," stated Tony.

"Agreed." With that he turned, the man who was standing behind him parted to allow him passage and all of them started walking back towards the two cars. Slowly the protection team collapsed back onto the cars. Kyle noticed Tony starting to relax. The blonde stopped at the door and turned to look Kyle straight in the eye, and then she blew him a kiss. Kyle smiled and winked with his right eye in return. The doors of the cars slammed shut and in seconds the cars were gone. Tony turned to his right and started back towards the town centre and to where the girls were waiting. Kyle caught up to him. They walked in silence for about twenty seconds then Kyle spoke.

"So, mucker, who and what were they?" They both walked on, "They are not human, are they?" Kyle asked, Tony stopped.

"Sapiens."

"What?" asked Kyle.

"We don't call them humans, we call them sapiens." Kyle looked at him not quite sure where this one was going, "as in *Homo-Sapiens...* you know, mankind."

"Yeah, I get that bit," answered Kyle, he pointed back at the car park, "but they weren't sapiens ... were they?" Tony turned and walked on, Kyle caught him up. He wanted some answers and Tony knew that he had to tell him something.

"They are Noc's," he said as they carried on.

"Knocks?" replied Kyle.

"*Homo-Noctraili-Vampari,*" There was another pause then Tony translated what it meant, "Man who walks in the night," Tony turned and looked at him. Kyle was still not any wiser then Tony said words that he thought he would never hear for real.

"Most sapiens call them vampires," Kyle stopped, Tony walked on for three steps then turned to face him.

"Vampires?" Kyle stated.

"The Noctrailis ... or Noc's, the only people who call them vampires are the sapiens," Kyle looked at Tony and knew that he wasn't lying.

"You are telling me that vampires are real?" Kyle asked.

"We are real," Tony turned to walk away then spoke again, "Come on mucker, I will tell you all you want to know tomorrow." Kyle caught him up and they approached the car in silence. They could see both the girls inside chatting away, Kelly didn't look very impressed.

"What do we tell them?" Kyle asked,

"About the Noctrailis? Nothing," that did not answer Kyle's question, "I knew a cousin of hers and called her and they came and collected her. Stick to the truth as much as you can, then you cannot go wrong." As they climbed into the car they were met with a barrage of angry questions from Kelly. Karen said nothing until the conversation changed, but by then they were well on their way out of Portrush.

∞∞∞∞

Back at the bridge outside the Harbour bar Cara-Marie was using her left hand to scroll through the pictures on her digital camera, then she was scrolling through the address book on her phone with her right. She put the phone to her ear and listened to the ringing tone, after the fourth ring it was answered by Mark's tired voice.

"If this isn't a page three girl I am hanging up!" she smiled as she then heard a yelp as Mark was obviously punched or slapped by Rachel.

"Hi'ya, it's me and no I am not a page three model and if you hang up I am ringing back," she heard him let out two short laughs.

"Err, yes I know it is you, this modern technology thingy allows you to see the name and number of who is calling you," there was a noise in the background that she could not make out, "why are you phoning me at nearly one in the morning?" There was more noise and movement in the background, Mark was obviously in bed and Rachel was annoyed that he had answered his phone at all, she ignored it.

"Yes, meet me in the office at nine tomorrow morning, there has just been a fight outside the harbour bar," she looked at the pictures that she had taken of Tony and Kyle on the camera's screen.

"SO?" Mark asked in annoyance, it was not unheard of a fight happening after a night out in Portrush.

"It's who is involved, who ran away from the scene, and" she let it hang in the air.

"And what?" Mark asked.

"I got the whole lot on camera," she said triumphantly, there was silence on the phone.

"Cara," stated Mark.

"Yes?"

"I love you," This was promptly followed by a yep from him, she was smiling.

"See you then," she said as she hung up the phone. The ambulance had arrived in the small car park and was blocking the exit of the taxi's and the other cars that were there, the two uniformed police officers that had been at the far side of the street were still waiting for more police to arrive as they had recovered a small pump action shotgun from the bag, several knifes and a group of men who now refused to speak English. On top of that there was a growing number of impatient people who were being denied a quick journey home, tempers were flaring but Cara-Marie continued to look through the pictures. She stopped at one of Tony and she zoomed in, the side of his face filled the screen. "What are you?" she asked aloud, the shouting from outside the pub brought her back to where she was, it was time to leave.

Chapter 56

Cara-Marie was staring at the screen of the desktop PC; her living room was silent. She was staring at the mutilated images in front of her, part of her should have been shocked, perhaps even wanted to be shocked but nothing in her stirred. Her right forefinger twitched as it hovered over the mouse and scrolled through to the next set of gruesome pictures. All had been taken locally since the killings had begun; all had been taken by their photographer and none had been printed in their newspaper. He had however, sold copies of almost all of them to daily newspapers, mostly across the water in England but the interest worldwide had started to increase quite dramatically, especially from France. Her phone started to ring and made her jump; the noise startled her into the present. She crunched her face as she looked at the name on the screen; with slight annoyance she pressed the green button and placed the phone beside her right ear.

"What are you doing awake at this time of night? I said we will meet up tomorrow!" she did not hide her annoyance, Mark paused before he spoke.

"Umm, Cara, it's nearly nine in the morning!" His statement made her turn and look at the drawn curtains in her living room, "and I am phoning to say that I am not going to make it into the office," the natural light from outside was trying it's hardest to force its way inside; her mouth fell open at the realisation.

"Cara?" Mark asked,

"Yes?" she answered.

"Have you been awake all night?"

"No," the lie was as obvious as it was sudden in its answer to the question.

"Car-a," Mark dragged her name over two syllables.

"What?" she answered,

"Nothing," he knew it was pointless trying to have an argument with her, so he changed the topic back to the reason that he was phoning her in the first place. "Well, being the news junkie that you are you probably know more about this than me," he paused as she heard a door shut in the background, Mark was now outside. She fought with her thoughts before he continued speaking, "you have seen the news this morning, haven't you?"

"Well, no," she was almost apologetic in her answer, "I have been busy, I got two main stories finished on Ballybogy and a separate witness interview and then I have collated the stories from everything else that happened around Coleraine over the weekend," her defence was quick and aggressive, "then there is the stuff from last night."

"Have you filed them in Kevin's mail box at work?" he was walking as he spoke.

"Of course, I have! What do you think I am?" she felt her anger subside as quickly as it has risen, "sorry, I didn't mean to bite your head off," she said apologetically, Mark paused, she recognised the sound of his car alarm deactivating.

"Yeah, no probs, it happens when you are that tired, speaking of things getting their heads bitten off, flick on one of the news channels," she glanced over at the dark screen of the TV before she slowly started to rise from her chair.

"And what am I looking for exactly?"

"You'll see," he was smiling as he spoke,

"Where are you going?" she asked.

"To get Rachel," he answered, she spotted the remote in the far corner of the sofa, her body unconsciously moved towards it.

"Rachel? Why where is she?" she could feel how uncomfortable he had just become, it sounded like things had taken a turn for the worse.

"Oh, she went to her Mum last night and I'm just going to get her now," she could tell what kind of Sunday morning that he was about to have,

"Wasn't she with you last night?" she asked.

"Was ... she stormed off after last night's phone call."

"No probs," she could not think of any advice to give him for the situation that he was in, "stay in touch."

"And you."

The TV came to life as she got comfortable on the sofa, her right thumb moved over the controls and the familiar background of one of the 24-hour news channels filled the screen. The news story was forest fires in Australia, she wasn't sure why that would be of interest to her, she watched on. The presenter introduced a report from a journalist who was nearby one of the fires; it had destroyed a small town that she could not pronounce and was making its way along the coast. This didn't really interest her and for the first time she felt the tiredness creep over her body, perhaps a coffee was needed.

"Or maybe even my bed," she said out loud as she closed her eyes briefly.

"The local fire fighters have been joined by crews from all the nearby areas and are presently trying to save the small hamlet of Coleraine." The words made her eyes spring open; she could see the obvious connection ... now that was something of interest. She watched until the reporter had finished, and the presenter had taken over again; in her mind she was already thinking of the link story they could do. She wondered how many people from the area had ever moved there. A search of the local newspapers of Coleraine in Australia could wait until tomorrow. She propelled herself upwards and headed towards the kitchen and as she flicked the kettle on; another story about the Ballybogy killing came on. Cara-Marie was lifting a mug down from her cupboard when her ears picked up the story. Her body turned, and she stopped in the doorway of the small kitchen. The reporter was at the edge of the police cordon, the tape stretched across the road behind him fluttering in the wind. The reporter was obviously cold and was wearing a thick outdoor jacket and seemed to be speaking quite quickly into the microphone. Was he trying to finish the story as quickly as possible, so he could climb back into the warm broadcast van they had?

"If you don't like the conditions then get another job," she said to the TV screen. He wasn't saying anything she didn't already know so Mark must have been talking about the forest fires down under. As she turned back into the kitchen the face of Mike Dear filled the screen as he made an appeal for witnesses to get in touch with the Muirdris team but wasn't giving away any other details. She felt how tired she was; the kettle was starting to boil so she opened the cupboard and started to make a mug of coffee. The news channel was now reviewing the morning papers, the anchor had already introduced the reviewer, and both were laughing at the story.

"Yes, this must be one of the funniest stories published this year, apparently there is a werewolf running around Northern Ireland," their words had her back in the living room glaring at the screen. The reviewer was holding up one of the Sunday newspapers and sharing the joke with the programmes anchor. "Well, according to an eye witness they spotted what they are calling a werewolf just after one of these killings near the town of Coleraine."

"Really? A were-wolf," the anchor had raised his eyebrows and had drawn out his pronunciation of 'werewolf' as if telling a scary story to a child at bedtime. Both of them were giggling as they spoke.

"Yeah, apparently the picture they printed is evidence," the reviewer continued, and a picture filled the screen, she felt her insides turn as she looked at the picture that she had been shown in the coffee shop on the phone; the anchor was laughing out loud as he was answering the previous comment.

"And this is from someone who admitted to taking drugs that night," she sighed, the character assassination had already begun. The programme continued but the two men on the screen finished off this story with comments of 'Ludicrous' and 'Fantasy', they moved on to the next story, but she was searching for her mobile phone and she didn't care if Kevin was awake or not.

∞∞∞

Kyle walked out of his bedroom and headed towards the kitchen. His eyes glanced at the clock on the wall, but he barely registered the time. It certainly didn't feel like nearly half nine in the morning. His body slowly moved around the kitchen; before the kettle had even boiled a few slices of bread were toasted and cheese was sliced. He spread the soft cheese over the still warm toast.

Kyle lifted the controller to the small TV attached to the far wall in the kitchen and scrolled through the channels until he found the morning news. The story of forest fires in Australia was the top stop but the rest faded into the background. His eyes stared out of the kitchen windows over the green fields that lay around his house and the taste of the cheese remained in his mouth. His eyes became vague as his mind zoned out.

The legionnaires were sitting around under the shelter that they had built at Brobo, near Bouake in the Cote d'Ivoire. Many people around the world still referred to it in English as the Ivory Coast but the small West African country had maintained close links with France since its independence in 1960. They had asked for French Troops to be stationed there permanently since the failed coup in 2002, a request the French President did not have a problem answering. Kyle ate more of the cheese on toasted bread as a young legionnaire stopped by the staff sergeant, who looked up at the youngster with an annoyed look on his face. The young legionnaire spoke first.

"Legionnaire Fessler, 1 year and 2 months served Staff Sergeant."

"What do you want?" replied the staff sergeant, as the legionnaire passed on the message, he had been given Kyle looked over at him. Fessler when asked would say he was from Berlin, yet he spoke French with an English accent and could not speak a word of German. The legion was a good place to hide if you didn't want to be found. Suddenly Kyle was one of six men carrying the large rubber bag that had three handles on each side; they walked slowly onto the rear ramp of the transport aircraft of the French Air Force. Legionnaire Fessler had been one of the nine legionnaires killed the previous day. Twenty-three Africans and one American had also died in the rocket attack but the Africans who had carried it out had all died when they struck back. This however would not lessen the grief of the family somewhere in England who would be getting the hand delivered letter from the French consulate.

The sound of the doorbell made Kyle jump as a piece of his half-eaten toast landed on the floor. He was back in his own kitchen. The door chimed again as Kyle reluctantly rose from his seat and bending over, scooped the toast up from the floor. The toast went into the bin and he made his way towards the front door. He readjusted the dressing gown as he suddenly thought that it may be Kelly. After the fight at the pub she had taken off in a rage soon after they had got back to his house. It wasn't until he had seen the red lights of the back of her car speeding away into the darkness that he realised that she shouldn't have been driving. She hadn't drunk much but the fact that she had drank, meant she was probably over the limit; however, nothing would have kept her there last night. She had started screaming at him at one point before she grabbed her keys. He could not tell her who those people really were at the car park, how could he? 'Yeah they were vampires and the chick with the dark hair is a princess who went missing a few months ago… we were just giving her back.' He wouldn't have believed it either. It was Tony's smiling face that greeted him when the door opened and not Kelly's. Kyle felt slightly deflated.

"Morning," he was cheerful, and cheerful in an annoying way. Kyle stepped back and let him enter. Tony lifted his nose and bounded towards the rich smell of toast, "that smells good, since there is only one car in the driveway," Tony glanced back as Kyle closed the door, "I take it you're alone," he nodded as Tony disappeared through the doorway. By the time Kyle got into the kitchen Tony was already munching away at one of the bits of toast with cheese on it.

"Nice," he said as he was nodding his head.

"That was my breakfast" stated an annoyed Kyle.

"I like how you used *'was'* as it is now mine," Kyle sat down and faced out the window.

"The kettle's not long boiled, help yourself," he said as Tony pushed the edge of the toast into his mouth. Tony nodded and mumbled an answer as he turned towards the kettle. Tony opened the cupboard and lifted down one of the mugs and proceeded to make himself a mug of tea; Tony cleared his throat before he spoke.

"They made four arrests outside the harbour bar," Kyle looked over at him.

"Really?"

"Yeah, possession of unlicensed firearms etc, turns out they were Bulgarian, not Polish as the arresting officer first thought.

"Who got the arrest?" Kyle asked, Tony still had his back to him as he was pouring the hot liquid into the mug.

"Mick Cullen," Tony answered.

"The part-timer?"

"The very same," Tony lifted the tea bag out of the mug with the teaspoon and dropped it in the bin.

"Good one for him, who was with him?"

"Dunno, didn't recognise the name, she must be new." Tony walked over to the table and took up the chair directly opposite him, Tony scanned the remaining toast and bits of cheese, the small grin on his face told Kyle what his intentions were.

"Leave the rest of my breakfast alone."

"What?" Tony feigned a mock hurt.

"Besides," said Kyle as he moved in his seat, "I have some questions for you" he paused, "it's about last night."

"What about last night?"

"These ... knocks."

"Homo Noctrailis," stated Tony. Kyle looked up and reached for the last pieces of toast.

"Yeah," answered Kyle,

"Well what do you want to know?" he asked, Kyle paused for a moment, ate some of the toast, then looked up at Tony.

"Where do I start? Who are they? Where do they come from etc and precisely how did Portrush manage to have a load of vampires without loads of bodies stacking up?"

"Well, those Noc's come from a coven near Salisbury in England and they were over here looking for the girl."

"Why?" Kyle asked before Tony finished speaking which made it more of a demand.

"She is one of their own. She went missing and they went all out to find her,"

"Why?" Kyle demanded again.

"Well, she is important to them, she is one of the daughters of the Queen of the Black Witches in Southern England, and they want her back."

"Queen of what?"

"The Black Witches, they are over most of continental Europe." Kyle's mouth dropped.

"And I am supposed to believe that?"

"Believe what you want, but they are real," stated Tony.

"So, witches are in fact vampires?" Kyle asked.

"Not at all, most witches don't even know that the Noc's exist," Tony paused then finished off what he was saying, "the larger covens, 100 plus will be controlled by at least one Noc, sometimes, but very rarely it can be a family of them, as it is in Salisbury."

"And the guy in the car park was her dad or something?"

"Ha," Tony laughed, "No, not a chance he is one tier down in their society, her father would not come onto our lands at all, unless,"

"Unless what?"

"Unless he wanted a war," Tony was very 'matter of fact' about his statement.

"And that happens a lot, does it?" replied Kyle.

"Not for about two centuries or so, no."

"So, the vamps,"

"Noc's or Noctrailis, only sapiens call them vampires," it was Tony's turn to cut Kyle off.

"So, the Noctrailis," questioned Kyle "don't do daylight, turn into bats and are immortal thingies," Tony laughed again.

"They would tell sapiens that,"

"So, what is true and what isn't then?" There was an irritation in Kyle's voice that Tony picked up on.

"No, they don't turn into bats, no they don't fly, and no they are not immortal."

"So, what are they then?"

"They are Hematophagic."

"Excuse me?" stated Kyle.

"Hematophagic, a dietary trait whose food source is blood, it is found in nature." Tony could see Kyle going over what was being said to him.

"And the daylight thing?"

"That bit is true; their body fibres react to ultraviolet light."

"How?"

"They normally combust."

"But how do they combust?" Tony could see that Kyle was trying to explain to himself what he was hearing.

"Did you ever do the sodium test in chemistry in school?" Kyle looked confused, "ask any chemistry teacher about it."

"I don't actually have any chemistry teachers on my phone presently," Tony wondered if the sarcasm from Kyle had been deliberate.

"There is an experiment that you can do with a lump of sodium; you drop it into a sink full of water,"

"And what happens?" asked Kyle.

"It explodes, much like the Noc's and sunlight."

"So, you two are at war then?" he asked,

"I would say we have an understanding,"

"An understanding?"

"Yes, we observe them, and they observe us; we have had wars in the past of course."

"So how come you don't get on so much? It seems every vampire film these days has werewolves and vamps ..."

"Noctrailis," injected Tony.

"Noctrailis tearing each other apart in them," Kyle finished his question.

"We control most of Europe and Asia but The Noctrailis control most of America, there are some wolves around there, but not many, they took care of that at the turn of the 19th Century, as I was saying the other day." Kyle remembered the conversation that they had in the car, "And you can tell how much they control Hollywood. It seems that nearly every TV drama or film nowadays portrays them with the latest hunk or model of the day." Kyle lowered the mug and gazed across at Tony as he carried on talking, "I mean when was the last time you saw an ugly Noc on the TV? It is very subtle but very effective."

"How?" Kyle was back to his one-word questions.

"Easy, it makes sapiens think that it is 'cool' to be a Noc, they are immortal, they can do what they want, it can be attractive to teenagers."

"So, what is the truth?" asked Kyle.

"The truth? That instead of being immortal you have just cut your life span in half, you can't go into daylight and if you don't get blood your vitamin D deficiency will kill you."

"Vitamin D deficiency?" retorted Kyle.

"Yes," replied a confident Tony, "They suffer from vitamin D deficiency from a severe lack of daylight."

"And that is why their skin is the colour it is?" asked Kyle.

"Right on," answered Tony as he moved forward again and lifted the mug of tea and emptied the rest of it in one mouthful.

"How do they feed?" Kyle asked.

"What do you mean 'how do they feed?' they kill sapiens for their blood."

"Why humans? Why not cows or something?" asked Kyle.

"No idea, I'm not a Noc," replied Tony.

"How can they kill people? There would be a police investigation?" Tony could see that the police officer in Kyle was surfacing again. Tony slowly nodded twice as he considered different answers until he settled on one that Kyle could relate to.

"One hundred thousand people disappeared in the UK last year alone," this was a statistic that Kyle would probably have known.

"So, you are saying they were all taken by vampires?"

"No, not at all," Tony paused again, "only some of them, the rest, well who knows," Tony could tell that he had hit a nerve with Kyle. This was something that he wasn't expecting so he quickly changed the conversation.

"Which reminds me," Tony started.

"What?" asked Kyle.

"Have you got a dinner jacket?"

"Eh?" this turn of events surprised Kyle.

"Well, have you?" Tony asked.

"Yes, why?" he answered.

"Brilliant you will need it Tuesday evening," said Tony as he rose from the table.

"And why will I need it Tuesday evening?" Kyle asked.

"We are having a Moon Dance at the farm and you are, of course, invited." Kyle had stopped moving as Tony looked back at him.

"A Moon Dance?"

"Yes, we have them throughout the year and the next one is on Tuesday evening."

"What is a Moon Dance?" asked Kyle,

"Now *that* will take all day."

Chapter 57

Mike was sitting on the chair beside the bubbling coffee machine in Sean's office. The folder was open in his lap and he was concentrating on the mass of paperwork the folder contained. The conversations coming from the main office were background noise to him as he focused on what he was reading. Mike glanced over when the sounds from the main room changed.

"Good morning sir," echoed around. Mike looked up as the stern-faced chief inspector walked directly through the centre of the room and was heading straight for the door of the office. Mike noticed he wasn't acknowledging the polite salutations that seemed to bounce off him. The Chief Inspector's uniform was immaculate, and his air of authority let everyone know that they were beneath him. The face was younger than what could be expected for someone who had served 20 years in the police. The crop of blonde hair didn't move as he glanced to his left then refocused on the doorway ahead of him. Mike placed his mug of coffee down on the table and stood up as he entered.

"Chief Inspector Anderson, good morning Sir, I ..."

"Lose the pleasantries," Chief Anderson almost pushed him out of the way as he barged past him and walked around Sean's desk. Mike paused as the Chief sat down behind the desk, the smell of coffee filled the small room as Mike closed the door and sat back down.

"Chief, would you like a coffee?" Mike asked, "it's Inspector Parrish's own ground Kenyan." The Chief Inspector looked over and glanced out to his left at the rest of the team in the main office.

"Aye, why not; white no sugar," Mike slowly poured the coffee then gracefully handed it over the desk to him, "where is Parrish?" The inspector had lowered his voice as he took the mug from Mike, he also noted that he had not used Sean's first name or rank and to him that showed disrespect.

"He texted me, he's on his way but held up by traffic, but he will be here for the start of the brief." Mike sat back down in the seat but the glare from across the room stopped everything.

"This is a major investigation and you are telling me that the inspector isn't here? You get him on the phone, and you tell him that he's here, now." Chief Inspector Anderson had started to tap the desk with his right forefinger as he spoke, it added menace to what he was saying, "Or I'm progressing this investigation," Mike tensed up as he knew the threat to replace Sean was not an idle one.

"Ok," Mike took out his phone and scrolled through to Sean's number as the Chief slowly drank from the mug. The Chief's facial expression did not change as Mike heard the engaged tone in his right ear, "His line is busy sir, but I know he'll be here shortly," Mike got a look of utter disgust in reply. The Chief didn't speak so Mike decided to, "Inspector Parrish has asked me to go through a few things with you,"

"I don't give a toss if he is stuck in traffic," Chief Anderson cut him off, "He's supposed to be the lead investigator in this here matter; I want to speak to him now! I'm not saying that this is your fault, but it is now your problem!" Mike saw the anger rising; he remained silent as the volume of the voice in front of him rose. "But since this is such an important investigation then given the priority that the chief ..." Mike listened as he continued, "That's the chief con ...." he was dropping in a direct reference to the chief constable so that Mike was sure Chief Anderson had access to him, "has given to this investigation I would suggest that Parrish gets his ass in this office right away."

"Ok Chief, I will try his number again," Mike still had his phone in his hand, so he scrolled through his numbers again. This time he switched the call over to the speaker-phone setting so that Chief Anderson could hear what was being said. For a moment, he hoped that Sean would answer the call but again he hoped that he wouldn't. The female voice that boomed out of the small phone had a very pronounced English accent and she repeated the words that Mike had heard countless times.

"I'm sorry but the number you have tried is switched off, please call again later or try sending a text," Mike wanted to smile but kept it to himself as his right thumb ended the call. Chief Anderson raised his right arm to dismiss the call.

"Right then," the Chief leaned back into Sean's chair and looked out over the rest of the team. Mike glanced over at the busy detectives, all of which knew that there was a chief inspector sitting in the office watching them. "While we're waiting, what are the things he wants us to go over then?" The Chief wasn't even looking at him now. His contempt overpowered the smell of the coffee; he had a reputation for being direct, but you don't get to be the youngest Chief Inspector by being otherwise.

"At the main briefing, we will go over each individual crime scene and get an update from those who are working them," Mike slightly paused as the Chief glanced over at him, the Chief didn't speak, he carried on, "we have had a good response, especially after the Crime watch programme,"

"Mmmhuh," the Chief made the sound without opening his mouth, Mike carried on.

"We had a massive response from that and because of the response we got more detectives from the M.I.T.s at Lisburn to come up and help ...."

"Which M.I.T.s did you get?" The Chief injected.

"Lisburn," answered Mike, Chief Anderson screwed up his face.

"Is that Fitzpatrick's crew?" he asked, Mike thought for a second before answering.

"I believe it is, aye," Mike knew of Detective Inspector Fitzpatrick but had never worked with him, Chief Anderson's face turned to one of disgust.

"That guy's an idiot," He turned and looked back out at the rest of the team, the smile dropped from Mike's face as that was not the kind of comment a Chief Inspector should say about another Inspector in front of Mike. It was very unprofessional and showed total disrespect. Mike moved the conversation on and tried to ignore the comment.

"Even though the Limavady murder would normally have come under the M.I.T. at Derry the outgoing Inspector up there was retiring so he handed the whole investigation over to us,"

"Sgt Dear," Chief Anderson turned his head and held up his hand to stop Mike mid-sentence, "cut to the chase, stop telling me things that I already know and tell me something that I don't," Mike breathed in and thought for a second then decided to say it out right.

"There are a couple of things that Sean wanted you to know about this investigation before we held the full brief and that is only between him, myself and the other Detective Sergeant, Simon McAllister ..." It had the desired effect, the Chief looked slightly surprised.

"Simon?"

"Yeah, Simon McAllister, a bit old and losing his hair," answered Mike who could see that the Chief was trying to picture him.

"Where is he from?" the Chief asked.

"He spent a lot of time up in Derry, Sean knew him as a section Sergeant," the Chief dismissed the comment and turned his head away again, so Mike carried on. "The first thing is a witness statement from a survivor from the Castleroe killings," Mike lifted the folder that he had been reading from and handed over a bundle of A4 witness sheets that had been stapled together. "It's quite interesting some of the things that she is describing, but ... this is an unreliable witness," The Chief cast Mike a very disapproving look at the 'unreliable witness' bit but didn't stop him so he carried on, "Sean still wants it part of the investigation, yes she admits to taking drugs, yes she was drinking alcohol, but it is her descriptions of what she saw that we are concentrating on."

"Pardon?" The Chief was annoyed again.

"Sean ..." Mike corrected himself, "Inspector Parrish still wants this to be a part of the investigation, but it is only between the senior members of the team." The Chief slowly sat back in Sean's chair and looked down at the copy of the statement.

"Go on," he instructed.

"It's her descriptions of what she saw, I mean for example when she said she saw the clouds change into horses..." The Chief's head shot up.

"She saw what?" his voice had raised a level as well.

"She said that she watched the clouds change into horses and then the grass turned blue and she saw two people change into dogs and they attacked the group and ripped everyone apart," the Chief was even less impressed now, "then she lost consciousness, next thing she knew there were two off duty coppers there with their personal weapons out," the Chief's face scolded at him.

"Who took this statement?" he demanded.

"One of the detectives..." answered Mike.

"Who?" repeated the Chief, Mike had to think for a moment. The name would be on the statement in the Chief's hand, but Mike made a best guess.

"Detective Constable Cargill," Mike shifted in his seat as the disapproving Detective Chief Inspector glared at him then glanced down at what was in his hand and Mike wondered for a second if it had been Cargill, he had taken so many statements over the last few weeks he could have got that bit wrong.

"Is Cargill giving the briefing?" the Chief asked.

"He will be giving that part of the briefing, yes," answered Mike, even if he had not been, he certainly was now, "the drugs that were found at the scene ... we found quantities of X and...."

"Not interested in that," stated the Chief without looking up, his right-hand finalising what he had cut in with.

"Right," Mike glanced down at the contents of the folder that was on his lap, "the other thing that we are keeping between us is ... do you know Dr Burns down at the forensic labs?" The Chief glanced up.

"Yes," his tone said it all, of course he knew him.

"He is putting forward a theory..." started Mike.

"I used to play golf with him," the Chief cut in.

"Right ..." Mike's eyes glanced over at the far door that was the entrance to the main office, still no Sean, "You were obviously standing on his right side as he is completely deaf in his left," Mike regretted it as soon as he had said it.

"He plays off sixteen, complete rubbish," the Chief didn't look up at all as he spoke.

"I don't play golf, so I have no idea what that means,"

"Keep going,"

"He's putting forward a theory that there is 'someone' or 'some people' out there that he says he can prove through their DNA that are able to change shape," Mike took a breath in. "But the direction that Inspector Parrish is pushing the investigation is that these murders are being committed by 'more than' one person and they are using either a single large dog or several dogs in their ... activities." Mike glanced down as his right hand moved through the first few sheets of printed statements that were in the folder on his lap, "initially we thought that the DNA was corrupted," he paused as his eyes found what he was looking for, "then Dr Burns' report supported this as it showed both human DNA and canine DNA."

"Sgt Dear," The Chief once again stopped him speaking, Mike looked up at him as the Chief continued speaking, "you are boring the pants off me... if I want to know what Dr Burns' evaluation of the professional forensic evidence is or what he is doing then ...." The Chief sat forward and put his left arm on the desk and pointed at Mike with his right forefinger, "I'll ask him." The Chief's firm tone was back. Mike could see what was coming next, so he threw it straight at him.

"He's about to go public with this and say that there is a werewolf running around Northern Ireland."

"No, he won't," The Chief cut Mike off again.

"Well ..." Mike started.

"He will not be going public with that," the Chief sat back in the chair and folded his arms letting Mike know that he was totally in control.

"Grand, cuz we tried stopping him," Mike tried to explain what had happened before, but the Chief showed him the palm of his right hand in a stop sign.

"Right." Mike stopped at the Chief's one-word sentence. There was a slight pause in the room before he asked his next question, "What lines of enquiry is this investigation actually following?" Mike breathed in and was about to speak but the Chief beat him to it. "So far you have told me what everyone else is doing... where the hell is this investigation progressing, that's the third time I've asked you," The Chief raised his tone, this time he added menace to it, "If you want to keep your rank I suggest you give me a direct answer right now!" The Chief started to tap the desk with his right forefinger as he spoke, adding weight to what he was saying.

"We had identified a Latvian man called Alexi Chernov."

"Ah ha," the Chief cut in again, Mike now knew that whatever he said the Chief would undercut him and there wasn't much he could do about it, "It's called *evidence* and you are starting to really piss me off now ..." Mike kept his first thought to himself or he could be a constable by this time tomorrow.

"From the evidence we gathered we have confirmed that this is the same DNA that killed Trotman, killed the young man in Coleraine and killed the five people at Castleroe."

"Right," The Chief relaxed slightly.

"However, the DNA is different for the killings in Limavady," he looked straight at the Chief.

"This DNA that you are talking about, is this 'low copy DNA' or is this 'positive DNA'?" he asked.

"Positive ... DNA," Mike answered.

"Continue,"

"We can confirm, 100% that those killings were carried out by the same person."

"Do you have any witnesses to those killings?" the question was almost insulting, but Mike didn't rise to it.

"No."

"Any CCTV?" The Chief was now in a quick-fire round of questioning.

"None that we can use, no."

"Any ballistics?"

"No."

"Any other medical?"

"Just the ...."

"Any toxicology?" The Chief didn't give him time to answer. Mike would rather be in court that in front of Chief Anderson right now.

"The medical that we got ...."

"I shouldn't have to ask these questions, you should be telling me this," the Chief really didn't like Mike; that much was obvious, so he tried to answer the questions asked.

"The medical that we have, which you will see later in the briefing includes a large cast, which Dr Burns took from one of the bodies showing the shape of the teeth of the animal that carried out the killings," The Chief gave him another look of disgust.

"Right, ok,"

"He had a dental pathologist look at this and he stated it is some type of cross breed...."

"For the second time if I want to know what Burns is going to say, I'll ask him." Mike noticed that he dropped Dr Burns' title, "I want to know what evidence we have!" The Chief paused and looked like he was going to say something else but when he didn't Mike spoke instead.

"We had a name and we moved in to make an arrest, but he committed suicide before we got there ..."

"Who was that?" The Chief was back to the quick-fire questions.

"Alexi Chernov," Mike answered.

"Where's he from?"

"Latvia."

"He's ..." Mike started but was cut off again.

"How long has been here?"

"He has been here approximately four months."

"Where does he work?"

"He wasn't working."

"What? Did he sign on the dole? How did he gain entry to the country?"

"He came over by ferry."

"Right, where? Which one? Belfast?"

"Larne," answered Mike.

"Larne, ok have we bothered our backsides speaking to customs?"

"He arrived in a car ...."

"Have we spoken to Harbour police?" Mike paused again. The Chief probably wasn't going to like what he had to say next.

"A member of Harbour police is coming down today to give a presentation,"

"You haven't spoken to them? Why the hell not?" the Chief was getting annoyed.

"I haven't spoken to Harbour police as another detective did ..."

"That is pathetic ... absolutely pathetic ...." Mike glanced over at the entrance to the main office as Sean walked in; it had been a long while since he was so relieved to see him. The Chief started saying something else but stopped himself as Sean approached. Mike rose from where he had been sitting and opened the door of the office as Sean passed through the main office, greeting several of the team members on the way. Sean swept into the office with a cheerful greeting.

"Morning," Sean was smiling as he looked at a very tense Mike, he guessed straight away what had been happening.

"What time does your watch say?" asked the Chief. Sean walked past Mike and went over to the coffee machine, he answered as he bent over and started to pour himself a mug of Kenyan coffee.

"Same time as yours probably, why?" Mike resisted smiling.

"You are late, you were meant to be here over half an hour ago ...."

"I was in with the Superintendent, bringing him up to date with the investigation .... By the way, why weren't you there?" he said as he turned around and lifted the mug to his lips. Chief Inspector Anderson's face slowly flushed bright red.

"What meeting? I wasn't informed of any meeting. I should have been informed immediately!"

"I sent you the email last night after I had spoken with him over the phone," Sean was smiling but the Chief was furious and close to exploding.

"Email? Why didn't you phone me?"

"It was late, and I didn't want to disturb you," Sean's tone was almost comical as he closed his eyes and took another sip of the hot liquid. "Ahh, a fine example of a good coffee ..." he opened his eyes and looked at Mike, "much in the same way that you are a fine example of a detective Sergeant!" Sean was smiling, Mike was trying not to.

"Fighting with a uniformed sergeant in the car park of a police station in view of members of the public is not what I call a good example," Chief Anderson nearly exploded in the chair, Mike now knew what had been eating at him, Sean's face changed.

"Well if you look at the station's CCTV you can see that Sergeant Dear was attacked 'from behind' by Sergeant Tattershall and he was defending himself."

"That's not what I heard," answered the Chief.

"I don't care what you heard. I know what I saw and the station chief at Coleraine agreed. Sergeant Dear was assaulted by someone who has a history of assaulting his previous inspector and was reprimanded for being overly aggressive while making an arrest," Sean had made his point well, the Chief Inspector reached forward and lifted the mug of coffee that was sitting on top of the desk.

"That will be all Sergeant." The Chief was dismissing him, Mike didn't need to be told twice. Without speaking he walked out of the office, as he turned to close the door Sean gave him a quick wink, in all the time Mike had worked for him he had never winked at him before. Inwardly Mike smiled, closed the door and walked over to the nearest desk that had three detectives around it.

"So, how was your course then?" Sean asked as the tension in the room lifted.

"Yeah, not bad."

"So that is you qualified up to Chief Constable then?" Sean watched as his eyes shot up and met his.

"Yeah ... I am."

"Brilliant, were you the only Chief Inspector on the course?" Sean wasn't moving, he just looked at the man who was sitting behind his desk.

"No, Bruce is from Hampshire," Sean noticed a movement of people out in the main office, most of the team had started to huddle around PC screens at one side of the office. A hand waved the others over towards them as more people started to become interested in what was going on. Sean felt his head turn back towards Chief Anderson who had just spoken to him.

"What?" Sean asked.

"I said, I will have a new Sergeant for you tomorrow."

"Why?" Sean was surprised by this.

"Why?" The Chief repeated back at him, "because the one you got does not know half of what is going on with this investigation!" The Chief drank from the mug, "not good enough."

"Not good enough?" Sean was starting to get annoyed, "that man is one of the best detectives in the service and if you are replacing him you had better replace me and Simon at the same time."

"What?" the Chief answered.

"You heard me, you are not breaking up my team, if you want this team to go forward in this investigation you will leave me alone to lead it the way that I want to." Sean gave him a look to ensure that the Chief would have no doubt that he meant every word that he was saying and the fallout from having a whole team replaced would not stop in this room. "Mike Dear almost single-handedly cracked the Henderson case and he has the best interview technique I've ever seen," Sean paused then went for him again. "You do know about the Henderson case, don't you? You were keeping up with what was actually happening back here while you were away, weren't you?"

"Of course, I was ..."

"So, then you're also aware that he got an excellent result and he got a compliment from the judge for the way he presented that investigation and you know how rare compliments like that are!" Sean was yet again making his point well.

"Really? Then how come he did not know what half of the staff in this investigation are doing?" It was a challenge and it was a challenge Sean could easily meet.

"What we are doing today answers that, once a month we get a representative of every part of this investigation together and they give a briefing to the rest of the team as to the progress of what is happening..." The Chief didn't like this, "so," Sean continued, "if we are missing anything then it will be picked up with these monthly briefings ... every 'i' dotted and every 't' crossed ...." Sean paused as he drank more from his mug of coffee.

"Well your super cop wasn't able to tell me anything about how this investigation is progressing!"

"There is a very good reason for that," answered Sean who paused as he drank more from the mug, the Chief looked up.

"And why is that?" he asked.

"Well I can give you the short version."

"And what is the short version?" he asked.

"We do not have a single thing that I am prepared to take into a court room." Sean's comment had the necessary effect as it brought it home to Chief Anderson how serious the situation was.

"What about the response to the Crime Watch programme?" Sean shrugged at the Chief's question.

"We got a good response but like I said, nothing I will take into a courtroom."

"You really don't have anything?" he asked.

"We have quite a few leads which you will hear about in a moment," Sean pointed out the office window towards the main office where the level of conversation had increased. Both heads turned as Mike came up and knocked on the door, Sean waved him in. Mike opened the door but didn't come in.

"Boss, you had better take a look at this." Mike turned towards the first of the desks, Sean followed him out with the reluctant Chief Inspector following. The group parted to let the three men pass. The detective sitting at the desk looked up at Mike.

"Show them," said Mike; the detective moved the mouse and the screen came to life.

"What is this?" asked the Chief Inspector.

"It's the BBC news website, our good doctor has published his papers ..."

"WEREWOLF ON THE LOOSE IN NORTHERN IRELAND," Sean read the headline out loud.

"It's already on the 24-hour news channels and they're saying we're investigating it," Constable Cargill was at a different desk, murmurs flowed through the team of detectives.

"Right, let's get this show on the road ..." Sean said. This was not the time or the place to go into anything like this. Everyone stopped talking as Sean got their attention, "Mike, are we ready to start?"

"Yes boss," Mike answered.

"Right then, once I have a fresh coffee we can begin the briefings." Sean turned and looked at the Chief Inspector, "Chief, would you like a fresh one?" He held up his mug. The question wasn't about coffee, Sean wanted to speak to him alone in the office and Chief Inspector Anderson knew that.

"Thank you, Inspector Parrish, I would."

Chapter 58

Cara-Marie was sitting at her desk working away at one of her stories. Her fingers were flying over the keyboard of the desktop computer and she held the stern look on her face. Kevin had her in the office first thing and had given her a real dressing down. Although the door was closed her co-workers must have heard it and the way she had slammed the door as she had stormed out told everyone what she thought. That had been over two hours ago, she hadn't spoken a word since. Her stories about the van on fire and the assault outside the Harbour bar in Portrush would be printed; her story about a werewolf in Coleraine would not. His words echoed in her head; the memories made every fibre of her body tense with anger.

The phone on Mark's desk started to ring. It had one ring at a time, so it was an internal call, probably from one of the reception staff, he reached forward and lifted the receiver to his ear.

"Coleraine Herald,"

"Phone call for Cara," it was one of the girls from the front desk.

"Coleraine Herald," he repeated, whoever was calling was outside, in the background he could hear passing cars and the unmistakable sound of wind that mobile phones seemed to amplify.

"Hello, could I speak to Cara-Marie McKenna please?" The quiet young female voice had a local accent and almost seemed nervous.

"May I ask who is calling please?" Mark glanced over at the side of Cara's lowered head. She was totally engrossed in what she was doing.

"Can I talk to Cara-Marie please?" The voice had raised an octave and this time was more assertive, whoever she was, she didn't want to talk to him.

"Yeah, hang on," Mark reached forward and pressed the secrecy button on the phone which lit the small red light; he passed the phone around his head and held it towards her.

"Phone call for you," she looked up and glared at him.

"Who is it?" she demanded.

"No idea, she didn't want to talk to me," she grabbed at the receiver as Mark touched the secrecy button again, he lifted the base of the phone from his desk and set it over on Cara-Marie's as she started speaking.

"Hello, reporters."

Mark was looking at his own desk but was glancing out the side of his vision as her expression mellowed, "Oh, hello …" she started, she obviously knew the caller. Mark moved the mouse and his PC burst into life; he wasn't doing much but he was listening to every word Cara was saying.

"Mmm, yes of course," the look on her face lifted slightly, "I could meet you this morning if you like?" she was smiling now, "Ok, that's no problem," the grin was getting bigger. "Ten minutes then, Ok, see you then," she dropped the receiver back onto its base. Mark looked over at her, but she didn't look back. Her right hand shot out and grabbed at the mouse and saved what she was doing.

"Going somewhere?" he asked.

"Yes," she replied as she was standing up and pushing her chair back at the same time.

"Oh, where are you off to?" she wasn't looking at him at all.

"Out,"

"Who are you meeting up with?" she was looking at her screen as it shut down as she went for her jacket on the back of the chair.

"Possible story source," she had her back to him as she pulled on her jacket, "back later," she said without looking back, the rear door flew open and as she went to walk out as he called after her.

"Cara!" She stopped and looked back at him, he had turned in his chair, so he was facing her; he hadn't shouted but it had been loud enough for her to hear.

"Mmmph?" she said through a closed mouth.

"I'm still with you on this …. OK?"

"I know," her eyes looked down then jumped up to meet him eye to eye, "I'll text you later then," and with that she was gone. He swivelled in his chair as he focused back on his screen again, behind him he heard Kevin's door open.

"Where is she going?" he asked, Mark turned his chair to face him.

"Out,"

"What?"

"Out."

"What kind of an answer is that?" Kevin demanded, Mark shrugged.

"It is what she said to me before she disappeared out the door," Kevin paused and thought for a second.

"Who was the phone call from?"

"No idea, she wouldn't tell me her name, but you could try reception. They put the phone call through"

"Mark, I want to go over the photos you emailed me, pop in, will you?" he knew that there was nothing wrong with the pictures from the scene at Ballybogy and the pictures of the burnt-out van. Kevin didn't want to discuss photos, he wanted to talk about Cara. Mark didn't answer, he just followed him into his office. Kevin walked around behind his desk and sat down, Mark stayed the opposite side as Kevin turned the monitor screen round so he could see. Mark took the seat opposite the desk as Kevin started complimenting him on the pictures, Mark was now on the defensive, he had never done this before, and he didn't like it. "So yes, we can use these, in fact I was going to ask you which one of the Ballybogy ones you think would make a good front page?" Kevin was being overly nice, not like him, and Mark was already waiting for the obvious question that was coming his way about Cara-Marie.

"Any of them, all those ones I have only sent to you, most of the others I have already sold on," Kevin glanced up as Mark knew he would.

"Anyway," Kevin looked back at the screen, "about Cara," here it came, before he could say another word the phone on the desk started to ring. The name of the editor of the whole newspaper group filled the small screen on the phone. Mark read it upside down as Kevin smiled and touched the loudspeaker button.

"Morning how ar…" Kevin was cut off before he could say another word.

"*WHAT THE BLOODY HELL DO YOU THINK YOU ARE DOING UP THERE?*" Mark rose and started to walk out of the office as the screaming editor continued, "*WE HAVE ONE OF THE BIGGEST STORIES THIS NEWS GROUP HAS EVER COVERED, AND YOU SUPPRESS IT? EXPLAIN*" Kevin was dumbstruck as Mark walked out through the door and headed back towards his desk, he however didn't close the door behind him as Kevin lifted the receiver to his ear and cancelled the loudspeaker.

"Look, I have no idea what you are on ab……" he had been cut off again. "What?" Mark didn't have to turn around to know the expression on his face. "Werewolves? Cara didn't …." he was cut off again. Mark smiled. Cara-Marie did save all her stories to the group mailbox and now that the story was out, another newspaper group had got the exclusive, but it was Cara who had tried to get it published weeks ago.

"Well done girl," Mark whispered to himself as Kevin continued to be cut off every time he tried speaking. She had been proved right. Mark waited until the call had finished before he started to text her, grinning as he did so.

∞∞∞

Cara-Marie walked on through the centre of town unaware of the happenings that were ongoing back in the office. Her eyes looked down then glanced up to avoid a man in blue overalls delivering a large cardboard box to one of the shops. His small white van was covered in dirt with the company logo just about visible on its side.

"Mornin' Cara," the voice was heading in the opposite direction, she smiled and lifted her hand, she didn't want to talk, she needed to be somewhere, and she really didn't have time to chat. She slowed on Church Street as she walked past the church, the door of the coffee shop at the far side of the street opened and an excited young couple walked out. She paused as they let the door close behind them. They wrapped an arm around each other as they turned and walked away. Joy burst from them and for a moment she wondered what they were so happy about. She felt a moment of jealously as she had not known pure joy like that in too long a time. The happy couple walked away from her engrossed in their own world in which for a while at least, they didn't have a single care in the world, she had come to a complete stop in the middle of the street. She wasn't hearing the surrounding sounds anymore as the sound of her own breathing drowned everything else out. For a moment, she felt herself start to float as if everything was no longer real, and the real world seemed to slowly drift away as if in a dream. A dream that she didn't want to wake up from, then just as suddenly, she was back. Her left hand tightened her grip on her shoulder bag, and she started to walk towards the entrance in the cast iron railings that surrounded the old church. She looked around the grounds as she slowly stepped forward through the gates and onto holy ground. For a moment, she stared at the heavy wooden doors that filled the entrance to the main building. People were moving up and down the street, but nothing seemed to be moving in the peaceful stillness of the churchyard.

"Cara-Marie?" The young female voice asked, she spun round to meet the woman who was walking towards her, she smiled, and they shook hands. She didn't know her well but recognised her as one of the staff from the coffee shop. She remembered the last time that she had seen her just after she had thrown the glass at the wall in the upstairs room, the woman in front of her now was not sobbing, wasn't as emotional as she had been before.

"It's good to see you again Rachel,"

"And you, so much has happened since they finally let us bury him." Rachel Boyd stepped past her and headed toward the entrance of the church. She had not seen her since her brother's funeral and even then, it was only at a distance. Cara-Marie stepped forward and slowly paced beside her down the pathway, she glanced around, it was open, but no one was close enough to hear what they were talking about, she suddenly realised why Rachel Boyd had chosen this place for their meeting.

"How are things getting on?" she asked, the young face turned and forced a smile.

"Well, they are getting better as the police seem to be leaving us alone now." Cara-Marie answered with a nod but didn't speak as she wanted Rachel to talk freely. "Mum has taken it the worst ... well you would, wouldn't you ..." Cara nodded again. Rachel went on to describe what had been happening with different family members since her brother's murder and spoke as if she knew them all personally. They stopped once they had reached the building and Rachel slowly turned to walk back up the pathway.

"But that's not why I asked to speak to you today," An excitement made Cara-Marie's body tense up as she listened to the young woman, there was something coming, and it was something good.

"Why is that?" she quietly asked. Rachel stopped and looked across the street at the people who were walking back and forth. Cara-Marie stopped as well but she was looking at the peaceful face that was standing beside her, a few seconds ticked by before Rachel spoke again.

"I think, I saw what killed him," it made Cara-Marie's eyebrows jump.

"And what do you think you saw?"

"I had been at a friend's house and I was coming back down the main road; the Jet Centre was off to my right when I first heard them," she could picture where she was but then her mind reacted to what had just been said.

"Them?"

"Yes, the two of them."

"Who?"

"Well, I heard the howling first then they ran through the trees in front of me." This was precisely what she wanted to hear, "they were about 40 or 50 metres in front of me and they ran straight across the road and away…" Cara listened, she felt her right hand tighten the strap of the shoulder bag.

Rachel was in full flow. "I didn't think much of it until I heard the news but then I realised what I had seen," Rachel was almost in a euphoric bliss as she described what she now knew to be the moments following her brother's death.

"What did you see Rachel? What ran across the road?" Cara-Marie asked.

"The wolves," Rachel almost seemed pleased with herself, the face flashed back into Cara-Marie's mind, the face that she herself had seen that night in the car park across the river.

"What did they look like?" she quietly asked, Rachel took a step away from her as she started to describe her memories.

"Well the first one was bigger than the second one, they were magnificent animals, really big … I've never seen a dog that big before."

"How big?" Cara-Marie asked, Rachel held her hand almost at her own shoulder height.

"About up to here," Rachel started to describe that different shades of the fur on their coats and used her hands to show how they ran.

"Did they have tails?" injected Cara-Marie. Rachel stopped for a moment, Cara-Marie looked straight into her face and could see the concentration.

"That did bother me," Rachel replied.

"What did?"

"That they didn't have any tails, what kind of a dog doesn't have a tail?" Cara-Marie felt a chill and it made her shiver. She wasn't cold, but her body reacted as if it was, Rachel continued to describe watching the two animals head off towards the Heights housing estate.

"Did you get a picture?" Cara asked.

"No," Rachel shook her head, "I had my phone on me, but I didn't think. It wasn't until the police came and told us he was dead that it really hit home," Cara-Marie nodded in understanding, it isn't something most people would consider straight away. Rachel talked on for a few minutes as Cara-Marie's phone started beeping with a text message. Rachel stopped and looked at her as she reached into her shoulder bag for her phone.

"You're never alone with a mobile," Cara-Marie reached for her phone.

"No, you're not," Rachel replied.

"And it's from the office," Cara's thumb paused over the phone as she considered reading the text from Mark now or later. Her thumb made the decision for her and opened the message. Rachel stepped forward and moved past her on her way towards the gates and Cara-Marie read the long text message. A triumphant smile spread across her face as she read it again, Rachel had stopped by the gates, whatever it was it was certainly good news,

Cara-Marie looked up at her. "Rachel?" she asked.

"Yes?" she replied, she took a step forward.

"If I was to interview you would you be OK with me putting that in print?" Rachel's face beamed a broad, happy smile.

"Yes, of course I would."

"Then may I suggest," Cara-Marie walked forward as she spoke, "that you let the Coleraine Herald treat you to lunch and we can go over the details."

"I like the sound of that, and that new cafe has just opened down there," Rachel pointed back down the street Cara-Marie had walked up to meet her, "and I have been meaning to try it out and this seems like the perfect time." Cara-Marie had started tapping in a message back to the office as the two of them walked almost arm in arm down the street. The interview would make a good spread in the paper and she could have that done by lunchtime, then she could go over what the other media outlets were now saying about the events in Coleraine.

Chapter 59

Sean was sitting in his office running over the facts of the investigation. The briefing yesterday had taken longer than he had wanted but the whole team had presented everything, most of the leads had produced nothing but they could at least show they had followed them up. The team still had very little to go on and since Dr Burns had published his article they had spent most of the afternoon fending off journalists from all over Europe wanting werewolf stories. Everyone wanted to know if the Police Service of Northern Ireland were investigating werewolf attacks. Sean had all the team sticking to the same story that they were looking for at least two people who had committed the murders.

He had Mike re-publish the pictures of the girl with the black hair and he had given the task of doing a full background check on Chernov to Eddie. This seemed to satisfy Chief Anderson who had now disappeared back down to Police Headquarters and was thankfully out of their space. Although he could be a help with dealing with the higher echelons of the police service he could also be a hindrance with the detectives who were 'at the coal face'. Sean scrolled through the story from an American news channel, 'IRISH WEREWOLVES KILL FIVE,' and sighed.

The main office was empty, Mike had set up the projector in the middle of the room; the military were due to arrive in less than half an hour to give their briefing. Sean collapsed the website and opened the email chain he had sent from Coleraine to Darren.

"You will get to meet 'The Duke' and the Unholy Trinity'..." Sean read out loud. Darren was obviously referring to the military personnel coming with him. Sean eyed the clock on the wall as Mike and Simon walked into the main office. He looked at their faces and thankfully the bruising had faded which was helpful since he wanted them to do the press interviews; he lifted his left hand in recognition as they approached his office.

"So, when are you moving in?" asked Mike as he entered, Simon was right behind him.

"I'm not moving anywhere," Simon retorted, Mike landed on one of the seats and Simon dropped down on the chair beside him.

"You'll be living together by the end of the year."

"I will not ..."

"Seen it before ..." answered Mike as he rested back into the chair.

"And I am telling you we are not moving in together," protested Simon,

"Simon was out on another hot date last night," he explained, Sean nodded.

"It was not a 'hot date'," Simon's voice raised an octave.

"What was it then?" Mike had a nefarious smile on his face as he continued to poke fun towards Simon, "Don't bother trying to tell us that you two are 'just friends' and went out for a bite to eat," Sean looked over as Simon visibly blushed.

"Suddenly got warm in here, hasn't it?" said Sean as he joined in the baiting.

"Don't you start, too," complained Simon as he folded his arms and sat back into the depths of the chair. Mike opened his mouth to speak but was cut short by the door to the main office opening and a group of men walking in. Sean recognized the leader.

The first one was shorter than the rest and certainly looked older; he had once had dark hair, but it was receding and turning silver. He was wearing trainers, jeans and an outdoor jacket. Sean immediately rose; he darted around the desk and the two of them met just outside Sean's office door. They obviously knew each other well; the greetings were warm and friendly.

"What about ye Sean?"

"I'm grand, howz you getting on up there?" Sean replied, the other man nodded then looked Sean up and down.

"I'm good, well things are obviously good here, look at the weight you have piled on!"

Sean stepped back and turned towards Mike and Simon. "Well here is my team," The man stepped forward with his right hand outstretched, Mike took the firm grip in his own. "Detective

Sergeant Mike Dear and Detective Sergeant Simon McAllister, this is Detective Superintendent Darren Forester," both Mike and Simon reacted at his name.

"Another Glentoran man ... good ta see ya."

"Good morning Sir," said Mike. Darren took Simon's hand in a firm handshake.

"Good morning Sir, it's good to meet you," said Simon.

"Ach, forget the 'sir,' please call me Darren," Darren turned to introduce the four men who were with him. The first was better dressed and had an air of authority around him. His fair hair didn't seem to move and was longer than what would have been expected of someone from the military. Mike noticed his crystal-clear blues eyes that let him know he was dealing with a professional. Darren started the introductions.

"Sean, this is Major Alan Dukesby, two SAS," Sean reached out his hand, the handshake was a firm one, Darren continued.

"Alan, this is Detective Inspector Sean Parrish."

"Pleasure to meet you," said the Major. His accent was a deep-set English, not upper class, but certainly not that far away from it.

"Good morning Major and thank you for the help you are providing for us at such short notice," Sean mixed the greeting with a thank you.

"No problem, any help we can be," the Major nodded once as he spoke, "and please, call me Alan, you're not military," Sean extended his hand and introduced Mike and Simon in turn. The Major shook each hand and introduced himself by his first name then turned to the other men who were with him. Mike made a quick assessment that they were all mid to late thirties, physically fit and although seemed pleasant enough so far, he was sure that these were the type of people you would want on your side and not against you. Alan introduced each one in turn.

"This is Sergeant Major Steve Minister," Sean shook the hands of each one in turn as they were introduced. "Staff Sergeants Chris Abbey and David Priest," Sean smiled as he heard the names and he got the comments from Darren's email, *"You will get to meet the duke and the un-holy Trinity!."*

"Gentlemen, please," Sean held out his right hand pointing towards several chairs that were sitting either side of the gap in the centre of the room. The desks lined the side, all of them were clear and tidy, the group made its way towards them.

"So how have you been with all this?" Darren started as Sean began moving the chairs into a small semi-circle, the others quickly follow suit. Sean glanced over at one of the soldiers who was looking at the pictures of the Castleroe murders.

"Busy, certainly busier than I have been in a long time,"

Sean invited everyone to sit. The soldiers removed their various outdoor jackets to reveal a series of different fleece tops among them, except for the Major who was wearing a thick woollen jumper. As they each took a seat Sean walked out up to the front.

"Right gents, the reason you are here," various people moved in their seats until they were comfortable. Sean noticed that the military were listening to every word he was saying, "We are currently progressing with a major investigation involving several murders with numerous suspects, although we cannot discuss the exact details, as I am sure you can understand," Sean's comment was answered with a series of nods, "we would like your professional assistance with the details of some of our enquires."

"Any assistance we can be ..." the Major stated.

"And it gets them out for the day," Darren injected, Darren's comment was immediately answered by comments from one of the soldiers.

"At least we work for a living," it was obvious that they all had a good working environment.

"Right, Mike have you got the laptop ready?" Sean asked.

"Yes boss," Mike stood up and walked over to the far side of the room. He lifted up a small table and placed it in the centre of the semi-circle, the power cables from the laptop and the projector hung out from behind them and led over to the power sockets in the wall.

"You have your stuff on pen stick?" Sean asked.

"Yes, all ready to go," answered Steve Minister. The wall behind Sean lit up as Mike knelt and booted up the laptop and projector.

"Right, our first question is that during our enquires we have come across several people who claim to have been part of a military formation that was known as Spetsnaz ..." the solders all looked towards each other, one of them whispered loud enough for the room to hear.

"Several?"

"And we would like to know first of all, what we may be dealing with," the Major and the Sergeant Major exchanged glances, "and I would appreciate that these requests not leave the room ..." Sean looked at the two men again then decided to reword his request, "or at least not leave your own circles."

"We can certainly do that," stated the major, the Sergeant Major looked over to one of the other men.

"Chris," Chris Abbey nodded and stood up to hand the pen stick to Mike. He inserted it into the laptop and within seconds the window for the usb port opened and Mike moved a mouse onto the icon.

"Which document is it?" Mike answered his own question when he looked at the screen, there only was one icon on the pen stick.

"That one will do fine," the English voice stated through a grin, Mike nodded and double clicked the icon and the first slide filled the screen, he stood up and handed the mouse over.

"It is infra-red so you can just right click through your slides from anywhere in the room," Chris nodded and took the mouse. The first slide just had the name 'Chris Abbey' on it. There was no rank or any other details, Chris started the presentation.

"Good morning gents, for those of you who do not know me, I am Chris Abbey," Sean and Mike took up their seats and Sean looked around, "this short presentation will be on 'Spetsnaz' and I will cover briefly who they are and what they do ..." Chris paused slightly, "if you have any questions could you keep them to the end of the presentation please," Sean glanced over towards the other soldiers, they would be accessing him as much as the police officers were listening to the presentation itself. The next slide appeared, and it showed a military patch that had a fist clutching an AK type rifle. The words around it was in a language that Sean couldn't read.

"So, Spetsnaz or 'Volska Spitsialnovo Naznatcenijel' to give them their full title ..." The words appeared on the slide; Sean was glad Chris had said it out loud. "Which translates to 'special purpose troops,' have been at the top of the tier for the Soviet Union and now the Russian Republic since at least 1974." Sean listened as Chris went through their involvement in Afghanistan in 1979 and Chechnya. "They are considered some of the best trained troops of the whole armed forces of the Russian Federation. They have created a reputation as one of the best in the world because of their very harsh methods of training." Chris looked around the room, "they train to the highest standards and their training is as realistic as possible ... it is not uncommon for members of Spetsnaz to be killed on training exercises," Chris let the comment sink in before he continued the presentation. Chris spoke for a few more minutes before he started taking questions. It was Mike who spoke first.

"Chris, these guys ... how brutal can they be?" Chris paused for a second and glanced over at the pictures on the far wall.

"They can be very brutal .... They have developed their own martial art called 'Sambo'."

"Sambo?" asked Sean.

"Yes, Sambo was developed by them for use when deployed on operations, it's the deadliest of all the martial arts, and they train to kill and to kill outright either with or without weapons ..." Sean and Mike exchanged a glance that did not go unnoticed.

"What size are they?" Sean asked.

"A deployed Spetsnaz group would normally be of approximately company strength, say anything from 80 to 120 soldiers," Mike's eyebrows rose.

"What about total strength, how many are there?" Sean asked. Chris paused before he answered.

"Exact numbers aren't known but it was estimated that in the mid 1980's there was approximately eight Brigades of them, say 30,000 men however that number has certainly fallen in recent times. It is estimated there are no more than 15,000 personnel currently," everyone heard Sean breathing in.

"Do they all know each other ... or is it confidential?" Everyone could tell why Sean had asked the question, Chris answered it as best as he could.

"Spetsnaz are split into several different organisations, but most will only serve in one unit ... if two people served in the same unit then it is possible that they could know each other, if not there is a chance that they do not," Sean nodded in thanks.

"So, who is Alpha Squad?" Simon asked, Chris paused,

"Alpha Group to give them their proper title is a counter terrorist unit that specialises in hostage rescue. They are highly specialised and number approximately 600 personnel ... their most famous rescue was in Moscow where Chechen rebels took over a theatre during an opera performance and held over 200 people hostage." Sean, Mike, and Simon all looked at each other, Chris continued. "Alpha Group went in, all the rebels were killed, but so were a large amount of the hostages ..."

"What else can they do?" Sean asked.

"Well, all operatives have special airborne training as well as mountain, special and foreign weapon training, counter sabotage, diver training etc."

"So just one of these people would not have a problem with a group of drunken teenagers," it was Mike who asked the question. Chris knew this question was relating directly to the police investigation.

"They would go through them all like butter,"

"And two police officers armed with just pistols at point blank range?" Sean moved in his seat as Mike asked the question, Mike's eyes glanced over at him, there would not be any more questions from him. Chris paused.

"I can only say that if they got away alive, they were doing well."

"Thank you, Chris," said Sean as he moved in his seat and turned towards Darren. "Is it two presentations or just one?" he asked, Darren looked over at Steve.

"Two, we didn't want Chris doing all the work," Steve answered.

"That makes a change," said Chris.

"I do more than you anyway," quipped Steve. Chris stepped forward as Mike leaned in and removed the pen stick and handed it over. The banter between the soldiers continued until the Major stopped it. Mike was now loading in the pen stick that had just been handed to him and like the first one it only had one item on it. Sean looked around. Simon had started to chat to the Sergeant Major and Mike was making notes.

The next presentation started much the same as the first as David Priest introduced himself and what he was going to be talking about. The first slide appeared with the words 'GROUPEMENT des COMMANDOS PARACHUTISTES GCP' the subtitle translated it to COMMANDO PARACHUTE GROUP. He started with the history dating back to 1965. Sean was confused so he asked the question that was foremost in his mind.

"Excuse me," he started, David stopped, and everyone looked at him. "I have to stop you there, this isn't what we wanted," Darren sat upright as the Major looked over at him. Sean continued, "We wanted to know about an organisation called 'Le CRAP'?"

"Yes, this is the same group, they had a name change a few years ago, GCP is what they are at the present," Sean's eyebrows rose.

"Ok, please continue," Sean sat back in his chair as the rest of the room relaxed.

"The GCP comes under the command of special operations for the French Army." The next slide appeared with the words '*Commandos de recherché et d'action en profondeur, LE CRAP.* "The entire organisation is administered by the 11th Parachute Brigade. Most work independently of the main French forces behind enemy lines as a harassment force etc," David continued with the history. Sean noticed that David had not attempted to pronounce what CRAP was in French. After a few more minutes, David finished his presentation and offered questions. Sean raised his hand.

"What does Le Crap translate to in English?"

"Deep Action and Reconnaissance Commando," he answered.

"Where do they recruit from?" asked Mike.

"The French Army,"

"Do they take people from the Foreign Legion?"

"Yes, but they would have to be of the highest standards ... you would probably not find them in a normal legion regiment, but they would probably take from the legions parachute force, 2 Rep."

"Second Foreign Parachute Regiment," Simon read from notes on his lap.

"The very ones," David replied.

"So, they are very good as a group, what are they like individually?" Sean kept the questions flowing, David paused.

"I'm not sure what you mean?"

"Are they, per man as highly trained as yourselves or the Russians for example?" David looked over to the other soldiers, it was clear he wasn't sure how to answer that one. The Sergeant Major spoke up.

"Well, each team would have a specific job and they would train towards that,"

"How good are their snipers?" Mike and Simon looked over at Sean as he asked the question, where was he going with that? The Sergeant Major spoke again.

"Just to be a sniper means you are already a specialist in staking, map reading, etc. To be a GCP sniper the soldier would have undergone a very tough selection course and completed advanced training courses in special operations."

"So, an individual with that background would be very good?"

"Very," the Sergeant Major confirmed.

"Could you give us an example to go on?" Sean asked, the Sergeant Major thought for a moment then answered.

"I think the most obvious one was their operations in the Ivory Coast."

"What happened?" Mike asked.

"The Ivory Coast was a former French colony and after a civil conflict they requested French Peacekeeping troops and after a couple of incidents the French suffered several casualties following a rocket attack by Ivory Coast aircraft ... the French president ordered them destroyed. GCP went in and within a matter of hours grounded the entire air force and completely uprooted the rebels."

"When was that?" Simon asked.

"Just a few years ago, they stormed the rebel positions and dealt them a blow that they never recovered from."

"So, they are good," Mike stated.

"Very good," the Sergeant Major answered.

"Do they have their own martial art as well?" Mike asked, the soldiers all turned and looked at him.

"No," the Sergeant Major answered, "but they are masters at unarmed combat."

"So, they can be dangerous," Mike added.

"All professional special forces are dangerous to an enemy," Mike looked over at the man who was staring at him.

"Not the kind of person you would want to upset then?" Mike asked.

"Not really," The expression on the Sergeant Major's face changed as if he was about to say something but changed his mind. Sean stood up and walked in front of the group.

"Well gentlemen I would like to thank you for assisting us with our investigation ..." Darren stood up and walked over beside him.

"Well we were in Belfast anyway," he stated.

"Do you have to shoot off somewhere?" Sean asked. Darren looked over at the Major who shook his head.

"Nope," Darren answered.

"Well I would like to invite you all to stay awhile and enjoy our coffee," the mood in the room relaxed as everyone stood up, and conversations started among them. Slowly chairs were placed back beside the desks and Mike closed up the laptop. Sean invited Darren down to his office, the Major followed. Mike watched them walk away and as he turned around the Sergeant Major approached.

"So, you guys have your hands full then?" Steve asked.

"Yeah, pretty much," Mike replied.

"I do hope it isn't 'Spets' doing this," Steve pointed towards the pictures on the wall.

"So, do I, after what you just said," answered Mike, Steve looked at him and frowned.

"Well if given the choice I would prefer one of them to what the newspapers are saying." the soldier looked away, "at least Spets are real," Mike nodded and smiled.

"Thanks again for this; asking questions saves a lot of guess work," Mike stated, the soldier turned and looked over his shoulder.

"That it does ... any help we can be please ask," he reassured.

"I don't think the Chief Constable would be too pleased about us requesting to deploy military personnel ... hopefully those days are gone," Steve nodded.

"Yeah, I don't think any of us want that again," Mike suddenly realised where he had seen him before.

"By the way ... when was the last time you were in Coleraine police station?"

Chapter 60

Kyle was waiting for Tony in his living room. The TV was on, but he wasn't watching it. He was toying with the cuff links that adorned his pressed white shirt. The black bow tie was slightly loose; he never had quite got the hang of how to tie one correctly. His black trousers were nicely pressed and had a gentle shine, and the dinner jacket was hanging off a coat hanger on the rear of the door of the living room. He wasn't anxious but there was a slight trepidation as to what exactly was going to happen tonight. If someone had told him a year ago that he was going to dinner with a room full of werewolves ... well it would have got the obvious response, yet, here he was, waiting for his friend who he now knew was a member of the furry and fang club, that, itself, was something else.

The evening was starting to darken; the headlights of the car cut through the approaching nightfall as they turned up the lane that led up to his house, he glanced at the watch on his wrist. Tony was exactly on time, it was almost as if he had been waiting down the road for the right time to arrive. He turned and walked out of the living room and headed towards his front door as he heard the car approach. Tony seemed to be out of the car even before it had stopped. He was excited, very excited in fact, he was already wearing his dinner jacket and he was beaming from ear to ear. Kyle opened the front door just as Tony bounded up to it.

"Ready to go?" he asked. Kyle took a step back and allowed Tony to fly past him and into his house.

"Yeah, just got to grab my jacket," he answered. Tony carried on past him and headed towards the kitchen. Kyle closed the front door and glanced down at the floor, Tony was wearing black leather shoes and a short trail of dirt from outside followed him into the kitchen.

"Brilliant," he said out loud, "Help yourself to a brew, the kettle isn't long off the boil," he tapped the door and it started to swing closed, as he reached for his dinner jacket Tony shouted back from the kitchen.

"No time, we need to get going." Kyle knew that Tony was in his biscuit jar and would already be munching. As Kyle slipped on his jacket Tony reappeared in the doorway, munching as he did so, Tony looked him up and down as Kyle crunched up his face.

"What?" Kyle asked, Tony paused chewing and spoke through a mouthful of biscuits.

"Mmph?"

"It's ok, you can hoover it up later," Kyle answered as he buttoned up his jacket.

"Hoover what?" Tony answered as he cleared his mouth, Kyle shook his head and lifted the small holdall that was sitting on the sofa.

"And where am I sleeping tonight? You said you had sorted a room for me?" Kyle pushed his way past Tony and headed for the door, Tony followed him.

"Yeah, remember the room you woke up in the last time you were there?" Kyle looked at him as he reached the front door, "in there,"

"Brilliant, any chance of you telling me what is going to happen tonight?" Kyle asked as the front door opened, Tony stepped past him and headed out into the night.

"Sure, dinner and entertainment," Tony paused, "It's going to be really good."

"Just as long as I am neither the dinner nor the entertainment," Tony looked away and walked around the car.

"You're not, no."

"Which bit?"

"What?" Tony asked as he opened the door.

"Am I not the dinner or the entertainment?" Kyle asked as he opened the passenger door. Tony climbed in and closed the door behind him while Kyle followed.

"Neither," he reassured, "we do not eat our own."

"Wow," said Kyle as Tony started the engine, "that makes me feel a whole lot better.".

"Whatever." He gunned the engine and the car jumped forward and headed off back down the lane. The twenty minutes that it took to drive to the farm seemed to pass very quickly. Tony had been telling Kyle how the evening would go.

"It all seems so formal." Kyle noted.

"It is," Tony answered as they turned into the lane that led up to the brightly lit farm.

"It is what?" Kyle replied.

"Formal, this is a formal dinner, which is the reason that you are in a dinner jacket after all." Tony still had the excited smile on his face, he was obviously looking forward to this evening's planned events. The courtyard was full of people standing around, there was an excitement that abounded. It had been quite a while since Kyle had felt so out of place but suddenly the enormity of his situation hit him. He was about to have dinner with a room full of mythical creatures, mythical creatures that he could hardly believe were real but real they were and here he was looking at a yard full of them. Tony was chatting away excitedly as he reversed, parked the car.

"What?" Tony asked as he took hold of Kyle's right arm.

"You are like a kid in a sweet shop."

"Yeah, pretty much," and without further warning he released his seatbelt and jumped out of the car. Tony was greeted enthusiastically by two men standing nearby. The older one was dressed in a dinner jacket, but the other was still wearing the clothes of a farm hand. Here was one person who wasn't going to the ball, he adjusted his jacket as he closed the door and for a moment he looked around at the near jubilant celebrations that were occurring around the farmyard. Most of the groups of people were dressed for a formal night out, the men in dinner jackets and black ties and the ladies in evening gowns, dotted among them were those who were obviously still working the farm. The excitement was evident in everyone's face. There were a lot of people who were looking forward to this. Tony turned to beckon Kyle over from the far side of the car. Kyle walked around as Tony stepped to one side, the man in the dinner jacket looked Kyle up and down and smiled.

"Kyle, this is Dermott; Dermott ..." Tony extended his arm towards Kyle as Dermott stepped towards him with his right hand outstretched. Dermott clenched Kyle's offered right hand in a grip with both hands. A small but firm handshake followed as Dermott looked straight into Kyle's eyes.

"So, the prodigal son returns?" Dermott's accent was a heavier county accent.

"What do you mean?" Kyle asked, Tony looked over at Dermott, these two were obviously comfortable with each other and knew each other well. Dermott slightly smirked.

"You probably won't remember, you were very young the last time I took you for a ride on one of the tractors," Kyle kept his face expressionless as he answered.

"I'm sorry but I have no memory of you," Dermott nodded as a cheer went up from behind them, everyone turned towards the opening door of the barn. Tony ushered Kyle with the sudden movement of people in the farmyard, everyone turned towards the doors as the cheering was mixed with applause.

"What's going on?" Kyle asked as Tony let out a loud cheer. Tony was clapping enthusiastically as five very happy people in track suits walked out of the barn and headed towards the farmhouse. The crowd swarmed around them like sports fans that are finally getting near to their team. Kyle could only see their heads as they formed a line, one after another and made their way through the crowd towards the door of the farmhouse. The man at the front looked like he was in his mid-forties and the one behind him seemed to be in his early twenties. A woman was third in the line and she was tying her dark auburn hair into a ponytail, she was slightly shorter than the others but was equally excited. The last two had the faces of teenagers, very excited teenagers at that.

"That is the hunting party," Tony answered, Kyle looked over at him.

"Oh yeah, and what are they hunting dressed like that?" Kyle asked.

"You will see," The crowd started to move forward towards the farmhouse as another cheer went up. The front door opened, and Carl walked out and greeted the first of the five. Slowly each one walked up to him, they exchanged firm handshakes, and quiet comments that Kyle could not hear from where he was. The applause increased momentarily as Carl shook hands with the last member of the hunting party.

"What's so special about him?" Kyle asked as the five turned about to face the crowd.

"It is his first hunt," the crowd moved forward again as Carl held up his right hand and in a moment the crowd was silent, all attention was focused on him.

"*BRING FORTH THE BEAST,*" Carl shouted. The large metal doors of the barn shuddered as they were forced open. Kyle didn't notice them being closed after the five people walked out. The crowd backed away and a space was formed in the front of the barn. The lights from inside the barn illuminated the whole yard as a stag was walked outside by a young woman. She was wearing a dark green sweatshirt, blue jeans and green rubber wellington boots.

Kyle looked at her. Her jet-black hair was nearly touching her shoulders and the smile on her pretty face matched the fire that burned in her dark brown eyes. He guessed that she could probably be early twenties and kept herself fit, the jeans fitted her perfectly. Kyle glanced over at Tony, he was more interested in the deer and was clapping again, Kyle looked over as the deer was led towards the house. The woman stopped half way across the yard, keeping control of the animal with the harness around its head as the five members of the hunt slowly walked forward and started to walk in a circle around. One would extend an arm and gentle touch the coat of the stag, another would lean towards him and take in a deep breath through their nose.

"What is happening now?" Kyle asked, Tony leaned over towards Kyle.

"They are gathering his scent," the applause started again, it was quieter than before and seemed to ripple through the crowd.

"Don't they have to cut it or something?" Kyle asked.

"No, they don't." Tony looked over the heads of the people around him. Excited chatter was flying between everyone as the deer was being led away, "and he isn't an '*it*', the beast is a '*he*'"

"He?" Kyle repeated.

"Yes, he, as in a male."

"Guessed that with the antlers," answered Kyle, the crowd started to move forward.

"A doe can grow antlers as well, mostly during the winter time," explained Tony.

"So how did he get chosen for this then?" The crowd of people were walking around the corner of the farmyard and away from the farmhouse, the rest of the buildings of the busy farm were situated around. Off to the right-hand side were two 4x4's. Both had several farmhands sitting on the top of them. Kyle looked at the rifles that were resting over their laps. They were bolt action rifles that could be used for hunting.

"He's at the end of his mating life, it is part of a cull that happens on every deer farm in the world, the only difference is how we cull them," the crowd gathered pace.

"And how exactly do you do that?" Kyle asked.

"We let them loose in the woods and give them a fighting chance, that is more than stalkers do."

"Has a deer ever survived?" Kyle asked as a hand landed on Tony's right shoulder. The hand belonged to a man who was about the same age as Tony and was dressed in a similar dinner jacket, and he was very pleased to see him. Excited pleasantries were quickly exchanged then Kyle was introduced. Kyle tried to place his accent, it was mostly local but there was a twinge of something else.

"Kyle Foster."

"Sean Lefebvre." Kyle's hand was firmly gripped for a few seconds then released. Sean looked him straight in the eye, so Kyle looked back. A moment of dominance reigned before Tony stepped into their line of sight.

"Lefebvre?" Kyle enquired, Sean looked around Tony, "that isn't a local name. Where are you from?" The group walked on past more buildings, somewhere made of bricks and others from corrugated iron. The smell of the abattoir hit Kyle's senses and he recoiled slightly before he composed himself and walked on beside Tony.

"Canada," Sean's one-word reply made Kyle's head spin round.

"Really? I lived in Ottawa for a while, where are you from?" Kyle asked. Sean's face relaxed slightly before he answered.

"Edmonton, let me guess you are a Blue Jays fan?"

"No, I'm more of a hockey man." Kyle's answer got a small grin from Sean.

"I would say 'Maple Leaf's' but the 'Edmonton Oilers' top the league." Sean walked confidently on, Tony glanced between the two of them. Kyle started nodding his head before he spoke.

"Well if I remember right 'Calgary Flames' were at the top of the league more than the Oilers were," Sean's head spun round and glared at Kyle.

"But anyway, since I have no idea what you two are on about can we talk more about what is happening tonight instead!" injected Tony. Sean paused then glanced at Kyle before patting Tony on the shoulder again.

"No problem, see you later," with that Sean disappeared back into the crowd. The crowd was slowing down and was gathering around the side of a 4-foot-high concrete wall. Kyle stopped beside Tony.

"Who is he?" Kyle asked.

"Later," Kyle nodded. "I take it you were touching a nerve with the hockey thing?".

"Oh yes, the British equivalent would be him supporting Manchester United and me saying I was a Manchester City fan." Tony smiled.

"Oh, by the way..." Tony started,

"What?" Kyle asked.

"To answer your earlier question, yes, one has fought them off," Kyle had to think for a moment before remembering his last question.

"And what happened there?" Kyle asked,

"He put three in hospital, so he was sent to private land in England to live out the rest of his life," Tony paused for a few moments as the excitement started to grow in the crowd again, "last I heard he is still alive, he earned the name Emperor."

"Never heard of him," stated Kyle as he looked over the landscape. The farm was at the top of a rise that gave them a panoramic view of the surrounding fields, over to the right was a wooded area that covered the far hillside. The woman with the stag walked out from one side, the applause started again, she was smiling and obviously enjoying the moment. She shared a shouted comment from a young male voice in the crown. She answered with a crunched-up look and a comment that Kyle could not hear. Carl came through the crowd with two men who looked out of place. They had an authority about them that commanded respect and for the moment Kyle wondered who they were. Carl ran his hand down the back of the very calm animal. Kyle wondered if it knew that it did not have long to live. The lights on the building behind them went out, and it was only then that Kyle could see how much the dark of the night was closing in and as if on cue some of the few clouds in the sky moved to one side and the land was illuminated by the moon.

Another cheer went up, Kyle glanced at Tony as he took a deep breathe in. His eyes were closed, and he seemed to be breathing in the moment. Kyle's eyes were pulled downward as the movement of Tony clenching his fists caught his eye, others around him where doing something similar in their own moments of ecstasy, the chatter of the people suddenly started again. Kyle looked around at the excited group of people. He didn't know the faces around him, but he would occasionally see a knowing nod of recognition from people who probably knew his Dad. He was glad that had not been brought up with every person he had met. Carl started on a prepared speech that quietened down the crowd. Kyle could make out he was talking but he could not make out the words.

"RELEASE THE BEAST!" he commanded as he finished, then he took a step back as the woman who had been holding the harness around the head of the deer undid the straps. The deer bolted off towards the middle of the empty field. The crowd clapped and cheered as the evening's events got underway. Kyle watched as the deer slowed to a walk, the animal lowered his head and started to graze.

Even though the evening was drawing in, Kyle could still clearly see him, the majestic creature slowly walked towards the small wood that lay ahead. The clapping and cheering rose as Kyle's eyes picked up on movement over to the right-hand edge of the field. The five large dogs walked forward, but their shape was larger and different from a normal dog. The larger one was in front, leading the others, its head looked over towards the crowd. Kyle was surprised to see the wolf lift its head as if to acknowledge the crowd. Tony was ecstatic, and Kyle suddenly knew that the five people they had seen earlier were now the five wolves starting to spread out in front of them, then they all stood up.

The small pack started to split. The lead wolf was walking straight towards the deer as the others stayed in pairs, each pair headed off to either side of the larger wolf as they started to gain speed. All five wolves edged up to a trot as the deer spun around and stared directly at the five animals that were coming across the field towards him. The deer bolted away, the wolves broke into a full sprint.

"Go on lad," said Kyle, Tony was clapping his hands above his head in excitement as the deer ran into the woods. Kyle watched as two of the wolves disappeared around the right side and the other two jumped into the woods through the left. The larger wolf slowed and turned his headfirst to the left then to the right and watched as the wolves went from view, then he lowered his head and jumped between the trees.

"Right then," said Tony as he slapped his hand down on Kyle's shoulder. Kyle turned towards him as the crowd started to disperse, everyone had broken down into smaller groups and was heading back towards the main barn.

"So, what happens now?" Kyle asked as he turned and started to walk in the same direction alongside Tony.

"Well," Tony started, "We will have to wait while they hunt," Tony was still smiling like a kid with a new toy. Another man in a dinner jacket landed off to Tony's right side. They quickly exchanged excited comments about how great it was, by their body language Kyle could see that they knew each other well. As quickly as he had arrived he had disappeared back into the crowd.

"So, we just hang around then?" Kyle asked as he glanced over to his right to watch three armed men climb into one of the 4x4's, the engine gunned into life and the headlights came on.

"No," reassured Tony, "we are off to the bar for a drink," Kyle's head spun around.

"The bar?"

"Yes, 'the bar', it is somewhere we can have a drink." Tony acknowledged a couple who were walking past. The young woman did not look older than 20 but was moving quite quickly for being in four-inch heels and a figure-hugging cocktail dress. The young man who was on her left arm was dressed in a pressed dinner jacket and looked about the same age as she did, Kyle could not translate what they were saying but recognised it as Irish. Kyle was introduced as they walked along, both gave knowing smiles at him.

"I've heard a lot about you," she said,

"And I have heard nothing about you," Kyle replied but then glanced at Tony as he finished the sentence, "Yet," Tony glanced at him, the 4x4 took off as the crowd of people passed by it heading towards the woods.

"So, this is your first dance?" she asked, Kyle paused, and side stepped around a man who had just stopped to answer his phone.

"Yes, yes, it is,"

"The first of many," Tony injected.

"Excellent," said the young face as the crowd turned around the corner of the barn. It looked to Kyle like the whole courtyard was heading into the barn. Excited and happy conversations filled the air as they slowly moved forward. The big doors of the barn had been pulled back. Kyle followed behind Tony as he had held out his right hand to allow the young couple past. The entrance to the barn had been swept clean and everyone was filing through a door on the right-hand side that Kyle had not noticed before. It opened into a well-furnished room with a long dark stained wooden bar with rows of shelves with wines and spirits. The three young men who looked like none of them were over 19 years old and were standing behind the bar, the light from the fridges behind them lit them up. Each of them was wearing a pressed white shirt and a black bow tie.

There were several tall legged round tables designed for people to stand around and place their drinks on, the rest of the room had large chesterfield chairs and sofas that had small coffee tables in front of them. All of these were arranged in groups around the bottom half of the room. The windows all looked out over the dark fields and were dressed in expensive looking thick draw back curtains the same colour as the carpet. The room was filling up quickly as most people headed for the bar, Tony tapped Kyle on the shoulder.

"Drink?" Tony held his right hand in a cup shape and motioned it towards his mouth.

"Yeah," Kyle answered as he walked forward into the room.

"Grab a seat, I'll be right back," Tony turned and headed off towards the bar. Kyle looked around the room as small groups of people formed and chatted excitedly with each other. He looked around at all the smiling faces, he had many expectations of what he thought he would find here, and none of his expectations were met, in fact, they were all being shattered. Kyle looked at the pictures that were hanging very neatly around the room. Some were of landscapes while others were of groups of people. He felt his legs move before his mind registered that they had as he seemed drawn to a black and white framed picture on the wall. As he got close to it he recognised the side of the farmhouse across the yard from where he was standing now. The picture had been taken quite a few years ago and showed a group of men standing around a very old Land Rover. By the style of their clothing and of the vehicle he guessed the picture had been taken in the mid 1970's. Suddenly his eyes focused in on one face, a man standing on one side of a group of smiling men. The features of the face had not been captured well and there was a slight blur on the picture, but Kyle Foster felt his heart beat a little bit faster as he looked at his Father's face.

He knew he was staring, but his eyes could not move. His father looked happy and he had the type of smile that he remembered. Kyle could feel his insides turn; his muscles tightened and for a moment sadness and mourning gripped him. The sounds of the busy room faded as he could almost hear the chatter of the men as they grouped together. Kyle scanned the other faces, none he recognised but he knew by their clothing they all must have worked at the farm. *Kyle breathed in through his nose as the sound of his brother's laughing filled his ears. The sun shone brightly in the sky as the two of them climbed over the old tractor that had broken down in the field. Kyle looked over the field at his Father as his brother suddenly pushed him off the top of the tractor. Suddenly he was grabbed and thrown back. Kyle jumped back and faced the figure in front of him.*

The heat of the sun was gone, and he was back in the bar at the farm.

"Whoa," said Tony as he held his hands up, each hand had a drink in it. Kyle looked at Tony and his head darted around him as he expected everyone to be looking at him. No one seem to notice that Kyle was tensed up and breathing heavily, he let himself relax as Tony took a step forward and offered him one of the pint glasses.

"What's in this?" he asked.

"Cider," Kyle accepted the drink as Tony drank from his own. Kyle stepped a bit closer, Tony glanced at the photo on the wall then looked back at Kyle who was composing himself very quickly.

"There are lots of couples here tonight," Kyle's statement was also asking a question and Tony didn't have to guess what the question was.

"She isn't feeling well so she decided not to come this time," Kyle nodded in answer.

"Did you see someone you recognised?" asked Tony, Kyle half turned towards the photograph and pointed with his finger.

"Yeah, that's Dad," Kyle turned back towards the crowd and drank some more from the glass in front of him, Tony paused before he answered. "Sorry,"

Kyle looked at him. "What have you to be sorry for? You didn't kill him,"

"And he did once own this place. You will find things here that bear his name or have his picture." Tony explained.

"Yeah, I guessed as much, but that one caught me a little off guard."

"You ok?" Tony asked.

"Yeah, I'm good," he paused "So how long do we have to wait?" he asked, a long howl echoed in through the windows from outside and the room exploded in celebration.

"The kill, they got the kill!" shouted one excited voice.

"Not long now," answered Tony.

Chapter 61

The door to the isolated farmhouse opened and Anders was met by Anna. She did not speak but stepped backwards to allow him to enter. She was dressed head to foot in black, black jeans, jumper and socks. Her hair was tied up in a pony tail and she wasn't wearing any make-up. Anders nodded and walked forward into the small room being careful not to hit her with the small backpack he had over his left shoulder. The heat from the fireplace felt warm and welcoming. Anders stopped by the wooden desk against the wall on his left. The centre of the room was occupied by a two-seater sofa and a matching chair that faced the small TV. Apart from that the room was bare, Anna walked past him and headed towards the only other door that was in the far corner of the room, she walked through and closed it behind herself. Anders looked out of the window at the green fields that spread out into the darkness of the evening from the rear of the farmhouse. He could still hear the sea crashing on the rocks at the foot of the nearby cliff. Normally he didn't notice the north Antrim Coast but over the last few days he had started to, which was something that he was keeping to himself as he did not want the others knowing something like that.

The door that Anna had walked through opened and Davidov walked in. Davidov smiled but it wasn't a warm smile.

"So, what have you found out?" Davidov went straight to business, Anders turned away from him and slid the small backpack off his shoulder.

"Quite a bit," he started to explain as he unzipped the top of the backpack. Davidov walked over beside him and looked on as he dropped the backpack on the floor and opened the black folder that he was now holding. Anders spread a collection of photographs across the top of the wooden desk. The photographs were all pictures of people and one picture of the deer farm, Anders started pointing at each photograph in turn and explaining who each one was.

"This as we know is Carl O'Brien, Alpha of the Northern Den," Davidov listened, "This is Dermott, he is head of security."

"Is he the one who leads their assault teams?" Davidov asked.

"Yes," Anders confirmed.

"Then he will be a problem," Davidov was staring at Dermott's photograph.

"Not when you know where he lives," Anders was smiling as he spoke, Davidov's head shot up and caught him eye to eye.

"Very good," he replied.

"Know your enemy and know yourself, know this and you will be assured the final Victory." Anders quoted.

"How many are there in total?" Davidov asked, Anders breathed in and paused.

"At least 30," Davidov knew that was a guess.

"How many in total work at the farm?"

"There are 76 employees plus a few family members," Anders was more confident with this answer.

"Can they expect any help from the Southern pack? There are over 300 of them there."

"No," Anders shook his head, "the main pack is split into three smaller packs, if O'Brien was to call for help it would be seen as a sign of weakness and he could be challenged from inside his own," Anders shook his head again, "and no Alpha will do that." Davidov and Anders shared a knowing smile, Davidov looked over the photographs and spotted a face he had seen before.

"Who is that?" Davidov asked as he pointed to one of the photographs. Anders paused and looked over at the photograph.

"That is Tony Fallon," Davidov stared at the face of the young man who was looking over to his left-hand side.

"And what does he do?" Davidov asked.

"Police officer."

"Where?"

"Here in Coleraine," Davidov started to slowly nod his head.

"Yes, he stopped us at a check point near the hospital."

"And he was part of the security team that assaulted the house!" continued Anders.

"Was he?" Davidov's eyes shot up, "Does he live at the farm as well?"

"No," said Anders, "He lives with a sapien woman in a house near Portrush."

"Do we know exactly where that is?" Davidov asked, Anders nodded his head, Davidov smiled then straightened up.

"We have most of their pack, the important ones anyway," Anders explained. Davidov moved his eyes up and looked at Anders before he turned and walked over to the window. Davidov lifted his hands and placed them on his hips.

"Is everyone organised?" he asked.

"Everyone paired off and has rented rooms or holiday houses."

Davidov glanced over his shoulder, "Do they all understand?" he asked.

"Everyone has obeyed you and we are ready to serve," Anders was smiling with pride as he spoke, Davidov looked back out the window.

"How far away are they spread?" Davidov asked.

"Along the coast from Bally...castle, Port...rush to Castle...rock." Anders still had trouble pronouncing the names of the local coastal towns.

"How quickly can they all come together?"

"On your orders,"

"Good," Davidov turned around to face him, "You know what I want you to do?"

"Yes," Anders was beaming with pride.

"Then carry out your instructions."

"I obey," Anders braced up, spun round on his heels and bolted for the front door. The door slammed behind him and seconds later Davidov heard the sound of the engine starting up then the vehicle speeding away. As the sound disappeared Davidov leaned back on the wall. The bedroom door opened, and he looked over towards it, Anna stood in the doorway with her left hand high up on the door frame and her right hand high up on the door. Her left knee was bent in towards her right knee, so she was standing in a Y shape. Her dark hair hung down over her shoulders and her seductive smile filled her face, Anna was wearing only her black silk underwear and her appearance had the desired effect on Davidov that she wanted.

"So ... everything is happening the way we want it to then?" she asked. Davidov smiled then walked over to her.

"Oh yes ... this land will be ours," and with one movement he picked her up and threw her onto the large double bed. The rear of his left foot kicked the door and it slammed shut; it would not open again until morning.

∞∞∞∞

Sean breathed in through his nose. With his eyes closed he slowly relaxed back into the sofa in his living room, he reached out with his left hand and picked up the controller of the TV. As he started scrolling through the channels, he heard the sound of footsteps coming from above him. His eyes followed the sounds as they crossed the ceiling. His wife was going for a long soak in the bath, she would be taking her time. He stopped at a 24-hour news channel, the headlines would be coming up in a few minutes, so he decided to wait. The English presenter was covering recent signings to a premier league football team. The presenter carried on; the screen changed into a countdown to the top of the hour. The countdown reached zero and the screen was filled with two presenters behind a large desk, they took turns going through each of the headlines. Sean's mind did not register any of them as none of them affected him. Part of him was glad that they were no longer national headline news, as they had been yesterday, but the local news would be different.

Before he had left the office, some of the new team members had been showing him a few of the stories that were starting to spring up over the web including one by a journalist up in Coleraine who had a witness who said she had spotted the werewolves running away from where the Castleroe murders took place. The detective was also able to point out that this witness was the sister of one of the victims. Sean had told the detective to interview her anyway, but he already knew that nothing would come of it. The phone in his pocket started to ring and he sighed out loud as he read Mike's name on the screen.

"Hi boss, sorry to disturb you ..."

"No, you're not, don't lie," Sean heard a female voice in the background and knew that Mike was at home.

"OK, I'm not," Sean couldn't help but smile, "but it sounds good."

"Where are you now?" asked Sean.

"The spare room,"

"What are you doing in there?"

"A bit of peace and quiet," Sean thought for a second then asked the question.

"Things OK with you and your missus?"

"Yeah, not too bad, but that's not the reason I am phoning," the lie was obvious as was the change in conversation away from what was going on at home with Mike, he was all too aware that things were still not good.

"No probs, so what's up?" he asked.

"Well it's about when the squaddies were up,"

"Which bit? We now know that the Latvian fella was equipped with the knowledge to commit the murders, but we can't connect him directly to any of them," answered Sean.

"Yeah, I agree with you on that, it was what one of the unholy trinity lot spoke about afterwards," Sean was now interested; the military had stayed for half an hour after the briefings finished and many had exchanged conversations, but he had not heard anything that they he would be interested in.

"What was said?"

"Well, it wasn't exactly what he said ... it was more what he didn't say,"

"And what was that?"

"It was just afterwards, and we were near the happy snaps on the wall and he made a reference that it was better that the Russians were real but 'other things' weren't..." Mike paused but Sean was confused, he didn't see any connection.

"Yeah ...so?" Sean asked, "What do you think he was saying?"

Mike paused for a bit as if he was gathering his thoughts. "Well ... these guys ... they are some of the best in the world, yeah."

"Probably why they are called 'Special' Air Service."

"Exactly," Mike paused,

"Mike, I'm not following you, what are you thinking?"

"None of us made any reference to anything other than the background of our suspects,"

"Yeah," Sean could not see where he was going with this,

"And I certainly had a hunch that he knew more than what he was saying,"

"What kind of hunch?"

"Same kind of hunch I had with Henderson," Sean was at full attention now.

"That's some hunch."

"There's only one thing I don't know."

"What's that?" Sean asked.

"What to do about it ... I can't really bring him in and question him now can I?"

"No, not at all,"

"So ... any ideas?" Mike asked.

Sean felt his shoulders fall at the question, the phone was silent for a few moments as he gathered his thoughts, Mike spoke first, "I'm stuck as well,"

"Well I do have one idea," stated Sean.

"What's that?" asked Mike.

"We both have a think about this and chat tomorrow."

"Yeah, maybe Simon will have more ideas," Mike added.

"Maybe he will,"

"Oh, remember when we had that big scare about the van with a bomb in it?"

"Yeah, didn't they eventually find it near Ballykinlar army camp?" Sean asked,

"Yeah, when that was all kicking off I passed one of the squaddies on the stairs in Coleraine cop shop," Sean thought about what Mike was saying, he thought for a second before answering.

"I would not put it past Special Branch using the military for surveillance in a job like that, it was probably nothing to do with us," Sean stated,

"Yeah, ... hadn't thought of that,"

"Only one of us has to,"

"Anyway, we can leave it until we chat to Simon in the morning."

"Yeah no probs ... yeah coming now," Mike wasn't talking to him anymore, so Sean pressed the red button on his phone. He dropped the phone on the sofa, the news presenters were discussing more stories, but he wasn't listening. Sean rested his head back on the sofa and thought over what Mike had said. 'What could the military know about what was tearing people apart?' Sean didn't want to think about it, what he did want was the breakthrough that they so desperately needed. So much work had been done with so little to show for it and yet there was still so much to do. How could they go into court with what they had? What he really needed was the girl with black hair, if they could find her that would be a step forward at least.

∞∞∞∞

Cara-Marie turned the news off and the screen on the TV went black. There was nothing in the news that she didn't already know; she should be feeling on top of the world as she had been proven right and also had a witness' story. Her idea of getting it all together in the paper and on the website, had been a good one, the number of views of the website had increased significantly since this had all started. Kevin, however, was livid but he could not say no to her story from Rachel Boyd. She had managed to move a story from page five as she agreed that it wasn't a front-page story. She should be feeling happy, she should be feeling like she deserved the praise from the rest of the newspaper staff, but she didn't. She walked over to her PC and started it up again. It seemed like she was spending more of her time sitting in front of the PC than anything else.

It didn't take long to get into her emails. She opened then deleted one after the other until she didn't have any new emails, she took a deep breath in and sighed, what could she do next? What else could she do? Her mind was blank as she clicked onto one of the worldwide news links in her email messages. She flicked through how it was all being reported overseas and yet again there was more reporting in France than anywhere else.

Her eyes focused in on a picture taken in France of a man being interviewed. She didn't read the text of the interview, but she did notice the smart police officer in the background. She thought for a moment then went over to her handbag, pulled out her phone and started to write a text message. 'HIYA, JUST HAD A THOUGHT, ARE YOU FREE FOR A COFFEE TOMORROW? IT SEEMS LIKE AGES SINCE WE HAD A CHAT' Cara-Marie scrolled through her phone's address book and selected Tony's name. After she added him, she scrolled back up to Kyle's name and added him as well, maybe if she could not get anything out of Tony, she may get something from Kyle.

Her mind replayed the events outside the harbour bar, Tony had moved with amazing speed then had ran away. She knew there was very little mention of him from the police about the arrests and the weapons they had recovered after that incident. All of those arrested had been remanded in custody and were awaiting their day in court; there was no doubt that prison awaited them. She waited for her phone to beep with a reply, but none came, she clicked on another website and scrolled through the stories, her eyes only just acknowledging the contents, in frustration, she closed the website down then went offline.

Cara-Marie walked round to the window in the living room, the TV was as silent as the phone remained and she wondered what they could be up to. She pulled the cord that moved the vertical blinds, so she could see what was happening outside. The street light didn't light up much of the street, but the clear night was illuminated by the moon. Her eyes looked up into the sky at the round face that was looking down at her, for a moment, she could almost feel warmth from the light that irradiated her. Her eyes darted around but they were drawn back to the only thing that was hanging in the sky. What was it about the moon that had such an effect on so many people? One of the French newspapers had plotted that all the killings had happened either on, or a day either side of a full moon. If that trend was to continue then something should happen over the next few days. The phone in her pocket bleeped with the arrival of a text message; her Mum was still keen for her to 'POP ROUND' but Cara-Marie wasn't going anywhere tonight. She really wasn't in the mood for company, no matter how good the intentions.

Chapter 62

The bar was even livelier now than it had been before; the excitement of the evening was building. Several people had introduced themselves to Kyle, but the polite conversations were short and never personal, he got the impression that he was being sized up by everyone.

"That is because you are," stated Tony.

"What do you mean?" he asked. Tony stepped a little closer.

"They all know of your father. It's because of that and the fact that you are my guest that you haven't been challenged,"

"Challenged?"

"Yes, challenged," Tony turned to look around the room.

"Any chance you could be more .... specific?"

"We are a pack, and every pack member wants to be higher in the pack than they are," Tony paused, "it is all about your standing and place in the pack. Your dad was much liked and very well respected and if one of the more junior of the pack was to put you down then they would jump a few places."

"You mean have a fight," Kyle's voice lowered into a more menacing tone,

"Sometimes; sometimes it's just verbal ... but I have no doubts that you can handle yourself. It happens in the sapien world too, it was very like that back in our battalion," Tony glanced over at Kyle, "I take it that life in the legion is something similar as well?" Kyle glanced around at the room full of people who were all enjoying themselves then he nodded. He looked at the large, expertly carved, wooden letters that hung behind the bar.

"So, what does, 'An Rua' mean?" he asked,

"The red hair,"

"And why are you called that?" Kyle asked, Tony smirked,

"Look around you," Kyle paused, Tony did not have to explain further.

"So, what's happening now?" Kyle asked, Tony acknowledged two women who were standing at the end of the bar, they smiled and one of them waved back.

"The hunters are getting cleaned up and the chefs are preparing the beast."

"Preparing?" Kyle enquired.

"Yes," he paused, "you will have to ask the chef about how he prepares the meal, it's too much for me." Kyle looked over as the two women approached. Both were quite tall but less than six feet, the first one had the same dark auburn hair and pale green eyes as most of the pack. Her red figure-hugging evening dress showed off her curves to the maximum. Almost hiding behind her was a woman who Kyle recognised as the farm hand who had walked out with the deer earlier. As she approached Kyle realised just how black her hair was. Her eyes were a very dark hazel which in turn suited her satin black dress, Kyle was impressed. Tony greeted them as if they were the oldest and closest of friends, all three soon turned towards Kyle.

"And I would like to introduce ..." Tony started.

"Kyle Foster, son of our last Alpha," the first woman interjected, she extended her right hand towards Kyle as she spoke. Her smile beamed an excitement that you would expect in a young child at Christmas. "Yes, I have heard lots about you," Kyle looked into her eyes as he firmly shook her offered hand.

"And who would you be?" Kyle asked as politely as he could.

"Eve McMurrugh," she answered,

"This is Dermott's wife," explained Tony. Eve stepped to one side and allowed the girl with the dark hair to step forward with her hand extended.

"Hi, I'm Amanda,"

"Amanda," Kyle repeated as they gripped each other's hands, Kyle asked the first question that came into his head.

"That's not a local accent, where are you from?" Both the girls raised their eyebrows then they exchanged glances before Amanda looked back at him.

"Yes, you are right, I'm not from round here, I am from Castlederg," she explained.

"Ah, a border girl," answered Kyle.

"You have been there?" she enquired, just as Kyle was about to speak a deep horn sounded from the far side of the double set of curtains by the far wall. The curtains were drawn back and revealed a set of double doors that were opened from the inside and a lone man dressed in a dinner jacket walked in. All conversation stopped, everyone turned to listen to him. He walked a few paces into the room and stopped, his hands were by his sides as his voice filled the room in a shout.

"RUA OF THE NORTHERN DUN, HONOURED GUESTS, FAILTE," He extended his arms and held his palms uppermost; a smile on his face. Kyle leaned towards Tony.

"Fal-shah?" Kyle asked quietly. Tony leaned his head over but never took his eyes away from the man by the doors.

"Irish, it means 'welcome,'" Tony refocused on what was happening.

"TONIGHT ...WE FEAST!" a loud cheer went up from all those in the room. The introducer moved over to one side and extended his hand to the open doorway behind him, *"PLEASE WELCOME OUR TOP TABLE,"* the cheers gave way and applause started as the two doors opened once again. Carl was happily chatting to one of the men that had been with him when the deer was released, and Paul was directly behind them talking to the other man.

"Who are they?" Kyle asked as the four men reached the bar and the applause died down. The room was engulfed in happy chattering as all the little groups of people who were around the bar started chatting away with each other.

"Council members," answered Tony.

"What ... as in Coleraine council?" Kyle asked, Tony flashed a glare at him.

"No," Tony relaxed a little, "they are from 'our' council." All four started chatting amongst themselves in what could best be described as polite conversation. Kyle was quite taken by this girl, Amanda, and for the time being forgot all about Kelly and the effect that she had on him; why was this one so different? Tony glanced at Kyle them looked at his own glass, both his and Kyle's were nearly empty. Kyle glanced over at the glasses that the women were holding and asked the obvious question.

"Would anyone like another drink?" the answer was universal. Kyle took their drink orders and headed towards the bar, weaving through people as he went. As soon as he was out of ear shot Eve turned around to Tony.

"So, tell me more about our latest addition?"

"What would you want to know?" Tony asked back.

"Well," Eve started, "Is he single?" Tony looked at her.

"You have someone, and I don't think he is your type anyway!" Eve mocked shock at Tony's response.

"Oh, it's not for me; Amanda here was too polite to ask," the reply got a powerless punch on Eve's arm.

"I can ask things like that myself," she answered.

"He is cute though, isn't he?" Eve lowered her voice slightly in a suggestive tone which got a staring look from Amanda.

"There is someone he does socialise with from time to time, no, she isn't from round here, besides," Tony lifted the glass to his mouth and finished it off, "I thought Sean had stated his claim on you already?" The question was directed at Amanda and it made Eve look over at her, her face changed to one of annoyed anger at Tony's question.

"What? That prick? I don't think so," Tony looked around the room, Sean was at the opposite end of the bar from Kyle. Tony caught Sean's eye as Sean glared back at him. Sean had not hidden how much he liked Amanda. However, Amanda didn't hide how much she couldn't stand to be anywhere near him. Sean had always reacted violently when any potential suitors approached. He looked over at Kyle who was turning back towards the three of them and slowly started to make his way towards them.

"It looks like Sean has taken a dislike to your friend as well," Eve commented.

"Kyle can look after himself," Tony answered.

"I am sure he can," Eve was smiling as she replied just as Kyle made his way around a small group of men who were standing talking near them.

"Here we go," said Kyle as he started to pass the requested drinks out. Amanda looked over to her right as another young woman waved her over. Amanda and Eve shared a glance before excusing themselves and headed over towards where the young woman had been joined by two others. Soon the group of five women were chatting away furiously together and occasionally one of them would look back at Kyle and Tony. Kyle spotted it.

"So, what's going on now?" he asked, Tony took another sip of his drink.

"It seems all the young girls want to know who the latest single male to join the pack is." Kyle looked around the room.

"It seems they are not the only ones who are paying an interest in me," Tony looked over at the end of the bar. Sean was glaring furiously at Kyle.

"No, they aren't" Tony looked over at the doors again as the presenter appeared again.

"RUA OF THE NORTHERN DUN, HONOURED GUESTS, WOULD YOU PLEASE START TO MAKE YOUR WAY THROUGH TO THE DINING AREA." The double doors opened once again, and several people started to slowly walk towards them. Kyle followed Tony as he made his way with the crowd towards the open doors. The room that they were entering was slightly darker than the brightly lit bar but was at least twice the height of it. For a second Kyle thought he had stepped back in time. The large room was longer than it was wide, large thick wooden beams stretched from the floor up the walls and into arches that ran the whole way down the roofline. The room looked like a medieval banquet hall but the modern chandeliers that hung down from the roof dispelled some of that.

"Wow," Kyle felt himself saying as he paused to look around the impressive room, Tony looked over at him and smiled. The crowd of people slowly streamed past Kyle as he looked around. Large red drapes hung down in the corners of the room with another smaller set covering what was obviously another set of double doors at the far end of the room.

The room was filled by tables that were all together and formed a large 'E' with all the legs coming down towards the end of the room. The tables were all set out for formal dining each with a place setting with cutlery for at least three servings and crystal glasses for white wine, red wine and a tumbler glass for water, every few places up the table were a selection of wines and water. People continued to walk past him, and they started to take their places standing behind the elegant chairs that lined the sides of the tables. Eve and Amanda were over at the far side of the room. Kyle looked over to his left and focused in on Tony's back, he was standing with several others and seemed to be enjoying their present conversation. When he turned around he had a joyous smile on his face, Tony walked forward and motioned with his head for Kyle to follow him. Tony had been looking at a large diagram of the layout of the room, each place setting had a name beside it and Tony's gap was soon filled by other excited people who were looking for where they were sitting.

"We are over here," he said as Kyle approached. They walked up the leg of the tables and came to a stop near the top. Tony stood behind a chair, so Kyle followed suit. Kyle looked down at the place names. Tony's name was written in full, but Kyle's simply said 'guest'. Slowly the room filled up with everyone standing behind the chairs, the room was alive with conversation. A woman in a long black dress came up beside Kyle and introduced herself. Kyle was, in turn, introduced to her husband. He had not realised yet that he had just instantaneously forgotten her first name.

"My condolences for your father," she quietly whispered.

"Pardon?" replied Kyle, the comment had completely caught him off guard, the woman turned her head and leaned slightly towards him.

"My condolences for your father," she repeated, "I was still a child, but I remember him well, like most in the room we mourned him."

"Thank you," he said before he turned and glanced over at Tony. Tony was chatting away to the man on his left side, both started laughing at whatever had just been said. Tony looked over at him.

"You ok?" he asked.

"Yeah I'm good."

"You know, you really should learn how to lie better." Kyle's eyes shot up to meet Tony's and for a moment they shared something unsaid, matching smiles broke out on both faces as the room suddenly fell silent. Kyle looked over his right shoulder at the small group of men walking through the entrance doors.

Carl was in a good mood and was happily chatting away to the older man that was with him. Several others followed in behind them, all of them chatting as if they didn't have a care in the world. The small group passed behind Kyle as they walked up towards the top table. Kyle noticed how the candles on the tables seemed to lighten their faces. Tony looked over at Kyle and guessed what he was thinking.

"The one on Carl's right is called Grishin and the other is called Tatamovich."

"And they are council members," recounted Kyle as Grishin looked directly at him.

"They also have very good hearing." The top table took their seats and slowly the rest followed. Once everyone was comfortable and helping themselves to the wine the double doors to Kyle's left opened, most of the room suddenly sprang to their feet and started to applaud the five people in track suits that had just walked in. Kyle started clapping as the hunting party formed a line behind the top table. They all looked out over the room, they were very happy and looked very proud of themselves.

"They are very clean," remarked Kyle.

"They have just showered," explained Tony out of the side of his mouth. Carl turned and held up his arms with the palms towards the room and ushered everyone to sit. Excited conversation shot around the room, most of it, Kyle noticed was directed towards the youngest of the faces in the line. Carl walked down the line and shook each one by the hand and exchanged a few words, at the bottom of the line he stopped and turned back towards the room.

"*WOULD EVERYONE PLEASE RISE FOR THE ARRIVAL OF THE BEAST!*" he shouted. Everyone pushed back their chairs and stood up. The chatter had stopped. All eyes were focused on the double doors. Carl turned towards them.

"*BRING IN THE BEAST.*" The doors opened once more, and the sound of bagpipes filled the air. The applause started again but quieter than it had been before. Kyle expected the piper to be dressed in a Scottish tartan, but he wasn't. The piper was wearing a dark green jacket with silver lacing over the chest. He was wearing a kilt of plain brown. Kyle had never seen one like that before. Near the piper's left knee was a large brooch on the kilt that had a crest on it Kyle didn't recognise. The piper made his way down behind where Tony and Kyle were standing and continued to march around the tables until he came up to the far end of the top table. The crowd had joined in with rhythmic clapping. The piper continued to play as he came to a stop and all heads turned towards the two young well-dressed teenagers who were carrying the large platter with the uncooked stag's head on it. The applause rose to a triumphant cheer as the two young men stopped near to where Carl was standing, again Carl quietened the crowd.

"*AS YOU ALL KNOW THIS WAS THE FIRST HUNT OF ONE OF OUR NUMBER ...*" The applause rose again until a very smiling Carl raised his hands again.

"*SO, IT IS AN HONOUR FOR ME TO INVITE OUR GUEST TO CARRY ON WITH THE MARKING TRADITION.*" The applause rose again when Grishin walked over to the stag's head. Kyle had to move his body so he could see what was going on. Grishin had lifted a knife that had been placed beside the stag's head and was cutting something. A cheer went up as he held high his left hand and showed off the piece of hide that he had just cut from the stag's neck. Grishin walk over towards the very excited young man standing at the end of the line of hunters.

"It's a very old tradition called 'marking'," Tony started to explain,

"Hunters of old would mark themselves with evidence of their kill," Kyle finished the sentence for him. Kyle looked over as Grishin wiped the flesh down both sides of the young man's face leaving a visible trail of blood. The cheer rose again as Grishin congratulated the young man; as Grishin moved away Carl stepped forward and embraced him. The two teenagers with the stag's head turned around towards the double doors as the piper started up again and the hunters followed the head out of the room with the piper at the rear, everyone sat down.

"So, what happens now?" asked Kyle.

"Well," he started, "they will quickly get dressed and return, so we can all eat." Kyle nodded as he reached for his glass of white wine. He looked around the room and realised he felt differently than what he thought he would. He was not uncomfortable or out of place, the natural warmth of the place seemed to comfort him and for the first time in a very long time he knew what it was he had been missing. He felt warm, he felt safe, he felt protected and most of all, although he did not know how, he felt like he belonged. He did not realise it at the time, but he was slowly stepping towards the pack.

The three-course meal came and went and as the small cups of very strong coffee were being poured for each place setting, platters of different cheeses and biscuits started arriving along the tables. Kyle had really enjoyed the food. He had remarked to the woman sitting next to him that he had never eaten venison before. It was near to the end of the meal and he still could not remember her name. His eyes searched for the name card but that had long since been removed and he was about to ask when the piper entered the room once again.

The piper stayed by the double doors this time and played through a selection of tunes, much to the delight of the gathered audience, as he finished, he bowed slightly towards the top table then turned and smartly walked out. Kyle turned back in his seat and spotted the area at the back was now occupied by a man with a large round drum.

"It's called a Bodhran," explained Tony. The drummer was sitting on a wooden chair with his back to the wall, he had a hold of the back of the instrument and started to play a rhythmic thump with the piece of wood in his other hand. Kyle thought the series of thumps sounded a little bit like a heartbeat. The double doors at the back of the hall opened once more. These were the doors that he had come through from the bar. Out of the darkness ran three beautiful women dressed in thick dark green dresses decorated with amazing Celtic patterns, the dresses stopped near the tops of their thighs and their legs were covered in thick black tights.

Kyle had not noticed that the floor where the dancers were was wooden and the sound from their shoes matched the rhythm of the drum. Each of them held their arms tight against their sides as the pace increased. The dancers went through a well-rehearsed dance that had them pivoting around the centre girl.

"This is amazing," Kyle had to raise his voice over the sound of the music towards a smiling Tony.

"I know," Tony leaned forward to speak into his ear, "keep watching." The dance stopped with a crash of shoes on the floor and pounding of the drum. Kyle thought that the applause could have raised the roof, he looked upwards.

"Are we underground?" he asked.

"Yes," replied Tony who then nodded towards the dancers. The drummer was joined by the piper who had changed into a plain white cotton shirt; it had lace ties at the front. He wore plain brown trousers that looked like they were from a few centuries ago. This time he was carrying what Kyle knew to be a set of Irish pipes. The three dancers had just about got their breath back as the two musicians started to play again. After a few moments the dancers started again, this time a little slower. They moved around the small dance floor with an elegance that impressed

Kyle. They weaved through each other then headed for the opening double doors. The applause started again as the tune ended; the dancers disappeared into the darkness of the bar as the two musicians started again. This time the tune was quicker and had the two of them bouncing where they were sitting. Kyle found himself tapping with his right hand on the table when suddenly a male dancer jumped out of the darkness much to the delight of the diners.

The dancer was wearing a light green silk shirt with black trousers and had the same tap dance type shoes on as the girls. His pace quickened and his kicks got higher as he danced around the floor. He was smiling with an excitement in his eyes, he was clearly enjoying himself.

"He won a world competition in New York a few years ago," Tony stated.

"Wow, it looks it," Kyle was transfixed. The display continued for several minutes as Kyle watched a master perform his craft, and then as suddenly as it had begun the dance ended. The dancer stood with open arms and received the thunderous applause from all who were there. Kyle, too, was cheering and clapping excitedly.

"That was amazing," he exclaimed to the woman beside him, she gave him a knowing look and continued to clap herself.

"He is the best I've ever seen," she said, "and I'm not just saying that because he is your cousin."

"Cousin?" Kyle looked over at her, she met him eye to eye.

"Yes," she nodded, "a few times removed but he is in your family tree somewhere." The surprise had Kyle spinning in his chair towards Tony.

"Yeah, probably," Tony answered, "You possibly have a few distant relatives here." The dancer gave a bow then turned and walked out towards the bar followed by the two musicians. The double doors closed, and a silence came over the room as Carl stood up.

"Honoured guests, friends," all heads in the room turned towards the top table. "I would like to invite you all first of all to show your appreciation to the catering staff who as usual have out done themselves," Carl started clapping as the double doors to Kyle's right opened and a single man walked in, he was wearing chef's whites and smiled and nodded as he received the applause. The noise died down and he turned to walk back through the doors that closed behind him.

"I would now like to invite our guest of honour, to say a few words, Mr Grishin, please," Carl opened his right hand towards Grishin who made one nod of his head, a light applause echoed around the room. Grishin adjusted his dinner jacket as he stood up then started to speak, his Russian accent did not overcome his use of English which was obviously not his first language.

"Rua of the Northern Den," a small cheer went up from some of those in the room. "It is our honour, as council members to be among you once again," he turned slightly towards Carl as he spoke, "and I thank you for your kind and very warm welcome. I congratulate you on the very fine food that was prepared, and I congratulate your young one on his first hunt." Kyle's eyes glanced over at the far side of the room where the young man who had been marked earlier now sat in a clean and pressed dinner jacket. He smiled with pride as those sitting around him passed on their own congratulations. The room quietened again as Grishin spoke once more. "I will not speak for long as I know you are all looking forward to the rest of the evening, so I will say one final thing." Kyle inwardly breathed a sigh of relief.

"Recently one of your own was taken," Kyle saw the immediate effect this had on everyone, "and even though we are one less tonight we have gained one more," Kyle noticed that he had said 'we' and not 'you', Grishin reached forward and picked up his glass of wine, "It's our absent friends we miss the most, so to them we give this loyal toast," Grishin raised his glass into the air, "Absent friends!" in unison the whole room stood up and raised their glasses.

"Absent friends," Kyle sipped at his wine as everyone started to take their seats again.

"Thank you, Rua," Grishin said as he sat back down. A ripple of applause came from the room as Carl stood back up again.

"Thank you for your kind words, now," Carl still had his glass in his hand, "We have one more thing to do," a bolt of electrical excitement shot around the room at Carl's words, "I would like to invite our guests to please return to the bar and the rest of us, please follow me," everyone again stood up as Kyle turned towards Tony.

"What is happening?" Tony gave him a smile and patted him on the shoulder.

"I will meet you in the bar afterwards."

"After what?" Kyle asked, Tony just looked at him then smiled and turned to walk away from him towards the opening double doors that Carl and the rest of the Rua were now all heading towards, the woman who was standing beside him placed a hand on his shoulder.

"Maybe another time Kyle, we have to go to the bar," he looked at her then looked around as the room soon emptied. Several people had gone back towards the well-lit bar, Kyle thought maybe twenty at most. To his surprise Amanda who had spoken to him earlier came up to him with a very pleased look on her face.

"Are you not running tonight?" she asked, Kyle looked at her confused.

"Running?" a realisation came over her as Kyle answered.

"Ah," she looked around the room before sipping from the drink in her hand.

"What do you mean 'ah' and what is running?" he asked, Amanda stepped closer then looked straight into his face.

"They are going to 'run with the pack' and answer their moon lust," he looked even more confused than he had been before, her eyes darted from one side to the other then he stepped a little closer again.

"I still have no idea what you are on about," he said quietly.

"Would you like to see them?" she asked. Kyle wasn't sure what she was talking about, but curiosity mixed with the alcohol he had been drinking brought about only one answer.

"Of course," he replied. Without moving her head, her eyes to pointed to the door.

"I need some air," she had slightly raised her voice before she turned and started to walk towards the door. She looked back over her left shoulder seductively, if it had been any other time the invitation would have been clear, but Kyle knew he wasn't about to be taken to bed. He smiled and followed her up the stairs.

At the top of the stairs she stopped and turned towards him and held a single finger to her lips. The message was clear, no sound. He watched as she knelt down and removed her 4-inch heels then pushed open the door that led back into the main barn. Kyle followed as she slipped through, then with surprising speed she darted along the side of the barn to the far end from the entrance. Amanda stopped by a single sliding door that had been cut into the main frame of the barn. He stopped just behind her as she moved her head slightly to the left. She was listening to whatever was going on at the far side of the wall.

Amanda looked at him and with her right hand pushed the metal door open a few inches then moved out of the way, so Kyle could look out over the courtyard that they had stood and watched the hunting party leave from. The 4x4's were gone but a small group of armed farm hands were standing by the metal gates that opened out to the field, they were happy about something. The lights of the courtyard lit up the whole area, but they were in darkness. She drew closer when the first wolf appeared.

He was on all fours but stood up to his full height as he entered the courtyard, the farm hands moved and started to open the gate as more appeared. Kyle's eyes widened as more creatures came out of the darkness. Each one was different, yet they were all the same. Some had darker coats, and some had very light ones. With their size, you could not mistake them for normal wolves, the pack grew until the courtyard was full. A few walked on four legs, but most remained upright on their hind legs, it was an amazing sight that had Kyle struck for words.

"Beautiful, aren't they?" she quietly remarked.

"Yes," Kyle's answer was a whisper as her head came closer, Kyle looked over at her.

"You're not a wolf, are you?" he asked. Amanda's head shot round and stared into his eyes. She did not answer at first; her face relaxed; she looked out the small gap once again.

"Nope, not entirely," her answer confused Kyle a little but before he could ask the next question she spoke again, "and the name is Garou, not wolf," she paused again. "I am like you; both my parents are Garou, but I chose not to become a full member of the pack." Kyle turned his head and looked out over the courtyard again. The pack was moving into the field and off into the darkness.

"There, by the gate post, standing up." Kyle's eyes followed the directions without even thinking about it and there standing on its hind legs was a majestic looking wolf. His coat had a mix of brown and grey that seemed to flow over his shoulders and down his back. High in the sky the full moon broke through the clouds and lit up the field. Kyle looked at the face of the creature that was now looking at him. He looked into the eyes and recognition burst in himself. Tony dropped a single nod of his head then he spun round to join in with the howl that had just started.

The sound echoed over the fields and washed into the barn. Kyle felt his entire body react as he closed his eyes for a second and let this beautiful feeling wash over him. He reopened his eyes and Tony was gone into the darkness. The pack started to run towards the wood, Kyle felt the feeling subside in him. The noise of Amanda's rapid breathing made him look at her, she had closed her eyes and was bathing in the same emotion as he had just been. As she opened her eyes a fire burned in them and then a look of gentle peace spread over her face. He smiled back at her, he was about to say something but was stopped by Amanda suddenly lunging at him.

Amanda locked her mouth on his as her fingers gripped the hair on the back of his head. Her other hand dug into his shoulders with the passion of the kiss, her tongue fought with his inside his mouth as he felt his hands moving around her waist. The kiss seemed to last for an age before she broke it off, they both opened their eyes together as she stepped backwards a pace.

"Wow," Kyle said.

"You seem to say that about a lot of things," Amanda said. Before Kyle could ask anything else, she turned and started to walk away from him, "It's called 'moon lust' for a reason," she said, then stopped after a few feet. "I'm going back to the bar to wait for them, it would be nice if you could join me for a drink," Kyle did not need to be asked twice.

Chapter 63

Cara-Marie was woken by her phone ringing. Her bedroom was still dark as she slowly focused on where she was, the phone continued to ring, she looked over with annoyance as the screen seemed to illuminate the entire room. As she propped herself up with one elbow she turned on the bedside lamp first and grabbed the phone. She paused as she looked at the screen to see two things, first what the time was and second who was calling. It was just after half six in the morning and the number was withheld, she was in two minds whether to answer it or not.

"Hello?" She still wasn't totally awake when she answered. The male voice at the other end was excited and blurted out a name she did not recognise and before she could ask him to say his name again, he started with his quick-fire questions.

"So, do you think werewolves are in fact real and if so, why have they suddenly started killing people around Coleraine?" This was the second question as she totally missed the first one; the caller wasn't really pausing for an answer, "It has been reported that you witnessed one of the murders, yet you are currently not part of any police investigation, do you think the officer in charge of the investigation should be replaced?" Cara-Marie went from sleepy to annoyed in one second.

"Excuse me, but who are you and how did you get my number?" The caller repeated a name she did not recognise but the accent was English. She couldn't place the newspaper group he said he worked for, but she was pretty sure it was one of the tabloids from London. He was the very type of journalist she hated! All they wanted was the scandal; they didn't care about the actual facts. His questions kept coming.

"Is it true all these murders are being carried out by a patient who used to be committed in a mental home and that he used to enjoy dressing up as a dog?" The stupidity of the last question was the final straw.

"Look you!" Cara-Marie was shouting down the phone now, "I don't know how you got this number but look at the bloody time, if you want to talk to me then get your facts straight and call me in my office..." she breathed in slightly before she continued, *"AND DON'T CALL THIS NUMBER AGAIN, GOT IT."* Cara-Marie didn't care if he had got it or not, she hung up the phone and slumped back on her bed. Her eyes started to look around her room before she started staring at the ceiling. The stare continued as the outline of shapes started to form above her, her breathing deepened and for a moment she was standing in the car park by the river. For a moment, she looked at the face of the creature as it stared back at her from round the side of the building; for a moment those eyes bored into her very soul that made her body suddenly jump. She was sitting up in the bed; the duvet was a crumpled mess on the floor and all the shapes and the wolf were gone. She closed her eyes and breathed in slowly as she calmed down. She flopped back on the bed and lifted the phone to her face; she read the time and knew she would not get back to sleep; the alarm would be going off shortly anyway so that would be pointless. "Right, decision," she heard herself say out loud as she got up and headed out of the room. Fifteen minutes later Cara-Marie was sitting on the sofa with most of her breakfast already eaten, some of the toast was left and the mug of tea mostly consumed. The TV was on and, as she watched the seconds tick by, she changed her mind and flicked the channel over to a 24-hour news channel. The headlines came on, car bombs in Iraq, floods in Pakistan and a tornado in America, thankfully people getting eaten in Northern Ireland wasn't mainstream international news. She glanced down at the time on the screen, finished off her tea in one mouthful, turned off the TV and headed for the shower. She would be ready for the phone call when it came from the tabloid later.

∞∞∞∞∞

Sean was already looking over papers in his office when Mike walked in.

"Morning," he said as he entered the small office. Sean glanced up at him and made a 'harrumph' noise from the back of his throat. Mike sat down as one of the younger detectives appeared at the door holding several 8" x 10" prints in his hands.

"Morning ..." he glanced from Sean to Mike.

"Morning," Mike replied; Sean said nothing.

"I got these printed off some CCTV footage that we got last night and ..." he held the prints out towards Mike who reached for them as the detective finished speaking.

"I think that this is the girl with the black hair that we have been looking for!" Sean moved in his chair, Mike was now very interested and flicked through the prints. He glanced up at Sean.

"I think you could be right," he said, Sean sat upright as Mike stood up and held the prints out to him, Sean reached out and took them. He spread them across his desk and looked at a girl walking past a petrol station with an older male.

"Where did these come from?" Sean asked, Mike looked over at the detective who paused before he answered.

"They came down from Coleraine yesterday afternoon," he replied.

"When was this recorded?" Mike asked.

"Two days ago."

"Where?" Sean asked without looking up from the prints.

"From the filling station in Castlerock," Mike looked over at Sean.

"That would explain why she hasn't been seen around Coleraine in a while,"

"It would," Sean looked back at the prints as a very cheerful Simon walked in.

"Mornin' all," Simon knew instantly that they had something. "What?" he asked. Sean handed him one of the prints.

"Where is this from?" Simon asked without looking up.

"Castlerock,"

"Two days ago," said Mike.

"Brilliant."

"Isn't it?" said Mike.

Simon looked at Sean. "I'll take a couple of the guys and head up to Coleraine today and follow this up."

"Do it," Sean's answer gave him all the authority he needed, Simon looked to his right.

"Right grab one of the others and we will head in a bit," the youngster nodded, "and can you copy all this to us before we go as well?" Simon instructed.

"It's already done," the detective answered, "the copies are on my desk."

"Good lad," answered Simon. The detective turned and left the office.

"If we can narrow down where this chick might be living then finding her just got a whole lot easier,"

"Indeed," said Sean.

"Who is the guy with her?" Simon asked.

"That is possibly who we could be looking for!" stated Mike.

"It could indeed," answered Sean who smiled for the first time.

"We find her, we find him."

"Do you recognise him?" Sean's question wasn't really directed at either of them, Simon looked over at Mike.

"Nope," answered Mike.

"Me neither," said Simon, "but we could circulate this among the other M.I.T.s and see if anyone else knows him," Sean nodded at Simon's suggestion, "never know what that might turn up," he finished off.

"Do it," Sean nodded, "then fire it out around the stations and see if any uniforms have had any dealings with this character."

The young detective reappeared at the door; all three heads turned towards him before he spoke. "We just had a phone call from the desk sergeant at Coleraine," he started.

"And?" asked Mike as the detective paused.

"They are dealing with a farmer who had half of his herd of sheep killed last night, apparently they were all torn apart … he thought we should know."

"Where?" asked Simon.

"He is in the station in Coleraine," answered the detective.

"No, where exactly did this happen?" Simon retorted with a slight annoyance. The detective had to look down at the notebook in his hand.

"Just the far side of Coleraine, … on the Castlerock road," It was enough to get a reaction from all of them.

"Right, we are all going," stated Sean. "Mike move the team back up to Coleraine, leaving one here to send this out to the other M.I.T.s. Simon?" Simon looked back at him from the detective that was filling the door, "You take two and follow this up this morning," Sean lifted one of the prints that was on his desk.

"Right boss," Simon answered.

"Are you going to tell the Super or the Chief?" Mike asked. Sean pushed his chair rearwards just before he stood up.

"When I have something definite to tell them, yes … in the meantime …. let's go."

∞∞∞∞

The lights changed to green and the small car in front of Cara-Marie pulled off in front of her and her own car roared forward.

"Easy tiger," Mark said from the passenger seat. He had his new camera bag that he had been showing off in the office. Kevin hadn't been particularly concerned about her early morning phone call or the fact that someone she didn't know had her number, in fact, he had been very nonchalant about the whole thing which just served to annoy her even more. The rest of the staff had been talking about her story. Kevin was happier about the amount of hits the website had and that he was now getting more calls for interviews from larger newspapers across Europe. Carla-Marie muttered something under her breath as they shot over the junction. The car carried on up Castlerock road and right up behind the car in front that had slowed to a stop as it started to signal to turn right. The flow of traffic coming the other way showed no sign of letting the car through and that just infuriated her more.

"Hey … it's only some sheep," Mark's sentence was cut short by a look of wrath from the driver's seat; he turned his head and held up his hands in mock surrender. "Sorry I spoke."

The car in front started turning so she took off around it, soon they were out in the rolling countryside on their way to the farm. They both recognised the two cars already there. Coleraine's other newspaper had got there before them.

"I wonder how long they've been here?" Mark's question wasn't really directed towards her as it was more of a statement.

"I'm sure we will find out soon enough." They climbed out of the car, she looked over the roof and out over the field; she caught his look and nodded in that direction. Mark turned around and spotted the two uniformed police officers walking down the side of the field towards them. A white van turned into the farmyard and drove up behind them. The farmer who was by the back door of his farmhouse stopped talking to the two other journalists and started walking over towards the van. A man in his mid-twenties got out and walked towards the farmer; they obviously knew each other.

Cara-Marie held back a bit and listened to the exchange between the vet and the farmer. Apparently the farmer had got up as he always did and after breakfast had got onto his tractor and headed out to check on both of his flocks. It wasn't long before she had been joined by the other two journalists and Mark.

"Hi Cara,"

322

"Hi," she replied,

"I really liked your story,"

"Which one?" asked Mark. It was obvious which one they were talking about and to Cara-Marie the question seemed unnecessary and pointless but to Mark it made perfect sense. She had done more than one story in the last week, even if it was just the one that got everyone talking.

"The witness, I think you may have something there," she was about to say something, but the vet and the farmer were now walking right towards them.

"And how many have you lost?" asked the vet.

"26," the farmer replied, the journalists all stepped to one side and allowed them to pass between them.

"How many were stolen?" he continued.

"None,"

"None?" the vet stopped and looked at the farmer.

"Yes, none. I have accounted for all of them, 26 of the black faced sheep were all killed … I've counted the bodies, the rest of the black faces were at the other end of the field all panicking, most stuck in the fence or the hedge … "

"They were trying to get away," Cara-Marie didn't realise that she had just said that out loud until the vet and the farmer looked back at her.

"Aye, the sooner we catch the beast the better," the farmer said with disgust.

"What beast?" the other journalist asked, the farmer looked at them with surprise.

"The beast of Ballycastle," the vet shook his head and turned and walked on, the rest followed him. Mark caught her eye and she raised her eyebrows then looked at the vet then back at Mark, the message was clear, follow him.

"So, you have black faced sheep?" Mark asked, trying to make conversation,

"Aye, white faced as well, got over 200 of them."

"But only the black faced were attacked?" the other journalist asked, the farmer had to turn to look over his other shoulder to answer that question.

"Keep' em in separate fields right now … don't want them cross breeding," he spoke as if the four of them knew exactly what he was talking about. The group arrived at a tubular metal gate that broke the lining of the hedge. The two police officers had turned back to the gate when they had seen them all approach. A tall female officer stopped the four journalists from entering the field.

"It is still a crime scene and until the investigation is complete it is going to stay that way," she insisted.

"But they are only sheep!" The fourth journalist hadn't spoken until now and his comment got a disgusted looked from the vet and a torrent of abuse from the farmer. The farmer opened the gate and allowed the vet through and slammed it shut behind him. He muttered some abuse directed at the journalists.

"Hi Alison," the other journalist said after the fourth one had made an excuse and returned to his car.

"Hi," Alison answered.

"How are you?" Both the police officers stopped and looked at each other as they listened in on whatever was happening in their earpieces. They shared a glance then Alison motioned with her head; the other police officer turned and followed the vet and farmer.

"Yeah, I'm fine," she answered.

"I'll see what shots I can get with my lenses," injected Mark as he strolled off down the hedge line. He was leaving Cara-Marie and the other journalists with the police officer, so she could find out more about what was happening in the field.

"Haven't seen you in a while?" the other journalist asked, the police officer thought for a moment before she smiled.

"Yeah, last time was up at the Mountsandel murder," Cara-Marie's body reacted.

"So, the police are treating it as murder, not suicide?" she asked, Alison glared at her for a few seconds before the other journalist stepped in.

"Sorry, should have done this sooner, Cara-Marie of the Herald … this is Alison of Coleraine DCU … we have known each other for a while." Cara-Marie had always wondered who her opposite numbers police source was, now she had a firm idea. Cara-Marie held out her hand and Alison shook it firmly. They hadn't been introduced by their surnames; she'd seen this police officer around but never had a reason to speak to her.

"I'm not sure what the investigation team is doing," Alison corrected, "Murder … suicide, I don't know,"

"I will have to ask them," Cara-Marie replied with a smile.

"You can when they get here," Alison stated.

"They are coming here?" Cara-Marie replied.

"Yes," Alison tapped her earpiece as she answered, "just heard," this had Cara-Marie's mind racing.

"What would the Muirdris team want with slaughtered sheep?" Again, she had spoken aloud, Alison shrugged.

"Well, that's something else for you to enquire of them," she had a sarcastic smile on her face now, "but don't expect much of an answer," just then Cara-Marie's phone bleeped.

"Oh, excuse me," she said as she dug into her jeans.

"Oh, that reminds me!" exclaimed the other journalist, "better get mine from the car!" They disappeared as she read the text, it was from Kyle. 'YES, NO PROBS SAY 2PM?' she had to think for a moment before she remembered that she had text him last night and asked if he wanted to go for a coffee.

"Good news?" Alison asked.

"Oh, just meeting a friend for coffee later," she said as she began typing a reply.

"A nice guy?" Asked Alison

"Kyle is …" Cara-Marie stopped herself talking as she pressed the send button, Alison's eyes widened.

"Yes, and he is on days off currently," Alison knew who she was talking about.

"Yeah, we do coffee from time to time; it's good to talk," Cara-Marie replied, she hoped for a second that she hadn't just revealed one of her sources, as she replaced the phone Alison's face burst in recognition.

"You weren't with him when he discovered the bodies at Riverside, were you?"

Suddenly she wanted to lie, and part of her felt like she had to…but something stopped her. She wanted the distraction of someone else, but Mark was sitting on a wall taking photographs and the other two were still at their cars.

"Yes, yes, I was," she felt herself speak without forming the words of her own accord, Alison looked away a little before she asked the next question.

"What did it look like?" Cara-Marie paused; she wouldn't say anything she hadn't already put in her police statements.

"Well the dog was ripped completely apart and …" she started.

"No, not the bodies … the killer … what did it look like?" she was totally taken aback. it, she had called it, 'it', Not he or her or them, 'it'. She paused then before she knew it Cara-Marie started to describe what had stared at her from around the corner of the building. Alison listened, she didn't move, she didn't immediately discredit her, she just listened, just as she was finishing Mark walked up to them.

"Maybe we can talk more later?" Alison asked, she nodded.

"Right, I got a couple of shots, maybe we can use some them," Mark almost shouted as he approached. Alison and Cara-Marie turned towards him and started a whole new conversation.

Chapter 64

"What did she say?" Tony asked as they drove towards Portrush. Kyle was sitting in the passenger seat and was engrossed in his phone.

"Which one?" he asked, "Kelly or Cara?"

Tony smiled. "Both, didn't you get Amanda's number?"

Kyle's head shot up. "No," he denied, "What?" Kyle asked, Tony smirked at him, "What?" Kyle repeated.

"I wish I could have seen it," Tony answered.

Kyle grinned. "Well he underestimated me,"

"Obviously!"

"I was surprised that your fella Paul only stepped in after yer man Lefebvre ended up on his back," stated Kyle.

"Talk me though what happened," Tony glanced over at Kyle as the car slowed down at a T junction.

"Well it was about an hour after you all had come back from your little ... *'run in the woods'*..." Kyle paused as the car picked up speed again.

"And?"

"And the bar had mostly emptied but the disco was in full swing when he came barging up and shoved me into the bar,"

"So how did he end up on the floor?" Tony asked.

"Well he told me to back off and that the girl was his and no one else could touch her,"

"How did that go down with Amanda?"

"She swore at him to go away and do things with himself," Kyle was smiling as he recounted what had happened. It was clear to Tony that Kyle was impressed by her, "then he went to hit her," the car slowed down for a sharp corner and the two friends momentarily met eye to eye as Kyle finished the sentence, "Well, I was faster than he was," Tony laughed as the car speeded up again.

"Then she took you to bed,"

"Then she took me to bed," repeated Kyle.

"You haven't actually answered my first question either," said Tony.

"Which was?"

"What did she say?"

"Cara wants to meet me for a coffee later today," Kyle started tapping a message into his phone,

"So, what about Kelly? What did she say?" Kyle stopped texting and looked up.

"Nothing," he answered.

"Nothing?" replied Tony,

"Nothing yet, anyway," Kyle confirmed,

"Are you thinking serious thoughts about her?" Kyle screwed up his face at the question.

"Kelly? No, not at all," Tony kept looking at the road ahead, the denial had been quick and total and was obviously a lie.

"What are we listening to anyway?" Kyle's change of conversation gave Tony all the answers he needed to know about how Kyle felt about the physiotherapist.

"If you don't like it, change it," Kyle picked up the iPod attached to the music system and started to scroll through Tony's playlist. Kyle reacted when he found one he really liked. Tony slowed the car down as they pulled into the short driveway outside his house, Kyle raised the volume a bit and sang louder.

"Do yourself a favour and don't go in for one of these talent shows on TV!" Tony parked the car and switched off the engine, Kyle closed down the iPod and they both pushed open the car doors and stepped out. Kyle turned to say something over the roof of the car towards Tony, but he stopped. His whole body tensed as he spun round towards the house. The house drew all his focus and every muscle was milliseconds from springing into action, there was only one word in his head.   *DANGER*

Kyle felt the same but for Tony the single word in his consciousness changed.

"KAREN,"

Kyle burst towards the steps that led up towards the front door, but Tony was already past him, and through the open door as Kyle reached the top of the steps. Kyle wasn't slow, but Tony was moving at amazing speed. Kyle had seen glimpses of this agility but nothing like this, Tony had screamed her name as he had burst into the house. Kyle bounced in through the front door and for a second, he stopped. The sudden smell of blood was overwhelming. Tony's scream came from the kitchen. Kyle stopped at the kitchen door.

The room was cold, the smell of blood filled his nose. Tony had Karen's body pulled up into his chest with her face up against him. Her dressing gown was drenched with blood. Her legs were covered in blood, her hands, her body, the floor, there was blood splattered everywhere.

"It's ok my darling, it is ok, I'm here," the pain in Tony's reassuring voice tore at his vocal cords. Tears carved their way down his face and for the next moment Kyle feared the worst but then she moved her left arm towards him. Her skin was the colour of white marble and her voice was very, very weak, she started crying as she spoke.

"I'm sorry, I'm so sorry," The scene in front of Kyle was choking him as she continued, "I've lost our baby," The words slammed into Kyle's shocked face. Tony's head shot up as he screamed at him.

"Put your fucking gun away and get her an ambulance!" Kyle hadn't even realised that he had brought his gun out, he looked down at it as he stepped back lifting it to his hip.

"AMBULANCE ... NOW" screamed Tony. Kyle nodded, and headed for the front door.

"It's ok, my sweet darling," Tony's voice stayed in the kitchen as Kyle stopped just outside the front door. Kyle pulled his mobile phone from his pocket and pressed the 9 button three times. It wasn't until he had the phone to his ear that he became aware of how fast he was breathing. The number rang, then rang and rang again.

"Come on!" he shouted out loud before the female voice answer.

"9-9-9 emergency, which service please?"

"Ambulance," Kyle fought to slow his breathing as a male voice came on the phone.

"Ambulance service," The voice was calm as Kyle stated that he was an off-duty police officer and he needed an ambulance.

"What is the incident?" The voice asked, 'Incident?' Kyle thought, it wasn't an 'incident'.

"It's Karen .... We think she had a miscarriage," Kyle for once didn't want to call it a domestic incident.

"What address is the incident at?" the voice asked, of all the things to get annoyed about it seemed trivial compared to what was happening in the kitchen.

"The address ... yes," Kyle had to think for a moment before he recited where he was.

"Where is the casualty now?" The voice was asking the set questions on the monitor screen in front of him.

"She is in the kitchen with her husband,"

"Is she breathing?"

"Yeah ... yeah she was talking."

"Is she still bleeding?" Kyle lost it completely and started screaming at the voice that his friend was lying on his kitchen floor with his wife and no he didn't know whether she was still bleeding or not and that he wasn't about to check.

"How long is the fucking ambulance going to take?" There was a pause before the voice answered.

"An ambulance has been tasked and should be with you in 20 minutes."

"20 minutes?" he was angry now.

"For the address, you are currently at it will take our nearest asset that time to get there, Constable," the voice had used Kyle's police rank and Kyle paused before he spoke again, all these calls were recorded.

"Alright, no probs."

"Will you stay on the line?" the voice asked.

"Of course, I will,"

"Can you reassess the casualty please?" Kyle turned and walked back up to the door of the kitchen and slowly peered in, Tony was cradling Karen, they were sobbing near to uncontrollably, he looked up at him.

"It's on the way, 15 minutes," Tony nodded, Karen moved her knees up towards Tony who kissed the top of her head.

"It's Ok darling the ambulance is on the way," Kyle took a step back then turned towards the front door. What he had just seen was repeated to the voice at the other end of the phone, the voice asked Kyle to say what had happened, Kyle started from them pulling into the driveway.

"How long has the casualty been lying on the floor?" Kyle had to think for a few moments. Tony had told him the reason she had not been at the moon dance was that she had been feeling unwell.

"I'm not sure ... it could have been all night ... the kitchen is freezing,"

"Ok," the voice answered.

"How far away is the ambulance?" Kyle asked, the voice was quiet again for a few moments,

"Not long now,"

"Ok," Kyle paced back and forth.

"Ok ..." said the voice, "Good luck,"

"Kyle?" Tony shouted from the kitchen, Kyle appeared at the door of the kitchen in less than a second.

"Yes mucker?" he asked, a very tearful Tony looked back at him.

"Would you grab the duvet from the spare room for us?" Tony was a lot more controlled and quieter, Karen was the same marble white, but tears were still streaming down her face.

"Yeah ... of course," Kyle darted into the room that he had slept in not that long ago and ripped the duvet from the bed. Kyle stepped inside the kitchen for the first time. Tony nodded his thanks and lovingly tucked the duvet around her. Kyle had never felt this uncomfortable in his life, so he slowly stood and went to walk out of the door when Tony's phone went off. Tony reached his right arm from underneath the duvet and threw it at him.

"Sort that for us, will you?" Kyle nodded after he had caught the phone. He looked at the screen as he walked away, it was a withheld number. Kyle answered it with a quiet 'hello' and as he returned outside the house. He recognised the female voice as one of the civilian controllers at the police station.

"Hiya ... it's me ... just a quick call, there has just been a 999 call to your house .... Are you ok?" she was speaking in a lowered voice; this wasn't an official call. Kyle wondered how to say what was happening. He knew her but that was just through the police; this wasn't someone that he would stop and have long chats with walking down the street.

"This is Kyle Foster ... Tony can't answer the phone,"

"Oh ... is he ok?" It sounded like the concern in her voice was real and that there was no way that this was going to stay quiet for long.

"Yeah he is .... May I speak to the duty inspector please?" Kyle was making it official and she would know that.

"Yes, of course, ... hold on please," Kyle looked out over the amazing view as he waited. The sun broke through the morning clouds and reflected off the waves of the sea as they rushed towards the shore. Portrush was in the distance and for a moment Kyle felt a little bit of peace as the sound of the ambulance came from the far side of the hill. As the ambulance appeared at the crest of the hill a male voice came on the phone.

"Constable Foster, this is Inspector Davidson ..."

∞∞∞∞

Grishin was sitting at the round table of the empty coffee shop watching as the people of Belfast walked past. It had rained earlier but the gusting Autumn wind was making sure everyone was keeping their jackets and coats buttoned up. The young waitress smiled as she made her way round the tables to where he was sitting; the tray with the two coffees was glided towards him. Tatamovich was still at the toilet so he would miss this chance for another quick conversation with the young Polish girl.

"Thank you," Grishin said as she leaned forward to position the coffee; she answered him in Polish then seconds later she was gone. Grishin didn't touch the coffee until Tatamovich returned.

"Well?" he asked.

"Well, what?" Grishin answered.

"When are we going home?" Tatamovich reached for the coffee in front of him as he asked the question, Grishin gazed out the window again. It was starting to rain slightly.

"We will hear what is to be said tonight, then decide after that." Grishin's response seemed to please him.

"Excellent, I want to get home to my own again," he muttered something else but Grishin chose to ignore it.

"Did you not like the last moon dance?" Grishin asked,

"Yes, the Rua always put on a good dance. Even the fight at the bar was good."

"What fight?"

"One of the Rua was moving in on a female that another wanted,"

"Nice," Grishin replied, the rain was starting properly as he reached for his coffee.

"So, what of the Noctrailis?" Tatamovich questioned while watching the supple movements of the waitress. Grishin took a deep breath in before he answered.

"The female they were searching for was returned to them and the Rua Fallon got a ruling worked into it for his family," Grishin looked over towards him, "not bad and," Tatamovich looked over at him, distracted away from the young waitress, "and once more the Rua have obeyed our laws ... so after tonight we can finally go home,"

"So, what time do we have to leave here by?" he asked.

Grishin looked at the watch on his wrist. "Not for another four hours at least," Tatamovich beamed a smile and pushed back his chair.

"Right, I will see you back at the hotel then," he lifted his coffee and walked over to where the waitress was standing and started a conversation. Grishin smiled then took a mouthful of the coffee before rising from the table and heading towards the door. As he walked outside, he paused in the doorway and looked up and down the street, then headed off leaving Tatamovich inside.

Across the street sitting in the doorway of an empty shop was a dishevelled figure of a man sheltering from the wind and rain; he shuffled as he tried to make his position more comfortable. A voice echoed in his right ear.

"November One Zero this is Zero Alpha confirm that X-ray One has left, over." The man didn't speak or move except for his right hand which pressed a small button deep inside one of his pockets twice. The effect was a deliberate noise that indicated a 'yes' response to the voice of Major Dukesby.

"Roger that One Zero stay in location, Two One, Two Two and Two Three stay on X-ray One, all other November callsigns stay in place around X-ray Two .... Out." The small earpiece went silent again as the rest of the unholy trinity went off to complete their own surveillance tasks around the Russian called Grishin. For the moment he was staying here, that was until the Russian inside moved off somewhere else.

328

Chapter 65

Mike cast a glance over at Sean who was leaning on the table of the coffee shop, he was staring out the window at a point further down the street. Sean didn't notice the people walking up and down Church Street, his mind was elsewhere. The woman in front of Mike was being served and that drew his attention back to where he was. He looked over the handwritten menu on the black chalkboard and guessed what his boss would want. Simon was still down with the farmer that they had just left along with the two others who had come up with them that morning. Unfortunately, the visit to the farm had been a disappointment and wasn't what they had expected at all.

"Morning …. What can I get ya?" The young female voice asked him from across the counter, Mike glanced at the name badge. 'Rachel' was spelt out in thick black letters on a piece of white plastic pinned to her black cotton uniform.

"Morning …" Mike paused to look over the menu again, "Two caramel lattes please," the young woman smiled and turned her back to him as she started to prepare the drinks. The counter staff shared a joke that Mike didn't understand, it was obviously an 'inside joke' with the staff.

"Of course, *Mister Flannigan."* She over emphasized her response to the joke.

"Quite naturally *Miss Boyd."* They smiled and shared the joke as they carried on what they were doing.

"Two caramel lattes?" asked the man behind the till.

"Yes?" answered Mike who handed over a crisp £5 note that he had got out of the cash machine only that morning.

"Thank you," was the response. As the two coffees were placed in front of him Mike suddenly realised who 'Rachel Boyd' was, he smiled and lifted the two coffees and returned to the table that Sean was at. Sean didn't register his return until Mike spoke.

"Do you know the girl behind the counter?" Sean lifted an eyebrow and looked at him, shifted in his seat then looked over his left shoulder.

"Can't say that I do, no,"

"Rachel Boyd," Mike held the mug up near his mouth as Sean crunched up his face.

"You say that like I am supposed to know who 'Rachel Boyd' is!"

"Rachel Boyd, sister of one of the victims from Castleroe and the one who did the interview that was published in the Herald the other day."

"Didn't we get a statement from her?" Sean asked.

"Yeah, but I haven't read it yet … don't think there was much in it. She claims to have seen the werewolves running away from Castleroe over towards 'the heights."

"Brilliant," signed Sean, "I can see that going down a treat in court." Mike smiled.

"I can just see it now," Sean continued, "I saw mythical creatures running across a road just after they ate my brother,"

"I think the story line was something similar,"

"I pity the journalist who printed that one," Sean replied.

"Well," said Mike, "you can pity her in person."

"What?" asked Sean.

"The journalist who printed that story, is walking the far side of the street," Sean raised his sitting posture as they watched Cara-Marie walking up the pavement, totally oblivious to the fact that she was being watched.

"Oh, and Simon had an idea about the squaddies," Sean looked over at Mike.

"And what was that?" Sean asked.

"The boxing event…" Sean looked slightly puzzled, Mike continued, "invite them down to the inter-police boxing event that is happening at the Europa Hotel in Belfast. Then when they relax see what you can get from them,"

"Ok, do it," Sean glanced over at the entrance door then back at Mike, hiding his face as Cara-Marie walked in. They waited for her to pass and start a conversation with Rachel before Sean stood and headed towards the door. Mike took a gulp of his coffee before following him outside and back towards the Coleraine police station.

∞∞∞

Yelina slowed the car down as Anders raised the camera to his eye. A few seconds later he turned and sat back in the passenger seat and she accelerated away from the farmhouse.

"How many is that now?" she asked, he looked at a notebook that was on his lap.

"Five … one more and we're done," he looked over at her and smiled, "by tonight, between us and the others we all will have plotted every single one of their homes," his grin became ghoulish, "when the time comes these Rua will not know what hit them!" He started grinning a defiant grin while Yelina paused before only smiling slightly.

"They have to be at home for us to find them all at once," she said.

"When the time comes …." Anders repeated, "we will make this 'our' land." Yelina knew from the tone that it was Davidov speaking and not him. Yelina for the first time was frightened about the future and it was obvious Anders was not. She had voiced her opposition to the move Davidov made to become Alpha and she still had the bruises to prove it. They had made her go to the Rua's den and that had frightened her, the road rose up in front of them and as they went over the crest of the hill she spoke.

"Where are we going next?" again he looked at the pad in front of him.

"Ballykelly," he answered.

"Where is that?" she asked.

"It is the far side of Limavady …. keep going straight, I will direct you from here,"

"You have been there?" she asked. It sounded like he knew exactly where he was going, he cast her a dominant look.

"Keep driving … I will tell you where to go." She looked out the front of the car and watched where she was going on the road. Why had she ever sided with Anders and Davidov and left her home back in Latvia? The question repeated itself night after night in her head. At first it had all been new, exciting, but now … now only danger lay ahead and from what she had seen of the Rua this was not going to be an easy fight. It had taken four of them to take down just one of them in the car park but against the whole pack? For the first time since she had been a child Yelina felt afraid.

"Did you not have fun last night?" he asked.

"Hunting sheep isn't normally what I call fun, but it was good to be ourselves."

"I agree," he replied, "hunting sapiens is more to my taste." She cast him a glance

"Our laws prohibit us from hunting sapiens, do they not?"

"Not at the cost of our own survival," he snapped, she stopped herself from asking the next question that was in her head as she guessed she probably didn't want the answer. "We will make this land our own," he repeated

∞∞∞

Cara-Marie had gone upstairs after she had got her coffee. Rachel had been pleased to see her and was still excited about seeing her story on the newspaper's website. Cara-Marie was just pleased at the Victory she had scored over the newspaper's editor about the whole episode. The downstairs of the coffee shop was quite busy, but the upstairs was quieter. There was a middle-aged man engrossed in a novel in the far corner and a young couple that probably should have been at school.

She positioned herself behind a table by one of the windows, both the man in the corner and the young couple were far enough away so she could have a conversation that wouldn't be overheard. She sat facing the entrance and the window to her right let the light of the day flood in. It looked like it may rain but it was staying dry for the moment. She glanced at her watch, Kyle Foster wasn't supposed to be here for another ten minutes. It was unlike her to be this early.

330

She found her phone in her right pocket easily and typed out a text. 'HI, GOT MY COFFEE ALREADY AND SITTING UPSTAIRS. WHAT WOULD YOU LIKE?' She pressed the send button and placed the phone down on the table expecting Kyle to answer almost straight away. She found herself staring out the window at the various people walking past, slowly faces came into focus…a mother from an event at one of the local primary schools, a farmer who had been convicted of drunk driving, a teenager that had been rescued from the sea by the lifeboat crew … 'there are disadvantages of being a local journalist' she thought to herself. Before she had left she wrote up the farm story and placed it in Kevin's mailbox. Mark was busy sorting through all his pictures before putting the ones that he didn't want up for sale. The phone bleeped with the arrival of a message, but it wasn't from Kyle. The screen was filled with the single word. MUM, she paused for a second before she opened the text.

'I AM MAKING DINNER AT 6 TONIGHT. IT WOULD BE VERY NICE IF YOU COULD MAKE IT' she read the text again, "it would be very nice if you could make it!" she whispered to herself. 'It would be very nice IF….' she knew what it really meant. 'You ARE to make it for 6 …' She breathed a deep sigh then typed in a simple reply.

'OK, MUM, SEE YOU THEN. CM x' She probably could have thought of several reasons why she had to be somewhere else but for once she thought she had better head around as she had in fact cancelled the last few attempts by her mother to get her around to the house for an evening meal. It was probably just her Mum wanting to spend some time with her, so she resigned herself to her fate this time. The phone bleeped again, she sighed again but to her surprise the screen said, 'KYLE FOSTER'

'HI RUNNING LATE, JUST LEAVING THE HOSPITAL AFTER DROPPING TONY OFF, BE THERE IN TEN.' Her fingers were tapping out 'OK' and sending but her mind was already racing. Why was he at the hospital with Tony? What had happened? And how come she didn't already know about it? She set the phone down on the table and waited before picking it up again. She sipped some of her latte before she started typing another message but this time it was to another 'contact' at the Coleraine police station. The background music from the coffee shop got a little bit louder, which was good as the others in the room would not hear anything that she was saying but then she could not hear what they were saying either. The ringing of her phone made her jump, she looked at the screen before answering.

"Hello?" she said, she recognised the female voice at the other end as the support staff from the police station that she had just sent a text to. She listened as she was informed about the ambulance call to Tony's house. His wife had miscarried.

"Oh my God … I didn't even know she was pregnant!" she exclaimed.

"No one did … total surprise here … oh … got to go," and suddenly the conversation was over. She felt a sudden surge of emotion and her heart went out to her school friend. She couldn't imagine what they were going through right now and she felt the tears well up inside her. A deep breath helped the feeling to subside before she picked up the phone to send him a text, but she suddenly paused. She decided it would be best to wait until after she had spoken with Kyle. Her entire plan for the conversation that afternoon just changed.

Cara-Marie rested her elbows on the wooden table, and she held the mug of coffee in both hands, she felt the warmth of the liquid from inside the mug. Today had not been a good day. First a field full of slaughtered sheep, an office full of tension and now this, maybe dinner with the folks wasn't so bad.

∞∞∞∞∞

Alan Dukesby walked into the small, bare office that was just along the corridor from the main operations room, the room did not have any windows and the single door was the only way in and out. The desk had a computer monitor, keyboard, mouse and a landline phone that was connected to the military network. Alan was carrying a file in his hand. Steve Minister walked in behind him and sat down on the only chair that was pushed up again the wall opposite the door; as he walked round the desk the Major placed the file down over the keyboard.

"Well?" Alan asked.

"Well," Steve started, "we can confirm that the two we have under surveillance in Belfast are not any of the group from Scotland."

"Definitely?"

"Yes boss, definitely," Steve confirmed, Alan sighed and relaxed back in the chair behind the desk.

"Right, if they're not who we are after then lift the surveillance on them,"

Steve nodded. "At least we know that we are on the right track,"

"The downside is that the police are looking for them as well,"

"Yeah," answered Steve, "that brief on Spets was the breakthrough we wanted,"

"How many of the Latvians have the police identified?" Alan asked.

"Just from what the boys and I spotted on the wall they have got pictures of the fit chick with the black hair,"

"Anna," injected Alan,

"Anna," confirmed Steve, "the suicide in Coleraine we have also confirmed is that fella Chernov but apart from that... we don't know."

Alan nodded his head slightly. "I'll ask Darren to see what he can find out without them knowing that we are after them as well."

"Mmm," answered Steve, "Yeah he could probably get a good look at their stuff." Steve pointed to the file on the desk, "are we going to share that with the police?" he asked, Alan looked at him, then glanced at the file.

"Nope," Alan breathed in through his nose loudly, "I don't think the head shed would be very happy if we let it slip what had been happening,"

"Isn't he moving on soon anyway?" Steve asked.

"Yeah, he has got a staff job at Whitehall," The phone in Alan's pocket buzzed, he shifted in his chair and pulled the phone from his pocket. He was quiet for a few seconds as he read the text message, "talk of the devil .... it's from Darren," he said.

"Must have known we were talking about him," replied Steve.

"It seems the coppers from the other day want to say thank you; we have been invited to an inter-police boxing competition down at the Europa hotel."

"Really?" answered Steve, "that would be good ... pour a little alcohol down their necks and we should find out more!"

Alan smiled. "My thoughts exactly,"

"Right," said Steve as he stood up and headed for the door, "I'll pull the boys back in." Steve was just leaving as Alan shouted after him.

"Oh, one more thing ..."

Steve stopped, "Yes boss?" he asked.

"Something I forgot to ask you."

"What's that?"

"How's the wife getting on?"

Steve smiled at Alan's question. "Enjoying being up the duff ... and enjoying being able to do what she wants to the house while I'm away!" Both men shared a short laugh before Steve turned and left the office, closing the door behind him.

Alan sat back in the chair and picked up the file, flicking it open to a group of surveillance photographs. The first photograph had been taken at night through a night vision lens in a forest. The tall figure was slightly out of focus, but you could still make out the head and shape of the werewolf running on its hind legs. The creature was carrying something in its left hand but from the angle that the photo was taken you were unable to make out what the object was, however, Major Alan Dukesby of the Special Air Service Regiment knew exactly what it was.

"Don't worry ... we'll find you," he whispered to the photograph, "Then it will be my turn to put your head on a pole in the forest."

Chapter 66

"Anyway, I had better be going," Kyle pushed his seat back and stood up.
"Are you heading back to the hospital?" Cara-Marie asked, he glanced at his watch.
"No, Tony said he would text me later,"
Cara-Marie forced a smile that didn't hide the sadness in her eyes.
"Tell him from me ...." she paused,
"I will," as he stepped back to give himself space to replace the seat back, Cara-Marie lifted her right hand from the table to stop him.
"Any help that I can be ..." she started.
"Just ask?" he finished off.
"Yeah," she nodded, this time the smile was more natural, "Enjoy your date tonight," she said as he started to walk away. Kyle stopped in his tracks and looked back at her.
"How did you know I have a date tonight?" he quizzed.
"Well for the last half hour you have been constantly looking at your watch and bang on the top of the hour you are nearly running out the door ... and since you aren't going to the hospital ..." she smiled,
"And you are a journalist after all,"
"I am a journalist after all," she repeated, as he walked away.
He shouted back towards her. "Not jealous that it isn't you that I'm taking out tonight, are you?" Kyle asked. Cara-Marie's shocked eyebrows jumped up.
"What makes you think I would have said yes?" she retorted. He smiled then disappeared down the stairs. Cara-Marie relaxed in her chair and looked out the window watching as he disappeared up the street. Something about the whole thing just wasn't right, something about this situation just wasn't adding up and it was annoying her. She gathered her things and shoved them into her shoulder bag then darted out the door. She was walking as quickly as she could, her mind was subconsciously taking her back to the office. She moved sideways around someone who was moving far too slowly, her mind all the time racing, the phone ringing in her pocket made her slow down.
"Yes?"
"That's no way to answer a phone!" it was Mark from the office.
"Ah ... brilliant, I was just on my way to see you."
"What?"
"Where are you right now?"
"Aaah .... sitting at my desk?"
"Perfect, meet me at my car in two minutes,"
"Wha...." his question was cut off and the phone replaced in her pocket even before the command had registered with him. It took her more than two minutes to get to the supermarket car park and Mark was already standing nearby, leaning up against her car with his arms folded.
"Hi,"
"Hi," Mark raised his right hand in greeting,
"Right, I'm on to something but I'm not sure what exactly," she started.
"Ok, hit me." Mark relaxed back on the car, he was not expecting the punch that landed on his left upper arm, "Aeow," he exclaimed.
"You said 'hit me' ... so I did,"
"I didn't actually mean ..." Cara-Marie raised her fist again but paused when he didn't say the words.
"Anyway ..." she relaxed,
"Remember the fight outside the harbour bar in Portrush?" she asked, he crunched up his face then glanced upwards.
"Technically I wasn't there, I was at home in bed with my soon to be ex ..."

"But you remember the incident, yes?"

"Group of Polish guys got arrested and a couple of sawn-offs were recovered."

"Bulgarian."

"What?"

"Bulgarian, they were Bulgarian, not Polish."

"Whatever .... What's your point?" Mark asked,

"Well nothing was said in court about the two policemen who were there and stopped whatever was happening at the time."

"Yeah, the pics that you took weren't great but there wasn't anything we could use."

"Yeah, I know .... What my point is that one of the coppers broke the whole thing up ... I mean the speed he moved at ..."

"Was like nothing you had seen before, yeah, I remember the phone call ... so?" Mark's question was both bored and sarcastic, "look, I can't see where you are going with this?"

"Ok, I said with everything going on here those two have to be involved somehow."

"Those two, ... one being your old school friend Tony what's his name."

"Fallon, Tony Fallon, yes. Every time something happens either one or both of them are around ... now come on what are the chances of that happening?" Mark shrugged his shoulders, so she explained, "I just spent an hour in a coffee shop with the other one, Kyle,"

"That must have been nice," Mark injected with raised eyebrows.

"He is a source, nothing more."

"Of course, he is ..."

"Look, normally he is chatty; I can usually get some info out of him but today ... zip."

"So? He isn't as chatty as usual ... doesn't mean he is running around killing people."

"I know," she started, "that's not what I am saying,"

"So, what are you saying?" Mark asked.

"If you could shut up for a few minutes I will tell you!" Cara-Marie had raised her voice to him, and it did have the intended result.

"Ok, I'm listening."

"Tony is over at the hospital as his wife has just had a possible miscarriage,"

"Didn't know she was preggers,"

"It seems no one did, but he just told me they found her this morning lying on the kitchen floor ... they think she had been there all night."

"That's awful," Mark paused, "but how does that tie in with anything?"

"So where were they last night? ... what were they doing 'all night' that they only found her this morning?" She now had Mark's attention, "and last night 'something ... or someone tore apart a field full of sheep."

"That wasn't that far away from where he lives ..." Mark continued.

She smiled and nodded in reply. "And anytime I asked, 'where they were last night' the answer was just 'out' ..."

"Just 'out'," Mark breathed in and looked around the car park then over at her.

"So, what do you want to do now?" he asked.

"Find out where they were," she answered.

"And how are you going to do that?" he asked.

"No idea."

"Where are they now?" Mark asked.

"Tony is still at the hospital with his wife ..."

"So, he's out, what about the other one?"

"Kyle is heading out somewhere with a physio, Kelly, who works for the police."

"How do you know that?" Mark asked.

"She was texting him while we were having coffee, his reaction every time she sent him a text was priceless."

"A physio who works for the police called Kelly ... that should narrow it down a bit."

"Now here is what I would like you to do ......" Mark unfolded his arms and listened to what she was saying, nodding occasionally to let her know he understood what it was she wanted. All of it possible and not too illegal. In a couple of days Mark would know more about 'Kyle Foster of Coleraine District Command Unit' than he probably knew himself.

"Not a problem," he said when she had finished, "What are you going to do?"

"Be a journalist," Cara-Marie was smiling as she spoke.

∞∞∞∞

The atmosphere over dinner with Kelly wasn't what Kyle had been expecting. The food she prepared had been very nice, but something was wrong.

"Nothing," she answered when he asked the obvious question. In the past she had been very friendly and making jokes but this time she was a lot more distant and had been giving him one-word answers. 'Yes' and 'No' had been the total of their conversation so far and this evening wasn't going the way that he had hoped. Kyle had accepted the offer of a glass of wine, but she was only drinking water. His eyes flicked up at the clock on the living room wall, it was only approaching half nine and time seemed to drag.

"So, what else has been going on in your world?" he asked. Kelly wasn't looking at him and seemed to be constantly checking the time.

"Not much .... got a lot on at work at the mo ..." Kyle didn't believe her at all as she shifted in her seat. The distance that she was sitting away from him may have only been inches, but she was making sure that it could have been miles. "Got a lot to do for tomorrow so I am going to have to kick you out in a bit," Kyle glanced over at his glass. He had drunk maybe a mouthful of wine, although he was well under the legal limit he was now aware that he would not be staying the night and would have to drive very shortly.

"Ok .... When would you like to meet up again?" he asked, something in his insides turned as she lifted the glass of water to her lips. Her eyes glanced up at the clock again as the second hand ticked slowly round the white face on the display.

"Oh ... we will have to do something ... but I can let you know when I am free." Kyle was now convinced that something else was up, but she wasn't going to tell him anything.

"Well if I am driving I better not have any more wine." Kyle placed the glass on the coffee table. Kelly smiled a false smile as she stood up.

"Well it was really nice to see you again." Kyle knew a slap in the face when he got one, and this was an obvious one, he stood up as well.

"Yeah it has been nice," he knew he was being shown the door. The look on her face confirmed she didn't want him here any longer. He slightly smiled as they walked out of the living room and headed towards her front door. Kelly's phone bleeped with a text message which she giggled as she read over.

"Good news?" Kyle asked as he opened the front door. Kelly looked up and had a spark in her eye that he had seen before but had been noticeably absent this evening.

"Mmm ... oh ... just a client wanting to book more sessions." Her eyes looked down and her right hand tightened around the phone as the coldness of the night air washed over him when he opened the door. Kelly stepped in behind the door to either shelter herself from the wind or to make sure that she wasn't seen from the outside. Kyle turned to face her and looked her deep in the eyes.

"Has it been a problem me coming around tonight?" he asked. Kelly stared at him for a moment then looked down as she stepped forward closing the gap of the doorway.

"No, no not at all, besides we arranged all this last week and there have been loads on at work ... I'm just snowed under that's all," he felt his eyes slowly blink as his face grimaced unconsciously.

"Ok, another time then."

335

"Yes, another time ... take care," then the door was firmly shut. Kyle slowly turned on his feet and as he started to walk away he heard her phone bleep from inside the house, but he kept walking. He had not been able to park his car outside her house as the street was quite full, he looked around as he slowly walked away under the street lights that managed to hide the low clouds of the night sky. The evening had been a disaster, in fact the day had just got worse at it had gone on. It was quite a contrast from the evening at the moon dance and then finding Karen on the floor, getting a grilling from a journalist and then this. This had not been a day he enjoyed at all. Cara-Marie had been at the farm where all the sheep had been killed and seemed transfixed on that. Yes, it had only been a few miles away from Tony's house, but it was a farm he had never been to and why was she so fixated on where Tony and he had been the night before? 'I was having dinner with a room full of werewolves!' he thought to himself, yes that would have gone down well.

Kyle walked around to the driver's door of his car and climbed in. For a few moments, he just sat there as his mind went over what he had seen at the farm then at Tony's house. His car keys found their way into his hand. He couldn't make sense of what had just happened at Kelly's, he paused again as he pushed the ignition key into place.

"Where could I take her that would impress her?" he said out loud, he had a 'Eureka' moment. In seconds, he had jumped out of the car and was bounding back up the street towards her house eager to share his idea that would no doubt be received with glee. Something made him slow down, maybe he was wrong, but for a second, he thought he had just seen her front door close. His pace slowed as he approached the small wall that was around her tiny front garden. She had not totally closed the curtains that hung in the front room. Kyle's pace slowed to a halt as his eyes focused in on the living room door that had just been pushed open as Kelly was moving backwards. The feeling of excitement had totally left him as the male who was with her pushed the door closed. Kelly threw herself at him as they met in a passionate embrace, their hands fought with each other's clothes as they fought to pull each other's garments off.

The man looked like he was early twenties and enjoyed body building. Kelly's top had already hit the curtains as she reached behind her back to unclip her black lace bra. The man moved forward and the two of them sank from view as Kyle felt his stomach tighten. Part of him wanted to bang on the door, part of him wanted to kick the door in and leave whoever the body builder was unconscious on the floor, part of him wanted to demand of her what she was doing, part of him wanted to claim what he thought was his. His body and mind were overcome with an intense rage. A low growl rose from his throat bringing him back to where he was.

What had just come out of him? That had never happened before! Part of him was filled with an angered sickness that made him want to fully give into rage. But another part of him was a police officer and the police officer tightened his fist and turned and walked back towards his car.

He would leave talking to her for a while, until she got in touch with him, he would be going to the police boxing event in Belfast alone. He would wait until she wanted him and not the other way around for once. Then his phone beeped in his pocket with the arrival of a text message. Kyle stormed back to his car and climbed inside before he took out the phone and stared at the screen. Tony's name made him take a deep breath in before he opened it. 'HI, COULD YOU COME AROUND TO THE HOSPITAL AND PICK ME UP?' Of course, he could. Kyle took a breath in and fought back the bile that had filled the back of his throat, as he fought back the anger and rage that struggled to get out of him. He sent a short acknowledgement back to Tony to say that he was on his way. His friend needed him. The car leapt forward and took off into the night.

Chapter 67

Sean Parrish walked into his office, the main office was slowly starting to fill with the rest of the investigating team. He closed the door behind him. The sounds became muffled as he slowly went through his morning ritual of hanging up his coat, switching on the coffee machine and his police net desktop computer.. He closed his eyes and let his mind wander.

The sound of a text message arriving brought him back to reality Sean reached into his pocket and pulled out his phone. It was a short message from Mike. 'HAVE A LOOK AT THE NEWS HEADLINES' Sean let out a sigh. He placed the phone on the desk and reached for the computer mouse. In a few seconds he was on one of the news channels. In a few moments, his screen was filled with a young woman standing in a news studio. He didn't recognise it but thought it looked American. The screen froze for a few seconds before the woman suddenly burst into life. Her accent was American. She had shoulder length brown hair with a nefarious smile that made her head tilt to one side as her voice came out of the small speakers under his desk.

"And a different story from Northern Ireland, once only known for conflict. Now has a new terror spreading across the land" he felt his eyelids slowly close for a moment, 'Oh no', he thought to himself as the presenter continued speaking, *"It seems that a 'Werewolf' has been running around and attacking people … in one recent incident five teenagers were mauled to death by the creature and that is not all. One local resident of the town of Coleraine claims to have seen the werewolf running away."* The screen changed, he recognised the background as the new bridge roundabout that wasn't far away from the Castleroe murders. The camera panned to a face that he did not recognise at first, but he did recognise the name of Rachel Boyd that was spread over the bottom of the screen.

The contrast between the two accents was vast as the very young-looking face spoke from underneath a woollen hat. Rachel smiled a lot during the interview and pointed up the road to illustrate the direction where she claimed to have seen them. A picture of Rachel and her brother was shown in the corner of the screen, the news team were making the story more personal, they were presenting that this had happened to real people.

"In events that evoke memories of a similar happening in Wisconsin several years ago it makes you ask the question … what else is out there we don't know about yet …." The screen froze, and the link ended. Sean felt himself release a heavy breath. They really didn't need this, and he didn't need to look over the other websites to guess what was on them. He closed the internet link and went back to his police net inbox that was again full of emails that meant nothing to him. A figure appeared outside the office and after a double knock the door opened and the well turned out figure of one of the detectives appeared.

"Detective Constable Cargill," Sean spoke without looking up.

"Good morning Sir, there is someone here to see you …." the young detective stepped back as the figure of an older man in a dark suit and a light brown raincoat filled the doorway, his police ID card hung around his neck and bounced around as he stepped forward into the office. Sean looked at the well-worn face looking back at him, they both smiled at the same time.

"Sean, me boy," the man held out his hand Sean stood and warmly shook the offered hand.

"He says he knows you," finished of the young detective who stepped back out of the way to allow the older man further into the office.

"Martin!" Sean exclaimed, they shared a warm greeting, "come in, come in … make yourself at home," Sean extended his hand to offer Martin a seat. Martin looked around the office then took off his coat and threw it over one of the chairs as the young detective left the office and closed the door behind him.

"Still drinking more coffee than water I take it?" Martin asked as he sat back in one of the chairs.

"Of course, is there anything else?"

"No, probably not," answered Martin as he reached over and poured some coffee into one of the mugs that were placed around Sean's coffee machine.

"So how are tricks over in London?" Sean asked.

"Aye ... not bad ... not bad at all."

"How is your missus getting on?"

"She is ... getting on, that is, enjoying having all three kids still at home," they shared a short laugh.

"How old are they now?" Sean paused before he asked the rest of the question, "it must be fun having a house full of teenagers."

"They aren't teenagers anymore ... two of them are in their twenties!" replied Martin.

"Where has the time gone?" Sean asked.

"Where has the time gone indeed," Martin replied, "so, who have you got on your team now?" Sean looked out over the main office.

"Mostly kids ... not one of them is over 25."

"And detectives already?"

"Oh yeah ... fast track careers, personally think that they are just pushing the last of the old RUC out as fast as possible," Sean lifted the coffee mug again.

"Yeah, I know what you mean," Martin relaxed himself back into the chair then raised the mug to his own face, "nice coffee," he stated, Sean glanced over at him.

"I know," he paused, "I buy it."

"Pity it wasn't like this when we started," said Martin.

"That was a long time ago," answered Sean.

"And not long to go before we are both on the scrapheap!"

"Yeah, the training depot was a long time ago."

"A lot of water has passed under the bridge since then,"

"It has ... a lot of changes ... some for the better...." Sean didn't need to finish the sentence.

"So, who are your sergeants?" Martin asked,

"Mike Dear and Simon Mc Alistair."

"Dear ...." Martin pondered.

"The Henderson case was his last high-profile result," said Sean, Martin sat up in the chair in recognition of the name.

"Of course, Henderson ... bad one that one .... How long did he get in the end?"

"Long enough ...." said Sean,

"I had a couple of run ins with him in the past myself."

"Yeah, I remember," said Sean.

"But we could never get anything on him to put him away for any real length of time," this polite conversation was good, but it was obvious that Martin wasn't just here to catch up on old times.

"But anyway, since I don't believe that you were just 'popping by' are you going to tell me the reason you are here?" Sean's question had the desired effect, Martin visibly flinched in his seat, whatever the reason was, it was uncomfortable for the very experienced senior detective that was sitting in his office.

"Actually, I was just up with Sutcliffe," Sean noticed he hadn't finished the sentence.

"And what would a Detective Chief Inspector of the Metropolitan Police in London want with a Superintendent in Belfast?" Sean paused again, "Or should it be the other way around ... what would he want with you?"

"He was after my advice," Martin answered, Sean didn't believe him.

"Really? Super Sutcliffe seeking advice! Martin ...." Martin looked at him as Sean leaned forward onto his desk, "we have known each other too long to come out with that crap ... now ... what is going on?" Sean demanded,

"How is the case going?" Martin asked, Sean stared at him.

"Not too good presently,"

"Really? I thought that you would be all over this one?"

"I will give you the same answer that I gave him last week."

"And what was that?" Martin asked.

"I haven't got a single thing that I am prepared to take into a court room," the smile had gone from Sean's face as he could now guess why Martin was here.

"That's what I thought," Martin replied.

"What did he offer you?" Sean asked. Martin didn't look at him and took a breath in before he replied.

"Your job,"

"And what did you say?" Sean asked.

"Not a chance in hell would my missus ever let me move back over here!" Martin relaxed into a short laugh which Sean smiled at as he watched him turn away.

"I bet she wouldn't ... is that the only reason?" Sean asked,

"No," he paused.

"What was?"

"It's really good to see you again mucker ... just wanted to pop my head around the door," Sean nodded as Martin spoke.

"You are always welcome as you know ... you will have to come around to the house for dinner 'my missus' would love to see you," Martin smiled and nodded his head as he looked down again.

"I just wanted to find out from you, yourself if what I have been hearing is true,"

"That depends on what you have heard?" Sean asked.

"Sean, neither of us has got long to do ... just do your time and get out with your pension ... you of all people deserve it!"

"I am aware of how long I have got ... you have less than two years as well by the way." Martin nodded; Sean had picked up on the veiled threat but wasn't going to answer it.

"Yeah, two years to go then I get my pension," Martin looked up, "and you will get yours."

"I intend to ... but you haven't answered my question!" Martin looked up with a look of 'don't talk to me like that' but the look passed as quickly as it had appeared. Martin finished off the mug of coffee and placed it on the small table beside the coffee machine.

"No, I didn't answer your question because I can't believe that I would ever have to say it," Martin answered.

"Say what?" Sean answered instantly.

"Really? ... *WEREWOLVES?* ... since when did we indulge in investigating fantasies?"

"I'm not investigating 'werewolves' or any other mythical creature ..." Martin sat back in the chair and continued to listen as Sean carried on speaking, "my team and I are investigating several very brutal murders and we are being thorough in that investigation."

"That is what I thought ... I just wanted to hear the words,"

"Glad I put your mind at rest," said Sean as Martin stood up, "is that why you said 'no' to the job offer?" Martin reached for his raincoat and smiled over at Sean.

"I have to go away, think about it and give him an answer tomorrow," Martin let his face relax into a full grin as Sean stood up behind his desk, "you do know that it's all over the newspapers that there is a werewolf running around Northern Ireland, don't you?"

"Yes, I do, I'm not interested in what the gutter press are printing, I am interested in putting forward physical evidence that will convict a murderer or murderers," Sean almost quoted their training manual in his response, Martin got the hint. "You will let me know what your decision is, won't you?" said Sean.

"You already know it mucker, I wouldn't do that to you," Martin reached out his hand to shake Sean's. Sean knew that any senior detective would be glad to sweep in and take over an investigation and scoop the rewards, if friendship didn't come into it.

"I know ... the invite to dinner still stands," both men shook hands as Simon walked in.

"Morning boss I ..." he was cut short by the figure of a man in a suit that he did not know who had just started to put a raincoat on.

"Morning ... Detective Sergeant Mc Alistair I would like to introduce a very old friend of mine from my depot days ..." Sean opened the palm of his hand towards Martin, "This is Detective Chief Inspector Mullen of the Metropolitan Police and this ..." Sean turned his hand towards Simon. "Is Detective Sergeant Simon Mc Alistair ... Simon was one of our uniform sergeants when I was out in Tyrone." The two men smiled, stepped towards each other and shook hands.

"DS Mc Alistair ... I have heard a lot of good things about you," said Martin, Simon smiled before he answered.

"The good bits are lies, the bad bits are probably true, Sir,"

Martin glanced over at Sean. "I may try to poach him from you Sean."

"He's not going anywhere ... he has too much work to do here,"

"The inspector keeps us all busy," answered Simon as he motioned towards Sean, Martin let out a short laugh and paused, he glanced at Sean.

"Simon would you check on Mike and confirm that the lads have finished the tasks that they were working on yesterday, if you don't mind." Simon nodded.

"No problems, just for your info Superintendent Forester was on the phone to reference the CCTV stills from Castlerock and he asks you give him a ring in a bit,"

Sean nodded. "I will." Simon turned and left the office saying his goodbyes as he went, Martin paused as the door shut.

"Darren Forester? From Special Branch?" he asked.

"The very same, you know him?" Sean asked, Martin looked out the door.

"Yeah, unfortunately,"

"Why 'unfortunately'?" Sean asked,

"Bitter experience,"

"Something I should know about?"

Martin turned his head away. "Watch your back with him,"

"Why?" Sean enquired,

"He doesn't play by the rules ... that one."

"What do you mean?"

"How is he involved with this?" Martin's right hand waved in front of himself.

"We asked him ... well his 'military' contacts for some advice and confirmation on some lines of investigation." Sean wasn't about to tell Martin any details of their involvement.

"Watch him like a hawk," Martin turned towards Sean and held out his right hand. Sean reached up and closed his hand in Martin's as Martin continued talking, "that man has ended more careers and destroyed more lives than anyone I know ... he is dangerous and if he is in any way connected to this ...." Martin paused again, "I want nothing to do with it." Sean nodded.

"Thanks, I will," he answered.

Martin released his grip and turned, opened the door of the office and walked straight out past the rest of the team of detectives. Most of them looked up, they all now knew exactly who he was and were eager to hear what he had wanted. Although they could not hear what was said they saw the body language, and that body language had not been good.

Simon walked back into the office as Sean sat down in his chair.

"So, what did he want?" Simon asked. Sean looked at him then shot a look at the door, Simon slightly turned and closed it. Simon took a seat and listened to what his boss had to say, he recounted most of the conversation and included the warnings he had been given.

"So, it seems people want us to 'go away'." Sean's statement made Simon nod his head.

"Is he going to take your job?" Simon asked.

"No, but ...I want to find out what the history is between him and Darren Forester!"

Simon smiled. "I'm on it."

Chapter 68

Kyle was standing in Tony's living room overlooking the impressive landscape. The sun was starting to set, and it was creating a breath-taking view over the Donegal hills. Kyle's eyes darted over to the expanse of the dark blue sea, he watched the small white shape slowly make its way towards the mouth of the Bann River and for a moment he wondered who would be onboard the sailboat at this time of year. His eyes fixed on the small craft, but his ears picked up Tony's voice talking on his mobile phone in the kitchen.

"No, I can't make it, but Kyle should be able to …… No, he will be fine, I assure you." he wondered what he was being volunteered for, he guessed that Tony wasn't speaking to the police control room, "Ok, no probs …… Yeah thanks … I will, slan," Tony was still trying to speak Irish to everyone, he turned his head towards the door of the living room as Tony walked in. Tony had changed into a pair of jeans and a plain sweatshirt, he forced a smile as he caught Kyle's eye. He looked exhausted. He had been on the phone constantly to both his family and Karen's family since the news of her being rushed into hospital had broken. It was clear both Tony and Karen had kept her pregnancy a secret.

"Well?" Kyle asked, Tony stopped beside him but kept the phone in his right hand.

"Well what?" Tony answered.

"Who are you 'assuring' me to and for what have I just been spammed for?" Tony's grin was more genuine this time.

"They need you out at the farm," he answered as he stared out of the window at the ever-decreasing sunset.

"What for?" he asked.

"Dermott needs some guys for a visit to the farm later, can you get there by 7?" Kyle stared at him this time.

"That's just over an hour from now," Kyle paused, "and that is assuming I want to go!"

"It's pack business, you are expected to go."

"Maybe I don't want to be a part of 'pack business' or whatever," Tony's head shot up and he stared Kyle in the eyes. Kyle felt that whatever had just risen in Tony backed away slowly and turned his head to looking back out the window.

"You *are* a part of the pack, maybe you don't realise it yet, but you will come to need the pack, need to be near the pack" Tony looked at his friend, "and the pack needs you."

"And why does the pack need me?" Kyle asked as his own head turned to stare at the fading sunlight that was turning the low clouds different colours and shades of red.

"We need each other if we are to survive … every year it becomes a little bit harder to survive in this … this modern world," Tony relaxed into what could have been a prepared speech, maybe it was or maybe he was repeating something he heard before. "To this world we are nothing but animals, monsters that should be hunted down and destroyed. Our enemies are very good at keeping the perception of us as something for the sapiens to fear." Tony lowered his head, "and as you know our enemies are certainly out there."

"Something I have been meaning to ask," said Kyle.

"What?" answered Tony.

"You and … 'the pack' have certainly shown off your strengths," he started.

"Yes," Tony glanced towards him,

"What about weaknesses? What about all that stuff about silver and crucifixes and all?" Tony let out a little chuckle.

"As I keep on saying, Dark Age paranoia has a lot to answer for."

"What do you mean?"

"I mean, yes as a species we do have reactions to silver but as things are with sapien kind it differs from person to person, some have mild reactions … other more severe."

"So silver bullets all round then?"

"Again, Dark Age paranoia, because silver was so rare it was thought at the time that it was the only thing to use against us," Tony was smiling as he spoke, "however, no self-respecting Garou would ever have any silver in their house, besides normal bullets cause the same amount of damage," he inwardly laughed at his own joke, Kyle didn't react.

"I spotted one of the girls at that moon dance thing wearing a crucifix, what is the story there?" Kyle asked. Tony breathed in through his nose before he spoke.

"The whole 'holy' thing has always surprised newcomers to any pack," he started.

"Why?" asked Kyle.

"Well, we can walk on consecrated ground and things like that."

"You don't explode when covered with holy water then?" Kyle's question made Tony's head dart over to stare at him.

"No, we don't."

"Your enemies, you mean those knock things?"

"The Noctrailis, yes, some of the legends and myths are true, but some are not." Kyle thought about what he was being told and remained silent as Tony continued to explain what to some people is the unexplainable.

"We don't know the full reason but one way that I like to think about it is that it is a battle against good and evil that has been going on for centuries."

"But who is the good and who is the evil? Is that not an individual perception?" his question raised Tony's eyebrows.

"Yes, it can be, but think of it like this ... God made sapien kind in his own image."

"If you believe in God for starters,"

"Yes ... but hear me out on this one," Kyle nodded,

"God made sapien kind in his own image but the Devil, after he was thrown out of heaven and cast down to earth declared war on all things that came from God."

"I remember this bit from Sunday school ..." Kyle injected.

"God made all things and the devil does all he can to destroy them."

Kyle looked confused. "I take it there is a point to this?"

"Yes ... sapiens only have one singular predator ... there is only one thing that specifically hunts them."

"Vampires," answered Kyle.

"Noctrailis," corrected Tony. "For example, God designed sex and gave the parameters for healthy sexual living and the Devil corrupted it with disease, rape etc."

"I am not following you Tony."

"Ok ... God made man," Tony and Kyle exchanged a look, "Ok, if you believe that," said Tony, Kyle nodded, "and the Devil took man and corrupted him, changed him into the very root of all things evil, a man that hunts only man, kills only man," Kyle breathed in as Tony continued to mentor. "An abomination that could never exist in heavenly realms."

"An un-holy creature," answered Kyle.

"That hides amongst its very prey."

"Mankind," Kyle said out loud.

"A prey that considers them 'cool' and 'sexy'," said Tony as Kyle lifted his head and stared out as the darkness engulfed the last rays of light from the sun.

"Hollywood does have a lot to answer for!" Kyle commented.

"Yes, it does, and we are nearly the only thing that stands in their way."

"So, this is all one big holy crusade then?" asked Kyle, Tony smirked.

"No, the people we defend are the ones who can and will turn on us just as quickly."

"So how do you explain your 'pack' then?" asked Kyle, "are they not 'abominations' as well?" Tony cast Kyle an evil look then relaxed; it was a genuine question after all.

"Not sure to be honest but we can walk on holy ground etc," Kyle and Tony shared another glance "We even have had one of our own go to Rome and join the priesthood!"

"So back to my original question, apart from silver what are the weaknesses? Is there anything that the Garry lot …"

"Garou," corrected Tony.

"Garou … are scared of?" Kyle noticed that Tony visibly twitched, he had obviously just touched a nerve.

"There is only one thing that terrifies our kind," Tony seemed uncomfortable.

"What is that?" Kyle asked.

"Never and I mean never mention this at the farm or you will get a very nasty response."

"Why?"

"Why?" Tony repeated, "because Garou only have one way of dealing with their fears … they attack!" Kyle looked away as Tony continued "and when we attack we do not stop until the danger is destroyed, is dead or we have won."

"So, what is this thing that I am not to talk about?" Kyle asked,

"We don't talk about this and we would not normally have this conversation with anyone," Tony repeated his stance, "Rabies," Kyle looked up, whatever he had been expecting, that wasn't it. "If one of us contracts rabies it could spread through an entire pack in weeks …" Tony's expression fell into deep concern as he explained further, "if one of us goes rabid then all the worst of sapien fears comes to life. If the wolf gets to take control and that wolf is rabid …" Kyle looked over at him, he had never seen that look on his friends face before. Kyle was watching real emotion. "It would take the whole pack to take a rabid down … if that rabid got near sapiens it would kill everyone they came across," Tony looked up and looked at Kyle once again, "it would be all the worst parts of all the werewolf films and stories that have ever been written," Tony started to shake his head, "it would be the worst possible time for us all, it could be the end of us all … well here in Ireland at least," Kyle knew that Tony didn't want to carry on talking about this as it was obviously too close to home for him and things at home were emotional enough with his wife still in hospital. He needed a change of direction and he could only think of one track.

"Well if I am going to the farm what are you going to be doing?"

"Well for starters I am going to get a lift from you back to the Causeway hospital to see how Karen is getting on."

"Have you finished packing a bag of her things to take in tonight?"

"Yes mucker, I have, shall we go?"

∞∞∞∞

Anna watched as the car pulled up outside the cottage, she didn't say anything as Anders walked towards the front door. Anders banged on the door once, she listened to the noise that came from the bedroom behind her. Slowly she turned and walked over to let Anders in. The door was pushed open and he barged into the room. Anders didn't acknowledge her as he stopped in the middle of the room.

"We are ready," he said, speaking towards the open door that led to the main bedroom, but he didn't approach it. Anna walked past him and stopped in the open doorway.

"Anders is here," she quietly said into the room, she stepped backwards to let Davidov enter the living room. Davidov was dressed in a black woollen jumper, black jeans and a stylish black leather jacket. Anyone who didn't know him would have thought he looked like a malicious gangland boss on his way to a business meeting. Their thoughts would not be far from the truth. Anders breathed in. Although he caught Davidov's eye he immediately looked down towards the floor before Davidov spoke.

"Well?" he asked quietly, Anders looked up to answer.

"We have two teams overlooking the farm and one will remain with the cars at the bottom of the lane, if anything happens, we will deal with it,"

Davidov nodded twice. "It is time to go then," Davidov walked towards the door and Anders followed behind him.

"I'll just get my ..." Anna started.

"You are staying here," said Davidov as he reached the door.

"No, I am coming as well."

"You will stay here until we return,"

"Why?" she protested.

"Because I said so," Davidov shouted, Anna stepped back at the volume of his voice.

 "I thought ..."

"I don't care what you think. I am telling you that you are staying here," Davidov pointed at the floor to reinforce his point. Anna was being put in her place, her Alpha had spoken and given an order, there was only one thing she could do as she looked towards the floor of the bungalow.

"I obey," she sounded almost sheepish, she continued to stare at the floor as the two of them left, if she had looked up, she would have seen Anders looking back almost laughing. In seconds, the car roared into life and with a screech of tires they took off down the road. Anger burst through her, this was not what they had agreed on earlier when the two of them were in bed together. This was not the plan at all, and she was supposed to be at his side as he went in front of the Rua. All the Rua were going to see that she was no longer Alexi's but Davidov's, things had changed with their pack, and for the better. They would be together, defiant before the Rua and dictate to them what the terms were going to be. Dictate from strength and strength was something that all Mongols had in abundance, especially in front of lesser Garou. Anna's anger burst out of her and she threw open the door to the cottage and ran out after the car. She ran up onto the road, but it was already gone. Her anger and mixed emotions were clouding her. She felt pain and hurt and both sadness and jealously that she was not going to be with him at his moment of triumph.

Slowly her breathing calmed down and she closed her eyes. She swallowed hard but could not stop the single tear that rolled down her cheek. She brushed it away as she became aware of how quickly the darkness was falling. The fields around her were slowly turning grey. Folding her arms in front of her, she turned back towards the open door of the cottage. Her feet dragged as she moved slowly to cover the short distance. Back inside she would be warm, back inside she would wait for her Alpha to return. Anna could not do anything else as he had given an order and every fibre of her would obey her Alpha.

DANGER!

The feeling threw her up against the wall beside the door, her back slamming into the masonry before her body jumped forward. Her wolf bore her teeth and she felt herself snarl towards it. She dropped down onto her right knee and her fists were clenched ready for the fight. Her wolf craved to be released, her eyes scanned through the darkness looking for whatever the danger was, but the danger was backing away. Anna's strength grew. There was something the far side of the green field opposite and it knew it had been spotted. It backed away as she stared at the hedgerow. Whatever had been there was moving away. She rose to her feet and closed her eyes to concentrate with her ears. There were footsteps, but the soft earth made them difficult to hear, she could easily follow them, but she had been given an order and could not leave. Her body relaxed, and she opened her eyes and stared off into the darkness. The feeling of danger had left as had the feeling of anger, even this was something she had not anticipated. She spoke the one word that was in her mind out loud; the one word that described her enemies and her enemies had just found her. She said the word softly,

"Noctrailis"

she knew it would be loud enough for them to hear in this quiet part of the coast, and she knew what they were just as they knew what she was.

Chapter 69

Kyle got out of his car and looked around the busy farmyard. People were going back and forth, everyone was busy with something. Kyle's eyes caught the shape of rifles that were slung off the shoulders of a small mixed group of yard hands. Their faces and hands were blackened, and their camouflage clothing was the same pattern that he knew the British Army used for their snipers. Something serious was afoot. He watched as the group with the rifles headed off round the barn and out of sight.

"Hello," the greeting was mixed with a smile as someone passed close to him but before he could answer they disappeared inside the barn.

"Kyle," his name was shouted from the far side of the yard. The voice had come from the rear of two 4x4s parked at the far side of the yard. His body moved on instinct, an automatic reaction to a word of command, something that all soldiers are trained to do. Kyle walked towards the vehicles as Dermott came from the rear, he was talking to two younger men.

"Is that all clear?" he said, they nodded, "great, off you go then." Without hesitation, they turned and shot off down the side of the barn. Dermott looked towards Kyle and held out his hand in greeting, the handshake was firm, and he wasn't smiling.

"So how is Tony getting on?" Dermott walked past him. Kyle had to turn to walk with him as he was heading towards the door of the farmhouse, he noticed that the first question was about Tony and not Karen.

"I dropped him at the hospital before coming here," answered Kyle, Dermott nodded.

"That's good."

"Can you tell me what is happening here? And what is my part in it?" asked Kyle as he turned his head and looked around the farmyard. Dermott stopped by the door of the farmhouse and looked at him.

"Yes, it is simple, we have some members of another pack coming here tonight to explain what they have been doing and a few 'restrictions' to be placed on them." Dermott went to speak again but Kyle cut him off.

"And who are these 'other pack members' exactly?" Dermott breathed in and Kyle saw it. If anyone else had spoken to him like that then they would have been knocked down by him, and the look on Dermott's face changed to express that.

"Only out of respect for your father I will let you get away with that, only once will I or can I allow that ... do not interrupt me again ... clear?" Kyle nodded. Dermott's voice changed to a more mellow tone once he knew he had established that he was higher up the pack than Kyle was. "Our Alpha and the two council members will meet with them at the top of the lane ..." Dermott looked directly at Kyle. You and I will be Carl's principal security team with one other, triangle formation. I will be number one and you will be number two. I've been told you are close protection trained?" Dermott was taking the lead as the main bodyguard and would directly control the immediate protection of the principle and ensure he was removed with speed from any hostile act and Kyle would be first to engage any hostiles. Kyle felt himself nod in understanding, much like the two young men at the 4x4s had.

"I will be at his right-hand side," Dermott paused and waited for Kyle to finish the sentence to confirm he understood what it was he wanted him to do,

"And I will be slightly behind you ready to move forward and cover the evacuation."

"Which will be from the top of the yard and back into here," Dermott turned and directed with his right hand. From here Dermott went on to describe the positions of the overwatch sniper teams and that there would be an assault team at the far side of the hedge row and another down the far side of the main road. Even though it was late evening Kyle could still make out all the sites that Dermott was talking about.

"What will their set up be?" Kyle asked, Dermott glanced at him and with his right hand directed towards the end of the lane that leads up from the main road to the farm.

"They will have two cars at the bottom of the road ... that will stay there ... and two possibly three of them will come up the lane, I will stop them there." Kyle nodded as he looked over the ground that was being described to him.

"Will they be armed?"

"I would be," answered Dermott, "Now let's do a quick walk through of all that ..." Kyle walked beside Dermott as he walked over to the end of the lane.

"Do we expect them to use firearms?" Kyle asked after Dermott had finished speaking.

"I do."

"Then should we inform the police?" Kyle's question made Dermott's head shoot over and Dermott glared at him.

"We don't need the police!" Dermott scolded.

"If a crime is committed then it is the job of police ...." Kyle looked over at him, "I am still a police officer and I swore to uphold the law."

"And uphold the law we shall ... your law and ours," with that Dermott turned and walked away from him, Kyle wondered what was going to happen next. Dermott paused as he approached the corner of the farmhouse.

"You better come with me to the armoury then," Dermott turned his back to Kyle and walked off. Kyle ran for a few steps then slowed to a fast walk until he caught up with him. Dermott led Kyle round by the first of the large barns then on past the granary. On the right-hand side of the granary was a small single storey building that was newer than most on the farm. The red brick building had no windows and only one door that had a red light above it. The thick security door was ajar, and Kyle didn't recognise the man who was standing there but he straightened up as the two of them approached. Dermott greeted him in Irish, the man replied, and a short and friendly conversation flowed between the two before Kyle was led inside. The single room had a corridor that ran from the entrance and along the wall to Kyle's right. It was only six feet wide and the rest of the room was dissected into three large caged rooms. Kyle had seen this type of armoury many times, it seemed they were the same the world over.

The fluorescent strip lights burned and hissed as they walked underneath them. Kyle was being taken to the cage at the far end. He glanced at the rows of weapons that were secured inside, most were the bolt action hunting rifles and shotguns that he had expected to find but the third cage was different, very different. Kyle paused as they stopped by the hatch that was hanging open. The door to the cage was firmly locked and had an older man inside who greeted Dermott in the same way that he had been greeted at the door. Instead of bolt action rifles this cage had rows and rows of very new looking G36 rifles. Kyle looked over the rows of the weapons and spoke without even thinking.

"So, what will happen if the police find out about you all having a large amount of military type assault rifles?" Dermott and the armourer shared a look and a laugh.

"They already know" the armourer smiled "we have yearly official police inspections!"

"What?" replied a surprised Kyle.

"Yes, we have our legally required inspection of the armoury and all our firearm certificates to ensure they are all legal," answered Dermott.

Kyle pointed towards the German made weapons, "But how? Those types of weapons are illegal outside the police and military," Dermott leaned on the hatch and spoke to the armourer.

"Pass us one out, will you?" said Dermott, the armourer nodded and retrieved the first rifle from the rack on the wall. Dermott took the rifle and pulled the cocking handle rearwards and showed Kyle that it was clear before he handed the weapon over. He took the weapon and looked it over; it was brand new.

"These are single shot only, military have fully automatic ... the military ones have the shorter barrel ... we have the barrel at the legal requirements and the military have magazines of 30 or 50 rounds .... We only have magazines that hold five rounds ... all totally legal," Dermott explained.

"But what is your justification?" Kyle asked.

"Justification?" Dermott repeated, "If we have to deal with a charging stag then we can defend life," Dermott and the armourer shared a glance as Dermott spoke again, "They are not for use outside the farm ... under any circumstances."

"How long have you had them?" he asked.

"Couple of months," replied the armourer.

"What did you have before that?" The armourer looked at Dermott who nodded in approval.

"MP5's but they were not powerful enough, so we had to improve." Kyle handed the rifle back to Dermott who in turn handed it back to the armourer.

"Have you got his FAC?" asked Dermott. The armourer nodded and lifted a file from under the hatch. He flicked through the pages until he came to what he wanted and turned the file to the open page. Kyle stepped forward and looked at the recently issued and valid Fire Arms Certificate with his name on it, everything here was in fact legal.

"Now let's get you back up to the farmhouse ... they will be here soon," with that Dermott waved goodbye and walked towards the door of the armoury. Kyle followed a few seconds later.

∞∞∞∞

Davidov was sitting in the back of the car. His eyes were closed, and he was breathing slowly. Anders was in the front passenger seat with Viktor driving, the second team were following behind them. There was silence in the car. A silence that Davidov was relishing, it had been the correct decision to leave Anna at the cottage. The car rose and fell in the country lanes, they had gone to a car park that was near a forest and they had walked through a slow practice of what they would do if the Rua tried anything. Training, training, training, 'The more you sweat in training, the less you bleed in battle,' Davidov had heard from his instructors during his army service. He felt himself breathe in and slowly exhale as his eyes opened. The car slowed down, they were approaching the entrance to the farm.

"We are here," Anders stated. Davidov waited for the car to come to a complete stop before he moved towards the door. Anders opened the door from the outside and stepped back to allow him room to exit the car. Davidov straightened up and looked around himself. Viktor was standing by the driver's door and was looking all around while Anders was beaming like a child on Christmas Day. The second car slowly drove past stopping at the side of the road at the far side of the entrance to the farm.

"What can you see?" Davidov asked. Anders tilted his head as he listened to his ear piece. Davidov looked over at the farmhouse and saw how brightly it was lit up. A group of several Rua standing at the far side slowly moved back out of sight around the building.

"They have a team at the top of the barn and another on the hillside 500 metres to our right." Anders was repeating what he was listening to, they had their own team that was behind them and was covering them as they attended the meeting.

"The council members are not to be harmed," Davidov stated.

"I obey," answered Anders who then repeated the command towards his jacket. A high-pitched noise suddenly came from his ear as he ripped the earpiece out, Davidov smiled, the Rua were using their counter measures again.

"Everyone knows what to do?" Davidov asked, Anders straightened up.

"Everyone understands and will obey your orders," Davidov nodded as the single figure walked towards them. The teenage boy was wearing a sweatshirt and jeans with neatly combed hair, he stopped about 10 metres away from them.

"You are to follow me," he said. He did not shout, nor did he look Davidov in the eye. He bowed his head slightly and turned and walked back up the path. He was being polite and courteous, much as Davidov would expect to be treated as Alpha. Davidov gained eye contact with each of the group that were there. Only Anders would come with him while the rest would pick out individual Rua and if anything happened they would be the ones that they would kill.

The job of their own sniper pair would be to take out the opposite sniper team before they could engage their Alpha. The game of chess had begun.

Davidov walked up the path, deliberately taking time with each step, as if each step was a message to those who were watching, and many would be watching. The CCTV cameras would have quite an audience tonight. The teenager stopped at the top of the lane and Davidov came to a stop as Anders walked forward to stand in front of him.

"My Alpha requests that you wait here," the teenager again looked down and was respectful, Anders went to speak but Davidov stopped him.

"Please inform your Alpha that we are here, and we wish to speak with him," Davidov was making the request formal, much to Anders obvious annoyance. The teenager nodded and turned and walked away. Davidov glanced over to his right, there were Rua in the hedgerow, five at least. Anders glanced over towards them, he had seen them as well. If the shooting started, this is where he would fire first.

The door of the farmhouse opened, and two Rua walked out and stood on either side of the door. A senior Rua came out and started to walk towards them. Davidov slightly moved to his right so he could see him clearly. This Rua was full Garou and held a position of authority in their pack, he stopped only a few metres away.

"Who are you?" Davidov asked. The Rua was not as respectful as the teenager, quite the opposite in fact, Davidov felt his wolf bear his teeth towards him.

"I am Dermott McMurragh of the Northern Dun of the Rua," his greeting was also formal. "During this meeting, you will not make any sudden movements towards my Alpha or any member of this pack, to do so ..."

"I know the rules, Rua," Davidov spat.

"We will go over them anyway so we ... 'avoid' ... any misunderstanding," answered Dermott, Davidov nodded.

"You will not make any movement towards my Alpha unless directly invited to do so." Dermott looked at Anders, "Your escort will not move at all," Anders glared back at Dermott as he continued speaking.

"The two council members will stand to your left and our right, half way between each of us ... their ruling is final." Davidov again nodded in agreement, "at the end of the meeting you both will walk back down the lane to the rest of your pack." Davidov didn't move this time. "During the meeting only, the council members and the two pack Alphas will be permitted to speak." Dermott was again looking at Anders as he spoke to drive the message home, "any non-compliance of these rules and none of you will leave here alive." Davidov looked at Dermott as Anders grunted. He went to speak but Davidov cut him off.

"I agree to these terms," said Davidov as he spoke to Dermott. The two Mongols stood in silence as Dermott turned and walked away from them as he headed back towards the farmhouse. Seconds later the door opened and one by one the small group of men gathered outside then walked towards Davidov and Anders. Davidov looked over the Alpha O'Brien, the Rua Dermott was in front of him with another behind him and to the right and then the two council members separated from them and slowly they formed a small circle. Davidov looked towards the council members and smiled.

"Godspodine Grishin ..."

"English," The demand came from O'Brien, all eyes looked over at him. "I am Alpha of these lands and all conversation will be conducted in English. Both the council members looked at each other then Grishin nodded once. Davidov started again.

"Mister ... Grishin and Mister ... Tatamovich," Davidov nodded towards them, both nodded once in recognition.

"Firstly, you will tell me exactly what happened to Chernov?" demanded Carl.

"He died," answered Davidov, Grishin let out a short laugh.

"How did he come to die?" Carl expanded his question. Davidov paused then took a slow breath in before he answered.

"He was weak and showed his weakness and he could no longer run our pack." The answer spoke for itself, no one there needed any other detail, and it was pack business.

"Now I want a ruling ..."

"You will listen to what I have to say Sprogis, no demands from you ... I am Alpha here." Davidov didn't move but Anders did. His body tensed and his arm flinched as if he was about to jump forward to protect his Alpha from this verbal attack, but everyone else flinched too and in less than a second Dermott's pistol was in his hand and it was pointing directly at Anders as were several other weapons.

"Stop," shouted Grishin. The moment froze in time until he spoke again. "Put your weapon away and you ..." Grishin looked at Anders, "You know the terms of this meeting ... Do that again and I will allow the Rua to act ... understand?" Anders nodded and visibly took a step backwards as an act of submission.

"We are Mongols ... we do not take kindly to orders from others," explained Davidov, "he was just protecting me," Dermott replaced the pistol back into the holster on his waist belt.

"What is it that you want?" Grishin asked.

"We have been hunted all the way across Europe, conflict after conflict and our numbers have suffered from that ..." Davidov looked over at Carl, "I only want what is left of us to be left alone so we can live out our lives here in the Green land in peace." Davidov had made his request quietly but he stared O'Brien in the eye. Grishin looked around him then looked over at O'Brien as he spoke.

"It is for the Alpha of the Northern Den to decide, it is a local matter," Carl nodded and stared back at Davidov.

"You will follow the terms that I set here tonight, and you will not stray from them or you and all your ... pack, will be destroyed." Davidov's eyes shot over to his right in the direction of the team in the hedgerow. There was no movement, but he acknowledged them anyway.

"What are your terms?" he asked.

"I have already stated my terms to the council members, and they agree all is fair," Davidov glanced over at both the council members who were expressionless and emotionless.

"And what are those terms?" Davidov asked again.

"You will inform me of all your movements around this country, you will inform me of all your residences and any interaction with the sapiens will first be sanctioned through me."

"What do you mean by that?" Davidov knew what he meant but was making it heard.

"You and your pack will not mate with any sapien in this land ... no offspring, understand." Carl raised his voice slightly to reinforce his point, Davidov paused before looking around himself. The Rua were putting a cap on the size of his pack.

"What other terms?" he asked.

"You will come here once a month to report on everything your pack does," Davidov's face crunched up.

"My pack business is my pack business, not yours," he answered angrily.

"If you want to live to see tomorrow you will do as I say, these are 'our' lands, not yours." Carl stared straight at Davidov, he could see the anger in his eyes starting to boil over.

"What about our own dances? We still have to celebrate them."

"You can, but you will inform me of where and when ... and you will avoid all contact with sapien kind."

"What if we are attacked?" Davidov asked.

"You can defend yourselves but only in sapien form ... you will not draw attention to our kind ...." Carl paused before delivering the end of the sentence, "like what you have done in Belfast, Coleraine and Castleroe ... that will not happen again ... understand?" Davidov nodded.

I have some terms of my own," he glanced over at Grishin, but Carl still stared at him.

"State your terms," Carl's voice had a hint of menace in it.

"I want my pack to be left alone, if I agree to these terms then you will let us be." Carl stared at him as he continued. "This is my only request, we are to be left alone to live our lives. Our pack business is our pack business, you will be kept informed, but my pack decisions are mine to make and mine alone." Davidov raised his voice slightly. "You leave us alone and we will leave you alone, we want nothing to do with your pack business, you know the reasons why we had to leave our own lands; we only want our peace. You have yours, let us have ours." Silence fell over the group as eyes bounced from one to another, the matter of Paddy M'Kane's death was not brought up but these terms would stop any further action over it. Before Grishin made the first move by nodding his head twice, Carl glanced at Grishin then stared back at Davidov.

"The council has approved these terms and we agreed to them, do you agree to the terms on your pack?" Carl had raised his voice, so everyone could hear him.

"I agree to these terms," he answered.

"If you break these terms then I will defend these lands and this pack as I see fit," Carl's threat left no doubt as to their full implication.

If you break your terms then my pack will defend itself from all aggression." Davidov's answer carried the same threat.

"Do you agree?" asked Carl.

"I agree," answered Davidov, at this Grishin stepped forward a single step and raised his voice to almost a shout.

"Then as of this night new terms exist between the Rua of the Northern Den and the Mongol Garou ..." Grishin looked at everyone standing there. "These terms are binding and let no Garou break them or they themselves will be broken .... It will be recorded in our history and brought into our law," Grishin first looked at Carl then over at Davidov.

"It is agreed, now go your separate ways." Davidov nodded towards Carl and both he and Anders turned and walked back down the lane towards the waiting cars. Carl turned and walked back towards the farmhouse with Kyle walking behind him. Dermott caught his eye and stopped him by the door as the rest walked inside.

"They've got a lot to talk about that is not for your ears," Kyle nodded as people appeared out of the darkness. The door of the farmhouse slammed shut as Kyle heard the raised voice of Carl shouting inside. Dermott motioned to follow him, Kyle turned away and walked through the gathering crowd.

"Was that not the result he wanted?" Kyle asked. Dermott looked over at him.

"If the council had not been there all 'that lot' would be dead ... you don't come onto someone else's land and make your own demands, it's not done," Dermott wasn't hiding his anger either, down the lane Davidov looked back up at the farmhouse.

"Are you really going to live by those terms?" Anders asked.

Davidov's head shot round. "Get in the car, they can still hear us!" Davidov finished off his command with a direct slap.

"Why was the sapien policeman behind O'Brien?" Anders asked out loud before Davidov looked away and climbed into the back of the car.

Chapter 70

Mike was already in Sean's office as Sean walked in through the main door of the team's office. Mike was sitting on one of the chairs facing Sean's desk. Sean knew he was early as none of the investigating team had arrived yet. Mike looked up and smiled as Sean walked towards the office door.

"Mornin'," he greeted, Sean grunted as he moved around the desk to take his seat.

Mike was chatting away about everything and nothing, but Sean wasn't taking any of it in. There was one topic that he had not mentioned so far so Sean asked directly.

"How are things at home?" Mike stopped at the question.

"Aye, ok," Sean knew that meant that they weren't.

"We got the stills from the CCTV footage that Special Branch gave us," Mike had changed the conversation straight away. Things were getting worse and Mike was focusing all his attention on work, which was good from a work point of view but bad from a marriage one. He had seen it before, in fact had been there himself but thankfully his marriage had survived, many police marriages didn't, "and we had clearly seen the woman and have good clear full facial prints of two other men and a blonde-haired woman."

"Have we seen them before?" Sean asked as he raised his hand to welcome Simon as he was walking into the main office.

"One of them yes, Mornin',"

"Morning all," answered a very cheerful Simon who walked past Mike and landed himself on the other chair. Mike looked at Sean they both looked at the smiling Simon.

"What has got you all happy?" Mike asked

"I don't know what you mean!" Simon replied.

"Were you out on a date last night?" Mike was fishing.

"What I do in my time off is up to me ..."

"So, you were then .... Where did you take what's her name?" the banter between the two men had started, Mike was deliberately baiting Simon, but the only person who couldn't see it was Simon himself. Sean brought it to a close when more of the team started to arrive. Waves and greetings were exchanged as the desks started to fill up.

"So anyway," Sean straightened up in his chair, "Where are we up to?" he asked. Mike handed out the 8" x 10" photos that had been sitting beside him.

"Right we got these yesterday from Special Branch, they were taken from a CCTV camera at a petrol garage in Castlerock last week. I believe it is the same woman that was at the scene in Belfast and near the Riverside murder in Coleraine." Simon nodded as he handed the pictures one at a time over to Sean, "we have placed the man with her also being nearby in Coleraine as well."

"But we haven't formally identified them yet?" asked Sean.

"Not 100%, no," answered Mike.

"So, what are we doing about this?" Sean asked.

"Well," Simon started, "Mike and I are going to head up to Coleraine today and run this through to local coppers there and see if any of them recognise any of these faces," Simon glanced at Mike before looking at Sean, "hopefully someone will have scooped or at least stopped one of them," Sean nodded.

"Any more on the Chernov fella?" Sean asked.

"Yep," replied Mike as he opened the folder again. "He bought a property on the Lodge Road in Coleraine and paid cash for a used car from a local dealer."

"His name was on the deeds?" Sean asked.

"Yeah, signed, sealed and delivered," replied Mike.

"The Latvian consulate in London wants the body handed over to them as soon as possible," injected Simon.

"Why is that?" Sean asked.

"It seems his brother owns a lot of the oil industry and has a lot of pull over some of the local establishment."

"That figures," said Sean as he looked through the window of his office, "have we got everything we want from forensics?"

"It seems so," answered Mike.

"Then release the body,"

"Are you still heading to the press conference this afternoon?" Mike asked.

"Yeah, don't really want to, but the Super wants me there." Mike and Simon exchanged a glance. Superintendent Sutcliffe didn't share the limelight with anyone unless it was to deflect flak. This was an open press conference being held at police headquarters, neither of them liked what it added up to.

"Oh, I found some stuff out about that Mullen fella from the Met police," said Simon. Sean looked at Mike and motioned for him to close the door of the office. Mike reached over with his right hand to gently push the door closed; things like this were not discussed in front of young detectives.

"Well it seems that Super Forester and the good inspector were sergeants at the same time here in Belfast some time ago," Simon started.

"Which station?" Sean interjected.

"Musgrave Street," he answered, "then 'it is rumoured' that when the Super was going for his Special Branch exams he was also having a bit of an affair with a female sergeant that was working with Mullen at the time ..." Simon paused.

"Go on," said Mike.

"Well ..." continued Simon, "The details are not exact but there was something of an irregularity with something Mullen was doing on the side and the Super found out about it and Mullen threatened to expose his affair ..."

"That would destroy his chance of getting into the branch!" said Mike.

"Possibly his whole career as well," said Simon, "and it appeared that they had a little 'set to' in the car park but it was the Super who got to the station chief first and before things really did 'explode' ...."

"One was off to Special Branch and the other off to London," Mike finished the sentence.

"What was the thing on the side that Mullen was doing?" Sean asked, Simon shrugged.

"A business or something, but whatever it was it was enough to get him moved to the training centre while his transfer to the Met went through."

"Which means it wasn't exactly legal then," suggested Mike.

"Possibly," answered Simon.

"Was there a connection between Mullen and the woman Sergeant?" Mike asked.

"Don't know," Simon shrugged, "but the Super was married at the time." Sean nodded his head and looked out over the main office.

"Are you going to the boxing match this Thursday?" Mike asked, Sean looked at him.

"Wasn't planning on it, why?" he replied.

"Well we have invited the military along ..." said Mike.

"And we can see if we can find out what they know?" continued Simon.

"Exactly!" said Mike.

"Are you going to be heading home that night?" Mike asked.

"Yeah, I..."

"I will give it a miss," the statement from Sean got the other two looking over at him.

"Ok," answered Mike.

"But keep me info'd on what you find out from them."

"Will do boss,"

"What time are you two heading to Coleraine?" Sean asked and changed the conversation entirely.

"I'm thinking right about now," Mike looked over at Simon, "you really did score last night, didn't you?" Sean was thankful that the mug that Simon threw at Mike was empty and that Mike caught it before it smashed on the wall behind him.

∞∞∞

Cara-Marie was scanning her notebook as she sat quietly behind her desk at the newspaper; she saw the words, but she wasn't reading them. Her mind had wandered after she had filed her last news story in the editor's mailbox. The story was fine, but her mind wasn't on the topic. Her mind was in fact far from any of the topics the editor had wanted her to cover since she walked in this morning. The wolf in her nightmares had returned, it was still staring at her and howling as it walked away. Was it protecting her or chasing her? She had never been one for trying to interpret dreams and for a long time she had thought it was all a load of nonsense, but then a lot of what she believed had been shaken over the last while. Her phone bleeped, Mark's name came up on the screen, she glanced over to her right and realised that she hadn't noticed him leaving. 'MEET ME IN THE COFFEE SHOP. I HAVE SOME INFO FOR YOU.' Her senses returned to her as her mind focused on the words. He had been sitting behind his desk earlier and they would normally share stuff openly. Whatever this was it wasn't for the ears of the rest of the team, she replied, 'OK, SEE YOU SOON, CM' and shut down her desktop. She reached for her coat and shoulder bag and darted towards the door.

"Where are you off to?" Her head shot round to see Kevin leaning up against the door frame of his office, he was holding several sheets of paper in his left hand, she paused before she answered.

"Just heading out to meet someone about the school story," and with that she was gone. The door shut behind her as he glanced down at the school story he had just printed off from his mailbox. It was the very story that she had just sent him, and he was about to say 'thanks,'; wherever she was going, it was nothing to do with local schools. She started to button up her coat as she walked along the side of the street. She felt her own pace quicken as she headed towards the coffee shop. She seemed to be spending a lot of her time there lately. As she weaved through the shoppers dotted along Church Street, Cara-Marie didn't notice that the street was quieter than usual. In her rush, she didn't notice the windows of the old Woolworths shop had been boarded up, nor did she notice the scruffy looking young man leaning up against the wall at the far side of the street who was paying a lot of attention to her as she marched up the street. He lifted a cigarette up to his mouth and sucked hard. The end of it glowed for a few seconds as he breathed the smoke in before exhaling and allowing the smoke to be forced out of his nostrils; his eyes followed her as she carried on then passed from his sight. He glanced at his watch and made a mental note of the time.

Cara-Marie walked into the busy coffee shop. There were a small group of mothers with their toddlers on their laps enjoying a morning coffee and gossiping, she walked on past the two people who were cueing at the till and waved at Rachel Boyd who was serving.

"Yes, I was," answered Rachel, she had obviously just been recognised by the two teenagers who were waiting for their order, "I was also interviewed by CNN as well," Cara-Marie tried not to look straight at her as she walked towards the bottom of the stairs. Rachel was enjoying her new-found status. She entered the quiet first floor to find Mark sitting alone at a table. He rose to his feet in a very polite way as she walked up and dropped her bag on the floor. There was a mug of coffee waiting for her. A copy of their latest edition was spread out across the table and Mark had a pen in his right hand as if he was making notes but there was no writing on the pages.

"Hi'ya,"

"Hi'ya ... oh thanks," she said as she sat down and lifted the still warm mug towards her face, "busy morning?" she asked as she motioned towards the newspaper with her head, he looked at the paper then quietly let out a short laugh.

"Oh no ... just going over a few things," Mark started to fold the newspaper up and this revealed one of his photographic folders and a couple of A4 manila envelopes. Protruding out of the top of one of these was an official looking document which Cara-Marie's eyes scanned over. The address at the top was of a letting agent in Portrush and she guessed that the contents of that envelope were a new letting agreement between them and Mark; things weren't good at home. Mark started by talking about some of the other bits he had been doing and problems with one of his cameras. He was especially pleased about a photograph he had sold for a nice sum. She was letting him talk, she didn't answer anything he said for a few moments and it was during this that she started to notice that he looked like he hadn't slept at all last night. He hadn't shaved, and his clothes were more unkept than usual.

"Great," she finally said, "but you could have told me all this back at the office ... why here?" she asked; he looked around at the empty room.

"I have found some stuff out for you," Mark reached under the newspaper again and brought out a new notebook. It had writing on it that clearly wasn't his. It was neat, tidy and well-spaced out; in fact, it looked quite feminine. She sat forward on her seat, both hands clutching the warm mug in her hands and studied Mark as he read.

"First of all, the physio that you were asking about is called 'Kelly Vixen' and she works for occupational health and welfare of the police down near Carrick ...." Mark studied the notes in front of him.

"Vixen?" she said out loud.

"Yes," replied Mark, "been down there a few years and ...." Mark paused.

"And what?" asked Cara-Marie.

"And she is well known through the police."

"What for?"

"How can I put this? ... 'liberal' with her affections ..." Mark grimaced, she nodded in understanding, "she works mostly down at Carrick but does do clinics at various stations around the province ..." Cara-Marie thought about what he was saying,

"Nothing there we can use though," she stated,

"Not really," he answered, "she also runs a private clinic out of her house down in Ballymoney."

"So, a copper could go there for perfectly legitimate reasons ..." Cara-Marie didn't finish her sentence.

"Yeah," nodded Mark.

"What else have you got?" she asked.

"You little friend Foster has had quite a busy life so far," Mark set the notebook down and reached into his camera bag to pull out a couple of photocopies. The first was a picture of Kyle looking a lot younger in a military uniform that she did not recognise, "Six years in the French Foreign Legion ..." Mark flipped the page over and started to read the notes on the second page, "His dad and elder brother were both killed in a car bomb in the early 80's" she looked up from the photocopy as Mark continued, "he was only a toddler at the time and was sent over to Canada to live with an aunt," Mark scanned the page as he paused, "came back when he was in his late teens then dropped off the map for a while before turning up in France." Cara-Marie stared at the young face on the page. She looked at the other photos, but they were all much the same, photos of Kyle in camouflage clothes and holding a rifle that she had never seen before. "Then two years ago got into the police and after training was sent to Coleraine for his first two years' probation."

"So, he is up for a move then?" she asked.

"Probably, but he could request to stay here … but a lot of coppers who come to here opt to go elsewhere after their two years are up," she nodded as she looked back down at the first page. Kyle was staring straight at the camera. He was wearing a brown dress uniform, clean and pressed, and a peaked white hat with large red epaulettes on his shoulders.

"Oh, and he got some commendation or something after doing something in the Ivory Coast a few years ago …" she looked, "but I couldn't find out any details," Cara-Marie looked back at the face on the page.

"All good …. but what does all this mean when it comes together?"

"Well the one thing I found that you may find 'of interest' is …." Mark scrolled through the pages of notes as she stared at him.

"What?" she asked, "stop procrastinating," she demanded, he smiled.

"Well you know the other copper … Fallon."

"Yes," Cara-Marie's face contorted with confusion, she couldn't see where this was going.

"As it turns out, in addition to being a copper here in Coleraine, he also works down at that Deer farm that is owned by that O'Brien fella that is away … you know," Mark was spiralling his right forefinger towards the window.

"It's down towards Kilrea," she finished for him.

"Yes, that's the place," Mark looked back down at the notebook, "Well, it has transpired that Foster's father used to own it …. it was left to O'Brien after his dad's death and he has been running the business ever since," her face widened in realisation.

"I wonder if he knows that?" she said out loud,

"Who and which bit?" Mark asked.

"I wonder if Tony knows that Kyle's late father used to own that farm and I wonder if O'Brien is aware that Kyle even exists and ……." a smile spread over Cara's face. Mark shut his eyes and shook his head.

"The last time you smiled like that my work load doubled …" Cara-Marie was looking out the window, her mind was racing with ideas. She finished off the coffee and stood up to leave.

"Thanks for all this," she said as she stood and walked away.

"No problems," answered Mark.

"Don't worry I will do the leg work on this one," she said over her shoulder, "you can spend the time with your other half." Cara-Marie was at the top of the stairs as she said the words, her head turned to look at him and share the huge smile that was over her face. The smile dropped when she saw the expression on Mark's face. Mark's eyes had gone red and he looked like he was about to burst into tears. She didn't know what was going on and she knew he probably didn't want to talk about it. "Thanks for all this!" she raised the photocopies. Mark nodded. Cara-Marie stepped back to let two teenagers pass then glanced back into the room. Mark was busy tidying things up and had just bent over to reach into his camera bag. Just as she reached the fresh air outside her phone started to ring, she fumbled through one of her pockets and pulled the phone out, it was Kevin, she paused before she pressed the green button to receive the call,

"Hello."

"Cara? Hi'ya, it's me …"

"Hi'ya …" she answered.

"When you're finished what you're doing come back here, I've got some details for you."

"Details of what?" she asked.

"The press conference today!"

"What press conference, where?" no one told her anything about a press conference.

"The press conference by the police in Belfast about the werewolf thingy," his words hit her like a brick, he was acknowledging these may exist, and he was giving her the job of covering it.

"I'm on my way, I will be there in a few minutes," and with that she took off like a shot. Cara-Marie didn't see Mark leaving or see he was nearly crying, nor did she notice the scruffy young man smoking another cigarette at the far side of the street watching as she ran off up the street.

Chapter 71

Davidov and Anders looked at each other then back at Anna. Davidov turned and sat down on the chair in the living room of the cottage; she was furious and was standing with her hands on her hips.

"Well?" she demanded.

"Well, what?" Davidov answered back.

"What are we going to do about them?"

"The Noctrailis?"

"Yes!" she shouted, Davidov shook his head.

"Nothing."

"Nothing?" Anna was angry she hadn't been taken to the Rua last night, angry that Davidov hadn't returned until this morning, and now she was getting angrier as it seemed he wasn't taking the Noctrailis seriously.

"Yes, nothing, you went over to where it had been this morning?" he asked very quietly.

"Yes," the question confused her.

"And it has gone, yes?"

"Yes,"

"Then there is no problem."

"What? There is a problem," Anna marched forward towards where Davidov was sitting, "We need to gather the pack; we need to go out and hunt it down," Anders glanced over at Davidov who hadn't moved, he just sat there. "We need to kill it, kill them all, they have to know that 'we' control these lands now, they need to know that they can no longer do as they please." Anna glared at Davidov, never taking her eyes off him. "To do nothing is weak." Davidov looked up at her as she glared back at him. "Alexi was weak, he would have bowed down and done nothing … he was weak …" Anders glanced between the two as Anna continued. "To do nothing is weak … you are weak." Anders face widened at her expression of defiance. Davidov looked over towards him.

"Anders," he spoke quietly, Anders looked at his Alpha.

"Yes," he replied.

"Wait for me at the car, I will be out shortly." Anders straightened up.

"I obey," with that, he turned and shut the door behind him.

"Well?" demanded the defiant Anna, her anger rising at him.

Davidov suddenly sprang up and lashed out catching Anna with the back of his right hand. The force of the strike sent her flying across the living room and slammed her into the wall. She landed on the floor and rolled onto her side. Her mind was frozen with the shock of what had just happened, she had not fully realised what was happening as Davidov's full weight came through his knees into her abdomen and pelvis as he landed on her. His left hand grabbed her right wrist and slammed it into her chest. Davidov's face was full of rage, his eyes widened with madness as he started to rein blows down into her face. He screamed at her, each word was followed by the full force of his physical anger.

"NEVER … TALK … TO … ME … LIKE … THAT … AGAIN … KNOW … YOUR … PLACE …" Davidov's face started to blur, his words started to slow down as her left arm tried to fend off the blows, but it was to no avail, the blows kept coming.

Anders was standing by the car and he could hear her screaming. Davidov was putting her in her place, she could not tell the pack Alpha what to do, what he should do, that was his decision and his decision alone. No one could do that for him, a small grin spread over his face, he was enjoying this. Davidov was the Alpha and no one doubted that. Anna had been acting as if she was the Alpha, ordering others what to do. This would never happen again and Davidov was making sure of that. His word was final, he was the Alpha. The sound from inside the cottage quietened and he could see Davidov moving around inside through the window. A small car sped past where the car was parked. The three teenagers had their music playing loudly and they were massively in over the speed limit. Davidov had told them all to obey the local laws as they were not to draw attention from the local police. He had said the Rua were in the police and had stopped them at a checkpoint. They were to avoid the police and most importantly avoid any contact with the Rua that he had not first approved. Davidov had a plan and the plan was coming together.

The front door of the cottage opened and Davidov walked out and nodded towards the car. Anders opened the driver's door and climbed in. Davidov got into the passenger's seat and slammed the door. Anders noticed that his hands were still wet after he had washed them. Davidov didn't mention Anna, he didn't have to.

"First, we will go to the house in Coleraine then out to Yelina's," Anders nodded and started the car. The car jumped forward and sped up the country road. Anders didn't speak, he would wait until he was spoken to. "Is Pet'er there?" Davidov asked. Anders felt his gut turn at the thought of Pet'er alone in the house with Yelina.

"Yes," he answered.

"Good, you two may have to sort this little Noc problem out sooner than we first planned." The grin returned to Anders face, it was an excited grin, it was anticipating what was going to happen and the grin stayed on his face all the way into Coleraine.

∞∞∞

Simon stared out the window of Mike's car; he was staring at everything and yet staring at nothing. Mike glanced over at him. Simon hadn't said a word since passing Antrim.

"I wonder how the boss is going to handle the press conference," Mike looked at the clock on the dashboard of the car, "It should just about be starting."

"Yeah, yeah it should; he'll be ok," Simon looked at Mike, "as long as he isn't asked any questions, he should be fine," they both smiled in an attempt to ease some of the tension.

"That's one thing he isn't going to miss about the job when he goes," said Mike.

"Very true," agreed Simon, "but the Super is there so he probably won't get a word in edge-ways anyway; that, I think, will suit him."

"So, what was the score with this fella from London?" Mike had been waiting to speak to Simon alone about it, without other ears listening in.

"Inspector Mullen of the Metropolitan Police," stated Simon.

"Until yesterday I had never heard of him, and ...." Mike didn't finish the sentence.

"Well the Super offered him Sean's job."

"Why him?" asked Mike.

"Well, he was RUC, so it wouldn't be that much of a change for him but from what I can gather as soon as he found out about the Special Branch involvement ...."

"He ran a mile," Mike completed what Simon had been saying, "but was that the only reason?" Mike asked,

"Let's hope so, how long is this going to take?"

"Probably won't get out of the station today so we will have to come back up tomorrow to do the last of the stuff at Castleroe," answered Mike.

"No problems," said Simon as he shifted in his seat, "No problems at all."

∞∞∞

Cara-Marie was furious. It had been a very long time since she had been so angry, and her little car was paying the price. She had connected her phone up to her car just before she had left and had fought her way through the traffic around Belfast to get herself up and onto the M2, once the motorway opened she called Kevin.

"Hello,"

"Hi'ya, it's Cara-Marie here," she said, her eyes caught the clock that was on the screen of the phone, it was just before 4PM.

"Oh hello," he seemed a little surprised to hear from her, "how did it go?" he asked.

"Well they've released CCTV footage from Castlerock showing three people that they want to talk to."

"Do you have copies of them?" Cara-Marie felt her face crunch up, what sort of a stupid question was that? Of course, she had copies, every journalist there got copies and they would be on the evening news tonight.

"Yes, got them."

"Good, no problems, see you when you get back," and the phone went dead. Cara-Marie's car suddenly sped up as she pushed down on the accelerator but released it just as quick. Getting caught speeding would only make her life more difficult and she could do without the hassle. She tapped the screen of the phone again.

"Hi Cara," Mark sounded sheepish.

"Sorry, did I wake you up?"

"No, I have been busy at work, did you have fun having tea and biscuits with the Chief Constable?" Mark laid on the sarcasm in his voice.

"Ha bloody ha, no, he wasn't there."

"Cool," he said, "did you get what you wanted?" he asked.

"Not exactly."

"Define 'not exactly', as that can mean a lot with you."

"Well," she paused, "I got copies of stills from the CCTV footage they released."

"Brilliant," he answered.

"But it all went kinda downhill from there." There was a laugh down the phone,

"What did you do?" Mark asked.

"Well ... it was all coming from that Superintendent that's up his own backside ..."

"Sutcliffe?"

"That's the one, so I asked that Inspector who is actually doing all the work 'is the police service looking for werewolves?" Mark laughed again.

"And what happened then?"

"Well the inspector said something about looking for those responsible for committing gross acts of murder etc etc."

"Bollocks, bollocks, bollocks," Mark interpreted.

"Exactly, then the Superintendent got on his high horse and started gobbing off about being professional and all that crap."

"So, what did you say next?"

"Well," Cara-Marie breathed in before continuing. "I asked about the witness statements and the stuff already done on TV and internet about werewolf attacks."

"I bet they didn't like that!" answered Mark.

"No, that prick gave me a lecture about sticking to covering fetes and school plays and I should leave investigating serious crimes to the police!" Cara-Marie felt the anger rise in her once again and she recounted what had happened earlier.

"Oh, go on, what did you do after that?" he asked between the chuckles of laughter.

"Told him what I thought," he could imagine how that went, "I mean, who the hell does he think he is?" she demanded.

"A senior detective in the police perhaps?" he injected.

"Yeah, he came out with some crap like that, then started on about writing fantasy and sticking to reporting the news,"

"Ah ... this is brilliant, so how did it all end?" Mark asked.

"Well there was a journalist from Germany also started asking about werewolves and when it started to descend into laughter she stopped.

"Really?" he said.

"Yes, really," she answered.

"Well I will have to watch that in a bit then."

"You can stay right there, mister. I have stuff for you to sort out before you go anywhere tonight."

"Oooooh, your place or mine," Mark made a silly voice as he said it. It had an immediate effect on her as she went from being angry to laughing in less than a second.

"Let's keep it at our work desks, shall we?" she answered back.

"Oh, boring,"

"You obviously have nothing better to do then?" she commented.

"Got loads now that you are on your way back, where are you now?" she looked around the scenery that was flashing past her car.

"Approaching Ballymena,"

"Ok, see you in a bit."

"Ok, bye then," Cara-Marie reached over to cancel the call when he spoke again.

"Shall I get Chinese in for you then?" he asked.

"After what happened last time we tried to have a Chinese do you think that's wise?"

"Err," Mark thought about it. "I was offering to pay!" was the only answer he could think of.

"Ok, deal," she cut the phone off before he could say another word. It wouldn't take her that long to type up a report on the press conference and Mark could sort out the photos that she got from the police. It wouldn't be a late one, but it would be late enough for her to miss her Mum calling round with another invite to dinner where she would be inviting some of her friends round as well. Since Cara wasn't taking an interest in developing her own social life it would have to fall to her mother to sort it out for her.

Chapter 72

Mike closed the door of their office in the Coleraine police station. Simon had left moments before to head down towards where the car was parked; as the door clicked shut his phone rang.

"What's up?" asked Mike as he started to walk through the police station.

"Are you two nearly done up there?" Sean asked, his question was almost an order.

"Yeah just about, got the pictures distributed around the uniformed sections up here and tied up a few other dead ends ...."

"Like?" Sean asked.

"Like there was no one at the house in Lodge Road, looks like whoever was there hasn't been there in a couple of days?" said Mike.

"What makes you say that?"

"Well," Mike started, he paused at the main entrance to let two uniformed police officer's past. As he stepped outside, he continued his sentence, "there was a pile of mail inside the front door that hadn't been picked up in quite a while." Mike looked over towards Simon who was standing beside the car chatting on his mobile. Mike could tell by the smiles and the laughter that he was talking to the new woman in his life. Simon didn't laugh like that normally, it was good to see him this kind of happy.

"Yeah, no problems," answered Sean

"How did the press conference go?" he asked, Sean made a noise that let out his annoyance.

"As well as expected I suppose," Mike knew what that meant. "That wee journo from Coleraine was there, started asking about werewolves and the Super shot her down."

"I bet she didn't take too kindly to that!" Mike replied. Simon walked around to the far end of the line of parked cars, he didn't want him to hear what he was saying.

"I wish I had been there." Sean could just imagine the Super's annoyance. "Well the cameras were there so it will probably be on the evening news!" Sean's tone lifted a bit as Mike glanced at his watch.

"Err, boss, it is half past 7, the evening news was an hour and a half ago," Sean had probably been in his office all that time. Mike glanced at the darkening sky as their conversation paused,

"Bugger," was Sean's reply, "he'll be here in a minute."

"Who will?" asked Mike.

"The Super. When you two have finished what you are doing up there just head on home and we can chat tomorrow."

"Ok boss," Mike was about to ask a final question when Sean hung up the phone. Mike returned his phone to his trouser pocket as Simon walked back towards the car in a very good mood. Mike walked down and stopped by the driver's door.

"Who was that?" Simon asked from the passenger side. They talked to each other over the top of the car. Mike was looking concerned.

"The boss."

"How is he?" Simon asked.

"Well from what I can gather the press conference turned into a bit of a shouting match and the Super is about to arrive in his office."

"Really?" Simon exclaimed, "Why? What happened?"

"You know that journo of Coleraine?"

"Cara what's-her-name?" answered Simon.

"The very one," confirmed Mike, "well she started asking questions about werewolves and apparently the Super launched into her and it's all on the evening news." Simon looked down at his watch.

"Really? Hopefully we can catch it later on."

"Yeah, he had no idea what the time is, told us to finish off and head home."

"That doesn't sound like him!" stated Simon, "What did the Super want?"

"He didn't say, told him about the house that seemed to mellow him slightly."

"He really doesn't like the press, does he?" Simon smiled as they climbed into the car.

"Fancy heading up to the Castleroe site for a bit before we head back down the road?" Mike shut the car door and looked over at Simon.

"Why do that now?" he asked.

"Well if we get the bits and pieces down then we don't have to come all the way back up here again tomorrow?" Simon was smiling positively now, it made sense, but Mike guessed he probably had ulterior motives for such a move.

"Yeah sure, we should get it done before dark."

∞∞∞∞

Alison had led the way out from the police station and back into town. They had chatted over two ready meals which were their excuse for dinner before they had to carry on with the town patrol. The evening was getting darker and the wind had picked up. They moved through the shoppers making their way in and out of the shops. The two police officers carried on walking through the town and headed towards the bridge, Alison glanced at her watch.

"What time is it?" Kyle asked.

"Ten minutes to eight," she replied.

"Only two more hours to go," smiled Kyle. Alison caught his look and smiled back. Kyle was looking over the bridge. "So, what do you do on your time off?" Kyle's question was cut short by the yellow car screeching around the corner towards the bridge. A young couple, who had just started crossing the bridge, jumped out of the way and were narrowly missed being hit by the car. Kyle sprinted forward as he heard Alison's voice in his earpiece shouting at the control room.

"Yellow hatchback jumped the lights at the old bridge, excessive speed near miss RTC"

"Control," the police station answered with just one word as Kyle reached the visibly shaken couple who were sitting on the pavement at the side of the road.

"Did you see that?" the young man looked up at Kyle as he knelt beside them, Alison's voice continued in his ear.

"Whiskey India Charlie nine zero five zero," Kyle glanced up at Alison who was following the progress of the car on the far side of the river. 'How did she read the registration plate?' he thought to himself before turning to the couple. Alison narrated what was happening with the car until it was out of sight, from across the new bridge the area car lit up its lights and siren and started to chase the car. As the police car disappeared from view Alison turned her attention to the people who had been on the bridge. Kyle was controlling the young couple, so she walked over to the pensioner. Hopefully this wouldn't take long as none of them seemed to be hurt. Alison's voice was replaced by a male voice, the passenger in the area car who was describing each turn and each road as they gave chase to the yellow hatchback.

∞∞∞∞

Yelina felt her foot press down on the accelerator of the small car as she drove towards Coleraine. Davidov had arrived with Anders and had thrown her out straight away. Anders had been grinning in an excited way, she hated when he was like that. All she wanted now was to be back home. The car in front of her slowed down before turning left as she approached the roundabout. The large yellow 'M' stood above the trees to her right, but she wasn't hungry at the moment. Right now, she wanted to find Anna. Anna wasn't normally more than a few feet away from Davidov now that she was with him and not Alexi. When Davidov appeared without her and ordered her out of the house Yelina instantly started to worry.

Over the far side of the roundabout a police car suddenly turned its lights on and started rushing towards her. Yelina pulled the car into the side of the road and slammed on the brakes, she released the seatbelt as fast as she could and shifted herself so she could reach the automatic pistol she had tucked into the back of her jeans. Yelina pulled the gun out and tucked it under her left leg and grabbed the door handle with her left hand. If they were coming for her she knew she had to be out of the car, she could move faster than they could, and she was better with a gun than they were. Her eyes darted over to the woods where she had been watching over Davidov and Anna when they had dealt with the teenagers who found them. 'Leave none alive,' she had heard Davidov shout. The police car sped around the roundabout in front her and started coming up the road towards her. Her left hand tugged at the handle and the door sprung open less than an inch. She was ready, they would be dead before she made it to the woods and there was safety in the woods. They could not follow her there.

Suddenly the police car swung round and took the road that went up to her left and sped up the hill. The road she had planned to take to go to the small house in Castlerock, to where Anna was, where the Nocs had been. She would take a different route now. Yelina paused for a few moments and slammed the car door shut. Other cars went past her, but she stared out over the front of the car and slowly breathed in. The police were not coming for her, she was safe. Then the fear of Anders returned, Anders was becoming stronger in the pack, would she ever be safe again? Yelina hadn't noticed but the car had stalled and after moving the pistol she turned the key and started the engine, just before she moved off her eyes caught a fleeting movement from the trees. She stared.

The trees swayed slightly in the wind, but the nearby street lights could not pierce the darkness from inside the woods. Yelina stared into the darkness, nothing moved there but she was certain something had. Yelina stared. The movement had been so quick that sapien eyes would have missed it. Yelina stared and took a deep breath in, looked up and down the road and pulled off into the traffic. She would tell Anna what had happened, Anna would be able to help, unfortunately, when she got to see Anna she would forget all about the encounter.

∞∞∞∞

Mike and Simon were walking together up the pathway towards the Castleroe crime scene. The woods were getting darker by the minute, but they didn't quite need torches yet. Mike glanced at his watch, he was already late for the evening meal with his wife, and this no doubt would be another argument waiting to happen.

"Don't worry this won't take too long," reassured Simon, Mike gave him a forced smile.

"No rush, 'dot the i's and cross the 't's'" Mike mimicked Sean. Simon smiled. Simon was carrying one of the folders that had copies of all the scene of crime photographs.

"Right then," he said as they turned off the track and headed up the hill towards where the bodies were found, "let's get this done ..." Simon opened the folder and looked at the first photograph. "Victim number one ..." Simon started going through the details, Mike didn't have to look at the photograph, the scene was still fresh in his head, behind them a police car turned on its siren and the blue lights lit up the sky.

"Someone is late for their dinner," stated Simon, Mike smiled that was the common phrase used by plainclothes police every time the uniforms use a siren.

"I wonder what they are responding to?" Mike asked as he was looking up at the sky.

"Hopefully nothing that concerns you," answered Simon. Mike looked across at him as he continued, "Because if it concerns you then it concerns me ... And if it concerns me that means I am going to be very late for a lovely lady," Mike smiled.

"From Garnerville by any chance?" he enquired, Simon looked up and just smiled.

"That would be tel ..." the noise cut him off, both men turned and looked up the hill towards the sound. They couldn't describe the noise, but a noise had come from inside those woods. Their joviality had gone, stern concentration overwhelmed them.

"What was that?" Simon whispered.

"No idea," Mike whispered back.

"You stay here, and I will go around to the left." Simon stated, both men stared up the hill, their eyes didn't move.

"Ok," replied Mike. Simon quickly moved off, his right hand was on the pistol inside his jacket. Mike's right hand unconsciously moved and touched the familiar shape through his clothes, and

362

then Simon was gone. Mike was now regretting them separating, his hand moved inside his jacket and gripped on his Glock pistol as his eyes scanned the area in front of him.

"POLICE … STOP!" the shout came from Simon somewhere over to his left in the darkness. Mike was already running back down to the path when Simon shouted again, this time there was anger in his voice.

"I said STOP," Mike was on the path and running as fast as he could, his head moving to see past the trees and into the darkness, he couldn't exactly tell where Simon was. The first gunshot was followed by two in very quick succession. Mike's pistol was in his hands as the air was filled with a terrified scream. The singular scream stopped as quickly as it started. Up ahead, Mike spotted two pensioners walking through the woods, arm in arm.

"Police officer!" Mike shouted, panic was starting to take hold, the old man pointed with his right hand.

"Up there, he went up there!" He pointed off to Mike's right, he crashed through the trees in the direction he had been sent.

"SIMON!" he shouted, "SIMON WHERE THE HELL ARE YOU?" Mike kept running, his eyes desperately searching for some sign of Simon. "SI—M-O-N." Mike slowed down to a walk, the silence of the woods brought him to a stop, he raised his weapon, so it pointed in the direction he was looking.

"Is there anything we can do?" the old man shouted from the pathway.

"Go back to the car park and dial 999, tell them shots fired, assistance required," Mike slowly walked forward as the couple moved off, "Simon …." Mike's voice had reduced to a whisper as he slowly moved through the woods, taking one step at a time, turning to the left and then to the right. He went around a large tree and spotted the folder that Simon had been carrying lying on the ground. The contents scattered all over the ground. Mike stopped and stared at the blood that was splattered all over them. For the first time he felt real fear, Mike felt his insides turn and he had to swallow to keep down the contents of his stomach. "Si-m-o-n," he whispered. Mike walked forward two more steps and he caught sight of Simon's police issued Glock pistol lying on the ground. He stopped. Now all that moved were his eyes. His ears strained at the silence. In the distance, the cars on the main road continued to drive up and down and there seemed to be no reaction so far. Mike was paralysed, he could not move.

The noise made Mike drop to one knee and he thrust his weapon out in front of him. Rapidly his fear exploded in anger as his whole being jumped forward screaming. Mike had never moved as fast as he did, charging through the forest, jumping from side to side. They had his friend. Mike's voice was screaming but his mind was not forming the words. Onward, onward, onward, his body threw itself through the branches, slashing at his face and body when suddenly his body was stopped as quickly as it had started. His eyes widened in horror, every hair on his body reacted and his voice turned into a scream of the upmost anguish at the marker they had left for him. Mike fell to his knees and nearly dropped his pistol; he was unable to control his tormented sobbing. Mike could not hear the police sirens coming closer, nor could he hear the police radio net that just exploded into life.

∞∞∞∞∞

"Shots fired, officer down," The voice in Kyle's earpiece made him look over at Alison who turned and started waving wildly at the approaching police car, trying desperately to get them to stop. Its blue lights were flashing and its sirens wailing. The brakes squealed in protest as the driver slammed his foot down on them.

"Get in," screamed the driver. They could hear what was being said through the radio that was connected to their earpieces, but what they couldn't hear was the nearly hysterical sobbing and wailing that was coming from the woods at Castleroe.

Chapter 73

Grishin glanced over at Carl who was looking around the living room of the farmhouse. Paul, Dermott and Grishin were standing in the room. Carl was annoyed, very annoyed.

"All of the Latvians are accounted for," Dermott confirmed, "none of them were near Coleraine this time."

"So, either one or more of them slipped past your surveillance," said Grishin.

"Impossible!" Dermott raised his voice in his own defence.

"Or we have another wolf running around," Carl looked at the floor as he spoke.

"So, what do you want us to do?" Paul asked.

Carl walked over to the far window away from the entrance door. "We cannot accuse the Latvians with no proof," Carl looked at Dermott, "Are you 100%?"

"100%, I knew exactly where they all were at the time,"

"But you said one of their women had been nearby, did you not?" Grishin quizzed, Dermott looked over at him.

"Yes, the female, Gurin was driving past, but she continued to the cottage where Nikitin is in hiding; the rest were all covered by our surveillance."

"And she didn't stop?"

"No," silence returned to the room only to be broken by Carl.

"Then we must find this wolf," Grishin remained still. Carl looked at the clock, "this only happened less than an hour ago, so we must find out more before we accuse anyone!" Suddenly there was a knock at the farmhouse door.

"Come," shouted Carl, the door opened, and Tony filled the doorway. Grishin walked towards the window and was passed by Carl moving towards the opening door. All three Rua moved to greet Tony with handshakes, smiles and greetings in Irish.

"How is Karen?" enquired Paul.

"She is good, now," answered Tony.

"Is she out of hospital yet?" Dermott asked.

"Yes," Tony confirmed, "she is at home and being well taken care of."

"She isn't alone now, is she?" Carl asked.

"No," Tony looked towards Dermott, "Eve is with her."

"She is well looked after then." Dermott answered with a smile.

"The pack is relieved beyond words!" said Carl.

"Thank you," answered Tony, Carl placed his hand on Tony's shoulder.

"I am glad that your family is safe, but I do mourn the loss of your child."

Tony's eyes welled up as if he was about to cry but he looked down toward the floor.

"Thank you," he spoke quieter than he had before.

"Next time you will tell us when one of ours is about to bless the pack with new life!" they shared a smile, Tony glanced around the room at the stern but silent faces.

"But I need to attend to things, so I will leave you all to it." Carl shook his hand and Tony left the room.

"He looks stressed!" stated Paul.

"He just lost his first child and nearly lost his wife," answered Carl quietly. Dermott murmured an acknowledgement, Carl was staring at the back of the closed door, "I want a watch put on every Latvian, where they are, what they do, who they speak to," Carl glanced over at Dermott, this was directed at him.

"It is already in place, but ......" Dermott started to answer before Carl cut him off.

"No buts!" Carl almost shouted, "I want to know everything they do."

"What are you thinking?" asked Paul.

"You do not want to know what I am thinking," Carl replied, Paul and Dermott shared a glance.

"Yeah, … I do."

Carl stopped, glanced over at Grishin then at Paul and Dermott. A silence hung over the room, "there is a fight coming …" Carl spoke softly. Paul straightened himself up and almost started to laugh.

"Surely you cannot think that they would possibly try something?" Carl placed his hands on the back of one of the chairs and lowered his head briefly, he paused.

"I think they have an agenda. I do not know what it is or what they are up to, but they have one," Carl answered.

"I don't trust them," Dermott injected.

"Neither do I my friend, neither do I."

"Well," Grishin asked, "what are you planning to do next?"

∞∞∞∞

Cara-Marie was staring at the text on her desktop screen, it was dark now and she was still in the office. Mark was busy scrolling through pictures when the sound of a police siren went past. Cara-Marie stopped typing and glanced over at Mark who had also stopped what he was doing.

"What?" he asked. Cara-Marie said nothing, shook her head and went back to adding to the text on her screen. Her eyes darted over her desk as her fingers momentarily stopped typing again. Her eyes picked up the disorganised paper and general mess. The half-eaten Chinese take-away sat to the left of Mark's desk. The sound of her mobile ringing broke her out of her trance. The phone was in her handbag, she registered the sound, but her body didn't move.

"Aren't you going to answer that?" Mark answered. She paused.

"Not if it's my Mum again I'm not," He smiled. Cara-Marie reached into her handbag and rummaged around until she found her phone, she looked at the screen, and glanced over at Mark who raised his eyebrows. She shook her head, it wasn't her Mum. Mark looked at her as she waved her hair to free up her ear, she placed the phone to it and said a simple 'Hello' the reaction of her body made him react as well.

"What? …" Cara-Marie sat bolt upright in her chair. Mark slowly closed down his screen as he listened to her talk. "Where?" … "Castleroe? What? Again? … Ok, thanks, I owe you." Even before she had finished speaking, she was out of the chair and had darted for her coat. Mark was quick to guess that they were going somewhere fast, "Come on!" she screamed at him as her coat flew around her, even before he was out of his chair she had the coat on, her handbag over her shoulder and was heading towards the door.

"What?" he had to shout after her as he grabbed his camera bag, Cara-Marie was already outside. Mark had to run after her to hear her reply.

"Policeman killed at Castleroe, shots fired …" She was saying something else, but he could not and did not hear her as she had broken into a full sprint towards her car.

∞∞∞∞

Sean Parrish felt the phone drop from his hand, it bounced on the floor of his living room, he could no longer hear the programme that was on his television, and he could no longer hear his wife in the kitchen. He was numb. His eyes lost focus, he lost feeling in his hands and the only sound he could hear was the sound of his own breathing. He could not laugh, he could not cry, he could not feel. All he could do was breathe. He didn't hear his landline phone ringing or his wife shouting at him to answer it. All he could do was breathe. Tonight would be a very long night; the type of long night he thought was long behind him.

∞∞∞∞

Darren Forester cancelled the call on his phone and took a deep breath in. He looked around the basic kitchen he was standing in as the kettle clicked off. He folded his arms and leaned back against the wall as Steve Minister walked through the door and towards the boiled kettle. Darren didn't speak as Steve opened a cupboard and removed a mug. Steve glanced over his shoulder at Darren and raised the mug in his hand.

"Brew?" he asked, Darren nodded once as Steve turned back to the kettle, it only seemed like a second when Steve had turned and offered the steaming mug to him. Darren reached out and took it in his right hand, he lifted the mug to his lips, "What?" Steve asked.

"Any sugar?" Darren asked.

"When did you start taking sugar?" he asked, "but that is not what I was asking."

Darren looked over the mug at him, he took a deep breath, "Remember the coppers that wanted the Russian brief?" Steve nodded in answer as he took a drink from his own mug, "Well one of the fellas, Simon McAllister," Darren paused as Steve acknowledged him, "He was torn apart earlier up in Coleraine ..." Darren noticed that Steve's facial expression did not change, that was something he always thought was amazing with these guys.

"Sorry to hear that," Steve replied.

"Thanks."

"Was it the same as before?" Steve asked.

Darren paused, "Yes." The pair stood in silence for a few seconds before Steve walked out of the room. Darren turned and walked to the open door and watched Steve take his mobile phone out of his pocket, tap at the keypad and hold the phone to his ear. Darren watched as he slowly stepped forward and paused before speaking.

"Hi, get the guys together. We're having a briefing...yes...now...no probs." Steve took another mouthful of tea before casting the rest of the contents over the floor of the hangar they were in, then Darren's phone started to ring, Steve turned and looked at him, Darren nodded, then Steve turned and walked out of the large hanger.

Darren's phone started to ring again so he took it out to look at the name on the screen.

"Yes?" he listened for a few moments before saying only one word before he hung up, "Ok."

Chapter 74

Sean looked up from his desk as Mike walked in, his eyes glanced up at the clock, it was still an hour before anyone should be there on any ordinary day, but today was not going to be an ordinary day. Mike was stern faced; he had not slept; his black suit looked like it had been tailored to fit him. He was walking with purpose through the team room and directly into the office. Neither of them exchanged pleasantries as Mike sat down. The two of them looked at each other the silence was broken by the ringing phone. Sean lifted the handset and held it to his ear, he did not introduce himself as he answered.

"Yes Sir," he paused as he listened to whoever was calling, Mike looked over at the coffee machine, it was not on, there was no smell, he had not noticed it as he first walked in, "Yes Sir," Sean repeated, "Thank you Sir, that is very kind," Mike looked back at Sean, "Yes Sir, I will pass that onto the rest of the team," Sean slowly nodded, "Thank you Sir, ... Yes of course, I will see you later then," Sean looked up at Mike, "I will Sir, yes, thank you again," slowly he replaced the handset. Mike glanced at the desk, it was empty except for his computer keyboard and the phone. Sean brushed his hand down his black tie.

"Who was that?" Mike asked.

"Chief Constable,"

"Oh," Mike did not know what to say as his eyes darted around the room.

"He was confirming that he will be at Simon's funeral,"

"Has that been set yet?" Mike asked, he knew the answer to that already, but Sean guessed that he was just fighting to find something to say. Part of him wanted to point that out, on a normal day he would have, but then it would probably have been Si.......... Sean stopped his thoughts.

"No, not yet, it will be next week at least, we will have to wait until the Coroner releases him for burial. Have you given your statement yet?" he asked, Mike looked up.

"No ... No, that will get done this afternoon ..." silence fell over the room again, the seconds slowly ticked by before Sean broke it with a single word.

"Coffee?"

"Yes, yes of course." The silence had been broken. Sean stood up and walked round to the coffee machine and the two men started to chat as they always did as the coffee machine started making a noise. Mike rose to stand beside Sean. They had spoken several times the night before over the phone and at length when Sean reached the Causeway hospital before Mike had been released. Neither of them had slept much that night. Time passed and Sean sat back on the edge of the desk as Mike busied himself pouring the coffee. The aroma filled the room.

"Kenyan," Sean answered anticipating the question.

"Nice," Mike whispered, the phone in his pocket bleeped, he reached into his pocket and read the text message, his face crunched in concentration.

"Now who could put that look on your face?" Sean asked,

"Ahh...Apparently, some of the military have accepted our invitation to the boxing," Mike was still reading from his phone as he spoke.

"When is that again?" Sean asked.

"Tonight" he replied, "at the Europa,"

"Yeah, I think I will give that a miss ...." Mike looked up and gave his reply some thought.

"Me as well .... I know the rest of the team is still going, we do have a table after all."

"We do?" asked Sean.

"Yes ... It's under Simon's name.............." Mike stopped himself and Sean looked back at him, both men shared another glance before they looked down. Sean placed his mug on the desk.

"I saw him," whispered Sean. Mike's head shot up.

"What?"

"I saw him," Sean replied as Mike's eyes transfixed on his boss, his friend.

"Where?" Mike's voice was quieter now, Sean looked over at him.

"Here,"

"When?"

"This morning, just as I first walked in," Sean turned and pointed to a spot just outside the office door, "He was standing just there, in that old suit he used to wear,"

"What was he doing?"

"Smiling, just smiling," Sean's body tensed up and he breathed in loudly through his nose as he tried to fight back the tears welling up in his eyes, "it was only for a second, then he was gone, he was just standing there, smiling," Mike almost dropped the mug on the floor and stood up. He stepped towards him and put his right arm around his friend. Sean initially tensed then stood up himself. The two friends hugged, they had never done that before and for a few brief seconds Sean broke down. His body shook with a burst of sobbing which lasted several seconds before he fought to bring himself under control. He released his hug on Mike, and Mike stepped back as well. Sean forced a smile before walking back round his desk.

"He was just letting you know he is OK," Mike smiled, and Sean smiled back.

"Yeah, yeah he was." The door to the main office opened and Eddie Cargill walked in, followed by another member of the team, both acknowledged Sean and Mike in the office, both were also dressed in black suits.

"Today is not going to be a normal day," Mike didn't realise at first, he had just said that out loud.

"No, it isn't," answered Sean.

∞∞∞∞

Kyle was putting on his uniform in the Coleraine police changing room where his oncoming shift had only one topic of conversation: the murder of the detective the night before. Most of them had been involved cordoning off the site in Castleroe, in fact most of this shift had been at the exact same spot that the teenagers were killed only weeks before.

"What time did M.I.T. eventually leave?" someone asked.

"Still there," was a reply.

"Great ..." came another voice.

"Why great?" another asked.

"Guess what we are going to be doing most of the day!" This was met with a chorus of groans and complaints. Tony walked in just as Kyle was about to close his locker. He was instantly met with a sea of greetings and requests about how Karen was getting on; this was his first day back since she had the miscarriage. The two of them met each other and exchanged an eye to eye look, they smiled and shook hands. The grip was firm, as it always was.

"Hey mucker," Kyle's greeting was cut short by the section sergeant shouting at the door of the locker room.

"Everyone, briefing 5 minutes, 5 minutes! We've got a very busy day today!" the door of the locker room slammed shut.

"I'll see you downstairs," replied Tony. Kyle nodded and started making his way past the other guys and headed towards the door. The section sergeant was already in the briefing room and was handling some sheets of A4 paper as Kyle walked in. Some of the section was already in the room and it would not take long for the oncoming shift to file downstairs for their morning brief. Kyle stood by the far wall and acknowledged everyone as they entered and either sat down on one of the chairs or formed into a small group. Alison walked in behind one of the other female officers, they were chatting away. She looked over and acknowledged Kyle with a nod before taking up a space on the far side of the room. Tony was the last to enter, he was greeted with several handshakes and a hug from one of the female officers, the conversation in the room stopped when the Inspector entered. He walked to the front and exchanged a short pleasantry with the Sergeant that Kyle did not hear.

"Right then, good morning," he started, Kyle folded his arms as he started the brief as he always did, going over the events of the night before; he was listing everything except the murder. This was obviously going to take longer than usual. The inspector started to delegate tasks to members of the section in follow-up to some of the incidents from the night before. He was saving himself for the main event, he paused, then looked around the room.

"Right then," he started again, "the events at Castleroe last night," his face was sullen. "As we all know Detective Sergeant Simon McAllister of Belfast M.I.T. was murdered while continuing his enquires as part of the Operation Muirdris team," he looked up from the paper in front of him and looked around the room. "If you are approached by the press then that is all you say," his eyes looked at each person in turn. "This story has gone international already and there is press from all over the place; if anyone wants more, direct them to the press office in Belfast. If you're getting 'pushed' by any press, repeat this and if they are getting in the way of you carrying out your duties then deal with them. If you cannot then let the control room know," he paused when a police officer raised his hand.

"Has the name been released yet?" the Inspector glanced at his watch.

"It should have been, but I will confirm that for you," the Inspector glanced over at the Sergeant who nodded. He continued, "We are getting personnel from Ballymoney and Limavady to help with the cordon today so that will free up more of you."

"How many?" came a question from the room, he looked to where the voice came from.

"Four from each," a murmur went around the room, then more murmurs mixed with a few louder whispers. "Right and something I want stopped right here are rumours!" He had raised his voice and it silenced everyone in front of him, "I know there is a story going around about a beheading and heads on poles, but I want this to stop!"

"But it was?" said one voice quietly yet loud enough for everyone to hear.

"I don't care!" The Inspector was nearly shouting now, "That is for the investigation team, NOT YOU, I do not want that getting into the press,"

An older police officer raised his hand. "But it will get into the press," he said.

"But not from one of you, IS THAT CLEAR," the Inspector looked around the room again, "IS THAT CLEAR!" he repeated, there was a chorus of acknowledgment. "You stick to what you have been told regarding the press. I do not want any of my officers being accused of breaking the confidentially of an active investigation." After a few moments, he then listed the rest of the duties to each officer, most would be at the crime scene, Kyle had been paired up with Alison again, they exchanged a glance and she slightly nodded towards him when their names were read out. "Does everyone know what they are doing today? Any questions?" he finished off. Kyle glanced over as Tony raised his hand.

"What about me? I think I'm the only one that has not been detailed a task yet," the Inspector and the Sergeant exchanged a glance before the Sergeant answered.

"Yes Tony, we have copies of the CCTV imagery that was released at the press conference in Belfast yesterday and I would like you to take the lead on that today." Tony nodded, he was being kept in the station today, he knew it and so did the rest of the section; no one complained it would be expected after losing a child. "I have been told that M.I.T. will have someone in their office upstairs today so they will be the point of contact," Tony nodded again and folded his arms. "Oh, and before I forget, are any of you going to the boxing at the Europa tonight?" Several hands were raised, "Right I will try and release you as soon as I can at the end of the shift. I will use the Ballymoney and Limavady crews to cover." The Inspector said his final comments, and everyone started filing out of the room. Alison tapped Kyle's arm as he walked past.

"See you upstairs in 5 mins. I want to have a chat with Tony," he nodded at her. They would be walking around the town again today. Just then his phone bleeped, he stopped in the hallway and pulled the phone out of his pocket; Cara-Marie's name on his screen. He paused before he pressed the green button and opened the very long text message.

∞∞∞

Davidov stared at Anders who looked apologetic, his eyes looked towards the floor of the bungalow.

"What?" his voiced raised as he repeated the question, Davidov slowly started to cross the room towards him, Anders tried to back away.

"I..." Davidov's fist connected with the side of his head and sent him slamming against the door, he slid down the door as his legs gave way, he fell to his knees, and he looked over to Davidov. He was going to try to stand but Davidov towered over him.

"If I tell you to do something then you do it!" Davidov was shouting at him now, Anders cowered into the door; another punch slammed down on him.

"I am sorry," he half whispered. He felt Davidov stand to his full height. Anders turned his face to look up at him, Davidov stared down at him.

"Get out … and complete the mission that was given to you!" Davidov stepped back as Anders rose to his feet and reached out to open the door. Davidov stared at him. Anders dropped his gaze and pulled the door open. As he stepped through the open doorway he looked back into the room, Davidov had turned his back to him. He saw Anna standing in the bedroom door, her face bruised and swollen, but that couldn't contain the devilish grin that was covering her face. Anders slammed the door behind him and almost ran to the car, the wheels spun, and he took off up the road towards Coleraine. Anna stepped forward into the room.

"Viktor is not up to being left on his own against them!" she stated, Davidov was still angry, he stared straight into her eyes.

"That is why Dusmanov was told to stay there and keep control of the situation." Anna took note that Davidov had used Anders surname not his first name, "Shelaev is only 23 years old and has no experience in dealing with them," Davidov stormed past her, pushing her out of the way. She watched him walk around the bed and get down on his knee. He pulled a large rucksack from underneath the bed and threw it on top. The grin had gone from Anna's face as he started to assemble the modified assault rifle.

∞∞∞

Cara-Marie was staring at the phone on desk. Kyle still hadn't answered the text message. She kept glancing back and forth from her computer to her phone.

"CARA," it was almost a shout, she looked over to her right.

"What?"

"You haven't heard a single word I said, have you?" said Mark.

"Sorry …" she went to say something when her phone rang, in less than a second, she had grabbed it and it was to her ear, her face dropped, and her shoulders shrugged as her gaze lowered. "Yes, hello Mrs McGiven … yes I got the details. Yes, of course." Her eyes looked over as Mark's own phone rang; he answered it with a single line, 'Coleraine Herald,' he started scribbling. Cara-Marie could feel her annoyance building. This wasn't the phone call that she had been waiting for; in fact, this was a complete waste of time. "Yes Mrs McGiven, I will." Mark replaced his phone and sat back in his chair and picked up one of his cameras that were cluttering up his desk, the camera beeped as he pushed different buttons on it. Cara-Marie felt her phone beep in her hand with the arrival of a text message, "Ok, Mrs McGiven but I really have to go … yes … yes … well, all that business up in Castleroe is keeping us busy … Yes, … Yes …. Thank you and yes of course I will," Cara-Marie had a fake smile over her face as if Mrs McGiven was standing in front of her, "Ok, Bye for now," Cara-Marie cut the conversation off then quickly read the text. "Right he is walking round Coleraine today, so I will get to speak to him," she stated out loud.

"Who?" he asked, she looked over at him.

"Oh, one of the coppers who is a good source," she was tapping away at her phone and didn't hear Mark's reply, "Oh, the one you fancy?"

"CARA, MARK" Kevin shouted from the door of his office, both turned around, he waved once with his hand beckoning them into his office. As they both rose Mark spoke again, "So, what was the 'brilliant idea that you had the other day … you never did tell me?" Both of them lifted notebooks and headed towards the door, she looked annoyed.

"It wasn't such a brilliant idea … in fact following him and Tony to see where they were always going was a complete waste of time!" Cara-Marie stomped into the office and Mark followed behind.

"Following people, now are we?"

Chapter 75

Kyle glanced at his watch again, he still had an hour to go before the end of the shift. Kyle and Alison were standing on the bridge in the middle of Coleraine and the rain had held off which was good. Their patrols around the town had mostly been minor calls and fending off journalists from around the world and of course, the horror fans looking for werewolves. He glanced over at a group of people crossing the road. He was trying to spot anyone that wasn't wearing a wolf inspired top. Many had headphones from different devices on, others chatted excitedly. Alison was just finishing off directing two 'freelance' journalists towards Castleroe, and she had done a good job in deflecting their questions about how the police were dealing with the werewolf attacks.

"Thank you, yes no problem … glad to help," she was ever the diplomat. The pair took off with speed in their steps over the bridge away from the town, she turned towards him and smiled and then she nodded towards the town centre, he nodded back. He glanced over his right shoulder and into the tall trees that filled the space over the granite wall and between him and the Chinese restaurant. He smiled wondering if Kelly would like to go there. Kelly. The very thought made his stomach tighten, Kelly, he couldn't get her out of his head. Kelly … the images of what he had seen through the window flashed back in front of him, she really had gotten under his skin. "Hey," Alison touched his arm, the smile had dropped from his face and had been replaced with an intense scowl. "Earth calling Kyle…" Alison's smile brought him back to where he was, "Seen anything nice over the wall?" she asked, her question initially confused him.

"What?"

"I said, did you see anything interesting? … you were staring over the wall!"

"No … nothing much," he answered.

"She must be pretty amazing!"

"Who?" he asked, a knowing smile spread over her face.

"Never mind … are you going to the boxing match tonight?"

"Ummm, … yeah, you?"

"No, taking anyone?"

"Errr … No," another smile spread across her face.

"I heard that one of the journos from the Herald had been following Tony …" Kyle's head snapped up.

"Really?"

"You didn't know?"

"No … and I'm pretty sure he doesn't know either! Where did you hear that from?"

"It was said at yesterday's briefing … apparently Tony does know but she seems to have backed off since his wife …" Alison did not get to finish her sentence as she was cut off by the voice of the duty controller in the radio piece in their ears.

"Seven two, control, receiving" Alison reached up and touched the side of the handset.

"Seven two,"

"Seven two, control return to the station,"

"Seven two, received, on route now."

"Control, many thanks." They made their way up Church Street in silence. As they were passing the coffee shop at the corner of Society Street something made Kyle stare towards it. He did not know why but there was something coming from the café; something was raising his defences. Kyle glanced at Alison as she was doing the same, her eyebrows had dropped, and her body had tensed up as if waiting for imminent action. Alison took a deep intake of breath and walked on, there had been someone, or something in the café that neither of them liked but Kyle knew this time it was not a 'cop's hunch'. It was something else but whatever it was it would have to wait, they had to be somewhere else.

∞∞∞∞

372

Anders could still feel the sting of the swelling and the bruise on the side of his face, he had not expected Davidov to react the way he had, anger grew inside of him. It was Anna, it had to have been Anna that was doing this, and his resentment grew. The darkness was falling and from where he was inside the leafy bush beside the large tree he could clearly see down the hill towards the cottage where Anna was. The small stone wall separating the different fields along the coast ran along the side of the tree and off down towards the road. Anders had not moved in hours. He lay motionless, the rifle an extension of himself. Pe'ter was a few feet away pointing in the opposite direction and like himself he had not moved in hours. They were here to watch for the Noc; it had returned, and they had to deal with it. Anders wondered why it had been so interested in Anna and not the others. No one else had reported any approach but this one had come back and Davidov wanted it dealt with, and he would deal with it. The sunset had long passed and the kind of darkness that you can only find outside of a city sheltered them. They had covered their scent trails and a sapien could walk past them both and not see them; but this time they were not hunting sapiens.

Anders eye's flicked over towards Pe'ter who pointed up the hill with his trigger finger. Something was coming. Anders winked an acknowledgement. Time passed and he became aware of slow deliberate movements. His senses picked up the presence of the Noc as it crept along the far side of the small wall. It was male in his late teens with a long black coat covering most of his thin body. It carried on for another twenty metres and stopped where the wall that crossed the field met the wall that was going down the hill. Anders looked at Pe'ter and motioned with his eyes back up the hill, Pe'ter paused and looked around then shook his head, there was no one else. In very slow deliberate movement that made no sound Pe'ter slowly raised himself and turned around towards the Noc.

The front door of the cottage opened. Anna walked out carrying something in her right hand, the alarm of the car beeped, and she opened the boot. Anders eyes darted back to the Noc who had his left hand on the wall and his right hand in his groin. His mouth was open, and he was taking deliberate, almost forced breaths. The Noc's sexual excitement was growing. Anders suddenly realised what the Noc was doing and his anger quickly turned to rage. Pe'ter aimed his weapon, at this range he couldn't miss but Anders slowly placed his right hand on Pe'ter's shoulder and shook his head, no guns. Anders looked down at the cottage as Anna walked back inside and shut the front door. The Noc was now panting excitedly as his body started to shake. Anders lay his weapon on the ground and with his right hand reached to his side and slowly withdrew a large hunting knife. No, no guns, Pe'ter did the same. Anders knew that once Davidov heard this he would be pleased, he would be pleased at what they had done, pleased at what he had decided. A knife would be better than a rifle. The Noc never heard them coming.

∞∞∞∞∞

Cara-Marie flopped down on the sofa in her flat. Drained didn't even come close to how she was feeling. Kevin had made them go over every article about the detective's murder, each lead, each item, again and again. It had taken up so much time. They had heard rumours about what had happened, but Kevin kept going back to 'confirmed sources' and if they didn't have one, then it was only a rumour.

Could it be possible that his head had actually been cut off? Add to that the newspapers from around the world arriving at the door, phoning, emailing but the bit that really got to her was the phone calls to her mobile. How did her number become so available? All the interruptions had kept her away from doing what she was supposed to be doing so instead of taking an hour it had taken her well past tea time, and even then she still wasn't finished. Cara-Marie closed her eyes and let the darkness of the room cover her like a warm blanket. She began to relax as her mind slowly eased itself away from everything going on, then, out of the depths of her mind he slowly walked towards her. The wolf. He was not threatening, not loving, but he just stood there and stared at her and she stared back. The ringing phone in the corner of the room made her jump, she fumbled for the lamp switch.

373

"What?" she asked as she placed the handset to her ear, "Mum!!! No, ... I do not want to meet whoever he is ...... no, I don't care how long he has been there, I said no!" and with that she slammed down the phone. She knew she would not hear the last of this and that the phone would ring again shortly with a very angry mother on the other end, or worse, she would appear at the door. Her phone bleeped, she opened the message without looking at the screen to see who was sending it.

'OK TO POP AROUND SOMETIME TOMORROW EVENING?'

∞∞∞∞

The 4x4 was speeding up the lane towards the farm. Dermott looked over at one of the younger Rua and gave the instruction. "Go get Carl, tell him the council members are back and something is up," the youngster nodded and ran towards the main farmhouse. Grishin was driving and did not acknowledge the wave from Dermott as he sped past. The vehicle came to a sudden stop beside the other parked 4x4's. Grishin drove straight in and slammed on the brakes. He was alone in the 4x4 but there was something in the back, something quite large and covered with a sheet of coloured plastic. Grishin jumped out of the 4x4. Normally well-dressed he was wearing an old jumper with rolled up sleeves and jeans that looked like they didn't belong to him. His hands and forearms were splattered with blood that was not his own.

"Where is O'Brien?" he shouted at Dermott as he approached, the sudden arrival was attracting attention.

"I have sent..."

"Get him NOW!" Grishin cut him off, shouting his demand and he turned and leaned back inside the open door of the cab of the vehicle. Dermott paused, normally no one spoke to him like that, no one except Carl; he felt himself tense up and he wanted to bare his teeth, but this was a council member. A council member who now looked back at him and with a gesture of his hand commanded him to do as he had just bid him. Dermott nodded and turned towards the farmhouse.

The door opened and Carl and Paul came marching out, something was wrong, both were furious. Carl led the way as he stormed towards the wagon where a small crowd was gathering.

"Just what the hell is going on?" Carl was almost shouting, Grishin leaned back and pointed into the back of the 4x4.

"Get rid of that!" Grishin commanded.

"Get rid of what?" Carl asked. Grishin walked around the vehicle and opened the back door. He pulled the plastic off to reveal a Garou, in fact it was a dead Garou. The arms were up, and the fingers clawed back towards the body and there was a lot of damage around the face and throat, "that is not one of mine," Carl stated.

"It isn't, it is one of the Mongols, a female... Her name is Mia," Grishin replied and walked back around to the front door. He reached inside to pick up a small daysack which he threw over his shoulder, he stopped and stared at Carl. Carl had been looking at the dead wolf in the back, as the small crowd grew closer to look inside.

"I want to know exactly what happened" Carl demanded. Grishin nodded.

"Yes, as soon as I have washed." Grishin walked forward sternly, the small crowd parted to let him pass on his way towards the farmhouse. Carl looked at Paul who nodded towards Dermott, Dermott nodded back again, he knew what to do. Carl and Paul followed Grishin and Dermott started barking orders at those who were nearby. The body would be disposed of and the vehicle cleaned to almost showroom standard. Carl's anger was growing, and Paul knew it, this time he would not hold back against Grishin, council member or not.

∞∞∞∞

Sean was sitting in his living room; the room was silent. The only sound in the rest of the house was his wife walking back and forth from the kitchen, going upstairs then back down again. He was not sure how long he had sat there but he now realised that it had been a while. His phone started to ring. He had been ignoring the calls he had been getting since he got home, and he would probably ignore this one but then he read Mike's name on the screen. Part of him wanted not to answer it but he pressed the button and held the phone to his ear. The background was loud and Mike was nearly shouting just to make himself heard.

"Hi boss."

"Hi Mike, what's up?" Sean asked, the background exploded in cheering, "Where are you?" Sean asked.

"At the Europa Hotel...the boxing match."

With everything else going on Sean had forgotten about that. "Thought you weren't going to go?" he asked.

"Yeah, did not really want to but Super Forester got in touch. We had actually invited the military and a couple of them are here, seemed a bit bad form if we didn't turn up,"

"Aye, you're right I suppose, got anything from them?"

"Well, the Steve fella is definitely interested in what we are doing and keeps going back to what we wanted to know about Chernov's background,"

"Casual interest?"

"No, definitely something else but he is not letting on," answered Mike.

"Keep working on them, see what you can find out, any more news about Simon?" Mike paused before he said anything else.

"Yeah, CSI are sending all the copies of the photos from the scene tomorrow, they kept asking what I had moved etc ..."

"And did you? Move anything?"

"No, he was exactly as I found him," Mike closed his eyes, he tried to get the image of Simon's contorted face on a pole out of his mind, his stomach turned and tightened as he carried on, "Simon is in the mortuary now, got moved a couple of hours ago, uniforms have had real trouble keeping the press away."

Sean's face contorted. "Isn't there a cordon in place?" he asked.

"Yes," replied Mike, "but they have had to almost double the amount all the way around, mostly press from overseas trying to get anything at all. I heard that one of the CSI girls was followed to a petrol station and approached with an offer of ten grand in cash for any photos at all," Sean could feel his soul sink.

"So, what happened?"

"Apparently, they got told to piss off and I gather there was some pushing and shoving going on by the end of it," Sean felt himself relax.

"Oh, one last thing, just found out this evening," Mike continued.

"What was that?"

"It's about that fella Burns and his scientific paper." Sean felt himself contort again,

"What about it?"

"It's been dis-proved," Sean's eyes widened with this news,

"Pardon?"

"Yeah, apparently there is a group in America and another in China that have disproved his paper, stating that parts of the theory could be proven but, the DNA could not ... blah blah blah etc and some crap like that ... short story ... They are not real!"

"At last some good news," Sean replied.

"Yeah ..." Mike paused, "some,"

"Right, go back to the boxing, see what else you can get, and we'll talk tomorrow."

"Yes boss," the call ended, and the room returned to silence. Sean sat there alone for a few more moments before the thump of his wife's footfall on the stairs brought him back to where he was. Even though she tried, she could not comfort him, nor did she understand why he was still part of this whole mess, 'could he not take early retirement' He was inside his last two years after all' ... yeah she wanted him out, but not for his sake, for hers. She was now constantly asked about her husband and the werewolves and she did not like that, not one bit.

Chapter 76

Kyle had been driving for a while, he had awoken early in his own bed long before the sun was up. The gut wrenching feeling from the night before still had not left him. He had left before the boxing match ended and with good reason. He could not sleep; what had happened the night before went around and around in his head, and it wasn't going anywhere else, so he had gone out for a drive. The green fields had given way to the built-up area of Coleraine. He had to pull over twice to wretch, as if he had been drunk the night before, but he had not been. The early Sunday morning saw very little traffic on the roads. Coleraine gave way to open fields again towards Port Stewart, but nothing was helping how he felt. The road rose and as he went over the crest of the hill sunshine lit up the inside of his car. As he drove past the large graveyard on his left and the newly built houses on his right, the traffic had slowly started to build. Still his insides turned and convulsed at what he had seen, what she had said and the way she had acted.

Most of the traffic was turning left into the large car park in front of the very large, very new looking Baptist Church. Kyle's body reacted, he turned, and the car followed others into the nearby car park. Kyle had taken the keys out and killed the engine, then he paused. He had watched as Kelly had thrown her arms around another and kissed him passionately, openly invited the guy back to her hotel room that night and in front of Kyle caressed the face with a promise of 'not much sleep' that night. The text message he had received from her arrived just before 1 a.m. 'by the time you read this, I will be having 'fun' with another.' The thought turned Kyle's insides, he hated the thought, hated the images of what they were doing. All the memories of the times he had been with her.

Then, sitting around the table listening to the other coppers from Coleraine talking about her, boasting who had been with her and the final bit that made him take off was the one who offered him the homemade DVD. He was boasting about the times when Kelly had done 'home visits' and exactly what that had meant.

"She let you video her?" one of the female coppers had asked.

"Well, she didn't stop me!" was the reply. Kyle had walked up to Kelly at the bar and asked for a quick word. The two of them had walked into the lobby of the hotel and he had told her about the DVD and the fact that it was now being offered around.

"Oh, they are watching me?" Kyle felt the stab as she reacted, "That's great!" She had actually been pleased about it. He couldn't stay to watch the end of the inter police boxing event, he had gone to his car and driven home.

"That isn't the kind of girl you want to be with," one of the older coppers had said to him just before he had left, "if she is under your skin you better sort it, sooner rather than later," had been the last of the advice he had been given, now the whole section knew how he felt about her, and what she was doing about it. The knock at the window of the car brought him back to where he was, the face of an excited mild aged woman filled the window.

"Are you coming in?" she asked, Kyle smiled, "OK, see you in there," she wandered off in the same direction as everyone else as they migrated towards the two open doors. Church. When was the last time he had been in a church? and what was he doing here? His body reacted and propelled him out of the car and off in the same direction as the others. He passed through the smiles and handshakes at the reception, greetings of 'hello' and 'nice to see you' seemed to be the order of the day. The entrance to the main room of the very new looking church was on the left, the two double doors did not give an indication to the size of what you were walking into. The rowed seating went from one side to the other and was already full, this was not a traditional old church, this was new, modern and he noticed a lot of young people who all seemed very happy about something. The service was just starting, and he found a space at the side.

The service was not like any he had been to before. First, there was a band on the stage at the front, two young guys with electric guitars, keyboards, a set of drums and a good-looking blonde who was sitting but still rocking out on the bass guitar. Kyle didn't know any of the songs they sang, at one point one of the songs had nearly everyone clapping. The minister was dressed in jeans and a jumper and spoke for a bit before introducing a visiting Baptist minister from Canada. The two embraced and exchanged a few words before the Canadian was alone on the stage. He read a short passage from the bible and explained a bit about what he had just read. The subject got Kyle's attention, 'WARFARE',

"For we battle, not against flesh and blood, but against this present darkness," for a moment his mind flashed back to the farm, what would they make of them? Was what he had seen 'this present darkness?' and what had Tony said about the knock creatures? Were they not the evil ones? This last few months had taken quite a toll on him, what he had seen, not just at the farm, the murders, the other wolves … Vampires … It was in fact all real … Was this the 'present darkness' that this guy was talking about? He doubted it. Kyle did not realise how quickly the time had passed before the service had ended. The crowd rose for the final song and Kyle found himself staring at the bass player. She looked lovely and seemed happy by the look on her face. He had looked away when the song finished as one of the others had walked up to her and the two of them exchanged a short kiss. Kyle slowly made his way with the flow of people back out the double doors and towards the main entrance. There had been the open invite for coffee and biscuits, but he had already decided to leave. They were all being funnelled towards the Canadian minister who was exchanging greetings with everyone as they left As Kyle passed him he held out his hand, Kyle took it and they exchanged a firm handshake. The minister stopped and looked Kyle directly in the eyes, there was a pause of several seconds before the minister spoke.

"May God be with you in the battles you have yet to fight, go … be safe from evil." Kyle nodded at him and released the grip of his hands and walked out the door. The Canadian watched him go as the local minister spoke to him.

"What was that about?" the Canadian looked back at the minister and paused again,

"That was what he needed to hear," and with that he took the hand of the next person who was eager to speak to him.

∞∞∞∞

Tony was sitting in the living room of his home, he had got back only an hour ago. Since Karen had been in hospital he had been there every night, and had not actually been home except to get a change of clothes. Karen was going to be OK, but they had lost the child, for some reason her body had suddenly rejected what was growing inside her. She had only told him the day before and they were waiting until the first scan before they started to tell anyone else, now everyone knew and all for the wrong reasons. He had not drunk any of the tea that he had made for himself but just sat there watching the slow movements of the ocean, and the cars moving back and forth over the roads that rose and fell with the hills, … without her this was just a house, an empty shell, without her … this was not a home.

His phone suddenly burst into life, he looked at the screen and read Dermott's name.

"Hi,"

"Hi Tony, can you get to the farm inside the next hour?" there was some urgency in Dermott's voice,

"Yeah sure, what's up?" Tony started to raise himself in his chair.

"Carl wants to chat to everyone as soon as possible."

"What about?" Tony enquired.

"Farm business," Dermott replied. Something was wrong.

"Ok, I am on my way."

"Can you get hold of Foster? The number I have is not connecting up," Dermott said.

"Sure, I know he was at the police boxing in Belfast last night, so he may still be down there …" Tony said it without thinking,

"Aye, no problems, see you then." Dermott ended the call before Tony could say anything else; something was wrong, his energy levels rose as he propelled himself out of the chair and towards the door of the house. It did not take him long to throw a few items into a small pack, ensure his weapon was on his waist, then head out to the car.

∞∞∞

At the far side of a hedgerow towards the back of the house one of the bushes slightly moved. The heavily camouflaged Viktor tapped out a short message on his phone before returning to the still position he had been in all night. It would be another hour before he got a reply to return to the small house the others were in. He had known why he had been picked. He knew why Anders was so keen after the congratulations that Davidov had shown him after they had taken out the Noc. He also knew that Pet'er would have been given a task to get rid of him for the night as well. Anders didn't hide that he had chosen Yelina after Mia had disappeared. Yelina had been with Viktor and Mia with Anders but everything had changed since Davidov had taken over. Objection or voiced opinion was met with a beating. Anders had climbed the pack, so he only answered to Davidov, Yelina did not have a say and for a moment he wondered what he would find when he got back to the house.

∞∞∞

Yelina's eyes opened and she looked at the celling. Anders was face down on the bed beside her breathing deeply. She slowly turned her head and looked at him, bile rose in her mouth, if she had venom she would have spat it at him. His face was turned away from her towards the far wall. She turned away from him and pain shot through her body. Her whole body hurt, every movement was painful, and each movement was deliberate and slow. The muscles in her shoulders, arms and legs ached as she moved quietly across the room towards the robe that hung on the back of the bedroom door. The robe may cover her bruising from his repeated blows, but her mind remembered.

"You .... Will .... Never .... Say .... No ...... To ... Me .... Again ...." How many times had he done that last night, five? six? Blow by blow between each word he shouted, after the others had gone. Davidov had been pleased with what they had done, everyone was, taking out a Noc so easily and the fact that the Noc was stalking Anna only made Davidov happier. She now knew that Davidov had been deliberate when he tasked Viktor to the watch at the house of the Rua and sending Pet'er to look for Mia again. Mia was gone, if she did not want to be found she would not be, why had she not taken her with her, surely, she knew what would happen to her? After they had left Anna had been chatting to her, she could still see the bruise on the side of Anna's face, but she was excited. Davidov was planning a feast for them later that evening. Yelina had looked out the window of the small house at Davidov and Anders talking by the car, there was a cruel smile on Anders face as he spoke and Davidov just nodded and agreed to whatever he had just said. It started the second they had left. Anders had also planned a feast, and she was it, at first, she had tried to say no, but she could never fight him off.

"You are mine now!" he had shouted as he grabbed at her arm and dragged her through the small house. Yelina had walked over her shredded clothes in the hallway, she turned into the small bathroom and let cold water start to fill the sink. She scooped up some in her hands and splashed it over her face. The cold water felt nice as it ran from her face and down her neck, she looked up into the mirror that was in front of her. There were no marks on her face, he had made sure of that. Her mind flashed at the anger in his face as he yanked her head back and hissed into her ear, 'You are mine'... she had never known anyone to be as brutal as he had been, and each time he seemed to get more brutal than the last; her whole body ached. She stopped the flow of the water and felt herself gently start to weep, she turned and closed the door and sat back on the toilet and allowed herself to weep some more. She did not want to wake him as he would want her again. He had told her last night what he was going to do today. The tears turned into sobbing and she buried her face into a towel to hide the uncontrollable sound that was now coming from her. Why had she left with them? If she had stayed nothing like this would have ever happened. She was trapped, and she could not see a way out of the danger she was now in. Viktor could not help; he could only obey what he was being told to do. Pe'ter would not and after Mia had gone Davidov had put controls on them forbidding any of the female to be alone, especially after the Rua had put controls on them taking any sapien females, not that she thought that would stop any of them. There was a reason it was called 'moon lust.'

Yelina wiped her face with the towel, adjusted the robe and walked through to the kitchen. She busied herself with making coffee and starting to prepare a small meal for breakfast. When the machine clicked, she poured herself a cup of coffee. The smell filled her nostrils and she lifted the cup to her lips, and for a moment the pain in her body was gone, but only for a moment.

"Excellent, just what I wanted!" Anders voice made her jump; she had not heard him approach. He was naked, and his hair was ruffled, he walked straight up to her and without asking grabbed the cup from her, without even blinking he tilted his head back and threw the liquid down his throat. He swallowed, placed the cup in the sink, and as he did so his left arm shot around her waist pulling her towards him. A ghoulish smile spread across his face, "Now my lovely," Yelina looked at him in terror, "Time to earn your place by my side in the pack!" Before she could say anything, his left hand grabbed a handful of hair pulling her backwards, she did not mean to let out a short high-pitched yelp of pain, but she did, her hands came up to try and release the grip he had on her but to no avail. He started to push her back towards the bedroom, "Oh, do not worry my lovely ... I will make you scream for me!" Yelina Gurin was already crying before the door of the bedroom was slammed shut and the robe torn from her body, today would be a long day.

∞∞∞∞

Mike had not really enjoyed his Sunday lunch. He had taken his wife to the boxing event the previous evening and although there had been lots of smiles, she had let him know that the constant jibes and jokes about him 'werewolf hunting' had gotten to her. The soldiers had been polite but defensive, he was now sure they knew something that they were not letting on. When he had chatted to Sean he had convinced himself of this. They had left the event before the final bout; his wife had made it clear she had enough, and it was time to go home. He was now getting the silent treatment; she was not talking and letting him know she was not talking. The constant walking past and getting him to move without her speaking or answering any of his comments was still in full force. Today was going to be a long day. He had exchanged numbers with Steve, the Sergeant Major, and he smiled at the thought of the 'unholy trinity' of their surnames, 'Minister, Abbey and Priest.' He had noticed that their Officer, 'the Duke' had not attended, he could tell that Steve respected him by the way he spoke about him.

Mike knew that he had made ground with them and had opened a little when they were asking about why the interest in Spetsnaz, and 'were spets running around over here?' Mike had noticed that question had been asked twice, they knew more than what they were letting on. At the start of the event there had been a minute's silence for Simon, which had almost brought him to tears, the kiss on his cheek as they sat back down from his wife had been the only affection he had got that evening. The sound of a text made him move in the seat to get the phone out from his pocket. The name on the screen was Steve Minister, Mike wondered what he could possibly want? The text was one line.

'HI, CAN WE MEET IN LISBURN TOMORROW, SO WE CAN CHAT' Mike smiled, now he may find out more of what they knew, he was already phoning Sean when his wife walked into the room.

"And there you go, on your bloody phone again! Never talk to me ... no ..." she turned and stormed out of the room.

Chapter 77

Tony drove up the lane and into a very busy farm, there were people everywhere; there was a lot going on here. He reversed, parked the car and was immediately met with greetings from those who were walking past him.

"What's going on?" he asked.

"Everyone to the arena! Carl wants to talk to us all," answered one. Tony glanced around, and it was everyone, not just pack members but families as well; everyone was heading into the arena. Tony spotted Dermott over by the front door of the farmhouse, so he headed towards him. Six younger members who were all dressed for the outdoors and had bolt action rifles over their shoulders all nodded as Dermott spoke.

"So, you all know what I want you to do then?" They nodded again. Dermott tapped his right ear, "check in every 30 minutes and let us know if you see anything." Again, they nodded and went on their way. Tony knew they always had at least one pair on overwatch at the farm, but three pairs?

"Hi," Tony said as he approached.

"Hi," Dermott replied as he moved his head to one side; he was listening to someone speaking in the covert earpiece. Dermott reached into the pocket of his jacket to use the attachment for the communication system that their security detail used.

"OK, no probs, let me know when you are all in position," Dermott then glanced over towards Tony, "You Ok? How is Karen getting on?" Tony paused,

"Yeah, she is OK, still in hospital, they are saying they think it was something she ate that caused something in her body to ...." Tony started to trail off as he looked at the ground. Dermott's right hand came up onto his shoulder and Tony looked at Dermott's face as he did so.

"Anything we can do ..." Tony nodded and looked down again as Dermott squeezed Tony's shoulder, "Hey we helped your Gurkha's friend's wife, he was just your friend, you are family and we are here," Tony felt himself start to well up, he needed to change the subject and fast.

"What is going on here?" he asked. Dermott released his hand and looked over at one of the families that were walking past and heading towards the open door of the arena.

"Well," he started, "Carl gave one of the council members a right earful last night," Tony glanced over, doing that to a council member was unheard of, but he did not intervene as Dermott continued to explain, "found out a load about the Mongols and how they ended up here ... and Carl wants everyone to know." Tony nodded. "Oh and one of the council members took out one of theirs,"

"What?" Tony exclaimed,

"Yeah brought what was left of her here last night, apparently, she tried to have a go at them,"

"A female trying to go for a council member? I do not believe that!" Dermott patted him on the side as he moved off towards the arena.

"Neither do I, but that is the story they are telling." Dermott left Tony standing near the farmhouse, more people walked past him, almost all greeted him and asked about Karen. Just as he headed off himself Amanda appeared beside him, and like the others asked about his wife. Tony was just repeating what he had already said to everyone else and unlike back at the police station here, he knew they meant what they were saying.

"So, is Kyle here?" she asked,

"Ah, no, no he isn't, tried calling him but his phone is switched off." Tony noticed that her face fell slightly in disappointment. As they filled into the arena Tony noticed the platform on the right-hand side that was up against the side of the wooden inner wall of the arena. Everywhere he looked there were faces he knew, nearly all the pack was here. There was movement over by the main doors then with one motion they were closed shut, Tony had turned around to face the platform so he could see what was going on. The small crowd parted, and Carl and Paul appeared. Paul stopped at the edge of the platform, and Carl jumped up onto it. He didn't look happy, all conversation in the group stopped as everyone turned to listen to what was to be said. Carl was quite smartly dressed, and he paused and looked over the assembled crowd.

"Dermott," he started, he was loud enough for everyone to hear.

"Here," came Dermott's voice from over near the entrance.

"Is the security in place?" Carl looked over towards the voice.

"Yes, overwatch and communication teams are in place," Tony knew that no one would be able to come near or listen in to what was being said.

"Good, good," Carl turned towards the main group and paused, "as you know we had an encroachment on our lands recently! But they were quickly identified and approached. They were part of a Mongol pack from Northern Latvia ..." This got a short muttering of comments that passed between the crowd, "nine of them arrived, but I can tell you now that they are already down to seven in number!"

"Take them all down," came a shout from the far side of the crowd, this was answered by several voices of approval.

"If that must happen, then it will happen!" shouted Carl. Some cheered and some clapped but when Carl raised his right hand it all stopped. "Their Alpha was killed by their own and the council members were recently attacked by one of them and they dealt with her ... Dermott," Carl looked over towards the door again, "has the Mongol body been dealt with?"

"Yes, no traces left," Dermott answered, Carl returned his attention to the crowd. Tony knew he was doing all this to keep the pack together.

"Good, as you know we all recently agreed terms and we have kept our side," Carl continued.

"They killed Paddy!" shouted the same voice from the crowd and again there was a wave of chatter.

"Yes, they did, and if they step out of line again, we will put them down permanently!" another cheer went up. "But," Carl paused, "we will keep a close watch on them; they have to report all their movements and contacts to us. Remember there are only seven of them."

"Do we know where they all are?" came the same voice.

"Yes," answered Carl,

"But what if they do not keep to the terms?" asked the same voice.

"To remind them 'these are our lands' and we 'defend these lands' we will show them our own strength!" Tony recognised the quotes from the pack as everyone here would also.

"Why are they here?" asked the voice again,

"This I have only found out last night ..." Tony glanced around, everyone wanted to know and everyone was listening, "Two years ago the pack Alpha of the Northern Latvian Mongol pack died and as their pack rules stated the eldest son, if not challenged, assumes the position of Alpha." The crowd was totally silent as their own rules were much the same, "But, he was challenged, and challenged by his younger brother, Alexi, who with a following of support from within the pack made his challenge." Most knew what that meant for the Garou. "It was to have been a fight to the death, as per the law, but!" Carl had stressed the 'but' "the elder brother after defeating his younger brother at the point of death could not kill his own," there was another murmur of comments that were again silenced by Carl raising his hand.

"Yes, they went against the law and instead of death he and his followers were banished for life from their lands," Carl paused again, "the challenge was done in front of two council members and the brother's decision was accepted by them, as you may know ... this had never been done before." Carl seemed to relax as he spoke, "this was something unprecedented, but they were given a formal ruling from the council members, which made it legal," Carl continued. "They were banished from their lands and moved from Belarus, to Poland, and then to Germany,"

"Bet the Germans didn't like that!" the voice shouted out.

Carl smiled, "No, they didn't, they were chased out of Belarus, Poland and Germany and their numbers suffered for it."

"How many were there?" the voice seemed to be asking what everyone was thinking, Carl glanced over at Paul who spoke quietly, Tony could not hear.

"Twenty-five were originally banished, they have lost numbers with each time they fight, their biggest loss was in Germany, the nine that arrived here were the only ones who survived." The crowd broke out in spontaneous conversation, nine arrived and only seven remain, are they a threat? If they challenged they would lose again, the comments flowed around where Tony was standing.

"Where are they now?" the voice asked again.

"Dermott!" he shouted, Dermott appeared from the edge of the crowd and looked towards his Alpha, "Do you know the house they are all present at?"

"Yes," Dermott shouted back.

"Then organise a security detail and search the house, confirm the location and presence of each Mongol and I want this done 'TONIGHT'" Carl shouted the last word of the command and a loud cheer went up. Dermott nodded and spoke a response. Carl returned his attention to the gathered crowd. "Then 'Rua', we will remind them that these are our lands, and we, defend these shores, 'Rua'," Carl shouted the last word again, which was met with another cheer, "WE HUNT AS ONE!" The cheer turned into rapturous applause. Carl had put the pack at ease; the pack was one. Tony would stay for a while before returning to the hospital that evening. Later when he got his phone from the car, he would see all the text messages from the other section members about Kyle and the physio from the night before; most of it scandal and probably abuse. He could tell that Kyle would be getting a ribbing from them tomorrow, but all his messages to Kyle had gone unanswered. Amanda appeared again and started to ask Tony more questions about Kyle. Most he would fend off, some he would only half answer, much to the annoyance of this beautiful woman beside him.

∞∞∞∞

Cara-Marie was staring at the screen of the desktop computer in her flat, she had been at it all afternoon and she was only interrupted by the sudden arrival of her very angry Mother. She was furious she had not gone to her house the previous evening. She had invited the new single Doctor from the local surgery, and in her Mum's opinion 'really good looking' but she was still not interested. Her mum had stormed out in protest, 'by the time I was your age I was already married and had your sister!' It had made her cringe, how many times had she heard that line, 'by the time I was your age ......' well she was not her Mum and she wouldn't have her Mum live her life through her now. She got herself through university not her Mum.

She looked at the notebook full of scribbles and notes, it was almost chaotic, nothing was in order and if you did not know what you were looking at, it wouldn't make much sense. She lifted the mug to her lips and took a small sip which she spat back into the mug, the liquid was freezing cold. Off she went to the kitchen to make another, as the kettle was boiling she stared out into the darkness outside the window. She knew she was missing something; she couldn't put her finger on it, but there definitely was a missing piece. The kettle clicked off. Cara-Marie stood and stared at the kettle and the empty mug that was sitting beside it. She didn't know what she could do next; what could she do to prove what she had seen and what she believed? And how could she convince others that myth and reality were closer than she had ever believed herself? The solid knock at her door brought her back to where she was; it was certainly not her Mum this time.

∞∞∞∞

Steve Minister was standing outside the as Chris Abbey walked up to him. They both nodded in acknowledgement of each other. Steve was looking towards the main civilian airport at the passenger jet taking off, it was Chris who spoke first.

"So, we are going to do this tomorrow then?"

"Yeah," Steve spoke, "the coppers obviously know more than they're letting on and ..." he paused, "from what we saw at their offices, we both might be searching for the same people."

382

"People?" Chris's voice had raised slightly, "I would not exactly describe them as 'people'," Steve nodded in agreement. "So, what are we going to tell them?" Chris asked.

"Tell them? What? That the United Kingdom's Special Forces are currently searching Northern Ireland for a pack of werewolves that killed three of our own? Don't think so,"

"So, what about Darren's offer?" Chris asked. Steve contemplated it.

"Yeah, a 'sneak and peek' at their stuff would be good,"

"And he said he could get us inside the station gone midnight tomorrow then it would be up to us to get into the offices … We could take two techies to do their stuff on the coppers' hard drives, so we can get everything … In and out in less than five minutes," Chris stated. 'Steve had always respected the techies ability, the things they could do with covert cameras, covert listening and surveillance devices and the speed it took them to take everything from a hard drive, normally less than one minute, nothing was secure anymore. He nodded towards Chris.

"Yeah, you take the lead on that one," Chris nodded and smiled at being given the job, as he turned to walk away Steve called after him, "Chris," Chris turned back towards him, "make sure you take Darren with you, if you get compromised then he can deal with the station coppers!" Chris smiled and nodded, then turned and walked back inside the hangar. Steve stood in the semi-darkness then glanced at his watch, it was nearly 11pm. Steve turned and walked back outside the hangar. He headed towards the unit bar, tomorrow he could take it all to the Duke then maybe he would be allowed to do what he wanted to do. This was the very same bar they had the wake for the three from the squadron who had died in Scotland; every time he walked into the bar; he would remember the 'absent friends' toast. He would always make the toast to each of them and the forth, the yank. It had not been him who had first found the four heads on poles in the forest, but they had all seen the footage and stills from the cameras. No one could believe what they had seen at the time, now everyone wanted to be part of the kill or capture.

∞∞∞∞

The darkness of the kitchen was broken by the light coming from outside the window and by the clock on the wall. The bright light green numbers stood out in the dark. It had just gone half past two in the morning. She had gotten her breath back and stopped sweating, the thin silk robe stuck to her body as she drank from the glass of water. The water was cold and tasted good. Slowly, she walked over to the window. Cara-Marie gazed outside, nothing moved; everything was still, the houses and flats lit by the street lights. She lifted the glass to her lips and finished the contents, slowly she placed the glass down on the side-counter. The sink still had the plates they had eaten from earlier. She would collect the empty wine glasses from the living room in the morning before she headed off to work. With a sudden movement, she turned and walked through the flat and back into the bedroom, he was still lying face down and with his head under a pillow, she prodded him in the side.

"Hey," she prodded him again, this time his body made a slow movement, "Hey, time to go … you're not staying the night!" She turned and walked back through to the kitchen and poured herself another glass of water. She listened to the slow fumbling coming from the bedroom. Again, she stared out the window with a little smile on her face. The sound of the toilet flushing made her eyes dart over to the side and she waited for him to come to her, she folded her arms and waited. The quiet click of the front door closing let her know that he was not coming to say goodbye, she stomped back through the flat and looked at the closed front door. Outside she heard a car starting up, and with that her heart sank, the smile had gone from her face and she stood there in the darkness. She slowly turned and walked back into the bedroom. She let the robe slide from her and got back under her duvet. The evening had not been a total waste of time. She had one thing she knew she needed to do a lot of research on; who were they? The one thing she knew he had let slip and did not mean to, by the way the conversation was instantly changed, she said the word out loud.

"Rua."

Chapter 78

Mike parked his car near the rear of the train station in Lisburn, Steve had asked to meet him at 10 a.m. at the town entrance to Wallace Park. Mike was early, he crossed the road at the T-junction then took a seat on the wall and waited. He took out his phone and started to go through the many text messages he had, deleting them as he went, conversation after conversation, his hands froze when he got to a text from Simon. Mike read the message about meeting up in Coleraine the night he was murdered, he read the text several times, he could no longer hear the traffic going back and forth, his mind focused on the message. His mind replayed his last moments, the gunfire then the scream. The scream he hoped one day would go away. He straightened up as he remembered the funeral was to be on Wednesday. There would be a big turnout for that, unfortunately they would be overrun with politicians and senior police officers who just wanted to get their face on the news. He would try to stay away from the cameras that were sure to be there.

"DS Dear?" the English accent made him look up at the scruffy face of David Priest.

"Yes," Mike rose and extended a hand that was taken in a tight handshake. David had dirt on his jeans and wore a blue patterned 'lumberjack' top that seemed to be a bit of a fashion craze at the time. Mike looked out of place in his two-piece suit.

"Hi, great to see you, can you follow us, Steve wants to chat over by the bandstand." The soldier turned away from him and walked through the entrance gates into Wallace Park, at the far side of the road that led through the park was Chris Abbey. David was already leading the way as Chris also extended a hand toward Mike.

"Hi, great to see you again," Chris took off after his friend and Mike had to speed up his walk just to keep up.

"Did you enjoy the boxing on Saturday?" Mike asked. Chris had been one of the soldiers that had attended, David had not.

"Yeah, it wasn't bad, we have our inter-squadron boxing event at the end of the year, always fun," Mike went to ask him something about why the meeting was happening so publicly and not in an office, but Chris beat him to it with a question of his own. "Can you settle a 'discussion' for us?" Mike saw the other soldier look over his shoulder at Chris.

"If I can, then yes," answered Mike,

"You are a detective, right?" Chris stated,

"Ah, yes," he answered.

"And I am telling you that he IS," stated David,

"And I am telling you that he is NOT," quickly answered Chris,

"Of course, he is, or he would not be who he is!" David Priest retorted.

"But how can he be?" Chris turned to Mike, "Right, is Batman a super hero or not?"

"Pardon?" he was taken aback by the question.

"Is Batman a super hero or not? I mean, what super powers has he actually got?" Chris started to put forward his case, this discussion was something that had never crossed Mike's mind before.

"Of course, he is, he IS Batman! And therefore 'super' at what he does!"

"But he has NO special powers?" Chris speeded up and caught up with his friend as the argument continued. The road snaked through the park with trees on either side, autumn had been, and winter is coming, the days had started to get colder. The bandstand was ahead of them on the left, as they approached Steve stood up from where he had been sitting and almost jumped down the small steps towards the three men. The conversation between David and Chris had stopped. Steve walked straight up to Mike Dear and again he was greeted with a firm handshake.

"Hi Mike, thanks for coming," Steve turned to the other two and spoke, "Right, I will give you a shout when we're done," Both nodded and walked in separate directions, Chris went back the way they had come, and David headed off towards the entrance on the Belfast Road. Steve turned and headed back towards the bandstand, "are they still arguing about 'Batman'?" Steve asked, it was an ice breaker and Mike knew it.

"Yeah, never actually thought of that before to be honest," answered Mike, "but yes, they are," Steve walked over to the side of the bandstand, Mike took up a space a few feet away. Mike could see why he had chosen this place to meet, you could see in every direction for quite some distance. Mike looked at Steve whose body language was becoming defensive, "So, why would you want to meet for a chat here? We could have met in our office?" Steve looked over at him.

"Yes, we could have, but walls have ears," Steve looked around, "may I ask you a question?" Steve started, it was Mike's turn to be defensive.

"Normally it is me asking the questions, but sure, go ahead," Steve turned his head and looked over his shoulder before starting a slow walk around the inside of the bandstand.

"It is about your friend, Simon."

"What about him?" Mike asked.

"Well, it is not about him, it is about what happened to him."

"I cannot comment on an ongoing police investigation in the murder in Coleraine," Mike gave his answer sternly, his defences were up. Steve knew where he stood and nodded his head before continuing his slow walk.

"Ok," he paused, "but you were there when it happened?" Mike glared at Steve, he did not answer, he didn't have to, Steve nodded again, "Ok," Steve was about to say something else when Mike butted in.

"May I ask, 'why the interest' in that part of our investigation? Is there some piece of information that you would like to pass on?" It was a statement, a challenge. Mike was taking control of the conversation and he wanted to know where Steve was going with this. Steve shook his head.

"No, no information," Steve was about to say something else and again Mike cut him off.

"Then may I ask, why is the British Army interested in the brutal murder of a police officer?" Mike was firm with the question, and it stopped Steve in his tracks. Steve paused as it was obvious that he wasn't used to people speaking to him like that. The silence seemed to go on for a while before Steve broke it.

"The British Army, as far as I am aware has no interest in the death of your friend," Steve had turned the words around, 'his friend' made it more personal, instead of the 'police officer' as Mike had used.

"So, why am I here?" asked Mike, "If you want to discuss the rights and wrongs of Batman then can you do it with someone else as I have other things to do!"

"Was his head on a pole?" The question stopped Mike dead, he spun around and was now only a few feet away from the soldier.

"Can I ask you Sergeant Major, how you know exact details in our murder investigation that have not been made public?" Mike had made it formal by using Steve's rank.

"I didn't …. But you just confirmed it for me," Steve slowly passed Mike and started his slow walk around the inside of the bandstand again.

"What do you know?" Mike's voice was a lot quieter now. Steve looked over at him as he slowly paced.

"About your friend? Nothing," Steve paused again before he came to a stop to ask his next question, "Did you see it?" Mike's mind raced, the images of what he had seen flashed through his mind.

"I …" he did not know how to answer, Steve looked at him then set off on his slow pacing again, "do not worry, I've seen them too!" Steve's words crashed into Mike.

"Seen who?" his voice was no more than a whisper.

"We were on exercise in Scotland last year," Mike relaxed as the soldier spoke, "we were hosting the yanks, and we were still in the live fire part of the exercise," Mike listened as Steve continued, "The first we knew something was up was when there were several emergency messages that suddenly went out from one of the locations, and when we got there ..." his voice trailed off.

"What did you find?" Mike asked. Steve looked directly at him.

"What was left of four soldiers that had been shredded and four poles, all with heads on them," Steve stopped talking, Mike could only remember what had happened to Simon. "You said you saw it, what did you mean?" Mike asked.

"When we got the remote cameras back in, some video footage, other motion capture ... that means when any time something moves in front of it, it takes a picture ..." Mike knew what it meant but did not interrupt him.

"And what did those pictures show?" Mike asked.

"A creature that was standing upright, on its hind legs, humanoid in shape but with distinctive wolf like features," the two men exchanged a stare.

"I would very much like to get copies of those photos," Mike stated, Steve broke off the stare and started walking around again.

"Not a chance in hell," Steve stepped off into his pacing again.

"I could get a court summons," Mike started. Steve glared at him.

"For what? Images from a Special Forces exercise, showing dead Special Forces soldiers, taken by surveillance equipment that is classified secret in a country from outside your jurisdiction, showing creatures that are not supposed to exist? ... I don't think so," Mike was fixed to where he was standing, he could not move but his mind showed him again what he had seen at the top of the hill at Castleroe, and Steve's description had been exactly right. Steve walked up to him, "You have seen it, yes?" Mike raised his head, he looked back into Steve's eyes.

"Yes," Mike whispered,

"And you want to find it, yes?" Steve replied.

"Yes,"

"And what will you do, when you do?" Steve's question was like a slap in the face, Mike knew they had to be caught, but what would he do??? Mike could not answer. "We tracked a group of them across Scotland, took out one of them, but lost them near Newtown Stewart, did not actually think they would come across to here."

"You 'took out' one of them?" Mike asked. Steve smirked.

"Yeah, guess what, you do not need silver bullets, normal ones do just fine,"

"I didn't hear anything about four soldiers being killed in Scotland?" Mike asked.

"It was on the news," replied Steve,

"Was it?"

"Yeah, the helicopter crash, happened the following day, the press release just left out the furry and fang club bit."

"You crashed a helicopter to cover up four deaths?" Mike could feel himself getting annoyed. Steve had stopped again.

"No, the crash was real, just happened the following day, pilot and crew got mangled, survived the crash but in a really bad way, it was all reported at the same time, like I said, we just left out the furry and fang bit,"

"So, what are you going to do if you find them?" Mike asked. Steve didn't answer so Mike continued, "We are still investigating several brutal murders and we will find them, arrest them and bring them to justice ... and may I advise you in the strongest possible terms not to interfere with that!" Steve looked at him sternly.

"We have no intention of 'interfering', quite the opposite," Mike slightly relaxed.

"And how can you help then?" Mike asked, Steve set off pacing again, "we can put surveillance teams out … These 'people' you are looking for, we can help find them for you," Mike considered the offer.

"I do not have the authority to request military support to a police investigation, in fact our Superintendent would point blank refuse!" Steve glanced over at Mike.

"Sutcliffe?" Steve asked.

"Yes," answered Mike, "he is not a fan of using the military, quite the opposite in fact."

"Then don't tell him!" stated Steve. Mike looked at him quizzically.

"And how would I do that? Everything we get, he sees,"

"Ok, a way around that is to let us have access to what you have so far, and we will do our own thing, and when we turn something up … you will be the first to know," Mike paused again.

"I will have to run this past the Inspector," Steve nodded, "I will pass your offer on to him and see what he says,"

"Yeah that is no problem," said Steve, "We want to help as much as we can," Mike did not believe that at all.

"Mike," Steve stopped right in front of him, "we have both seen something that is not supposed to exist … it has killed mine and now yours and we want to help you do something about it."

"And what do you get out of it?" Mike asked.

"The sound knowledge that there will be no more 'heads on poles',"

"That is not much, after what happened to your team."

"Well, you do not get a lot of thanks in this job!" Steve said. "Besides, most of what we do, people never find out about anyway!"

The two men said their goodbyes and Mike left in a hurry. Steve watched as Mike walked away and when he was over 100 metres away he spoke out loud, "All stations, all stations, this is Three Three Alpha, subject moving away from my location, heading towards Green One, One Two Acknowledge," Chris Abbey's quiet voice came over the small device in Steve's ear.

"Confirmed, Subject One is passing my location, heading on to Green One and returning to Charlie One." There was a slight pause before Chris's voice came over the radio net once again, "Confirmed, Subject One is now complete in Charlie one and now mobile, heading towards, Green Three," Mike was back in his car and driving away. Steve spoke again.

"Roger, all stations, close down, RTB, out."

∞∞∞∞

Back at the hangar Darren Forester looked away from the screen and removed his headset. He leaned back in his seat and looked over as Alan Dukesby, the techie who was the third person in the room. started giving instructions about the collection of the covert equipment that had been used to record the meeting into his headset, the shutdown would not take long.

"Well?" asked Darren,

"Well, what?" Alan replied.

"Well, what do we do next, that was exactly what we expected!"

"We do the sneak and peek tonight and take copies of what we need," the techie was chatting away as the feed from different screens started to go blank as each camera was collected. "You will go along as well to fend off any of the station coppers." the Major added, that it had been an excellent idea on Steve's part. Darren nodded.

"Are we going to help them?" Darren asked as the Major stood up.

"Not if they are going to get in the way, no." Alan started to walk towards the door as Darren shouted after him.

"And what if they do, 'get in the way'?" Alan did not look back as he shouted his answer just before he got to the only door in the room.

"Then our police Special Branch will have to sort the police out then, won't they!" The door slammed shut behind him. The techie glanced over at Darren. Darren shrugged.

387

"He is a bit angry," Darren stated; the techie raised his eyebrows.

"He got the book thrown at him for the chopper crash … then the massive 'D' notice about the three dead." The 'D' notice, a Disclosure notice, an injunction that only happens in the specialist military or intelligence communities, utter a single word and you are looking at 30 years behind bars! And they were enforced.

"Four dead, you mean?" stated Darren, the techie spoke into the head set as the last screen went blank.

"Three of his, yes, the Americans went mental at losing one of theirs, all the footage was shared with them, then … zip."

"What?" asked Darren.

"Zip," repeated the techie, "all the yanks who went back to the US suddenly disappeared, all social media, all friendly contacts, dead, gone, nothing … Zip," The techie closed down one of the two laptops in front of him as Darren sat in silence. The techie jerked his right thumb towards the door that Alan had walked out of, "The boss's opposite number, stateside, suddenly replaced, there was supposed to be some social function … or something, the two of them had been friends for years then, …. nothing, the yanks even stopped referencing the exercise completely, the boss was taken off somewhere and was not heard from for nearly two weeks, then straight over here." Darren nodded as the technician continued to explain, "He was supposed to make Colonel but that got canned. I heard there was a five-year promotion ban, it was the CO who saved his career by giving him this" Darren Forester nodded as the techie went back to closing down the equipment. He looked at his watch, it was lunch time, they would get the official 'No' from Inspector Parrish the following day, but Steve would continue to push to help them in some way.

Chapter 79

Carl was sitting in the large chair in the front room of the farmhouse, he was concerned. Paul was standing over by the door and the other furniture from the room had been pushed back to give Dermott space to lay out the weapons they had brought back with them. They were not normal rifles, 'AK-74 with very up to date modifications, scopes, rangefinders, etc.' Dermott had said as he had laid the four of them out on the floor.

"Three sets of series four body armour, with plates, three tactical helmets with integrated communications ..." Dermott had looked up at Carl, none of the Mongols had been at the house when they got there.

"And it looked like they haven't been gone long?" Paul asked.

"I think we surprised them, there was still clothes, personal items, food in the cupboards, found this lot under one of the beds,"

"And what have you found on the hard drives of the laptops?" Carl asked. Dermott turned and opened the first laptop.

"You will want to have a look at this," Carl rose and was joined by Paul as Dermott clicked on one of the folders that was full of pictures, Carl recognised himself in the first picture. Dermott started to scroll through the pictures, Carl looked angry, Paul looked surprised, "They have been busy," Dermott stated.

"What is all this?" Paul asked,

"They have pictures and briefing notes on every member that lives off site,"

"Every member?" Paul asked, Carl glared at the screen and Dermott continued to scroll the different images.

"Every member, every house, family member, names, addresses ... which schools the kids go to ..." Carl slammed his fist down on the desk.

"Damn!"

"But the one that really concerns me is ..." Dermott came out of the folder that he was in and clicked on a different folder.

"Was this not encrypted?" Paul asked,

"Yes, quite well in fact, gave these to the communications team when we got back last night, took them several hours but they got in," Dermott looked back at the screen, "here," The image was of Anders smiling in a kitchen and holding a plastic bottle in his right hand.

"What is so concerning about this?" Paul asked.

"It is in Tony Fallon's kitchen," Dermott paused, "inside his house,"

"What is in that bottle?" asked Carl.

"A mild type of rat poison," Dermott answered.

"Rat poison, but that would have no effect on Tony?" Paul stated, Carl straightened up.

"No ... but it would on a sapien," Paul looked shocked as Dermott stood up and finished what Carl was saying,

"Especially a pregnant sapien,"

"But wouldn't that kill her?" Paul stated.

"No," answered Carl, "but it could cause a miscarriage!" Carl was now angry, "Paul, can we accommodate every single member that lives off-site here?" Carl asked.

"Certainly," Paul replied.

"Right I want everyone back here, TODAY!" Paul nodded, "Dermott, I want them found ... found and dealt with ...... FINALLY!"

"It will be done," Dermott answered as he tried to suppress his smile.

"Get your teams together!" Carl shouted as he turned and marched out of the room and into the rear of the farmhouse, "And get Grishin on the phone, NOW!" Paul and Dermott exchanged a smile.

"At last," Paul almost hissed.

"That isn't all," he said as he closed the folder, "found something else that is not good either,"

"What is that?" Paul asked. Dermott search through more pictures before clicking on the one he had been looking for; the picture filled the screen of the laptop. Paul recognised the coffee shop in Society Street in Coleraine, it had been taken from across the street and showed Davidov sitting at a table by the window and to his surprise Paddy M'Kane, "When was this taken?" Paul asked.

"Looking at the date on it, just after they first arrived here,"

"What!" Paul exclaimed, "does Carl know?" Dermott shook his head, "No, I will show him when he comes back downstairs."

"Why would Paddy be meeting a Mongol in a coffee shop?" Paul asked.

"And why would they keep a record of it and if he was helping them, why kill him?" Dermott stated. Paul straightened up before answering.

"Because he was no longer any use to them ... and possibly a liability," Dermott glanced over at him.

"That isn't what I am thinking,"

∞∞∞∞

Davidov was standing outside the front of the bungalow with Anders, everyone else was still inside.

"They found the weapons and everything else we left for them?" he asked. Anders smiled before he answered.

"Yes, they took the bait well, they arrived just as we expected, they got the weapons, armour and the laptops,"

"So, they think we are now unarmed and, on the run?"

"Of course, when they came to the first house in Coleraine that is what they saw, so, that is what they got!" Anders was almost beaming with pride at what he had done, "They are totally fooled, they do not know how strong we are!" Davidov looked over at him.

"I'm not so sure," Davidov spoke quietly, "Are the laptops encrypted?"

"Yes, it will take them sometime to get into them, possibly days!" Anders boasted, Davidov did not look impressed, "What about Mia?" Anders asked,

"What about her?" Davidov replied.

"Did you believe what Tatamovich said about her attacking them?" Davidov sat back on the side of the car.

"No ... but she is dead and therefore not able to serve the pack, therefore I don't care," Davidov stood and started to walk back towards the front door of the house, he stopped and looked back up the hill to where the Noc had been dealt with. Anders looked at him then followed his gaze up the hill as well, "if they could find us here then so can the Rua,"

"We will fight them if they dare!" Anders boasted, Davidov glared at him.

"We will fight them on 'our' terms, not theirs," Davidov turned back towards the front door, "do we have everything we need for tonight?" he asked, Anders started to follow him towards the door.

"Yes, we are ready!" again it was a boast but this time Davidov was not impressed with Anders. Davidov opened the front door of the bungalow and walked in, everyone in the room stood up as he did so. Anders closed the door as he followed him in. Yelina was closest to them, she lowered her head as he passed her. Davidov walked a few steps and stopped in the middle of the group. Anders stopped beside Yelina and with the forefinger of his left hand drew a line down her right arm, she looked up, the bruises on her face could not be hidden by the makeup. She looked at the floor again as Anders smiled. Davidov looked around, Viktor and Pe'ter looked stern but Anna had an excited look on her face.

"Right, Anders, Anna, Viktor and Pe'ter with me, we will go to the meeting," Davidov started, it was a command and everyone knew it, he glanced around at each one as he spoke their names, "Yelina, go back to the house and see what they have left, search it, bring everything you find with you to the meeting," Davidov again looked around at them, "Full weapons, ready to fight, understand!" There was anger in his voice this time.

"I obey," they all responded.

"OK, let's go then," It only took a couple of minutes before both cars were full of the Mongol pack as they were racing away from Castlerock leaving the bungalow empty. Up the hill near the base of the tree was a small opening in the ground, you could walk past it and not see it as it was less than four inches square. The lens of the observation device was the only part visible, the rest was more than two feet underground. The two soldiers lay, weapons by their sides, looking at the screens in front of them. There was just enough space for them to lay side by side, the observation equipment was in front of them with their personal Bergan rucksacks lying at their feet. In between the rear was the small tunnel they would have to climb out of to exit the hide; but that would only be done later tonight, under the cover of darkness. One of them lifted a dark green box that was two inches deep with a cable extending out the back of it; on top was a keypad with a small screen that showed what he was typing before he pushed the send button. Everything was done in silence. Back at the hangar the techie pressed the intercom button and asked Alan Dukesby to return. It did not take him long before he re-entered the room. Darren Forester was long gone.

"What's up?" he asked as he approached the desk, the techie looked at him.

"Data message from X-Ray One Three," he replied.

"Where are they?" Alan asked.

"Overwatch on the bungalow," the techie was tapping away on the keyboard of the terminal built into the desk he was sitting at, the message appeared on the screen. 'BRAVO ONE AND TEAM COMPLETE IN CHARLIE ONE, FIVE UP, CHARLIE TWO, ONE UP, NOW MOBILE ON BLUE SEVEN, ALPHA TWO EMPTY,' Alan let a little smile spread over his lips before he spoke.

"OK, let all the team know that Sprogis and his little pack are all in the two cars heading towards Coleraine, the first car has five in it and the second only one. I want the cut off teams to pick them up and see where they are all going," The techie nodded as he started to type what Alan was saying, "task overwatch to do a sneak and peek inside the house and see what they have left then get support to do a technical attack on the house now that they are all out of it." The techie smiled, he knew the two other techies that would be taken into the bungalow and in less than half an hour the entire property would be bugged with some of the most sophisticated surveillance equipment in the world. "When are the team from Lisburn expected back?" he asked, the techie looked at his watch.

"They are on their way now, so probably not long,"

"Right," Alan stated, "I want them back in and sorted for heading out to the police station tonight as soon as possible!" the techie nodded again as Alan turned and walked back out of the room. The techie had watched him go, he did not comment but he had paused before turning back to the terminal and starting to furiously type out all the instructions that he had just received. He knew the Castlerock team would be busy the rest of the day as would the team that were on their way back from Lisburn.

∞∞∞∞

Cara-Marie was still annoyed, and it was getting worse. Nearly every time now when the door opened it was more tourists looking for werewolf stories. The reception staff had soon got sick of it as well and just directed them over to her and Mark. Mark did have pictures to sell, but nothing anyone could use. All of this was a waste of her time, she had so many other things to do. Every time she typed the word 'Rua' into the search engine there would be another person at the door, and everyone seemed to be wearing clothing with images of wolves on them. The phone rang again on the desk, thankfully Mark answered it.

"It is for you!" he said, holding the handset towards her, she scowled over at him.

"Who is it?" Mark looked away as he answered but still held the phone towards her.

"Did not get the name, German newspaper this time." Angrily she snatched the phone and soon found herself saying the same thing again that she had been doing all morning. Her stories of the werewolf sightings and witness reports had now gone international, and the international media was responding. It seemed like everyone wanted to talk to her, but she didn't want to talk to them; she wanted to find out more and all of this was holding her up. As she spoke on the phone, she looked at the inbox of her work email address, she heard the ping of the arrival of another email. She glanced at the figure in the corner, that was 100 emails for her to work through, and they were just from today, she was going to be at work late tonight. As she replaced the handset of the phone she heard her name come from Kevin's office. She turned and looked over at him, he beckoned her over, her annoyance was starting to turn to anger. She pushed the chair back and went and stood in the doorway, he was reading something on his computer screen, he glanced up.

"Ah, Cara," he motioned with his head for her to come forward.

"What?" it was almost a demand; Kevin did not look up from the screen as she walked the few paces towards his desk.

"Right, just heard that there is going to be an update on a Crime Watch programme tonight ..." he looked up at her, "cover it will you!" she almost exploded.

"What? Are you kidding me?" Kevin stopped what he was doing, as did the rest of the office who were now listening to her outburst, "I have been fending off everyone, from London to Tokyo, every head bin who thinks they are a werewolf has either been knocking the door, emailing or phoning, I have not got time for that! Give it to someone else!" She was about to turn around and storm off when Kevin shouted at her.

"WHAT? Listen here you ..." both his hands were flat on his desk as he started to propel himself upwards, "All of this ... Wolves etc ... IS YOUR DAMN STORY IN THE FIRST PLACE! YOU PUT YOUR NAME TO DIFFERENT STORIES AND HAD ME PUBLISH THEM SO GUESS WHAT MY GIRL ... WHEN THE CRAP COMES TO THE DOOR GUESS WHO IS GETTING IT ... AND IF YOU DON'T LIKE THAT ..." there was a pause as he let the threat hang in the air, "YOU CAN ALWAYS HAND YOUR NOTICE IN AND PISS OFF AND DO SOMETHING ELSE! ... NOW DO YOUR BLOODY JOB AND RIGHT NOW YOUR JOB IS WHAT I SAY IT IS AND I SAY IT IS THIS ... NOW DO IT!" he waved his hand to dismiss her from the office as he sat back down. It was a slap in the face, and it took Cara-Marie a few seconds to recover before she could turn around and walk back to her desk. Everyone had heard it, including the tourists who were standing at the front desk. Cara-Marie sat back down at her desk and stared at the screen, everyone in the office had their heads down busying themselves with work so no one had to look at her, that was except for Mark who was staring at her.

"What?" she demanded as she grabbed the mouse for the desktop computer and brought the screen back to life.

"Did we not get a lot of sleep last night?" she glared at him for several seconds. Mark turned in his chair and tapped the keyboard of his computer, he turned his head to face the screen, "Obviously not then."

One of the reception staff suddenly started shouting, she was holding a phone to her ear as she repeated what was being said to her, "THERE HAS BEEN ANOTHER ATTACK, SEVERAL SHEEP KILLED ... THE FARMER SAYS HE HAS KILLED THE BEAST!" and with that, the office exploded in activity and shouting.

∞∞∞∞

Mike Dear looked at his watch, it was ten minutes to six in the evening as he stood outside the airport. When he had got back to the office from the meeting he had told Sean everything about what the soldier had said, and what he had offered. There was no point in taking that request to Chief Anderson, never mind Super Sutcliffe, both would refuse. After that, it had been a rush to get the last of the presentation together and then make a run for the airport to catch the flight, it had been close. Now they waited to be collected from where they had landed. He had read over his notes several times and looked over the images from the CCTV that they were going to re-release during the programme. He had asked just for him to go as he knew that Sean was exhausted but his wife had been shouting down the phone at him since he had told her he was heading to London again and would not be back until the following day, just in time for the funeral. To be honest he could do without this, but there was no-one else to lead it. Eddie Cargill appeared beside him, chatting on his phone as a tall man approached him.

"DS DEAR, PSNI?" the tall man asked; there was no handshake offered.

"Yes," Mike half turned and motioned towards Eddie, "And this is Detective Constable Cargill ..." the tall man nodded towards them.

"Would you follow me please, I am to take you straight to the studio," the tall man had not introduced himself or who he worked for, all they had been told was a driver would pick them up outside the main entrance.

"Well, it is either the right guy, or we are on our way to a shallow grave!" Eddie commented, Mike looked at him and smiled, before he extended the handle on his wheeled case.

"Come on then," as they started to follow the driver Mike's phone started to ring.

Chapter 80

Sean was sitting in his living room staring at the TV screen; the Crime Watch programme was due to start just after the advertisements. He was glad he was not there. After Mike left, he had spent most of the afternoon helping finalise the arrangements for Simon's funeral. Like a lot of the police funerals he had been to before it was not just the family mourning, the Chief Constable and several other senior officers along with local Politician's, although not invited, would turn up anyway, he hated them for it. They had no idea who Simon McAllister was, they didn't know him, hadn't watched him work, or even know what he had achieved.

The phone in his pocket started to ring, he looked at the screen, it was one of the younger team members that had been sent up towards Coleraine, Sean was waiting for this call as it would decide if he had to leave for Coleraine or not; he hoped not.

"Evening boss," greeted the excited young detective,

"Hi, what's the score, what have we got at Ballybogy?" Sean asked.

"Nothing,"

"Nothing?" repeated Sean,

"Nothing for us anyhow! Remember those stories of 'the beast of Ballybogy?" the detective asked. Sean was perplexed.

"No, what has that got to do with a possible murder? I want to know what's happening not fairy tales?" the detective now seemed a bit sheepish.

"Sorry boss, no, nothing for us at all, this is an animal attack, several sheep and a farm dog killed by a puma,"

"A puma? As in ..."

"A big cat! The farmer shot it with a shotgun, it's dead alright, so nothing for us!" Sean was now confused.

"How did a large cat end up outside Coleraine?"

"Well, I am originally from around here and I know the stories ......"

"What stories?" Sean asked.

"About the beast of Ballybogy! There have been sightings over the last few years that there was a large cat on the loose somewhere around here, some photos, witnesses you know, ..." The detective paused again as a car went past behind him, "well, it looks like it has finally been found!"

"Great ... but nothing for us?,"

"Ah, no,"

"Right then, I will see you in the morning,"

"Yes, bo" Sean cut him off and reached for the TV control to increase the volume, the tall blonde female anchor started with a very stern look on her face as she covered the crimes that they were hosting this evening, a pensioner mugged in their own home in London, a robbery of machinery from a farm that was worth over £5 million in Kent, a violent rape in Manchester, but so far, no mention of their case. The female presenter handed over to a male colleague who as he started speaking a map of Northern Ireland appeared behind him.

"Yes, thank you, first to Northern Ireland and an update on a series of very extreme murders that we first aired several months ago ..." Mike was introduced, he was sitting beside a clear plastic table and on a clear screen behind him Sean spotted the list of names of those who had been killed, 'Edgar Trotman, 'Septic' Simpson, the list went down the right-hand side of the screen. Mike seemed quite at ease, but Sean knew he would not be. The face of Alex Chernov appeared on the screen and details of his apparent suicide. Mike kept on stressing that it had been an apparent suicide and that it was still being investigated. More pictures appeared of the green BMW that had been recovered at Castleroe, then the CCTV images; there were three different ones of someone the police believed may be called 'Anna', but they did not have a confirmed surname. The last picture that had been taken at the petrol station showed Anna with two other men and another woman. Enlarged images of each face were shown in turn on the screen. The TV anchor kept on stressing that if you knew these people, or where they were you were not to approach them. Mike gave out the number for the Muirdris team again as it appeared across the bottom of the screen. Mike reviewed the killings in Belfast, then Limavady, then Coleraine,

"We would very much like to interview the woman with the black hair as we believe that she has vital information that will help us with this investigation!" Sean smiled briefly, "we believe that the group may be Latvian, and I would like to repeat that they should not be approached, we believe they are very dangerous people," the host smiled and asked the awkward question.

"So, the stories about werewolves, that have been everywhere, what is your approach on that?" Mike let out a small laugh that the host matched.

"Well, we are not interested in conspiracy theories, little green men or furry and fanged beasts from horror films!" and the two of them shared another laugh, "We are looking for some very dangerous people that need to be caught and brought to justice!" The host took back control of the programme and went over what Mike had been saying and the number reappeared on the screen, that was it, it was done, he then handed back to the female host.

"Right, now we move to Kent, where a very brash robbery has taken nearly all the farm machinery that has brought a crop producer to a standstill... Sean was no longer listening, he reached for the TV remote and switched it off. Silence filled the room. Sean thought over what Mike had done. There was so much that he did not mention, the cast from the dental pathologist, Mike's own statement, and what Mike had described to him at the top of the hill.

"They cannot be real," he found himself saying out loud.

"Pardon?" his wife called from the kitchen.

"Nothing," he replied.

∞∞∞∞

Cara-Marie watched the programme to the very end before she opened her laptop, it would only take her a few minutes to type up the story for Kevin; she looked at her email number, there were still 62 she hadn't opened, and that was just from today. The story would keep him happy, there was nothing new, but she did quote what the detective had said about 'little green men' and the 'furry and fanged beasts.' She ended the article with what she remembered about the paper that Dr Burns had published and that it had been rubbished by nearly everyone in the scientific community around the world. He had lost a lot of face and several Politicians had been calling for him to be replaced in the Forensic labs as 'how can any of his work be trusted now?' She filed the story into the drop box that he could access in the morning. Hopefully that would keep him off her back for a bit.

She had just made it back for the start of the programme. Both her and Mark had gone to Ballybogy but once they knew what was happening she left Mark there, and Mark seemed happy to stay. The farmer had been quite pleased with all the attention he was getting, especially when the story broke over social media. It had been reported as a werewolf attack and most of the visiting 'werewolf enthusiasts' had descended on the farm very quickly. Cara-Marie looked at her watch, it was nearly 10 p.m. She could, she thought, continue with the emails; they all did need reading at least, but that was going to take time. She paused as she looked at the screen. Cara-Marie picked up her phone and typed in a text message, 'HI, ARE YOU BUSY? BEEN A CRAP DAY AT THE OFFICE, I CAN DROP BY,' She had not heard from him since he had quietly left her flat the previous morning; she pressed the send button. She placed the phone on the arm of the sofa and moved the laptop from her legs onto the sofa; which email should she open first? The phone beeped with the arrival of a text message that had only one word. 'SURE.' The chill had left her and had just been replaced by a mild excitement. She would quickly shower and only apply a little make up as she knew he did not like loads of it. It would take another ten minutes before she was reversing her car away from her flat, she would not return until the following morning.

∞∞∞

Tony Fallon's fist missed Dermott's head, but it did hit the wall behind him. Tony was fast but so was Dermott. Tony was in a rage, Paul tackled Tony from the side, and it would take both Dermott and Paul several minutes to restrain and calm Tony down to a level where they could let him go. Tony was curled up on the floor of the front room of the farm, his rage had turned to sobbing at the picture that Dermott had just shown him.

"You could have warned him!" said Paul, Dermott stood up wiping the trickle of blood that was coming from his nose. Dermott glared at Paul as Carl walked into the room. He stood at the far side of the room. He didn't have to ask what had just happened, he knew. He nodded to both Paul and Dermott and motioned towards Tony who was starting to get control of himself. They went either side of him and helped him up into one of the chairs, the tears were still streaming down his face as he looked over at the picture on the screen of the laptop.

"*THEY DID THIS!*" he screamed as he jumped to his feet,

"I only found out this evening," Carl said, and he went to place his hand on Tony shoulder, it was batted away as he also shoved Dermott out of his path. Tony stopped at the laptop and sobbed again at the image of Anders on the screen. He turned around with both tears and rage in his eyes. Tony and Dermott shared a glance, at any other time doing that to the Alpha would be cause for punishment, but Carl did not move.

"I WANT THEM DEAD, I WANT THEM ALL DEAD!" Tony screamed, Carl then stepped forward and placed his arms around Tony's shoulders. Tony accepted his embrace and held it for a few moments before letting go. Carl stood back and looked at him.

"You will have what you desire, I promise you that." Suddenly there was a frantic banging at the door; Dermott opened it to see one of the young farm hands, his face and clothes were muddy. He had a bolt action stalking rifle over one shoulder, he was almost shouting into the house.

"THERE IS A MONGOL FEMALE AT THE BOTTOM OF THE LANE!" Carl shouted at Tony to stay where he was as they ran out of the door after the farm hand. Carl had stopped by the side of the house with Paul only a few feet away from him along the hedge row, Paul had his right hand on the pistol that was on his belt. Dermott was in the centre of the very active yard shouting instructions to those that were running in different directions. Several people who were armed ran towards Dermott, others who were not were ordered to go the other way. Tony could feel the anger inside him, but he had been told where to stay, his Alpha had told him. He did go to the doorway so he could see what was going on. He wanted to be over with Dermott, but he could go no further. Several members with bolt action rifles had been directed to the far side of the hedgerow at the opposite side of the lane. They all had perfect line of sight down the entrance to the farm, others were clambering up ladders the far side of the barn, so they could be on top; there was a lot of movement. Dermott had drawn his pistol, walked over and stopped at the top of the lane.

Tony looked over the field that separated the farmhouse from the road and the entrance, the single car was parked at the far side of the road and a lone woman stood at the mouth of the entrance. Tony looked over the fields and hills behind her, there was no obvious movement, but if there were more Mongols then it would not take long for the guys on the roof to spot them. Tony glanced over at Dermott who was speaking into the communicator, others moved at his command, very soon the yard was quiet; the woman had not moved. Tony knew that she was waiting to be called forward, if she just started towards the farm she would not make another five feet. Dermott glanced over at Carl and Carl nodded. Dermott looked back down the lane.

"ADVANCE" he shouted. Slowly the lone figure walked up the middle of the lane with her hands-on top of her head with the palms uppermost. Dermott stopped her when she was ten feet away from him, he was now aiming his pistol at her; she was in tears.

"I am not armed ..." she stuttered. There was a silence then Dermott spoke again.

396

"REMOVE YOUR TOP, KEEP IT IN ONE HAND AND FULLY TURN AROUND! Dermott commanded. Tony watched as she did as she had been told. Her movements were slow. The top she had been wearing was pulled over her head, she shook her hair to allow it to settle, she held the top in her left hand and slowly started to turn around. The white bra she was wearing did not hide the severe bruising that mottled her body, she did not have a weapon around her upper torso. She stopped and looked back at Dermott who continued to aim his weapon at her. "Replace your top," Dermott had lowered his voice, with his left hand he made a wave motion and two farm hands with rifles walked forward, both were up in the aim at the Mongol. Tony looked at the woman, his rage was calming and for a moment there was a pang of pity, she had suffered a severe beating, and recently. She was beautiful, but her face was still streaming with tears and her face burst back out the top of her clothing. "Keep your hands in the air." Yelina nodded. Dermott waved with his left hand again and the farm hand on his left moved forward and lowered his weapon, he moved around the back of Yelina and started a rough search around the belt of her jeans, her groin, then her legs and all the way down to her feet, as he stood up he nodded to Dermott. Dermott flicked his head and commanded the farm hand to retake his place on Dermott's left-hand side, without uttering a word the hand did as he had been commanded. Yelina just stood there, gently crying, Dermott lowered his weapon and stared at her.

"What do you want?" he asked, Yelina was still crying as she spoke.

"Please ..." Slowly she knelt, and lay face down with her arms out spread on the lane, this was total submission. "Please ..." she repeated, Carl started to walk over towards Dermott, he turned and motioned with his head for Tony to follow him, as he started to follow Carl, Tony's right hand touched the grip of his own pistol. Carl marched forward and as he approached the small group, the hand that was on Dermott's right lowered his weapon and backed away. Carl glared at the weeping woman that was lying on the ground.

"WHY HAVE YOU COME HERE!" he demanded, she did not look up, she continued to face the ground, she started saying something, but Dermott butted in,

"ENGLISH, SPEAK ONLY IN ENGLISH!"

"I'm ... sorry,"

"You were asked a question, answer it!" Dermott demanded. Yelina choked before she spoke again, her voice was broken and stuttered.

"Alpha of the Northern Den of the Great Rua ..." Dermott glanced at Carl, he could see the anger in Carl's face, with one word he would end the life on the ground and Dermott would not have a problem with that. "I come to beg for my life ... Whatever that may be worth."

"Just you, or your entire pack?" asked Carl; this time he was not shouting.

"Just me ..."

"Why?" Carl cut her off, Yelina paused before she answered.

"My life is in danger,"

"Why is your life in danger? That is a matter for your own!" Carl's voice was stern.

"My life is in danger from my own," she replied.

"That is still a matter for your pack," Carl paused. Yelina sobbed gently.

"Godspodine ... please ... I have done you no harm ... If I stay they will kill me ..."

"Why would they kill you. What have you done to deserve that punishment?" Carl asked. There was another pause,

"NOTHING ..." She protested, "Things changed since Davidov killed Alexi ..."

"Why did he do that?" Carl asked.

"He wanted Anna," Carl looked over at Dermott before looking back at her, "after that he could take her, and ..."

"And what?"

"And since Davidov has become our Alpha things have become worse." Yelina had now stopped crying but she had still not looked up, Tony became aware of the fact that Paul had joined them.

"How?" Carl demanded.

"Well after Anders killed the Noc I was given as a gift..." Carl looked at Paul, then back at her.

"YOU KILLED A NOC! WHY WAS I NOT INFORMED, THOSE WERE THE TERMS!" Carl shouted at her, Dermott's hand gripped his weapon.

"Davidov has never intended to meet your terms," she replied.

"What is he going to do?" Paul asked, Carl glanced over his shoulder.

"Challenge you," she replied, there was an obvious reaction from everyone standing there, everyone except Carl.

"When?" he asked.

"I do not know," she replied.

"When and where was this Noc killed?" Carl asked.

"Last week, it was stalking Anna ... Anders stalked it and killed it,"

"How?" Carl asked.

"With knife," Tony picked up on her heavy accent and the misuse of English. "Davidov very pleased with him,"

"What do you mean, you were 'given'?" Yelina paused and again started to cry.

"Anders had given Davidov a gift, he asked him what he wanted, Anders picked me,"

"Are you not already with someone?" Carl asked.

"Yes, Viktor, ... but Davidov said he could take me, Viktor, ..." Her voice trailed off, everyone knew what she meant. "Anders .... Brutal .... If I stay ...... he will kill me ... I know it, Viktor can do nothing." They had all seen the bruises when she had removed her top for the security search.

"Why should we believe you?" asked Dermott. Yelina was searching for something.

"Well," she stuttered again, "you were meant to find the weapons at the house yesterday, also ..."

"How did you find all of us, the families, how?" Carl demanded. Yelina again paused before she answered.

"We had the list of all your pack, where they all are,"

"How?" Carl asked.

"We were given it," she replied,

"Who by?" Carl demanded,

"The one called M'Kane,"

"Paddy?"

"Yes,"

"When?" Carl asked,

"Davidov and M'Kane met several times; coming here from Scotland was M'Kane's idea,"

"Why?" asked Carl.

"M'Kane wanted to be Alpha, knew he could not by himself, contacted Davidov a year ago, all arranged, met in coffee shop in Coleraine and bus station in Limavady" she explained. Tony reacted.

"The bus station, that was Davidov?" he asked, Carl looked at him, the stare said, 'be quiet,' Tony backed down.

"No, it was M'Kane, thought they had been seen ..." Yelina looked up from the ground before finishing her sentence, "Dead men do not talk!"

"Then why kill him?" Carl asked,

"Davidov wants to be Alpha, used M'Kane and by killing a Rua the other Mongols will follow him!"

"What about the others?" Carl asked.

"Others?" Yelina asked.

"The other killings, who was that?" Carl demanded again.

"That was Davidov and Anna ... Davidov could never follow rules .... send Anna out, attract men ... lead them away ... and feed," Tony could feel the resentment building up in him again, "Alexi tried to stop him ... could not,"

"Rise," commanded Carl. Yelina slowly stood up, the tears were still running down her face and cut tracks in the dirt that covered her face.

"Please ... Rua ... spare me my life ..." Carl stared at the woman in front of him then looked at Paul.

"Take her inside," Carl looked her up and down, "allow her to clean herself up then, Dermott," Carl looked over towards Dermott, "I want to know everything about where they are and what they have been up to." Carl turned towards the farmhouse; Tony stepped back to allow him to pass. "Tony, with me," he commanded.

Chapter 81

It seemed to Kyle the sun was up later in the day than usual. He looked out over the back of his house. He liked the view and the hot buttered toast he was having for breakfast. He had stayed in bed a little longer today. He was on the afternoon shift and in no rush. He lifted the TV remote and clicked on a 24-hour news channel. The big news was some kind of financial crash that was happening in banks all over the world, images and footage of people queuing outside of banks filled the report. The gut-wrenching feeling came back; the previous day most of the guys of the section had been relentless in making comments about Kelly:

"Oh, in love, are we?"

"Well, he was not the one getting the 'loving' on Saturday night!"

"Have you seen that DVD she made? Wow, I mean, wow!"

He had tried not to react, but each one had the same effect, they hit hard. He had been with Alison most of the day and she had not mentioned it until the shift was nearly over. He denied everything; she had not believed him.

"You need to take time to get her out from under your skin," Kyle had looked over at her as she had spoken, "it will take time and ..." she had paused, "it will hurt, but you need to back off from her. What feelings you may have for her, she doesn't have for you, and that, Kyle, can only end in disaster for you!"

Thinking about it made his guts turn, he knew he had to get away from her; the TV brought him back to the kitchen.

"And in other news the funeral of police officer Detective Sergeant Simon McAllister will take place later today ..." Kyle glanced up at the screen, then looked back out the window, he did not hear the rest of the report. His phone started to ring in the living room, it was still ringing as he picked it up. It was a withheld number, which normally only meant one thing, it was the control room at the police station.

"Can you get into the station in an hour please?"

"Why?" Kyle asked, "Our shift does not start until 2 pm?" Kyle could picture which controller he was speaking now to.

"Operational requirements, briefing by the Inspector as soon as everyone has arrived," she was not going to say the real reason over the phone but, 'operational reasons' meant that there was a job on and the morning shift would all get offered overtime; they would not.

"OK, I am on my way," Kyle ended the call but before he dropped the phone, he noticed that there was a text message from Kelly; his guts turned again as he opened the message. 'WHO DO YOU THINK YOU ARE? I WILL GO WITH ANYONE I WANT, WHERE DO YOU THINK YOU HAVE A SAY IN THAT?' Kyle read the message again, he was confused, he had not said anything to her, but possibly someone else had, the police was a small organisation and scandal travelled fast. Kyle tapped in a short reply before heading for the shower, 'WHAT ARE YOU TALKING ABOUT?' It would be answered with anger.

∞∞∞∞

Mike was dressed in a plain black, pressed suit, he walked through the main office in Belfast, the rest of the team were all dressed the same, the quiet conversations stopped as Mike entered. He nodded in recognition to those who were in the room, he headed for Sean's office. Sean was sitting behind the desk and seemed to be staring at the screen of the desktop computer, his jacket for the black suit he was wearing was draped over the rear of the chair, his white shirt was clean and pressed as was the plain black tie that extended down from his neckline. Mike stopped and knocked at the door.

"Hi boss," Mike stepped into the room, the first thing he noticed was the lack of the smell of coffee. He looked at the coffee machine, it was off and looked like it had not been switched on that morning at all.

"Hi Mike" Sean looked exhausted as he moved himself in the chair, "well done on the Crime Watch, from what I can tell the Chief and Super are happy," Mike sat down.

"Thanks,"

"What time did you get back?" Sean asked.

"6 a.m. flight this morning, straight home, changed then here," Mike looked up at the clock on the wall, "nearly time we were getting a move on," he said. Sean nodded.

"I am not looking forward to this," Sean almost whispered it.

"Neither am I," Mike replied,

"Well," started Sean and he went to stand up, "we had better get a move on." Suddenly Eddie Cargill appeared at the door with a large brown envelope in his hands.

"Ah, boss, you 'need' to take a look at this!" Eddie walked in and emptied the 8" x 10" colour photographs onto the Sean's desk. Mike picked up the first photograph of Anna.

"What are these?" Sean stated as he started to go through the pictures himself, everyone in the room recognised the faces from the CCTV in Castlerock, each one a portrait.

"Look what's on the back!" Eddie excitedly said. Mike turned the picture he had over and read out loud what was there.

"Anna Nikitin, Latvian national ... and this is an address near Coleraine!" Mike looked up at Sean who was reading the back of another one.

"Davidov Sprogis, Latvian national, former member of Alpha Group of the special forces of the Russian federation ... do we know this address?" Sean asked.

"No, it isn't any of the registered addresses we have for them, look," Eddie spread the other pictures out, "This one, Anders Dusmanov ... here, Viktor Shelaev, ... Yelina Gurin .... It's the whole bloody lot of them!" Eddie was getting excited.

"Where did these come from?" Mike asked.

"In the post this morning, post marked here in Belfast, and looks like they were posted yesterday" Sean lifted a picture he did not recognise.

"This one just says 'Mia', no surname,"

"She must be a part of the group; just haven't seen her yet," Mike and Sean exchanged a glance, this could be the breakthrough they had been waiting for.

"Right, Eddie, I want these names and addresses confirmed," Eddie was already nodding, "Get in touch with the Latvian embassy and get confirmation of these names and pictures, I want them ID'd before we go public with them, then get in touch with Coleraine. We will need uniform support this afternoon if we are going to these addresses," Eddie smiled and turned to leave the office.

"Eddie!" Eddie looked back.

"Yes boss?" he asked,

"Pick somebody to stay and help you with this, phone me when you're done," Eddie nodded, he would not be going to the funeral.

"Where the hell did these come from?" Mike asked,

Sean shrugged as he stood up, "I have no idea, looks like someone wants to help." Mike picked up more of the pictures, looking at each one. Sean pulled the jacket from the back of the chair, "Anyway, we should be somewhere, so let's go,"

ooοοoo

"Did they say why the meeting was moved by a day?" Anders asked, Davidov glared at him.

"Moving the meeting is not what is concerning me right now." It was a scowl, "I want to know where she is and what she thinks she is playing at!" Davidov's anger was growing. She had defied his order, when they had got back to the bungalow she was not there, and the car was gone. They went to look for her at the other house, but she wasn't there either. Some of her clothes and things were missing, and that could only mean one thing, like Mia, she had run. Davidov paced up and down outside the front of the bungalow, he hated waiting. Viktor appeared at the front door,

"We have the programme from last night," he said, Davidov turned and walked directly inside as Anders followed. Pe'ter was kneeling in front of the large TV as Viktor closed the door behind him. Davidov took his place first in one of the single chairs. Anna moved and perched herself on the armrest as the others sat back to watch the sapien 'Crime Watch' programme to see what the local police knew about them.

∞∞∞

In the hangar, the techie looked at both the active screens, one from inside the living room and the one covering the front of the house. Alan was sitting back from the console looking at what was happening on the screens. On the opposite side of the techie was a smartly dressed young man who was wearing one of the headsets.

"How long have you been in the intelligence corps?" Alan asked.

The smartly dressed man looked over at him, "Two years." Alan cringed, that meant limited experience.

"What language are they speaking?" he asked. The young man looked at the screen.

"It is a dialect of Muscovite Russian..."

"You can understand it, yes?" the techie asked, the young man gave him a disgusted look.

"Of course, I can. I can speak several distinct types of Russian!"

"So, what are they saying?" Alan asked.

"Bravo two and Bravo three were commenting on the female presenter. Bravo two would like to have aggressive sex with her ..." The techie looked around at Alan who met his look then turned back to the screen,

"Bravo one has just told them to shut up," the only sound coming from the feed now was the Crime Watch programme. Alexi's picture appeared on the screen.

"Bravo three has just asked why are they still looking for him, he is dead?" the translation continued, "Bravo four, the girl, has just reacted to her picture, it is a type of swearing," the young man stared at the screen and listened to what was happening in his headset, "Bravo two has just asked again about a meeting that is happening later ...... Bravo One has just shouted at them all to shut up."

Alan looked over at the door as Steve opened it and stood in the doorway, he motioned with his head for Alan to come outside, Alan nodded and looked at the techie,

"I want a full audio transcript of this as soon as it is done, OK!" the techie nodded.

"Yes boss,"

Alan walked outside the room and followed Steve towards the main entrance, Steve stopped as he got there.

"So, what did you get from last night?" Alan asked. Steve shook his head.

"Nothing we did not know already, they do not have as much as we first thought ... they have a great cast from a dental pathologist though!" Steve smiled, "got a great picture of it ... it will look good on the wall of the bar!" Alan smiled. From across the road came the sound of gun fire, neither men moved.

"Is that our guys on the range?" Alan asked.

"Some, just doing some grouping and zeroing with the new scopes we got the other day," Alan nodded.

"You know what I want done?" Alan asked,

"Yes boss,"

"So, it begins!" Alan stated.

"So, it ends!" replied Steve.

∞∞∞

Tony looked at his watch, the sun was setting and there was a chill in the air, he was standing at the front of one of the two police minibuses with Kyle, who was busy with text messages and was angry. Two other uniformed police officers from their section stood in front of them and chatted but Tony hadn't said much all day. The briefing they had earlier was from a man with

402

scruffy, black curly hair who looked like he, and his clothes, had not been washed in sometime. He stated that he was from the drug squad and they had been tasked with helping them secure a major arrest that day.

"As you are aware, large quantities of crystal meth have arrived in the northwest and are causing major problems," the drugs officer got several comments from the crowd about being around the night club in Portrush on a Saturday evening and experiencing 'major problems', the morning shift sergeant had got them all to shut up. A major shipment was due to be exchanged that very afternoon near the Downhill at the far side of Castlerock. The drugs officer had shown them photographs of the main players, one they all knew, and his silver BMW! Tony had wondered why he was at a drop off. It wasn't like him to be so involved with the drugs themselves. He normally got teenagers to carry the drugs so he could deny all knowledge if stopped by any of them. He knew the law and knew it well.

"We want to take these people and these drugs out of circulation," the drugs officer had continued. Their inspector brought up a slide of the area. Most would be in two groups at either end of the beach out of sight, they were to be used for securing the scene as the team made the arrests, supported by several police officers already picked from the morning shift.

"They're late," stated Kyle who moved beside him as he replaced his phone back into his pocket. The small area they were parked was out of sight from the rest of the beach. When called they were all to wait behind the two small hills for the different cars to arrive, the minibuses would block the only exit.

"Did you think they would be on time?" Tony asked, Kyle shook his head, he had tried to get a conversation out of Tony since the briefing but hardly got two words. Tony desperately wanted to be somewhere else as Karen was still in hospital. Kyle had overheard two of the staff talking about 'mild poisoning' and the complications with the miscarriage. Tony believed she would be coming home shortly and would be relieved when she did.

"You still missing your girlfriend?" one of the coppers asked; it got a chuckle from the others as well.

"I have no girlfriend," Kyle replied,

"Yeah, not anymore," Tony folded his arms and shuffled where he was standing, the other police shared a laugh at Kyle's expense.

"Did you hear about the werewolf squad?" one of them asked the group, both Tony and Kyle looked up.

"What, 'werewolf squad'?" Tony asked.

"You know, the M.I.T. lot that are looking for the werewolf!" he replied.

"I doubt they are looking for a werewolf," Tony replied as he slightly lowered his head to look at the ground. The minibus behind them exploded with laughter, and they all turned around. Just as quickly as it had happened a voice came over the police radio earpiece telling them to all shut up. They could be heard from where the other team and the drugs squad were hiding. As it quietened down the policeman continued,

"Well, I heard that this afternoon they got onto Coleraine demanding a load of coppers for a raid on a house, but we were all committed to this, so they got told to 'piss off'," he was smiling as he recounted his story,

"Where did you heard that?" Kyle asked.

"Oh, from one of the other sections!"

"And you believed him?" Tony asked his question quietly, but before he could answer the voice came back on the earpiece,

"All officers into position, all officers into position!" There was a frantic move from inside the minibus as Kyle and Tony almost ran past them to take up their positions lying on the ground, under the crest of the hill. The sun was setting, and the view of the hill looked beautiful. For a moment Kyle enjoyed what he was doing. Tony did not. Beside them a line of police appeared, ready to jump up and run forward.

"Haven't heard a car!" stated a voice,

"Neither have I," the chattering was really getting to Tony, if this was a military ambush there would be no talking whatsoever.

"Shut up," crackled the radio net again and they all fell silent. Kyle lifted his head slightly, a cool breeze blew into his face, along with a foul smell that made him wince. Nobody else seemed to react but Tony glanced over at him.

"Body odour," he whispered.

"What?" whispered Kyle back,

"Body odour," Tony repeated, "Someone up wind has not washed in a while ..."

"How can I smell it?" Kyle asked quietly and Tony smiled for the first time that day.

"Another part of you is waking up!" It took Kyle a couple of seconds to realise what he was talking about but before he could say anything else, the radio suddenly barked into life. The voice was shouting, and it sounded like they were already running.

"EVERYONE, GO GO GO!!!"

Chapter 82

Anders drove the car over the rise and Davidov looked to his left. The trees had given way to a small stone wall with wooden gates; it was an old cemetery. It had been raining earlier but thankfully it had stopped now. Davidov had told Viktor to take Pe'ter and get another car, but not from a dealership this time. They were to go to a smaller private vendor, hopefully one without CCTV. Anna sat quietly in the backseat. She hadn't said a word since they had watched the programme. She had been spotted and they knew her first name, now that was going to be a problem. She had accusations thrown at her and, to her surprise, Davidov did not defend her. She was left to answer for herself. The edge of the forest came right up to end of the stone wall and the forest blocked the view to the left. The view to the right opened into fields and grassland. Up on the hill to the right was the ruin of an old building. It had likely been a manor house many years ago. Davidov looked ahead, the road started to dip down the hill and slowly the sea came into view. Anders slowed the car at the black metal gates with spikes, supported by a large stone pillar on each side, and what at first glance looked like a wolf on top. Davidov lowered his head and Anders started to turn into the gate.

"They are not wolves!" Davidov stated.

"It's called 'Lion's Gate!'" Anna said from the backseat, Davidov turned to look at her.

"How do you know that?" he hissed, Anna looked sheepish.

"Alexi brought me here once when …"

"Enough!" Davidov held his right hand up, she knew not to continue speaking. As they drove through the entrance the road turned around to their left and opened into a car park. Anna looked over the wooden gateway that led up towards the ruins and Anders continued down into the empty car park. The small wooden shed on the right was locked up, there was no one here at this time of night. Just past the shed was the main car park where Anders parked the car with the rear of the car pointing back up towards the ruins. In front of them was the forest and it spread over the hills on the far side of the road. Davidov released the seatbelt and jumped out of the car followed by Anders and Anna. Davidov stopped at the front of the vehicle staring off into the darkness that covered the forest. He closed his eyes as he took a deep breath in. "We will make this land our own!" he said out loud. Anders let out a small yelp of excitement. Davidov didn't move, the wind blew in from the ocean and filled with the smell of the sea; he kept his eyes shut. Suddenly all three of them turned to face the stone wall at the far end, a smell had just hit them, all of them got ready for danger, but as soon as it had come, it went; whoever it was, they were quite far away.

Anders walked around to the back of the car to open the boot. He beckoned Anna to join him as he started to lift out the body armour vests and lay them on the grass behind the car. Davidov stood motionless.

"How long before Viktor and Pe'ter get here?" Anna asked, Anders looked at his watch before answering.

"As soon as they can if they know what's good for them!" Anders placed a helmet on top of the five sets of vests then reached for the first rifle, as he checked it Davidov spoke.

"Keep the weapons out of sight, only bring them out when we need them." Anders paused placing the rifle back into the boot of the car. As quietly as he could he closed the boot. All three looked towards the road as a line of vehicles suddenly went past. Some had flashing blue lights, which lit up the dark countryside, others did not, but as fast as they had appeared, they were gone, heading off towards Castlerock. Anna smirked.

"If they are looking for us then they are going the wrong way!" Davidov turned his head over his shoulder towards her.

"No, they were doing something down on the beach …" he looked forward again, "go down there and look and see what they were doing."

"Me?" Anna asked as she started to walk towards him, Davidov's head spun around to glare at her.

"Yes, do as you are told!" he commanded.

"But if there are any sapiens down there, I may be recognised from that programme!" she pleaded, Davidov thought for a moment, he turned and started to walk towards the rear of the car.

"Good point," he looked over at Anders, "You go," Anders looked around, there was no one else for him to pass the order to.

"But ..." he started, Davidov cut him off.

"Keep your hood up and hide your voice, do not use it unless you have to." Davidov looked at the neat line of body armour on the ground, he looked up at Anna, "Put this away, keep it out of sight until the others get here," Anna started to move straight away but Anders was stood still, Davidov glared at him, then motioned with his right hand in an 'away' gesture, "Do as I say!" he commanded.

"I obey," Anders nodded and quickly left. Anna opened the boot of the car and replaced the first set of armour and helmet, Davidov was deep in thought and obviously distracted. She walked up behind him and slowly wrapped her arms around his body, she was pushed away in annoyance.

"Stop that, we do not have time," Davidov was angry, Anna stepped back, then turned and carried on with what she had been told to do. She worked in silence until Davidov spoke again. "Have you heard from her?" Anna stopped and looked at the back of Davidov's head.

"Who?" she asked, Davidov spun around and glared at her.

"Who? Who else would I be asking about? Have ... you ... heard ... from ... her?"

"No," she replied, Davidov was about to say something else when a small car turned and drove in though the Lion's gate. It followed the same route as they had done and as the headlights of the car lit up the car park they were switched off, it was Viktor and Pe'ter.

"Why is it called the Mussenden Temple?" Davidov asked.

∞∞∞∞

Sean walked from the kitchen into the living room, the stairs thundered as his wife trotted up them to get changed out of the black dress she had worn for the day. Mike had told him about Coleraine turning down their request for uniforms because of 'other operational duties'. Sean had watched the news headlines before he had switched off the TV. Twenty kilograms of uncut crystal meth and a large amount of money had been recovered; and two Bulgarians and three teenagers had all been arrested. Sean listened to the story, the two Bulgarians where probably the suppliers and the teenagers were just the donkeys for the dealers; someone in the drugs squad would be celebrating tonight.

Celebrating, that was something he could not do. 'Celebrate Simon's Life' had been said several times today. He thought the comment stupid; this was not a celebration; it was a mourning. He understood things like that were mostly for close friends and family but 'celebrate'? No, not him. Mike had been standing beside him when he had asked Super Sutcliffe and Chief Inspector Anderson about early retirement; he was nearly in his last year and there had been several politicians that had called for him to be replaced when they were being interviewed on the news. The Super had turned him down flat. Chief Anderson had a go at him, in front of most of his team, which, as an Inspector, is something that should not happen. Afterwards, Mike had taken him to one side and asked if he had been serious. Yes, he had, but it looked like he was staying where he was. He had heard one thing during the day that made him smile. The new nickname, 'werewolf squad'. It did have a ring to it; gave them something different. Sean sat back down in his chair. His phone buzzed with a message, reluctantly he reached into his pocket and looked at the screen. It was Chief Anderson.

"Oh God, what does he want now?" Sean heard himself speak out loud, then he opened the message. 'BE IN MY OFFICE AT 10 AM' that was it, nothing else, no please or thank you, just 'be

406

in my office' but he would not care, everything would have to be on hold until after this meeting. Sean was going to phone Mike but decided against it, he would tell him in the morning what it was all about. The trip to Coleraine would have to wait until later for them to check out the addresses that they had been given. It was time to go to bed.

∞∞∞∞

Davidov smiled as the three minibuses slowed then turned into the Lion's gate, each dimmed their lights as they did so.

"They are here," he said, everyone moved. Anna was sitting in the driver's seat of their car with her legs hanging out the door and Anders was at the far side of the car park while Viktor and Pe'ter were at the rear of the two parked cars. It had been two hours since they had arrived in a hatchback that looked like it was over twenty years old, 'perfect' Davidov had commented; they listened to Anders tell them about the police and the drugs down near the beach, 'that will keep them all busy and away from here' Davidov had said. Anders was pleased with himself. Davidov was standing at the front of the two cars, with Viktor and Pe'ter on either side at the rear. Anna was standing on his left while Anders had trotted over and was now on his right. The three minibuses stopped end to end opposite them, the doors opened and the men inside all got out. They were well-built, had short or no hair and looked angry and they formed a collective group that was staring at Davidov. Anders looked them over. From around the side of the group walked a larger man, who unlike the rest of the group had hair that was nearly on his shoulders, his outdoor jacket seemed to make him even bigger in the darkness. They looked at each other, then Davidov let a huge smile burst over his face; the man did the same.

"Vanya!" Davidov shouted, he held his arms up as did Vanya, the two men embraced.

"Davidov," Vanya's accent was even stronger than Davidov's and he stood a good two inches taller, they knew each other and knew each other well. The rest of the group relaxed and slowly moved closer, "And who is this?" Vanya asked as he looked Anna up and down.

"She is mine," Davidov smiled "so stay away!" both men shared a laugh, Vanya looked back at Anna.

"Little Anna Nikitin, I remember you when you were but a child!" he was smiling as he spoke, Anna smiled back.

"Uncle Vanya, it is so good to see you again," she stepped forward and they both shared a short hug. Vanya looked around at the rest of Davidov's group.

"But where is the lovely Yelina? I have not seen her for ..."

"She is mine!" Anders cut him off before he could finish his sentence. Anders did not see Vanya's fist as it hit him square in the chest, the power of which sent him flying backwards and tumbling into a ball. Anders got himself onto all fours, gasping for breath.

"Not for long she isn't" Vanya almost shouted, most of his group smiled while some chuckled, "and never interrupt me again Dusmanov." Vanya stared at Anders who was struggling to stand. No one moved to help him; he was on his own.

"she is not here," Davidov said, "she fled yesterday,"

"Fled?" asked Vanya, "Fled where?"

"Not sure, she may be with two council members." Vanya's face went deadpan.

"Which council members?" he asked.

"Grishin and Tatamovich," Vanya nodded,

"Ok," Vanya raised his right hand and placed it on Davidov's shoulder, "this has been a long time in the planning ... What are we here to do?" he asked. Davidov face smiled with excitement as he turned to Viktor and Pe'ter, he clicked his fingers and the two of them walked to the front of the car and stretched a large hand drawn map over the bonnet. They switched on hand held torches that lit up the map of the farm complex. Davidov stood with Vanya beside him, the rest of the group closed in around them.

"This is the main farm of the Rua's northern den..." he started, "You should have seen the pictures we sent you already!" Vanya nodded, "so to confirm each building," Davidov took out a

407

pen from his pocket and started to point to each one in turn, "this is the front and main entrance onto the farm, and here, is the farmhouse where O'Brien will be,"

"How do you know he is there?" Vanya asked,

"During the day, he is out on the farm but every evening he is in here, unless they have a dance on,"

"And the Rua love to dance," came a voice from the group, the comment was answered by several of them laughing.

"Yes, they do," replied Davidov.

"How many Garou are there?" Vanya asked.

"Thirty, but less than a quarter of them will be there," answered Davidov.

"Why?" another asked, Davidov looked over at the voice.

"Because we put a deception plan in place and they're out at the homes of all the members that live off site" Vanya patted Davidov on the shoulder.

"Very good work, how did you do that?" he asked.

"Simple," he said, "we left decoy weapons and laptops for them to find that pointed to us assaulting the homes offsite, then they deployed to protect them and the families ... thereby taking their main focus off the target!" Davidov smiled at Vanya, "making your mission easier!" Vanya nodded.

"Who is their mission commander?" he asked.

"He is Dermott McMurragh," Davidov looked over at Viktor, "You have his picture?" Viktor took the small bag from his shoulders and took out a file; he started flicking through the plastic covers before stopping and held up a picture of Dermott. Dermott was standing near the front of the barn with several people around him.

"Who is the red-head on the left?" another voice from the group asked.

"There are plenty of Rua females for you once this is over," Davidov replied. This got a collective cheer and started comments about what they'd do when the Rua were theirs.

"Enough!" shouted Vanya, all conversation stopped. "We have a job to do first," Vanya looked back at Davidov, "Talk me through the rest of the buildings, how many do we expect guards." They both shared a look, "Everything," Vanya added. Davidov smiled.

"No problem, the assault will be in three directions, ten members each, the first will go to here ,The farmhouse ; The second, here; the main barn, there is a bar and main dining area on the lower floor," Davidov paused and looked up from the map, "you should have already seen the pictures from there!" Vanya nodded, "Good. This is the armoury" Davidov's briefing continued for several more minutes before he stopped and looked at Vanya who was studying the map and everything he had just heard.

"We may not get them all." he spoke quieter than he had before, and shook his head,

"We don't want to get them all, just the important ones, once they are dead, I will challenge what is left and then take over the northern den!" Vanya smiled again, then placed his hand on Davidov's shoulder.

"One question," Vanya stated.

"Go ahead," replied a pleased Davidov.

"How did you get Alexi to challenge his brother in the first place?" Davidov smiled before he replied.

"I didn't" Davidov smiled again and looked over at Anna, who was smiling in the darkness. Both Vanya and Davidov shared a laugh.

"What really happened in Poland?" Vanya asked, the smile faded from Davidov's face.

"Alexi led us into a trap ... We were lucky to get out alive," Vanya looked at

"Da, that is what I had heard," Vanya turned to face the group of men around him.

"You all know what to do, Group One in the first bus," Vanya pointed to the first mini-bus, "Two and Three in there and there," the group was already starting to move back "I want full assault weapons and equipment ready to move in three minutes!" with that, there was an outburst of activity. Vanya took a step forward then looked back at Davidov.

"Give us one hour, then ..." he paused, "come and make your challenge," Davidov nodded and tried to suppress his feeling of euphoria; his time had come.

It was less than three minutes before the three groups of men were standing beside each minibus, everyone was dressed in black clothing, with kneepads, communications equipment, body armour, tactical helmets and pistols in holsters strapped to their sides. Most of them had the same AK-74's as Davidov, but each group had one with a sniper rifle and another with a large shotgun. All the rifles had suppressors, range finders and different types of scopes, everyone was eager to go. Vanya barked one command and they clambered onto the minibuses. The doors slammed shut and Vanya walked around to the far side and got into the lead vehicle.

"I will give you O'Brien's head!" he shouted Victoriously, Davidov lifted his right fist into the air. As the vehicles left there was an excitement within the rest of Davidov's group, all except Anders who stared in hatred.

"Dusmanov!" Davidov shouted at him, Anders snapped around to look straight at him.

"Do you know your mission?"

"Yes," Anders shouted.

"Then," Davidov spoke quietly, "carry it out,"

Chapter 83

Kyle had just opened his front door when his phone rang. He kicked the door shut with his foot and dropped the holdall bag on the floor beside the entrance, his police kit could wait until the morning. He shoved his hand into his pocket, pulled the phone out, and smiled when he read the name on the screen. He pressed the button as he let his jacket slide from his shoulders. He held the phone to his ear by lowering his head on to his right shoulder.

"Hi Cara!" he said as he tried to wrestle the jacket from his arms, the jacket dropped on the floor behind him.

"Hi'ya, right, I know you were involved at the downhill!" she started.

"What makes you think that?" Kyle asked,

"Well, your phone was off and when I phoned the station, I was told you had 'operational deployed'!" Kyle smiled, this girl knew her stuff, "and we both know what that means!"

"Well," Kyle started, "all I can say is what was already on the news, a large volume of drugs and cash was recovered and five were arrested, that's about it"

"Hmm," she was not convinced, "was one of the arrested a driver of a silver BMW?" Kyle laughed, "Really?" she laughed as well

"Does every person in the north west know who he is?" Kyle asked,

"Well, was he there?"

"No, no he wasn't." just as Kyle spoke car headlights lit up the front of his house, someone had just turned into his driveway. "Hang on," he said as he walked into the living room. The hallway light was on, but the living room was dark.

"What's up?" she asked,

"Someone has just driven into my drive," Kyle answered as he looked out from the darkened room as the car pulled in beside his own.

"Who is it?" Cara-Marie asked,

"It is ... Tony, for some reason," Kyle was confused,

"Have you not just been on shift with him?" Cara-Marie stated,

"Yeah." Kyle saw Tony climb out of the car and walk towards the front door,

"Is Karen OK?" Cara-Marie asked. Kyle paused as Tony rang the doorbell.

"I don't know ... I'll call you back." Kyle hung up and raced around to open the front door; as he opened it Tony was backing away.

"Alright, grab your stuff, let's go ..." Tony had already turned away from him and was walking back towards his car. Tony had been very quiet today and anytime anyone, including himself had asked about Karen they got a very short answer, something seemed wrong. Kyle picked up the bag he had dropped by the front door and seconds later threw it into the rear of Tony's car. His house alarm had beeped as he slammed the front door shut. Tony was already in the driver's seat and he seemed like he was in a hurry. Kyle jumped into the passenger seat and as he was doing up the seatbelt Tony reversed and spun the car around. Kyle wanted to ask about Karen, but he was sure he would find out soon enough, so he tried something different.

"What happened, back there, on the beach?" he asked, Tony was gunning the car down the driveway and he looked over at him as they reached the main road.

"We made important arrests and recovered drugs and cash." Tony had a 'that was a stupid question' look on his face as he turned the car onto the main road, and they raced off. Yes, Tony definitely wanted to get somewhere fast.

"No, I meant with me and that smell thing? I could never have done that before?" Tony nodded, Kyle continued "I mean, am I getting the 'powers of a wolf?' he asked, Tony again looked over at him with same stupid question look.

"No, dickhead," Tony started, "a wolf, like any dog, has a scent gland that is seven times bigger than yours is, you will never be able to 'smell' like a wolf,"

"So, what happened then?" Kyle asked.

"Your scent gland does not get bigger, but it does become more active, that is why you picked up the body odour on the wind ..." Tony glanced over at him again, "You are waking up, young one!" Kyle thought for a moment.

"What do you mean, 'I am waking up?'"

"Your wolf, it is slowly waking up, with time you will learn," Tony answered.

"What does that mean?" Kyle asked, "Look, I am totally confused, can you tell me straight! Am I actually a werewolf?!! I just don't know it yet or something?" Tony smiled, "and what do you mean, 'young one?" Tony almost laughed at the question.

"That is what she calls all new members," he answered.

"Who does?"

"Tyler," Kyle looked over at Tony, waiting for him to continue, but he didn't.

"OK, can you kindly tell me who this 'Tyler' is then?"

"Tyler Reynolds runs a stable with several horses on the Isle of Skye," Kyle listened as Tony continued, "and ... all Rua must go there,"

"Why?" Kyle asked.

"Why? ..." Tony repeated the question, "Why, because she will teach you how to control your wolf, she will teach you how to control your moon lust, and ......"

"And what?"

"And there is no one in the Rua that can beat her, Northern Den or the main pack .... she will also teach you how to fight!"

"I know how to fight!" stated Kyle,

"As a sapien, yes, you do, but Garou fight differently," Kyle looked puzzled by what Tony had just said. "As a sapien, unarmed, your main weapons are your hands, yes?" Tony asked. Kyle nodded. "As a Garou, your main weapon is your mouth ... we fight very differently." Tony stated.

"So, it is like a training academy or something?"

"Yeah, something like that,"

"I take it she isn't, small, green, 900 years old and talks funny then?" Kyle let a small grin appear on his face, Tony got the reference.

"No, ... And I would advise you not to say anything like that to her, ... you do not want to upset her!" Tony stated.

"Why?" Kyle asked.

"Because ... she can kick your arse unarmed or with any weapon you care to mention, plus, she is tall, slim, very fit and she is a red head ..." Tony glanced over at Kyle as he finished what he was saying, "and you never upset a red head!"

"Oh," answered Kyle, "so she is a master she-wolf then?" Kyle felt the car jolt as Tony had touched the brakes, there was nothing on the road. Kyle realised he had reacted to the question.

"Tyler has," Tony paused as he tried to find the words, "been through a lot, she has done so much for us, but ..." he paused again, "piss her off and you will know about it!"

"Bet her other half just loves that?" Kyle remarked, the look on Tony's face dropped.

"And, DEFINITELY never mention that!" he stated, Kyle glanced over, he did not have to ask the 'why?' question, it was already there. "She was married to a sapien, who knew what she was, they had a brilliant time, they moved around the world for a while, when ......" Tony stopped talking, after several seconds Kyle spoke.

"What happened?" Kyle asked, Tony was obviously uncomfortable with whatever was coming next.

"Well, this is never discussed ... AT ALL, WITH ANYONE!" Tony stated, "They were living in Canada, somewhere quiet and fairly remote at the time. She was out running up a mountain nearby when a group of Noc's found the house, when she got back, the house was on fire and her other half was staked out in the back garden. They had done some ceremony or something on him," Tony paused, "cut his heart out,"

"Bloody hell," Kyle whispered,

"Yeah, the local police were already there, they did have CCTV which the police took but it did not do much good."

"So, what did she do?" Kyle asked,

"Spent three weeks tracking them,"

"Did she find them?" he asked.

"Oh yes," Tony replied.

"And what happened then?"

"When she found them, they had joined in with another group so there were either ten or fifteen of them," Tony paused, "None survived," Tony glanced over at him, "so don't piss her off!"

"When did that all happen?" Kyle asked,

"About twenty years ago,"

"And she moved to the Isle of Skye?" Kyle stated.

"Not at first, no, do not let her accent fool you, she was born in England, both her parents were English but raised in Lisburn, so quite broad 'Norn Iron like,' but we are not sure where the DNA comes from. As far as we know there were no Garou in her family tree going back several generations."

"How can that happen?" Kyle asked,

"Well, it can lie dormant and pass down through children until it is activated, that is why we investigate every dog attack that happens, just in case,"

"Just in case," Kyle repeated.

"And she has a thing for Capybara's"

"What?" Kyle asked.

"Capybara, it looks like a large beaver, but it is actually a rodent ... she had four of them last time I was there, so, don't make any jokes about Bar-bee-queuing them,"

"Why?" Kyle asked.

"Because it makes your nose bleed!" Kyle smiled as Tony laughed at his own joke. It was the first time today that he laughed; it was obviously a good memory for him.

"Ah, Tony?" he asked.

"What?"

"Since we are not obviously going to the hospital, can you tell me where we are going?"

∞∞∞∞

Vanya was in the passenger seat of the first minibus as it slowed down. On the left was the farm, exactly laid out as Davidov had said; also, nearly in total darkness, just as Davidov had said. The phone in his pocket shook slightly as a message arrived, Vanya read it. It was cramped inside the vehicle but there was no sound. Vanya looked over his right shoulder at his team in the backseat, everyone was dressed the same. Black boots, fire resistant overalls with pads at the knees and elbows, body armour, the front of which had pouches for magazines for their weapons, grenades, communications and other assault equipment. Everyone had the same black gloves that had reinforced armour over the knuckles, helmets and face shields so you could not actually see their faces, and the shields were thick enough to stop the effects of explosions. Everyone had a long primary weapon with a pistol on their thigh as a backup. All their weapons had suppressors, no one would hear them when they opened fire, unless you were standing right beside them, and if you were, you were already dead. They were trained and trained well; everyone knew what they had to do. No one spoke. Vanya tapped his watch and held up a finger. One minute to go until they were on target. The driver of the minibus braked once to let the vehicle behind him know, the message was repeated back to the third minibus. All three had turned their lights out once they had turned into the top of the road. The driver had what looked like a set of binoculars attached to the front of his face, with these night-vision googles he could see as if it was daylight. At dawn and dusk, they could see better than a sapien but at night, they saw better, but not much. The driver slowed to a crawl. Vanya nodded and

412

while the minibus was still moving the side doors opened, and without making a sound, the minibus emptied.

Vanya crouched by the hedge, his team were all in a line along the hedgerow, the second minibus went past, and the doors opened and they jumped out and formed up at the far side of the entrance, all in a line and all without a sound. As the third minibus passed them the small car behind them did the same. Vanya looked at the small hatchback that had been in the car park. Davidov had sent Anders Dusmanov along as well, he had messaged him twice during the journey there, Vanya had agreed. The car was being driven by Pe'ter and had no lights, again it slowed, the passenger door opened and Dusmanov got out without a sound. His body armour was the same, his rifle and helmet were the same as most of his team, but the rest of his clothing was different. The car, like the minibuses did not accelerate away as the engine noise may alert the target that they were there. Anders stopped by the roadside and looked straight into the visor of Vanya's helmet; their eyes locked. Vanya pointed at him then pointed to the ground beside him. Anders was to stay by his side during the assault. Two of the three teams ran across the road, the second one had a long sniper rifle and Vanya watched as they disappeared into the darkness. It would not take them long to get into their position; they could take out the Rua sniper that may be on the roof of the barn. Vanya waited for the single click in his ear, overwatch was in position. Vanya looked down the road then over to the other side of the entrance, he held up his clenched fist and without a sound all three teams started to move. The team at the far side of the entrance went through the hedge and in a line started up the far side of the lane. His team moved up the lane and team three went up the side of the hedge and silently made their way towards the farmhouse. As he got to the top of the entrance his team sprinted over the yard and formed up in a line along the entrance to the barn, team three were stacked up along the side of the farmhouse waiting for the signal to assault. Vanya looked over at the second team as they arrived quietly, the first one stopped and went down onto one knee. Vanya watched as the second one placed a hand on his shoulder to let him know that they were all in position. Vanya paused, then held up his fist, as he dropped his fist the entrance to the barn was pulled open and his team rushed in, as the last one went in the other team followed, one team would clear the barn and the arena and the other would go through and clear the bar and the dining area that was underground. Both Vanya and Anders turned around at the entrance with their weapons raised looking for any dangers that may be there, protecting those that were completing the assault.

There had been a small crack as the door of the farmhouse had given way and team three went in with their weapons up, again leaving two members facing outwards protecting the assault teams. Vanya smiled, the surprise was complete. Vanya kept his weapon up with the stock back into his shoulder and he looked over it at the area along the side of the barn past the farmhouse. He slowly turned his body so the weapon and he moved as one, looking for any possible threat that may be there. Everything was still. In his ear, he heard the first of two clicks, team one had completed their assault, everything was done with no problems. A few seconds later it happened again, the bar and the dining area had been swept, any Rua that were there were dead. He looked across at the farmhouse as the team reappeared and formed up in a line along the front of the house. That was all clear as well. Vanya looked over at the one who was in the middle, he raised the thumb of his right hand, it was done. Vanya could feel himself smile as the two other teams reappeared and formed up in the front of the barn, in his ear a whispering voice spoke.

"Team one complete, no enemy,"

"Team two complete, no enemy,"

"Team three complete, no enemy," Vanya smiled again, Davidov had been right they were all out protecting their own off-site. Vanya pressed the small button on the side of his weapon then spoke.

"All teams, phase one complete, phase two, GO!" at that the team that had been at the front of the farmhouse sprang up and ran across the yard to the far wall. The teams in front of him all suddenly rose and sped around the corner of the barn, the team in front was heading for the two smaller buildings by the granary and his team crossed the yard heading towards the communications building. It was manned 24 hours day, and there would be targets for them there.

Suddenly his earpiece shrieked with a deafening pitch that forced him to rip it out, as that happened the head of the team member in front of him exploded, propelling him backwards. Several members of his team started shouting and the large lights of the farm came on. They were in the open. He raised his weapon and started firing at the lights when the first bullet hit the side of his helmet, then his left leg, then his left shoulder. The force spun Vanya around. He twisted then rolled over his right hand grabbing the pistol attached to his leg; all around him team members were firing and being cut down. The volume of fire that was coming at them was immense, and in that second Vanya knew they had walked into a trap. The Rua also had suppressed their weapons and they had used countermeasures to block their communications, for the first three seconds his teams could not have responded, it was all the Rua had needed. The seconds seemed to go by slowly. He glanced over towards the granary as the last two of the team there fired off their weapons at the unseen enemy as the volley of shots hit them, sending them rearwards like dolls. He looked over to the team member by the wall, his helmet was off, and his face was covered in blood, there was blood coming from his left shoulder, and his left arm was hanging by his side. He had his pistol up and was firing towards a target that Vanya could not see. Vanya felt pride, it was one of his and he was fighting to his very last. Vanya knew him, he knew his family, he watched as he fired again then again before a shot found its target and the last team member fell.

Vanya felt a searing pain in his legs, his left arm, his shoulder, the side of his head. He felt a warm liquid pour over the side of his neck as he lay on the ground, he knew he was bleeding from somewhere. He lifted his pistol and pointed towards the communication building but before he could fire another bullet found its mark, throwing the weapon away from him and shattering his right hand. Then there was silence. Vanya looked up at the night sky and became aware of movement beside him. Anders was still alive. Vanya looked over at him, he had been hit several times as well, and he had started to weep, disgust and bile filled Vanya's mouth, disgust at him for his weakness at the time of his death, disgust and hatred for him.

"Clear!" was shouted in English from across the yard. Vanya tried to look up. He saw the line of Rua, dressed very similarly to them but their weapons were different. He recognised the western weapons and the professional way the Rua were checking each one, one at time, one covering and the other checking to see if they were alive. He had taught his teams to do the same, he suddenly heard movement from all around him.

"Clear,"

"Clear,"

"Look who we have here?" Vanya looked up at the blackened but smiling face of Dermott. Dermott was wearing body armour and was holding a bolt action stalking rifle. "Vanya Moiseyev, of the Latvian Mongol Pack!" Vanya rested his head on the ground, it was becoming hard for him to breathe now.

"Dermott McMurragh of the Northern Den of the Rua," he whispered.

"I see we have heard of each other," Dermott replied, "something you should remember!" Dermott walked up and leaned over him, "These are 'OUR LANDS' and we WILL defend them,"

Vanya smiled up at Dermott. "Not for long," he whispered.

Carl walked up beside Dermott and stopped to look at him just as Vanya Moiseyev took his last breath. Dermott walked over to the struggling Anders, he looked down into the pale face filled with fear.

"Now you have been a naughty boy, haven't you!" Dermott said, Anders quivered as he held his hands to one of his wounds, the blood freely flowed.

"Please!" he whispered.

"Yeah guess what, my wife said exactly the same when I found her in a pool of blood on my kitchen floor!" shouted Tony as he kicked him with fury, Anders rolled over in a ball squealing in pain. Tony raised his pistol to fire, but Dermott jumped forward and grabbed him by the shoulders. Tony's eyes burned with rage and passion. Dermott embraced Tony and looked over at Carl, Tony did the same. Carl paused and nodded once. Dermott stood back and unzipped his smock, pulled out a small pistol and handed it to him.

"No, do not use your own," Tony looked at Dermott then the weapon that was in his outstretched hand. "Use this one, this one can't be traced!" Tony's eyes filled with tears again as Dermott stepped out of the way. Tony replaced his own pistol. Tony could not see all the movement going on around the yard, all the dead were having their weapons and body armour removed then placed in a line beside the barn. Tony could not see the others who were carrying bodies by the feet and hands, almost dragging them over the yard toward the ever-growing line of dead Mongol wolves. He could see the picture taken in his own kitchen, the smiling face holding the bottle of poison, the face of what was laying on the ground in front of him.

"P-p-please," Anders whispered again, Anders tried to raise his blooded right hand to appease Tony,

"You killed my child!" Tony almost shouted,

"P-p-please," Anders repeated as Tony raised the weapon. Tony looked into the right eye of what was there, he raised the blade of the foresight, so it was in the middle of the eye and adjusted the pistol. The rear sight was in alignment, it was a perfect shot. Anders looked back at him, then suddenly he looked over to Tony's left. Yelina glared at him,

"Yelina, please?" his voice was no more than a whisper, Yelina spat towards him.

"You killed my child," Tony repeated. Anders Dusmanov did not feel the single bullet hit his right eye and pass through his head. Tony relaxed and lowered his arm, Yelina looked at Tony, his eyes were full of tears.

"I am sorry,"

"What for?" he asked, Yelina looked down then raised her head again,

"I am sorry for the life of your child," Carl and Dermott walked over beside the two of them but before Carl could speak a farm hand ran up with an excited look on his face.

"Report," ordered Dermott,

"We got them, we got them all!" as the young man spoke the first of the minibuses drove into the yard, the windscreen in front of the driver and the driver's door had been smashed out, there was blood over the outside of the door.

"Any of ours hurt?" Carl asked, the young man shook his head.

"No, no injuries so far!"

"What about the overwatch?" Dermott asked, the young man shrugged,

"Looks like they took off as soon as the shooting started, left their weapons and everything!" Dermott looked at Carl. Carl nodded his head.

"Get Grishin from the woods ... we need to talk!" Dermott smiled, turned and started shouting orders.

Chapter 84

Kyle wasn't sure how he felt, the bar at the farm was packed; everyone was excited about what had happened. The Mongols had come to wipe them out and they had fought back, never had a fight been so one sided before, the whole pack had been taken part. They had just enough time to get the message to the main pack down south before the Mongols arrived. Kyle and a team of five had been tasked with protecting the two council members in the woods. They had not been too happy about that, but Carl had stamped his authority down, he was Alpha here, and both Russians had reluctantly agreed. Once the all clear message had gone around, they had walked back up towards the farm; there was excitement everywhere. Kyle recognised the euphoria; it had been the same in the Ivory Coast after their assault on the airfield. The French Forces were not touched again for the rest of that tour. He lifted the drink to his lips and took a look around at the excitement and pure joy he saw on all the faces.

"Hey, there you are!" Kyle looked to his right as Amanda came towards him. Her black leather boots and camouflage trousers were covered in mud, but her red fleece top was clean as a whistle. Her face had been blackened but was now mostly clean. Kyle noticed the bits she had missed under her ears and in her eyebrows.

"Hi'ya," he smiled, she stepped forward and threw her arms around his neck and pulled him into a tight hug, Kyle held the drink in one hand and held her with the other arm, the hug lasted for several seconds before she let go. She was excited, very excited; in the whole room there was only one topic of conversation.

"So, did you get any?" she asked,

"No, I was part of the team protecting the council members down at the woods," she looked surprised.

"Really? I thought with your background you would have been up in one of the towers!" Kyle smiled,

"No," he paused, he did not know what to say.

"Well, I got two," she was grinning, "I could clearly see his face ... you know the first one, and when the lights came on I let him have it, right in the face," Amanda was touching Kyle's right arm as she spoke,

"Is that the first time you have killed someone?" he asked when she paused, she glanced at him, by the look in her eyes he knew it was.

"Well," she hesitated, "a person ... yes, killed plenty of animals before, not got a problem with that," Kyle smiled, "also, wasn't it great that Tony got to kill the one that nearly killed Karen!"

"What?" Kyle almost spun around with the shock of what she had just said.

"You know, Tony,"

"Yes, I know who Tony is, but someone tried to kill Karen?"

"You didn't know about the photographs?" he shook his head, "well, we raided their house on the far side of Castlerock and found two laptops ..." Amanda took a drink before continuing, "and when we got into them we found out that they had done close target reconnaissance not just here at the farm, but on every single member who lives off site, you know," she drank again from her drink, "They had lists of family names, car details, the lot ..." she paused then looked up at Kyle, he was deep in thought at what he had just heard, "Except you, they didn't have your address ... knew you are in the cops though, I spotted a photo of you in the middle of Coleraine," Amanda smiled but Kyle did not.

"But what about Karen?" he asked,

"Oh, yes, well we found a photo of that one, Anders, taken in Tony's kitchen with a bottle of mild rat poison ... apparently, he spread it over her food and that caused ......" she stopped.

"I know what it caused. I was there when we found her," Kyle sipped at his drink, "when did Tony find out?" he asked.

"Last night, Dermott showed him the photos" Suddenly the way Tony had been acting all day made sense, she went on to describe, with joyful glee, the last moments of the crying by the pitiful Anders Dusmanov at Tony's hand. Kyle's eyes searched the room for Tony, but he couldn't see him. Dermott had told Kyle to go to the bar with the others while the teams completed the clean-up. He had said 'all traces of this will be wiped away' and Kyle believed him. Amanda pushed her left hand around his right arm and pulled herself close.

"So," she smiled, staring into his eyes, "are you still in love with that physiotherapist?"

"What?"

"You know who I mean, the one that when she texts you, you stop what you are doing and answer her back; the one that you are in love with?" Amanda was teasing, and he knew it, but he felt a sick twist in his stomach; he looked away. Amanda felt his body tense up and almost start to pull away from her, she smiled deviously, "Yeah, that's her, the one you're thinking about now," she relaxed herself, "things not going well I take it,"

"We are not dating if that is what you mean!" Kyle stated emphatically.

"That was not what I asked!" she replied. Kyle was uncomfortable with the way this was going and Amanda let out a short chuckle as she leaned in and kissed him on his cheek, "Well, we are just going to have to get her out from underneath your skin then, won't we!" Kyle opened his mouth to say something when shouting came from outside the bar. The angry male voices had an immediate effect on the bar, all conversation stopped, and the bar was still. It soon burst into activity with everyone rushing towards the exit, they both joined the direction the crowd was going.

"What is happening?" Kyle shouted towards her.

"OUTSIDE, EVERYONE OUTSIDE!" a voice shouted,

"What's going on?" another voice asked, no one knew but they all rushed outside to find out. The yard was already full of people. There was a rush of armed men and women heading across and into the field to the right, three were already scrambling up the ladder, rifles across their backs. Kyle made his way around the two 4x4 vehicles parked with the rear of them up against the side of the barn. There was a jostling for position as some clambered up and onto the tops of the 4x4's to get a better look. Kyle could hear Dermott shouting commands at the top of the lane, he was still dressed the same way he had been when Kyle had come up from the woods.

"There you are," Tony's hand landed on Kyle's right shoulder, Tony seemed a lot happier now. Tony stood at Kyle's right shoulder looking over towards the farmhouse as the door opened. Carl walked out and stopped by the hedge, he looked across the field towards the entrance to the lane. He was followed by four wolves, fully changed, fully upright. They position themselves around him, protecting him. A cheer rose up from the crowd as they did so and for a second Kyle thought they looked like magnificent creatures. Carl had not moved. Paul walked out the door followed by the two council members, then the group walked towards the end of the lane.

"What the hell is going on?" Kyle asked, Tony nodded towards the end of the lane.

"A challenge,"

"A what ..." Kyle didn't finish what he was saying as he spotted what was at the bottom of the lane. The group started to make their way up the lane. Davidov Sprogis was topless. He was determined as he marched up the lane. A smaller wolf was walking upright beside him. Two in sapien form stood behind him that Kyle didn't recognise, but Tony did,

"They were the overwatch for their assault; they got away," the excitement of the crowd gathered until Carl silenced them. In the quietness Kyle could hear the footfall of the four as they continued up the lane.

"STOP!" shouted Dermott, his pistol was in his hand, Davidov stopped, defiance chiselled into his face. Carl walked forward until he was nearly in line with Dermott, the four wolves around him did the same, keeping up their protective shield. Kyle watched as the two council members made their way around the group and stood between Davidov and Carl. Davidov started speaking in a language that Kyle did not understand but was stopped by Carl shouting.

"ENOUGH! ONLY ENGLISH, THESE ARE OUR LANDS AND YOU WILL SPEAK ENGLISH." Grishin looked at Carl and nodded once.

"He is right, English if you please." Davidov stared at Carl.

"I am Davidov Sprogis of the Northern Latvian pack of the Mongol Clan and I hereby challenge you to be Alpha of this den!" Davidov spoke with venom in his voice, although everyone was silent Kyle could feel the tension rising.

"I am Carl O'Brien of the Northern Dun of the Rua, and these are our lands!" Carl shouted. Grishin turned to him.

"You have been issued a lawful challenge ..." Grishin was staring at Carl, "Do you accept, or do you forfeit?"

"What does that mean?" Kyle whispered to Tony,

"If Carl does not accept then Davidov automatically assumes Alpha of the Dun," Tony whispered very quietly

"Is that likely to ..."

"Of course, I accept!" the crowd cheered with one voice and applause started, Grishin turned to face the gathered crowd and raised his right hand, the crowd fell into silence. Grishin turned back towards Davidov but it was Carl who spoke loud enough for everyone to hear.

"Vanya is dead, as are all of his hunting party," Carl was triumphant. Davidov stared at him again, there was a growl from the wolf beside him.

"Who is that?" Kyle whispered again, and again Tony leaned in close to his ear.

"That is Anna Nikitin, his mate, niece to the late Vanya," Kyle nodded, he could see a smile spread across the face of Davidov.

"I never liked him anyway," Davidov answered.

"Why is he shirtless?" Kyle asked,

"It is to let everyone know he is making a challenge."

Grishin turned to Carl, "Carl O'Brien, you have been challenged for the right to be Alpha of your Den," Carl nodded, Grishin looked back towards Davidov, "In your challenge, do you accept a yield?" Davidov shook his head, Grishin looked back towards Carl, "in your acceptance, do you accept a yield?" like Davidov, Carl shook his head, Grishin looked at Tatamovich who nodded in agreement, Grishin continued. "It has been agreed in the presence of two council members that this will be a fight to the end!" A sudden chill went over Kyle, he understood what that meant. Grishin turned towards Carl again, "Carl O'Brien!" Kyle noticed that Grishin was being very formal in what he was saying, "These are your lands, and you have accepted the challenge, it is up to you to pick the form!" A buzz of excitement went through the crowd.

"Pick the form?" Kyle asked,

"He can choose to fight in sapien form or as a Garou," Kyle looked at him, "he will pick his wolf, no Garou would do any differently!" Kyle looked back at what was happening in front of him. Carl shouted his reply.

"I CHOOSE OUR TRUE FORM!" and another cheer went up from the crowd.

"What if he had picked the other?" Kyle asked as the cheering died down. Several heads turned towards him, some looked puzzled others looked in disgust.

"Then they would fight with swords," Tony replied,

"Swords?"

"Yes, swords, you know those long sharp things with a pointy end!" Kyle gave his friend a small punch in the side; it was good to see him smiling again.

"PREPARE!" shouted Carl, this was supported by another cheer. The crowd parted as Carl and the four wolves turned and walked towards the entrance to the barn, Davidov followed several feet behind them. When the two parties had passed inside the crowd swelled forward. Amanda, Kyle and Tony all went along with the flow; everyone crowded around the outside of the arena. Kyle stopped when he was about the middle of the barrier; the entrance was now to his right, and as the last of the crowd entered the large doors were pushed shut. Grishin was standing in the middle facing everyone. Kyle looked over at Carl, who was now naked and kneeling on one knee with his head bowed, he was starting to change. Davidov jumped up in his wolf form and spreading his arms wide let out loud roar, Anna and the other two joined in, clapping, applauding in appreciation and support for Davidov. There were hisses and jibes coming from the crowd, their local hero was the popular choice. Paul and the four wolves walked backwards towards the far side of the arena, Davidov's group did the same. Kyle noticed that several members of the crowd had begun to change, more followed, barking and yelling their hostility towards Davidov.

"What happens now?" Kyle asked, Tony had been chatting to someone behind him, the question turned him back towards the main event.

"Grishin will call them forward, to start the challenge," Kyle couldn't believe what he was watching. Carl stood upright, like Davidov he looked magnificent in his wolf form. Carl took deliberate steps towards the centre of the arena as did Davidov.

"Looks like a boxing match!" Kyle stated. Grishin waved towards Paul who walked forward, he was cradling something in his arms. Carl and Davidov stopped several feet from each other, both growled, both tensing up their bodies, ready to fight. "So, what happens now?" Kyle was still looking ahead as he asked the question.

"They will be offered a sword ... neither will take it,"

"Why not?"

"They do not need it, Garou have three weapons, sapiens only two."

"So, how does it end?"

"Badly for one!" Tony retorted, Kyle glanced over at him as Paul reached Grishin's side. Grishin lifted what looked like a short staff, he held it aloft, with one hand gripping the end, the other gripping the middle. Slowly he withdrew the sword from the scabbard.

"That's a katana!" Kyle said out loud, "Why a Japanese sword?" Kyle asked.

Tony shrugged. "They are the strongest, nearly everyone has their own, each one is specifically made for an individual person, it is marked then it is theirs,"

"Have you got one?" Tony nodded.

"Sprogis!" Grishin shouted, "I offer you this sword for combat!" Davidov shook his head, Grishin turned to Carl, "O'Brien, I offer you this sword!" Carl shook his head.

"What if the other guy wins?" Kyle enquired,

"Well, if he does, that means Carl is dead, it will be put to an open challenge and anyone can take up the challenge to defend the pack," Kyle nodded, "but I will be very surprised if it comes to that,"

"Why?" Kyle asked,

"There is a reason why Carl is Alpha ..." Tony was grinning, "he is really good!" Grishin continued. "The Challenge was made without yield," he nodded towards Davidov, "and was accepted, also without yield," Grishin nodded towards Carl, "This is a challenge to the end, NO ONE CAN INTERVENE!" Grishin raised his voice for the last part; no one could help if it was going badly for one. Both wolves nodded towards each other. Grishin handed the sword back to Paul and Paul walked away, "Move back ten paces," Grishin commanded, as the two started to back away from each other a hush fell over the arena. Grishin started to back away himself, never turning his back, as the two stopped. They crouched, ready for the off. Grishin continued to back away until he was at the side. The arena was almost silent.

"BEGIN!!!" shouted Grishin.

At the command the arena exploded in noise, everyone shouting and screaming their support. The two wolves launched at each other with incredible speed, they collided in the middle with a great force. Kyle was mesmerised, he had never seen anything like this! It was a fury of teeth, claws and force. Powerful blows and counter blows were struck sending either back, each jumping forward again to continue their own assault. Skin was shredded and slashed, teeth sunk into fur, and fur ripped out. Kyle felt a frenzied emotion building up within, he heard himself starting to shout, the rest of the arena was in uproar at what was happening in front of them; it was an amazing sight.

Even though they were in wolf form Kyle could easily tell the difference between the two; lacerations and bite marks were now visible on both. It was a bloody match, and both seemed to be as fast and as strong as each other. Carl lunged forward but the swipe of his claws that came from the end of his fingers missed their target. Davidov ducked and grabbed Carl's wrist yanking him forward, turning he threw him to one side. Carl skidded and rolled across the floor of the arena. Davidov jumped towards where he had landed. Carl was up on all fours and was ready for the attack. He threw himself into Davidov sending him rearwards and onto his back. Carl pounced and dived towards Davidov but just before he struck, Davidov rolled out of his way.

The two fighters jumped to their feet and launched at each other again, this time swipe after swipe was fended away. Carl gripped Davidov by the side of the throat and pulled him from his feet and over onto his side. Davidov's neck was wide open, a thunderous cheer went up from the crowd, the killer blow was about to be struck. As Carl went to bite down on Davidov's neck, Davidov extended the fingers on his right hand and rammed them straight into the right side of Carl's chest. Carl let out a squeal of anguish and pain as his heart was pierced, Davidov pushed him over onto his side and jumped up. Carl shook for a second and was still.

Carl O'Brien was dead!

The arena was stunned into silence except for Anna and her two pack members; their cheering was the only sound heard. Davidov staggered back, then stood upright and howled, he had won. Crying and shrieks of 'NO' could be heard from all around the arena. Davidov staggered back and Grishin marched forward. There was movement from all around the arena, Grishin lifted his right hand into the air.

"STOP!" Grishin looked around the arena, "THE CHALLENGE IS NOT YET OVER!" Grishin knelt beside the curled-up body of Carl O'Brien, he placed his fingers on his neck then looked across to the side of the arena where Tatamovich was standing. Grishin signalled with a single nod. Davidov started to walk around in a small circle with his arms held high in celebration, barking and jeering as he went. Anna jumped forward but was shouted back by Tatamovich. She retreated almost dancing with excitement, her dreams for so long were becoming a reality. Grishin stood up and walked towards the centre of the arena, he looked over at Tatamovich who nodded in reply. Grishin turned, there was crying and dismay coming from the crowd. Anna was still celebrating as Davidov walked over, turned and stood beside Grishin. The two exchanged glances. Davidov was grinning, he knew he had won, this was now his. Grishin turned to the crowd and shouted.

"RUA OF THE NORTHERN DUN ..." A quietness descended as he spoke, "A LAWFUL CHALLENGE WAS MADE, AND WAS ACCEPTED BY BOTH PARTIES," Kyle could feel the resentment in those around him, but it was absolute hatred coming from Tony.   Kyle looked into the face of his friend; he had never seen him this angry before. "AND DAVIDOV SPROGIS HAS WON THAT CHALLENGE!" The cheering from the corner went up again, but there was hissing and disgust from the rest of the crowd. Grishin turned to Davidov and looked at the wolf that was standing beside him. "AS THE VIKTORIOUS CHALLENGER, YOU NOW HAVE THE RIGHT TO ASSUME THE POSITION OF ALPHA OF THIS PACK ......" Grishin turned back to the crowd, "UNLESS ANOTHER CHALLENGER COMES FORWARD, IF SUCH A CHALLENGER COMES FORTH WOULD YOU ACCEPT SUCH A CHALLENGE??" Davidov was gleeful in the acceptance.

"What does that mean?" Kyle whispered,

"It means anyone can step forward and challenge him, but, it would be to the death as well, no half measure's," Tony replied, almost spitting as he did so.

"DOES ANYONE CHALLENGE SPROGIS FOR ALPHA OF THE NORTHERN DEN!" Davidov stepped forward, beckoning with his right hand for someone to come forward, he was obviously enjoying his moment, "DOES ANYONE CHALLEGE SPROGIS FOR ALPHA OF THE NORTHERN DEN!" Grishin repeated.

"I will," it was almost a whisper, Davidov spun around to look towards where the voice had come from, Grishin had not heard it.

"FOR THE FINAL TIME, DOES ANYONE CHALLENGE SPROGIS FOR ALPHA OF THE NORTHERN DEN!"

"I will." This time the voice was louder, Grishin turned and looked at the direction that Davidov was now pointing. Tony looked at Kyle,

"What the hell are you doing?" Tony was shocked by what he had just heard. Kyle looked at him.

"If Dad were here, what would he do?" Kyle asked.

"A CHALLENGE!" Grishin shouted, a cheer from the crowd went up, those standing around Kyle backed away. "COME FORWARD" Grishin commanded. Kyle felt his body move a step forward. He climbed over the wooden side wall of the arena and felt himself march towards the centre, towards the staring Grishin and the smiling, beckoning wolf that as Kyle approached leaned forward and snapped his mouth in a gesture of what was to come. Kyle hardly flinched. Grishin stopped him when he was only feet away by holding up his right hand. "You are not a Garou?" he asked, Kyle shook his head.

"No, I am not,"

"Then what makes you think you can challenge Davidov?" Kyle thought before answering, almost shouting so everyone could hear,

"I AM KYLE FOSTER, MY FATHER WAS JOHN FOSTER, GAROU AND ALPHA OF THE NORTHERN DUN, THIS WAS HIS DUN," a wave of shouts of approval, howls, claps and cheers came from around the arena, "MY FATHER DEFENDED THESE LANDS ......" Kyle looked over at Davidov, "AS I INTEND TO DO AS WELL!" Grishin stood back, he looked at Davidov.

"DO YOU ACCEPT THIS CHALLENGE?" Grishin shouted, Davidov nodded eagerly, "THE TERMS ARE THE SAME AS THE FIRST CHALLENGE AND CAN NOT BE ALTERED," Grishin looked over at Kyle, "DO YOU UNDERSTAND?" Kyle nodded as he turned to face Davidov, Grishin looked around at Paul, "BRING HIM A SWORD!" Grishin looked straight at Kyle, there was no emotion on his face, "Remove your top, this is a challenge," Kyle understood and as he dropped his top on the floor of the arena Paul arrived with the Katana sword. Paul held it out horizontally towards him, Kyle turned and gripped it with his right hand, Paul did not let it go initially, there were tears in his eyes and his face was contorted with grief. Paul glanced over at where Carl lay motionless on the floor before his eyes darted over towards Davidov.

"Fuck him up!" Paul stated quietly before releasing his grip on the sword. Paul took a step backwards, turned and walked away. Kyle turned the sword around and gripped the wooden scabbard with his left hand, he looked closely at what was now in his possession, his right hand gripped the handle and slowly he pulled the blade uppermost. The scrapping noise quietened the arena, Kyle smiled, he twisted his wrist and the blade whooshed through the air. The perfect blade itself had almost no weight. Kyle looked over at the near drooling Davidov and cast the scabbard away to his left. Grishin held up his hand and the arena fell silent once more. Kyle gripped the handle with both hands and breathed a slow intake of breath to calm himself. His vision blurred as he concentrated on the only thing that was in focus, the werewolf in front of him, the werewolf whose hands were outstretched, whose fingers beckoned him in.

"BEGIN!!!" shouted Grishin. Davidov lunged forward, his mouth open and going for the bite. Kyle dropped to one of his knees as the attack passed over his head, he twisted his wrists and swiped the sword horizontally across the creature. Time passed slowly. Everything moved in slow motion. Davidov was already launching his next attack with his left hand, fingers outstretched and aiming for Kyle's head. Kyle looked into his eyes and the surprise that burst in them as the end of the blade parted his abdomen. Everything moved so slowly, the blade drew a line across Davidov's stomach, and it opened like a ploughed field. Davidov's right arm slammed into the wound in an attempt to keep the contents inside, his left came down as well in support as he fell to his knees. Kyle jumped up and in one motion the blade swept free. He stepped past him and pointed the blade directly at Davidov. Launching an attack, he jumped forward slamming the sword into Davidov's back, Kyle felt the ribs part as the blade passed between them and smashed its way out of Davidov's chest. Davidov let out a pronounced yelp as his left hand tried to grab at the blade. Kyle stepped back and withdrew the sword. Davidov's outstretched left hand tried to stop himself from falling forward. He managed to push himself back up, so he was almost kneeling, his right arm was across his abdomen, the contents of which were starting to protrude passed his arm. His left hand found the hole in his chest, he stared at his hand and at the blood pumping up through his fingers. Davidov could not hear the crowd or the shriek from Anna, he became absorbed in his own moment, and for a moment it was peaceful. The sapien had been quick, quicker than any sapien he had seen before. He glanced down to his left where Kyle had planted his own left foot. Davidov had not seen Kyle move around behind him so quickly, he watched as the foot started to turn in the ground and he became aware of Kyle taking a step a forward. Davidov did not hear the sword as it passed through the air, nor did he feel it as it sliced through his neck.

With one movement it was done. Kyle stood with the tip of the blade almost touching the ground as Davidov's body straightened up then fell backwards. His head bounced like a ball in front of them then stopped, the face of a handsome wolf looked upwards with a look of total surprise on its face. Kyle relaxed and straightened up.

"STOP!" shouted Grishin, "I SAID STOP!" he shouted again, Kyle spun around and with both hands on the handle thrust the blade forward just as the wolf of Anna Nikitin pounced towards him, eyes filled with rage, mouth open in attack. The blade passed in through her mouth and out the back of her head, which stopped halfway down the blade, her body shook violently for several seconds then stopped. Kyle released the blade as he couldn't hold the weight of the dead wolf any longer and Anna fell to the ground. Kyle knew that Grishin was shouting something, the arena had exploded in a roar, none of which Kyle Foster could hear. He glanced over at the two who had been with Anna, both had ripped off their own tops and both had started to change. The Rua pack descended on them, jumping over the arena wall and charging towards them. Some wolves, others in human form, the two had their backs to the wall and were snarling and shouting, one had a knife and other yelled at the coming attack. In a fury of fur and fangs, it was all over in seconds; all parts of the challenge had been settled.

Kyle stood there as Grishin walked up to him, Kyle could not hear what was being said, as he was looking at the crowd that had gathered around Carl's body. Tony suddenly appeared and placed his hand on Kyle's shoulder.

"Where the hell did you learn to do that?" Tony was joyous,

"What?" answered Kyle as his senses brought him back to where he was.

"Use a sword like that? Where the hell did you learn it?" Tony was almost hugging him now; the joyous crowd had closed in around him. He was surrounded by a sea of smiling and tearful faces. Kyle started to accept the congratulations but Grishin shouting stopped them all.

"In the Legion," answered Kyle, Tony looked surprised.

"They teach you how to use a sword in the foreign legion?" he asked, Kyle smiled,

"No, it was a Japanese guy in our company; we did it in our spare time, it was fun"

"You lot fought each other using swords?" Tony asked,

"No mucker, we had brush handles," Kyle shrugged, "but the theory was sound"

"STAND BACK!" shouted Grishin again, the crowd parted and backed away from Kyle. Paul was at his left side with the scabbard, he was smiling but still had tears in his eyes as he took the sword from the dead wolf and retreated back into the crowd. "FOSTER OF THE RUA, DO YOU ACCEPT THE POSITION OF ALPHA!" Grishin was smiling towards him, Kyle let the words sink in.

"He cannot!" came a voice from the crowd, a rush of questions flowed over the crowd.

"STEP FORWARD!" commanded Grishin. Sean Lefebvre stepped out from the crowd, he was glaring at Kyle.

"He cannot," Sean repeated his statement.

"HE HAS WON A RECOGNISED CHALLENGE; THE POSITION IS HIS ... UNLESS YOU ARE CHALLENGING HIM!" Grishin shouted towards Sean, Sean looked over at Grishin.

"He can't be Alpha. He is not full Garou! He can't rule!" Grishin paused.

"My father ..." Kyle started, Sean cut him off,

"Was a Garou, ruled the Garou. You are not! Therefore, you cannot rule!"

"He is a Garou," Tony injected, "we called to his wolf several weeks ago, and his wolf answered!" Sean shook his head,

"He cannot rule when he is not a full Garou ... what message does that send out about the pack? ... anyone can challenge as our Alpha is not a full Garou, the Southern Pack will not allow it," there were nods and voices of agreement.

"So, how does this happen? If this is my father's gift, then so be it," Kyle said,

"You have to have the wolf inside you activated, then you will be a full Garou!" Tony said it loud enough for everyone to hear.

"IS THAT WHAT YOU WANT?" Grishin was still shouting; everyone was silent as he spoke. Grishin was staring straight at Kyle, Kyle nodded. "So be it," a wave of excitement went around the group, Kyle looked over at Tony,

"So, how does this happen then?" Kyle asked.

"You have to be bitten," Sean shouted from where he was standing. Kyle nodded then looked at Grishin, "Ok, let's get this done!" Kyle answered, there was an explosion of cheering and applause, except from Sean, who looked at the rapturous Amanda as she fought her way to the front of the crowd to see what was happening, then back at Kyle, he turned and disappeared into the crowd.

"AS ALPHA, YOU MAY CHOOSE WHO TURNS YOU!" Kyle paused, then looked at his friend, Tony understood.

"Give me a minute," Tony turned and walked away through the crowd, he was starting to undress as he did so. The excitement in the crowd was mixed tears and lament for Carl. It didn't take long before the crowd parted. Kyle turned towards the creature that was walking towards him, and Kyle turned to Grishin,

"It's in the saliva, right?"

"Yes, it is," Grishin smiled and nodded, Tony walked in front of Kyle and stopped. Kyle was unsure about what exactly was about to happen next, the crowd fell silent.

"KNEEL" commanded Grishin, Kyle went down on one knee, the wolf that was his friend knelt before him. Kyle looked into the eyes of his friend and they shared a smile.

"BEGIN!" commanded Grishin, and with that Tony pounced and sunk his teeth into the top of Kyle's shoulder, his mouth was over both the front and the back of the top of the chest, his teeth bit down on the scapula at the back and the clavicle at the front. Kyle shrieked in agony. He had never known pain like this before. Tony had thrown his arms around him and Kyle sunk his head into the fur around Tony's neck, the pain shot through his body as Tony's mouth moved almost in an attempt to get a better grip as Kyle felt the world around him go dark.

Chapter 85

The sun was just rising over the hills and the sky was clear as Viktor pulled in front of the bungalow. The Rua knew about the other houses, but they did not know about this one and he was glad about that. Viktor jumped out of the car, slamming the door, he was in a rush. He opened the boot of the car and grabbed the shopping bags full of everything he had just bought from the 24-hour garage near Castlerock, this should be everything they needed to get out of here before the Rua found them. Viktor used his elbow to close the boot and fumbled his way to the front door, trying not to drop anything. He had to drop one load so he could reach into his pocket to get the front door key. He lumbered his way in. Pe'ter was still where he had left him, sitting upright in the chair with a duvet wrapped around him. His face was still as pale as it had been when he left a few hours before hand.

"Hey, I got everything," Viktor walked past him and dropped the bags on the floor, he looked into two of the bags before lifting the one he was looking for, Let's have a look at you." Viktor sat on the arm of the sofa beside the chair and dropped the bag beside him, Pe'ter hardly moved as the duvet was pulled back to reveal the state that he was in. Pe'ter was topless but had dressings and bandages wrapped around his right shoulder and a large cotton dressing on the right side of his chest. Pe'ter had to raise his right arm so Viktor could look at it. The blood had seeped through and had stained the duvet, Pe'ter had a slight shake over his body as he started to peel back the dressing. Viktor was trying to be as cheerful as he could, "This dressing will need changed to be changed." The dressing peeled away quite effortlessly to reveal the open puncture wounds underneath. "You're lucky that does not go all the way through your chest!" Viktor stated, Pe'ter took a breath in.

"Is he dead?" he quietly asked, Viktor didn't have to ask who he was talking about as he opened the shopping bag to reveal it was full of first aid items, different sizes of dressings, tape, cotton wool, clear packets with liquid in it, latex gloves, scissors. Viktor opened one of the larger dressings and placed it over the wound on Pe'ter's chest. He looked at the dressing on his shoulder, the blood had not only gone through the single dressing but through the elasticated bandage that covered it; it needed to be changed as well.

"Yes, he is dead."

"How do you know?" Pe'ter whispered, Viktor continued to unwrap Pe'ter's shoulder and remove the blood-soaked dressings. His open wounds would need cleaning as well; blood still seeped from several of them.

Viktor started to explain, "If he was still alive that would mean he had won and Anna would have summoned us by now," Pe'ter winced as Viktor poured the liquid from the sachet over the open wounds,

"I don't know how I got away," Pe'ter looked up at Viktor, "They knew we were coming; they were waiting." Viktor nodded, the two from the overwatch had said the same. "It was as if they wanted me to get away." Pe'ter tried to sit up, but Viktor gently pushed him back into the chair, "The guy with the shotgun should not have missed at that range!
I saw him aim at me ... he could not have missed ..."

"But miss he did," Viktor answered as the first dressing went over his shoulder; Pe'ter reacted to the pain. "Don't worry we are safe here," Viktor continued. Pe'ter's eyes widened and he gently shook his head. Viktor looked confused. Pe'ter's eyes looked over at the small green military looking box with the keyboard and a very small display. Viktor wondered why Pe'ter was looking at the hand-held counter-measures device. Pe'ter looked straight into Viktor's eyes then again at the box, he was being told to look at it. Viktor placed the last dressing onto Pe'ter then reached over and lifted the box from the table and looked at it, it was on standby mode. Pe'ter nodded once and without speaking Viktor pressed the ready button. The screen lit up and in one corner a small green light started to blink, this would take less than ten seconds, if the light went to permanent green there was no problem. The light stopped flashing and turned red. Viktor and

Pe'ter exchanged looks, this time Viktor was alarmed, there was at least one surveillance device inside ten metres of them and they were transmitting, someone, somewhere was listening to them.

"I think we need to go," whispered Pe'ter, Viktor nodded,

"Yes, back to the house in Belfast, I think," Viktor said louder for the benefit of those who were listening, "Come let's get you dressed and ready for the trip". It took them less than ten minutes to get Pe'ter dressed, have a small breakfast that Viktor prepared, then manhandle him out to the car; the whole thing was done in silence. Viktor walked around the small house and collected some of the items and placed them into the last shopping bag; the rest were already in the boot of the car. Viktor went through the drawers in the kitchen, but when he opened the cupboard he stopped, in between the mugs and cups was the postcard. Viktor slowly lifted it out and stared at it, after a few seconds he rushed through the house, taking the bag then slamming the front door behind him. Viktor threw the bag onto the backseat and jumped into the driver's seat. Pe'ter was wrapped up in a different duvet and was belted into the passenger seat as the car took off.

"What?" Pe'ter asked quietly, Viktor tossed the postcard over to him. The card dropped onto Pe'ter's lap. He picked it up but there was nothing written on the back of it; on the front was a picture of a hill with 'Welcome to Scotland' printed on it. Pe'ter was confused. Viktor was driving quickly, he wanted to get away from the house.

"Where did you find this?" Pe'ter asked,

"It was placed in with the mugs," Viktor was driving as fast as he could on the country roads. Pe'ter was still none the wiser.

"What is it and why would you want it?" he asked,

"We first left it for them as a message back in Scotland," Pe'ter spotted Viktor tightening his grip on the steering wheel, still Pet'er did not understand, "and they have given it back!"

"What do you mean, 'we left it for them'?" he asked.

"It is a message for us," he stated.

"Who from?" Pe'ter asked, "it is not the Rua?"

"No, it is not," Viktor confirmed.

"Then who?"

"It seems that the British SAS have a sense of humour!"

∞∞∞∞

Cara-Marie looked at the clock on the wall, it was nearly half ten in the morning and today was dragging by. She didn't care that there was some sort of financial crash going on that every single news outlet was reacting to. Her story, the story she wanted and needed to prove was being shelved, and she knew it, but the emails still kept coming.

"I hear they caught the werewolf!" said one of the reception staff, Cara-Marie's head spun around as did Mark's.

"What?" she asked, the receptionist was laughing as she spoke,

"Yeah, this loon walked into the police station with a wolf costume on and admitted everything ... got arrested for wasting police time," both the receptionists laughed and shared the joke. Cara-Marie went back to the list of emails that she had to answer, after all this was 'her story' so she could deal with all this. She glanced over at Mark, but he had hardly said anything since he got in.

"You Ok?" she asked,

"Pardon?" Mark looked lost.

"Are you OK?" she repeated, Mark nodded and returned his attention to the laptop, Mark was not ok.

"Fancy a coffee?" she asked,

"What?" he replied,

425

"I want to get out of here for a bit and you are coming with me!" she spoke quietly so no one else could hear,

"Oh," he replied,

"Oh!" she repeated, Mark was flustered so she finished his sentence for him, "Yes, I would love to, Cara-Marie that is a great idea, I am just getting my coat!" Cara-Marie was smiling as she stared at him, he smiled back, "and it is MY treat!" she said,

"And it is your treat," he repeated as they both started to gather up their personal items. Mark's went into his pockets, Cara-Marie's went into her handbag, and they were out the back door before anyone else had noticed they were leaving.

"So," she started, "What is up with you today?" she asked as they started down the street, she noticed his face fall with sadness.

"Rachel moved out two nights ago," her head spun around, she touched him on the arm,

"Mark, I'm so sorry,"

"Her Mum came around as well to help move her stuff ... she had a right go at me,"

"What about the baby?" she asked, he shrugged, "got told that I will never see it, etc"

"They cannot stop you, you will still be able to get to see your child," Cara-Marie was not sure what else was happening inside his head, but he was concerned about something, she waited for him to speak.

"I knew a while ago that it was a mistake, I should never have left her," suddenly she knew he was talking about his ex, not Rachel but the previous.

"Have you spoke to her?" she asked, Mark nodded,

"Late last night," they walked on towards Church Street, "We were texting each other a few days ago and she suggested we meet face to face ..."

"How did that go?" she asked, Mark welled up, she thought he might burst into tears,

"Can I ask you a female point of view?" Cara-Marie nodded, "Well, it was friendly enough until,"

"Until what?"

"Well, it was her response when I asked her out again," Mark was obviously upset, "and I'm not sure what she meant by what she said. Like, what are you, as a girl, saying when you give the old line?" Cara-Marie smiled then answered,

"What did she say?" she asked,

"Well, I got the 'I see you only as a friend, I really like you, but I don't want to hurt you, and you are more of a brother to me now," he looked at her, "honestly, if you were saying that to someone what exactly are you saying?" she thought about lying but then decided against it.

"She has someone else," she looked at him as he slowly nodded, "I know that is not what you want to hear but it is the truth." at that her phone started to ring, it was a withheld number. "Hello," Cara-Marie slowed down to single steps as she listened to whoever she was talking to; she suddenly looked up at him, whatever it was it was serious, "Right, yes ... I know who that is." Cara-Marie nodded at Mark and turned around and started to head back to the office, her speed suddenly increased, "Right, yes, yes, that is first class ..." she was nodding again, he had to speed up to catch her as she ended the call.

"Ok, what is going on?" he asked, she gave him a serious look,

"Carl O'Brien, the owner of the deer farm was killed in an accident last night ... the police are there now,"

"The deer farm? ... that one the far side of Kilrea where you followed yer man Fallon to?"

"Yeah, same as where Paddy M'Kane worked,"

"M'Kane? the fella that was killed at Ballybogy?"

"The very same .... so, your love life will have to wait,"

∞∞∞∞

Mike Dear was sitting in the office at the Coleraine police station; he had come up to try and organise the properties that they had searched for, but to no avail. He had all the correct

426

paperwork, it was all there, but 'operational reasons' kept being put in his way. First assisting with a drugs seizure and now someone getting killed in a farming accident. It was so frustrating but there was nothing he could do about it. The office was empty. He had sent them all home over an hour ago. He had wanted to go himself but that would mean having to go back into the office in Belfast and that was something, for today at least, he did not want to do. The funeral yesterday had gotten to him, it really had; he had been standing only feet away when it was pointed out to the families that he had found Simon. He had been warned by Chief Anderson not to give any details, especially that he had been beheaded and placed on a pole, 'those kinds of details a family does not need to know, remember that!' Mike had taken the warning, but it had still got to him, he could not have stayed in Belfast today.

After the desktop had shut down, he made his way through the police station, which was mostly empty, everyone was still at the deer farm. He went down the stairs and out the main entrance, his car was parked on the right as he walked outside. His body was in automatic, he was in the car, seatbelt on and driving out of the station before he even knew it. The car turned right out of the station onto the Lodge Road.

The fire station beside the police station seemed quiet and traffic was light as he slowed by the traffic lights beside the Lodge Hotel. Mike was almost in a daze as he sat there, the red light holding the car in front, his eyes, normally looking everywhere just looked straight ahead. The sound of a car horn brought him back, he was in the flow of traffic making his way around the round-about. He only had to get across this then he would be on his way back to Belfast. He looked up at the sky, it was starting to get dark already. The flow of traffic coming from the right had been stopped at the lights at the other junction, and the last few cars were passing. Soon he would be on his way, but he would be late home again. He cringed at the thought of another argument with his wife. His eyes looked at the red hatchback driving past him. The person in the passenger seat was wrapped up in a duvet, it was cold but not that cold. He watched as the red car kept driving around to the right. Suddenly his mind flashed, he was back in the moment, he suddenly recognised the young face of the driver, his mind fought for the name that he had memorised:

"Shelaev," he heard himself out loud, "Viktor Shelaev!" The lights in front of him turned to green and he felt his car jump forward, but not that far as the car in front of him seemed to be going slower than everyone else. He spotted the red car again as it carried on around past the exit to Belfast taking the exit towards Limavady and Castlerock. The car in front started to indicate they were heading to Belfast, but as soon as they started to turn Mike pressed his foot down, the traffic in front of him was keeping him at the speed he was. He took the same exit as the red car. Coleraine Rugby Club was on his left as his eyes searched forward, he glimpsed a red car up ahead, he was now fighting to get through the traffic. As he was slowing down on the bridge for the traffic lights up ahead he spotted the red hatchback again over to the right heading towards Castlerock. The lights changed to green and he shot past the car on his left. He caught glimpses of the top of the red car up ahead as he made his way along the riverbank then up through the traffic lights and out of Coleraine towards Castlerock, 'why were they going back there?' he wondered. Mike fought with his phone, first he tried to phone Sean, but he got his answering machine.

"Hi Boss," Mike looked at the small digital display on the dash, "it's just past 6 pm and I was leaving Coleraine when I spotted Viktor Shelaev and one other in a red hatchback, they seem to be going towards Castlerock, I'll phone again when I know more," Mike turned the car turned onto Castlerock road, he went past the petrol station that was on his left, he stared at the driver of the white car that was trying to pull out onto the road, "Stay!" he willed, the driver did not move, the car in front of Mike slowed and indicated that they were turning left. Mike manoeuvred his car around them, the top of the red car had disappeared up ahead, Mike accelerated, he had to find them!

∞∞∞∞∞

Pe'ter coughed and Viktor reached over and patted him on the shoulder.

"It is OK," he reassured, "she said she would meet us there," Pe'ter nodded,

"Do you believe them?" Pe'ter asked, as he pulled the duvet closer around him. Viktor had turned the heating up in the car.

"Possibly, but I do believe her," he answered,

"Where was the name of that place we met?" Pe'ter asked.

"Ballycastle," he replied,

"It was good to see her. Where did she say she would meet us?" Pe'ter asked.

"At that Mussenden temple place,"

"Do you believe the Rua will let us go?" Pe'ter asked,

"If she says they will, then I think they may,"

"As long as we leave tonight," Pe'ter coughed again.

"As long as we leave tonight," Viktor repeated as Pe'ter closed his eyes and fell asleep. It did not take long before Viktor was reverse parking the car in the car park by the Lion's gate, he shook Pe'ter awake. "Come on, it's not too far," Viktor was smiling now. Pe'ter climbed out of the car, leaving the duvet behind. Viktor looked up at the low dark clouds, "I think it will rain later," he said.

"It always rains here!" Pe'ter answered and he was slowly pulling on the outdoor jacket that had been on the backseat.

"Yes, it does," he nodded, "so for that alone it will be good to get away from here!" Viktor lifted a small daysack from the back of the car, he had packed some of the food and a bottle of lemonade, as well as two pistols and the last two grenades that they had left, 'just in case' he had said to Pe'ter earlier. Pe'ter agreed it was a good idea.

"How far is it?" Pe'ter asked, Viktor pointed past the old wall, it is just over there." The place was now in darkness but there were still two cars they he did not recognise in the car park, that meant that there was someone still on the site. Pe'ter was walking quicker than he had been, his strength was returning, and quickly. "Hey, is she here already?" Pe'ter asked, he was trying to smile but he was still in pain and it showed.

"Not yet, but she will be here soon,"

"Then you two can be together again," Pe'ter answered, Viktor felt his stomach tighten, 'Yes,' he thought to himself, 'Yelina and he would be together again.' They followed a path with fields either side of them. The ruins up on the hill were covered in darkness, they could make them out clearly. The sound of the ocean was not that far away and as they reached the top of a small rise they could see the round building down near the cliff edge that they were heading towards. "Why could we not meet in the car park?" Pe'ter asked.

"Well, if we waited there, we may be recognised," Viktor glanced over at him, "and the last thing we want is the police arriving!" Pe'ter nodded as Viktor continued to explain, "Plus, here we can see anyone coming." Suddenly a breath of wind swept down the hill and brushed around them. Both men stopped, their bodies tensed up and turned towards the old ruins, ready for the attack. That smell, sapien smell. There was at least one sapien up wind from them right now. They lowered themselves, reducing their silhouette, making it harder for anyone to see them. The two men stared up the hill and the smell was decreasing, whoever it was they were moving away.

"Must have been the sapiens with the cars!" Pe'ter said out loud, Viktor relaxed.

"Yes," he agreed as he raised himself upright again, "Come on, let's go," he said as he walked towards the small gate in front of the round building that had only one entrance.

"What is this place?" Pe'ter asked as they got closer, Viktor looked at the stone steps that led up to the single doorway. Pillars stood either side of the door and more were equally placed around the building. Viktor thought they were more for decoration than actual support, the doorway looked straight out the window on the far side of the circle. The dome on the roof had a large monument on it. A stone wall ran along the cliff edge, and waves crashed on the rocks below. Pe'ter poked Viktor in the side.

"What?" Viktor asked,

"I said, 'what is this place?'" Viktor nodded as they slowly walked through the gate of the small wire metal fence and stepped towards the steps and for a moment it was a bright sunny day with no rain. Yelina took his right hand in her own and smiled at him, lifting his hand to her lips she kissed it gently,

"I love you," she whispered, the sun surrounded her and seemed to make her even more beautiful,

"I love you too," he whispered back, then suddenly she was gone, it was dark and about to rain. Viktor looked over at the wall where they had made love that day, that happy day. "It was built by an aristocrat; a gift for his lover as a library," Viktor stared at the spot where he had been with Yelina and smiled at the memory, Pe'ter grabbed at the bag on his shoulder.

"I am hungry, let's eat."

Chapter 86

Kyle woke and looked around the room; it was the same bedroom in the farmhouse that he had slept in before., He went to move but the pain in his left shoulder struck him like a bolt of lightning. He didn't mean to yell out loud, but he did. His right hand moved over to the dressing, he could barely move his left arm. The door opened, and a smiling Amanda walked in,

"Hi'ya,"

"Hi," Kyle fell back on the bed exhausted, he had real trouble moving. Amanda held out a steaming mug, "What is that?" he asked.

"I hear you like tea with hot buttered toast!" she replied.

"I don't see any toast!"

"That is on the way up," she smiled,

"What time is it?" he was feeling too tired to even speak as she placed the mug on the small dresser beside the bed, she looked at her watch,

"Nearly 6," she answered as she walked up and sat on the edge of the bed.

"In the morning?" he said trying to turn over but the pain in his shoulder forced him back again; she let out a short laugh,

"No, silly, 6 in the evening, you have been out cold for nearly a day!" Kyle closed his eyes, her felt her fingers slowly caress his right arm then play with his fingers before taking his hand in a tight grip. Kyle opened his eyes; the emotion was bursting in her eyes and excitement was all over her face.

"I need to get to work?" he whispered.

"Tony has taken care of that for you," came the male voice at the door, Paul stood in the doorway holding a small plate. Kyle could smell the toast from the other side of the room, "you do not have to be anywhere for the next two days," Paul walked forward and placed the plate beside the mug, smiling as he did so.

"What has happened?" Kyle whispered,

"Well," Paul began, "After you were bitten, your wounds were cleaned and dressed and you were brought here; you have been here all day," Paul looked at Amanda, "and this one here has been keeping a close eye on you." Kyle turned his head and looked at Paul,

"I mean what happened with Carl?" he asked. Paul straightened up, then nodded, he could not, not answer, this was his Alpha now.

"Well, the police were notified about a farming accident. Carl was found with three puncture wounds from the antlers of a stag this morning; the police have only just left. The Health and Safety people are coming back next week." Kyle closed his eyes. It was a fight to open them as Paul spoke again, "and there is someone here that needs to speak to you." Paul stepped back to reveal a middle-aged man in a grey suit. Kyle somehow knew that this was a sapien, there was no wolf here.

"Mr Foster, may I come in?" he asked. The man was very polite and had a brown leather briefcase in his left hand. Kyle nodded. Paul motioned with his head for Amanda to move. She did so and stood over behind Paul as the man walked over to the bedside. "Allow me to introduce myself, I am Neil McAndrews of Anderson, Henderson and McAndrews." Kyle looked up at him. He had a small smile, but the rest of his face did not look happy.

"That sounds like a bunch of solicitors!" Kyle remarked.

"We are a bunch of solicitors!" Neil answered.

"Neil has represented the farm for nearly 20 years," Paul added. Kyle glanced over at Paul then back at Neil who laid his briefcase on the edge of the bed and opened it to take out a handful of A4 sheets of paper.

"Right, just a few things to go over first now that you have taken the farm over from the late Carl O'Brien," he started.

Kyle again started to sit up, "What?" he asked before the pain forced him back again, Amanda stepped forward but was stopped by Paul.

"Oh, I am sorry, Mr Foster, was that me?" Neil asked, he looked over at Paul who shook his head. Kyle opened his eyes and looked back at the three people who were standing in the small bedroom. "Well," Neil continued, "I have to read to you the part of Mr O'Brien's will that pertains to you," Neil focused in on what was written on the page, "I leave all the farm, assets and all connected with the farm, it's business and all assets to Kyle Johannes Foster," Neil looked up, "and I have already confirmed that is you," Neil looked back down "Kyle is to take over the running of the business as soon as practically possible," Neil looked down at Kyle, "So Mr Foster, you are now in the venison business!" Kyle looked over at Paul who was smiling,

"Congratulations!" Paul remarked with a nod, Amanda had a huge smile on her face as Neil lifted an envelope out of the briefcase.

"And Mr Foster, Mr O'Brien has left you this letter." Neil stepped forward and handed the envelope to Kyle. It took Kyle a great effort to raise his right hand to take it, "right, now that is done, we can do the rest of the paperwork when Mr Foster is feeling better!" Paul nodded, Neil said his goodbyes and left. Paul walked over to the door, they exchanged a few words then Paul turned back into the room. Amanda sat back down on the bedside and retook Kyle hand.

"So, boss," Paul was smiling, he stepped forward and held out his right hand for a handshake. Kyle released Amanda's hand and gripped the offered hand. Paul did not let go as he suddenly knelt down on one knee. Amanda stood up to move out of the way, Paul bowed his head. "Kyle Johannes Foster," he started, "Alpha of the Northern Dun of the Rua of the Garou," All Kyle could do was stare at the top of the bowed head in front of him, "I am Paul Hawkins of the Northern Dun, I make this sacred oath that I will serve you and the pack unto death, to defend these lands, from all enemies and will follow all lawful commands as you have directed me to do so," Paul released Kyle's hand and clenched his fists and placed them on the floor of the bedroom. Kyle looked at Amanda, who lifted her right hand with the palm uppermost and mouthed the word Kyle had to say, he nodded and gave the command.

"Rise," Paul did so; as he stood Kyle noticed that there were nearly tears in his eyes, Paul turned to her,

"We need to leave him in peace," Paul looked at the envelope then at Kyle, "when you are done, just shout and we will be here." Kyle nodded, "Right," he said as he turned towards the door, lifting his left arm around Amanda as he did so, "the Alpha needs his peace and his rest, there is a lot to do tomorrow," Kyle watched as they both left the room, Paul closed the door behind him. Kyle listened as they both trundled down the small wooden staircase. He picked up the envelope with his right hand. His name had been handwritten on the front of it, he guessed by Carl, it was easy to open, he unfolded the single sheet of typed paper, and started to read.

'Kyle, well if you are reading this then things have not gone well for me. You have no idea how much it meant to me that we had found you. Your father meant a lot to nearly everyone here., He protected us when we could not protect ourselves and helped establish the Northern Dun separately from the rest. He once wrote me a letter much like the one you are reading now. I was to take care of you until you were old and ready enough to run the farm, but your family took you off to Canada before we could really sort things out. This is your home, by now you will start to realise who, and what you are. Some say it is a curse. We, the Rua, do not believe that; we have always seen it as a gift. Your ancestors have defended these lands for centuries, now it is up to you to carry on what we have maintained down through the centuries. Listen to Paul, he knows so much. You will have to go to Scotland, that is, if you have not already done so. Listen and learn from Tyler, but do not underestimate what she can do!

You have your father's strength. I see it every time we meet, so, Kyle, the only command I have for you is what we have always done, 'Defend these lands'

Carl

Kyle read over the letter again, then felt his strength start to leave him, he closed his eyes and drifted off to a very deep sleep. The toast and tea would go unconsumed; Amanda would come in later and clear them away.

∞∞∞

Mike slammed on the brakes of his car as he passed the Lion's gate. Over in the car park for the Mussenden Temple was the red hatchback; thankfully the road was clear or there would have been a collision. He reversed the car at speed back up the road then once he had gone past the gate he stopped; the car jumped forward in through the Lion's gate and down into the car park. It was the red hatchback he was looking for! Mike parked the car as quickly as he could then he jumped out and nearly ran over to the car. Mike walked around the car looking at every detail. Apart from his car and the red one there was only one other car in the dark car park; but he was not interested in that one. There was no external damage to the car and no sign of forced entry. Mike took out his phone to get hold of Eddie Cargill; he cursed when he realised that there was no phone coverage where he was. He looked around to see where they may have gone. He walked around the car again then he spotted it. He knelt down to get a closer look. It was a small pool of fresh blood, there was not much; it had not been there long. He found another a few feet away and it led off towards the temple. Someone was still bleeding, not a lot, but enough for him to see where they were going. Mike started off towards the path that led up to the temple. He reached onto his belt and withdrew his pistol; no phone coverage, no one was coming, he was on his own, these were very dangerous creatures, but he knew he could not stop ... his feet knew the way.

∞∞∞

"She is late," Pe'ter scowled. The wind picked up and the sea seemed to grow louder. Viktor was leaning over the wall and looking out to sea. The long beach off to their left stretched down around Magilligan point and to the ferry that would take them over the border into the Republic of Ireland and away. They had been given 24 hours to leave the island and they had said that they would; they would have left already if they had not been waiting for Yelina, he looked at his watch,

"She is only 30 minutes late," Viktor turned back around towards Pe'ter who was just changing his dressings. The bleeding had stopped now, his body was already repairing itself and it would not take him long to fully recover. Pe'ter was topless in the darkness and with each passing hour his strength was returning, that was good. He would not need any more dressings.

"It is time for you to get dressed before she gets here!" Viktor said with a smile,

"Well, the sooner she gets here the quicker we can leave," Pe'ter took the phone out from his pocket, the light from the screen lit up his face, "and why pick somewhere where there is no phone signal?" Pe'ter looked up puzzled, "that is just stupid," he said, Viktor smiled then the wind blew around them again. Both men reacted to a different smell, someone was coming. "That is not Yelina!" Pe'ter dropped to one knee as Viktor grabbed at the daysack, his hands fought with the contents until he found the familiar grip of the pistol then he too was on one knee. Over the rise near the ruins walked the shape of a man that was not swinging his arms as he walked.

"Male, sapien," whispered Viktor. Pe'ter nodded,

"He is armed with a pistol and it has a two-handed grip," Viktor nodded as Pe'ter described what he saw, Pe'ter turned towards Viktor, "and he is coming here!" There was silence as the figure slowly walked forward. "We have to take him!" stated Pe'ter who looked from the figure to Viktor then back at the figure.

"Yes," whispered Viktor, "we do," Viktor was about to say something when he noticed that Pe'ter had started to change and in a moment, Viktor frantically pulled off his clothes and also began to change, this would be no problem for them.

∞∞∞

Yelina turned the car in through the Lion's gate, then into the car park where her headlights lit up three cars. She didn't recognise two of them, but she smiled when she spotted the red hatchback. She turned the car around and parked on the same side as Viktor's car, her excitement was building, and for the first time in a long time she felt safe. The Rua had kept their word, so would they, Viktor had agreed that they would leave tonight and never return, finally they were free from Davidov and she was free from Anders. She had enjoyed watching him die, but she regretted that she hadn't killed him herself. Anders had gone after the Rua's woman and killed their child. The Rua had his revenge, Anders was dead, and he would never place his hands on her again. Yelina climbed out of the car and closed the door quietly, she had picked somewhere no one would be looking for them. Viktor had sounded pleased when they had met, finally they could have a future and that made her happy. Yelina walked around to the rear of the car and opened the boot. She lifted out a small daysack full of hot food she had picked up at the chip shop in Coleraine. She threw the daysack over her shoulder and closed the boot, the only other thing in her bag was a small pistol the Rua had let her keep. They had taken all of the other weapons and equipment. She had not complained, she never wanted any of it anyway. She walked into the darkness towards the temple that held good memories for her.

∞∞∞∞

Mike had his weapon in both hands and his arms were out in front of him, exactly as he had been taught to do; he turned his body keeping the pistol as an extension of his arms. He wasn't sure what he was looking for but there shouldn't be anyone around here at this time of night. Slowly, step by step, he moved forward. The ruins of the old manor house were on his right. The path led down to the temple but in the darkness, he could no longer see if there was any blood on the ground; the path had given way to grass and the direction had been cut out so people could easily follow. The Temple was up ahead.

MOVEMENT.

Mike dropped to one knee and brought his weapon up. He looked over it and stared into the darkness. The clouds had started to part, the light of the moon lit up the entire area, it was beautiful, but there were two figures quickly running towards him, he raised his weapon.

"POLICE OFFICER, STOP!" he shouted as the two figures came into focus. He had seen them before, in Castleroe. He knew he was looking at werewolves and they were real. Two of them were charging at him as he made his decision and aimed at the one on the right.

Suddenly, there was a blinding flash mixed with a loud bang followed in quick succession by several more. The force of it made him unstable, he couldn't see, and he covered his face with his hands to try and stop the pain in his eyes. Something collided with him with a lot of power sending him tumbling over. Hands grabbed at him and spun him over forcing him face down on the ground. They were not gentle, everything was done with great strength, his head was pushed into the ground, and a heavy weight on his back prevented him from moving. His arms were forced twisted behind his back, his weapon was gone, the wolves had him, and he was a dead man.

As suddenly as this all happened, it stopped. His ears were still ringing from the loud noise as he was hoisted up by two armed men on either side of him, both wore dark 'military tactical gear', the kind he had seen in the movies. Their helmets had four tubes coming out of the front of them that looked like the eyes of an insect; and mesh covered their faces. Mike knew that these were not normal soldiers. Mike glanced around to several movements to his left and his right as other armed soldiers raised their weapons and then stopped. A single figure came out of the darkness towards them. As he got close, he raised his right hand, pressed a button at the side of his helmet and raised the night vision equipment so it locked above his head.

"Mike," Mike looked at the figure as he came closer, it was not until he was only feet away, and the soldier removed the mesh from his blackened face that Mike recognised Steve Minister. Mike was dumbfounded, "Well, of all the places I never expected you to show up!" Steve was smiling,

"How did you ......" Mike started, he was still trying to take everything in,

"Know?" Steve finished the sentence for him, "like I said the last time I saw you; we have run into this lot before!" A soldier came out of the darkness.

"Area secured boss," he said. Steve nodded,

"Right, you know what to do?" the soldier nodded, "right get on with it,"

"Hey," Mike started, "What about ..." Steve looked over at him.

"The wolves? Well let's just say they will not be bothering you again," Steve turned to walk away, Mike went to step forward but the soldier on his right grabbed his shoulder,

"Hey!" he protested,

"Let him go," Steve commanded, the soldier released his grip, "there is someone who wants a word with you." Mike looked around in the darkness, the two soldiers who were behind him turned and walked away. Mike looked at the ground and spotted his weapon, as he was picking it up another figure walked towards him. This figure was different. He was not dressed the same as the soldiers. Mike recognised the police issued overalls and police body armour, but he was wearing the same kind of helmet and night vision as the soldiers. He had his thumbs tucked into the space of his body armour under his arms, he lifted the night vision and a blackened face smiled at him.

"Mike me boy," Mike again was taken aback.

"Superintendent Forrester," Mike said formally. Darren put his arm around Mike's shoulder and started to lead him towards the ruins, "I've told you before, call me Darren,"

"Just what the hell is going on here?" Mike demanded, "They are suspects that we wanted to question as part of our investigation!"

"Well," Darren started, "from the look of things they did not want to do much talking ... speaking of talking, we need to talk ... you are going to be served with a 100-year disclosure notice ..." Mike suddenly slowed down as Darren let go of his shoulder,

"I want to know what happened here!" he demanded, in the darkness he could see that Darren was smiling,

"That is no problem me boy, happy to do that ... just you will not be able to tell anyone for the next 100 years!" Darren started walking away from him, "and as you know, break a 'D-notice' and it is straight to prison for you me boy ..." The realisation of the situation he was in suddenly was apparent, he would not be getting the breakthrough that the team so desperately needed.

∞∞∞∞

Yelina Gurin was down on one knee by the side of the stone wall, she had heard the policeman shout, she recognised the flash-bang as it had gone off and the noise of suppressed weapons. She could not tell if it had been Pe'ter or Viktor she had heard yelping, but she knew at least one of them was dead. She watched as the soldiers continued their sweep of the area, tears slowly started to run down her face, her dreams were gone. She watched as a soldier took up a defensive position that was forming part of their inner cordon. She had to get out of here or she would be caught. She would mourn Viktor later. As quietly as she could, she raised herself up and ghosted her way back around the stone wall to the car park. She almost broke into a run, fumbling for her car keys; she must get away or they would kill her too. Yelina was at the driver's door and just about to push the key in when she heard a small noise. The noise made her slowly turn and face the trees at the other side of the car park, there was someone there. Her body tensed up, ready for the attack when something hissed towards her, striking her in the left shoulder with such force that she spun around and fell to the ground. Yelina tried to get up but could only manage a crawl. The bullet had struck just underneath her clavicle and pain shot through her body. As she was crawling she could hear the noise of someone approaching, she turned in defiance to face the soldiers, she would fight them to the last. It was not a soldier who approached but a tall blonde woman, the supressed pistol in her right hand.

"Who ... Who are you?" Yelina asked, the bullet had entered the top of her lungs, each breath was becoming more difficult.

434

"My name is Alison, but that means nothing to you," Alison Wallace stopped at Yelina's feet, she looked at her with disgust, "What did you expect to happen? Coming over here and thinking that you are taking over?" Alison's face had slightly changed, Yelina, sniffed, there was no Garou here. She sniffed again as Alison opened her mouth wide, Yelina could see into her mouth and watched as her incisors grew. Yelina recoiled with fear.

"Noctrailis!" she whispered as Alison holstered her weapon and jumped at Yelina, Yelina tried to fight off the Noc, but struggle as she might, the Noc overpowered her and started to feed on her neck.

∞∞∞

At the side of the car park the small surveillance camera looked on. There was no noise, no lights, nothing to show that it was working. It just looked at the frenzy that was occurring behind one of the cars in the car park. Just over 100 metres away the two soldiers looked at their monitor, one slowly moved and lifted the small green keypad and started to tap in a message, seconds later they got the reply. Major Dukesby was also watching. The soldier showed his friend the message and he nodded, he looked at the monitor, without speaking he mouthed one sentence 'What is that?' he asked, the second soldier shrugged, they could debate it later when they got back to the hangar.

Alan Dukesby was looking at the monitor from the camera in the car park, the techie was monitoring all the screens on the different laptops. The split screen showed the shots from the helmet cameras of the deployed team, and the other screen was the area cameras. The door to the room opened and a young female face poked in,

"Boss, they are here,"

"Good," said Alan as he stood up and walked towards the door, the Land Rover came to a stop outside. Chris Abbey had been driving and stayed in the driver's seat, but the passenger and the two men in the back got out. Alan walked straight towards them, holding out his hand in greeting, it was taken firmly.

"Good evening, I am Major Alan Dukesby, Twenty Second Special Air Service Regiment,"

"Hello, I am Paul Hawkins of the Northern Dun of the Rua," both men released their grip, "is it done?" Paul asked,

"Yes, just," Alan replied, "would you like to come into our mess, I feel we have a lot to discuss," Paul nodded and as he followed the soldier he looked back at the other two and gave a single nod towards the Land Rover, they were to stay there.

"Dukesby?" Paul asked as he caught him up,

"Yes,"

"Any relation to John Dukesby who fought in the Radfan in the 1960's?" Alan smiled,

"Yes," he confirmed, "my Father," Alan was now curious how this man he had only just met could possibly know that.

Paul smiled, "Then my Father fought with your Father," Alan was leading Paul towards the bar as he thought for a moment,

"Would that be 'Paddy Hawkins? The man who could track anyone across nearly any terrain?" Paul nodded,

"Yes, there was a very good reason he could do that," Alan opened the door and allowed Paul to enter,

"So, I am finding out, we do have a lot to discuss!"

Chapter 87

Tony walked into the living room of the farmhouse. "Well?" Tony asked, excitedly, Kyle nodded in return. Tony bounded over to him with is hand held out, Kyle sat forward and took his hand. Tony pulled him from his seat and threw his arms around him in an embrace. "Well done mucker, well done indeed, so, what are you going to do next?" Kyle paused at Tony's question.

"Well that is me out of the police," he said,

"Really?"

"You really don't expect me to stay in after this, do you?" Kyle answered,

"Ha, no, no not really," Tony paused, "so that is both of us out then, what's next on the cards?"

"Well I am off down to Belfast tonight, I have booked into a hotel then going to meet the Southern pack tomorrow" he paused again, "and I am meeting up with Kelly tonight," Tony gaped at him.

"I thought you had finished with her?" he questioned.

"I'm giving her one final chance., I think this should change things."

"I will never tell you what to do, especially now, after everything you have achieved," Kyle looked at his friend as Tony spoke, "but she is a mistake! You can do so much better, and ... better is waiting." Kyle didn't have to ask who he was talking about.

"Probably," said Kyle as his phone beeped; he reached forward and picked up the phone to read the message. He looked up at Tony, "And she wants to talk to me as well!" Tony's shoulders relaxed, his eyes blinked, it was almost like an 'I told you so' moment, but he could not say anymore apart from the obvious question:

"Are you sure you want to meet her tonight?" Kyle nodded, his phone beeped again, "Well, she is keen," Tony stated, Kyle looked at the screen and shook his head,

"It is from Cara-Marie," he said,

"You two, still 'just friends'?" Tony asked,

"Yes," Kyle replied,

"Well, she has a friendly name,"

"She has a what?" Kyle asked,

"Her name, the first part of her name, 'Cara – it is Irish for friend, as in 'An Cara', my friend" Kyle opened the message and a look of shock burst over his face, Tony leaned forward, "What is it?" he asked,

"I think we may have a problem!" Kyle said, handing the phone over to Tony who read the single line, 'SO, HOW IS LIFE AS THE NEW ALPHA OF THE NORTHERN DUN?'

∞∞∞∞

The drape covered the body, Sean and Mike walked into the room after the pathologist. All three of them stopped beside the open door to the fridges that held the bodies awaiting a post mortem. The pathologist pulled the drape back to reveal the upper torso of Carl. It was obvious that he had been prepared for the viewing. The pathologist lifted a manila folder that had been lying on top of the drape and as the three police officers looked down at the cold face staring up into the heavens the pathologist started to read from the folder.

"Mister Carl O'Brien, 52, died late, last Thursday evening on his farm..." He paused as he read through the notes on the page, he spoke without looking up, "this body was healthy and there was no disease to accelerate death..." The pathologist continued to describe the wounds and injuries; he was mid-sentence when Sean interrupted him.

"Excuse me Doctor," The pathologist stopped talking, the only part of his body to move was his neck to lift his head up and looked emotionless in his annoyance at being interrupted, he didn't hide his disgust at the living! Sean continued "would you be able to tell us how these injuries occurred?" Mike looked at Sean then back at the pathologist whose face did not move.

"Yes," The single word hung in the air as the police officers waited for him to speak again, Mike broke the silence.

"Well Doctor would you be able to share that with us please?" the Doctor flicked over more sheets of paper then started reading aloud.

"Death was caused by catastrophic bleeding into the thoracic cavity following three penetrations to the chest; these were done with force…" Sean glanced down at the body that was lying before him and the pathologist continued reading from his written report.

"Could these injuries have been caused by a bladed weapon?" he suddenly asked out loud. Everyone stopped to look at him.

"Where did that come from?" Mike asked, the pathologist looked straight into his eyes.

"No" came the one-word reply.

"Why not?" asked Mike.

"The three penetrations were caused by something solid that was a lot thicker than a blade; all are of different lengths as well." The detectives looked at each other again, this was a conversation that would continue later. "What happened to him?" the pathologist asked, Mike answered for Sean.

"The farm hands said that he was out tending his deer when a stag charged him, and he was caught by the antlers." The pathologist looked down at his notes, flicked through the file, looked over the body and then lifted his head towards the others.

"Well his blood gases show that he had been exerting himself just prior to death so, yes, that is feasible!" Sean asked for a copy of the report and the pathologist nodded. Sean said his thanks and they turned and left. Mike waited until they got outside the building and were nearly at the car.

"What are you thinking boss?" he asked, Sean stopped by the door of his car, he turned and leaned up against it.

"Carl O'Brian wasn't killed by any deer,"

"I was thinking the same," said Mike, "Ok, so how do we prove it in court?" he asked, Sean looked down at the ground.

"I do not know,"

"So, what happens now?" Mike asked, Sean shrugged,

"Well, they have confirmed the bodies in the Mussenden forest were Sprogis, Shelaev and Shimikov … The girl, Gurin was found in the car park with her throat slashed. Their DNA puts them at the murder scenes in Belfast, Castleroe and Coleraine. The weapons that killed them were all recovered at the scene with a blood trail of 'at least' one other heading away from there …" Sean paused, "and all Dr Burns' research rubbished by nearly everyone, so as far as the Police Service of Northern Ireland is concerned, werewolves do not exist and we solved a case of serial killers! And ……"

"And?" asked Mike.

"And from the Chief Constable that is what we report, everything we have as long as there is no mention of werewolves, unicorns or the loch ness monster!"

"That does not answer my question?" Mike asked again,

"It does for the Super and the Chief, case closed!"

"There is something going on at that farm!" Mike protested. Sean nodded as Mike continued, "Paddy M'Kane worked there, O'Brien was not killed by any deer and the two coppers from Coleraine that seemed to be involved with all this suddenly leave the police and set up there!"

"Both of them?" Sean asked, Mike nodded,

"Apparently that fella Foster, his late dad owned it and it was in O'Brien's will that if he was ever found it all goes to him."

"Very convenient," stated Sean, "but not our problem anymore,"

"So, it is true then …You asked for early retirement again?" Sean opened the door of the car and climbed inside, Mike joined him seconds later.

"Yes, and ..."

"And you got it." Sean looked at his friend and nodded.

"We have not seen the last of these," as Sean spoke his phone started ringing. He dug into his pocket and pulled the phone out, he looked at the number, it was one he did not recognise. He pressed a button and turned the keys in the ignition of the car, the phone went to loud speaker and the voice boomed over the speakers inside the car.

"Good morning," the voice was male, and one Mike would describe later as 'Very English'; it was a crisp upper-class accent that was very hard to impersonate. "May I speak with Inspector Parrish please?"

"Speaking," Sean replied.

"Excellent, great to finally track you down, Inspector," Sean screwed up his face, he had no idea who this was, "I have been trying for a few weeks to get hold of you but the numbers I kept on getting were just not the right ones!" The voice laughed at his own joke, Mike shrugged, "Anyway," the voice continued, "It is really good that I have finally gotten a hold of you,"

"Ah, excuse me," Sean butted in "but can I ask who you are?" The voice paused,

"Oh yes, sorry, kinda used to people already knowing who I am. I am Rupert, nice to finally speak to you Inspector. Right, like I said, I have been trying for several weeks now," Mike shook his head and adjusted his seatbelt.

"Sorry to cut in again, 'Rupert', but what can I do for you?" Sean asked.

"Oh, well, more of a social call really you see we both have been tackling the same problem, but it seems from different ends!"

"I am sorry Rupert, I have a lot going on so exactly who are you and exactly what do you want?" Sean asked. The phone went silent for a few seconds then Rupert spoke again.

"Yes, of course, how could you possibly know me Inspector," again Mike mouthed the words 'this is a waste of time!' Sean nodded, "well let me introduce myself formally, I am Rupert Baskerville, 27th Earl of Baskerville hall, and well, not to put too fine a point on it but these creatures have been plaguing my family for over 150 years!"

"You are kidding me?" Mike said out loud, "Baskerville?"

"No Inspector, I am not, 150 years ......"

∞∞∞∞

Four hours later Kyle was standing outside the restaurant in Great Viktoria Street in Belfast, he looked up at the clear night sky, no clouds, it would be cold tonight he thought to himself. The street was busy, busy with people walking back and forth; busy with traffic and busy with ignorance of what was going on around them. Kyle would never look at a city with the same eyes ever again. His head turned up the street in the opposite direction, his eyes scanned the far side of the street and his eyebrows lowered. He could not see them, but he knew that they were there, and they were keeping their distance and that, after all, was fine.

Kyle spotted Kelly at the far side of Great Viktoria Street, behind her was the glass fronted 'Europa Hotel'. Kelly was looking left and right and was searching for the space to cross. Kelly had picked the restaurant and booked the table, Kyle quite liked her choice. She was wearing black four-inch heels with jet black jeans. Her white cotton top had a wide neck that revealed one of her shoulders. It was covered with a small black jacket that matched her jeans. Her hair was down, nearly touching her shoulders, and was slightly shorter than the last time that he had seen her. The crossing started beeping and the traffic came to a halt as the small mass of people on both sides of the street surged forward. Kelly strode towards him, she wasn't smiling. Kelly stopped about three feet away from him and Kyle smiled at her, but it wasn't returned.

"Hi" he said in greeting. Kelly lifted her head and met him eye to eye; the look however wasn't returned either. She looked from side to side then ushered him inside. There was another couple waiting to be seated. Kyle stood behind her right shoulder as the tall waiter approached; he was dressed head to foot in black and was over polite to the couple in front. Kyle tried to open the conversation with the brick wall that Kelly had become. "It is nice to see you." Kelly turned her head and just looked at him and answered with two simple words.

"Oh, please," The sternness returned to her face. Kyle was sure that it would change when he told her his news, whatever her problem was he felt sure that he could solve it. She looked magnificent standing there in the shrouded darkness at the entrance of the restaurant. Kyle could feel his heart beat just a little bit faster. She still had this effect on him, there was a part of him that wished that she didn't, but another part was overjoyed that she did. The waiter returned. Kelly spoke before Kyle could and asked for the table that she had booked for them. The waiter backed away, picked up two menus, then turned and led the way into the main seating area. The waiter walked on turning to his right up a small set of steps that opened onto a small section with four sets of intimate tables. The waiter stopped at a small table; the only one that was unoccupied. The other three tables already had couples at them. Kyle noticed that two of them were already eating a starter and the third couple were scanning the large menus and laughing over a shared joke. The waiter pulled the far chair back from the table and allowed Kelly to sit down and face the entrance. The waiter placed the menus on the placemats and asked through his smiles what they would like to drink. Kyle picked up his menu and flipped over to the wine list when a stern Kelly ordered for both of them.

"Two small Cokes with no ice, thank you." The waiter smiled, made a note on the small memo pad and left. Kyle looked up and slowly lowered the menu. Kelly had not picked hers up and sat back in the chair with her arms folded. The three other couples were engrossed with each other. Kelly's body language was telling him they would not be doing the same.

"Coke?" Kyle asked, "I was going to get us a bottle of wine." Kelly unfolded her arms and sat forward, the stern look never leaving her face.

"Yes, Coke. I'm not sharing a bottle of wine with you," Kyle lowered his voice as she increased hers. Kelly hadn't noticed but the levels of conversation at the other nearby tables had suddenly become quieter.

"May I ask why?" he asked,

"Look, I think it is time we cleared the air." Eyes around them darted. "There is something I want to tell you that will affect the way we are!"

"There is something I want to tell you as well," answered Kyle.

"Well I will go first," Kyle heard a whisper from a table to his right as Kelly continued, "I am moving in much higher social circles nowadays." Kyle's eyebrows raised as another whisper passed, this time to his left.

"Social circles?" he asked, his eyes caught the look of the bloke to his right who, as soon as they made eye to eye contact, looked away.

"Yes," continued Kelly, "much higher than someone of say, *'your'* standing!"

"And what may I ask, is my standing?" The waiter appeared and deposited two tall glasses of Coke with ice; he left before either of them had noticed.

"Well come on, you're not in the best paid job in the world now are you!" She stated, he knew from that who she was taking about now, he looked down at his right hand as he took a loose grip on the cold glass.

"I am not in that job anymore. I resigned today," his eyes looked up and into her eyes, she looked away, not holding the gaze.

"Well that is not a surprise," Kelly said slightly triumphantly, "I have my sights set much higher and I aim to get there."

"With a footballer!" stated Kyle, she got very defensive.

"Who is up for trials with FOUR premiership clubs next year, then after that, who knows!!" Kyle just looked at her, Kelly let out a little giggle as her smile broke over her face, she did not hide her excitement.

"So, what about us?" he asked.

"Us?" Kelly coughed as she said it, "are you taking the piss?" Kelly smiled even more as she sat back in her chair, "us? there never was an 'US'… I think you need to get your head out of the clouds!"

"And the times we made love?" he stared into her confident face.

"It was just sex, not making love, there 'is' a difference!" Kelly lowered her chin and tilted her head and let out a little laugh, the woman over to Kyle's right whispered a single word to the man that was sitting opposite her.

"Bitch,"

"So, this is about money then?" he stated.

"Ha, love is good, and love is nice but, it doesn't pay for my new Rolls Royce! You'll learn that one day." Kyle slowly nodded his head as the waiter reappeared.

"Are you ready to order?" Kelly smiled back at him and gave an answer that drew gasps from those around them.

"No, not yet, 'WE' will not be ordering as my friend here is leaving shortly but when my boyfriend arrives, we will be ordering then!" Kyle calmly lifted the glass of Coke to his lips. He could hear the whispers that were now bounding around the other couples, and 'Bitch' was being used more than once. Kelly spoke again. "Yes, he *is* coming here, and you will not be here when he gets here!"

"You had this all planned?" Kyle stated.

"Of course, I did!" Kelly let out another chuckle as she spoke. Kyle could tell that she in fact truly loved this, she sipped at her drink. "I am going to be a kept woman soon and that is something that an EX-police officer cannot do!" The whispers were louder, but Kyle doubted if Kelly could hear any of them and guessed that even if she could she would not have cared, "So, it is nearly time for you to be on your way then!"

"I was in love with you," he stated, eyes around them darted back and forth, Kelly chuckled again as she spoke.

"That will always be your problem," she answered.

"You don't feel anything for me then?" Kyle asked,

"Have you not been listening?" Kelly sat back in her chair, "Well," she paused "Yes, you have been fun."

"Fun?"

"Look, you are a really nice guy and you are a gentleman; you just don't do it for me," Kyle took a mouthful of Coke, as he placed the glass down he asked his final question.

"So, don't you want to know what I have to say?" Kelly looked at her watch before looking back at him.

"Look, I don't really care what you have to say," Kelly looked at her watch again, "Just make it quick then piss off will you, he will be here in a few minutes." Kyle finished off the drink and let a few seconds tick by before he folded his arms on the table and let a small grin appear over his face. Something flashed in her eyes and all conversation at the other tables had stopped to listen to what he had to say. She butted in, "if it is '*I love you*' well I think that we have covered that!"

"No, it's not that," smirked Kyle, he looked deep into her eyes before he spoke as he wanted to see the pupil reaction. "I just came into some money," her pupils widened as she took a sharp intake of breath.

"How much? £10 on the lottery?" she sarcastically asked.

"No," he answered, Kyle paused before he finished his sentence, "I just did a deal where I have taken over a firm that runs deer farms, here and in Scotland." Kelly's face contorted as if she didn't understand what he was saying so Kyle said the one line he always wanted to say. "I just made a profit of Eight point seven million pounds to be exact!" The man sitting at the table to his right burst out laughing, the couple to his left giggled out loud and the third couple moved in their chairs at what Kyle had just said. Kelly just stared at him, not knowing whether or not to believe him. Kyle pushed his chair back and started to stand, "So, you enjoy your struggling footballer," he stood up to his full height "and I will see you around."

Kyle turned to walk away and he didn't look back at the table as he walked towards the door. Kelly would sit there for another twenty minutes before her phone beeped to let her know she would be alone tonight as work had got in the way and the footballer was unable to get there. 'What work would he do at this time of night?' she shrugged the thought off but it would be another month before the story broke in one of the daily newspapers as to what the 'work' had actually been; she was tall and a model; an under-age model at that. Kelly was not going to have the life she most desperately wanted with a footballer.

∞∞∞

Out in Great Viktoria Street Kyle paused for a few seconds then turned left and started walking up towards Shaftsbury Square. He pushed his hands into his pockets and weaved between the people on the pavement as a smile spread across his face.

∞∞∞

Across the street, Dani and Sabine watched him from the edge of the car park, they were hidden by a large wooden billboard advertising cheap flights around Europe. Alison walked up and stopped beside them; they each shared a glance before Sabine spoke.

"So, that's the new Alpha then!" It was more of a statement than a question, "out by himself, all alone," she finished off. Dani smiled before looking across the street, "Why don't we just kill him tonight then?" asked Alison. Dani and Sabine looked at each other then back to Alison. Sabine opened her mouth to speak but was cut off by the male figure that came out of the darkness behind them. He was just less than six feet tall and had what would be described as a 'Normal' build, his hair was dark blonde and his accent American.

"Look down the street behind him, 40 feet," All their eyes scanned back down the street. "Two males, that is his protection," Alison didn't recognise the men and probably would not have spotted them if she had not been told.

"So that makes three of them," stated Alison. "We could still take them!" The girls were quiet as they knew a put down was coming. The American slowly walked around them. He was dressed quite stylishly, more so than them.

"That is the three we can see, no, an Alpha will have more security than that," he paused then looked straight at Alison, "and that my friend is not a fight we could win tonight!"

Dani watched as Kyle crossed the road, her eyes moving over his body, she could feel saliva pour from her glands. "Still, very nice," she said. Sabine agreed.

The American spoke as if reading from a book. "Then a warrior will rise from a green land and the blood of his enemies shall flow from his sword; many legends shall be told of his feats and daring and from him all Garou shall see new strength,"

"Where did that come from?" Sabine asked.

"It is written in their sacred scrolls," answered the American. Dani snapped at the comment; her contempt clearly visible.

"Sacred scrolls? Why should we take notice of any crap they come out with? We are higher than them, not the other way around!" The American stepped forward again and watched Kyle walk on up the street.

"Because a wise man studies his enemies!" He stepped forward again, the girls came up on either side of him, "and study him we will."

"Why should we?" asked Alison.

The American paused, none of them ever expected to hear the words he said.

"Because war is upon us; war with the Garou."

A slow smile spread over Dani's face...

"At last."

www.ingramcontent.com/pod-product-compliance
Lightning Source LLC
Chambersburg PA
CBHW072037190726
48294CB00005B/1293